D0567023

OATH OF THE RENUNCIATES

OATH OF THE RENUNCIATES

THE SHATTERED CHAIN
THENDARA HOUSE

Marion Zimmer Bradley

Nelson Doubleday, Inc.
Garden City, New York

THE SHATTERED CHAIN
Copyright © 1976 by Marion Zimmer Bradley

THENDARA HOUSE
Copyright © 1983 by Marion Zimmer Bradley

All Rights Reserved

Published by arrangement with
DAW Books, Inc.
1633 Broadway
New York, New York 10019

Printed in the United States of America

Contents

OATH OF THE RENUNCIATES

THE OATH OF THE FREE AMAZONS

From this day forth, I renounce the right to marry save as a freemate. No man shall bind me *di catenas* and I will dwell in no man's household as a *barragana*.

I swear that I am prepared to defend myself by force if I am attacked by force, and that I shall turn to no man for protection.

From this day forth I swear I shall never again be known by the name of any man, be he father, guardian, lover or husband, but simply and solely as the daughter of my mother.

From this day forth I swear I will give myself to no man save in my own time and season and of my own free will, at my own desire; I will never earn my bread as the object of any man's lust.

From this day forth I swear I will bear no child to any man save for my own pleasure and at my own time and choice; I will bear no child to any man for house or heritage, clan or inheritance, pride or posterity; I swear that I alone will determine rearing and fosterage of any child I bear, without regard to any man's place, position or pride.

From this day forth I renounce allegiance to any family, clan, household, warden or liege lord, and take oath that I owe allegiance only to the laws of the land as a free citizen must; to the kingdom, the crown and the Gods.

I shall appeal to no man as of right, for protection, support or succor; but shall owe allegiance only to my oath-mother, to my sisters in the Guild and to my employer for the season of my employment.

And I further swear that the members of the Guild of Free Amazons shall be to me, each and every one, as my mother, my sister or my daughter, born of one blood with me, and that no woman sealed by oath to the Guild shall appeal to me in vain.

From this moment, I swear to obey all the laws of the Guild of Free Amazons and any lawful command of my oath-mother, the Guild members or my elected leader for the season of my employment. And if I betray any secret of the Guild, or prove false to my oath, then I shall submit myself to the Guild-mothers for such discipline as they shall choose; and if I fail, then may every woman's hand turn against me, let them slay me like an animal and consign my body unburied to corruption and my soul to the mercy of the Goddess.

THE
SHATTERED
CHAIN

DEDICATION

for Tracy
in return for
Telling me the joke about
the spaceman, the *leronis* and
the three Dry-Towners.

(Twelve years elapse between the first part and the second.)

Part One

ROHANA ARDAIS,
Comynara

Chapter One

Night was lowering across the Dry Towns, hesitating as if, at this season, the great red sun were reluctant to set. Liriel and Kyrrdis, pale in the lingering daylight, swung low over the walls of Shainsa.

Inside the gates, at the outskirts of the great windswept marketplace, a little band of travelers were making camp, unsaddling their mounts and off-loading their pack animals.

There were no more than seven or eight of them, and all were garbed in the hooded cloaks and the heavy tunics and riding-breeches of the mountain country, the faraway land of the Seven Domains. It was hot in the desert lands of Shainsa, at this hour when the sun still burned with some force, but the travelers still wore their hooded cloaks; and though every one of them was armed with knife and dagger, not one of the travelers carried a sword.

This was enough to alert the crowd of Dry-Town loafers, hanging around to watch the strangers pitch camp, to what they were. When one, sweating under the weight of laden saddlebags, slung back hood and cloak to reveal a small shapely head, with dark hair close-cropped as no man—or woman—of Domains or Dry Towns ever wore it, the hecklers began to collect. So little goes on, ordinarily, in Dry-Town streets, that the watchers behaved as if the arrival of the strangers were a free show arranged for their benefit, and they all felt free to comment on the performance.

"Hey, there, come have a look at this! Free Amazons, they are, from the Domains!"

"Shameless bitches, that's what they are, runnin' around like that with no man to own to 'em! I'd run the lot out of Shainsa before they corrupt our decent wives and daughters!"

"What's the matter, Hayat, you can't keep hold of your own wives? Mine, now, they wouldn't run loose for all the gold of the Domains. . . . If I tried to cut 'em loose they'd come back cryin', they know when they're well off. . . ."

The Amazons heard the remarks, but they had been warned and were prepared for this; they went quietly about the business of making camp, as if their observers were invisible and unspeaking. Emboldened by this, the Dry-Town men came closer, and the jokes flew, free and ribald; and now some of them were addressed directly to the women.

"Got everything, haven't you, girls—swords, knives, horses, everything except what it takes!"

One of the women flushed and turned, opening her lips as if to reply; the leader of the group, a tall, slender, swift-moving woman, turned to her and said something, urgently, in a low voice; the woman lowered her eyes and turned back to the tent-pegs she was driving into the coarse sand.

One of the Dry-Town idlers, witnessing the little exchange, approached the leader, muttering suggestively: "Got your girls all right under your thumb, haven't you, then? Why not leave 'em alone and come along with me? I could teach you things you never dreamed about—"

The woman turned, pushing back her hood to reveal, beneath graying close-cropped hair, the gaunt, pleasant face of a woman in middle years. She said in a light, clearly audible voice, "I learned everything you could possibly teach me long before you were housebroken, animal. And as for dreams, I have nightmares like everybody else, but thanks be to the Gods, I've always waked up so far."

The bystanders guffawed. "One in the eye for you, Merach!" Now that they had turned their jokes on one another instead of on the women, the little band of Free Amazons went quickly about the business of setting camp: a booth, evidently for buying or selling, a couple of sleeping tents and a shelter to guard their mountain-bred horses against the fierce and unaccustomed sun of the Dry Towns.

One of the onlookers came forward; the women tensed against further insult, but he only asked politely enough: "May one inquire your business here, *vahi domnis?*" His accent was thick, and the woman addressed looked blank; but the leader understood, and answered for her: "We have come to sell leather goods from the Domains; saddles, harness and leather clothing. We will be here for trading at daylight tomorrow; you are all invited to come and do business with us."

A man in the crowd yelled, "They's only one thing I'd ever buy from women!"

"Buy it, hell! Make *them* pay for it!"

"Hey, lady, you going to sell them britches you're wearing so you can dress like a woman?"

The Free Amazon ignored the jeers. The man who had come to question her said, "Can we direct you to any entertainment in the city this night? Or"—he hesitated, looked appraisingly at her, and added—"entertain you ourselves?"

She said with a faint smile, "No, thank you very much," and turned away. One of the younger women said in a low, indignant voice, "I had no idea it was going to be like this! And you *thanked* him, Kindra! I'd have kicked his dirty teeth down his throat!"

Kindra smiled and patted the other's arm soothingly. "Why, hard words break no bones, Devra. He made an offer with such politeness as was in him, and I answered him the same. Next to these"—she swept the crowd of loafers with an ironic gray glance—"he was the soul of courtesy."

"Kindra, are we really going to trade with these *gre'zuin?*"

Kindra frowned faintly at the obscenity. "Why, yes, of course. We must have some reason for staying here, and Jalak may not return for days. If we have no apparent business here, we will be prime objects for suspicion. Not trade? What are you wearing for a head, today? *Think,* child!"

She moved on to a woman who was piling saddlebags within the shelter, asking in an undertone, "No sign yet of Nira?"

"None so far." The woman addressed glanced uneasily around, as if fearful of being overheard. She spoke pure *casta,* the language of the aristocrats from Thendara and the plains of Valeron. "No doubt she'll seek us out after nightfall. She would have small liking for running the gauntlet of these folk; and for anyone dressed as a man to enter our camp openly and unchallenged—"

"True," Kindra said, looking at their watchers. "And she is no stranger to the Dry Towns. Yet I cannot help being a little fearful. It goes against the grain to send any of my women in man's dress, yet it was her only safety here."

"In man's dress . . ." The woman repeated the words as if she felt she must have misunderstood the other's language. "Why, do you not all wear man's dress, Kindra?"

Kindra said, "Here you betray only your ignorance of our customs, Lady Rohana; I beg you to keep your voice low when we might be overheard. Do you truly believe I wear man's dress?" She sounded affronted, and the Lady Rohana said quickly, "I meant no offense, believe me, Kindra. But your dress is certainly not that of a woman—not, at least, a woman of the Domains."

Deference and annoyance mingled in the Free Amazon's voice as she said, "I have no leisure now to explain to you all the customs and rules of our Guild, Lady Rohana. For now, it is enough—" She broke off at another outbreak of guffaws from the bystanders; Devra and another of the Free Amazons were leading their saddle-horses toward the common well at the center of the marketplace. One of them paid the watering fee in the copper rings that passed as currency anywhere east of Carthon, while the other led the animals to the trough. As she returned to help Devra with the watering, one of the idlers in the crowd laid hands on her waist, pulling her roughly against him.

"Hey, pretty, why don't you leave these bitches and come along with me? I've got plenty to show you, and I'll bet you never—*eeyah!*" His words broke off in a howl of rage and pain; the woman had whipped a dagger from its sheath, slashing swiftly upward, laying open his filthy and tattered clothing to expose bare, unhealthy flesh, a line of red creeping upward along the quarter-inch-deep slash from lower belly to collarbone. He stumbled back, staggering, falling into the dust; the woman gave him a contemptuous kick with one sandaled foot, saying in a low, fierce voice, "Take yourself off, *bre'sui!* Or next time I'll spill your guts, and your *cuyones* with 'em! Now get the hell out of here, you filthy bastards, or you won't be fit for anything but selling for he-whores in the Ardcarran bordellos!"

The man's friends dragged him away, still moaning more with shock than pain. Kindra strode toward the woman, who was wiping her knife. She raised her eyes, grinning with innocent pride at how well she had defended herself. Kindra slapped the knife out of her hand.

"Damn you, Gwennis! Now you've made us all conspicuous! Your pride in knife-play could cost us our mission! When I asked for volunteers on this trip, I wanted *women,* not spoiled children!"

Gwennis' eyes filled with tears. She was no more than a girl, fifteen or sixteen. She said, her voice shaking, "I am sorry, Kindra. What should I have done? Should I have let the filthy *gre'zu* paw me?"

"Do you really think you were in danger, here in daylight and before so many? You could have freed yourself without bloodshed and made him look ridiculous, without ever drawing your knife. Your skills were taught you to guard against real danger of rape or wounding, Gwennis, not to protect your pride. It is only men who must play games of *kihar,* my daughter; it is beneath the dignity of a Free Amazon." She picked up the knife where it had fallen in the dust, wiping the remnant of blood from the blade. "If I return it to you, can you keep it where it belongs until it is needed?"

Gwennis lowered her head and muttered, "I swear it."

Kindra handed it to her, saying gently, "It will be needed soon enough, *breda."* She laid an arm around the girl's shoulders for an instant, adding, "I know it is difficult, Gwennis. But remember that our mission is more important than these stupid annoyances."

She left the women to finish the watering, noticing with a grim smile that the crowd of idle watchers had evaporated as if by magic. *Gwennis deserved every harsh word I gave her. But I am still glad she rid us of those creatures!*

The sun sank behind the low hills, and the small moons began to climb the sky. The square was deserted for a while, then some of the Dry-Town women, wrapped in their cumbersome skirts and veils, began to drift into the marketplace to buy water from the common well, moving, each of them, with the small metallic clash of chains. By Dry-Town custom, each woman's hands were fettered with a metal bracelet on each wrist; the bracelets were connected with a long chain, passed through a metal loop on her belt, so that if the woman moved either hand, the other was drawn up tight against the loop at her waist.

The Free Amazon camp was filled with a smell of cooking from their small fires; some of the Dry-Town women came close and stared at the strange women with curiosity and contempt: their cropped hair, their rough mannish garb, their unbound hands, breeches and low sandals. The Amazons, conscious of their stares, returned the gaze with equal curiosity, not unmingled with pity. The woman called Rohana finally could bear no more; leaving her almost-untouched plate, she got to her feet and went into the tent she shared with Kindra. After a moment the Amazon leader followed her inside, saying in surprise, "But you have eaten nothing, my Lady. May I serve you, then?"

"I am not hungry," said Rohana, stifled. She put back her hood, revealing, in the dim light, hair of the flame-red color that marked her a member of the telepath caste of the Comyn: the caste that had ruled the Seven Domains from time unknown and unknowable. It had been cropped short, indeed, but nothing could conceal its color, and Kindra frowned as the Comyn woman went on:

"The sight of those women has destroyed my appetite; I feel too sick to swallow. How can you endure to watch it, Kindra, you who make so much of freedom for women?"

Kindra said with a slight shrug, "I feel no very great sympathy for them. Any single one of them could be free if she chose. If they wish to suffer chains rather than lose the attentions of their men, or be different from their mothers and sisters, I shall not waste my pity on them, far less lose sleep or appetite. They endure their captivity as you of the Domains, Lady, endure yours; and truth to tell, I see no very great difference between you. They are, perhaps, more honest, for they admit to their chains and make no pretense of freedom; while yours are invisible—but they are as great a weight upon you."

Rohana's pale face flushed with anger. She said, "Then I wonder you ever agreed to this mission! Was it only to earn your pay?"

"There was that, of course," Kindra said, unruffled. "I am a mercenary soldier; within reason, I go where I am hired to go, and do what I am best paid to do. But there is more," she added in a gentler tone. "The Lady Melora, your kinswoman, did not connive at her own captivity, nor choose her form of servitude. As I understand what you told me, Jalak of Shainsa —may his manhood wither!—fell upon her escort, slew her guards, and carried her away by force; wishing, for revenge or sheer lust of cruelty, to keep a *leronis* of the Comyn enslaved and captive as his wife—or his concubine, I am not certain."

"In the Dry Towns there seems no great difference," said the Lady Rohana bitterly, and Kindra nodded. "I see no very great difference anywhere, *vai domna,* but I do not expect you to agree with me. Be that as it may, Lady Melora was carried away into a slavery she had not chosen, and her surviving kinsmen could not, or did not, choose to avenge her."

"There were those who tried," Rohana said, her voice shaking. Her face was almost invisible in the darkened tent, but there were tears in her roughened voice. "They vanished without trace, until the third; he was my father's youngest son, my half-brother; and had been Melora's foster-brother, reared as her playmate."

"*That* tale I have heard; Jalak sent back the ring he wore still on his fingers," Kindra said, "and boasted he would do so, and more, to any other who came to avenge her. But that was ten years ago, Lady, and if I were in the Lady Melora's slippers, I would not have lived to endanger any more of my kinfolk. If she has dwelled for twelve years in Jalak's household, surely she cannot be in any great need, by now, of rescue. By this time, one would imagine she must be resigned to her fate."

Rohana's pale face stained with color. "So in truth we believed," she said. "Cassilda pity me, I, too, reproached her in thought, wishing her dead rather than living on in Jalak's house as a shame to us all."

"Yet you are here now," Kindra said, and although it was not a question, Lady Rohana answered. "You know what I am: *leronis,* Tower-trained; a telepath. Melora and I dwelt together, as young girls, in the Dalereuth Tower. Neither of us chose to remain lifelong, but before I left the Tower to marry, our minds were joined; we learned to reach one another's thoughts. Then came her tragedy. In the years between, I had indeed all but forgotten; learned to think of Melora as dead, or at least gone far beyond my reach, far, far beyond my touch or my thoughts. Then —it was not more than forty days ago—Melora came to me across the distances; came to me in thought, as we had learned to do when we were little maidens in the Tower at Dalereuth. . . ."

Her voice was distant, strange; Kindra knew that the red-haired woman was no longer speaking to her, but to a memory; a commitment. "I hardly knew her," Rohana said, "she had changed so greatly. Resigned to her place as Jalak's consort and captive? No; simply unwilling to cause"— Rohana's voice faltered—"more death and torment; I learned then that my brother, her foster-brother, had been tortured to death before her eyes, as a warning lest she seek rescue. . . ."

Kindra grimaced with horror and revulsion. Rohana went on, steadying her voice with a fearful effort. "Melora told me that at last, after so many years, she bore a son to Jalak; that she would die before giving him an heir of Comyn blood. She did not ask rescue for herself, even then. I think—I think she wants to die. But she will not leave her other child in Jalak's hands."

"Another child?"

"A daughter," Rohana said quietly, "born a few months after she was taken. Twelve years old. Old enough"—her voice shook—"old enough to be chained." She sobbed, turning her face away. "For herself she asked nothing. Only she begged me to get her daughter away; away, out of Jalak's hands. Only so—only so could she die in peace."

Kindra's face was grim. *Before I bore a daughter to live in the Dry Towns, captive, chained,* she thought, *I would lay hands on myself and the life within me, or strangle the babe as she came forth from my womb! But the women of the Domains are soft, cowards all!* None of this showed in her voice, however, as she laid a hand on Rohana's shoulder, saying quietly, "I thank you for telling me this, Lady. I did not understand. So our mission is not so much to rescue your kinswoman—"

"As to free her daughter; that is what she asked. Although—if Melora can be freed . . ."

"Well, my band and I are pledged to do all we can," Kindra said, "and I think any of us would risk our lives to save a young girl from living chained. But for now, Lady, you will soon need all your strength, and there is neither courage nor wisdom in an empty belly; it is not fitting that I should lay commands on a *Comynara,* but will you not join my women now and finish your meal?"

Rohana's smile wavered a little. *Why, beyond her harsh words, she's kind!* She said aloud, "Before I joined you, *mestra,* I pledged myself to conduct myself in all ways as one of your band, and so I am bound to obey you."

She went out of the tent, and Kindra, standing in the doorway, watched her take a place by the fire, and accept a plateful of the stewed meat and beans.

Kindra did not follow at once, but stood thinking of what lay ahead. If it came to Jalak's ears that anyone of the Domains was in his city, he might be already on guard. Or would he so despise the Free Amazons that he would not trouble to guard against them? She should have insisted that the Lady Rohana dye her hair. If any spy of Jalak's should see a redheaded Comyn woman . . . *I never thought she would be willing to cut it.*

Maybe courage is relative; for her, maybe it took as much courage to cut her hair as for me to draw knife on a foeman. . . .

It is worth risk, to take a young maiden from Jalak's hands, from chains to freedom.

. . . Or such freedom as any woman can have in the Domains.

Kindra raised her hand, in an automatic gesture, to her cropped, graying hair. She had not been born into the Guild of Free Amazons; she had come to it through a choice so painful that the memory still had power to make her lips tighten and her eyes grow grim and faraway. She looked at Rohana, sitting in the ring of Amazons around the fire, eating, listening to the women talk. *I was once very like her: soft, submissive to the only life I knew. I chose to free myself. Rohana chose otherwise. I do not pity her, either.*

But Melora was given no choice. Nor her daughter.

She thought, dispassionately, that it was probably too late for Melora. There could not, after ten years in the Dry Towns, be much left for her. But there was evidently enough left, of what she had been, to spur her to an enormous effort to get freedom for her daughter. Kindra knew only a little of the telepathic powers of the Comyn; but she knew that for Melora to reach Lady Rohana, over such distance, after so long a separation, must have taken enormous and agonizing effort. For the first time, Kindra felt a moment of genuine sympathy for Melora. She had accepted captivity for herself rather than allow any more of her kinsmen to risk death by torture. But she would risk anything, to give her daughter a choice; so that her daughter would not live and die knowing nothing but the chained world, the slave world, of the Dry-Town women.

Lady Rohana did well to come to me. After so many years, no doubt, her Comyn kin wished Melora dead, wished to forget she dwelt in slavery, a reproach to them.

But that is why the Free Amazons exist, in the final analysis. So that every woman may, at least, know there is a choice for them . . . that if they accept the restrictions laid upon women, on Darkover, they may do so from choice and not because they cannot imagine anything else. . . .

Kindra was about to leave the tent, to return to the fireside and have her own meal, when she heard a small, strange sound: the whistle of a rain-bird; such a bird as never cried here, in the Dry Towns. Quickly she turned, nervously alert, seeing the small, slight form that wriggled under the back flap of the tent. It was very dark, but she knew who it must be. She said in a whisper, "Nira?"

"Unless you think some rain-bird has gone mad and flown here to die," said Nira, rising to her feet.

Kindra said, "Here, get out of those clothes; another woman around our fire will never be noticed, but in men's clothes you would collect another crowd here. We had quite enough of that while we were off-loading."

"I heard," Nira said wryly, slipping out of her boots, unbuckling the shortsword she wore—contrary to Domain law—and concealing it in the clutter of the tent. Kindra flung the younger woman a shirt and loose Amazon trousers, saw that she was very faintly silhouetted by firelight, and turned the tiny lamp lower still until they were in darkness. Nira was folding up her disguise; as she stepped into her clothes, Kindra came and asked in a whisper, "Was there any trouble? What news, child?"

"No trouble; I passed for any trader's lad from the mountains, any apprentice; they thought me a beardless boy with his voice still unbroken. For news I have only gossip of the marketplace, and some from the ser-vants at Jalak's door. The Voice of Jalak, who keeps his Great House when the Lord is away, has received a message that Jalak, and his wives and concubines and all his household, will return before noon tomorrow; and one of the slave-girls told me that they would have returned tonight, ex-cept that his Lady is heavy with child, and could not ride so far this day. Jalak has sent word for the midwives to be in readiness at any time after his return, and his servants are making bets about whether this will be the son he wants . . . it seems he has begotten nothing but girls, whether by wife, concubine or slave-girl, and that he has promised that the first of his women to bear him a son shall have rubies from Ardcarran and pearls brought from the sea-towns at Temora. Some old midwife says that she can tell by the way Lady Melora carries her child, low and broad, that it is a son; and Jalak will do nothing to endanger her while he has this hope. . . ."

Kindra's face twisted in distaste. She said: "So Jalak is camped in the desert? How far away?"

Nira shrugged. "No more than a few miles, I gathered. Maybe we should have arranged to attack his tents. . . ."

Kindra shook her head. "Madness. Have you forgotten? The Dry-Town-ers are paranoid; they live by feud and combat. On the road, take my word, Jalak will be guarded so that three cadres of City Guardsmen could not come at him. In his own house he may be a little more relaxed. In any case, we cannot stand against open attack. A quick strike, a guard or two killed, and ride like hell; that's the only kind of chance we have."

"True." Nira had dressed in her own clothes again; they were about to leave the tent when Nira laid her hand on Kindra's arm, detaining her. "Why must we have the Lady Rohana with us? She rides but poorly; she will be no use at all in a fight—she hardly knows which end to take hold of a knife—and if she is recognized we are all dead women. Why did you not demand that she wait for us at Carthon? Or is she like those men who hire a watchdog and do their own barking?"

"I thought so myself at first," Kindra said, "but the Lady Melora must be warned, and ready to leave with us at a moment's notice; the slightest delay could ruin us all. The Lady Rohana can reach her mind, without warning Jalak, or rousing his suspicions as even the most cautious message could do." Kindra grinned wryly in the darkness of the tent. "Besides, which of you wants the task of caring for a pregnant woman on the journey back? None of us have much taste for it—nor any skill should she need nursing. Or do you want to try?"

Nira laughed ruefully. "Avarra and Evanda forbid it! I stand reproved!" she said, and went to join the other women around the fire. After a moment Kindra went to join them, taking the plateful of food they had saved her (it was cold by now, but she ate without noticing), listening to the women talking softly as they cleared away the dishes, set a watch. Mentally, she checked them over.

She had handpicked this group from volunteers, and with all of them except the young girl Gwennis, she had worked before. Nira, who could pass as a man when she must, and had even, only the Blessed Cassilda knew how, learned to use a sword. *Against Dry-Towners we may need it.* By the Charter of the Guild of Free Amazons, it was not lawful for any Amazon to bear a sword. *Too threatening to the men of the Domains, for women to play with their precious toys!* Yet that law was not always honored; Kindra felt no guilt that she had allowed Nira to teach the others what she could of handling a sword. Then there was Leeanne, who had been neutered at fourteen and looked like a slim boy: breastless, hard-bodied and spare. Another who had known the neutering operation—which was illegal, but still turned up sometimes as a *fait accompli*—was Camilla, born of a good family in the Kilghard Hills; she did not use her family name Lindir, for they had long disowned and disinherited her. Camilla was nearing middle age, and like Kindra, had spent most of her life as a mercenary fighter; she was scarred with multiple knife-scars. Also Kindra had chosen Lori, who had been born in the Hellers and fought with two knives, mountain style; and Rafaella, Kindra's own kinswoman. Not all the Free Amazons were fighters, of course, but for this mission

Kindra had chosen, mostly, the best fighting women she knew. Then there was Devra, who was not a great fighter, but skilled beyond anyone Kindra had ever known at reading the trackless lands of mountain or desert, so that Kindra had chosen her, warning her to keep out of any close-quarters fighting. And Fat Rima, who was altogether feminine in appearance and manner, and so heavy she could ride only the biggest horses; but Kindra knew she was skilled at making and managing a campsite, and their comfort was valuable, too, on a trip like this; and like all Amazons, Rima was completely able to defend herself. *And she has other skills that may be needed before we reach Thendara!* Kindra reflected. Then there was the girl Gwennis, and Lady Rohana.

Anyone who knew the Free Amazons, Kindra thought, could tell at once that the Lady was not one of them: her walk, her speech, her riding. But there was no one here, the Goddess be praised, who knew that much about them!

They had finished putting away the supper gear; Kindra surrendered her empty bowl, to be scrubbed with sand by Fat Rima. Rafaella brought out her small *rryl* and laid it across her knees, striking a preliminary chord or two. "Kindra, will you sing for us?"

"Not tonight, Rafi," she said, smiling to soften the refusal. "I have plans to make; I'll listen to the rest of you."

Devra began a song, and Kindra sat with her head in her hands, her mind not on the music. She knew she could trust every one of these women with her life. Lady Rohana was an unknown, but she had more reasons than the others to work at Kindra's command. The others had all volunteered; partly, at least, because like every Free Amazon from Dalereuth to the Hellers, they hated the Dry-Towners with a deadly hatred. The Domains themselves had made an uneasy peace with the Dry Towns, and kept it; there was no love lost between Domains and Dry Towns, but there was a bitter memory of the long wars they had fought, without any conclusive victory on either side. The Domains might accept the present state of truce out of political expediency; and their women with them. *The Domains live under men's laws. They accept the enslavement of the Dry-Town women because it pleases them to think how benevolent, by contrast, they are to their own women. They say all men must choose their own life-styles.*

But no woman who had ever cut her hair and sworn the oath of a Free Amazon would ever accept that compromise!

Kindra had early freed herself from a life that now seemed to her as enslaved, as weighted with invisible chains, as that of any Dry-Town woman who walked in her ornamental bracelets and fetters of possession; she felt that any woman who truly chose, and would pay the price, could do as much. *Yes, even the women of the Dry Towns.* Yet, for all her lack of sympathy for any woman who bowed her head to a man's yoke, she felt a surge of hatred and loathing for the men who perpetuated this kind of slavery.

Should I tell them my plans now? She raised her hand and listened. Lady Rohana, who had a sweet, small, untrained voice, and Gwennis, who had a very light, true soprano, were singing a riddle-song from the Domains. Kindra decided not to disturb them. *Let them have a night's undisturbed sleep first.* "Set good watch around the camp," she said. "Some of these Dry-Towners may have ideas about how Free Amazons might like to spend their nights, and I doubt we'd care for their notions."

Chapter Two

At high noon the marketplace of Shainsa lay sweltering under a direct sun, beating down on the dry stone, the sun-bleached stone walls of houses and buildings that turned blind faces to the light.

In spite of the insults and jeers that the loafers of the streets had flung at the Free Amazons, their booth, a light woven-wicker affair intended for transport on horseback, had been doing a flourishing business all morning; the mountain-tanned leather commanded a good price in the Dry Towns, where few animals could be husbanded and leather and textiles were scarce. Their stock was vanishing, in fact, so quickly that Kindra was beginning to fret; if any happenstance delayed Jalak's return, and their wares for sale were exhausted, their lingering in the town might cause some suspicion. *Must I lay the groundwork for an accident to one of the pack animals?* she wondered. Then there was a stir in the marketplace, an almost visible murmuring of rumor, and idlers, passersby and children began to drift toward the great gates. *Jalak,* she thought. *It must be Jalak returning, nothing else could create so great a stir.*

Leaving the booth in the hands of Devra and Fat Rima, she moved idly with the crowd toward the gates, Rohana at her side. She muttered, in a tone that could not be heard six inches away, "Now, if ever, you must get a message through to your kinswoman. Tell her to be alert to move at a moment's notice; we may have only a few minutes to strike and we must take it when the occasion offers. It will not be until after nightfall; thereafter, she must be ready. Also, find out precisely where she sleeps, and if she is guarded and by how many; and where her daughter sleeps, alone or with other royal daughters."

Rohana leaned against the Free Amazon's arm, feeling suddenly sick and faint with the enormous responsibility. Now it was suddenly all on her shoulders. Someone jostled them; Kindra glared, steadied Rohana on her feet and the jostler flung a jeering phrase at them that made the Comyn woman blush with indignation, more for Kindra's sake than her own. She knew the Free Amazons were often accused of being lovers of women; she supposed some of them were. Yet all Kindra's kindness to her had been entirely impersonal, almost motherly, and Rohana felt a surge of anger that Kindra should suffer such insult on her behalf. *How absurd to be thinking of that now! As if I—or Kindra—could possibly care what some Dry-Town nothing thought of either of us!*

There was a blare of horns, a strange, hoarse fanfare. First came a dozen of his guards, in trappings so alien to Rohana as to make little impression on her except the general one of rude splendor: sashes and baldrics, elaborately gilded tunics, high headdresses. Then *cralmacs,* furred and tailed humanoids with great gold-colored eyes, wearing only their own fur and elaborate jeweled sashes, riding on the great shambling *oudhraki* of the far deserts: a legion of them, it seemed. More guards, less elaborately and ceremonially dressed this time, but armed with the long, straight swords and daggers of the Dry-Towners. Rohana thought, *Just as well that Kindra's band did not try to strike him encamped by night.* And then came Jalak himself.

Rohana had to turn away before she had more than a sight of his thin, hawk-keen face, sun-bleached under thick pale hair, fierce bristling mustachios; there were times when it seemed to her that so immense a force of hatred *must* somehow communicate itself to its object, that he could not fail to be aware of her thoughts. Rohana, a telepath since girlhood, lived with that as reality; but Jalak seemed impervious, riding amid his guards with a set, impassive face, looking neither to left nor right.

Near him rode—she supposed—a couple of his favorites, slaves or concubines; a slim girl with lint-white hair, chains jeweled, her body muffled in a scant fur smock, but her long legs bare to the fierce sun; she leaned toward Jalak and murmured and cooed to him as they passed. On Jalak's other side a thin, elegant boy, a pretty minion: too curled, too jeweled and perfumed to be anything else.

Behind Jalak and his favorites rode an assembly of women, and among them, outstanding for her flame-red hair (now, streaked faintly with gray), rode Melora. Rohana felt faint. She had been prepared for this; Melora had come to her in thought. But seeing her like this, in the flesh, changed beyond recognition *(And yet, Cassilda pity us, I would have known her anywhere, anywhere . . .),* Rohana felt that her pain and pity would overwhelm her and she would sink down, fainting.

Kindra's hand closed painfully on Rohana's arm, the nails digging into the flesh; Rohana recalled herself. This was her part in the rescue, the thing only she could do. Deliberately, she reached out and made contact with her kinswoman's mind.

—*Melora!*

She felt the shock, the start and flutter. She was suddenly afraid lest Melora should see her, make some sign of recognition.

—*Betray nothing; do not look for me or try to see me, darling, but I am near you, among the Free Amazons.*

—*Rohana! Rohana, is it you?*

But Rohana, from her place in the crowd, saw—and felt a sudden, fierce pride in her kinswoman—that Melora rode on without making any visible sign; her eyes fixed, apparently, on nothing; slightly slumped in her saddle; the taut, thin, careworn face beneath the graying red hair showing nothing but weariness and pain. Suddenly Rohana was struck with fear and compunction. She thought, *She is so heavy, so near her time, the child weighs on her so. How can we possibly get her away in safety?* She sent the concerned question.

—*Can you ride, Melora, can you travel, so far in pregnancy?*

The answer was almost listless. —*It is easy to tell you do not know the Dry Towns; I would be expected to ride even closer to my time than this.* Then the answering thoughts were fierce with hate. —*I can do what I must! To be free I would ride through hell itself!*

Painstakingly, then, bit by bit, Rohana relayed Kindra's message; received Melora's answer, even while the caravan passed on, passed by the marketplace. At the rear came a few more guards, who indifferently tossed small coins, copper rings, wrapped fruits and sweetmeats into the crowd, watching with dead eyes, as the beggars scrambled for them. Kindra and Rohana, not staying to watch the painful spectacle, turned back toward their booth. Once safely inside it, Rohana relayed the information she had received.

"Jalak sleeps in a room at the north side of the building, with his favorites of the moment, and Melora; not that he has any interest, at the moment, in sharing her bed, so she told me; but at the moment she is his most prized possession, bearing his son, and he will not let her out of his sight. There are no guards within the room, but there are two guards, and two *cralmacs* armed with knives, in the antechamber. Until this last pregnancy, Jaelle—that is her daughter—slept in her mother's room; now she has been moved to a room in the suite set apart for the other royal daughters. She complained that the noise the little ones made kept her from sleeping; Jalak is indulgent with girl-children if they are pretty ones, and allotted her a room to her own use, with a nurse there. It is at the far end of the royal children's suite, and looks out on an inner courtyard filled with blackfruit trees."

She anticipated Kindra's next question, saying, "I have the plan of the building so clear in my mind that I could draw it for you from memory."

Kindra laughed and said, "Truly, Lady, you would make a Free Amazon someday! Perhaps it is our loss that you did not choose our way, after all." She went to the women still in the booth, saying in an undertone, "Sell what you can; but what cannot be sold by nightfall, be prepared to abandon. Do not strike the booth; if we leave it standing they will expect us to be here come morning. Be sure the horses we used as pack animals are ready to be saddled for Melora and her daughter. . . ."

That afternoon seemed endless to Rohana. The worst of it lay in that she must behave exactly as usual—or at least as near to usual as was possible for her, here in the Dry Towns, far from her accustomed ways of occupying herself. She tried not to fidget visibly, knowing it would only disturb the Amazons, who seemed quite calm, selling their wares, tending their animals, idling around the camp. And yet, as the afternoon wore on, it seemed to her that she could see small signs that they were not, after all, quite so indifferent as they seemed to the coming battle. Camilla sat crosslegged at the back of the booth, sharpening her great knife to a razor edge, whistling an odd, tuneless little melody that, after a time, began to set Rohana's teeth on edge. Kindra sat drawing patterns again and again in the sand and quickly rubbing them out again with the toe of her boot. Rohana wondered how Melora was passing the time, but resisted the temptation to follow her in thought. If Melora could take some rest before sunset, let her do so, by all means!

How will she travel? She looks not more than three days from her time— if so much!

Slowly, slowly, the great red sun declined toward the hills. It seemed to Rohana that no day in her lifetime had worn away so wearily, with every hour stretching into lifetimes. *Not even the day my second son was born, when I seemed to lie for hours stretched on a rack of pain tearing me asunder . . . even then, something could be done. Now I can only wait . . . and wait . . . and wait. . . .*

Kindra said quietly, as she passed, "This day must seem longer still for your kinswoman, Lady," and Rohana tried to smile. That, at least, was true.

"Pray to your Goddess that the Lady Melora does not go into labor this day," Kindra said. "That would be the end of hope. We might still rescue her daughter, but if the Great House was ablaze with lights, midwives running here and there to attend to her . . . even that would be made more difficult than we could manage."

Rohana drew a deep breath of apprehension. *And she is so near to her time.* . . .

She tried to form, in her heart, a prayer to the Blessed Cassilda, Mother of the Seven Domains; but her prayer seemed to hang on the dead air, waiting, like everything else. . . .

And yet, as all things mortal must, even the day wore to an end. The Dry-Town women, veiled and chained, came to buy water at the well, and again they lingered, fascinated even through their scorn, to watch the Amazons moving about, tending their horses, cooking their meal. Rohana offered what help she could; it was easier if her hands were busy. She watched the Dry-Town women come and go in the marketplace, thinking of Melora, her hands weighted by the jeweled chains, her body weighted with Jalak's hated child. *She had been so light and quick, as a girl, so frolicsome and laughing.* . . .

They finished their meal, and Kindra signaled to Rafaella to take her harp, strike a few chords. She said in an undertone, "Come in close, and listen; act as if you were only listening to the music."

Rohana asked in a low voice, "Can you play 'The Ballad of Hastur and Cassilda'?"

"I think so, Lady."

"I will sing it. It is very long, and my voice," she added, with a self-deprecating smile, "is not so strong that anyone passing by would think it odd if you kept very quiet to listen to me—but not so soft that Kindra cannot talk more softly still, and be heard."

Kindra nodded, pleased at Rohana's quick comprehension of her plan. Rafaella played a short introduction, and Rohana began, hearing her own voice wavering:

> "The stars were mirrored on the shore,
>   Dark was the dim enchanted moor;
>   Silent were field and tree and stone. . . ."

The other women clustered in close, as if to listen to the ancient ballad; Rohana heard her own voice falter, fought to steady it. She must somehow collect herself to remember all the seemingly endless verses, string it out while Kindra gave soft, detailed instructions to every one of the Amazons. *Get hold of yourself,* she ordered and commanded herself: *This is something you can do, while they do the real work . . . the dangerous work, the fighting.* . . .

Yet they are women. I learned to think fighting was for men; I could never carry a knife, strike, see blood flow, perhaps suffer wounding, die. . . .

Sing, damn you, Rohana! Stop thinking, sing.

> "He lay thrown up along the shore,
> The sands were jeweled evermore,
> And to the shore Cassilda came
> And called him by a mortal name. . . ."

Struggling to remember the next lines, she heard Kindra, in a low, tense voice, detailing the information she had been given, pointing to the pattern she had scratched in the sand by firelight.

"Jalak sleeps here, with his favorites and Melora; there are no guards in the room, but just outside . . ."

> "Cassilda wept and paled and fled,
> Camilla knelt and raised his head,
> He left his high immortal fire
> For mortal man's entranced desire;
> White bread and wine and cherries red . . .

"—No, damn it, I skipped a verse," she said, breaking off in vexation, then realized it did not matter; no one was listening anyway.

> "Brought by her doves through morning bright,
> Camilla came, and bowed her head;
> He ate and drank by mortal light;
> And as his brilliance paled away
> Into a dimmer earthly day
> Cassilda left her shining loom:
> A starflower in his hand she laid;
> Then on him fell a mortal doom. . . ."

"Are the windows accessible by ladders?" asked Gwennis, and Kindra snapped, "They might be, if we *had* ladders. Next question, but no more stupid ones, please! We have time to kill, but not *that* much time!"

> "Into the heart of Alar fell
> A splinter from the Darkest Hell,
> And madness raging on him came,
> He cried again on Zandru's name,
> And at the darkened forge he made
> A darkly shining magic blade;
> An evil spell upon it cast. . . ."

"Devra and Rima, you will stay here, and the moment we come in sight, get moving! Be sure that the guards at the gate make no outcry. . . ." Kindra looked meaningfully at Rima.

The fat woman laid a hand on her knife, with a grim nod. Kindra said, "Camilla, you ride lighter than any of us; you will carry the child on your saddle. Lady Rohana—*no, go on singing!* You must be ready to ride close to Melora, to be alert for anything she needs; we shall all be busy enough evading pursuit and dealing with anyone who might come after us."

Rohana felt a shudder take her, seize her body and shake it like a rabbithorn in the grip of a wolf. Her voice faltered; she tried to cover it with a cough, and doggedly went on, knowing she was garbling the words horribly:

> "He could not see the—something—plan
> That gave a God to mortal wife,
> That earthly love with mortal man—
> Should bring to man a—something—life,
> Camilla fell without a cry—"

Damn, damn, I've skipped two whole verses again. . . .

> "And Hastur, shielded by her heart,
> Knew he could die as mortals die. . . ."

"Lori, you handle the *cralmacs;* I understand you know how they fight. Those long blades . . . anything else? Leeanne?"

"Remember that sometimes the Dry-Towners poison their swords. Don't neglect even a scratch. I've got some ointment that is supposed to neutralize their worst poisons. . . ."

> "Then Hastur son of Light had known,
> (For so had ruled the Shining Sire
> When first he left the Realm of Fire)
> Once more his star must burn alone . . .
> For on the earth he might not reign
> If he should cause one mortal pain,
> Or in that hour he must return
> To the far realms that were his own. . . ."

"We'll never be readier than now," Kindra said softly. "Finish the damn song, Rafaella, and get your dagger."

Gratefully Rohana began the last verse:

"And ever more the cloud waves break
Along the fringes of the lake,
And tears and songs still whisper there
Upon the still and misty air. . . ."

It was an unnerving experience, knowing they were all listening now, but impatient of every note, eager for her to finish. *Damn it, no more eager than I!*

"They built a city in the wild,
Fit for his rule, the kingly child,
And singing of Camilla's doom
They wrought for her an opal tomb."

She skipped the little postlude and rose impatiently, letting Rafaella put her harp away. Earlier in the afternoon she had packed the few possessions she had brought on this journey into a small bundle. Inside the tent the Amazons moved quickly and efficiently by the light of a single shaded candle, stowing food and necessary belongings in their saddlebags. Rohana watched, keeping out of their way. Devra and Fat Rima moved away toward the city gates, and Rohana felt another shudder take her; their business was to assure that those gates would be unguarded when they came back this way in a hurry, fleeing. . . .

Don't be squeamish! The guards there are Dry-Towners; they've probably deserved death a dozen times over. . . .

But they have no quarrel with any of us! There must be some good men among them, who have done nothing more than live as their forefathers have lived for centuries. . . .

Angry at herself, Rohana stifled the thought. *I hired Kindra's band to get Melora and her child away. Did I really believe it could be done without bloodshed? You cannot take hawks without climbing cliffs!*

Kindra beckoned the red-haired woman to her side. She said in an undertone, "I had thought to leave you here with these; but we shall need you, in case your kinswoman must have help—or reassurance. Come with us, Lady, but look to yourself if there is fighting; none of us will have time or thought to protect you, and Jalak's men may think you one of us and attack. Have you any kind of weapon?"

"I have this," Rohana said, showing the small dagger she carried, like all Comyn women, for personal protection. Kindra looked at it, trying to conceal her scorn. "It would be small service in a fight, I fear. But if we fail —I do not think we will fail, but nothing in this world is absolutely certain but death and next winter's snow—if we fail, at least it will keep you from falling alive into Jalak's hands. Are you prepared for that, *vai domna?*"

Rohana nodded, hoping the Amazon could not see that she was trembling. And again it flickered fleetingly through her mind, as had happened more than once during the twenty days she had been in their company, that perhaps Kindra had some small spark of psi power, that she followed Rohana's thoughts a little more than might happen by chance, for the Amazon's hard-boned hand descended briefly on her shoulder; only for a moment, a light touch, and hesitant, lest the noblewoman angrily refuse her sympathy. "My Lady, do you think none of us is afraid? We have not learned not to fear; only to go on in the face of fear, as women are seldom taught to do on our world." She turned away, her voice brusque again in the darkness. "Come along. Nira: to the front, you know the way step by step, we know it only from my Lady's drawings and maps."

Thrust to the rear of the small group of women, Rohana followed, hearing her pounding heart, so strongly it seemed to her that the thumping must almost be audible in the dusty, deserted streets. They moved like ghosts, or shadows, keeping in the lee of buildings, stealing along on noiseless feet. Rohana wondered where they had learned to move so silently, found she was afraid to speculate. For a panic-stricken moment she wished she had never begun this, that she were safe at home in Castle Ardais, on the borders of the Hellers. She wondered how her children fared without her, how the cousin who had managed her estates after her husband's death a few years ago was dealing with the business, what was happening far away in the mountain country. *This was never any place for me. Why did I ever come here? War, revenge, rescue, these are matters for men!*

And the men were content to let Melora pine away and die, captive! She hardened her resolve and stole along at the rear of the little column, trying to pick up her feet and put them down as silently as the Amazons, not to stumble against a chance stone.

The city was a labyrinth. And yet it was not very long before the women in front of her stopped, drew close together in a knot, seeing across an open, windswept square the loom of the Great House where Jalak of Shainsa ruled. The house was a great squared building of pale bleached stone, glimmering faintly by the light of a single small gibbous moon: a blind windowless barrack, a fortress, the two doors guarded by tall guards in Jalak's barbarous livery. Silently the Amazons turned, slipping through the shadows and along the side of the building. Rohana had heard Kindra's plan, and it seemed to her a good one. Every outside door into a Dry-Town house was guarded; against direct attack at the doors a couple of guards could hold it indefinitely. But if they could somehow get through the small side gateway into the courtyard, make their way through the garden—hopefully deserted, at this hour—and get into the house through the unguarded *inside* doorways, they might get into Jalak's chamber.

She had heard Kindra say, through her singing, "Our best hope is that there has been peace in the Dry Towns for many moons. The guards may be bored, not as alert as usual."

She could see the guard at the side gate now. *Evanda be praised, no more than one.* He lounged against the wall; Rohana could not see his face, but she was a telepath, and even unsought, his thoughts were clear enough: boredom, dullness, the sense that he would welcome anything, even armed attack, to relieve the monotony of this watch.

"Gwennis." Kindra murmured. "Your move."

(When this plan had been put forward, Gwennis had protested, sullenly. "Does it have to be me?" and Kindra had said, "You're the prettiest.") Now there was no protest, the band's discipline held. As Gwennis deliberately scuffed a stone loose against the wall, Rohana felt the Amazon leader thinking, *This is the worst moment of risk.* . . .

The guard straightened, alert to the noise.

He's alert, we can't take him unawares; so we have to get him away from the gate, get him out into the center of the square, Kindra thought.

Gwennis had swiftly divested herself of knife and dagger, torn her tunic slightly down the front. She sauntered out into the moonlit square, and the guard was instantly alert, then relaxed, seeing a woman alone.

We are taking advantage of him, yes. Of the centuries-old Dry-Town contempt for women as helpless, harmless chattels. Victims, Kindra reflected bitterly.

The guard did not hesitate more than half a minute before stepping away from his post at the door, moving purposefully toward the young girl. "Hey, pretty thing—are you lonely? One of the Amazons, huh? Have you got tired of them and come looking for some better company?"

Gwennis did not raise her eyes. Rohana had heard the argument about that, too. ("I won't seduce him to his death. If he minds his own business he is safe. I won't use a feminine trick.") But the guard had already left his post, and Gwennis' silent indifference to him had provoked his curiosity; he came swiftly toward her, saying, "Ha—caught you without that knife you wear all the time, huh? Now you'll see what it's like really to be a woman. Who knows, you might even like it better. Here, come here and let me show you a thing or two. . . ." He reached for the girl, roughly pulled her against him, spun her around, one hand covering her mouth to stifle a cry . . . his words broke off in a strangled gasp. Lori's long knife, thrown with deadly accuracy, went straight into his throat. A moment later Lori herself bent over him, delivering a swift, fatal death-stroke to the great vein below his ear. Kindra and Camilla dragged him into the shadow of the wall, out of sight of any chance passerby; Gwennis scrambled up, fastidiously wiping her mouth as if she could wipe away the guard's rude touch. Kindra rummaged at the dead man's belt, found his keys and began to try them one by one in the heavy lock. *Locked on the outside, not within. Less against invaders than against the escape of one of his women. . . .*

The lock was stiff; it seemed to Rohana, quaking in the quiet street, that it creaked loudly enough to alarm the whole town, but after a moment it gave and the door swung noiselessly inward. The band of Amazons crowded inside, shrinking against the inner wall, pushing the door closed.

They stood in a quiet and deserted garden. Here in the Drylands little grew unless it was planted, except thornbush; but Jalak, tyrant of Shainsa, had spared no expense to create an oasis for himself and his pampered women and favorites. A multitude of fountains splashed, tall trees towered overhead, flowers grew in lush profusion, with a sweet, damp, rank smell. On silent feet, guided by the sketch Rohana had made after the rapport with Melora, the women threaded their way along the bricked pathway, and paused in the shadow of a grove of blackfruit trees.

"Leeanne," Kindra whispered.

As the slender, sexless figure moved away toward, Rohana knew, the chamber where Melora's twelve-year-old daughter slept with her nurse, Rohana found herself wondering incongruously how a neutered Amazon thought of herself. *Not as a woman, surely. A man? Some indefinable third thing?* She dismissed the thought impatiently. *What nonsense to be thinking about now!*

They moved toward the unguarded garden door; a moment later they were actually inside. Rohana, moving now from memory of her rapport with Melora, began to move directly toward the guarded room where Jalak slept.

Was Melora awake, alert for them, expecting them? All this afternoon she had resisted the temptation to reach out for telepathic contact with her cousin, but now she yielded; reached for rapport, more easily as the long-neglected skill came back.

—*Melora, Melora!* And suddenly, in a half-forgotten sensation of blending and merging, she *was* Melora, she . . .

. . . She lay silent, facing the wall, every muscle tense and alert, willing herself to relax, be patient, wait. . . . In her body the heavy child kicked sharply, and she thought, with weary patience, *You are so strong and lusty, little son, and, Avarra pity me, I have not even the heart to wish you more like to die. It is not your fault but your ill fortune that you are Jalak's son. . . .*

Will it truly be tonight? And the guards . . . how, how? The memory that had been with her, night and day, for ten years now of her foster-brother Valentine, broken, writhing, his fingers cut from his living body, covered in blood, after atrocities too many and too dreadful to think about. . . . *Oh, Evanda and Avarra, Aldones, Lord of Light, not Rohana, too. . . .*

No! I must not remember that now! I must be strong. . . .

Painstakingly, muscle by muscle, she forced herself to relax.

Jalak slept now, deeply: the first, sated sleep of the night. Beyond him she saw, by the dim moonlight from the courtyard window, the pale forms of the two favorites who shared his bed. They, too, slept; Danette—pale, nude, her long scattered hair enfolding her; Garris snoring a little, lying on his back, folded against Jalak's long body. At first this had infuriated and humiliated her to silent tears and passionate rebellion; after ten years she was only wearily relieved that *she* need no longer share his bed. During these months while she carried his son, Jalak, proud, and as near to kindness as he ever came, had yielded good-naturedly to her plea and allowed her to have a bed of her own, that she might sleep in peace and rest well. For years now she had been freed at night, like other Dry-Town women, from the chains she wore by day; only while she was still a rebellious prisoner had she been forced to wear them night and day. More than once, in that first faraway year, she had flown at his throat . . . ceasing only when she knew her furious resistance excited, amused, stimulated him. . . .

Poor Danette, how she hates me, how she gloated when she took my place in Jalak's bed, never guessing how willingly I would have resigned it years ago—and she hates my child worse than she hates me, she knows she is barren. If only I were. . . . I wish Garris no ill. His parents sold him in the brothels of Ardcarran when he was no older than Jaelle . . . he loves Jalak no more than I . . . perhaps less. Cruelly as the Dry-Towners treat their women, there are at least laws and customs to protect women to some degree, and not even such laws protect such as Garris. Poor little wretch . . . he still cries. . . . How slowly this night seems to pass. . . .

She stiffened, every nerve in her body alert. *What sound was that?* The next moment the door came crashing inward and it seemed all at once that the room was full of . . . *of women?* Jalak woke with a bellow, snatching up his sword where it lay ready, night and day, to his hand; he yelled for the guards . . . a yell that went unanswered. Already on his feet, he yelled again, naked, leaping at the first who came against him; they crowded him against the wall, and Rohana, seeing through her own eyes now—although she shared Melora's thought, *Where are the guards?*—saw the Amazons force him against the wall, saw him disappear behind what looked like a wall of women, slashing, darting in with their knives; saw the long ripping cut with which Kindra darted in, slashed, the tendons at the back of his knee. He fell, howling, struggling. Danette, wide-eyed, kneeling upright on the bed, shrieked.

"Garris! Garris! Get his sword! They're only *women*. . . ."

"Silence that bitch," said Kindra, and Camilla's rough hands muffled Danette's shrieks with a pillow. Garris sat upright, looking down at the writhing, howling Jalak with an unholy joy. . . . Rohana caught up a furred cloak from the foot of the bed, wrapped it over Melora's scanty nightgown. "Come—quickly!"

Guided between her kinswoman and the Amazon leader, Melora stumbled into the hall; her foot slipped in the blood of the guards who had been killed there. *Are they all dead? All?* Even Jalak's howls had stopped. *Dead, or unconscious from loss of blood?*

She saw through the still-open door that Garris had caught up Jalak's sword; Nira whirled, her own sword at the ready, but Garris rushed past them, not even looking at her, disappearing down the hallway, with—evidently—no thought in mind but his own escape.

Rohana hurried Melora along, out into the silent garden. It was so silent that it took her breath away; fountains splashed, trees rustled undisturbed in the wind, no sound or light to show that somewhere inside there in the Great House, eight or ten of Jalak's fighting men and perhaps Jalak himself lay dead.

None but Jalak himself had had opportunity to strike a single return stroke; but that single slash had gone to Nira's thigh and she limped, leaning heavily on Camilla's arm. Lori came and bent beside her, roughly wadding the wound with her kerchief, wrapping it hastily with the belt of her tunic. Leeanne came out of the darkness, carrying in her arms a small form in a long nightgown, barefoot. She set the little girl on her feet, and in the dim light Rohana caught a glimpse of a small, surprised, sleepy face.

"Mother—?"

"It's all right, my darling, they are my kinswomen and our friends," Melora said in a singing voice; she stumbled, and Kindra put a hand under her elbow.

"Can you walk, Lady? If not, we can carry you somehow—"

"I can walk." But Melora stumbled again and put out her hand to clutch at Rohana's arm, thinking, *For the first time in a dozen years I am outside that wall with unbound hands—walk? I could run, I could fly.* Hurrying along between them, stumbling, she lost track of where her steps were taking her. *Anywhere. Anywhere away from here. Like Garris. . . . Poor little creature, I hope they do not hunt him down for Jalak's murder. . . .*

She felt the knives of pain in her side and back, felt the weight of her unborn child dragging at her, not caring. *Free. I am free. I could die now, happy. But I must not die and delay them.* . . .

The deserted marketplace was a silent wilderness of empty stalls, deserted booths. Rima and Devra came out of the dark, near where the horses waited. "The gates are clear," Rima said, with a suggestive gesture —a finger drawn across her throat.

"Come, then. Leave everything but your own saddlebags and food for travel," Kindra said, leading Melora to a horse with a lady's saddle. "Before you mount, *domna*, get into these clothes; they may not fit well, but they will be better for riding than that nightgown."

Melora felt Rohana slip her gown over her head, under cover of the darkness; help her into the long, loose trousers, tie them around her waist; slip a fur-lined tunic over her head. The faint smell in their folds made her want to weep with recognition and thankfulness: the spices and incense used to sweeten the air in every home in the Domains. She caught back a sob, letting Rohana help her to her saddle, slip suede boots—far too big— on her feet.

She looked around anxiously for Jaelle; saw that one of the Amazons had wrapped her in a cloak and lifted her to a saddle behind her, where she sat alert, amazed, her long straight hair streaming down her back, too excited and astonished even to ask questions.

Kindra took the reins of Melora's horse, saying, "Sit your horse as best you can, Lady; I will guide her." Melora clung to the saddle-horn (unfamiliar, after so many years, to ride astride again!) and watched, tensed against the pain of moving, as Kindra moved to the front of the little column of riders. She said in a low, tense voice, "Now ride like hell, all of you. We may have as many as five hours before the sun comes up and somebody finds Jalak in his blood; but we won't have more than that no matter how lucky we are, and from this day on for the next three dozen years, no Free Amazon's hide will be worth a *sekal* anywhere in the Dry Towns. Let's *go!*"

And they were off. Melora, clinging to her saddle, bracing herself as best she might against the jolting of her horse's gait (though she realized that Kindra had indeed provided a horse with an easy gait, the best available for a pregnant woman), looked back for an instant at the black loom of the walls of Shainsa.

It's over, she thought, *the nightmare is over. Thirteen years of it. Jalak lies crippled for life, hamstrung, perhaps dying.*

I hope he does not die. Worse, oh, worse for him to live and know that a pack of women has done this to him!

I am avenged, and Valentine! And Jaelle will live free!

They rode into the night, unpursued.

Chapter Three

To the end of her life, the Lady Rohana Ardais never forgot that mad ride, fleeing from the walls of Shainsa; alert at any moment for some small sound behind them that would mean Jalak—or his dead body—had been found, and the hunt for them was up.

For the first hour it was very dark, and she rode blindly after the sound of hooves from the other horses, with only dim shadows ahead. Then Kyrrdis rose, a brilliant half-circle above the horizon, so bright that Rohana knew it was not more than an hour or two ahead of the sun; and by its blue-green light she could make out the forms of the other horses and their riders.

They were traveling more slowly now. Even the swift horses from the plains of Valeron could not keep up the pace of those first hours. She wondered how Leeanne had found their road in the darkness; the Amazon's reputation as a tracker was evidently well-deserved. She could see Jaelle, a huddled, dark small form, collapsed in sleep against Camilla, clinging drowsily to the saddle. What did the child think of all this?

She was reared in the Dry Towns. Perhaps, to her, all this is quite normal: murder, midnight raids, the stealing of women. What if her loyalty is to Jalak? After all, he is her father.

None of us has any idea what Jaelle is like. . . . We have thought only of Melora's wishes. . . .

Melora is a telepath. She must know her child's heart. . . .

In the final hour before dawn they stopped to breathe the horses; Leeanne went to the top of a nearby hill to spy out any sign of pursuit. Rima came and put some bread and dried meat into Rohana's hand, poured wine into the cup at her saddle-horn.

"Eat and drink while you can, Lady. There won't be much time for breakfast if we are being pursued. There are a few hiding holes between here and Carthon, and Kindra knows all of 'em, but mostly our safety lies in a good long start. So you eat now."

Rohana chewed a mouthful obediently, although her mouth was dry, and the stuff tasted like stale parchment. She thrust it into a pocket of the unfamiliar Amazon trousers; maybe later she could manage to swallow it. She sipped at the wine, but it was too sour to drink, almost; she rinsed her mouth and spat it out again.

She led her horse slowly for several steps, hearing its deep, panting breaths slowly quiet to normal; rubbed its head absently, leaning against the warm, sweating body. She thought, not for the first time since she had undertaken this long journey, how fortunate it was that she was hardened to long riding, hunting with hawks in her distant mountain home. *If I were the kind of woman who did little more than sit over her embroidery-frames, I would be half dead of saddle-sores.* This made her think of Melora again *(How weary she must be!)* and she made her way through the Amazon crew: dismounting, slumped to rest, eating, talking in low tones. She noted that Jaelle had been lifted down and was sleeping heavily, curled up on someone's cloak, and covered with another. *At least they seem to be looking after her well. I do not suppose any of them know much about children.*

She looked around for Melora, seeing that Kindra was helping her kins-woman out of the high saddle; but before she could approach them, Nira, the crude bandage loose around her thigh, intercepted her. "Can you dress this wound by moonlight, *domna?* It hinders my riding more than I thought, or I would wait for the light."

Rohana felt a moment's impatience; then, remembering that Nira's wound had been incurred in their service, felt ashamed of herself. "I'll try. Come here, away from the shadows, where the light is brightest." She rummaged in her saddlebag for the few items of women's gear she had brought, found a clean, unworn shift and tore it into strips. Like every-thing else it was gritty with the sand of the Dry Towns, but clean.

She had to cut the bandage, and then the trouser leg, away with a knife; it was stuck to the wound with clotted blood. Nira swore under her breath, but did not flinch as Rohana washed the ugly cut with the sour wine—*At least the stuff is good for something,* she thought—and bandaged it tightly, pressing the hard pad of bandage against the wound. "It should be stitched; but I cannot do that by moonlight. If it begins to bleed again, I will do what I can when it is light."

Nira thanked her. "Now, if that bastard Jalak doesn't poison his weapons—one hears such things of Dry-Town men—"

"He does not," Melora said quietly beside them, and Rohana rose, folding what remained of the torn shift, to see her cousin standing there. Her face was dim in the moonlight, but even so it looked swollen and unhealthy. "Jalak would think that a coward's way; it would mean he did not believe his blows were strong enough to kill, and he would lose *kihar*—lose prestige, you would say, be shamed before his peers, if he stooped to a poisoned blade."

Nira got up awkwardly, grimacing as she put weight on her wounded leg. Her boot crunched on sand as she drew it on. She said wryly, "That is a comforting thought, Lady, but is it fact, or is it a sentiment seemly for a loving wife?"

"It is true, on the honor of my House," said Melora quietly, but her voice trembled, "and only my own Gods know how little I was a loving wife to Jalak, or anything else but a pawn to his filthy pride."

"I meant no offense," Nira said, "but I make no apology either, Lady. You dwelt in his house a full thirteen years, and you did not die. I would not have lived to shame my kinsmen so, even though my father is no great Comyn lord but a small-farmer in the Kilghard Hills."

"You have shed blood in my service, *mestra;* could I take offense, unless my pride were as great and evil as Jalak's own? As for my own life—can you see in the darkness?" She thrust out her wrists, took Nira's fingers in her own and guided them. Rohana, watching, touching, saw and felt the rough callouses from the metal bracelets on the chains; and above them on each darkly tanned wrist, a long, ragged, seamed scar. "I will bear them to my death," she said. "And after that, I was chained day and night—chained so tight I could not feed myself and had to be fed by the women and carried to the bath and to the latrines." Her voice shook with anger and remembered humiliation. "By the time I had healed, my child had quickened in me, and I would not kill the unborn with my own death." She looked at the dark form of her daughter, huddled and lost in sleep, saying, "How did you get her away? Jalak had given her into the charge of his fiercest woman-guard. . . ."

Leeanne had come back from the hilltop in time to hear this last; she said: "There is no sign of pursuit so far; not even a sand-rat seems to be stirring between here and Shainsa. As for your daughter's nurse, Lady, she sleeps past any waking; I do not like to kill women, but she came at me with a dagger. I was sorry to kill her before the child's eyes, but I had little choice."

"I will not weep for that one," said Melora with a grimace. "Indeed I think there will be small weeping for her, even in Jalak's house. She was my chief jailer before Jaelle was born, and I hated her worse than Jalak's own self. He was cruel because it was his nature and he had been reared to be so; but she was cruel because she found pleasure in the pain of others. I trust Zandru will delight in her company in hell; to be sure he will be the only one who has ever found such pleasure. Had I ever been trusted with a weapon again, even at table, I would have sunk it into her throat before turning it on myself." She turned to Rohana; for the first time there was a moment to exchange a quick, awkward embrace. *"Breda . . .* I am still not sure this is no dream, that I will not waken in Jalak's bed."

With the touch of Melora's swollen hands in hers, Melora's wet face pressed against her own, the rapport wakened again; Melora's mind lay open to her, and more: sharp physical discomfort, pain. Rohana thought, panicked, *Can she ride? Will she go into labor here and now, in the desert, far from help, delaying us . . . ?*

Gently, Melora loosed Rohana's hands and the contact lessened. "It is easy to see you know little of the Dry Towns. May you never have cause to know more! I would have been expected to ride, even nearer to my time than this. Don't worry about me, *breda."* Her voice broke in a sob. "Oh, it is so good, just to speak to you in our own tongue. . . ."

Rohana was desperately uneasy about her; she was not highly skilled in midwifery, but as mistress of Ardais she had seen many births; she knew Melora needed rest and care. But the Amazons, at Kindra's signal, were already mounting again, and indeed there seemed no choice.

Kindra came to inspect, briefly, Nira's bandaged wound. "So far there is no sign of pursuit, but with dawn someone will certainly find Jalak—or his corpse. And I would greatly prefer not to fight Jalak's men, or end my days chained in a Shainsa brothel."

Even in the dim light Melora's smile was perceptible. "It may be there will be no pursuit; most likely Jalak's heirs have found him dead and are already squabbling over his property and his wives, and the tenancy of the Great House. The last thing they would want would be to recapture a son of his with a valid claim!"

"Aldones grant it be so," said Kindra, "yet some kinsman of Jalak might seek *kihar* by avenging him—or some rival might want to make very sure any son with a valid claim did not survive him."

Melora gave Rohana's hands a convulsive squeeze, but her voice was calm. "I can ride as far as I must." Her eyes went to her sleeping daughter. "Can I have her with me on my own saddle?"

"Lady, you are heavy; your horse should not carry such a doubled weight," Kindra said. "Those of us who ride lightest will take turns to carry her, so that she can sleep a little longer. Can she ride? We have a spare horse for her, if she can sit alone on a saddle."

"She could ride almost as soon as she could walk, *mestra.*"

"That will do for when she wakes, then; for now, she can sleep," said Kindra, and lifted Jaelle, still sleeping, to her own saddle; she clambered up beside her, while Rohana assisted her cousin to mount. She was fearfully clumsy, and seemed unsteady in the saddle, but Rohana said nothing. There was nothing to say; Kindra was right and they both knew it. She gathered up her own reins, took the reins of Melora's horse to lead it onward across the desert.

Melora was gazing wistfully toward the sunrise. "At this hour, I always long for—oh, I don't know—some snow, or rain, anything but the eternal sand and hot dry wind."

Rohana said softly, "If the Gods will, *breda,* within a tenday you will be back again in our hills and see the snow at every sunrise." Melora smiled, but shook her head. "I can ride now, and guide my own horse, if you think it better."

"Let me lead it, for now at least," Rohana said, and Melora nodded and leaned back in her saddle, bracing herself as best she could against the motion of the beast.

The sun rose, and Rohana saw, as the miles went by under the feet of their horses, that the character of the land had changed. Flat, barren sand-desert had given way to low, rolling hills as far as the eye could see, and a low scruffy ground-cover of thorn-trees and gray feathery spicebush. At first the smell was pleasant, but after a few hours of riding through it, Rohana felt that if she ever again ate spicebread at Midwinter Festival it would choke her. Her throat was dry; she almost regretted the wine she had not been able to drink. Hour by hour Melora seemed more unsteady in her saddle, but she made no word of complaint. Indeed, she did not speak at all, riding head down, her face stony-gray with effort and patience.

As the sun climbed the light grew fiercer, and the heat. Some of the Amazons drew loose folds of their shifts or tunics over their heads; Rohana did likewise, finding the heat preferable to the direct glare. She was beginning to wonder how long Melora could continue to ride—and she herself was weary and saddle-worn almost to the point of dropping from her saddle—when Leeanne, riding ahead, turned back, held up her hand and called to Kindra, who rode quickly ahead to join her, while the others came to a gradual halt.

After a moment Kindra came riding back. "In the next ravine there is a water hole; and some rocks for shelter from the sun. We can lie there during the heat of the day." As they followed her along the path Leeanne indicated, Kindra dropped back to ride beside Rohana and Melora.

"How is it with you, Lady?"

Melora's attempt at a smile only stretched her mouth a little. "As well as I can hope for, *mestra*. But I don't deny I shall be glad to rest a little."

"So shall we all. I wish I could spare you this. But—" She sounded apologetic, and Melora gestured her to silence. She said, "I know perfectly well that you and yours have put your heads in jeopardy for me, and more. God forbid I should complain about whatever you must do for your safety and ours."

Something about the words made Rohana's breath catch in her throat. Melora had sounded, for a moment, almost precisely her old self: gracious, gentle, with the winning courtesy she had shown to her peers and inferiors alike. *She spoke as she would have spoken when we were girls together in Dalereuth. Merciful Evanda, is there really any hope that one day she will be herself again, live out her life happy and free?*

The water hole was a dull, glimmering sheet of water, less than twenty feet across; it looked pallid and unhealthy, but Kindra said the water was good. Behind it were a cluster of blackish-red, forbidding rocks, casting purple shadows on the sand, turning the omnipresent fluff of spicebush to a lavender shadow on the barren space. Even the shadow of the rocks made Rohana think more of snakes and scorpions than cool, inviting rest, but it was better than the burning glare of the Dryland sun at midday.

Rohana helped Melora to dismount, steadying her uneven steps. She guided her to a seat in the shadow of the rocks and went to lead her horse to the water, but Kindra stopped her. "Care for your kinswoman, Lady," she said, taking the bridles of their horses, and, lowering her voice, "How does she, really?"

Rohana shook her head. "So far, she is managing. There is really no more I can say." She knew perfectly well that anyone skilled in such matters would say that Melora should not ride at all. But Kindra knew that, too, and there was simply nothing to be done.

She said, "Are there any signs of pursuit?"

"So far, none," said Leeanne, and Jaelle, who had slid down from her horse, came up to them, and stopped, shyly, at a little distance. She said, "How do you know we are not pursued, *mestra?*" She spoke the language of the mountain country with a faint accent, but understandably; and Kindra smiled at the child.

"I hear no sound of hooves with my ear to the ground; and there is no cloud of sand rising where men ride, within the distance my eyes can see."

"Why, you are as good as Jalak's best trackers, then," said the little girl in wonder. "I did not know that women could be trackers."

"Living in Shainsa, little lady, there is much you do not know about women."

Jaelle said eagerly, "Will you tell me, then?"

"Perhaps when I have time; just for now, do you know enough about horses to know that these must be watered, and cooled?"

"Oh, I am sorry—am I delaying you? Can I help, then?"

Kindra handed the small girl the reins of the horse Melora had ridden. "Walk him slowly back and forth, then, till his breathing quiets and the sweat is almost dry around his saddle. Then lead him to the water and let him drink what he will. Can you do that, do you think?"

"Oh, yes," said Jaelle, and walked off, holding the horse's reins. Kindra followed with Rohana's horse, and Rohana stood, looking after Jaelle. She seemed tall for her age, lightly built, with delicate bones, her hair flaming red, hanging halfway down her narrow back; she wore the nightgown in which she had been wakened—fine-spun Dryland linex, smoothly loomed and embroidered—although one of the Amazons had put a short jacket, much too big for her, around her shoulders. Her feet were bare, but she walked on the hot sand without apparent discomfort. Rohana could not see that the child resembled Melora, except for her flaming hair; but there was no discernible resemblance to Jalak, either.

She returned to Melora, who had stretched out her clumsy body on her riding cape, and closed her eyes. Rohana looked at her with disquiet, then composed her face hurriedly as Melora opened her eyes. "Where is Jaelle?"

"She is helping Kindra to water the horses," Rohana said. "Believe me, she's quite safe and well, and seems not over-wearied by the ride." Rohana lowered herself to the shade beside her cousin. "I wish I had even a little of her energy."

Melora stretched out her thin fingers, clasping Rohana's hand in hers as if hungry for the reassurance of the touch. "I can see how you have wearied yourself for me, too, cousin. . . . How came you into the company of these—these women? *You* have not deserted husband and children as they do . . . ?" The question was evident without words, and Rohana smiled in reassurance. "No, love. My marriage—as I knew it would be—is well enough: Gabriel and I are as happy as any other couple."

"Then how—"

"It is a long story," Rohana said, "and not easy in the telling. It seemed to me that everyone had forgotten you; I had all but forgotten myself, thinking you dead or—or resigned to your life." She added, half defensively, "It had been so long."

"Yes, a lifetime," said Melora with a sigh.

"When you came to me, at first I thought it a dream. I made the journey to Thendara and spoke to some of the Council; but they said they could do nothing, the time was not right for war with the Dry Towns, and they would send no others to die. I had all but resigned myself to thinking that nothing could be done, when by chance—or who knows, by the work of some Goddess—a little band of Free Amazons met with me on the road. They were hunters and traders, and had a mercenary soldier or two to protect them; and in talk with them, I learned that while their band did not venture into the Dry Towns, they knew of one who would. So I went to their Guild-house and spoke with Kindra; and she agreed to attempt the rescue. And so—"

"So here you are," said Melora, almost with wonder, "and here I am. It was true. I had resigned myself, and when I knew I bore Jalak's child again, and that child a son—I was ready to die." Her eyes went to her daughter; Jaelle had finished walking the horse, and was standing beside him as he drank from the water hole. "She is past twelve; at thirteen she would have been chained. I think if you had not come I would have killed her, somehow, and then myself. . . ."

Rohana saw the deep shudder that ran through her cousin's body. She put out her hand quickly to clasp Melora's. "It is past, love. All past. Now you can begin to forget."

Forget? While I bear Jalak's son? Melora did not speak the words aloud, but Rohana heard them anyway. She said very gently, "Well, for now you can rest, and you are free, and safe for the moment. Try to sleep, dearest."

"Sleep." Melora's smile was wry. "I cannot remember when I really slept last. And it seems a pity to sleep now, when I am with you again, and safe . . . and I am happy. . . . Tell me all the news of our kinfolk, Rohana. Does Marius Elhalyn still rule in Thendara? What of our people, our friends—tell me everything," she said yearningly, and Rohana had not the heart to silence her.

"That is a long story and would take many days and hours in the telling. Dom Marius died the year after you were taken; Aran Elhalyn keeps the throne warm from year to year, and as usual the Lord of Hastur is the true ruler; not old Istvan, he is senile, but Lorill Hastur, who was his heir. You recall that Lorill and his sister Leonie were with us at the Dalereuth Tower, when we were girls; I thought perhaps Lorill would move against Jalak for your sake—"

Melora sighed. She said, "Even I knew better than that; the Hasturs must think of more important things than the dues of kin, or how are they better than the Dry-Towners with all their feuds and little wars? There is peace otherwise?"

"Peace, yes . . . Lorill has brought the Terrans from Aldaran to Thendara; they are building a spaceport there, and he has defended his move before the Council; some of them fought it all the way, but Lorill prevailed, as the Hasturs usually do."

"The Terrans," said Melora, slowly. "Yes, I had heard; men like us from another world, come on great ships from the stars. Jalak told such tales only to laugh at them; in the Dry Towns they do not know that the stars are suns like ours, lighting worlds not unlike our own, and Jalak loved to scoff at such tales and say these so-called off-worlders must be clever rogues indeed to fool the Seven Domains, but that no sensible man from the Drylands would be caught so. . . ." She shut her eyes, and Rohana thought, for a moment, that she slept; and was grateful. Knowing that she, too, should try to rest, she closed her eyes, but a shadow fell across her face, and she opened them to see Jaelle standing there, looking down at them. She said in a whisper, "It is you who are my—our kinswoman, Lady Rohana?"

Rohana sat up and held out her arms; Jaelle gave her a quick, shy embrace. "How does my mother, kinswoman? Is she asleep?"

"Asleep; and very weary," said Rohana, rising quickly to her feet. She drew the child away so the sound of their voices would not disturb Melora.

"I will not waken her, but I wanted to see—" and her voice trembled. Rohana looked down at the small serious face, the wide green eyes.

Comyn, she thought; *she does not look like Melora, but her Comyn blood is unmistakable. It would have been wrong, entirely wrong, to leave her in Jalak's hands; not only inhuman but wrong!*

Jaelle said, almost in a whisper, "She should not ride now; the baby will be born so soon. . . ."

"I know that, dear. But we are not safe here, except for a little rest. When we reach Carthon, we will be back in Domain country; and out of Jalak's reach forever," Rohana said quietly.

"But—what will it do to her? The riding, the weariness—" Jaelle began hesitantly, then dropped her eyes and looked away. Rohana thought, *Has she laran?* Even in the telepath caste of the Comyn, the Gift did not begin to show itself much before adolescence; a trained *leronis* could make educated guesses about a child Jaelle's age, but it had been so long since Rohana had used her telepath training that she could not even guess about Jaelle. *Now, when I need to know, the Gift deserts me. . . . Why must women have to choose between the use of* laran *and all the other things of a woman's life?*

She looked down at Melora, wiped out in exhausted sleep, and thought of the time when they had been young girls together, in the Tower at Dalereuth, learning the use of the matrix jewels that transformed energies; working as psi monitors, in the relay nets that kept communications alive in the vast spaces of Darkover, learning the technology of the Seven Domains.

There had been three of them, all the same age: Rohana, and Melora, and Leonie Hastur, sister to that Lorill Hastur who ruled now behind the throne at Thendara. Rohana's family had insisted that she marry, and she had left her work in the Tower—not without regrets—and gone to marry the heir to the Ardais Domain, to supervise the great estate there, to bear sons and a daughter to that clan. Leonie had been selected Keeper; a telepath of surpassing skill, she was now in charge of the Tower at Arilinn, controlling all the working telepaths on Darkover. But Leonie had paid the Keeper's price; she had been forced to renounce love and marriage, living in seclusion as a virgin all her life. . . .

Melora had been given no choice. Jalak's armed men had seized her and carried her away to imprisonment and chains . . . rape and slavery and long suffering.

Rohana's weariness was giving her strange thoughts. *Did Jalak really change her life so much? Do any of us have choice, really? At our clan's demand, to share a stranger's bed and rule his house and bear his children . . . or to live isolated from life, in loneliness and seclusion, controlling tremendous forces, but with no power to reach out our hand to any other human being, alone, virgin, worshiped but pitied. . . .*

Jaelle's small hand touched hers lightly, and the little girl said, "Kinswoman . . . you are so white. . . ."

Rohana quickly returned to reality. She said matter-of-factly, "I have eaten nothing. And in a little while I must wake your mother and see that she eats something, too." She went with Jaelle to where the Amazons were sharing out food and drink; this time she diluted the wine with water from the well and found it sour but drinkable. Kindra went to look at the sleeping Melora and came back, saying, "She needs rest more than food, Lady; she can eat when she wakes," and looked at Jaelle, saying, "You will be sunburned and saddle-sore if you try to ride in that nightgown, *chiya.* Gwennis, Leeanne, Devra, you are smallest, can you find the little one some clothes?"

Rohana was surprised and warmed to see how immediate the response was; all but the tallest of the women went at once to their saddlebags, searching, sharing out what they had: an undervest here, a tunic there, a pair of trousers (Leeanne's, and even these had to be rolled up almost to the knees). Camilla, whose feet were slender, brought out a pair of suede ankle boots, saying, "They will be too big, but laced tightly, they will protect her while she is riding and keep her feet from the sand and thornbushes." They were embroidered and dyed, evidently her own holiday gear, and Rohana was more surprised than ever; a neuter, she would have thought, could hardly have maternal feelings.

Jaelle let Rohana undress her and clothe her in the strange garments, looking around hesitantly toward her mother but forbearing to disturb her. She did say shakily, as Rohana belted in the bulky long trousers, and began to lace up the pretty, dyed-leather boots, "I have always been told it is not seemly for a woman to wear breeches, and—and, I am *almost* old enough to be called a woman."

"Better breeched than bare, Jaelle," Rohana said, adding more gently, "I know how you feel. Before I came on this journey, I believed nothing could force me to wear breeches and boots, but necessity is stronger than custom; and, as for seemliness—well, you cannot ride in that tattered nightgown with your bare haunches in the wind."

Camilla came and checked the fit of the boots. "If they are too loose and make blisters, child, tell me and I will find an extra pair of thick stockings. How do women manage to ride in the Dry Towns, little lady?"

"The saddle is made like this"—Jaelle demonstrated—"so that a woman can sit sidewise and her skirts are not disordered."

"And will slip and fall if her horse stumbles," said Gwennis, "while I can ride as fast and far as any man, and I have never had a fall. But in the Domains, little one, you can wear those clumsy riding-skirts your kinswoman prefers to wear."

"Clumsy they may look," Rohana retorted, "yet I ride well enough in them that I can hunt with hawks in the mountains; in a bad season, when the men cannot spare time for the hunt, the little children or sick people have never had to go without birds or small game for their table, riding-skirts or no; I ride as well in them as in these." *And I wish I were wearing them now,* she thought, but knew the Amazons would have had small sympathy for that.

Gwennis ran her hand along Jaelle's long tangled hair. "It is a pity it should snarl so."

Jaelle's eyes filled with tears; she looked up at Rohana's cropped head and said, "Do you have to cut it?"

Rohana said firmly, "No indeed. But let me comb and braid it tight, so it will not tangle while you ride." She made Jaelle sit down and began to comb the waist-length, fire-red hair. She felt again a pang at the thought of her own hair, which had been her pride, her one claim to beauty. *Gabriel will be angry when he sees my hair, hacked short like an Amazon's.* She thought defensively, as if answering her husband, *I had no choice, it was for Melora's sake.* But Jaelle's should not be sacrificed.

Kindra came and looked at Jaelle, dressed in the too-large odds and ends of Amazon garb, but she made no comment. She drew Rohana aside for a moment and said, "Do not tell the child, and do not disturb your kinswoman, but there is a small cloud of dust at the horizon. It probably has nothing to do with us—it is not in the direction of Shainsa, from which pursuit would come; but I must warn my women, and you, Lady, should be wary."

"Should we be ready to ride again?"

Kindra shook her head. "No. In the heat of the day we dare not; we would die of heat prostration as painfully as on a Dry-Towner's sword. We will hide ourselves among the rocks and hope that this dust has nothing to do with us, or with Jalak and his men; sleep if you can, Lady, but stay near to Melora and the little one, and caution her, if she wakes, to stay hidden in the shadow of the rocks." She signaled to Devra and Rima, saying, "I shall set you two on watch; Leeanne and I have been leading and tracking all the night, and Nira has lost enough blood that she needs rest. But call me at once if that dust seems to turn in our direction. Lady, go now and try to sleep. And you too, *domnina,*" she added to Jaelle.

"May I bring my bread and finish it before I sleep?" Jaelle asked, and Kindra said, "Of course," as she went away to rest. Gwennis, reaching into her pocket, smiled at Jaelle and said, "Are you hungry, *chiya?* Here is a sweet for you; suck it before you sleep, and it will keep your mouth from getting too dry in this heat."

Jaelle accepted the candy with a small, shy inclination of her head. She looked around at the Amazons with curiosity—though Rohana could see that she was trying hard to repress it and, in politeness, ask nothing. At last she said to Gwennis, "Some of you look—almost like men. Why is that?"

Gwennis glanced at Rohana; then said, "Yes; Leeanne and Camilla. They have been neutered; their bodies are not actually those of women. There are some women who feel that womanhood itself is too great a burden to be borne, and choose this way, even though the laws forbid it."

"But you are not like that," Jaelle said, and Gwennis smiled.

"No, *chiya.* It is troublesome to be a woman, from time to time—I imagine you are old enough to know so much—but all in all, I think I would rather be a woman than not, even if it were easy or simple to find anyone, in these days, who will risk the laws against that sort of mutilation. All in all I find it more pleasure than trouble."

Rohana, too, had been curious about this; like all women reared in the protective, pampered world of the Domains, she had always thought—when she had thought about the Amazons at all, which was seldom—that they were mannish women, or plain girls such as would burden their families to find any sort of husband. But, except for the two neutered women, and the mountain tomboy with the two knives, none of them were anything like that. Kindra was gentle and almost motherly, as was Fat Rima; and the others seemed none too different, clothing and cropped hair apart, from her own waiting-women. As for Gwennis, she seemed almost like a little girl herself, not much older than Jaelle, or Rohana's own daughter.

Jaelle smiled at Gwennis and said, "You would be beautiful if you let your hair grow long."

It was Rohana's own thought. Gwennis said with a kindly smile, "Why, perhaps so, little sister, but why should I want to be beautiful? I am not a dancer, or an actress, or a lyric performer, that I should need so much beauty!"

"But if you were beautiful, you could make a good marriage," Jaelle said, "and you would not need to be a soldier or a hunter to earn a living."

"But, little one," said Gwennis, laughing, "I do not want to make a marriage, not even a good one."

"Oh?" Jaelle pondered this for a moment; it was easy to see that this was a new idea to her. "Why not?"

"For many reasons. Among others," she said deliberately, "lest I should find that my husband sought to keep me in chains."

Rohana felt it like a blow; Jaelle put her hand to her mouth and bit at the knuckle. Her face went white, then a desperate, agonized crimson. She made a small strangled sound, turned away and ran to her mother's side, flinging herself down on the blanket beside her and burying her head in her arms.

Gwennis looked almost as dismayed as the child. She said, "My Lady, I am sorry, I should not have said that."

Silently, Rohana shook her head. She said at last, "She had to know."

Suddenly Jaelle has realized what this is all about. Before this it has been an adventure, safe because her mother is here; but she has not truly understood. And now—now she knows.

And a shock like this, to a girl just on the threshold of womanhood . . . a girl with extraordinary telepath potential . . . Rohana was not sure just how she knew this, but she was sure of it. *What will it do to her?* Slowly, Rohana went and laid herself down in the shade beside Melora and Jaelle. Melora slept heavily. Jaelle's face was buried in the blanket, her thin shoulders trembling violently. Rohana reached out to draw her close, comfort her, as she would have done with one of her own children; but Jaelle resisted her stiffly, and after a moment Rohana let her be. *I am almost a stranger to her,* she thought in despair. *I can do nothing for her. Not yet.*

Chapter Four

Three days and nights had passed, and Rohana had given up expecting pursuit or capture. If there had been pursuit at all, it had taken the wrong direction or been left hopelessly behind. Or else Melora was right, and Jalak's heirs, finding him dead or wholly disabled, were busily dividing up his remaining wives and his property.

Gradually the character of the land had changed: the first days had seen dry, burning, gritty sand, broken only by scruffy thornbushes and feathery spicebush; now there were endless, trackless leagues of low, rolling dunes, covered by grayish Dryland bracken, with now and again a sharp black outcrop of rock. *As if,* Rohana thought, recalling the old tale, *when Zandru made the Drylands, even the very rocks rebelled and broke through their cover, thrusting up in rebellion . . . the very bones of the world refusing to be covered in these barren leagues of desert and sand. . . .*

It was nearing twilight; the fierceness of the sun was tempered by the lengthening angle of the shadow. All that day they had seen no living thing, and Kindra had cautioned them to drink sparingly from their waterskins. "Should anything delay us," she had warned, with a sharp glance at Melora, "we might not reach the next water hole this night . . . and we cannot carry too much in reserve."

Melora rode just ahead of her, head down, braced stiffly in her saddle. She had not spoken since they left the site of their noonday rest, and when Rohana would have felt her forehead for fever, she had turned away, refusing the touch, refusing even to meet Rohana's searching eyes. Rohana was desperately worried about her. This trip was far too long, far too arduous for any pregnant woman. Melora had not complained; Rohana had the chilling sense that she had ceased to care. She seemed to have expended all the effort of which she was capable in making the original contact with Rohana that had resulted in her rescue; that accomplished, it seemed to Rohana that Melora no longer cared. She had not even asked any further questions about her home, about their kin, about what lay ahead when they should leave the Dryland country and return to the Domains.

The sun descended, a great blood-colored orb, blurred at the horizon with the first clouds Rohana had seen since they crossed the river at Carthon. Kindra, riding ahead, stopped to let Rohana come up with her, and pointed to the purpled sunset. She said, "Those clouds hang over Carthon; and beyond Carthon we are in the Domains again. Even if Jalak came so far, he would have to come with an army. Safety lies there. How does the Lady Melora?"

"Not well, I fear," Rohana said soberly, and Kindra nodded.

"For her sake I shall be glad when we cross the river and we can travel at a pace more fitting her condition. It goes against me, to force the pace this way, but there is no safety for any of us in this country."

"I know," Rohana said, "and I am sure Melora understands. She knows, better than any of us, the dangers for women of the Domains, here in the Dry Towns."

Kindra said, "Well, we will make camp yonder"—she pointed to one of the great black tumuli of rock, upthrust like jagged teeth against the low horizon—"and there, if the Goddess is good to us, we will cook some hot food, and perhaps even wash the dust from our faces."

"Do you know every water hole in this territory, Kindra?"

The woman shook her head. "I have never traveled here before, but I can see the *kyorebni* circling as they do only over water. And tomorrow before midday perhaps we will ford the river, and be safe in Carthon." She grimaced. "I am hungry for hot roast meat and good hot soup instead of this unending porridge and dried meat and fruit, and some fresh-baked bread instead of hardtack."

"Me too," Rohana said, "and I shall stand surety for the best meal we can buy in the best cookshop in Carthon, believe me, once we cross the river!"

Kindra looked back and said slowly, "Pray to your Goddess, Lady, that *domna* Melora is able to enjoy that meal. Ride back to her, Lady Rohana, and reassure her that we will make camp just a little farther on. She seems almost ready to fall from her saddle." Her face, in the gathering darkness, was deeply troubled.

Rohana did as she was bidden, sighing. It seemed that never in her life had she known such prolonged and incessant fatigue. The thought of sleeping in a bed under a roof, eating hot, fresh-cooked food, bathing in a hot tub of scented water, comforts she had taken so much for granted that she never even thought about them, made her whole body ache with an almost sensuous longing.

She supposed the Amazons would think such longings soft and weak. Well, she would show them that she could endure hard living if she must; she was *Comynara* and she would be strong as any man of her caste. But she wished there were a few comforts for Melora.

Melora was riding next to Fat Rima; as Rohana neared them the big Amazon lowered her voice and said, "Look to your kinswoman, Lady. No, she has not complained, but I earned my bread for a time as a midwife in the Lake Country, and she has a look to her that I do not like."

It's good to know there is a midwife among us, at least. Rohana drew her horse even with Melora's; Melora raised her head, slowly and wearily, and her look shocked Rohana. Her face was swollen, with a dull pallor; even her tight lips were colorless. She tried to smile at Rohana, but could not quite manage it. Her face contracted in a sudden spasm of pain, and Rohana knew at once what her kinswoman had been trying to conceal.

"Breda, you are in labor!"

Melora grimaced. "For some hours, I fear," she said apologetically. "I had hoped we could reach a campsite near to water. I am very thirsty, Rohana," she added, in the first hint of complaint Rohana had heard from her lips.

She leaned over and took Melora's hands in her own. She said, "We are very near to water, love; can you ride just a little way farther, just a few hundred steps more? See?" She pointed through the falling dusk. "One or two of them are already dismounting; see there? Listen; I can hear Jaelle laughing."

Melora said softly, "She is like a little animal let out of a cage. I am so glad that they are so good to her. Poor little rabbit, I have had so little strength to spare for her, on this journey. . . ."

"I am sure she understands," Rohana said softly.

"I hope she does not," Melora said, and in the twilight her face twisted. They were near to the place where the others were dismounting; again Rohana heard Jaelle's light merry laugh. In the days of the journey she had quickly become a favorite with all the Amazons; laughing, chattering, full of endless questions about the world and the life before her. They had competed with one another for the privilege of carrying her on their saddles when she grew weary, saved her such tidbits and choice morsels as they could scrounge from their sparse meals, told her stories and sang songs to while away the tedium of the trip, even fashioned her small toys and playthings from odds and ends.

If nothing else, we have freed Jaelle, and she is a daughter of whom any of the Domains could be proud. Jalak's blood may be a handicap when the time comes for her to make a good marriage, but that can be overcome. She has laran, *I am sure; I will have her tested when we come to Thendara.* . . .

She slid from her horse, relinquished it to Rima, who came to lead it away, and tenderly helped Melora from her saddle. Melora's knees buckled and Rohana had to support her cousin's weight in her arms; she held her upright, but suddenly frightened, called to Kindra. After a moment the Amazon leader came from the shadows, took in the situation with one appraising glance. "So your time has come, *domna?* Well, only two things in this world are sure, birth and next winter's snow, and both come when they will and not when it is convenient. Thanks to the Goddess, we are near to water. A pity we had to abandon the tent; no child should be born with only the sky for a roof."

"Better under the free sky than in Jalak's Great House," Melora said fiercely, and Kindra held her hand for a moment. "Can you walk just a little, Lady? We will prepare a place for you to rest."

"I can do what I must," Melora said, but she leaned very heavily on her kinswoman, and Rohana felt an all-encompassing dread. Here, in the black night, in the desert, with no skilled hands to help . . . *Rima had been a midwife, perhaps; but the Free Amazons renounced womanhood.* . . .

"I had hoped that I could hold out till we reached Carthon," Melora said, and Rohana realized that her kinswoman was sharing her sense of unease and dread. Rohana must somehow manage to be strong and confident.

She said, "Look. They are making a fire, we will have light, and some hot food, and there is water near," as she guided Melora's steps toward the kindled blaze. "And we are in luck; one of these women was once a midwife!"

She was dismayed, now that she could see Melora by firelight: hands and ankles swollen, eyes red and feverish. *She should have told us hours ago; we should have stopped . . . but then the child would have been born without water near.* . . .

Melora sank down gratefully on the pile of blankets that the Amazons had arranged for her. For a moment she buried her face in her hands; Rohana could hear her breathing, loud and hoarse like an animal. Then she raised her head and said plaintively, "I am thirsty, Rohana—will you bring me a drink?"

"Of course." Rohana began to rise, but Melora clutched at her hands. "No, no stay with me. Did I tell you why I suddenly knew I must escape, get Jaelle away, or kill her myself before this child was born?"

"No, dear, you didn't tell me—"

"When I found her—playing with Jalak's other little daughters—they had all of them, even Jaelle, tied ribbons about their hands, playing at being grown up, and in chains—"

Rohana felt herself shudder, deep down in the bones. She said quickly, "Dear, let me go. I will fetch you a drink; do you think you could eat a little?" She left Melora lying on the pile of blankets and went to the darkness near the water hole, kneeling to rinse the cup, trembling, glad to hide her face in the darkness.

After a little she managed to control herself and come back. Kindra said from the fire, "Tell her we will have some hot food soon, and something to drink; it may strengthen her for what lies ahead. And I think we can manage torchlight later, if we need it."

Rohana somehow managed to thank her. She came back and knelt beside Melora, who was lying with her eyes closed; Rohana held the cup to her lips, and Melora gulped it thirstily. Rohana said, "We shall have some hot food for you soon; try to rest." She went on talking, saying anything that crossed her mind, trying to sound encouraging; after a few minutes, Melora put out a hand to stop the flow of chatter.

"*Breda*—" She used the *casta* word for "sister"; in the intimate inflection it also meant "darling." "Don't lie to me. In memory of what we both were, once, don't try to pretend, as if I were still an outsider; what is going to happen?"

Rohana looked at the sick woman, heart-wrung. *So after all she is still Comyn, still telepath; she can read me so easily.* "What can I say to you, Melora? You know as well as I that no woman so far in pregnancy should travel so far or so fast. But other women have survived worse than this, and lived to frighten their granddaughters with the tales of what they endured. And I'll be with you."

Melora clasped her hand. "Better you than the evil crone who brought Jaelle into the world," she said, clinging to her cousin's fingers. "She would not even free my hands. . . ." She ran her fingertips, as with a long-habitual gesture, along the jagged scars at her wrists. "Jalak swore if I bore a son he would give me whatever I asked, save my freedom; I had it in my mind to ask for her head."

Rohana shuddered, was grateful when Fat Rima approached them; she said, "Here is our midwife; she will do what she can for you, *breda.*"

Melora looked up at her; she felt—Rohana sensed it—skeptical and more than a little frightened. But she said (and again, poignantly, Rohana was reminded of the lighthearted and gracious girl Melora had once been), "I thank you, *mestra;* I did not know any of the Free Amazons would choose such a womanly trade."

"Why, Lady, we earn our bread at any honest work," Rima said. "Did you truly think we are all soldiers and hunters? The Guild-house in the city of Arilinn, where I was trained, has a specialty of training midwives; and we compare everything that is known about the problems of birth from Temora to the Hellers, so we are the best of midwives; even on the great estates, sometimes, women will send for us. Now, my Lady, let me see how far this thing has gone, and how long you must expect to wait here." She knelt, feeling all about Melora's body with gentle, expert hands. "Well, it is a strong child, and a big one, too."

She broke off as Jaelle came running toward them. The child's face was drawn and white in the firelight. "Mother—oh, Mother—" she said and burst into tears.

Rima said firmly, "Come, my child, that will not help Mother. You are almost a woman now yourself; you must not behave like a baby and trouble us."

Melora dragged herself upright, letting herself lean heavily on Rohana. "Come here, Jaelle. No, let her come to me, I know she will be good."

Struggling to fight back her sobs, Jaelle came and knelt beside her mother; Melora seized her in a fierce embrace and said, not to any of them, "It was worth it all. You are free, you are free!" She kissed the small wet face hungrily, again and again; then laid her hand under Jaelle's small quivering chin and looked at her a long time in the wavering firelight before saying, "You must go now, my darling, and stay with the other women. You cannot help me now, and you must leave me to those who can. Go, my dearest love, try to sleep a little."

Crying, Jaelle let Gwennis lead her away into the darkness beyond the campfire. Rohana heard the child sobbing softly for a long time; then she was quiet and Rohana hoped she had cried herself to sleep. The night wore on slowly. Rohana stayed with Melora, holding her hands, now and then sponging her sweaty face with cold water. Melora was still and patient, doing what she was told, trying to rest between the spasms; now and then she talked a little, and after a time Rohana, with a shudder, knew Melora had lost track of where she was and what was happening. She talked to her own mother, years dead; once she started up with a shriek, crying out curses in the Dry-Town language; again and again she sobbed and entreated them not to chain her again, or cried out, over and over, "My hands! My hands!" and her fingers went again and again to the long ragged scars at her wrists. Rohana listened, murmured to her soothingly, tried now and again to break through the delirious muttering. . . . *If Melora knew she was here and free, here with me.* . . . She tried, with all her telepathic skill, to reach her cousin's mind, but all she could feel was horror and long dread.

Blessed Cassilda, mother of the Domains . . . Evanda, Goddess of light,

Goddess of birth . . . merciful Avarra . . . what she must have endured, what horror she must have known. . . .

None of the other women slept, although Kindra had ordered them all to bed; Rohana could sense, like a tangible vibration in the air, their awareness, their concern. *At times like this it is a curse, to read the thoughts of others. . . .*

Once, when Melora slept for a moment, in exhaustion, Rima met Rohana's eyes over the struggling body and shook her head briefly. Rohana closed her own eyes for a moment. *Not yet! Don't give up hope yet!*

Rima said, pityingly, "She has no strength left, I think, to be free of the child. We can only wait."

Rohana suddenly knew if she stayed there another moment she would break into hysterical screams and sobs, herself. She said thickly, "I will be back in a moment," and rose, plunging away, around the campfire, toward the crude latrine the Amazons dug at their camps. She leaned against the harsh rock-face, covering her face, struggling not to vomit or scream. After a moment, controlling herself a little, she went to the fire, where a pot had been left with the hot drink of fermented grain, which the Amazons used in place of bark-tea or *jaco,* just simmering. She dipped herself out a cup and sipped it, fighting for self-control. Kindra, tall and almost invisible in the darkness, stopped and laid a hand on her shoulder.

"Bad, my Lady?"

"Very bad." Rohana felt for a moment that the hot bitter brew would choke her. "She is not—not a woman who could ever have borne children easily; and here, without skilled help, after so much suffering—after this hard journey—without care or comfort . . ."

Kindra's sigh seemed to come from the very depths of her being. "I am sorry, truly sorry. It is cruel that she should suffer so much for freedom, and never live to enjoy it, after so much courage. It must add greatly to her suffering, to know that even if her child is born alive, there will be none to suckle him or care for him."

A resentment she had not known she felt, against these women who had chosen to spare themselves the pains of womanhood, surged up in Rohana, out of control. She had forcibly to restrain herself from flinging the scalding contents of her cup at the older woman. She said bitterly, "You! What would *you* know of that fear for a child?"

"Why, as much as you, Lady," said Kindra. "I bore four children before I had turned twenty. I was given in marriage very young, and my first child died before I could bring him forth; the midwives said I should not try to bear another, but my husband was eager for an heir. My second and third children were daughters both, and he cursed me. I came very near to death with my fourth child—he was three days in the bearing—and this time, instead of curses, when he saw our son, he showered me with gifts and jewels. And then I knew a woman's lot in our world was wholly accursed. I was of no value; the daughters I bore him at risk of my life were of no value; I was nothing but an instrument to give him sons. And so when I could walk again, I left my children sleeping, one night, and cut my hair, and made my way alone to the Guild of Free Amazons, and there my life began."

Rohana stared at her in horror. She could think of nothing to say. Finally she stammered, "But—but all men are not like that, Kindra."

"No?" Kindra said. "I rejoice you have not found them so, Lady, but that is luck and good fortune, and no more." She glanced at the reddening sky, and said, "Hush," listening to the sounds that had changed, in the last few minutes, from long, patient sighs to harsh, gasping breaths and hoarse short grunts of effort. She said quickly, "Go to her, Lady. It cannot be long now."

There was enough light in the sky now so that Rohana, coming to kneel beside Melora, could see her kinswoman's face, strained and swollen as she fought, panting, for breath.

"Rohana—Rohana—promise me—"

Rima said, imperatively, "Don't talk, dear; pay attention now. Take a good deep breath, and hold it. Come now, dear, that's right, another nice long breath. Now, bear down—come on, hold on tight, just push—"

Rohana let Melora take her hands, cling to them with agonized strength as the inexorable process of birth seized her body, wrenching her into spasms. Rima said, in the singsong that Rohana supposed was common to all midwives, "Come on, now, sweet, that's a good girl, another nice big push, hard now. That's right, *that's* a good girl, come on now, just a little bit more—"

Rohana felt Melora's nails dig into her hand; the contact wrung her with agony. Wide open to her cousin, she felt the tearing pain wrenching at her own body, gasped with the weight of it. *Too much, too much . . . worse than when Kyril was born. . . .* She felt the smothered scream Melora was fighting back, thought in dismay, *Gabriel stayed with me; now I know how he felt . . . I know now he felt all I was enduring. I never knew . . . too much, too much. . . .*

She felt the pain ebb away, felt Melora relax for a moment. Rima said authoritatively, "Come on, now, breathe deep, get ready for the next one; a few more good ones like that and it'll be all over." But Melora ignored her, clutching at Rohana's hands. She gasped, "Rohana, promise—promise—if I die—care for my children. My baby, take my baby—"

She gasped, and arched her body again under the fierce, wrenching pain.

Rohana could not speak; she reached for contact with Melora again, directly to her mind.

—I swear it, darling, by the Blessed Cassilda and by the Lord of Light. . . . They shall be as my own children, may the Gods seize me if I make any difference between them and the children born of my own body. . . .

Melora whispered, "Thank you—I knew—" She collapsed again. Over her head, dark with sweat, Rima looked up, and Rohana met Kindra's eyes. Kindra said quietly, "I had better fetch Jaelle now."

Rohana looked up indignantly; looked at the swollen, unconscious body, the spreading bloodstains, feeling the wrenching agony seize Melora again, and herself flinched before the terrifying assault on body and mind. She said in violent indignation, "How can you? Is this any place for a little girl . . . ?"

Kindra said gently, but inexorably, "It is her right, Lady. Would you wish to sleep through your mother's death-bed? Or are you still lying to yourself, Lady Rohana?" She did not wait for Rohana's answer. Rohana, kneeling, letting Melora grip her hands with that anguished death-grip, heedless of Melora's nails digging into her and drawing blood, was seized again by that moment of terror she had known at the climax of her own child-beds. . . . *Breaking, tearing, splitting, coming apart . . . dying.* . . . Rohana struggled to keep herself a little apart from Melora's terror, to give her kinswoman some strength, something to cling to outside her own agony and fear. She held Melora, murmuring endearments, whispering, "We're with you, love, we're right here, we're going to take good care of you . . ." but she did not know what she was saying.

For the first and last time Melora shrieked aloud, a long, terrible cry of anguish and dread; and then, just as the sun was rising, into the terrible silence there was another sound: a strange, sharp, shrill sound, the uplifted howling of a newborn child.

"Praise to Evanda," said Rima, holding up the naked, bloody child, feet first. "Listen to how strong he is! I didn't have to slap *this* one into life—"

Melora whispered, almost inaudibly, "Give him to me," and reached out for him, her face changing. *The never-failing miracle,* Rohana thought. Always, no matter how hard and terrible the birth, there was this moment of joy, when the face changed, alight and glowing. *Melora looks so happy, so happy; how can she?* Rohana wondered, not remembering her own happiness. Rima wrapped the baby in a fold of clean towel she had laid ready, and placed him on Melora's flaccid belly. She said matter-of-factly, "He will do well enough."

"Jalak's son," Melora whispered, and the joyous smile slipped away. "What will become of him, poor little wretch?"

Rima said sharply, "My Lady—"

Melora reached out her hands. She said, "Jaelle—Jaelle, come here and kiss me—oh, Jaelle—"

Rima cried out in consternation; blood came forth in a great gush, and Melora sighed and fell back, her face white and lifeless. And there was no sound in the sunrise except the crying of Melora's motherless children.

"Will you truly have Jalak's son to foster, Lady Rohana?" Kindra asked.

The sun was high in the camp. Jaelle had cried herself to exhaustion and was lying on the sand between them, limp, like some bedraggled little animal. Rohana was half sitting, half lying against a pile of saddlebags. She had wrapped the naked child and thrust him inside her tunic against her breasts, where he squirmed and nuzzled, already lively and seeking the nourishment he did not know would be denied him. Rohana patted the warm bundle tenderly. She said, "What else can I do, Kindra? I swore to Melora that her children should be to me as my own in all things."

Kindra said fiercely, "He is a male of Jalak's blood; do not your kinsmen and your foster-brother's blood cry out for revenge, that you should cherish him? Is there not blood-feud and a life between you and Jalak's son, my Lady?" She bared her knife, handed it to Rohana, hilt first. She said, "He cost Melora her life, so she came never to her hard-won freedom; and he is Jalak's son. Avenge your kinsmen, Lady."

Chilled, sick with horror, Rohana knew that Kindra spoke no more than simple truth. The men of the Ardais and Aillard Domains would have echoed her words: Jalak's son must pay for Jalak's crimes.

She felt the child move against her body, warm and strong. *Melora's child; and I took him up from her dead body.* She looked at Jaelle, who was curled tight beside them, her eyes shut in rejection. *She is Jalak's child, too. Must she pay?*

Kindra said earnestly, "Rohana, he will die, whatever you do now. There is no nurse for him, no food, no proper care. Don't wring your heart for him; let him lie here beside his mother."

Slowly, Rohana shook her head. She handed back the knife, meeting the Amazon's eyes. She said, "Blood-feud and revenge are for men, Kindra. I am glad to be a woman, and bound by no such cruel law. Let this child's life, not his death, pay for my foster-brother's death; Ardais lost a son in Valentine, so this boy shall be called Valentine." She laid her hands, as if in ritual, on the small squirming body, "And he shall be foster-son to Ardais, in place of the one who died at Jalak's hands."

Kindra put the knife away, raised her face with a grim smile. She said, "Well spoken, my Lady. An Amazon would say so, indeed; but I had not thought you were so free to discard the laws of your clan and caste."

Rohana said violently, "I hope I will always feel free to ignore any law so cruel! It may be that he will die, as you say; but not at my hands, and not if I can save him!"

Kindra nodded. "So be it," she said. "I will speak to Rima; she has fostered motherless babes before this. Our women sometimes die in bearing, too, and Rima is skilled in all the secrets of the Arilinn Guild-house." She rose, saying, "There is another child of Melora's who needs your care; look to her, Lady."

She went off to join the other Amazons, who were burying Melora in the hill behind the water hole. Rohana turned to Jaelle and began to stroke her hair gently.

"Jaelle," she coaxed, "don't cry any more, darling. I know nothing can heal your grief, but you must not make yourself ill with crying. I swore that I would be a mother to you, always. Come, darling, look at me," she pleaded. "Don't you want to see your little brother? He needs someone to love and comfort him, too." She added, *"You* had your mother for twelve years, Jaelle; this poor little mite lost his mother before she had ever looked into his face. He has none but his sister; will you not come and help me to comfort him?"

Jaelle pulled away with a shudder of violent revulsion, her sobs rising again to a frenzy, and Rohana, in despair, let her go. Jaelle had not spoken since Melora's death; Rohana feared that in those last few moments of Melora's life, spent in terror and dread, in the fear of death, the child's mind had been roughly opened to the terrifying telepathic rapport, her latent Gift wakened in that dreadful instant of shock and agony.

No one could have blamed Melora for reaching out, with her last conscious thought, in the only way for which she still had strength—for one last, desperate attempt to touch her beloved child. But what had it done to Jaelle?

As if he sensed Rohana's desperate unease, the baby began to stir and fret and whimper inside her tunic again. She stroked him, thinking of the long leagues that still lay between them and Carthon, where she might at least find a wet-nurse for the child. For him it was a simple matter of survival; handled, fed, carefully cared for, he would survive. But what of Jaelle? She would not die, but what had that shock done to her? Only time would tell.

Perhaps the Amazons can do more for her than I. I am, in her mind, still part of that moment of terror and death. But perhaps they can comfort Jaelle and help her.

She must leave it to them, at least until Jaelle was calm and recovered her senses. After that—Rohana looked longingly at Jaelle's soft tangled hair, but dared not touch her—after that, only time would tell.

Chapter Five

Twelve days later, Rohana looked down from the top of the pass that led away into the valley of Thendara.

"Jaelle," she called, turning back, "come here and see the city of your forefathers!"

Obediently the young girl rode forward, looking at the ancient city that lay in the valley below them. "This is the city of the Comyn? I have never seen so big a city; Shainsa is not half so large." She looked down with fascination and, it seemed, with dread, at the wide-flung buildings, the Comyn Castle beyond. "Tell me, kinswoman; is it true that the Comyn are descended from the Gods? My—I have heard it said, and I have heard—I have heard it denied. What is the truth?"

How deftly she avoids either her father's name or her mother's! In twelve days she has spoken of neither of them. Rohana said, "I can tell you only what I have heard myself. The story goes that Hastur, son of Aldones, Lord of Light, came to our world at Hali; and that he wooed and won Cassilda, daughter of Robardin, mother of the Domains; and thus all those of the blood of Hastur are kin to the Gods. If it be true, or only a beautiful fable, I know no more than you; but this much is true beyond question. All those of the blood of the Hasturs, all the kin of the Seven Domains, have the *laran* powers, the psi gifts that set them apart from all other men born on this world."

"Are all of the Comyn of Hastur blood, then?"

"In the beginning, yes; although in the great days of the Towers they were separated into the seven families we now call the Domains. All are of the blood of Hastur and Cassilda. But it is sure that none of us are Gods or anything like it, my child."

Would that we were. I should know better what to do with you, little one. Rohana sighed, touching the warm sleeping weight where Melora's baby slept, tucked inside her tunic for warmth; it was cold at these heights, even in summer. Jaelle was no longer openly hostile to Rohana, but she had not turned to her for comfort, either. Nor had she been willing to touch her little brother, or so much as look at him.

Every one of the Amazons—even the two neutered women, Leeanne and Camilla—had shared the burden of the newborn child in those first dreadful days, before they reached Carthon and found a wet-nurse for him. They had all spared sugar and meal to make gruel for him, and, knowing that Rohana was exhausted and burdened with grief, had taken turns to carry him and try to soothe his fitful crying. Only Jaelle had steadfastly ignored her brother; had refused, even when urged repeatedly by Kindra, whom she adored, to hold him in her arms or even look at him.

As if her thoughts had reached him, the baby Valentine began to stir and fret, and Rohana beckoned to the wet-nurse from Carthon; she rode forward, took the child from Rohana, and opening her dress, lazily put the child to her breast. She was, Rohana thought, a singularly stupid woman —*I would not let her rear a pet dog, let alone a child*—but he throve on her milk, and for now that was all that mattered.

Should any woman alive be allowed to live so ignorant that she is no better than a dairy-animal? The Free Amazons openly despised her, and with the pride seen in the invincibly stupid, the wet-nurse treated them with contempt. Rohana—sharing their contempt for the woman, but needing her services—tried to mediate an uneasy peace.

Rohana stretched her back (the sling in which she carried the baby during the day gave her cramps in the shoulders) and tried to think ahead. She had pledged Melora that she would rear the children as her own. Her husband would not object; he had said often that he would welcome more children, regretted that Rohana had borne only three. But now reaction had set in, after Rohana's first elation at saving Melora's son alive. *What have I taken upon myself? My eldest is already almost grown; my daughter is already five, and since two of our children are sons, Gabriel agreed I need have no more. And now when I thought I was done with it, again I have all the worry and trouble of rearing a very little one! No doubt Gabriel will begin to talk, again, of having another so he will not be brought up alone.*

Am I only an instrument to give him sons? she thought, and was horrified at herself. Quickly she turned her thoughts elsewhere: *What place can we make in the Domains for the son of a Dry-Towner? And Jaelle, so cold and withdrawn, will she ever accept me?*

It was too much to expect, that she could find comfort in the child. I am a mother myself, that was the greatest comfort to me, that something remained of Melora . . . but Jaelle is a child. She sees only that poor little Val robbed her of their mother. . . .

Kindra drew her horse close to Rohana's. She said, "Lady, is that where the Terrans are building their spaceport? What do they want here, these men from another world?"

"I do not know." Rohana gazed at the great dirt-colored slash beyond the city of Thendara, where, it seemed, several miles of the valley had been ripped open by their enormous machines and smoothed to an eerie, unnatural flatness. Part of the area had been paved, and buildings were sprouting in strange, unlikely shapes. "I have heard that our world is at a crossroad of their travel roads among the stars; they seem to have trade caravans between the many worlds as we have between the towns in the Lake Country. I don't know what their trade may be, no one has bothered to tell me, though I think Gabriel knows." She fancied a look of contempt from Kindra. *Why should I be content with ignorance? Oh, damn these Amazons, they are making me question everything: myself, Gabriel, my very life!*

It made her voice edgy. "These people, they call themselves the Terran Empire, came first to Caer Donn, near Aldaran, and began a spaceport—a small one, they could not build so wide in the mountains there—and dealt with the accursed Aldarans. Hastur offered them a place here to build their spaceport where the climate would be more to their liking—I have heard that to them our world seems cold—and so we can keep watch over their doings; but of course we have nothing to do with them."

"Why not?" asked Kindra. "I should think that a race which can travel from star to star as readily as I can ride from here to Nevarsin would have a great deal to teach us."

Rohana said stiffly, "I do not know; Hastur has willed it so."

"How fortunate are the men of the Domains, that they have the son of Hastur to teach them," said Kindra, her gray eyebrows lifting. "A stupid woman like myself would have felt that a race which can make trade caravans among the stars might outreach even a Hastur in wisdom."

Rohana was annoyed by the sarcasm, but she felt too deeply indebted to Kindra to take her to task for it. "I have heard it explained thus: Hastur feels there is much in their way of life that might be more of a threat than we can know at once. They have, for a beginning, leased the spaceport here for five hundred years, so that we will have plenty of time to choose what we can learn from them."

"I see," said Kindra, and was silent, thinking it over, studying the enormous slash on the horizon, where strange machines crawled and unknown shapes grew against the horizon.

Rohana, too, was silent. As they rode this last mile, it seemed that she was, in a curious way, changing worlds. For near to forty days she had lived in a world as alien to her as the world of the Terrans below; then she had grown used to it, and now she must again change worlds, make ready to reenter her own.

At first the world in which the Amazons lived had seemed hard and comfortless, strange and lonely. Then she had realized that most of the strangeness was not the physical lack of comfort at all. It was quite different. It was easy to get used to long hours of riding, to unfamiliar and ugly clothes, to bathing as one could in stream or river, to sleeping in tents or under the sky.

But it was not nearly so easy to give up the familiar support of known protections, known ways of thinking. Until she came on this journey, she had never quite realized how much all her decisions, even small personal ones, had been left to her father and brothers, or, since she married, to her husband. Even such small things as *Shall I wear a blue gown or a green? Shall I order fish or fowl for the table tonight?* had been dictated less by her own tastes and preferences than Gabriel's wishes. She had not realized, until Jaelle and the newborn Val were hers for fostering, how much even what she had said to the children or done for them had been based, openly or not, on how well Gabriel would think of her for her dealings with them.

A strange, painful, almost traitorous thought kept returning: *Now that I know how to make my own decisions, will I ever be content again to let Gabriel decide for me?*

Or, if I do go back, is it only because it is so much easier to do exactly what is expected of a woman of my caste?

They had ridden through the great city gates of Thendara now, and people came out to stare at the sight of a Comyn lady in the company of an Amazon band. Inside the city Kindra dismissed most of the Free Amazons to the Guild-house in Thendara. Accompanied only by Kindra, Jaelle, and the wet-nurse with the baby, Rohana rode on to the Comyn Castle.

In the suite that had belonged to the Ardais clan for uncountable years, Rohana summoned the skeleton staff of servants who remained there all year round—most of the Ardais retainers returned home to Castle Ardais, with their masters, when Council season was over—and ordered that comfortable quarters be found for the wet-nurse and the baby; that Kindra be treated as an honored guest; and that Jaelle, whom she introduced as her foster-daughter without going into details, be made comfortable in a room near her own, and provided with suitable clothing.

Then she dispatched a message to the Princess Consort announcing her return, and summoned her own personal maid, bracing herself for the inevitable: the woman's shocked reaction to her hacked-off hair, her completely unsuitable clothes, the state of her hands and complexion, roughened with riding and outdoor living.

It will be worse than this, when I return to Ardais. Why should I need to be always beautiful? I am not a dancer, or a lyric performer. And I have long ago made my good marriage. But there are those who would think Melora's rescue too dearly bought at the cost of my hair and my complexion!

Just the same, even while she chafed at the woman's cluckings and scoldings for getting herself in such a state, it was good to lie again at full length in a hot bath, scented with balsam; good to soothe her roughened and chapped skin with creams and healing lotions, to be dressed again in soft feminine garments.

When she was ready, word had come that the Lady Jerana would receive them; and that the Lord Lorill Hastur wished to receive the Free Amazon leader as well. When Rohana relayed this royal command—for, though veiled in exquisite courtesy, that was what it was—Kindra smiled wryly.

"No doubt he wishes to be certain I have not committed the Domains to war with the Dry Towns."

"Nonsense," said Rohana irritably. "He is Melora's kinsman too; I am sure he wants to thank you!"

"Well, Lady, whatever it is, it is for me to obey the Lord Hastur," said Kindra, "so we shall see."

When Jaelle was brought to them, Rohana drew breath in amazement at the child's surprising beauty. The grime of travel, and her ill-assorted cast-off garments, had obscured it before. She was tall for her age, her skin very pale, dusted with a few faint amber freckles; her hair had been washed and hung below her waist, the color of new copper. She had been prettily dressed in a delicate green gown, just the color of her eyes. Truly, Rohana thought, a daughter of whom any Comyn household could be proud. But would they see it? Or would they see only that she was Jalak's daughter?

The Lady Jerana, Princess Consort of Aran Elhalyn (she had been born an Aillard and was Rohana's cousin), a languid, fair-haired, spoiled-looking woman, greeted Rohana with the embrace due a kinswoman, kissed Jaelle coldly and spoke graciously to Kindra.

Why shouldn't she be gracious? It's all she has to do in life, Kindra thought.

"So this is our dear Melora's child," said Jerana, looking the girl up and down. "A pity she is Jalak's daughter as well; it will be hard to arrange a marriage for her that suits her station. Has she *laran?*"

"I do not know. I have not had her tested." Rohana's voice was cold. "I have had other things to think about."

Lorill Hastur said, "Such brilliantly red hair often indicates an extraordinary degree of psi power; if she were so gifted, she could be sent to a Tower, and the question of marriage need not arise."

Rohana thought that in any case it was too soon to worry about the marriage of an orphan only twelve years old, who had not yet recovered from multiple shocks; but she did not say so. She suspected Lorill picked up the thought anyway. He was a slightly built, serious-looking man about Rohana's own age; like many of the Hasturs, his flaming hair had already begun to turn white. He frowned in Jaelle's direction, and said tactlessly, "I suppose there is no doubt she *is* Jalak's child? Now if Melora had been already pregnant when she was captured, or if we could put it about that this was the case—"

Jaelle was biting her lip; Rohana feared she would cry. She said coldly that, unfortunately or not, there was no doubt about the girl's parentage.

"I assume Jalak is dead?"

Kindra said that they did not know for certain. "But there was no pursuit, Lord Hastur, and when we reached Carthon, there were already rumors of change in the Great House at Shainsa."

"Of course you know what troubles me," Lorill Hastur said. "Your rash act—I am speaking to you, Rohana; I know the Free Amazon only did what you employed her to do—your rash act could have plunged us into war with the Dry Towns."

Kindra's eyes met Rohana's in a brief, vindicated grin. She might as well have said, aloud, "I told you so."

"Lorill, you are Melora's kinsman, too! Should I have left her to die in slavery, and her child in Jalak's hands?"

The man looked deeply troubled. "How can I say that? I loved Melora; I cannot express my grief that she did not live to enjoy her freedom. As a man, and her kinsman, what else can I say? But the peace of the Domains is in my hands. I cannot go to war to right one person's wrongs, or I am no better than the Dry-Towners with their endless tyrannies of blood-feud and revenge. I must try to do what is best for everyone within these Domains, Rohana; Comyn and commoner alike. What of our farmers and peaceful citizens who live along the borders of the Drylands? Must they live in fear of revenge and reprisal by the Dry-Towners? And if the truces we have worked so hard to make are broken, that is all they can hope for."

Suddenly Rohana felt sorry for him. He was speaking only the truth. His personal feelings could not be allowed to conflict with his duty as Councillor. He was Melora's nearest living kinsman; the duty he had shirked, for whatever good reason, had been done instead by women. That could not be easy for a Hastur to swallow.

"Kinsman, that is of little moment now. What does matter is the guardianship of Melora's children."

"Children?" Jerana asked. "Has she others?"

"The son she died in bearing, Lady." Rohana glanced uneasily at Jaelle. Jerana should have had tact enough to send the child away before discussing her future before her; but it was not for Rohana to suggest it.

Jerana said, "Oh, they can be fostered somewhere. If Melora had lived, I suppose we'd have had to do something for them, but we can't be expected to take any kind of responsibility for the children of some Dry-Town tyrant. Put them out to fosterage somewhere and forget about them."

Even Lorill flinched at the brutal tactlessness of that. Rohana said firmly, "I pledged Melora before she died that I would rear her children as my own." *Melora knew our kinfolk better than I, it seems.*

Jerana shrugged. "Oh, well, I imagine you know best. If Gabriel does not object, I'll leave it to you." Rohana realized that Jerana was glad she could dispose of it so perfunctorily.

Lorill Hastur turned to Kindra and said, "Was it you who accomplished the rescue, *mestra?*"

"My women and I, Lord Hastur."

"We are deeply in your debt," Lorill Hastur said, and Rohana realized he was trying to soften Jerana's indifference. "You did what my kinsmen and I failed to do. What reward will you ask of me, *mestra?*"

Kindra said with dignity, "My lord, the Lady Rohana has paid my women generously; you owe me nothing more."

"Still, there is a life between us," Lorill said.

"No, for I failed. My appointed task was to restore the Lady Melora to her kin," said the Free Amazon.

Rohana shook her head. "You did not fail, Kindra; Melora died free, and she died happy. But it is for me, not you, Lorill, to offer her what extra reward she will ask."

Kindra looked up at them both, and moved to Jaelle's side. "Then, since you both offer a gift," she said, "I ask this: give me Jaelle to foster."

Lorill Hastur said, in shock, "Impossible. A child of Comyn blood cannot be reared among Free Amazons!"

Rohana, too, had felt a moment's shock at this request—such presumption! But Lorill's words angered her as much as Jerana's rudeness had done. "Fine words, Lorill. But you were willing to sit uncaring in Thendara, and let her be reared in chains by Jalak." She beckoned Jaelle to her, and said, "Jaelle, before your mother died, I swore to her that I would rear you as my own daughter, born of my body. I know she meant I should keep you in my house, bring you up as my own child. But you are twelve years old; and if my own daughter, at twelve years old, came to me and said, 'Mother, I do not want to live with you, I want to be fostered by such and such a one,' then—if her choice of foster-mother were such a one as I could trust—then I would consider carefully her wishes in the matter. You have heard Kindra ask for you, and"—she looked with angry defiance over Jaelle's head, at Lorill Hastur—"it is *mine* to decide. But will you not come with me to Ardais, and be *my* daughter?" she pleaded. "I loved your mother, and I will be a mother to you as well. You will have my daughter and her friends for playmates and sisters, and you will be brought up as your mother and I were reared, as a *Comynara,* as is fitting for our caste."

Jaelle, darling, you are all I have of Melora. . . .

The hard little face was unyielding, strangely set. "And when I am grown, kinswoman?"

"Then, birth or no, Jaelle, I will arrange for you a marriage as good as for my own daughter—" and then she knew, suddenly, that she had lost. Jaelle's face went cold.

She said, "I want only to live where I will never be in subjection to any man. If Kindra will have me to foster—" She went and laid her hand in the Free Amazon's, and said, "I do ask it, kinswoman."

Rohana thought, almost in despair, *It is too late to treat her as a little child. She has known so much that would age her before her time.*

Still, she was a Comyn daughter, and might have *laran.* She said gravely, "Kindra, she must not be neutered. Promise me that."

Kindra's face held outrage. "I see you have understood all too little of the Amazons, Lady. We do not neuter women."

"I saw the two of your band—Leeanne and Camilla—"

"We do not neuter our women," Kindra repeated implacably. "Now and again, a woman will be so maddened with hate for her own womanhood that she will persuade or bribe some healer to break the law for her sake; often they come to us afterward, and we cannot cast them out; there is usually nowhere else they can go, poor souls. But women who come to us first, instead, usually learn self-respect, not self-hate. I do not think—if she is fostered among us—that she will come to such hatred." She put her arms lightly around the child's shoulders, turned to Jaelle and spoke directly to her, but not as if she spoke to a child at all; she spoke as if to an equal, and Rohana felt a strange emotion that after a moment, incredulously, she identified as *envy.*

"You know, Jaelle, you cannot, by the laws of our Guild, be accepted yet as an Amazon; even our own daughters must wait until they are legally old enough to be counted as women, to marry, or to choose. When you are fifteen, you will be permitted to make that choice; until then, you will be only my fosterling."

Lady Jerana said querulously, "I think this whole business is outrageous; can't you stop it, Lorill?"

Rohana thought, with anger she did not know she possessed, that it had been outrageous enough to discuss the girl before her face as if she were deaf, dumb, blind and feeble of wit. Lorill Hastur seemed to echo her indignation as he said, "It is Rohana's right to choose where Jaelle should be fostered, Jerana; she first consulted you, and you chose not to exercise your privilege of decision. Now I will defend Rohana's right to choose."

Oh, good for you, Lorill! She looked at him gratefully, thinking that being Chief Councillor couldn't be the most pleasant of jobs. Jerana's pretty, vapid face was spiteful.

"Well, Rohana, at least you need not worry about finding someone to marry Jalak's daughter; I have always heard that the Free Amazons are eager to find pretty young girls whom they can convert to their unnatural way of life, turning them against marriage and motherhood, making them haters of men and lovers of women. It was clever of you to let Jaelle among them. . . ."

White with anger, Rohana felt that she would like to slap Jerana's sneering mouth, silence the filthy implication of those words. Then, as she saw Kindra smiling, she knew her sojourn with the Amazons had changed one thing forever.

She would return to her old life, and the world of women. For the rest of her days she would tune her decisions to the invisible winds of Gabriel's whims, perhaps. But one thing would never be the same; and it was a difference that changed the world.

Rohana knew, now, that she was living that life *by choice;* not because her mind was too narrowly bounded to imagine any other life, but because, having known another life and weighed it, she had decided that what was good in her world—her deep affection for Gabriel, her love for her children, the responsibility of the estate of Ardais that demanded the hand of its lady—outweighed what was difficult, or hard for her to accept.

And so nothing that any woman like Jerana might say could ever hurt her or make her angry again. Jerana was simply a stupid, narrow, unimaginative and spiteful woman; she had never had any opportunity to be otherwise. Kindra was worth a hundred like Jerana. *I am free. She could never be,* Rohana thought.

She said, almost gently, "I am sorry you feel that way about it, Jerana, but this seems to me a happy choice for Jaelle; you did not choose to foster her yourself, and since you do not love her, it is just as well. I would be selfish indeed to keep Jaelle tied to the ribbons of my sash, just to comfort me in my bereavement."

"You will give her to that—that Free Amazon, that shame and scandal to womanhood?"

Rohana said serenely, "I know her, Jerana, and you do not." She held out her arms to Jaelle and said, "I told you that if my own daughter made such a choice, I would listen to her. Be it as you wish, then." She folded Jaelle in her arms, and for the first time the little girl hugged her, hard, kissing her on the cheek, her eyes shining. Rohana said, "I give you to Kindra to foster, Jaelle. I bid you be a dutiful daughter to her; and do not forget me."

Then, letting Jaelle go, she stretched her hands to the Free Amazon. The older woman's calloused, sunburned hands met her own; the level gray eyes looked straight into hers. She said quietly, "Lady, may the Goddess deal with me as I with Jaelle."

Rohana's mind lay open to the touch. Again, and for the last time, she felt the Amazon's immense kindness, steadiness; she knew she would trust Kindra with her life—or with this other life so precious to her. She was surprised to feel that her eyes were filling with tears.

She thought, *I almost wish I were coming with you, too. . . .*

Kindra said softly, aloud, "So do I, Rohana." There was no formal "My Lady" now; they had gone too deep for that. Rohana could not speak, even to say good-bye; she laid Jaelle's hand in Kindra's and turned away.

The last thing Rohana heard, as they left the audience chamber, Jaelle skipping along at Kindra's side, was the little girl asking eagerly, "Foster-mother, will you cut my hair?"

Part Two

MAGDA LORNE,
Terran Agent

(Twelve years elapse between the first part and the second.)

Chapter Six

If there was a noisier job anywhere in the Galaxy than building a spaceport, Magda Lorne hoped she'd never have to listen to it.

And a *long* job. This one, it seemed, had been building most of Magda's life. She had been born at Caer Donn, the Terran Empire's first foothold on Darkover; had been eight years old when the HQ had been moved here to Thendara; and the spaceport had been under construction ever since.

Even the violence of the autumnal storm had only dulled, not silenced, the roar of the building machines, although the mountains behind the city had disappeared into a blur of white snow, and even the old town beyond the HQ was all but invisible. Magda went through the heavy storm doors into the unmarried women's quarters and simultaneously slammed out storm and noise. Inside it was soundproofed. The lights here were yellow Earth-normal. At least this building was finished, she thought, and *quiet.* All during her brief marriage to Peter, they had lived in Married Personnel Quarters; unfinished and the soundproofing still not complete. And she wondered, sometimes, just how much the perpetual tension of the noise had contributed to the breakup of that marriage. She shrugged the thought off, opening the door of her room. *It would never have worked, no matter what the conditions. I don't think I was ever in love with Peter, and I'm perfectly sure he was never in love with me. We'd just been together too much,* her thoughts ran on the familiar track, *and not quite enough, not quite enough to get it out of our systems. When that wore off, we realized there wasn't anything else to hold us together.*

Recalling her marriage to Peter, her thoughts continued along an annoying, smooth and familiar groove. *Where is he? He's never been away so long before. I hope nothing's happened to him.*

She sternly admonished herself not to worry. Like herself, Peter Haldane was a graduate in Alien Anthropology from the Empire University; like herself he had been brought up since childhood on Cottman IV, which the natives called Darkover; and like herself, when they returned to the planet that both was and was not their home world, they had gone directly into Empire Intelligence work. The Empire might call the work they did *Intelligence* and think of it as elaborate spying, but to Magda, and Peter, and the others like them—not many, here on Darkover—it was the best training for an alien anthropologist: to mingle with the people of their world, to get to know them in a way anthropologists not reared here never could. Peter was evidently on a lengthy assignment somewhere. But this time he had been gone so *long!*

And there were the *dreams.* . . .

Magda knew she should report the dreams. In the course of her Alien Psychology credentials, she had been tested for psi potential; and had tested very high. Just the same, she was reluctant to make an official report of her recurrent dreams—all of which, without exception, warned her that Peter Haldane was in trouble—as if to do so might give them some reality. *Dreams are just dreams, that's all.* . . .

Nevertheless, when she finished shedding her heavy outer layer of clothing, she went to the communicator button.

"Personnel? Lorne here. Is that you, Bethany? I don't suppose Haldane has reported back, or sent word, has he, in the last twenty-eight?"

"Not a word, Magda," the woman in the coordinator's office replied. "I knew it; you're still carrying around a yen for Peter, aren't you? You've been on the button every twenty-eight, asking for news."

"Yen be damned," Magda said irritably. "In case you've forgotten, I've known Peter since I was five years old; we grew up together, and I worry." *And that,* she thought, cutting the connection, *is why I don't report the dreams. I'm sick and tired of every bored woman here speculating, out loud, how long it will be before Peter and I get together again! Is it going to get so bad that one of us has to put in for a transfer and leave Darkover? Damn it, I grew up here, this is my home, too!*

I wonder if Peter feels that way too? We never talked about it. We never talked much about anything, outside of bed. That was half our trouble. . . .

She still felt irritable as she took off the Darkovan outfit she wore for her work outside the HQ gates. She wore the ordinary dress of a woman of Thendara: a long, full skirt of heavy cloth, woven in a tartan pattern, a high-necked and long-sleeved tunic, embroidered at the neck, and ankle-high sandals of thin leather. Her hair was long and dark, coiled low on her neck and fastened with the butterfly-shaped clasp that every woman wore in the Domains. Magda's was made of silver, a noblewoman would have worn copper, a poor woman's clasp would have been carved of wood or even leather; but no chaste woman exposed her bare neck in public.

She hung the Darkovan clothes away, first rubbing their folds with an aromatic mixture of spices; it was as important to smell right as to look right, in the Old Town. She showered and got into Terran clothes, thin crimson tights and a tunic with the Empire emblem on the sleeve. They felt chilly, and she thought it made no sense to wear thin synthetics here and heat the buildings to a temperature that made them practical. It just made the Terrans unfit for the climate.

It's like the yellow Earth-normal lights everywhere in the HQ: it just keeps everyone from adapting to the red sun. I know, it's Empire policy everywhere; and when spaceport personnel are likely to be transferred all across the Galaxy at a few days' notice, of course maintaining a stable set of standard conditions makes sense.

But it's hard on those of us who really live here. . . .

She was trying to decide whether to have food sent to her room, or to go to the HQ cafeteria and eat in company, when the communicator summoned her again.

"Lorne here," she said, in no pleasant temper. "I'm off duty, you know."

"I know—Montray here. Magda, you're an expert on the Darkovan languages, aren't you? Isn't there a special inflection for speaking to the nobility, and a feminine mode of address?"

"Both. Do you want a capsule lecture, or a library reference? My father compiled the standard text, and I'm working on a revision."

"Neither; I want you to translate," the coordinator said, "You're our only resident female expert; and I'm mortally afraid of offending the lady by some improper form of speech. I've heard about the various gender taboos, but I don't know half enough about them, and that's a fact."

"The lady?" Magda's curiosity was piqued; noblewomen were rarely seen even on the streets of Thendara.

"A lady of the Comyn."

"Good God," Magda said. She had rarely set eyes on a single member of this royal and aloof caste; even the men of the Comyn, if they felt the need to speak with one of the representatives of the Empire—which didn't happen often—did not hesitate to summon them into Thendara instead. "One of the women of the Comyn has summoned you?"

"Summoned, nothing! The lady's in my office right now," said Montray, and Magda blinked.

She said, "I'll be there in three minutes." Her normal duties did not include working as a translator, but she could understand why Montray was unwilling to use the regular staff.

This was completely unprecedented; a woman of the Comyn, in Montray's office . . .

Magda put on her outdoor clothing. She had removed her butterfly-clasp; she started to coil up her long hair on top of her head. The Darkovans certainly knew that Terrans went, in Darkovan clothing, into the Old Town, just as the Terrans knew that a considerable number of the Darkovans who worked at construction jobs on the spaceport were paid to pass along information about the off-worlders to the Darkovan authorities. But neither side took official notice of it. It was important for Magda to look like any other Terran translator. But her bare neck prickled at the exposure.

I ought to act as if I didn't even know about the proper degree of exposure for a Darkovan woman. But she felt bare and immodest; she took the braid down and let it hang loose down her back.

The noise had shut down now to a nighttime roar; her feet, in thin shoes, slid on the slippery, sleeted sidewalks. She was glad to get into the Temporary HQ building, where Temporary Coordinator Russ Montray—Darkover wasn't important enough in the Empire, yet, to be assigned a proper Legate for liaison with the native residents—met her in the outer office.

"It's good of you to do this for me, Magda. It won't hurt to let them know we have some people who can speak the language the way it really ought to be spoken." He was a plump, balding man in his forties, with a habitual worried look; even in his centrally heated office, with the thermostat turned up to the maximum, he always looked, and was, cold. "I took the lady into my inner office," he said, and held the door for her.

He said, in his poor and stumbling *cahuenga* (the lingua franca of the Trade City), "Lady Ardais, I present to you my assistant, Magdalen Lorne, who will speak with you more easily than I can do." He added to Magda, "Tell her we are honored at her visit, and ask what we can do for her. She must want something, or she'd have sent for us instead of coming here herself."

Magda gave him a warning look; she guessed, from the flash of intelligence in the lady's eyes, that she understood Terran Standard—or that she was one of the occasional telepaths rumored to be found on Darkover. She began, *"Domna,* you lend us grace. How may we best serve you?"

The woman looked up, meeting Magda's eyes; Magda, who had spent her life on Darkover and knew the nuances, thought, *This woman is from the mountains; the women of the lowlands are more timid with strangers.* As custom demanded for all of the Comyn, she had brought a bodyguard—a tall, uniformed man in the green and black of the City Guard—and a lady companion, but she paid no attention to either of them. She said quietly, "I am Rohana Ardais; my husband is Gabriel-Dyan, Warden of Ardais. You speak our language well, my child; may I ask where you learned it?"

"I spent my childhood at Caer Donn, Lady, where the citizens mingled more with the Terrans than is the custom here; all my playmates were Darkovan children."

"Ah, that explains why you speak with the accent of the Hellers," Rohana said. Magda, studying her with the eyes of a trained observer, saw a small, slightly built woman, not nearly as tall as Magda herself. It was hard to tell her age, for there were no telltale lines in her face, but she was not young; the heavy auburn hair, coiled low on her neck and confined with an expensive butterfly-clasp of copper set with green gems, was liberally streaked with gray. She was well and warmly clad in a heavy dress of thick green wool, woven and dyed and elaborately embroidered. She bore herself with great poise, but her hands, clasped in her lap, moved nervously on one another.

"I have come here, against the will of my kinfolk, to ask a service of you Terrans. Perhaps it is foolish, a forlorn hope—" She hesitated, and Magda told her that it would be an honor to serve the Lady Ardais.

Rohana said quietly, "It is my son; he has disappeared. We feared foul play. Then a workman who is employed here in your port on one of your great buildings—surely it is no secret that many of these are paid by us to tell us what we wish to know about your people—one of these workmen, who knows my son slightly, reported to us that he had seen my son here, at work. This was some months ago; but it seemed to us, at last, that any rumor was worth investigating. . . ."

Startled, Magda relayed Rohana's words to the coordinator. "It is true that we employ many Darkovans. But—your son, Lady? Most of those we employ are put to work as common laborers, running machines, doing carpentry and building—"

"My son is young, and eager for adventure, like all men his age," Rohana said. "To him, no doubt, it would seem a great adventure, to mingle with men from another world. He would not hesitate to work as a layer of bricks or a pavement-maker, for the sake of that. And as I say, he was seen and recognized here." She handed Montray a small packet wrapped in silk; he unwrapped it, slowly, glancing at Magda as she translated Rohana's words.

"I have brought a likeness of my son; perhaps you could ask those of your men who are responsible for the work crews of our people, when he was last employed here."

Inside the silk was a copper locket; Montray opened the clasp to reveal a miniature painting. His eyebrows rose as he looked at it.

"Take a look at this, Magda."

He handed it to her, and she looked on an elaborately painted likeness of Peter Haldane.

"I can see by your faces that you both recognize my son," Lady Rohana said. Magda's first thought was, *This is impossible, insane!* Then sanity came to her rescue. *A chance resemblance, no more. A fantastic coincidence.*

Montray was on the communicator. "Get me a personnel solido and photos of Peter Haldane, Bethany. Magda"—he turned back to her—"you can explain."

Magda tried. She could see faint beads of perspiration along the lady's hairline; whether from nervousness or from the heat of Montray's office— or both—she could not tell.

"Chance resemblance? Impossible, my child. He was recognized by the color of his hair, and that color is borne by none but Comyn, or those of Comyn blood."

"It is not rare among Terrans, my Lady," Magda said. (She had known this; Peter had made jokes of it. "On the Darkovan side they think I must be some nobleman's bastard!") "It carries among us no claim to nobility, but means only that one's parents had red hair, and a certain racial makeup." She broke off as Bethany came in, took the small solido and personnel printout that bore a color photo of Peter Haldane. She handed them to Lady Rohana without comment.

Rohana studied them a moment, then looked up, her face gone white. "I cannot understand this. Are you very sure he is not one of ours, in some disguise that has misled you?"

"Very sure, my Lady; I have known Peter Haldane since childhood."

"How can this be? One of your Terrans, so like to one of us . . ." Her voice wavered. "I can see that anyone might be deceived, if this man wore Darkovan dress. And your man is missing, too?" Not until hours afterward did Magda realize that she had not told Rohana this. "Strange. Well, I see I must search elsewhere for news of my son."

When she had taken leave of Montray, formally, she turned to Magda, lightly touching her hand. She looked at her, a long and searching look. "Somehow I think I have not heard the end of this matter," she said. "I thank you for your courtesy. A day may come when I can help you, my girl; until then, I wish you well."

Magda was almost too surprised to speak; she managed a formal word of thanks, but Rohana kindly waved her away, summoned her companion and the sweating Guardsman and departed.

Left alone with Magda, Montray exploded, "Well, what do you think of that!"

"I think the poor woman is worried to death about her son."

"Almost as worried as you are about Haldane, huh?"

"A lot more. Peter is a grown man, and entirely on his own. Why should I—"

"Damned if I know *why* you should, but you are," Montray said. "And I gather her son is a grown man, too. But on a damn feudal world like this where fighting duels is the most popular indoor sport, I gather there's real cause for concern if the man of the house doesn't come home."

"Feudal is hardly the proper description—"

"OK, OK, Magda, you're up on all the little nuances and fine points; I'm not, I don't want to be. All I want is away from this damn place; you can have my job any time I can get a transfer out—or you could, except that on a world like this a woman wouldn't be allowed to take it. I should think you'd want out, too. The point is: I understood most of what the lady was saying to you. It looks like you've made a useful contact. It's not easy for a woman to do anything much on this world, but if you have an in with someone on the top levels, in the Comyn—"

Magda found she did not want to explore this point just now. She reminded Montray, rather tartly, that she had come here in off-duty time; he told her to put in a voucher for the extra pay, and let her go.

Yet, back in her own quarters, removing her heavy clothing, she thought about what he had said. Rohana had spoken formally at first, and when she had called Magda "my child" she had spoken in the inflection normally used to a servant or an inferior—or someone like a translator. But at the end she had called her "my girl," in the intimate mode she would have used to a young woman of her own caste. Was it only random kindness?

Outside, the snow had turned to heavy sleet; Magda went to the window, drawing aside the curtains to look out through the doubled, soundproof glass into the silent raging of the storm.

You're out there somewhere, Peter, she thought. *What are you up to? If there's really any such thing as ESP, I ought to be able to reach you somehow. Damn it, Peter come home, I'm worried, damn you.*

She thought, *How Peter would laugh at me. He's somewhere, following some obscure lead he's found.* Magda knew she was a good Intelligence officer; knew Peter was considered a gifted one. A woman could not do too much in the Intelligence line on a planet like Darkover, where strong codes and taboos regulated female behavior; Magda knew that elsewhere, on a less strongly patriarchal planet, where men and women were equals, she could have had more scope for her talents. *Yet Darkover is my home. . . .*

One of the messier moments, during the tense weeks before the showdown that had ended their brief marriage, had been Peter's accusation that she was jealous, jealous because he was allowed to accomplish more than she was on a world like Darkover. And of course, it was true. . . .

Oh, Peter, come home. I'm worried. Feeling foolish, yet taking it seriously, Magda strained in concentration—as she had done at the New-Rhine-Rakakowski Institute on Terra, making her significantly better-than-chance scores on her ESP cards—to try to send a message, if such a thing were possible. *Peter, Peter, we are all worrying. At least let us know you are safe.*

But there was no sense of contact, and at last, drained and weary, feeling it had been an idiotic endeavor, Magda gave up and went to bed.

That night she dreamed of Peter Haldane, but he was laughing at her.

Chapter Seven

The season drew on, and the cold thickened. Magda, who had been born in the mountains, did not mind the cold; at least, not when she could wear suitable clothing for it. But most of the Terrans burrowed indoors like animals in their winter holes, venturing out only when they must; and the crews of the starships that touched down here confined their stay to the minimum, seldom venturing out even into the port and never going into the Old Town.

Even Magda, careless of official disapproval, wore her Darkovan dress more and more around the HQ, suffering the inconvenience of long skirts and heavy petticoats for their warmth. One afternoon when she came in from a day spent in the Old Town, it was snowing so heavily that the idea of changing into the thin Terran synthetics seemed insane; she went directly to Personnel, and the station where her observations were recorded. Montray's pretty assistant, heavily sweatered, looked at her with envy. "I don't blame you for going native. I'm almost tempted to transfer to your section so I can dress for the climate! I don't know how you manage to get around in those things—but they do look warm!"

Magda grinned at her. "Usual question."

"Usual answer, I'm afraid," Bethany said soberly. "No word from Peter. This morning the boss took him off the active-duty list; he's officially reported PMOD—provisionally missing on duty. Pay suspended subject to official contact, and so forth."

Magda flinched. The mechanism was in motion for having him declared *Missing, presumed dead.*

Bethany said, trying to comfort her, "Nothing's final yet. Maybe he found a friendly place to stay and just settled in for the winter. He couldn't travel in this, even if he was all right."

Magda's smile only stretched her mouth. "It's not nearly winter yet. The time when travel becomes impossible and all business shuts down for the spring-thaw is almost four months away. The passes aren't even closed into the Hellers."

"You're joking!" Bethany looked into the raging storm and shivered. "But you should know, you've been out in it. Summers, I think you have a peach of a job—nothing to do but mix with the crowds in the city and listen to gossip. But in weather like this—I'm surprised they didn't name this planet *Winter.*"

"They couldn't; there's already one called that. Read the records someday. Speaking of records, I'd better get mine set up."

"Is that really all you do—listen to gossip?"

"That, and a lot more. I take note of the fashions being worn by women, make linguistic notes on new expressions and changes in the local argot . . . languages change all the time, you know that."

"Do they really?"

"Do you use the slang expressions now that you did when you were seven years old? It doesn't matter if an agent uses some outdated expressions; people do pick up little tags of speech from their parents, and everybody tends to use expressions that were common in their own teens, when peer relationships were being established. The one thing no undercover agent on the Darkovan side can do is speak as if he'd learned the language from a book; so I work all the time keeping us all up to date. Montray gets away with it because he's meeting people as a Terran, and it's a compliment for him to go halfway by speaking their language at all; speaking it too well would be a subtle form of one-upmanship that would rouse all kinds of psychological resistances in the Darkovans he meets. They're *supposed* to be able to speak better than he does. But the agents who work on the Darkovan side can't make mistakes even in slang. And everybody has to keep up with common usage."

Bethany looked puzzled. Magda elucidated: "Well, look. For instance; there's a word which means, literally, 'entertainer,' or 'singing woman.' It's in the standard texts. But if you called a ballad-singer, or one of the soprano soloists with one of the orchestras in Thendara, by that word, her father or brother would call you out in a duel—call a man out; a woman using such a term would simply be regarded as very vulgar and ill bred."

"An *entertainer?*" Bethany repeated the word in amazement. "Why? It sounds inoffensive enough."

"Because for decades that particular word has been a polite euphemism —the kind of word you can use in front of a lady—for 'prostitute.' No respectable woman on Darkover would soil her mouth with the word *grezalis*—that's vernacular for 'whore'—and no man but a boor would use it in front of her. The respectable concert soprano is a 'lyric performer,' and don't forget it if you go to a concert in Thendara!"

Bethany shivered. "I had no idea a translator's work was so complicated."

"It's true; you have to take extra pains to avoid giving offense. One of my main jobs is to check through official speeches to make sure our translators and speech-writers avoid words with accidentally offensive connotations. For instance: you know how our standard official speeches—not just on Darkover—are full of expressions of friendship and brotherhood? Well, the commonest expression for 'friend and brother' in the *casta* language—that's the official language in Thendara—is red-flagged as an absolutely taboo term for official speeches here."

"Why, for heaven's sake?"

"Because the commonest expression meaning 'friend and brother,' if you don't get the inflection just right, can get you in an *incredible* amount of trouble. In the impersonal inflection it expresses the purest sentiments of fraternal charity and humanitarian concern, and is perfectly suitable for official and diplomatic use. Just the same it's red-flagged, because a lot of our officials simply cannot *pronounce* the language well enough, and even if they *mean* to use the impersonal inflection, they're likely to *sound* like the wrong one. And if you use that word—the same word—in the personal inflection, it means 'brother' in the sense of family intimacy and closeness, and is too familiar; while if you happen to use it in the intimate inflection, you're defining the person addressed as a homosexual—and your lover. Do you see now why it's an absolutely forbidden term in official language?"

"Good God! I certainly do." Bethany giggled. "No wonder Montray has his own private linguist to write his speeches!" The women exchanged a conspiratorial chuckle; Montray's ineptitude in the Darkovan language was a standing joke in the HQ. "And so that's why you go over all his speeches personally? You know everything about Darkover, don't you, Magda?"

Ruefully, Magda shook her head. "No, certainly not. No Terran can." *And if any Terran could, no Terran woman could.* The thought was as bitter as ever. But she put it aside.

"It would have been different, if the Terran HQ had stayed at Caer Donn. There, the Terrans and Darkovans met more or less as equals, and we could mingle with them *as* Terrans. There was no need for undercover agents. But here we have to work undercover; the Comyn have completely refused to cooperate. They leased us land for the spaceport, let us hire workmen for construction jobs and allowed us to build the Trade City, but beyond that—oh, hell, Beth, didn't you get all that in Basic Orientation?"

"Yes, I did; Class B Closed, very limited trade, spaceport personnel restricted to the Trade City. No fraternization."

"So, you see? No other Terran children will get the kind of chance that Peter, and Cargill, and I did—to grow up playing with Darkovan children, learn the language from the ground up. That's why there are so few of us who can actually pass, on the Darkovan side, *as* Darkovan—and I'm the only woman."

Bethany asked, "Then why didn't they keep the HQ at—where was it—Caer Donn? If they were so much friendlier there?"

"Partly the climate," Magda said. "If you think this is cold, you should see what winter's like in the Hellers. Everything comes to a dead stop, from midwinter-night to the spring-thaw. The climate of Thendara is pleasant—well, moderate anyway—by contrast. Then there was the problem of roads and transport. There's just not enough *room* at Caer Donn for the kind of spaceport the Empire wanted, not without leveling a major mountain or two, and the Ecological Council on Terra wouldn't have given permission for that even if the locals hadn't objected. Then there's the question of trade and influence. The Aldarans back at Caer Donn rule over miles and miles of mountains, forests, valleys, little villages, isolated castles and a few thousand people. In the Domains there are five good-sized cities and a dozen little ones, and Thendara alone has almost fifty thousand people. So there really was no choice at all, for the Empire. But it means Empire agents, anthropologists and linguists, have to work undercover, and we're still working out the parameters. There are literally thousands of things we don't know yet about this culture. And the Comyn's policy of not helping us at all is a terrific blockade; they don't *forbid* people to work with us, but the people here just *don't* do anything the Comyn disapprove of. And that means that those few of us who can pass as Darkovan can practically name our own terms; because even keeping up with the language is a difficult and complicated undercover job. Of course I can't do *all* the things, here, that a male agent would do. One of a male agent's prime tasks, in linguistics, is to keep up with the dirty jokes; and of course I don't hear them."

"Why would anyone need to know dirty jokes? Is this for the Folklore Reference section?"

"Well, that too. But mostly to avoid accidentally offensive—or unintentionally funny—references. You grew up on Terra; would you say, in a serious and formal context, that somebody or other was *always in the middle?*"

"Not unless I wanted my audience to crack up and start snickering and leering. I see what you mean; you have to red-flag the punchline of the current dirty jokes or any specially notorious old ones. But you don't hear the dirty jokes—"

"No; I have my own specialty. I mentioned that some expressions aren't used by women—or in front of them, among the polite. There are also special expressions used mostly *by* women. Darkover isn't one of those cultures that has a special women's language—there are some of *them*, Sirius Nine for instance, and *there's* a real translator's nightmare! But no culture is ever completely free of 'women's talk.' Not even Terra. For instance, I came across a footnote in my language history text saying that women in one of the major prespace cultures used to refer to their menstruation as 'the curse.' "

"Did they really? Why?"

"God knows; I'm a linguist, not a psychologist," Magda told her. "Listen, Beth—this is fun, but it isn't getting my work done."

Magda bent over her keyboard and began to type her day's notes into the computer terminal for analysis, programming and storage by the computer experts who would later code them.

A joke is making the rounds in Thendara, she typed. *Heard on three occasions in the last five days. Details vary, but basically concerns two (three, five) Terrans who were on an outdoor escalator on the port, which malfunctioned, stranding the Terrans for several hours (three days in one version) between the first and second level pending repairs. Implications: Terrans are so addicted to mechanical transport that walking down a half flight of unmoving stairs is physically or psychologically impossible. The implications of this: Darkovan concept of Terrans as physically weak, incapable of effort. Secondary implication: envy of Terran access to machinery, the ease of Terran life-styles? The growing frequency of jokes about Terrans, most of which appear to concern our life-style with special reference to its physical ease, would imply . . .*

"Magda," Bethany interrupted, "I just got a flash from Montray; do I tell him you're here?"

Magda nodded. "I'm still officially on duty."

Bethany spoke into the communicator, listened a moment and said, "Go on in."

Inside, Montray frowned irritably at Magda's Darkovan clothes. "A messenger just brought word from the Comyn Castle," he said. "One of the Big Names over there—one Lorill Hastur—has just sent for me, and included a request that you—you personally—be brought along to translate. I imagine your friend, the Ardais lady, has been talking about your special skill with the language. So I have a problem." He frowned. "I know perfectly well that it's not according to protocol, and probably improper, too, to take along a woman as official translator on the Darkovan side. On the other hand, I understand one simply *doesn't* ignore a request from the Comyn. Who are the Hasturs, anyway?"

Magda wondered how Montray could live on Darkover, even in the Terran HQ, for as much as a year, and still not know precisely who the Hasturs were, and why. "The Hasturs are the most prominent of the Comyn families," she said. "Lorill Hastur is the real power behind the throne. The prince, Aran Elhalyn, is popularly referred to as 'keeping the throne warm with his royal backside, which is the most useful part of him.' Most of the Hasturs for the last two hundred years have been statesmen; they used to sit on the throne as well, but they found it interfered with the serious business of government, so they gave up their ceremonial functions to the Elhalyns. This Lorill is the Chief Councillor—roughly equivalent to a prime minister, with a supreme court judge's power thrown in."

"I see. I suppose it's important not to offend him, then." Montray scowled at Magda. "You can't go as an official Terran translator in *that* outfit, Lorne!"

Magda said, "I'm sure it will offend them far less than what I'd normally wear around here. You do know, don't you, that a Terran woman's ordinary dress would be considered, on the Darkovan side, indecent even for a prostitute?"

"No, I didn't know that," Montray said. "I suppose I'd better take your advice, then; you're supposed to be the expert on women's customs."

But as they went through the great gates, past the black-leathered Spaceforce man on duty, Montray scowled. "See what you've let me in for? He probably thinks I've picked myself up a Darkovan girlfriend."

Magda shook her head, reminding him that the Spaceforce guards knew her, and were accustomed to seeing her in Darkovan clothing; she never went into the Old Town without it. But, too late, it occurred to her that she had, perhaps, let Montray in for trouble on the Darkovan side. Terrans were not precisely popular in the Old Town, and the sight of a Terran escorting a respectable Darkovan female could indeed cause some trouble, if some Darkovan hothead wanted to take advantage of it.

This is idiotic. I know fifteen times as much about Darkover as Montray ever will; yet by strict protocol I'm not even qualified to be an official translator, far less for any position more advanced than that; just because I'm a woman, and Darkover is a world where women don't hold such positions.

So by accident of birth, I'm permanently disqualified from the work I know best, while an idiot like Montray needs a specially qualified linguist to write his speeches, and two more to hold his hand in case he gets lost or has to ask his way a hundred meters outside the gates! I should have Montray's job. He isn't even qualified for mine!

Montray was shivering; Magda had no sympathy for him. Montray knew what the climate was like; he had authority to dress for it, or modify the official uniform in some more suitable way, but he didn't even have the imagination for that.

I ought to get right off this damn world. There are plenty of planets where I could do the kind of work I'm best fitted for.

But Darkover is the one I know best. And here, I'm only fit for a woman's job!

And I can only do even that because I'm a Terran. Darkovan women don't even do my kind of work!

At the gates of the Comyn Castle, a man in the green-and-black uniform of the City Guard asked their business. He used the derogatory mode, and Magda bristled.

Montray would not have noticed, but Magda told him stiffly that they had been personally summoned by Lord Lorill Hastur. The Guard went away, returning almost immediately; this time he spoke in the respectful mode, saying that the Lord Hastur had given orders for them to be conducted at once into his presence.

The hallways of the Comyn Castle were drafty, cold and all but deserted. Magda knew that at this season of the year, most of the Comyn had withdrawn to their own estates throughout the Domains; they gathered here only in Council Season, near midsummer. The Hastur Domain was far away on the borders of the Hellers; she supposed Lord Hastur had stayed here only because events in the capital city required his presence. She carefully studied the corridors, the hangings and ornaments, wanting to make the most of an opportunity which, for her, might never come again; no woman could hold an official post on Darkover, and she would probably never again enter the Comyn Castle.

At last they were led into a small audience chamber where Lorill Hastur awaited them: a slight, serious man, with dark red hair winged with white at the temples. He greeted them with courteous phrases, which Magda translated automatically. She had seen that the only other person in the room was Lady Rohana Ardais.

Magda would have said, if asked, that she did not believe in precognition and was skeptical about ESP. Yet the moment she saw the slender, copper-haired woman, in a dress of violet-blue, seated quietly on a cushioned bench, she *knew*.

This has to do with Peter. . . .

"My kinswoman has made the long journey from Ardais purposely to speak with you," Lorill Hastur said. "Will you explain, Rohana?"

"I came to you from a sense of obligation," Rohana said, "because you were kind to me when I came to you in deep trouble about my son." She spoke to Montray, apparently, but it was obvious that the words were meant for Magda.

"My husband and I have just received a message from Rumal di Scarp." Magda could not quite control a shudder as she translated. "Sain Scarp is the most notorious bandit stronghold in the Hellers," she explained to Montray. (As a child, that word had been used to frighten her little friends into good behavior: "The men from Sain Scarp will get you!")

Lady Rohana continued: "Rumal hates the men of Ardais with a deadly hatred; my husband's father hanged half a dozen of his men from the walls of Castle Ardais. So now Rumal has sent us a message: that he holds our son Kyril prisoner in the *forst* of Sain Scarp; and he has named a ransom which we must pay before midwinter, or Kyril will be sent back to us"— Rohana shivered slightly—"in pieces."

Montray said, "Lady, my deepest sympathies. But the Terran Empire cannot entangle itself in private feuds—"

Rohana's eyes blazed. She did not wait for Magda to translate. "I see you still have not understood. When, after I spoke with you, I returned to Castle Ardais, I found my son safe and well at home; he had delayed because of frostbitten feet, and came when he was able to travel. When we received the word from Sain Scarp, he was in the room with us, and he thought it a tremendous joke."

Magda turned pale, knowing what Rohana's next words would be. "I knew, then, having seen the portrait you showed me, just who is being held in Sain Scarp. Your friend," she said to Magda. "Is he your lover?" She had used the polite term, for which the nearest Terran equivalent was "promised husband"; the derogatory mode would have implied "paramour."

Magda forced her words through dread. A whole childhood spent hearing tales of bandits in the Hellers made her throat tight. "He was my"— she searched for the precise Darkovan equivalent for "husband," for there were at least three forms of Darkovan marriage—"my freemate. We have separated, but we were childhood friends and I am deeply concerned for his safety."

Montray, who had followed all this with difficulty, was scowling. "Are you certain? It is rare for any of my men to go so far into the Hellers. Could it not be some other kinsman with a resemblance to your son, Lady?"

"Rumal sent this with his message," Rohana said, and held out a man's neck-ornament on a fine copper chain. "I know it is not my son's; it was made in Dalereuth, and such work is not sold in the Hellers, nor worn much."

Montray turned it uneasily in his hands. It was a carved medallion of

some blue-green semiprecious stone, encircled in finely worked copper fili-
gree. "You know Haldane better than I do, Magda. Do you recognize it?"

"I gave it to him." Her mouth was dry. It had been shortly before their
short-lived marriage; the one and only time they had traveled together to
the plains of Dalereuth. She had bought it for herself, but Peter had admired it so extravagantly that Magda, who after all could not wear a man's
ornament, had made him a present of it, in return for— She raised her
shaking hands to the nape of her neck, touching the silver butterfly-clasp
she always wore.

*He took off the one I had worn, and pinned this one there . . . as only a
lover would dare to do . . . and I let him. . . .*

"That's pretty conclusive," Montray said. "Damn him, he knew better
than to try to get into the Hellers alone. What chance is there that this
bandit—di Scarp—will turn him loose, if he finds out he's got the wrong
man?"

"None," Hastur said. "The mountain bandits remember all too well
those first few years at Caer Donn, when Aldaran deceived the Terrans
into believing it was permitted to use your weapons against them. I hope,
for his own sake, that your young man does not reveal his identity."

Montray said, "Doesn't that just prove that we were right to help the
Aldarans, and that you were wrong to stop us? They are still ravaging your
people worse than ever, and your Darkovan Compact makes it impossible
to attack them effectively. You should have let us finish wiping them out!"

"I must respectfully refuse to debate the ethics of Compact with you,"
Hastur said; "it has kept Darkover free of major wars for hundreds of
years, and is not open to debate. We still remember our Ages of Chaos."

"That's all very well," Montray said, "but doesn't it mean anything to
you that an innocent bystander may be murdered in a quarrel that is none
of his, and that you are condoning their actions by making it impossible
for our people to rescue him?"

"It means a great deal," said Hastur, and his eyes glowed with sudden
anger. "I might remind you that he is hardly an innocent bystander, having walked into this situation of his own free will. We did not require him
—for that matter, we did not even give him leave—to travel in the Hellers.
He went of his free choice and for your purposes, or his own—not ours.
But we did not forbid him to go, either; and it is really none of our affair if
he suffers the same fate that our own men risk whenever they go there. I
might remind you, also, that there was no compulsion upon us ever to tell
you of his fate. Nor do we refuse you leave to rescue him, if you can do it
as secretly as he went there."

Montray shook his head. "In the Hellers, with winter coming on? Impossible. I'm afraid you're right; he knew the risks he was taking, he knew

what would happen if he got caught. I'm afraid he'll have to take whatever he brought on himself."

Magda said in horror, "You're not going to—to abandon him, just write him off?"

Montray sighed heavily. "I don't like it either, Magda. But what else can we do? He knew the risks; you all do."

Magda felt her spine prickle, as if the small hairs on her body were all standing on end. Yes, that was the rule of the Intelligence service. *The first law and the last is secrecy. Get into trouble, and there's no way to pull you out again.*

"We can ransom him," Magda flared. "I'll stand surety for the ransom myself, if you begrudge it!"

"Magda, it's not that. We'd gladly pay to get him loose, but—"

"Impossible," Lorill Hastur said. "Rumal di Scarp would never negotiate with the Terrans; the moment he knew his prisoner was a Terran he would take pleasure in killing him out of hand—by means I would prefer not to describe before women's ears. Your man's only hope is to conceal his origin." He turned to Magda and said, courteously not looking at her (a gesture which spoke a great deal about the quality of Magda's Darkovan dress and manners), "Not knowing otherwise, I would have taken you for a woman of the Hellers. Does your friend speak the language, and know our customs, as well as you?"

"Better," Magda said truthfully. Her mind was racing. *We must think of something! We must!* "Lady Rohana, they evidently still believe he is your son. Can *you* negotiate with them for his ransom?"

"It was my first thought. I would gladly do this to save a life. But my husband has forbidden me, once and for all, to go near Sain Scarp on any such mission. It was only with difficulty that I won his consent to come and tell you this much."

"Magda, it's no use. The only hope would be for Peter to escape on his own," Montray said. "If *we* go, and try to ransom him, as a Terran, we are only hastening his death-sentence."

She said fiercely, "If I were a man, I would go myself and negotiate for his ransom! There is no man alive in the Hellers who would know me for a Terran! If I could use the lady's name, and negotiate as if for a kinsman . . ." She turned, appealing directly to Rohana.

"Help me think of a way!"

I know she can do it, if she will. She is a law to herself, this lady of the Comyn, she will do what she thinks right and no one will forbid her. . . .

Rohana said to Hastur, "I told you this girl had spirit and strength. I will not disobey Gabriel—it is not worth the argument—but I will help her, if I can." She turned to Magda, and said, "You would be willing to go yourself into the Hellers? With winter coming on? Many men might shrink from such a journey, my girl." Again she spoke as if to a younger woman of her own caste. Magda set her chin, and said, "Lady, I was born near Caer Donn; I am not afraid of the mountains, nor of their worst weather."

Montray said harshly, "Don't be a damned fool, Magda! You're supposed to be the expert on women's customs on Darkover; but even *I* know that no woman can travel alone and unprotected! You may have guts enough—or damnfoolishness enough—but it's impossible for you to travel alone, here on this planet. You tell her, my Lady," he appealed to Rohana. "It would be impossible! Damn it, I admire her spirit, too, but there are things women just can't do here!"

"You are right," Rohana said. "Our customs make it impossible for a woman. An ordinary woman, that is. But there is one way, and only one, in which a woman can travel alone without danger and scandal. The Free Amazons alone do not accept the customs that bind other women."

Magda said, "I don't know much about the Free Amazons. I've heard the name." She looked straight into Rohana's eyes, and said, "If you think I can do it . . ."

"Once before, I employed a Free Amazon on a mission no man would undertake. It was a scandal, at the time." She looked at Lorill with a mischievous small smile, as if, Magda thought, she were evoking a shared memory. "So it will evoke no great scandal—or if it does, no more scandal than I can bear—when it is known that I have sent a Free Amazon to Sain Scarp to negotiate in my place for my son's release. And if Rumal di Scarp should chance to hear it rumored that my son Kyril is safe at Ardais, then he will only think that he has captured instead some kinsman or fosterling of our house, whom we are redeeming out of kindness or a bad conscience; and he will sneer at us for being so gullible, but he will take the ransom anyway and be glad to get it.

"I think I know enough of the Free Amazons to make it possible for you to pass as one, unchallenged. But there may be dangers by the way, child; can you defend yourself?"

Magda said, "Everyone in Intelligence—man and woman alike—is trained in unarmed combat and knife fighting."

Rohana nodded. "I had heard about this," she said, and Magda wished she knew *how* this information had come to Darkovan ears. *Probably the same way we learn things about them!*

"Go back, now," Rohana said. "Arrange for the journey, and for the ransom, and come to me at dawn tomorrow morning. I will see that you have the proper clothing and necessities, and that you know how to carry yourself as a Free Amazon."

Montray burst out, "Are you really going to do this harebrained thing, Magda? Free Amazons! Aren't they lady soldiers?"

Rohana laughed. "It is easy to see you know nothing about them," she said. "Indeed, it is comforting to think there is something you Terrans have not managed to discover about us!" Magda had to grin ruefully at that. "Yes, many of them are mercenary soldiers; others are trackers, hunters, horsebreakers, blacksmiths; midwives, dairy-women, confectioners, bakers, ballad-singers and cheese-sellers! They work at any honest trade; for one to serve as a messenger and negotiate in a family feud is completely respectable, as such things go."

"I don't give a damn whether it's respectable or not," Magda told Montray, and Rohana smiled approvingly.

"Good," she said. "Then it is settled." She gave Magda her hand, with a kindly smile. "It is a pity, but you will have to cut that lovely hair," she said.

Chapter Eight

Magda woke in the gray dawn, hearing the thin patter of sleet on the roof of the travel-shelter. It was her seventh night on the road, and until now the weather had been fine.

She had till midwinter-night. With anything like reasonable weather, she had ample time. But could anyone expect reasonable weather in the Hellers, at this season?

From the far end of the shelter she could hear the soft stamping and the rustling breaths of her saddle-horse and the pack animal, an antlered beast from the Kilghard Hills, better suited to the mountain weather than any horse. She wondered what time it was; it was still too dark to see.

It did not occur to her to regret—or even to think about—her chronometer. Like all Terrans allowed to work undercover on any planet anywhere in the Empire, she had undergone a long and intense conditioning, designed to make it virtually impossible for her to act in any way not consonant with her assigned character; and there was no item, in all her luggage and gear, of off-world manufacture. This was a habit of years; everyone in Intelligence learned the almost hypnotic mechanisms which meant that the moment she left the Trade City, Magdalen Lorne of Linguistics was gone, left wholly behind her; even her name was gone, packed away in a very small corner of her unconscious mind. *Magdalen* had no precise Darkovan equivalent; when she was a small girl in the mountains near Caer Donn, her Darkovan playmates had called her *Margali.*

She turned over restlessly in her sleeping bag, raising nervous fingers to her shorn head. It felt cold, strange, immodest.

Lady Rohana, in the long briefing session that had preceded her departure, had been sympathetic about that, too.

"I traveled once, in disguise, with a band of Free Amazons," she said, "and I had to cut my hair; I can still remember the shock I felt. I remember that I cried, and how they laughed at me. It was worse for me, probably, than for you: you are accountable to no one, but I knew how angry my husband would be when he knew."

Magda had asked, "And was he angry?" and Rohana smiled, a reminiscent smile. "Terribly. It was already done, so there was nothing he could do about it; but I felt his anger for almost a year, till it had grown to what he called a respectable length."

Magda heard the sleet beginning to abate and crawled out of her sleeping bag. Shivering in the fireless hut, she dressed quickly in the clothing Lady Rohana had provided: loose trousers, a long-sleeved and high-necked undertunic of embroidered linen, a fur-lined overtunic and riding-cloak. She had even measured Magda's foot and sent a servant to buy boots in the marketplace. Magda laced the high boots and led her animals outside, feeding them from the stacked fodder in the nearby shed and slipping the prescribed amount of coins into the padlocked box there. She led them one by one to the watering trough, breaking the ice there with the small hammer on her saddle. While they munched and drank, she went inside, quickly made a small fire and boiled some water, stirring it into the precooked, powdered mixture of grains and nuts that made a kind of instant porridge. Mixed with a few shreds of dried fruit, it was edible when you were used to it.

The ransom was safely hidden in her saddlebags, converted into the copper bars that were the standard Darkovan currency. In Terran exchange it was no more than a couple of months' salary for a good agent; they probably wouldn't even bother to take it out of Peter's "hazard" pay.

Why am I doing this? Peter's a grown man, able to take his own risks. I'm not his guardian. I'm not even his wife anymore. I don't love him that much, not anymore, not now. So why? But she had no answer, and it nagged at the back of her mind as she set off down the trail. She stopped at the indicator post near the travel-shelter, locating the next three shelters along this trail. One was at a reasonable distance for a large caravan with heavily laden pack animals; a second was located at a good day's ride for a party traveling at an easy pace but without much gear; the third was about at the limit of a long day's hard ride for a solitary traveler. *Maybe I can sleep there tonight.* . . . She turned from the post and started along the trail, feeling a faint unease she could not identify; then it came to her.

I'm out of character, reading the travel-post. Most Darkovan women can't read. . . . Literacy even among men on Darkover was by no means universal, though most men could spell out a placard or scrawl their own names; among women it was extremely rare, and her small Darkovan playmates at Caer Donn had been astonished and slightly shocked—and a little envious—when they discovered that Margali could read, that her own father had taught her. *Out of character. Damn it, this whole trip is out of character.*

Magda clucked to her horse, and started along the trail. Rohana had warned her: "I traveled with the Free Amazons, but not as one of them; I do not deceive myself that I know all of their ways and customs. If I were you, I would avoid any meeting with real Amazon groups; but most of the folk in the hills where you will travel know *nothing at all* about them. So no one will question your disguise, if you are careful."

And in seven days she had not been challenged, though once she had had to share the travel-shelter with two men, traders from the far hills. By law and custom, these shelters, put up centuries ago, and kept inspected and stocked even in wartime by the border patrols, were sacred places of neutrality, and must be shared by all comers; anything else would have condemned other travelers to die of cold and exposure. By law, even blood-feuds were suspended in the shelters, as Magda had heard was the custom during forest fires. The men had glanced briefly at Magda's short hair and Amazon clothing, spoken a few formally courteous words, and ignored her entirely after that.

But since then she had met no one; the advanced season had sent most travelers home to their own firesides. The clouds had thinned and gone, and the great red sun of Darkover, which some poet in the Terran Zone had christened The Bloody Sun, was rising between the peaks, flooding the high snowfields with flaming crimson and gold. As she rode up into the pass, it seemed that a sea of flame bathed the high snowcaps, a brilliance of solitude that exhilarated and excited her.

But the sunrise subsided, and there was nothing but the lonely silence of the trail. Silence; and too much time to think, to ask herself again and again: *Why am I doing this? Am I still in love with the bastard?*

Pride, maybe, that a man who shared my bed—however briefly—should not be abandoned and left to die, with no one to help him?

Or maybe, when we were growing up in Caer Donn, just the few of us among all the Darkovan children, we absorbed their codes, their ethics. Loyalty, kinship's dues. To the Empire, Peter is only an employee, expendable. To me, to any Darkovan, that's an outrageous notion, an obscenity.

She crossed the path before the sun was more than an hour high in the sky, her ears aching with the altitude, and began to descend into the next valley. At noon she stopped at a little mountain village and indulged herself by buying a mug of hot soup and a few fried cakes at a food-stall. Some

curious children gathered around, and Magda guessed, from their eagerness, that they saw very few outsiders; she gave them some sweets from her
saddlebags, and lingered, resting her animals before the climb to the next
pass, enjoying her first taste of fresh food since she had left Thendara.

They were all curious as kittens; they asked where she had come from,
and when she told them "Thendara," they stared as if she had said "From
world's end." She supposed that to these children, never out of their own
hills, Thendara *was* the world's end. But when they asked her business, she
smiled and said it was a secret of her patroness. Lady Rohana had given
her permission to use her name. "I will give you my safe-conduct, too,
under my seal. In the foothills there are many who owe service to Gabriel
and to me." She had also cautioned her against any but the most casual
contact with genuine Amazons, but had advised her that if she met any by
chance, she would be asked for her Guild-house, and for the name of the
woman who had received her oath. "In this case, you may say Kindra n'ha
Mhari; she is dead these three years"—and a fleeting sadness had touched
Rohana's eyes—"but she was my dear friend, and I do not think she would
grudge this use of her name. But if the Gods are kind you will get to Sain
Scarp, and, hopefully, back again, without using it."

She had finished eating, and was watering her animals at the village
trough when she saw a pair of men riding into the square. By the cut of
their cloaks she knew they were from the far Hellers; they were bearded,
and wore wicked-looking knives in their belts. They looked at Magda and,
she fancied, at her laden saddlebags, with a regard that made her uneasy.
She cut short the watering, clambered hastily into her saddle, and took the
trail out of town. She hoped they would stop there for a good, long rest,
and she would not see them again.

For a long time the trail led upward between heavily wooded slopes. The
ice and snow were melting in the noon sun and the trail was slushy underfoot; Magda let her horse find its own pace, and when the road grew
steepest, dismounted to lead it. She paused at a bend in the trail, where the
trees thinned at a giddy height, looking down at the narrow line of road far
below. There she saw, with consternation, what looked like the same two
men she had seen in the village. Were they following her?

*Don't be paranoid. This is the only road northwest into the Hellers; am I
the only one who could have legitimate business along it?* She stepped to the
edge, careful not to slip on the muddy, slushy cliff, and looked down at the
men riding the trail. Could she even be sure they were the same two men?
Yes, for one man had been riding a roan horse; they were not common at
any latitude, and to see two in the mountains in the same day's ride was
entirely unlikely. As if to dispel her last doubt, one looked up, apparently
saw Magda silhouetted along the edge, and leaned over to speak urgently

to his companion; they drew at their horses' reins, edging in toward the cliff where they would not be visible from above.

Magda felt panic grip and drag at her, a physical sensation like a cramp along her leg muscles. She hurried back to her horse, ordering herself sternly to be calm. *I'm armed. I've been combat-trained since I was sixteen, and first knew I was going into Intelligence.* On any other world, she knew, she would have been expected to take this kind of chance routinely, man or woman. Here she'd been sheltered by Darkovan custom.

If it came to a fight—she laid her hand on her knife for a moment, trying to reassure herself—it would be better to make a stand in the pass. She could defend herself better there than on the downslopes. But need it come to a fight? Terran agents were trained to avoid confrontations when possible. And she would have bet that even Free Amazons didn't go around looking for trouble.

Suddenly she knew that she could not, *could not* force herself to make a stand here and face them. She commanded herself to stay here and think it through, but even while she tried to form her thoughts clearly she was guiding her horse away down the slope, down the trail, hurrying and urging it more, she knew, than a good rider would ever do (there was a mountain proverb of her childhood, "On a steep road let your horse set the pace"), yet she knew she was almost racing downhill, hearing small stones slip and slide beneath the horse's hooves.

It was not long before she realized she could not go on like this; if one of her animals should fall and break a leg she would be afoot and stranded. She drew the horse to a stop, patting its heaving sides in apology. *What's wrong with me, why did I run away like that?* Behind her, the road to the pass lay bare and unoccupied. *Maybe they weren't following me at all. . . .* But she felt the vague unease, the "hunch" she had learned, in years of successful agent work, always to trust; and it said, loud and clear: *run, hide, disappear, get lost.* The woman who had trained her, far away on another world, had said: "Every good undercover agent is a little psychic. Or they don't survive long in the service."

Now what? She couldn't outrun them, burdened as she was with luggage and pack animal. Sooner or later they would come up with her, and then it would come to a fight.

She looked at the ground, covered with melting snow and mud, an amorphous trampled brownish mess. *Lucky. In new snow they'd see my tracks . . . and see where I left the trail, which would be worse. . . .* But in the running, muddy water and slush all tracks vanished as fast as they were made. She turned aside from the road, leading the animals through a small gap in the trees; turned back to obliterate, with a quick hand, the marks in the snow where she had crossed the edge; led them some distance from the road and tethered them in a thick grove of evergreens, where they could not be seen.

Then she slipped back, found a concealed vantage point where she could conceal herself between trees and underbrush, and gnawed nervously on some dried fruit as she waited to see the success of her trick.

It was nearly an hour before the riders she had seen came down the slopes, hurrying their mounts as much as they could in the mushy trail underfoot. But neither of them even glanced in Magda's direction as they hurried past. When they were out of sight, she crawled shakily from her hiding place. She noted peripherally that her knees were weak and trembling, and that the palms of her hands were clammy and wet.

What's the matter with me? I'm not behaving like a trained agent—or even like a Free Amazon! I'm behaving like a—like a bunny rabbit!

And why am I panicking now, anyway? I did the sensible thing. Any of our agents, man or woman, on any world, in that situation, would have done just what I did. Kept out of trouble. . . .

Yet she knew, no matter how she tried to rationalize it, that her flight had not been a considered thing, based on her standing orders to avoid a fight where possible. It had been, quite simply, a rout. *I panicked. That's the long and short of it. I panicked, and I ran.*

I behaved like . . . like. . . . Realization flashed over her. *Not like a Terran agent. Not like a Free Amazon. Like an ordinary, conventional Darkovan girl.*

The kind I've taught myself to be, in Thendara. The kind I was brought up to be, in Caer Donn. . . .

The short winter day was drawing to a close, and she thought, *I'll camp here tonight, in the woods; I'll let them get a good, long start. By tomorrow they'll have gone through two or three of those little villages, and with luck they'll think I just found a place to stay in a village, and give up.*

Or, possibly, they were respectable traders on their own lawful business and in a hurry to get home to their wives and children, she considered.

She put up her small tent. It was a compromise, the maximum possible protection in bad weather combined with the minimum possible in weight and size; a combination of an undersized tent and an oversized sleeping bag. It was the standard Darkovan traveler's model. She knew already that no sane person ever spent a night outdoors if he could possibly help it, which was why the roads were lined with the travel-shelters and huts and why they were sacred places of neutrality.

But she spent that night in the open anyway. By good fortune the weather kept fine, even the predawn snowfall unusually light; but Magda knew, as she emerged shivering, this was a bad sign. Clouds scudded thick and black, away north, and a high wind had already begun to toss the tips of the evergreens, promising a severe storm on the way.

In the lonely silence of the trail she went over and over her failure. However she rationalized it, it *was* a failure; she had panicked.

I've taught myself always to behave that way, whenever I step on the Darkovan side. It was the standard Intelligence conditioning: build yourself a *persona*, a character for whatever planet you're working on, and never step out of it, even for an instant, until you're safely back inside the Terran Zone.

But the personality I built for myself in Thendara won't work here. Because of the particular society on Darkover, and the way women live. It was different for the men. But I was the only woman; and I never realized how far I had come from ordinary agent's training. . . .

She tried to think it through, to analyze just what basic changes she would have to make in her basic Darkovan *persona* for this assignment, but the attempt made her so overwhelmingly anxious that she had to give up the effort. *The trouble is, I've been trained never to think of Terra outside the Zone.* Now she was trying to bring a process as automatic as breathing under voluntary control; and it wasn't working.

I can't be a Free Amazon. I don't know enough about them. Even Lady Rohana said she didn't know enough about them. So I can be only my basic Darkovan persona, pretending to be a Free Amazon. Lady Rohana seemed to think it would be effective enough to fool people who didn't have much to do with Free Amazons; but I'd just better hope I don't meet any real ones!

This caused another of those weird small repercussions which, for years, she had thought of as "hunches" and learned to trust. Oddly, this one iced her blood; she had physically to pull her cloak tighter about her shoulders against the sudden runnel of cold down her spine. *It would be just my luck, to meet a couple!*

Peter always said I had a talent for bluffing. Better get used to thinking of him by his Darkovan name.

She had a sudden moment of blank terror when the name refused to come to her mind, when she wholly blanked on it. It lasted only a few seconds, and the panic ebbed away as the name came back to her. *Piedro. That's in the Hellers. In the lowlands they'd call him Pier . . . why did I blank on it like that?*

It was an hour past noon when she passed one of the shelter huts; it was empty, and she hesitated, tempted to stay there overnight. But she had already lost half a day, and always, at the back of her mind, was the thought of the midwinter deadline. She must not only be at Sain Scarp by midwinter, but she must leave some leeway for return to Thendara before the winter storms closed the passes. *I can't see us camping on Rumal di Scarp's doorstep all winter.*

Nor did she particularly want to spend the winter cooped up anywhere, alone with Peter. *Once I used to daydream about something that would isolate us, so we had time only to be alone together. . . . Even now, it might be . . . pleasurable. . . .* Exasperated, Magda told herself to snap out of it. She wondered, half annoyed, if Bethany had been right all along; *was she still half in love with Peter? I should have taken another lover right away, after we separated. God knows I had enough chances. I wonder why I didn't.*

She checked the notice board, and discovered that there was another shelter just about half a day's ride distant. As she turned her back on the shelter she felt again the curious, almost physical prickling of the "hunch," but told herself fiercely not to be superstitious. *I'm afraid to go on, so I find reasons, and call it ESP!*

The trail steepened and grew rough underfoot; by midafternoon the thickening clouds lay so deep on the mountain that Magda was riding through a thick white blanket of fog. The dim gray world was full of echoes; she could hear her horse's hooves sounding dimly, behind and before her, like invisible, ghostly companions. The valley was gone, and the lower slopes; she rode high and alone, on a narrow trail above the known world. She had never been afraid of heights, but now she began to be afraid of the narrowness of the dim trail, of the white nothingness that hemmed her in on every side and might hide anything—or worse, nothing. Her mind kept returning to the cliffs and crags below, where an animal, putting a foot down wrong, might step off the trail, go plunging down the mountainside to be dashed to death on the invisible rocks far below. . . .

As the darkness deepened, the fog dissolved into fine rain and then into a thick, fast-falling snow, wiping out trail and landmarks. The snow froze as it fell, and the slush underfoot crunched and crackled under her horse's hooves; then the wind began to howl through the trees and, where they thinned, to roar across the trail, driving icy needles of sleet into her face and eyes. She pulled up her cloak's collar and wrapped a fold of her scarf over her nose and chin, but the cold made her nose run, and the water froze on her nose and mouth and turned the scarf to a block of ice. Snow clung to her eyelashes and froze there, making it impossible to see. Her horse began to slip on the icy trail, and Magda dismounted to lead it and the faltering pack animal, glad of the knee-high boots she was wearing; a woman's soft low sandals or ankle-high, tied moccasins would have been soaked in a moment.

I should have stayed in that last shelter. That was what that hunch was all about. Confound it, I ought to listen to myself!

Her feet were freezing, and she was seriously beginning to wonder if her cheeks and nose were frostbitten. Normally cold did not bother her, but she was chilled now to the bone; her thick fur-lined tunic and cloak might have been dancing silks.

She sternly told herself not to be frightened. The woman who had trained her in Intelligence work had told her that human stock was the hardiest known in the Empire. Man's home planet, Terra, had contained extremes of temperature, and, before civilization, ethnic types had developed who could, and did, live in unheated houses made of ice blocks, or on burning deserts sufficient to blister the skin. She could survive outdoors, even in this storm.

But frostbite could delay me, beyond the midwinter deadline.

The light of her saddle-lantern glinted on one of the small arrow-shaped signs of a travel-shelter. Her antlered pack beast threw back its head and whickered. Magda turned off the trail and trudged down the narrow path, leading toward the dark building she could just see. The road crunched with rutted and frozen sleet, much trampled. As she came through the trees, she saw the loom of two buildings; it was one of the large shelters, with a separate building for animals. Then she swore softly to herself. Through the crack of the door a faint light was visible: the shelter was occupied.

Oh, damn. I should go on. Why take chances? But the next shelter might be another half-day's ride away; and she was soaked, chilled and freezing. Her cheeks felt numb beneath her hand, and her eyes smarted. *Just to get out of the wind for a minute or two. . . .*

While she delayed, her horse and pack animal had made up their own minds; they tugged at the reins, plunging ahead of her inside the dark barn. There was a good, dusty smell of fodder and hay. It seemed warm and pleasant. She set her saddle-lantern in a safe place, and set about unsaddling the horse, off-loading her pack beast. *I wouldn't have the heart to take them out in this storm again.* Several horses and pack animals were already chomping on fodder and grain; Magda fed her animals, then sat down by the light of the saddle-lantern and pulled off her boot. She drew a sharp breath of dismay as she saw the whitish patches along the reddened flesh under the wet stocking. *I need fire,* she thought, *and something hot to get the circulation going.* She had lived on Darkover much of her life, and knew the danger signs. There could be no question, now, of camping outdoors.

She would simply have to rely on the traditional neutrality of the travel-shelters, and on the disguise she wore. After all it had excited no comment or question from the traders she had met that other night.

She gathered up her saddlebags and started into the main building.

Almost automatically she drew up her cloak collar to cover her bare neck; then, self-consciously, put it down where it belonged. Her Amazon's dress and short hair were the best protection in this situation; ordinary female dress and manners would make what she was doing unthinkable.

She pushed the door open and stepped into the light of several lanterns. There were *two* parties of travelers in the long stone-floored room, one at each end, around the fireplaces. As she saw the men near the door, her heart sank; she almost wished she had taken her chances in the woods. They were a party of big, rough-looking men, wearing strangely cut cloaks, and Magda fancied there was something more than impersonal curiosity in their eyes as they turned to look at the newcomer.

The laws of the road meant it was for Magda to speak first. She spoke the formal, almost ritual words, hearing her voice, light and almost little-girlish in the huge echoing room:

"As a late-comer I crave leave from those who have come before to share shelter."

One of the men, huge and burly, with fierce-looking reddish-gold moustaches, spoke the formal greeting, "Be welcome; enter this neutral place in peace, and go in peace." His eyes rested on her with a look that made her skin crawl. It wasn't just that the man was unshaven, and his clothes far from clean; that could be bad weather and traveler's luck. It was something in his eyes. But the laws of the travel-shelter should protect her. She clutched her saddlebags and edged past. Both fireplaces had been pre-empted, but she could build a small fire near the stone shelving along the center wall. She need not even struggle with tinder; she could borrow a light. (But not, she resolved, from the big man with the moustaches!)

At the far end, five or six figures were gathered; they turned when Magda spoke, and one of them, a tall, thin figure, lean to gauntness, came toward her.

"Be welcome, sister," the figure said, and Magda heard the voice in astonishment. A woman's voice, low-pitched and almost husky, but undeniably a female voice. "Come and share our fire."

Zandru's hells, thought Magda, involuntarily calling on a Darkovan God in her dismay, *what now?*

They're Free Amazons.

Real ones!

The tall gaunt woman did not wait for Magda's acquiescence; she said, "I am Camilla n'ha Kyria, and we are traveling on a mission to Nevarsin. Come, lay your things there." She relieved Magda of her saddlebags, led her to the fire. "You are half frozen, child! You had better get out of those soaked things, if you have dry ones to put on; if not, one of us can lend you something, till your own garments have felt the fire." She pointed to where the women had strung cords and hung spare blankets over them for privacy; by the light of the lantern they had hung there, Magda saw the stranger, Camilla, clearly. She was tall and emaciated, her face deeply lined with age—and what looked like knife scars—and her hair all gray. She had taken off outer cloak and tunic, wearing only the embroidered linen undertunic of a Thendara woman; beneath it her body was so spare and flat that Magda knew her for what she was: an *emmasca*, a woman subjected in adolescence to the illegal neutering operation.

Magda went behind the curtaining blankets, and got out of her wet clothing, slipping into spare trousers and tunic. She was glad of the privacy of the blankets, less because of the rough-looking men at the far end—they could hardly have seen her in the dim shelter—than because of the other women. Had Lady Rohana been right about every detail of her clothing and gear?

A slight woman, with hair the exact color of new-minted copper bars, put her head around the blankets. She said, "I am Jaelle n'ha Melora, elected leader of this band. Are your feet frozen?" She bent down to look carefully at Magda's feet and toes.

"No, I don't think so," Magda said, and Jaelle touched one foot with careful fingers. "No, you were lucky. I was going to say Camilla has some medicine for frostbite, if you need it, but I think even your cheeks are all right; you got out of the wind just in time. Put your stockings on, then, and come to the fire."

Magda gathered up her wet clothes and hung them on the poles the women had rigged there for drying their own garments. On a small grille over a bed of coals, some small birds were roasting, and they had slung a hook and kettle, in which some kind of hot steaming soup was cooking. It smelled so good that Magda's mouth watered.

Jaelle said, "May we know your name and Guild-house, sister?"

Magda gave her alias, and said she was from the Guild-house at Temora; she had purposely chosen the farthest city she knew, hoping that the distance would cover any small differences in dress and manners.

"What a night for travel! I do not think there will be so much as a bush-jumper stirring in these hills between here and Nevarsin," Jaelle said. "Have you journeyed all the way from Temora? Surely your clothes are of Thendara make; that leatherwork and embroidery is found mostly in the Venza hills."

There was nothing to do but brazen it out. Magda said, "They are indeed; such warm clothing cannot be bought on the seacoast—it is like trying to buy fish in the Dry Towns. My patroness was generous in providing me with clothing for my journey, and well she might be, sending me into the Hellers at this season!"

"Will you share our meal?"

Prudence dictated having as little to do with the strange women as possible. Yet they seemed to take it so much for granted that it might cause comment and arouse suspicion. Besides, the food smelled too good, after days of powdered porridge, to refuse. She made the usual polite reply: "Gladly, if I may be allowed to contribute my share."

Jaelle gave the expected answer, "It is not necessary, but will be welcome," and Magda went to her saddlebags for some confectionery with which she had provided herself for just such an occasion. The woman who was cooking accepted the sweets with a little cry of pleasure. "These, too, are made in the Thendara valley. I have not tasted this sort for years, and I am afraid we shall all be shamefully greedy! Except for Jaelle, who hates sweets like a true Dry-Towner!"

"Shut your silly face," said Jaelle, turning harshly on the cook, and the older woman bridled and looked sullen. Magda could see now that all the women were older than Jaelle, though most of them seemed young, except for Camilla. *So young; and their elected leader. She is younger than I, I am sure! And beautiful. I don't think I have ever seen any woman so beautiful!* Jaelle, like the rest, wore the shapeless Amazon clothing: loose trousers, tunic; but this did not conceal the slender, feminine body, the delicate poise of the flame-colored head on her shoulders, the features delicate and pale, and so regular that they would have been almost ordinary, except for the eyes, which were very large and framed in thick dark lashes.

"You have met Camilla," Jaelle said. "That is Sherna"—she pointed to the woman who was cooking their meal—"and that is Rayna, and that is Gwennis. And in a few minutes, we will have something to eat. Oh, and there are two latrine closets in this shelter; we have taken this one"—she pointed—"for our own use, so that you need not go down among the men to . . ." She spoke, with complete insouciance, a word Magda had never heard a Darkovan woman speak; she had seen it only in textbooks, for no man would have used it before her.

I'd better not talk much. Among themselves, at least, they don't use the euphemisms thought polite for women!

She noticed, too, that a roughly printed sign hung on the outside of the latrine the women had preempted, warning the men away. The trained anthropologist made another assumption at the back of her mind: *They expect me to know how to read. And some of them, at least, can write.* That, too, was a faint shock.

"Here, come and eat." Sherna ladled hot soup into Magda's own cup; divided one of the roast birds with a knife and handed her a share. Like the others, Magda sat on her unrolled blankets to eat. She told herself not to be nervous; she had eaten in Darkovan company often enough before this.

The Amazon Jaelle had pointed out as Gwennis—Magda thought she must be about thirty, a slender pretty woman in a blue linen undertunic—asked, "May we know the nature of your mission, Margali, if it is not secret?"

Magda had begun to suspect that among strange bands of Amazons this kind of polite interrogation was customary. In any case, after accepting the invitation to share their fire and meal, she could not retreat into churlish silence. *I was a damn fool. I should have camped in the woods.* But outside the walls of the shelter she could still hear the howling of the storm, giving her the lie.

"It is not secret, no; but it is a family matter of my patroness."

Rayna, a tall, slender woman with hair so curly that it frizzled all about her head like a small halo in the firelight, said, "And no doubt you will be proud to name her for us?"

Lady Rohana foresaw this. Bless her; I'd never have dared to name her without her permission. "It is my privilege to serve the Lady Rohana Ardais on a mission to Sain Scarp."

Camilla, who was sitting next to Jaelle on her rolled-out blankets, pursed her lips and glanced quickly at the rough-looking men, now sitting around their fire and talking loudly as they gobbled food from a big kettle.

Magda thought, *Can those men be bandits? Is it possible they are from Sain Scarp?* The thought set her to prickling with her "hunch" again; she did not hear Jaelle speaking to her and had to ask her to repeat what she had said.

"I said: the Lady Rohana, is she still so very lame from that fall she took from her horse? Poor old woman, and so soon after losing her husband, too; what a tragedy!"

After an incredulous moment, Magda realized what was happening. Nothing to do but brazen it out boldly. She set down her plate with a good display of offended pride.

"You have had later news than mine, or you are testing me, *sister.*" She spoke the customary address with heavy irony. "When last I saw the Lady Rohana she was hearty and strong, and to call her old would have been grave insult; I do not think she is twenty years older than I. As for her husband"—she rummaged quickly in her mind for his name—"I have not been privileged to meet dom Gabriel, but she spoke of him as alive and well. Or is there another Lady Rohana in the Ardais Domain whom I have not been privileged to know and serve?"

Jaelle's lovely face looked troubled now, and contrite. She said, "You must not be angry with me, Margali; the Lady Rohana is my kinswoman, and the only one of my kin who has been kind to the family disgrace. As you can guess, her honor is dear to me, and I would not hear her name bandied about without her leave. I beg you, give me pardon."

Magda said stiffly, "You had better see the safe-conduct I carry."

"Oh, please"—Jaelle looked very young now—"don't trouble yourself. Sherna, pour her some wine. Drink with us, Margali. Don't be angry!"

Magda accepted the wine, sweat breaking out on her palms; she wiped them furtively on her tunic. *Just my luck. But I managed that one. What else are they going to throw at me?* She sipped the wine, nibbling at some sweets and the nuts Rayna was passing around; they had been pickled in something tart and highly spiced, and she noticed that Jaelle, who had refused Magda's confectionery, ate the spiced nuts with relish.

She's young. But I'd better not underestimate her!

A burst of noise from the men around the other fire interrupted her, and she twisted around to look at them. They were drinking hard, passing a bottle from hand to hand and laughing uproariously; loud enough to drown out the howling of the storm outside. She strained her ears to listen, thinking, *If they are from Sain Scarp, they might know something of Piedro. . . .*

Camilla's hand came down on her wrist like a vise; Magda almost cried out with the pain of it. *"For shame,"* said the old Amazon, in a voice that cut like a knife. "Is this how Temora House teaches her daughters to behave, shameless girl, staring at drunken men like some harlot of the streets? Turn your back on them, you ill-mannered brat!"

Magda pulled her hand free of the wiry old fingers. Her eyes filled with tears of outrage and humiliation. She said in a whisper, "I was only wondering if they are bandits. . . ."

"Whatever they are, they are nothing to us." The old woman spoke with firm finality. Magda rubbed her wrist, wondering if there would be a bruise.

I'm doing everything wrong. I'd better keep my mouth shut, and go to bed as soon as I can. She lay back on her unrolled blankets, pretending sleep. The drunken laughing and singing of the bandits went on. Around the women's fire there was a little more soft-voiced conversation, some quiet laughing and joking—they were teasing Sherna about something that had happened at midsummer-feast. Magda understood none of it. The women waterproofed their low suede ankleboots, tidied saddlebags, cleaned and put away eating utensils and began to ready themselves for bed.

Someone said, "I wish Rafi were here with her harp; we could have a song, better than that noise!" She flicked a quick, oblique glance over her shoulder at the drunken crew at the far end, but, Magda noted, did not turn to look. Amazon etiquette?

Camilla said, "Rafi was with me when we punished those two women in

Thendara city. You are new-come to us, Rayna, Sherna, you have not heard? You, Margali, you came here from Thendara; has the tale made the rounds yet in the marketplace?"

"What tale?" Magda did not dare to pretend sleep too deep to answer.

"You have not heard, either? Well, it came to our ears that in the Golden Cage—you know of the Golden Cage?" she asked, waiting, and Magda nodded. The Golden Cage was a notorious brothel not too far from the Terran Zone; she knew that it was patronized by spacemen and Empire tourists sometimes.

"It came to us that there were two *entertainers*"—she spoke the polite term with irony—"who had cut their hair short and were nightly presenting an exhibition of a particularly indecent sort—I am sure that every one of you can imagine the details—which the old freak running the place announced as 'Love Secrets of the Free Amazons.' So Rafaella and I—"

"Dear aunt," said Jaelle, yawning, "I have known since my fourteenth year, and so have we all, that there are lovers of women in this world, and that there are pretended lovers of women, and that some men have nothing better to do with their manhood than indulge in naughty fantasies about them. Do you think we are so bored that you must entertain us with dirty stories, Camilla dear?"

"Then you haven't heard how we punished those bitches for pretending to be Amazons, and bringing scandal and disgrace to our name? Can you guess, Margali?"

Magda said "No," not trusting herself to say any more. *This is being told for my benefit. Somehow I've given myself away. That old* emmasca *has eyes like a gimlet.*

Camilla said, savoring the words, her eyes lingering on Magda, "Why, Rafi and I went there by night when their leering audience had gone, we dragged those shameless wenches out into the main square, we stripped them naked and shaved their heads bald as an egg, and their private parts, too, and smeared them in pitch, and rolled them in wood shavings."

"I should have been there," said Jaelle, her eyes glistening with savage relish. "I would have put a torch to them and watched them sizzle!"

"Oh, well, we left them there in that state to be found by the guard; somehow I do not think, after being so shamed, that they will pretend to be Amazons for their filthy charades. What do you think, Margali?"

Magda tried to make her voice steady, but there was a lump in her throat, and she knew what caused it: stark fear. She said, "Probably not; but I have always heard that a *grezalis* follows her trade because she is too stupid to learn any other, so it may have been a lesson wasted."

"You were too hard on them," said Sherna. "It is the foul old pervert who runs the place that I would have treated so. He staged that filthy show; it was not the women's fault."

"On the contrary, I think you were too easy on them," Jaelle said. "Shaming such women is useless; if they were not dead to shame, they would never have been in such a place."

"All women are not made harlots of their free will," Sherna argued; "they must earn their bread somehow!"

Camilla's voice was harsh, rasping like a file. "There is always an alternative," she said, in a voice that effectively shut off comment.

Magda, watching the grim old face, wondered again, *What kind of awful experience could make a woman hate herself so much that even neutering seems preferable to retaining any trace of female function?* The neutering operation had been illegal on Darkover for centuries; not even the strictest enforcement of the laws had managed to stamp it out.

Jaelle yawned again, asking Rayna, who was the tallest, to put out the lantern. Another woman banked the fire so it would keep a few coals through the night. Magda pillowed her head on her saddlebags as she saw the others doing, laid the knife from her boots beside her head.

Now that the danger seemed over, and the acute fear of discovery had subsided, she found herself elated. She had learned more about Free Amazons in one evening than twelve years on the Darkovan side had taught all the agents. She knew that because before leaving her post she had read through everything actually known about them, including folklore, rumors and dirty jokes, and it all fitted on a printout she could hold in one palm. *If I carry this off, I'll have something to brag about for the rest of my life; that I could spend the night with them and get away undetected.*

One after another, the Amazons dropped off to sleep. Old Camilla snored very softly. Sherna and Gwennis, who lay side by side, talked for a few minutes in whispers, then slept. Magda, in spite of the long day's hard riding, was too tired and tense to sleep. The noise around the other fire did not subside, but grew louder; Magda wondered if it was deliberate, a way of expressing hostility the men dared not show. There was loud talk, drunken singing, some of the songs of such a bawdy nature Magda knew they would never have been sung directly before any woman with the slightest pretense to respectability.

For a time she listened, then grew bored and irritable. Were there no laws of polite use for the shelters, to determine how late one party might continue to carouse when sharing a shelter with another group of travelers? Damn them, were they going to keep up that racket all night? It was surprising the Amazons put up with it, but then, their code evidently forbade them to take notice of the band of men.

The songs came to an end; there was a brief lull, a minor fight broke out and was settled, and in another lull Magda heard one of the men say loudly ". . . held at Sain Scarp . . ."

Magda went tense, straining herself to hear even one more word, but the loud drunken talk started up again. *They do know something about Peter! If I could only hear!*

Blurred by the conversation she seemed to hear the word *Ardais*—she was never sure—and her resolve stiffened. She *must* hear! The Amazons were all sleeping now. She would slip very quietly along the dark wall. . . . She had partially undressed; she sat up and drew on trousers and undertunic in the dark; slid quietly from her blankets and went barefoot along the wall, clinging to the shadows. She could see Jaelle sleeping on her stomach like a child, her face on her bent arm. Magda tiptoed toward the far end of the room, holding her breath; was rewarded by hearing one of the men say ". . . Ardais cub . . ." and ". . . send him back at midwinter . . ."

"And what answer did the lady . . ."

"You think he tells me all that? All I can . . ." It was drowned out in a burst of drunken laughter, then one of the men stiffened.

"What's that?"

"Mouse or rat, probably. Pass me the jug, you—"

Magda froze, but the first speaker got up, suddenly strode straight toward where Magda huddled in the shadow; she turned to slip away, missed her footing and fell full length. Above her she heard a great shout of laughter. The next minute hard hands came down on her and she was picked up bodily and carried into the center of the circle of men.

The man holding her set her on her feet, guffawing loudly.

"Some mouse or rat, Jerrall!"

Magda saw that her captor was the big burly mustachioed man whose eyes had frightened her when she first came into the shelter. He bent toward her, taking her chin in his ham-sized hand.

"Tired of sleeping alone, *chiya?*" He used the word for "little girl," which in family intimacy is affectionate; elsewhere, contemptuous. "Which one of us you got the hots for, hey? Bet it's me; saw you looking at me before."

Magda was wildly trying to get her breath, to *think*. She *would* not, she *could* not struggle and plead with these men!

"Yeah, we've all heard about the Free Amazons," said a big, black-bearded man, digging Magda's captor in the ribs with a wicked leer. "Let's wake up the rest of the girls and get them to join the party! What about it, little rabbit, did you come to ask if there was a drink for you here?"

Oh, God, what have I done? I've been responsible for breaking the shelter-truce, if I've involved the other women in this, made these men think. . . .

Furtively she felt for her knife; realized, in horror, that she had left it lying by her saddlebag.

"What's wrong, *chiya?* Not a word to say? Well, we'll loosen up your tongue, soon enough," said the big man who had grabbed her, and she felt his fetid, drunken breath hot on her face, the evil, bristling mustachios brush her cheek. He jerked her undertunic down around her shoulders. "Hey, a pretty one, too. Stop shoving, Rannar, you'll have your turn soon enough—I caught this one. You want a girl, go wake up one for yourself!" He ran his hands down her bared body. Magda jerked away, caught him by the arm, tried to wrench him in a judo throw; he sidestepped, with a leering shout. "Hey, pretty, I know a trick worth two of that! So you're a fighter, too? We can *really* have some fun with this one," he said, leering. Magda's arms felt numb.

What's the matter with me? She felt him take her shoulder, twisting it cruelly; she could not keep back a cry of pain.

"Now let's not have any more nonsense, precious. Just be a good little girl and we won't hurt you, no, we won't hurt you at all," he muttered, running his hot hands down across her breasts. She backhanded him, hard, across the mouth; rearing back in drunken rage, he struck her a blow that flung her, half stunned, to the floor. "Damn it, you bitch, none of that! Hold her, Rannar—"

She fought and struggled, gasping, silent, afraid if she opened her mouth that some word of Terran Standard would escape her. The men clustered around, shouting encouragement to the men who held her. Magda had been trained in unarmed combat since her sixteenth year; she tried to catch her breath, to find the strength to strike effectively, but she found herself held too hard.

Why can't I defend myself? How did I get this far? Suddenly, as a drowning man's whole life is said to flash before his eyes, Magda knew the answer. *I've psyched myself, for years, into behaving like a normal Darkovan girl. And they're too timid to fight—they expect men to protect them. I'm conditioned to that, and it canceled out my Terran agent's training. . . .*

She hardly knew it when she started to scream. . . .

Chapter Nine

Suddenly a light flared in Magda's eyes; a torch came down, blinding the man who held her. He reared back, yelling. Then there were half a dozen knives, it seemed, bared and leveled at Magda's captors.

"Let her go," said a low, level voice; Magda saw Jaelle's face above the torch. The man who held her backed away; Magda pushed the other man aside, pulled herself free and scrambled to her feet, clutching her torn tunic around her. The mustachioed man yelled something obscene, rushed forward, grabbing up his sword; there was a blur of blades, a clash, a howl, and the man fell, clutching at a slash across his thighs. Magda saw blood on Jaelle's knife. One of the women helped Magda to gather her torn clothing around her, while the men clustered together, muttering.

"Look out," Gwennis said sharply; the women fell back, braced, knives like a wall in front of them. Magda, thrust unregarded to one side, watched the slow, grim advance of the bandits, the unflinching barricade of the women's knives. Everything seemed sharply focused as she stood there waiting for the clash: the rough, menacing faces of the men, the equally unyielding faces of the women; the torchlight, the dark shadowed beams, even the patterns of the stone-flagged floor, seemed etched forever on her memory. Later she never knew how long that taut, sharply focused *waiting* lasted—it felt like hours, days—for the inevitable rush, clash of swords, tension drawn tighter, tighter. She felt like shrieking, *Oh, don't, don't, I didn't mean . . .* and physically raised her hands to cover her mouth so that she would *not* cry out.

Then one of the men swore roughly, dropped the point of his sword. "The hell with all this. Not worth it. Put your knives down, girls. Truce?"

None of the women moved, but the bandit leader—the big, black-bearded man who had held Magda down—gestured to his men, and one by one they lowered their swords. When the last one was down, the women slowly relaxed, letting the points of their knives drop toward the stone floor.

Jaelle said, "You have broken shelter-truce by laying hands on one of ours. If I reported this at a patrol station you could all be outlawed, with any hand free to kill you for three years." The strange beauty of her face in the torchlight, copper hair haloed around her pale features, made a strange contrast to her hard words. The leader said drunkenly, "You wouldn't do that, would you, *mestra?* We weren't hurting her none."

"We could all see how much pleasure she took in your advances," Jaelle said dryly.

The mustachioed man said thickly, "Ah, hell, she came to *us;* how'd we know she wasn't looking for a bit of fun?" The wound across his thighs still oozed blood, but Magda could see now that it was no more than half an inch deep: painful perhaps, and humiliating, but not disabling or dangerous. Jaelle wasn't even trying to kill him.

Jaelle swung around to Magda; her eyes glinted like green fire by torchlight, and Magda felt sick with shame and dread. *I am responsible for all this.*

"Did you come to them of your free will? Were you looking, as he says, for a bit of fun?"

Magda whispered, "No. No, I didn't." She could hardly hear herself speak.

"Then"—the Amazon leader's voice was a whiplash that cut—"what were you doing that they could think so?"

Magda opened her mouth to say, "I wanted to hear what they were talking about," but stopped before a single word could get out. Camilla had warned her: spying on men was not proper behavior for an Amazon. She could not disgrace these women, who had protected her without any obligation to do so, by bringing shame or contempt on them. They had welcomed her to their meal and fireside; dressed as an Amazon, she had violated one of their strictest codes of behavior. Now she knew she must lie, quickly and well, a lie that would not involve the Amazons in her misbehavior. She said shakily, "I—I had a cramp, and I turned the wrong way in the darkness, looking for the privy. When I saw I was wrong I tried to get away before they saw me, and I slipped and fell."

"You see?" said Jaelle to the men. Her eyes flicked Magda's face like the blow of a whip.

She knows I'm lying, of course. But she knows why. It was all the amend she could make.

Jaelle said, "You have broken shelter-truce, for which the penalty is three years' outlawry. And you have attempted to rape a woman here, for which *our* penalty is castration. Think yourselves lucky that your man did not succeed. And now gather up all that is yours, and be gone. By law we need not share shelter with outlaws and rapists."

Blackbeard said, and the drunken dismay in his voice was actually comical, "In this storm, *mestra?*"

"You should have listened to the voice of the storm before you broke shelter-truce," Jaelle said, and her face was like stone. "Outside, like the dirty animals you are! And if one of you sets foot over the threshold while we are still here, I swear, I will cut out his *cuyones* and roast them over the fire there!" She gestured with her knife. "Out! No more talk now! Out!"

Fumbling, drunken, muttering obscenely, they gathered up their belongings; grumbling and angry, but before the gleam of the women's knives, their massed, indomitable *waiting,* they went. When the door had closed behind the last of them, Jaelle said, "Rayna, Gwennis, go and be sure they do not disturb our horses and gear." She handed the torch to Sherna, and came slowly toward Magda. "You. Are you hurt? Did they do anything worse than tear your clothes and maul you?"

"No." Magda's teeth were chattering with shock and reaction. *I've been false to everything. To the Amazons, by behaving immodestly before men. To the mission I came on, by not finding out what I risked so much to know.* She felt sick, shamed, exhausted with the violence of her emotions.

Jaelle put an arm around Magda, supporting her. The action was not kind, but contemptuous. She said, "Give her some wine before she finishes this by falling in a faint at our feet!"

She shoved Magda down on a bench; Camilla held a cup to her lips. Magda pushed it away. "I don't want—"

"Drink it, damn you!" Camilla forced the cup against her mouth; Magda gulped, choked, swallowed again. Camilla said viciously, "You! I warned you, you bitch! Who let you out of the Guild-house in this state, with no notion of how to behave? If they had not all been as drunk as monks at midwinter-feast, it would have come to a fight, and we could all have been raped, or killed. You deserve to be beaten and sent back to the Guild-house!"

Sherna had built up the fire again; the women came in from the barn, and Rayna said, "They have gone; good riddance. I hope they freeze in the storm."

Jaelle was standing with her back to the fire, looking formidable. Camilla shoved Magda toward her.

"Jaelle, you are our chosen leader; it is for you to deal with her. If you say so, I will beat her bloody for you; it would be a pleasure!"

Jaelle said at last: "Let her go, Camilla; if I decide she should be beaten, I can do it myself. Well," she said to Magda, "what have you to say for yourself?"

It's not over yet. I've got to go on bluffing. She said, with a spurt of defiance. "You are not *my* chosen leader. Do I owe *you* an explanation of my conduct?"

Jaelle said angrily, "You could have involved us all in your stupidity— or your wantonness, whatever it was! What is one of our first basic rules? Never get yourself *into* anything you can't get yourself out of again! No one forces a woman into danger; but having taken a risk, you should be able to meet it. Now you have reinforced one of the old dirty stories about us, that we fight only in wolf packs and never meet our enemies fairly! Yes, damn you, I think you owe me an explanation; not me alone—all of us."

That was fair enough. She said at last, truthfully, "I heard a part of what they were saying; and it seemed to me that it bore on the business that brought me into these hills. I felt I had to hear it."

Jaelle considered that for a moment, frowning. Magda noticed, incongruously, something she had not seen until that very moment; Jaelle, standing there so secure and confident, was wearing nothing but her underwear. They all were. And somewhere at the back of her mind, the trained anthropologist, never off duty, was making notes: *So that's what Free Amazons wear for underwear.*

Old Camilla's voice was sharp. "Don't listen to a word she says, Jaelle. Men's boots, with a knife in them? And who let her out of the Guild-house in this shape, to disgrace us all? Any girl from the Guild-house, even a girl of fifteen, would know how to defend herself against rape, even unweaponed. There is something wrong here!"

"Yes, very wrong," said Jaelle. "Someone has behaved irresponsibly, allowing her to go about alone before she knew how to behave. You shame whoever took your oath," she said to Magda. "Who was she? Name her to us; she is responsible for your conduct!"

God help me, now I'm in for it! Well, the woman is dead, so Rohana told me, and it won't involve any living person in trouble. She said, "I took the oath at the hands of Kindra n'ha Mhari."

"You lie!" Jaelle raised her arm and struck Magda a blow that made her head ring. She slapped her again and again across the face. "You lie, you bitch," she said, trembling. "Kindra n'ha Mhari was my foster-mother; I dwelt with her seven years before her death, and every one of her oathdaughters is known to me by face and name! How dare you slander a dead woman? You lie, lie, *lie!*"

Magda's head was pounding with the pain of the blows. What now? *What now?*

Old Camilla thrust her face at Magda; she was white and shaking. She said, "If you were a man, I would call challenge upon you. Kindra n'ha Mhari took me in when I was alone and desperate; I have been a member of her band for thirty years, and I loved her as a twin sister! I don't know who or what you are, that you think you can misuse her name, but you will not do so again! Rayna, Gwennis, get her saddlebags; we will see if there is something in them to give us a clue to this filthy bitch of an impostor!"

Rayna got down and started to go through Magda's belongings by torchlight. Finally she pulled out the safe-conduct, handed it to Jaelle.

"It bears the Lady Rohana's name and seal. A forgery, no doubt, but you had better see it, Jaelle."

Jaelle turned it curiously in her hands, held it closer to the fire to see better. "Light the lantern, Rayna; we need light for whatever is going to happen," she said. "I cannot read in this murk." When the lantern was lighted she stood examining it for some time and finally said, "It is not a forgery; I know my kinswoman's handwriting too well for that. And the seal is genuine." She read aloud: ". . . Call upon all those who owe loyalty to the Domain of Ardais to give such aid as is in their power . . ."

"Stolen," said Camilla, her mouth lifting in a sneer.

"No, for it bears her name and a good description." She went to Magda and handed her the safe-conduct. "Did my kinswoman truly give this to you?"

"She did."

"No one can force Rohana to do anything she does not want to do," Jaelle said, "and I have never known her to lend her name to any wickedness. Are you truly on a mission in her name?"

Magda nodded. Jaelle said, "But you are not an Amazon, are you? How came you to try to pass yourself off as one, Margali—if that is truly your name?"

"It is the name I bore as a child." Magda blinked, for a moment afraid she would cry. But she spoke without faltering. "My mission is an honorable one, and it was the Lady Rohana who suggested to me that I dress and bear myself as an Amazon." She raised her head, still stinging with Jaelle's blows. "I have disgraced no one! If I had avoided your camp, no harm would have been done; but in this storm I did not want to sleep out of doors."

"No," said Jaelle. "You narrowly escaped frostbite as it was. So you thought you could get through the night without betraying yourself—"

"And then it seemed to me that those men knew something of importance to my mission. Something so important that nothing else seemed to matter."

"What prompted you to wear men's boots? Was it only ignorance?"

"Lady Rohana provided the boots," said Magda, "but I knew no better."

Camilla laughed suddenly. "I told the Lady Rohana that her ignorance of our customs would make trouble sometime; but it came many years later than I thought it would! Well, she meant well; I suppose if you had met no real Amazons you might have passed, indeed, as one of us."

Jaelle said curiously, "But, were you not afraid to travel in the Hellers, alone, and with winter coming on?"

A few hours ago Magda would have said, "No, I was not afraid." Now, having tasted fear, she was more honest with herself. "I was afraid, yes. But it seemed to me that my mission was more important than fear."

For the first time Jaelle's eyes were a little kinder. "So you felt the dress of an Amazon would protect you? Well, the disguise even deceived us, for a little while, and it seems to me that in general you tried to conduct yourself in such a way as to bring no disgrace upon our dress and name. It is not your fault you failed. But what put it into your head to come alone on such a mission, my girl? Was there no man to whom you could turn, no relative, no father, no warden, overlord or guardian? What is the mission on which you must travel alone?"

Having no better idea, Magda told the truth; or as much of it as she dared. "A near kinsman"—*(A husband is related, damn it, related by marriage at least . . .)*—"is held at Sain Scarp for ransom; if he is not ransomed by midwinter, he will be tortured and killed."

"And no man in your family or household would help you? But I do not understand this," Jaelle said. "If you had the right to appeal to the Lady Rohana, you would have had an equal right to appeal to her husband or to her sons for their aid."

Magda said steadily, "I have no right to appeal to the Lady Rohana. She aided me out of kindness and charity, because I had none other to help me."

"Ah, that is like her," said Jaelle. "No lame dog of the mountains ever came limping in vain to her doorstep." She sighed and yawned, covering her mouth with a small hand, so graceful it was hard to believe she had wounded a man, had beaten Magda with those same small hands. "Well, I am not your guardian, and your affairs are none of my business; normally I would feel bound to help anyone under the shelter of my kinswoman's patronage. But there is a more serious point at issue here. It seems to me, truly, that you have shown a spirit almost worthy of a true Amazon, venturing alone into the Hellers in the decline of the year, instead of calling upon some man for protection. You were stupid, yes, and you were unlucky; but if stupidity were a crime, half the human race would be outlawed at every crossroad, and—how says the proverb? *If ill luck were cheese, dairy-women would go wanting work.* Just the same"—she frowned —"no one may be allowed to impersonate a Free Amazon. Camilla has told us how one such impersonation was punished!"

Magda shuddered, but forced herself to say boldly, "You have said it yourself: I did nothing to disgrace you. And I know that Lady Rohana was allowed to travel with your band, dressed as one of you."

"True. But the law requires that before this is allowed, the woman must have the permission of the elected leader, and the consent of every one of the women who is to travel in their company."

"Then give me such permission," Magda challenged, and Jaelle broke into an unexpected smile.

"I almost wish the laws of our Guild permitted it," she said half aloud. "A thousand pities Rohana did not know how inflexible is that law. Had she sent for me, and asked that leave, *before* you had shown yourself in Amazon's dress, I almost believe—" She sighed, and said, "Well, the law does *not* allow me to give you that permission once you have invaded the privacy of my women in disguise: unknowing, perhaps, in ignorance of your crime, but invaded nonetheless. There was a day—and if we are not vigilant it could come again on Darkover—when we were invaded constantly by enemies, spies, seeking to learn something of our ways and weaknesses, or to carry tales about us, hoping to slander us to our disadvantage. The penalty for a man who invades us in disguise is death or mutilation, as we may choose and as circumstances dictate. For a woman the penalty never changes. Before you depart from us, the lie must become truth: You must take the oath of the Free Amazons, here and now."

Magda's first reaction was, *Oh, is that all?* Jaelle saw the relief in her face, for her voice hardened. "Don't dare to take it lightly," she said, "for if you swear it, and later betray it, any Free Amazon on Darkover may kill you where you stand; you are a dead woman the moment you put your nose out your own window!"

It flashed across Magda's mind: *An oath under duress is not valid.* That was the Terran Magda; in the next moment the Darkovan girl Margali, who had grown up at Caer Donn, absorbing the way of life, the codes, the beliefs of her Darkovan playmates almost more deeply than those of her parents, thought, *An oath I cannot betray; how can I do this?*

The conflict was terrible; she felt as if she were being wrenched apart. *I have come and gone between two worlds with impunity; now I must pay the price, and I do not know if I can!* She put her hands over her face, in a futile attempt to conceal her emotions. *If I refuse, will they kill me here and now?*

"Will you take the oath?"

Magda said, "What choice have I?"

"None, I fear. I owe it to my women, and to every woman of the Guild, that none shall invade us and carry our secrets outside. If you will not swear, we will simply have to carry you, as prisoner, back to the nearest Guild-house, and there keep you until you are willing to be sworn, or until midwinter-night when all our Guild meet in reunion and our judges can hear your story and decide what is to be done with you. It may be that no penalty will be exacted, that you will be sworn to secrecy about what you have seen and you will be allowed to depart."

"To that much I will swear willingly," said Magda, and meant it.

"But I am not empowered to take *that* oath from you. That can be given only by a judge, and at midwinter-night, and only after hearing everything that bears upon the case; if, for instance, you had several young children and there were none else to assume their care, or you had already sworn a Keeper's oath to a Tower. If you prefer, then, we can take you now to Neskaya Guild-house—it is only a tenday ride from here—and leave you to be judged at midwinter."

And by that time Peter would be dead by torture!

I guess I'll have to take their damned oath. It will give me time to decide what to do. . . .

Probably all it entailed—she remembered the few Darkovan oaths whose content and form she had heard—was a pledge not to harm any Free Amazon, and not to betray any of their secrets. *And I don't know any of them, so that's safe enough to promise! I can do that much honorably.*

But if there is more? She felt a kind of despair. "I will take the oath," she said, fighting to keep her voice steady.

Jaelle nodded. "I thought you would," she said. "Come, let us get it over with, then; we are all weary, and you more than any, I should imagine. Come here to the fire and stand among us."

Magda obeyed. Jaelle was standing directly before the fire, her back to the flames; Magda noticed again how very young she looked. How old could she be? Twenty-two, twenty-three . . . hardly more than that! The women made a circle around them. Camilla came to Jaelle and said in an undertone, "You are young for this; do you want me to take her oath?"

Jaelle patted the lined old cheek. "Dear aunt, you are always ready to spare me or shield me, but if I am old enough to be elected leader of a band, surely I am old enough to punish intruders, or to take an oath."

She said to Magda, "Bare your breasts before us."

Startled, confused, Magda fumbled with the laces of her torn tunic. Part of her, at this moment, the trained agent who never stopped taking mental notes for later use, was excited—the graduate anthropologist participating in an unusual and secret tribal custom; but the rest of her was just a frightened girl, ashamed as any girl reared in Caer Donn would have been ashamed, to stand with her body bared before strangers. She fumbled with the laces; Sherna came and pulled the tunic down so that she stood before them, bare to the waist, shivering. She clenched her fists at her sides, resisting the impulse to cover herself with her hands, as one by one the women came and solemnly inspected her bare breasts.

This must have been an ancient way of making sure they were not invaded by men in disguise. I'll bet there was a time when the candidate—or the intruder—had to strip herself bare, head to foot. She bit her lip hard to keep from breaking into nervous laughter—or tears. *I feel like a horse in the market!*

When every one of the women had looked her over, Jaelle said, "Have we all verified that this is in truth a woman, and not a man come in disguise to mock us? If there are any doubts we shall have this one stripped naked; any of you has the right to demand it." Magda was no longer able to be elated at this verification of her guess; she stood shivering, her eyes cast down. But no one demanded it, and Jaelle nodded.

"So be it; we accept you as a woman. Now, you have cut your hair and come among us of your free will; so I call upon you to repeat the oath given in the days of Varzil the Good, to the Guild of Free Amazons, in accordance with the Charter kept at Nevarsin. In the presence of these witnesses, repeat after me: From this day forth I renounce the right to marry save as a freemate. No man shall bind me *di catenas* and I will dwell in no man's household as a *barragana.*"

Stumbling over the words, Jaelle prompting her at intervals, Magda repeated the words. "No man shall bind me . . ." *Nothing,* she thought, *is less likely than that I should ever want—or any Terran-born woman should be allowed—to marry* di catenas, *by the old religious ritual. And a* barragana *is simply a kept woman, a concubine.*

"I swear that I am prepared to defend myself by force if I am attacked by force, and that I shall turn to no man for protection."

Magda repeated the words; again, feeling that she was actually disintegrating. *Two of me—the Terran Magda, the Darkovan Margali—and they're breaking apart! Who am I? Who will I be after this?*

". . . Turn to no . . . no man for protection. . . ."

I've been taught to defend myself since I was sixteen years old. On any other world I would have been doing it all along. Here I was sheltered, and when I finally had to try, I couldn't. Without Jaelle's band I'd have been beaten up and probably gang-raped. I might have survived it—people do—but it would have been a hell of a thing to live with!

"From this day forth I swear I shall never again be known by the name of any man, be he father, guardian, lover or husband, but simply and solely as—" Jaelle broke off. "What was your mother's name?"

Magda rummaged wildly in her mind for the Darkovan equivalent of "Elizabeth." *What's wrong with me? I heard it often enough. I'm disintegrating!* She said, after a perceptible pause, "Ysabet."

". . . As Margali *nikhya mic* Ysabet," said Jaelle, speaking the words in full without the common abbreviation, and Magda repeated them, biting her lip, fighting for self-control. Nothing so far in the oath had troubled or frightened her, but this did. Known only as Margali n'ha Ysabet. *Oh, Dad, do I have to give up your name, too? I didn't mind giving up Peter's, when we separated. But you, Dad, do I have to renounce you, too?* The face of David Lorne, graying, gentle, scholarly, seemed to swim in her mind, to shake his head at her in reproach. *Oh, God, Peter, are you worth this?* Margali n'ha Ysabet . . . Magdalen, daughter of Elizabeth. No more than that?

"From this day forth I swear I will give myself to no man save in my own time and season and of my own free will, at my own desire; I will never earn my bread as the object of any man's lust."

Well, no woman in her right mind would object to swearing an oath not to become a prostitute. Then she suddenly felt troubled. If a woman had no occupation of her own, that could also mean—a wife?

"From this day forth I swear I will bear no child to any man save for my own pleasure and at my own time and choice; I will bear no child to any man for house or heritage, clan or inheritance, pride or posterity; I swear that I alone will determine rearing and fosterage of any child I bear, without regard to any man's place, position or pride. . . ."

The Terran Magda thought, *Well, that makes sense.* But the girl reared in Caer Donn discovered that she was choking as she spoke the words. *Peter wanted a child. I didn't, then, but I was ashamed of not wanting it; I was almost as disappointed as he, to find I was not pregnant. I wanted so to please him. I knew I'd failed him—and now I can never . . . never make it up to him. . . .* She heard herself, to her own shame and horror, sob aloud. *He wanted that so much, and I failed him in that, I failed him in everything. . . .*

Jaelle waited for her sobs to quiet, repeating inexorably, ". . . Any man's place, position or pride. . . ."

Magda repeated the words, but found that she was crying as she spoke them. She ordered and commanded herself to be calm. *What's happening to me? Why am I coming apart like this?*

"From this day forth I renounce allegiance to any family, clan, household, warden or liege lord, and take oath that I owe allegiance only to the laws of the land as a free citizen must; to the kingdom, the crown and the Gods."

Magda repeated the words mechanically. She was almost too exhausted by emotion to hear them or understand their sense.

"I shall appeal to no man as of right, for protection, support or succor: but shall owe allegiance only to my oath-mother, to my sisters in the Guild and to my employer for the season of my employment."

And what of my loyalty to the Empire? Magda repeated the words, forcing them past the lump in her throat.

"And I further swear that the members of the Guild of Free Amazons shall be to me, each and every one, as my mother, my sister or my daughter, born of one blood with me, and that no woman sealed by oath to the Guild shall appeal to me in vain. . . ."

Magda discovered that her throat was thick again with unshed tears. She thought, *My mother is long dead. I never had a sister, and I shall never have a daughter. Yet I swear. . . .*

Jaelle reached out her hands, clasped Magda's cold hands in her own. She said quietly, "Margali n'ha Ysabet, I accept you before the Goddess as oath-daughter; henceforward you shall be as daughter and sister to me and to every one of us in the Guild. Here in the presence of these witnesses, I declare that you are from this moment sealed by oath to the Guild of Free Amazons, subject only to our laws, and I give you freedom of the Guild: and in token I exchange with you this greeting." She drew Magda close and solemnly kissed her on the mouth. "Kneel," she said softly, "and repeat: From this moment, I swear to obey all the laws of the Guild of Free Amazons and any lawful command of my oath-mother, the Guild members or my elected leader for the season of my employment. And if I betray any secret of the Guild, or prove false to my oath, then I shall submit myself to the Guild-mothers for such discipline as they shall choose; and if I fail, then may every woman's hand turn against me, let them slay me like an animal and consign my body unburied to corruption and my soul to the mercy of the Goddess."

Too late to retreat. Numb, desperate, Magda heard herself stumble through the words that condemned her to betray someone. *Whatever I do now, I am forsworn. What shall I do, what shall I do?*

Jaelle raised her to her feet, hugged her close. "Don't cry, my sister," she said softly, using the word in the intimate mode. "I know, it is a great and solemn step to take, and few of us have taken it without tears."

Camilla wrapped her in her tunic. "Poor little thing, you are chilled to the bone! Jaelle, how could you let her go through that long oath, standing there almost naked? When we had once seen her, you might have stopped to let her cover herself!" She wrapped a blanket over the tunic, drew her to the fire.

Jaelle laughed in apology and said, "Forgive me, Margali; I had never accepted an oath before, I was nervous, afraid I should forget some of the words—"

"Drink this, it will stop your shivering." Gwennis handed her the cup they had given her before, which she had not finished. She heard her teeth chattering against the rim of the cup; she sipped slowly, trying to get control of herself. They all crowded around her, hugging her, comforting her. Rayna murmured, "Don't feel bad, we all cry, you didn't cry nearly as much as I did!"

Jaelle said, "Now you must forgive us for being so rough with you before; now we are all your sisters. From tonight, every Amazon is your sister, but those who witnessed your oath are your family, and special, always." She looked affectionately around the circle, saying, "Are you not? Camilla cut my hair for me, nine years ago."

Gwennis said, in an undertone like a private joke, "How dare you chide her for crying, Jaelle? *You* didn't cry, I remember!"

"But I was fostered among you," Jaelle said. "Now we will finish this bottle of wine in our sister's honor, then we must all sleep. Tomorrow we must think how best to send her to the Guild-house, but for tonight we will celebrate."

They are all so kind to me now. I don't deserve it. Magda, calm now and exhausted, asked Gwennis, "Where am I to be taken?"

"To Neskaya Guild-house, or perhaps to Thendara, which is our own house," said Gwennis. "Every newmade Amazon must spend half a year in the Guild-house, learning our ways and unlearning the vicious old ways you have been taught since girlhood—all the things you were taught about seemly behavior for a woman. Your childhood put chains on you; there you will be taught to free yourself, to be what you best can be."

Oh, God! I took this oath to escape being sent to the Guild-house, to gain time! Am I forsworn for nothing, then?

Each of them had something to say to her. Sherna, who was a plump and pretty girl, came and knelt beside her. "I came to the Amazons two years ago, when I fully realized that I had no share in my father's estate; all my brothers shared, but not I; for me there was nothing ahead but marriage to some man who could help my brothers to manage my father's lands. They refused two men I liked because, they said, they would not dwell under one roof with them; and would have forced me on a friend of theirs. So when I knew I had no right to refuse, but could be made to marry at their wish and not mine, I cut my hair and came to the Guild-house. Do you know what I feared most?" She grinned, such a droll grin that Magda had to smile. "I feared they would tell me I could never lie with a man again! But, I thought, better that than marry to please my brothers. . . ."

Jaelle sat beside her. "It is customary for oath-mother and daughter to exchange gifts. I have no gift for you, Margali; I had not foreseen this. I must think of something."

They're so kind to me. So overwhelmingly kind. They act as if I were their long-lost sister. The oath means so much. . . .

Magda said, "My mission—I had told you it was life and death. . . ."

Jaelle said, "We will discuss that in the morning. It may be that you owe no loyalty to any man, even to a kinsman. But for now we must all sleep."

The women finished their wine and went to their sleeping rolls again. Rayna put out the lantern. It was very quiet, except for the diminishing, faraway howl of the storm. Camilla, who lay next to Magda, reached out her hand in the darkness and patted her gently on the cheek.

"You were not the first to shiver through the oath," she said. "When my oath was taken, I—you know I am *emmasca*—I had nothing like to a woman's form, and so three of the witnesses refused to believe I was not a man and I had to be stripped. Kindra was so distressed by that, that she, too, forgot to have me covered afterward. I was so humiliated, I wept for hours; but it was half a lifetime ago, and now I can laugh about it. Someday you will laugh, too, sister. Sleep well."

"You, too—sister," Magda said with difficulty. It was the first time in her life that she had ever spoken the word in the intimate mode.

One by one the women dropped away into sleep. Magda was almost too weary to think straight. *I can't go to a Guild-house and let Peter die by torture! An oath under duress is not valid . . . my first loyalty is to the Empire.*

She was very weary; sleep began, against her will, to steal over her. Bits and pieces of the oath seemed to echo in her mind. *Bear no child except at my own will . . . did I want Peter's child, then? If not, why did I cry that way? Or did I only* want *to want it . . . because I had failed him so?*

She thought, at the very edge of sleep, that she would rather like to go to a Guild-house, if it were not for her mission. *I could be as strong and effective here, as an Amazon, as on any planet where women are free.*

Whatever I do, I am forsworn. I can betray my oath to my sisters—or betray my first allegiance to the Empire. All my life, never knowing it, I have been two women: one Terran, one Darkovan. And now I am torn. I must betray someone, or Peter dies by torture.

Is Peter worth the sacrifice of my integrity? Can I give up that, too? With a life at stake?

Sleep took her suddenly, and she plummeted into it like bottomless darkness.

She dreamed of Peter Haldane; he was lying in the dark, on stone; cold and alone and frightened. And it seemed to her that as he had done only once or twice in the brief term of their love, he held out his hands to her, laid his head against her breast: off guard, vulnerable, no longer concerned to keep up the mask of strength, of masculine infallibility. She kissed him and soothed him in her dream, and he whispered to her, "You are the only one I can trust, Mag. I trust you. Everybody else is out to cut my throat, but you don't compete. I'm not afraid of you, Mag, you're the only one I'm not afraid of." And she wanted to cry but knew she could not, that it was for her now to be strong enough for both of them. . . . In the dream she wiped away his tears and comforted him, saying, "Darkover is not an easy world for men, either." But when she woke she was alone, in her lonely and solitary bed.

Chapter Ten

Magda woke late; it was full daylight in the shelter, and the Amazons had built up the fire and were cooking breakfast. She closed her eyes, pretending sleep, knowing that she could delay the decision no longer.

I took the oath to gain time. I do not want to break it. I have learned— and learned too late—that I am almost more Darkovan than Terran, and an oath is sacred. But that does not matter now. I cannot let Peter die, alone and by torture. I am an agent of Terra, and Peter is my colleague.

Once she had formulated that clearly, all the emotional reasons on the other side surged up inside her; but she forced them down with a great effort, her face set in rigid calm. *I have made my decision. I will not even think about any other possibility.*

Even if it's a wrong *decision?*

Stop that! No more wavering!

She set about wondering how she could carry it out. They were planning to send her to the Guild-house at Neskaya, which was a good long way from here. But it was in a different direction from Nevarsin, which was their immediate mission. Surely they would not alter their route to take her to Neskaya; one or, at the most, two would be detailed for that. She would pretend submission until they were off guard and trusted her—*How skillful I am at betrayal!*—then slip away and take the fastest route back to Thendara. *They will be looking for me at Sain Scarp, and if I go directly there, having betrayed my oath to them, they will have a legal right to kill me on sight, and Peter will die, under torture. Once in Thendara—what then?*

All I can do is to tell Montray I've failed, that—literally—he sent a

woman to do a man's job, and on this world, a woman couldn't handle it.
He will have to send someone else. There will still be time, just barely.

And what's ahead for me, on this world, after that?

Nothing. . . .

Magda accepted the fact that this meant exile from her own world, which was Darkover. She could never again take up her old work in Thendara; once she stepped into the Darkovan zone, any Free Amazon was legally entitled to kill her on sight. She would have to put in for a transfer, go somewhere else.

To a planet where a woman can have something genuine to do. She thought, bleakly, that at least her coup with the Free Amazons—*I've qua-drupled all existing knowledge about them*—would bring her an offer wor-thy of her capabilities.

The thought of leaving Darkover brought sharp, tearing pain, almost a physical agony. But there was no other way. She knew she could no longer endure the ordinary life of a woman on this world, nor the limited work that a woman could do here for the Empire.

If I could live here as a Free Amazon . . . but the price of keeping her oath was Peter's death by torture.

He is Darkovan, too. Would he accept his life, knowing I had bought it by oath-breaking and the sacrifice of integrity? The thought was too painful to endure. Magda forced herself to get up, to break off the endless, useless self-questioning.

Jaelle, already dressed, was standing by the fire, making up a hot drink from roasted grain; Magda had tasted it a few times in Caer Donn. She dipped up a cup for Magda, and said, "I made them let you sleep; you must have been wearied to death. The others are out with the horses, making ready to go. This morning you and I take the road for the Guild-house, where your name will be written on the rolls of the Charter."

Magda said, in a last desperate attempt to get through to her, "I have told you my mission is life and death; my kinsman will die by torture if I do not ransom him at midwinter."

Jaelle looked sympathetic. But she said, "By oath, sister, you renounced loyalty to any man, and to any household, family or clan. Your loyalties are to us now."

Magda clenched her fists in utter despair. Jaelle said gently, "When we reach the Guild-house, you may lay your case before the Guild-mothers; it may be that when they have heard all, they will decide that your claim does not violate the oath, and send someone in your place to ransom him. There would be time for that. But I am not empowered to make that decision."

Magda turned abruptly away. *So be it,* she thought grimly; *on your own head, Jaelle, even if I have to kill you.*

The other women came from the barn, laughing, chattering, talking of the ride ahead. Jaelle said, "The rest of you may ride when you will, but you must choose another leader; Margali and I must ride for Neskaya."

"Oh, Jaelle," Gwennis protested, "you took this mission because your brother is there, and you have not seen him in years! Appoint one of us to take her to Neskaya for you! I will gladly change with you."

Jaelle laughed, shaking her head. "Why, I just reproved Margali, reminding her that our first loyalty is to Guild, not kindred! As for my brother, a boy of ten has little need for a visit from a grown sister; I can see him at Ardais in midsummer, and anyway, no doubt dom Gabriel has taught him enough about the family disgrace that I am sure he would rather be spared my visit!"

Magda asked, "Is your brother a monk, then?"

"Oh, no! But he has been sent there, like many Comyn sons, to learn to read and write and to hear something of our history. He is Rohana's fosterling; I have seen him but once since he was three years old."

Pretending interest, she asked the nature of the mission.

"At Nevarsin, the monks keep the records of much knowledge lost elsewhere since the Ages of Chaos. They will not teach women, and we are not even allowed to stay in the guest-house, but we have leave to use their library. Our best scribes, a little at a time, are transcribing their books on anatomy and surgery, as well as those on birth and the diseases of women —books you would think they would turn over to us entirely, since the monks can make no use of them. We are allowed to have only two scribes there at a time; Rayna and Sherna are going there to change with two women who have been there for half a year, and Gwennis to keep house for them in the village, while Camilla will escort the others home."

Magda toyed with a bowl of the powdered porridge. She was curious, but asked no more questions. It went against the grain to pretend friendliness with a woman she might have to kill.

Soon after, the other women rode away, leaving Magda and Jaelle alone. While they were saddling their horses, Jaelle discovered that hers had a loose shoe.

"I wish I had discovered it before Gwennis left," she said. "She is no blacksmith, but I have seen her make emergency repairs. Well, we must stop in the nearest village. Just look at that!" She handed the shoe to Magda, who stood weighing it in her hand as Jaelle bent to examine the horse's hoof.

I could stun her with it and get away now. . . .

But she waited too long; Jaelle turned back and held out her hand for the shoe, dropping it into her saddlebag.

It was a bright morning, almost cloudless, with a brisk cold wind blowing. Jaelle sniffed the wind, started to throw a leg into her saddle—and at that moment Magda heard a savage yell and two men rushed them from the woods, knives drawn. In split-second shock, Magda recognized two of the bandits from last night: the black-bearded bandit leader, and the big man with the mustachios whom Jaelle had wounded. Magda heard herself shout a warning; Jaelle whirled, half out of her saddle. Then she was fighting, backed up against her horse, the two men almost hiding her from Magda's sight. Magda thought, *Run! Get away now, they're saving you the trouble of killing her—*

But already she had her own knife out, was running toward them. Blackbeard whirled and Magda felt his knife graze her arm, a pain like fire, as she plunged her own knife deep into his chest; felt it turn on bone and slip. He slithered, with a groan, to the ground. Jaelle was still fighting with the other man; she saw that Jaelle was bleeding from a long slash on the cheek. Then she heard Jaelle scream with agony as the bandit's knife drove down toward her breast; she fell to the ground and at that instant Magda felt her knife sink into the man's back.

He fell with a harsh sound, air escaping from lungs already no longer breathing. Slowly, feeling sick, she pulled out the knife.

I haven't fought anyone since combat training, ten years ago. Now I've killed one and wounded another. She looked at Jaelle, unconscious on the ground, almost under the body of the man Magda had killed. *Is she dead?* The thought did not bring relief, but a wrenching agony. *She fought for me, last night. And I would have betrayed her. . . .*

Jaelle stirred, and Magda knew that Jaelle's life still stood between her and her mission. She was still holding the bloody knife with which she had killed the bandit. She saw Jaelle's eyes move to the knife; she lay still, looking up at Magda without a word. Magda suddenly knew that she could not kill anyone in cold blood; above all she could not kill this woman who lay bleeding and helpless in the snow at her feet.

What good is Peter's life if I buy it with another death? I will save him honorably if I can; not otherwise.

She knelt beside Jaelle. Her face was covered with blood; more blood was soaking through her shoulder. She lifted the sticky clothes clinging to the wound.

The bandit's knife had gone under the collarbone and sliced down toward the armpit; a bad wound, painful and dangerous but not, Magda thought, necessarily fatal. She got out her knife again and cleaned the blade, saw that one of Jaelle's eyes was open—the other was clotted shut—

and that she was watching the knife. Magda said irritably, "I've got to cut these clothes off so I can stop the bleeding." She slit Jaelle's tunic and eased it gently away from the skin; Jaelle gasped with the pain but did not cry out. She only said, wetting her lips, "Did you—kill them both?"

"One is surely dead. I don't know about the other, but he isn't in any shape to harm us," Magda said.

Jaelle said, her breath coming loud, "Bandages . . . in my saddle-bags. . . ."

Magda got up, edging between the dead bandit and Jaelle's horse, which, smelling the blood, shifted its feet uneasily. She led the horse away and took down the saddlebags, hunting in them; she found two or three rolls, and what looked like a small, primitive first-aid kit. *That cut probably needs stitches, but I can't do it.* She made a pressure bandage, strapped it around Jaelle's shoulder, turned her attention to the long, hideous gash along Jaelle's face; it had laid her cheek open to the bone. Jaelle said, in a hoarse, frightened voice, "Can't see out of . . . this eye. . . ."

Magda went to the well behind the shelter, dipped up the icy water, came back and sponged the dreadful gash. The eyelashes parted; a little more sponging showed that the eye had only been stuck shut with blood from a small nick in the eyelid. Magda pushed the eyelids open; Jaelle gasped with relief.

"Can you walk? You can't lie out here in the snow." Magda knelt, slipped an arm around the woman, managed to hoist her to her feet; Jaelle tried to walk, but collapsed against Magda. Magda managed, somehow, to get her inside the shelter and lay her on one of the stone benches. She started to build a fire, put some water to boil, thinking that some bark-tea, or some of the Amazon grain-brew, would do them both good. And if Jaelle was in shock—and she looked like it—she had better be kept warm. Not knowing how Jaelle had stowed her own blankets, Magda got out her own and wrapped Jaelle up in them; shoved one of the stone slabs into the fire, thinking she could heat it, wrap it in something and put it at the hurt woman's feet. When the water boiled she poured it on the bark for tea, and went out to put the animals away—they wouldn't be going anywhere right away. The second bandit was definitely dead. She had to drag him out of the way to get the horses and her pack beast into the stable again.

When she came into the shelter Jaelle was conscious. She whispered, "I thought you had gone."

Remotely, like something someone else might have thought, it occurred to Magda: she could have escaped. After doing her best for Jaelle, she could have left her here to recover, and felt no particular guilt. Now it was something she could never have done. *I swore to treat every Amazon as my own mother, sister or daughter. . . .*

She fumbled for words, saying, "We are oath-bound—sister."

Jaelle put out her hand, a groping gesture that made Magda's heart ache, remembering how quick and skillful those hands had been. She whispered, "I told you—oath-mother and oath-daughter exchange gifts. I did not ask for such a gift as this."

Magda felt embarrassed. "You'd better not talk anymore. Are you cold?" She got another blanket, put the hot stone at Jaelle's feet, propped her up to sip a little of the boiling tea. Jaelle touched her sleeve. "Tend your own wound."

Magda had forgotten it. "It's only a scratch."

"Just the same. Some mountain bandits . . . poison their blades," Jaelle said with difficulty. "Do as I say."

By the time Magda had finished Jaelle was asleep or unconscious again. And asleep or unconscious she remained all that day. Magda made herself some soup from dried meat, late in the day, and tried to rouse Jaelle to eat, but Jaelle only moaned and muttered and pulled away from her hands; Magda knew that she was feverish. Once she woke and asked quite clearly for a drink of water, but when Magda brought it she was stuporous again and would not swallow.

Are there injuries I did not see? Or were the wounds poisoned after all? Magda found that she was fighting terror and dread. *I don't want her to die! I don't!*

By nightfall Jaelle's skin was blistering hot, and Magda could not rouse her even for a moment. Jaelle muttered and flung herself around; once she began with her free hand to tear at the bandage on her face. Magda pulled her hand away, but a few minutes later Jaelle was clawing at the bandage again. Magda, thinking that if she got the bandage loose she might hurt herself, make the scar worse, took a roll of the bandage and tied Jaelle's hands at her sides. She was not prepared to hear Jaelle begin to scream: wild screams of panic and terror.

"Oh, no, no, no, no . . . don't chain my hands, don't— Mother, mother . . . don't let them . . . oh, don't . . . oh, no, no!" and the thin tearing screams again. Magda had never heard such terror. She could not bear it. Quickly she cut the bandage, lifted Jaelle's hands one after another to show that they were free. Somehow that penetrated Jaelle's delirium; she stopped shrieking and lay back quietly. About an hour later she began restlessly to tear at the bandage on her face again, but Magda had no notion of repeating whatever had terrified her so; instead she took the unconscious woman's hands firmly between her own and held them tight. She said quietly and firmly, "You must not do that; lie still, you will hurt yourself. I will not tie your hands, but you must be still." She repeated this over and over, several times, with variations.

Jaelle opened her eyes, but Magda knew she did not see her. She muttered, "Kindra," and later, "Mother," but let her hands rest in Magda's without struggling. Once she said, to no one present, "It hurt. But I didn't cry."

Most of that night Magda sat beside Jaelle, listening to her delirious mutterings, holding her hands tight whenever she tried to tear at the bandages or, as she started to do later, to climb out of bed, under some agitated impression—Magda gathered from her raving—that she was needed somewhere else, at once. Magda had nothing to give her for the fever; there were some medicines in Jaelle's saddlebags, but Magda did not know how to use them or what they were. She sponged her several times with the icy water from the well, and tried to make her drink, but Jaelle pulled away and would not swallow. Toward morning she sank into quiet; Magda did not know whether she was asleep or had lapsed into a coma and was dying. In either case there was nothing she could do. She lay down at the unconscious woman's side and closed her eyes for a moment's rest; suddenly the shelter was full of gray light and Jaelle was lying with her eyes open, looking at her.

"How do you feel, Jaelle?"

"Like hell," Jaelle said. "Is there some water, or tea, or something? My mouth has not been this dry since I left Shainsa."

Magda brought her a drink; Jaelle gulped it thirstily and asked for more. "Did you stay by me all night?"

"Until you fell asleep; I was afraid you would tear off your bandages. You tried."

"Was I delirious?" When Magda nodded, Jaelle said with a wry grin, "That explains it; I dreamed I was back in the Dry Towns, and Jalak— well, it was frightful nonsense, but I have rarely been so glad to wake up." She put a tentative hand to the bandages.

"You will have a dreadful scar, I am afraid."

"There are some women in the Guild-house who think their scars a good advertisement for their skill," said Jaelle, "but, then, I am not a fighter."

Magda had to smile at that. "I should say you were quite a fighter."

"I mean, not a professional fighter. I do not normally hire myself out as soldier or bodyguard," Jaelle said, and shifted her body uncomfortably. "I don't remember much after you cut off my tunic."

"I'll tell you more after I dress your wound," Magda said. Jaelle had run so high a fever that Magda feared to find infection; but there was at least no renewed bleeding, though the edges of the wound looked ugly. Poisoned? Jaelle said, "I have some *karalla* powder in my saddlebags; it will keep the wound from closing too soon with rot beneath." At her directions Magda sprinkled the wound with the gray stuff before rebandaging it. Jaelle was exhausted and pale, but coherent; she ate some of the dried-meat soup, with Magda's help, and drank more water.

"You killed both of them? That does surprise me!"

"It surprised me, too," Magda confessed.

Jaelle uneasily fingered the bandage on her face. "I am not one of those who make a fetish of displaying their scars, but I may have to pretend that I am. Better scarred than buried—or blind! Camilla told me, once, that there were some men who found knife-scars on a woman irresistible." She sank back wearily against the rolled saddlebag under her head. "It was a fool's wound, really. Gwennis, or even old Camilla, could have driven them both away without taking a scratch."

She closed her eyes and slept again. She was somnolent, or sleeping, most of that day, but the fever did not return. Magda had little to do, after the animals had been tended. She thought about burying the dead bandits, but that was a task entirely beyond her strength. She stayed near Jaelle, in case the wounded girl should need anything. The sight of the bandage on Jaelle's face troubled her deeply. *She was so beautiful! In the Terran Zone they could repair that ugly slash as good as new; here, I suppose, she will bear that terrible scar until she dies!*

It occurred to her again that now, with Jaelle well on the way toward recovery, she could make her escape, leave her to recover at leisure, and not even have the other woman's death on her conscience. But by now the thought was very remote.

On the next day Jaelle was able to get up and walk about a little, moving her arm cautiously; swearing at the pain, but moving it, nevertheless. "I don't want the muscles to freeze and the arm to lose its strength," she said irritably, when Magda urged her not to risk tearing it open again. "I know what I am doing." Now that she was no longer somnolent with shock and exhaustion, she was in a good deal of pain, and it made her irritable and restless. Late in the afternoon Magda woke from a brief doze to find Jaelle staring at her as if trying to remember something. *Does she remember thinking I was going to kill her?* She remembered, with some shock, the moment when she had stood over Jaelle, not yet sure herself what she intended. Jaelle had been as still as a wounded animal awaiting the hunter's death-stroke. . . .

Jaelle said quietly, at last, "I did not expect you to stay with me, Margali; I knew you took our oath unwillingly. It is customary for oath-mother and daughter to exchange gifts; you have given me my life, I know."

"Don't!" Magda could not bear to start thinking again about her indecision. She got up and went out of the shelter, looking at the lowering gray sky, heavy with unfallen snow. Midwinter was only a few days distant; and on that day Peter Haldane would meet a dreadful death, suffering the penalty of Rumal di Scarp's blood-feud with the Ardais clan. Magda leaned against the outside wall of the shelter and gave herself up to helpless, desperate weeping.

After a long time she felt a soft touch on her arm; Jaelle stood there, looking very pale and troubled.

"Is he so dear to you—the kinsman of your mission?"

Exhausted, struggling for self-control, Magda could only shake her head and say, "It is not only that."

"Then tell me what it is, my sister." Jaelle took Magda's hand. She said, "Don't stand here in the cold."

More because she remembered that Jaelle herself must not be kept in the cold with her unhealed wound, Magda let herself be led inside. Jaelle stumbled, fell heavily against her; Magda caught her, eased her down on one of the stone benches.

"Now tell me, sister."

Magda shook her head, exhausted. "I told you all."

"But this time," Jaelle said, "the truth, will you not? I do not understand you, Margali. You were lying when you took the oath; you were not lying. You were telling the truth; you were not telling the truth. Even your name—it is your name; you have another name. Tell me."

Magda's defenses were down. "How did you know?"

Jaelle said, "I was born daughter to the Comyn; I have some *laran.*" Magda did not know the word as Jaelle used it; it usually meant a gift or talent. "I have not had the training to use it properly. Lady Rohana—she is my mother's kinswoman—wished me sent to a Tower to be trained in its use; I would have none of that crew. So my gift is erratic; I cannot use it when I would, and when I would not, it thrusts itself on me, undesired. It was so when you took the oath; I could feel, within myself, that you were torn two ways, and in such fear . . . there was no need for such terror as *that.* And now I can read your thoughts, but only a little, Margali—if that is your name. You are oath-bound, but so am I; as you are sworn, so am I oath-bound to you, never to hurt or betray you. Tell me, my sister!"

Magda said wearily, "I was born in Caer Donn. My true name—the name my parents gave me—is Magdalen Lorne, but the Darkover children with whom I played could not say that name; they called me *Margali,* and that is my name as much as the other."

"The—the *Darkovan* children?" Jaelle whispered, and her eyes were wide, almost with fear. "What *are* you, then?"

"I am . . . I am . . ." Magda struggled, the words sticking in her throat. This was basic. *You never tell any outsider who you are. Never.*

Jaelle is not an outsider. She is my sworn sister. Suddenly all conflict was gone. The lump in Magda's throat dissolved, and it seemed that she drew the first free breath she had drawn since she first entered this shelter several nights ago. She said, and her voice did not falter, "My mother and father were Terrans, subjects of the Empire; I am Darkovan, born in Caer Donn, but I am an Intelligence agent and linguistics expert for the Empire, and I work from Thendara."

Slowly, Jaelle nodded. "So that is it," she said at last. "I have heard something of the Terrans. One of ours in Thendara Guild-house—an *emmasca* who can pass herself off as a man: they all can, but many of them will not—hired herself out with the workmen among those building the spaceport, and she told us something of your people. But I did not know the Terrans were human, except in form."

Magda smiled at that way of putting it. She said, "The records of the Empire say that Darkovan and Terran are one stock from the far past."

"Does Lady Rohana know you are *Terranan?*"

"Yes; she saw me first there."

"This explains why you had to appeal to her," said Jaelle; she was just thinking out loud. "Your kinsman, is he Terran, too?"

"Yes; but taken prisoner by Rumal di Scarp because of a chance likeness to Lady Rohana's son."

"He is like Kyril? That will not endear him to me," Jaelle said. "I love Rohana well; Kyril is another matter entirely. But that does not matter now. You love this man so very much? Is he your lover, then?"

Magda said slowly, "No; although for a time we were"—she hesitated, used the Darkovan word—"freemates. But it is more than that. We were children together, and he has no one else. To my superiors in Thendara, he is—expendable; so I took this duty upon myself to save him from death and torture."

Jaelle bit her lip, frowning, idly fingering the bandage on her cheek. She said, "I must think. Perhaps—you are in the employ of your service, under bond for a legitimate service? A Free Amazon is bound by law to fulfill any work she hires herself of her free will to do, and it could be legally said you must complete this pledge and honor your conditions of employment." Again, she was thinking out loud. "You say you do not love him. How *do* you feel about him, then?"

"I don't know." Magda searched her mind; surprised herself by saying, "Protective."

Jaelle looked at Magda with that intense, frowning stare which made Magda wonder if the girl was really reading her thoughts. She said, "Yes; I think no man has ever meant more to you than that, not yet. You have, I think, the true spirit of an Amazon, and if you had been born among us, I think you would have come to us in the end. This must have been what Rohana saw in you."

She was silent for some time, thinking; suddenly she laughed.

"There is only one man living whom I love less than Rumal di Scarp," she said. "I would love to cheat Rumal of his prey! And you are oath-bound to obey all lawful commands of your employer. And there is a life between us; and it is required of me that I give my oath-daughter a gift. I will come with you, Margali, to Sain Scarp!"

Magda said, again with that sense of conflicting loyalties, "Jaelle, I can never thank you for this, but first you should know: it will cause much trouble for you in Thendara. Lorill Hastur has forbidden anyone in the Domains to take part in this affair."

"You do not listen very well," Jaelle said. "I do my own thinking, not the blind will of Hastur. Like all people, I must obey the laws of the land; but the whims of Hastur are not yet the laws of Thendara, and Lorill Hastur has no right to forbid any Free Amazon, under the Charter, to accept any lawful work. Lorill Hastur is my kinsman—though the only time he saw and spoke with me he seemed not very eager to accept the relationship—but he is not the keeper of my conscience! The Free Amazons owe no allegiance to any liege lord, even if he calls himself the son of Hastur. And it seems to me that if the Terrans could give you, a woman, and born in Caer Donn, the strength and spirit to venture alone into the Hellers, and the—" She hesitated, looking away. "And at the same time, the integrity to honor an oath, even under such conditions of strain, then it seems to me that these *Terranan* might have something to teach even a Hastur, and that the Free Amazons should be their friends and allies. So I will give you leave, and I will help you, to rescue your friend."

Magda said hastily, "It must not be known that Peter is a Terran!"

"No, indeed! Rumal would take delight in hanging him from his castle wall that same day!" She held out her hands to Magda and said, "I think I can ride tomorrow; we will ride, then, for Sain Scarp."

Chapter Eleven

Before leaving the shelter, next morning, Jaelle insisted on stripping the bodies of the dead bandits; an unpleasant task, as they had frozen hard in the bitter cold. They dragged them away from the path. "The *kyorebni* and the scavenger wolves will do the rest," Jaelle said cheerfully. "We could never have buried them with the ground frozen hard, so they can do our work for us."

The day was overcast and grim as they set forth, and Magda was anxious about Jaelle; exposure to cold, with an unhealed wound, could be dangerous. Yet once the pass of Scaravel was closed, no amount of haste could bring them to Sain Scarp before midwinter-night.

They made good time for the first three days; but on the fourth day it began to snow in earnest, and Jaelle looked troubled as they began to ride upward along the road to the pass.

"If we get through before dark, there is nothing to fear; Sain Scarp is a two-day ride beyond it, and there is nothing else so high as Scaravel. But if we are delayed today, or if we have to pass Scaravel in the darkness . . ." She was silent, frowning, obviously worried.

Near midday they came to a little village on the mountainside, where they bought some hot soup at a food-stall, and bargained for fodder for their animals. They were about to ride on when the lashings on Magda's pack animal suddenly gave way, and the pack slipped; the beast snorted and neighed, frightened by the bumping of the heavy pack hanging under its belly. Magda slid down and ran to free it from the swaying, bumping burden, but the frightened animal kicked and reared, and it was half an hour before, even with Jaelle's help, Magda could quiet the creature enough to get the remaining strap unbuckled and the pack off. Then they had to find a harness-maker who could mend the strap or make a new one; and when Jaelle came back after talking at length with the harness-maker (his dialect was so thick Magda could not understand him), she looked grave.

"Lady Rohana, with her escort, crossed Scaravel three days ago, on her way to Ardais," she said, "and the pass was open then; since then, no traveler has climbed toward the pass. We may find it blocked already; if not, this storm will surely close it till spring-thaw. Come what may, we must cross Scaravel tonight, or we cannot reach Sain Scarp in time. Let us find some more of that woman's good bean soup before we take the road; we'll get little warm food tonight."

Less than half a mile out of the village, Magda looked back down the trail and saw that the thickening snow had already blotted out the lights behind them. Jaelle wrapped a fold of her scarf across her bandaged cheek; her voice sounded muffled through it. "If these folk were not all living in the very shadow of Sain Scarp—and probably in their pay, or at least in fear of them—I think I would have left the horses here and tried the pass on foot. But I would not put such a strain on their honesty. There is a saying in the hills: 'Don't trust your bone to another man's dog.' "

It was less than an hour before they had to light their saddle-lanterns; the small lamps, fueled with resin, cast dim light for a few feet in every direction, but beyond that the light scattered into fog against the curtain of the falling snow. The trail was beaten deep between rocks, and Magda was glad, for the snow blotted out landmarks, and they might stray from the trail and never find it again. But when she said this to Jaelle, the other woman laughed through the muffling of the scarf.

"Just keep going up until there's no farther you can go! Myself, I'm glad of the snow; so near to Sain Scarp, Scaravel is no pass to travel alone in good weather. I have no doubt that is how your friend was taken! But on a night like this, even a bandit would be home by his own fireside!"

Higher and higher they rode, and Magda began to feel the dull, internal ache in ears and sinuses, born of the high altitude, which no amount of yawning or pressing her fingertips against her ears could completely dispel. The cold was bitter, and they began to feel the wind of the heights, which set the thick snow streaming almost sidewise against their faces and heaped it under their feet till they sank knee-deep in drifts and they had to dismount and lead their protesting horses. They moved slowly against the wind, each woman isolated in her own cocoon of darkness and silence. To Magda the world had shrunk to a circle less than ten feet wide, containing herself, the front half of her horse, the tail of Jaelle's saddle-horse just ahead and the soft crunching of the antlered pack beast that plodded along on his broad hooves after her lantern. Outside this narrow circle was nothing; only darkness and a wind that screeched like all the demons of Zandru's legendary ninth hell. Up, and again up, with the protest of knee muscles with every step, and her breath short. She wrapped her thick scarf heavily over her chin, and felt the wind freezing it, from the moisture of her breath, to an ice-mask.

She felt herself bump into something hard and soft at once, recoiled from the intrusion of something else into her private cocoon, and discovered it was Jaelle, who had turned her horse somewhat so it stood sidewise of the trail to block it. She put her head close to Magda's and shouted, "Let's stop for some food; it seems hours since we ate, and higher up it's dangerous to stop!"

They formed the animals into a triangle, nose to tail, and stood at the center of this crude windbreak, chewing on some dried-meat bars and fruit, which were the first things Magda could find at the top of the saddle-bags. The world had shrunk so small that Magda found herself staring at the small pattern of blue birds knitted into the back of Jaelle's woolen mittens, and wondering if Jaelle had knitted them herself.

Then above them, sweeping down from the heights and even drowning out the shrieking wind, came a shrill, eerie cry; a long, paralyzing howl that made Magda's ears ring and almost physically paralyzed her. She gasped with the sound, then knew what it must be, even before Jaelle said: "Banshee. I was afraid of that; let's just hope the wind distorts its sense of direction. And remember it would rather have the horses than us, so keep in their shelter."

Magda had heard about—but never actually *heard*—the shattering, paralyzing scream of the great flightless carnivores who lived above the snow-line and were attracted by the warmth and movement of their prey. Again the ghastly screech came, and it seemed to her that the meat-bar she was chewing had turned to leather in her mouth.

Jaelle was trying to make herself heard above the howl of the wind again. "What, Jaelle?"

"This is where we have to decide. I'm not an expert on Scaravel, but I *have* been over it in daylight, and I gather you haven't. Above here the trail narrows, so we can't turn around, and there's not even a level spot to spend the night. Beyond here, we're committed, because there's no stopping till we're on the other side. But it seems to be open now. It's a risk either way, but it's *your* risk, and your neck. Try it in the dark, or wait here? It's not a particularly good trail even by daylight."

Magda thought of the narrowing trail, the terrible carnivores of the heights, her own aching legs and wind-burned face. And Jaelle, beside her, was not really well enough to travel. *It's not Jaelle's mission at all. If I lead her to her death* . . .

"What would you advise?" Magda asked.

"I wouldn't advise; I'd try not to get into such a spot. But being in it, I'd probably go on. Just the same, I didn't want you to go at it thinking it's easy or safe, because it's not. This is your last chance to lose your nerve."

And this was the last chance. If they did not make it across Scaravel tonight, and it proved to be blocked by daylight after the night's snow . . . She said, "But what about you, Jaelle? You're still not strong—"

"There's almost as much risk to turn around here and go down," Jaelle said, "and if we stay here, we might freeze. I can make it if you can."

Magda was not so sure; but having come so far, she was unwilling to retreat or give up. She swallowed the last of the dried meat, and said, "All right, then, we'll try. Want me to break trail? You've been doing it this far."

"From here on we don't break trail; we let the horses do it," said Jaelle, "and we stay between them, in case any banshee is prowling around looking for a midnight lunch!"

The trail was really steep now, but between the two saddle-horses, crowded together on the narrow path, the howling of the wind reached them less fiercely. The snow crunched hard underfoot, and they clung to the saddles on the horses to keep their footing. The trail twisted and turned between great rocks that gave some slight shelter from the wind, but now and then Magda caught, between the horses' legs or over their backs, a faraway and eerie glimpse of great chasms and cliffs, of dizzy gulfs of space dropping away from the trail; and, hastily turning her eyes back into the enclosing world—the horses on either side, Jaelle pressed close against her elbow—she was glad of the darkness that concealed the giddy heights to either side. They struggled along side by side, so close that Magda could hear the other woman's labored breathing; again and again, from the heights above them, they could hear the eerie, demoralizing banshee cry. The horses stirred and stamped; Magda's horse tossed its head, and she hauled on the bridle, trying to calm and quiet the frightened animal.

"Won't the saddle-lanterns attract the banshees, too?"

"No, they're blind," Jaelle said. "They sense warmth and movement, that's all. I remember—"

Magda never heard what she remembered. In the next moment there was another high, chilling banshee scream—this one almost on top of them—and a screech from the pack animal behind them, and Magda's horse reared, struggling, at the very edge of the cliff. The pack beast went down, screaming, plunging, kicking in the snow, and over its struggling body Magda caught a blurred glimpse of a huge, naked, buzzardlike head, an enormous ungainly body, the beak plunging into the pack animal's soft underbelly and rearing up, dripping gore. Magda pulled out her knife, backing away, waiting for the moment to strike. The naked head whipped around in her direction, weaving, darting, and Jaelle caught her wrist and dragged her back.

She said in a harsh whisper, "Let it eat! It's too late to save the animal, and if it's full it won't turn on us!"

Magda knew that made sense, but the screaming of the dying beast, the terrified screams of the other horses and the foul stench of the great predator turned her sick. She covered her face with her hands as the wicked talons struck down, scraping, raking, and the evil beak plunged down, again and again, as the banshee gorged his fill. Jaelle pulled Magda down behind the horses, and the women lay there concealed, trying not to hear or to see as the creature ate with little growling clucks and snarls.

God, those talons! One blow from them almost ripped the animal in half! Magda thought.

It seemed a long time before the banshee jerked up its huge head, darting it from side to side without interest, then plunged back once for a final tidbit and lumbered heavily away. The talons left great sloppy prints of blood and filth on the snow. Magda, struggling to control her sickness, got up slowly. The antlered pack beast lay almost still, and—this was the ultimate horror—whining thinly, still alive. Magda could not stand it. She bent swiftly, drew her knife across its throat, and with one final twitch, it lay still. Behind the horses Jaelle was lying in the snow, retching weakly, helplessly.

Magda went to her. "Come on! Help me get the pack off that thing, and onto our horses! And then let's get the hell away from here before all that thing's brothers and sisters come around looking for another helping!"

Jaelle came, wiping her face on her sleeve. Her face looked grotesque, red and blotched. "Oh, that was horrible—horrible—"

"It was. But it could have been a lot more horrible if it had grabbed one of us instead," Magda said, and bent over the dead animal to cut the straps that held the pack to the half-eaten carcass. *The same strap we so carefully had replaced in the village!* With Jaelle's help she managed to haul it off the dead animal, though their hands were slimy with blood and entrails before they finished. Magda hoisted it to the back of her horse. "We can divide up the load tomorrow," she said. "Right now we'd better get moving."

Numbed by fatigue and horror, the women stumbled upward, higher and higher; and suddenly, rounding a curve in the deep-beaten trail, they were not climbing anymore. They stood in the top of the pass of Scaravel, and there was no way to go but down. Magda was too weary even to feel relieved. Jaelle was stumbling with fatigue and weariness, and Magda wished it were safe for her to ride. Certainly she could not go on much longer.

The going was easier now, although the horses had a tendency to slip and stumble; before long Magda felt the lessening ache in her ears that told they were losing altitude. She recalled hearing that banshees nested only above the timberline; when they reached the first clump of gnarled trees, thick wind-tangled evergreens, she could feel the tension running out of her like water. She stumbled along for another hundred feet or so, found a thick grove of trees where the horses would be a little protected from wind and the still-falling snow. Jaelle was dazed, out on her feet; she stood blinking, unaware what was going on. Alone, Magda tied the horses and blanketed them, managed to get up one of the tiny tents, got Jaelle out of her snow-caked riding-cloak and boots and shoved her into her blankets. She fell into her own without stopping to take off anything but boots. The tent was much too small for two—Magda had thought it was too small for one—but claustrophobia was better than taking the time to get up the other one; besides, they needed the warmth. She thought, as she fell asleep, *I'd bring the horses in if I could get them in.* Even the faraway wail of another banshee—or the one who had attacked them?—could not keep her awake.

The weather cleared in the night, and they looked on a dazzling white world, with evergreens bent almost double under their weight of snow. When Magda dressed Jaelle's wounds, they looked dull-white and macerated; they had been frozen, and this would make the scarring worse, but there was nothing to be done about it. She used some of the water she had boiled for porridge to try to clean them, but there was not much she could do. Jaelle ate listlessly, but she did eat, and Magda was glad; that glazed, numb look of exhaustion had frightened her. When she had done, she pointed to a low peak in the next range.

"Sain Scarp," Jaelle said. "If the weather holds we will be there tomorrow." Magda's eyes were sharp, but try as she might, she could see nothing but trees.

Jaelle laughed. "I doubt Rumal di Scarp will entertain us, so we may not have much of a midwinter-feast this year! But no doubt your kinsman would rather eat porridge on the open road than feast with Rumal! And if the weather holds fine, we might reach Ardais by midwinter; you cannot see it from here, though if you have good eyes you can see it from the very top of Scaravel. But I am not going back up to look now!"

Now that they were actually within sight of their goal, Magda found herself wondering about Peter again. How would he feel, to be rescued at a woman's hands? An hour later, as they rode down the trail through the melting snow, Jaelle voiced the same question.

"Your kinsman, will it damage his pride too much, to accept rescue at a woman's doing? Or don't the *Terranan* have that kind of pride?"

"Not usually. On other worlds men and women usually share the risks equally," Magda said. *But Peter was reared on Darkover, like me. And I found my Darkovan training too strong even for the Empire. Will it damage him, destroy him, as it might a Darkovan man?*

And suddenly Magda understood something about herself that she had never realized before.

Brought up as I was, at Caer Donn, only a Darkovan could have attracted me; they say the way you react to the opposite sex is conditioned before you're seven years old. None of the Terran men I knew seemed right, none of them had the right sort of emotional—or sexual—wavelengths for me. The sexual cues were all wrong. So Peter was literally the only man I knew to whom I reacted as to a male at all.

And when I was ripe for a love affair, he was the only man I knew; literally the only one. It wasn't that I cared more for him than others: it was that there were no others.

She realized that this might very well be the most important insight of her life, and resolved that she must somehow manage to hold on to it, even after she met Peter again.

Sain Scarp was an enormous fortress, isolated beyond a long rock causeway. The next day at noon the two women rode across the causeway, and Magda, at least, had the sense of eyes watching them from the tower at the far end. At the end of the causeway a big, rough-looking man stopped them, demanding their business.

Now. This is the culmination of it all; everything else that has happened— even the Amazon oath, dividing my life in two—was all for this. Strangely, Magda had almost forgotten that. She said, "I am the Free Amazon Margali n'ha Ysabet"—(how strange that sounded)—"come on a mission from the Lady Rohana Ardais. There is a prisoner and a ransom to be paid. Carry this word to Rumal di Scarp." They waited, shivering in the bright cold air, until the bandit chieftain came.

Afterward she could never remember what Rumal di Scarp looked like, except that he seemed a small man to carry such weight of rumor and horror tales: a small, wiry, hawk-faced man with fierce eyes. Behind Rumal, his hands bound, Magda saw a slender, familiar figure. *Peter!* He was thin and pale, dressed in shabby and torn mountain garments; a narrow fringe of coppery-red beard shadowed his face, but Magda knew him.

Rumal di Scarp came slowly toward them. "Well, *mestra*, I hear there is a ransom to pay. Who are you?"

Silently, Magda held out her safe-conduct; Rumal took it, handed it to the huge bandit at his side, who overshadowed him physically as much as the little man seemed to dwarf his giant companion in every other way. The man read it aloud to Rumal. "Lady Rohana Ardais . . . empowered to deal in a family matter . . ."

Rumal took the safe-conduct, crumpled it contemptuously and tossed it back to Magda. He said, laughing, "Gallant are the men of Ardais, that they send women to pay ransom for their menfolk! Why should I deal with you?"

Jaelle said, "Because I am the Lady Rohana's kinswoman, and if you do not honor your word I will spread it far and wide, from the Hellers to Dalereuth, that Rumal di Scarp does not honor his bargains. And then you may sit here in Sain Scarp and make soup from the bones of your captives for all the good they will be to you, since no one will ever again pay a single coin in ransom!"

Rumal made a gesture of contempt, signaled for Peter to be brought forward. "Well, there he is, heir to Ardais, whole and well, sound in wind and limb as a horse in spring market. And so, my ladies"—he used the intimate inflection, which made it sound even more contemptuous—"let us see the color of that ransom, then."

Magda knew her hands were trembling as she counted out the copper bars. Rumal shrugged, signaled to his giant henchman to wrap the ransom money in a cloth and take it away. "You have your kinsman. Take him away, then."

Jaelle looked at him defiantly, and said, "His horse and gear?"

"Oh, that," said Rumal. "That I kept to cover the cost of feeding him between snowfall and midwinter-night, lest the ransom grow too great for one horse to carry." He said ironically to Peter, "Farewell, my Lord; fortunate is that man so loved by his kinsmen that they entrust him to a woman's ransoming. See that you repay these ladies well for their courtesy, my Lord, since no doubt it was only their pleas that persuaded the menfolk of your clan to ransom you at all. And now—" He made a deep, graceful bow, whose very courtly grace sent a shudder of horror through Magda, much worse than if he were ugly or deformed. "Farewell, dom; a safe journey and a fortunate homecoming."

Peter made him a deep, equally ironic bow. "My thanks for your hospitality, messire di Scarp. May I sleep the night in each of Zandru's hells in turn before I taste of it again."

"A churlish speech," Rumal drawled, "but the color of money is not brightened by courteous words—nor dimmed by boorish ones." He turned on his heel and walked away, not looking back.

Peter reached out and seized Magda's hands in a hard grip. His own were shaking. "It *is* you," he said. "I dreamed—I dreamed—" His voice caught, and for a moment she thought he was about to weep, but he managed to control it, clutching her fingers painfully hard in his own.

She said, and her heart was wrung with pity, "You are so thin and pale! Have they been starving you?"

"No, no, though the fare was not what I could have hoped for in the Hellers," he said, still clinging to her hands.

Jaelle broke in: "There is a horse for you at the end of the causeway; we traded for it in the last village. I thought Rumal would keep yours, as he did. I hope it suits you."

"*Mestra,* I would ride a rabbit, or walk from here to Thendara in my bare feet, it is so good to be beyond these walls," he said. "Come, let us get out of bow-shot. . . . How came this to be? I had utterly lost hope that you would ever know where I was, or how, even, I had died."

Jaelle was studying him curiously as they came to where they had left the horses. "I cannot believe it! This is not a joke? You are not my cousin Kyril? Are you truly—*Terranan?*"

"I am," Peter said, and glanced curiously at Magda. "Who—and what—?"

"She is my friend and sister, Peter," Magda said quietly, "and she knows who we are, so there is no need for pretense."

Peter bent over her slender hand. He said, "How can I speak my thanks, *mestra?* Midwinter-night is too near for me to pretend I was not afraid."

Jaelle looked back, saw that Rumal and his men had turned to watch them from the end of the causeway. She said, with a hesitant laugh, "Now, indeed, I believe you are not my cousin Kyril. I think he would rather be hanged in fragments from Rumal's walls than confess himself afraid!" She added, after a moment, "No doubt they are watching and wondering why you do not greet me as a kinswoman."

From anyone else Magda thought that would have sounded almost unbearably flirtatious; Jaelle only sounded embarrassed. Peter said, "That will be my pleasure, then—kinswoman." He bent forward and made as if to give her a brotherly embrace and kiss on the cheek. Jaelle colored and lowered her eyes; suddenly, gently, Peter took Jaelle's slender hand up in his again, bent and laid a light kiss on her wrist.

Magda, watching, thought unexpectedly, *I'm free of him. Before, I would have been unendurably jealous—to see that look in his eyes, turned on any other woman. I nearly went mad when he danced with Bethany at a New Year's party last year. Now I do not care.* Her love, her guilt, her concern, had been a part of her so long that she felt cold, flat and empty. Now she looked at him with sympathy, with concern for his thinness and pallor. . . . *As if he were my brother, my child. But not a lover. Not now.*

Jaelle started to move away, then suddenly reached out and caught Peter's hand. She said, "I cannot believe it. You are so like to my cousin Kyril, and yet . . . let me see your hands! How many fingers have you?"

"Normal number," said Peter, "four and a thumb—oh, my God!" He was looking down at Jaelle's slender hand, lying in his own. "You have six fingers on each hand," he said numbly.

"Yes. The Ardais and the Aillard blood—those who bear it have the extra finger," Jaelle said. "Is it wholly unknown among Terrans? Rohana is Aillard by birth, and her husband an Ardais; and all of her children have the Aillard hands." She began to laugh hysterically. "If Rumal had—had bothered to count your fingers—" she got out between spasms, "you would now be hanging—in pieces—from his castle wall."

She could not seem to stop laughing; Magda came and tried to calm her, and at last, really frightened, reluctant but afraid that it was the only way to stop her, took her shoulders and shook her hard. Jaelle began to cry as hysterically as she had laughed. "You'd be dead," she got out between sobs, "you'd be dead—"

She has ridden too far; she is still not strong. Magda said to Peter, "Can you take her on your saddle? We must get away from here before night-fall," and watched as Peter tenderly lifted Jaelle on his horse, got on and supported the drooping girl, his arm holding her upright against him. Magda mounted her own horse, and took the reins of Jaelle's, leading it after them. And already—she realized a long time afterward—she knew then what was going to happen.

Part Three

JAELLE n'ha MELORA, Free Amazon

Chapter Twelve

The ceiling was painted blue, with a border and a design of little stars in gilt. At first Jaelle could not imagine where she was. Then she remembered that she had slept in this room during her one extended visit to Castle Ardais, in her sixteenth year.

"Before you renounce your heritage as *Comynara,*" Kindra had warned her, speaking more seriously than she had ever before spoken to her foster-daughter, "you must first know what it is that you are renouncing." So to Ardais Jaelle had gone, protesting, to remain a full half-year. She had not been happy there; she had felt, she told Rohana once rebelliously, like a fish in a tree.

But I am not sixteen years old anymore! Why am I here? She shifted her weight, and at the sharp stab of pain in her wounded shoulder, remembered. Where were her Terran companions? They had come late at night, she remembered, and she had told the servants at the gate to bear word to the Lady Rohana that her kinswoman had come to spend midwinter-night, bringing two friends. She remembered Rohana, graciously welcoming them all, and her dismay when she saw Jaelle's bandaged face. The rest was blurred.

Jaelle was lying in a big bed, wearing a long-sleeved nightgown, trimmed with lace at the neck and wrists. She supposed it belonged to Rohana, or to her daughter; she herself possessed no such garments, and it was too fine for a servant. One of the sleeves had been slit to accommodate the folds of bandage at her shoulder; her face, too, had been bandaged freshly. She looked around the room and saw a second bed near the window, and the Terran woman asleep in it, but at that moment Magda turned over and looked at her.

"You look better," she said. "When you were carried up here the night before last, I thought you were dying." Magda got out of bed and came to Jaelle's side. She, too, was wearing one of the lace-trimmed gowns, though she was so tall it came only midway down her calves. Her dark short hair had been washed and was curling around her cheeks.

Jaelle said, "I really don't remember anything after we got here; did you carry me here, or—" She hesitated, not remembering his Darkovan name, unwilling to use the Terran one where they might be overheard.

"No; dom Gabriel himself did you that honor."

Jaelle smiled wryly. "Poor dom Gabriel! How my kinswoman's husband dislikes me! Or, at least, dislikes having a Free Amazon in the family!"

"He seemed genuinely anxious about you," Magda protested, and Jaelle laughed a little. "Oh, anything belonging to Rohana he will treat kindly— pet dogs, Free Amazons, even Terrans, I suppose." She felt the smile stab ferocious pain through her bandaged face. "Does he know?"

"Rohana told him only that we were friends of yours," Magda replied. "She warned me afterward that the house was full of midwinter guests, and we must be careful. Of course, when dom Kyril met Peter, he was tremendously curious. He asked who Peter was, and Peter told him his usual tale—that he was born in Caer Donn, that he did not know his father's name. Dom Kyril said after that, 'Having seen you, I think I could put a name to your father's clan, at least.' And, like you, he looked at once at his hands."

Jaelle lay back, astonished at herself. *So weary, after sitting up only a few minutes?* Her shoulder throbbed as if it were afire. "Where is—where is he?"

"Asleep in the next room," Magda said, pointing to the connecting door. "Lady Rohana apologized that she could give us only these rooms; I told her that in any case you should not be left alone at night. You slept all of yesterday; you did not wake even when domna Alida came to dress your wounds."

"So I have lost a day," Jaelle said. Now she remembered, fuzzily, how they had come here. Rumal di Scarp would be expecting them to head at once for Ardais; would find it suspicious if they turned in any other direction. In any case, Scaravel was blocked behind them by the snow. Magda had felt that since Lady Rohana had arranged this mission, she had a right to know of its success.

Jaelle remembered, too, how Peter had ridden at her side, had helped her whenever they stopped to rest the horses. Much of that time, she had been in a daze of pain and weariness, but she remembered how when they stopped, he had coaxed her to eat, and how, when she could no longer sit in her saddle without falling, he had taken her again before him on his saddle and held her against him. All else was blurred, but she could remember, with a sharp tactile memory, the feel of his arms around her. She had been ashamed of her weakness and secretly a little glad of it, for it let her lean against him, rest her head on his shoulder through the swaying dizziness of pain and fever. . . .

She thought, with a sharp sting of guilt, *Appeal to no man for protection* . . . and closed her eyes, feeling tears of weakness sliding down her cheeks. She felt Magda's gentle hand on her wrist. "I will let Lady Rohana know you are awake," she said.

Rohana came before long, small and queenly in a fur-trimmed gown; she bent and kissed Jaelle on the cheek not covered with the bandage. "How are you feeling, my child? And how came you by this dreadful wound? Margali has told me very little, only that you fought for her."

"I suppose she did not tell you that she saved my life," Jaelle said, "nor that she is oath-bound to the Guild, and my sister."

Rohana asked very seriously, "Is this allowed, my child, that a *Terranan* should be accepted by oath into the Guild?"

"The Guild-mothers must give the final decision on that," Jaelle said, "but the Guild Charter excludes no woman; it is the oath, not the parentage, which makes an Amazon under the Charter. And my sister chose to honor her oath; to stay and fight for me, and to care for me afterward, when she could easily have abandoned me to die."

Rohana said gently, "Then she is kinswoman here, too, my darling." Relieved, Jaelle slipped back into exhausted sleep—or stupor—again, and over her head Rohana's eyes met the Terran woman's. "Someday you must tell me how this came about."

"I am not sure myself," Magda said with a troubled smile, "but I will honor my oath, whatever comes."

"For her sake? Only for friendship?"

"No. Not entirely. Perhaps—" Magda hesitated, searching for words. "Perhaps because I have two worlds to serve, and I think I can best honor both loyalties this way."

"And your husband? What will he say to this?"

"He is not my husband in law; we parted more than a year ago. Certainly he is not the keeper of my conscience."

"I thought—" Rohana stopped. Like all telepaths, she had a horror of seeming to intrude in any personal matter. But it had seemed to her, when she met Magda in the Trade City, that the Terran woman was wholly committed to her former lover; and she had had misgivings when she saw Magda in Amazon garb. It had seemed to her that in spite of the spirit and strength she had admired, Magda was all too feminine for the part she must play. It had seemed to her that Magda was much like herself, committed to taking a man's part for a woman's reasons.

She felt completely at a loss; and that was a new sensation for Rohana. It also roused questions she thought she had settled, completely and without any doubts, years ago. She was glad to put her self-questioning aside when Magda asked, "Is it right for Jaelle to sleep so much? Is she worse than I feared?"

"I do not know: Alida says that neither wound is healing as it should. She will know more today."

"It is my fault," Magda said, looking down at Jaelle with dread. Asleep or unconscious again? "She exhausted herself trying to help us."

Rohana's hands closed very lightly over hers. Magda did not yet know enough of the telepath caste to know how very rare a gesture it was, or what trust it indicated. "My dear child, don't blame yourself. Since Kindra died, there has been no one, no one at all who could make Jaelle do anything she did not want to do, or prevent her from doing her own will; so whatever she did was freely done." She looked down at Jaelle with a detached, sad tenderness. She said, and Magda felt that Rohana was not really speaking to her at all, "In many ways she is dearer to me than my own daughter. Yet I have known for many years that I must let her take her own way."

She turned to go. "Domna Alida will see her this morning; she is Tower-trained, and has great skill in such matters." She went away.

Shortly after, Peter came through the connecting door. "How is Jaelle?" he asked, in a low, troubled voice.

Magda repeated what Rohana had said, and he shook his head, dismayed. "I hate to think she would put herself in such danger for us," he said. "But listen to me, Magda; we have to leave here, as soon as we can. You know we can't stay here for midwinter, as Lady Rohana expects, when there might be someone here who recognizes us!"

"Rohana won't tell."

"Perhaps not. But among the household there are two or three men from Caer Donn who may recognize me . . . . remember me from the days when Terrans and mountain men could mingle freely. If they do . . ."

Magda was sympathetic, but for the moment another concern seemed more important. She said, "I cannot go without Jaelle's leave; perhaps I cannot go at all. Certainly I would not go while she is ill and needs me." She flung at him, in sudden rage, "Does an oath mean nothing to you?"

"Not one wrested from you by force," Peter said, "and in any case you had no right to give it. I know you were forced into it, but still—"

It was her own reasoning, and it made her angrier than ever, as he went on, persuasively, "I know you have always had a great love for pretending yourself Darkovan, and a pride in your skill at it. But there is a time to forget all that. Your first loyalty is to the Empire—do I have to remind you of that?"

He had taken her hands in his; she wrenched them away. "Then say I *chose!* I feel I can serve best this way, but if it comes to choice . . . !" She was trembling all over. He said, trying to conciliate, "I didn't realize you felt like that; you know I would never interfere in a matter of conscience, Mag. But why does this girl mean so much to you? It's not like you to have this kind of—this kind of emotional attitude over another woman. It's not quite—" He hesitated, unwilling to say it, and Magda, guessing what he refused to say, was angry again.

"Think anything you damn please! If you believe that, you'll believe anything!"

"Mag, I didn't say I believed—"

"You're a fool, Peter," she said in disgust. "Do you really believe no woman could be loyal to another woman out of common humanity and integrity? Jaelle saved my life; and do I have to remind you that if she had not risked hers to cross Scaravel Pass with an unhealed wound, you would still be counting the days to midwinter-night in Rumal's dungeons? And you want me to leave her, not even knowing if she will live or die, or be scarred for life?"

"Do *you* need to remain? I thought these people were her closest kin-folk!"

"Yes," Magda said, "but by oath she has had to renounce all her kin-folk; as her oath-daughter I am the closest kin she has beneath this roof." She said this with absolute certainty, knowing that, in spite of Rohana's deep affection for Jaelle, she would have said the same thing. Rohana had taken it for granted that Magda had a duty, and a right, to stay with Jaelle and care for her; more than Rohana's own right. Camilla had said, jesting, that Rohana was still ignorant about the ways of Free Amazons. But she had her finger on the very pulse of what they meant to one another; more, Magda knew, than she herself did.

Peter's anger had been short-lived, as always. He said, "Probably you know best, Mag; you usually do. And midwinter-feast is the time for hos-pitality; probably a couple of extra guests will never be noticed." He walked to Jaelle's side, and stood looking down at her.

"How beautiful she is," he said softly, "or how beautiful she would be, without that terrible scar! How could a woman like that renounce love and marriage?"

Jaelle opened her unbandaged eye; her vision was blurry and unfocused.

She said, "It is not love we renounce . . . only marriage . . . bondage. . . ." she stretched out her hand, and Peter knelt beside the bed, taking her hand in his. Her eyes fell shut again, but she kept hold of him.

He was still kneeling there when the door opened again and Lady Rohana came in, with dom Gabriel's sister, who had been described to Magda as a *leronis.* The title translated, usually, as "sorceress" or "wise-woman"; Magda suspected it meant, in this case, "healer." Her name was Alida. She was a small, slight woman with flaming red hair, younger by some years than Rohana, and with a kind of indefinable arrogance which made Magda, for some reason, think of Lorill Hastur.

Lady Alida inclined her head in the faintest of courteous greetings to Magda. She ignored Peter. She pulled back Jaelle's blankets and began to unfasten the cutaway nightgown; then looked, in unmistakable command, at Peter. He had been brought up in the mountains near Caer Donn and understood perfectly well; actually it was even somewhat scandalous that he should have been in the room when Magda was not fully dressed. He let go Jaelle's hand, but she quickly clasped it again, opening her eyes.

She said, "I want him to stay!" She sounded like a child, and Magda wondered if she were delirious again.

Lady Alida shrugged. "Stay, then, if she wants you. But take her other hand, and keep out of my way." Peter obeyed, and Alida, with some minor help from Rohana, got the bandages undone to examine the ugly wounds. Even Magda could see that they were not healing properly, but were swollen and festered. The clean slash on the face had spread and reddened, the nick in the eyelid so swollen that Jaelle's eye was shut.

"This is a poisoned wound! How came she by it?"

Briefly, Magda recounted their fight with the bandits. Lady Alida made a fastidious grimace. "That is no work for women!"

Jaelle flushed with anger. She said pettishly, "I do not need to be told you do not approve of my way of life, kinswoman, but courtesy should prevent you from insulting my sister and guest before me!"

Rohana said in haste, "Alida meant no offense—did you, kinswoman?"

Alida paid no attention to either of them. "What has happened to *your* wound, *mestra?*"

After a moment Magda realized that she was being addressed, and pushed up the long sleeve of the nightgown she was wearing. "It is healing."

"But not as it should," Alida said, her light, cold fingers gently touching the red seam, still puckered and inflamed. "A cut like this should long be closed and sealed, with not even an itch remaining. This still gives you some pain, I can tell—does it not?"

"Yes, a little," Magda said. She had so little experience with such cuts that she had thought it natural. She saw Peter looking up, in surprise and consternation, at her bare arm and the red seam there, and she pushed her sleeve down to cover it.

Alida said, "Jaelle must have been wounded first, and got most of the poison."

Rohana sounded anxious. "Can you help it, Alida?"

"Oh certainly. I learned to treat such wounds at Neskaya Tower; it is nothing much. You were Tower-trained in Dalereuth as a girl; can you monitor for me?"

Rohana nodded. "Certainly."

But Rohana watched, faintly troubled, as Alida uncovered her matrix jewel. She knew she should send the two Terrans away. This, she knew, was one reason why Lorill Hastur had interdicted any serious contact between Terran and Darkovan; he was unwilling they should learn anything about the ancient matrix sciences. Yet, if she should make a point of dismissing Magda and Peter from the room now, she must explain why.

She had told no one here that they were Terrans, but she was sure Gabriel guessed. When he had seen Peter's almost unbelievable likeness to their son Kyril, and heard that he was the prisoner from Sain Scarp, he must have known; but he did not really want to know, Rohana realized, that she had gone against his wishes again. *Because then I would have to tell him, in so many words, that he is not the keeper of my conscience; and even now I do not think Gabriel wants to know that in a way he cannot pretend to ignore.*

And the woman, Magda, was Jaelle's oath-sister and had a right to remain. As for the man—she saw Jaelle clinging to his hand, saw the tenderness in his eyes, and knew what neither of them knew themselves, as yet.

"Put that away, Lady Alida. I will have none of your sorcery," Jaelle said weakly.

"I must, child. There is poison in the wound and it is spreading to your eye; it can damage your sight. If I do not treat it now . . ."

"I do not care," said Jaelle in great agitation. "I will not allow—"

Rohana said sternly, "Stop it, Jaelle. You are behaving like a frightened child who will not have a cut bandaged! I had not believed you so cowardly!"

Alida's voice was kinder. "I know you were afraid of me when you were a child, Jaelle, but I hoped you had outgrown your fear."

"I am not afraid," Jaelle said, shaking with anger, "but I will not have you meddling with my mind! Once is enough for a lifetime!"

Suddenly Rohana recalled what Jaelle was talking about. On that single extended visit to Ardais, which she had demanded before allowing Jaelle to take the Amazon's oath, she had insisted that Jaelle be tested for *laran;* Melora's child, and with the flame-colored hair that marked the telepath strain, would surely have one of the Comyn gifts. Jaelle had been frightened and helplessly reluctant, but on this point Rohana would not be moved. Alida had done the testing, and Jaelle had come away white as a corpse and looking deathly ill. It was the only time since her mother's death that Rohana had ever seen Jaelle in tears. When Rohana had sent her away, a little calmed and comforted, Alida had said:

"Yes, she has *laran;* I think she is a powerful telepath, but for some reason she is blocking it. I could break her defenses, of course; but whether I could ever put them together again afterward—that is another matter. And since you have allowed her to be fostered among the Amazons, I think she would find life intolerable in a Tower. Let her take her own way."

Rohana had left it at that. She had complied with the law that every child of Comyn blood—legitimate or illegitimate; and in law Jaelle was illegitimate—must be tested. More was not necessary. She was sure it was the shock of rapport with her dying mother that had forced Jaelle to barricade her own *laran,* but she had not tried to find out.

But was Jaelle's fear still so acute? Domna Alida only said, unoffended, when Jaelle swore at her, "You are ill, Jaelle. You do not know what you are saying. Shall I really put you to the indignity of having your hands tied?"

Magda almost cried out: "No, you mustn't!"

"Jaelle," Rohana persuaded, "you are not one of those Amazons who makes a great thing of swaggering and comparing scars."

Alida said coolly, "If she wishes to end her days looking like a battle-scarred veteran of the campaigns at Corresanti, that is her affair; I am only concerned about her eyesight!"

Peter was still holding Jaelle's hand in his. He raised his free hand to Jaelle's cheek, caressed the smooth skin below the red slash. He said, as if there were no one in the room but himself and Jaelle, "You are so beautiful. It would be so dreadful to let that beauty be spoiled."

Jaelle moved her other hand, clumsily, toward his; and Magda knew—they all knew—that she would not protest further.

That wasn't fair, Magda thought. *Jaelle is too vulnerable. Peter should not have done it. . . .*

Lady Alida moved her hand, and Magda could see the blue stone in it—a jewel? A brilliant flash, a twisting, sickening *glare* . . . Magda turned her eyes away, unable to endure the sight. The *leronis* said quietly, "You were too busy cursing me to let me explain, Jaelle, but I need not touch your mind for this. I am going to be doing some very delicate cell-reconstruction work, so you must lie as quietly as possible, and try to make your mind as blank as you can, so that your thoughts will not interfere. You can sleep if you wish; it will be all the better if you do. I do not think you will feel any pain, but if you do you must tell me at once, so that your pain will not blur what I am doing."

Magda listened, in amazed curiosity. Hypnosis? All that about making her mind a blank . . . ?

"Rohana, you must monitor," Alida instructed. "And you must warn me if I come too close to the nerves, or to the small muscles near the corner of the eye," Alida warned, and again the blue jewel flashed in her hand. Magda felt a little, twisting ripple deep in her body, almost a sickness. Alida looked up, her face now remote and masklike, looking at Magda without really seeing her.

"Do not look directly at the matrix, *mestra;* many people cannot endure the sight."

Magda turned her eyes away, but found them drawn back. *Fakery, nonsense; but what are they going to do to Jaelle?*

Rohana approached Jaelle, bending over her; ignoring Peter, who still knelt on the far side of the bed, holding Jaelle's hands. Jaelle's eyes had fallen shut again. Rohana ran her fingertips along Jaelle's face, not quite touching her; down across the bared shoulder and the swollen, horribly festered wound there. It seemed to Magda that a line of light followed Rohana's fingertips, began to glow along Jaelle's skin . . . *As if I could see the bones through the skin. . . .*

Rohana said, —*No, not the bones, the nerve currents that lie among them.* . . . But Rohana had *not* spoken, not raised her head; she was bending intently over Jaelle.

Alida was holding the jewel stone before her eyes with one hand, her face set in an almost inhuman calm. Now Magda could see, around the two wounds, a dull pulsing, a kind of glow around the inflamed flesh.

Alida said, "Now," and Rohana began to move her fingertips along the wound in the collarbone and shoulder. She did not touch Jaelle, but as the small lines of light followed her fingers, the swollen flesh seemed to move and ripple, dull colors swirling inside it; to heave, tremble and change color, from angry inflamed red to thick festering purple and then, almost, to a dull black, the lights in the flesh dimming, pulsing. Magda caught her breath; was this some ghastly hypnotic illusion? Blood oozed from the wound.

"Careful," Rohana said tonelessly.

The rippling surface of the open wound slowly paled, turned purple again, and as the lights around it brightened, turned red, then a smooth, healthy pink. . . .

Rohana shifted her hands, drawing her fingertips above the repulsive open gash across Jaelle's face. Alida brought the blue jewel stone close, and Magda, seeing it without sickness this time, found herself caught up in what was happening. She saw with a curious double vision those nerve currents under the skin, the slashed and broken and infected layers of skin and muscle and escaped, oozing blood, the seeped poison around the eye . . . she *felt*, with an inner itch and tension inside her mind, what Alida was doing: lowering her consciousness farther and farther, *into* the cells, exerting the tiniest pressures *(How! How?)* on each cell, so that she actually *felt* the blood and poison as pressures against the light-lines of the nerves, sensed the tiny, delicate membranes, the pressures against them. . . .

"Careful," Rohana said again, a low soft neutral sound, but to Magda, deep inside Alida's awareness, it was like a shriek of warning; and with infinite caution, Alida eased the carefully intricate pressures, moved her touch away from a small ruptured blood vessel, felt and almost *saw* the tiny tensions of fluids so near the eyeball, the glowing inner mechanism of the eyeball and tear ducts, so near, dangerously near. *Ease up just there.* . . . Something in the back of Magda's mind said, *Psychokinesis:* the power of the mind to exert delicate cellular changes. Her consciousness seemed wholly sunk inside that light, bending pressure. She looked at Jaelle from a great distance. *As if I were up somewhere near the ceiling and looking down.* . . . Giddy shifts of perspective.

Magda thought, somewhere back in her mind, *I can do that, too,* and found her attention focused on the healing slash in her own arm, sensed the inner pressures, somehow *wrenched* them into consciousness, feeling a faint sting of violent pain, somehow *outside* herself, which vanished without trace. . . .

She shook her head as if to clear it. She was standing firmly on her own feet, and Alida had covered the blue stone. She blinked as if dizzy, and looked down at Jaelle in amazement and shock. There was now no hideous, festering slash crisscrossing Jaelle's cheek; only a narrow, bright red seam, still jagged and raw, from which one drop of clean blood oozed. The nick in the eyelid was gone, and the closed eye, beneath its fringe of lashes, was no longer swollen.

Alida drew a long sigh of weariness. Mechanically Magda pushed up her sleeve, staring in puzzlement at where the bandit had gashed her arm with his poisoned blade. There was no puckered red line there now; only a firm white scar, which looked long healed. *Did I dream it?*

Alida thrust the wrapped stone inside the front of her dress. She looked at Magda, with a questioning frown, but did not speak to her. "Jaelle?"

Rohana touched Jaelle's forehead lightly. "She is asleep, I think."

"Good; while she sleeps the healing will be finished," Alida said, and gestured to Peter. "Leave her."

He tried gently to withdraw his hand, but the fingers were locked around it. He settled himself into a comfortable position on the floor and said, "I'll stay."

Magda tiptoed to Jaelle's side and drew the nightgown up over the girl's bare shoulder and breast, covered her with a blanket, then followed Rohana and Alida out of the room. Alida stumbled, almost fell against the door; Rohana caught and steadied her on her feet. She said, "Go and rest, Alida. And I thank you for Jaelle's sake."

Magda's mind was whirling. It was *not* illusion! That terrible, festering wound, like a great open, oozing sore . . . and now, as she covered Jaelle with her nightgown, it had not even needed a bandage, but was clean and almost healed. There was also her own arm; it looked like a scar a year old. And somehow, with the aid of the blue jewel, this had all been done through the powers of the mind. *Psi power. I never believed in it, not really. But I saw it.* . . .

Rohana saw Magda trembling, reached out and gently steadied her as she had done with Alida. She said, "Rest, my girl, that is strenuous work. Why did you not tell us you had *laran?*"

And Magda could only stammer, confused and dismayed, "I don't even know what the word *means!*"

Chapter Thirteen

On the eve of midwinter-day, the long-delayed blizzard swept down from the Hellers, a thick white wilderness of snow and howling wind that effectively damped the preparations for the festival. The house-party guests had already arrived, but Lady Rohana told her guests, with some disappointment, that the usual festivities would have to be suspended. Normally, everyone who lived within a day's ride would have visited Castle Ardais at some time during the day to share in the merrymaking there.

Magda expressed polite regrets for the spoiling of the holiday, but was herself secretly relieved not to have to face more strangers. She had no personal fear. Dom Gabriel would not make trouble for his wife's guests, whoever they were; and the strong tradition of hospitality in the Hellers made it unlikely that they would meet with any personal unpleasantness. But it might well mean that other Terrans, after this, would be more carefully watched and restricted in their travel.

Lady Rohana had holiday gifts for them both: long riding-capes trimmed with fur. She also tactfully offered them garments more suitable for the festival, pointing out that they had only traveling clothes with them, and those much the worse for wear. Magda accepted with relief, Jaelle with a wry laugh. She said when Rohana had gone away, "My kinsman is cowardly, to make Rohana do his errands! Margali, you are a translator by trade; see if you can interpret this as I do! I may not have the words quite right, but the music is very clear, and the tune is something like this: 'I refuse to have two Amazons in trousers at my banquet-table!'"

Magda politely refrained from comment on her host, but she felt Jaelle was probably right. Jaelle was up and around now, though until today confined to her room, but she was recovering so swiftly that Magda still doubted the evidence of her own eyes. But there it was before her: the healed scar on Jaelle's collarbone, the red line—perceptible, and a little startling, but no longer disfiguring—across her cheek.

It makes Terran medical science look primitive! Magda thought.

But if it was psi force, what was the function of the blue jewel? Was it only a focus? Magda knew she would never rest till she knew the answer to these questions. The key seemed to be the strange word *laran,* which was colloquially translated as an art, skill, gift or talent; she surmised that a *leronis* was one who used *laran,* and that the meanings of "wise-woman" or "sorceress" were ancillary. Jaelle verified this guess, adding that *laran* meant an inborn gift for psi power, and that while she herself had a little of it, she had not wanted to be trained in its use. When Magda repeated Rohana's remark—that she herself seemed to have *laran*—Jaelle shut up and could not be persuaded to say another word.

In midafternoon the promised festival dresses arrived, brought by one of Rohana's women. Magda's was a rust-colored gown with narrow sable fur trim, and trailing sleeves lined with golden silk; it was one of the prettiest dresses she had ever seen, and fitted her well enough. She felt a twinge of regret as she put it on and brushed her dark smooth hair, thinking of the silver butterfly-clasp that she would never wear again.

Jaelle said, "Among Terran women, is close-cropped hair thought a disgrace?"

"Oh, no. Most women in Empire service wear their hair little longer than men; but I have lived on Darkover most of my life, and kept mine long to be able to mingle unnoticed with women here, so I am accustomed to long hair," Magda said. "I had half expected to be told that Amazons were not allowed to wear women's dress! Is this simply a courtesy to dom Gabriel, then, Jaelle?"

Jaelle laughed merrily. She had put on the delicate green gown Rohana had sent her. She said that it had been made for her cousin, Rohana's seventeen-year-old daughter, whose name was Elorie but who was usually called Lori. With a little pinning at the waist, it fitted Jaelle beautifully. As she brushed her own hair into a burnished coppery helmet and fastened it with a pair of gold bar-clasps from her saddlebags, she said, "Oh, no! Do you think we wear trousers compulsively, like men, you silly girl? We wear them when we have to ride, or work like men, but in the Guild-house, or when working indoors, we wear whatever seems comfortable to us. We are not *required* to wear anything in particular; we simply refuse to accept the social rule that *forbids* women to wear any comfortable garment for reasons of modesty or custom. The only thing we *may* not wear—by our Charter—is a sword." Again, she laughed. "Kindra chided me, now and then, that I spent so much of what I earned on finery; I probably have as many pretty gowns as Rohana, or more, because I need not account to anyone for what use I make of my money!"

Magda felt a little relieved; she was not fond of fine clothes, in particular, but she would have felt strange to think of spending the rest of her life in rough and unattractive work clothes!

Jaelle said delightedly, when they were ready to go down, "I had no idea you were so pretty! When I first saw you, you looked like a half-frozen rabbit, and after that I have not been able to notice!"

Magda herself had been aware of Jaelle's astonishing beauty, even in rough Amazon dress; in the green gown, she was breathtaking. She saw her own opinion confirmed when Peter joined them in the hallway, outside their connecting rooms; he looked at Jaelle in delighted amazement. She smiled at him shyly, and lowered her eyes; Magda knew Jaelle was embarrassed at recalling how she had clung to him when she was weak and ill. Jaelle did not offer him her hand as she had done readily during her illness; strangely, the very omission seemed to create a greater closeness than the frank gesture. *She reacted to him as a child reacts then. Now she is very aware that he is a man and she a woman,* Magda thought.

Peter said softly, "I am very happy to see you recovered, Jaelle," and with something of her own constraint, turned to Magda, and offered her his arm. She took it, mostly because she sensed his embarrassment and tension and it was an old habit, to cover his indecision.

"Have you noticed how like our own celebrations this is? The halls decorated with greenery, the great fire, the exchanged gifts—even the smell of the spicebread!"

She knew he was only saying the first thing that came into his head, to cover embarrassment; it roused an old emotion, a mixture of tenderness and exasperation, so familiar that she felt an old, inner trembling.

"You are lovely, Magda. But I miss your lovely long hair—" He put up his hand to touch the bare nape of her neck: a gesture of intimacy, permitted only to lovers. Magda felt embarrassed. She said in a low voice, "Don't, Piedro." She used his Darkovan name deliberately, to remind him of where they were. Yet she knew it had had exactly the reverse effect; it had recreated the old intimacy.

He said, "Margali," speaking her Darkovan name like a special caress. She saw Jaelle's eyes on them and dropped his hand as if it burned her, so that they went into the Great Hall side by side, but not together.

The kindled midwinter-fire burned on the great hearth, and dom Gabriel, Lord of Ardais, stood before it, a tall, soldierly man, with graying russet hair, dressed in green and scarlet. When Jaelle stepped toward him with a formal bow, he clasped her, briefly, in a kinsman's embrace, pressing his lips to her cheek.

"I rejoice that you are well enough to join us, Jaelle. A pleasant year to you, and all happiness."

"I thank you for your hospitality, for myself and my friends, Uncle," Jaelle said, and stepped along, to be warmly hugged by Rohana and to exchange greetings with her cousins. Magda and Peter stood before the Ardais lord; he bowed over her hand, raising his eyes to hers with a puzzled, kindly smile. Magda thought of what Jaelle had said: "Anything belonging to Rohana he will treat kindly—pet dogs, Free Amazons, even Terrans . . . !" It seemed to her for a moment that Jaelle had been hard on him; from the very touch of his hand she sensed he was a decent man and a kind one, if a little narrowed by the prejudices of his caste, and without much imagination. Anyway, if Rohana loved and obeyed him, he must have more virtues than Jaelle could see in him.

"Welcome, *mestra*, as my kinswoman's friend; a pleasant holiday to you, and a fortunate year."

Magda, recalling the New Year's greeting of her Caer Donn childhood, said, "My year will be brightened by the memory of your hospitality; may the fires of your hearth never grow cold, Lord Ardais," and saw the puzzlement grow in his eyes. As she moved on to exchange formal greetings with Rohana and her grown children, she thought, *He obviously knows we are Terrans. Is he surprised that we can manage ordinary politeness?* She wondered if the Ardais lord really thought that a race which could create a Galactic empire were all ignorant boors without any sense of good manners. . . .

Lady Alida, at one of the long tables, raised her eyes, looked directly at Magda and beckoned; Magda could think of no polite way to ignore the invitation. The Comyn lady wore a festival gown of pale blue; her red-gold hair was coiled low on her neck. She gestured to Magda to sit next to her, and Magda felt the little prickles of "hunch" touching her again. Alida was a Comyn lady, a *leronis*, and gifted with psi power. A mere trace of this, in Jaelle, had given Magda away. How could she manage not to betray herself?

For a time, everyone's attention was on the small delicacies of the table: a clear soup with golden slices of some delicious mushroom floating in it; small, hot savory tidbits of different kinds; spicebread in all sorts of ornamental shapes, gilded and decorated. But as these were taken away, and the servants—in their holiday garments, and joining in the feast they helped to serve—brought the main courses, Alida turned to Magda and said, "While your sworn sister was ill and needed your care, I would not call you from her side, *mestra*. But now she is well," and she looked at

Jaelle, laughing between Peter and her cousin and obviously teasing them about their resemblance. "I wanted a word with you. Have you never been tested for *laran,* Margali?"

"No. Never."

"But surely you were aware of your inborn talent, were you not?"

"No," Magda said again, and a faint frown furrowed the lady's high pale forehead.

"But surely . . . as you know, it wakes normally at adolescence; had you no hint of this gift? Or were you committed so early to the life of a Free Amazon that you did not ask for this testing?"

That would have been a good escape, but the lie was too easily discovered; it was a matter of record that she had only recently been made a Free Amazon. She fell back on the literal truth. "Until the other day, my Lady, I had no idea that I had the faintest trace of *laran.* It came as a great surprise to me."

"Well, when Midwinter Festival is over, we must have you properly tested," Alida said, as if the matter were settled. How, Magda wondered, would she get out of *this?* With definite relief, she remembered something else. She never would have believed herself capable of putting this forth with positive pleasure. "After midwinter, Lady, my duties commit me to the Guild-house."

Lady Alida brushed that aside. "Something will be arranged. An untrained telepath is a danger to herself and everyone around her, and that would apply to all your sisters of the Guild-house." She said no more, politely calling her guest's attention to the musicians who had come to entertain them, and would play later for the dancing.

But enough had been said to ruin Magda's appetite. What was she going to do now?

When the meal ended, the older guests gathered around the midwinter-fire for gossip and reminiscence (Magda knew these house parties, held when the weather brought all outdoor work to a standstill, were reunions of friends who often did not meet from year to year) while the younger people descended into the lower hall for dancing. Magda had learned to dance as a child—a girl could not reach her eighth year in Caer Donn without learning to dance, and to dance well—and knew most of these dances.

Although she took part with pleasure when Jaelle and Lori drew her into a ring-dance with a dozen other girls, she did not know what the rules of Amazon etiquette were for dancing with men after the group dances gave way to dancing in couples. But after a time, seeing Jaelle laughing and flirting and dancing with all comers, she grew less hesitant. She accepted the invitations, enjoying it on two levels: the Terran agent making mental notes (But would she ever really be that again?), and, to her own surprise, the young girl she had been in Caer Donn, mingling for the first time with young men. It was, literally, the first time since childhood when she had felt herself actually in the company of her own kind.

Magda had never realized until this moment quite how much her curious, between-worlds childhood had robbed her of the ability to mingle with people her own age. Childhood in Caer Donn had prepared her, emotionally and socially, for adolescence and maturity in the same world; instead, before adolescence, she had been torn away and isolated in the Terran Zone with children whose background was only that of the Empire; and at sixteen she had been sent off-world for training. She had felt isolated and completely at a loss with girls or boys her own age in the Empire. Later, when she could mingle with Darkovans in the course of her work, there were many inhibitions against allowing any purely personal contacts; and in any case Darkovan women met men only in their homes and under the proper sponsorship of their families.

But now, as Rohana's guest, she could join in freely. *If I had been exposed to a little of this when I was twenty I would never have married Peter.* The thought troubled her for some reason, and she was glad to turn to a young man of dom Gabriel's household who came up to her, asking for a dance. After a time he said, "Is your name—Margali?"

"Yes, that is what they call me."

"I thought so! You had another name, but none of us could pronounce it, so we called you by that one. You are *Toroku* Lorne's daughter, are you not?" The title was the equivalent of "learned man" or "professor," and had been given her father by the local children. "I knew you when we were children; you used to have dancing lessons with my sisters, Tara and Renata. I am Darrill, son of Darnak."

Now she remembered Darrill, and his sisters. She had once spent midwinter-night with Renata when she was quite small; she had played with them, visited in their home, and brought them to her own home in the HQ. Darrill had been an older boy, out of their orbit.

He said, "I thought all of you Terrans had gone to Thendara and would not return to the Hellers. What are you doing here?"

"I am Lady Rohana's midwinter guest—or rather, the guest of her kinswoman Jaelle."

Darrill demanded, "Do they know who you really are? I am dom Gabriel's sworn man, and if you are here under false pretenses, Lord Ardais should know!"

Magda said, trying to control her inner trembling, "My true name and my purposes are known to Lady Rohana; you may ask her if you wish. And I suppose, since she knows, that dom Gabriel knows as well."

He said with a faint grin, "I suppose so; but if the lady knows, it does not really matter whether dom Gabriel knows or not, since it is well known from here to the Kadarin that the lady rules the estate, with dom Gabriel's assistance when he feels so inclined."

She asked after his sisters; he told her the names of their husbands, and how they fared. She wondered if it was really safe to spend time with anyone who knew who and what she really was. But it might be worse to make a point of avoiding him; that would be suspicious conduct indeed. His fear that she was a spy once overcome, he seemed to accept it as quite normal that she be here.

It ought to be normal! Darkovans and Terrans should have a chance to be together, then they will not have a chance to build barriers of ignorance and distrust! Lorill Hastur is wrong, wrong, wrong!

When he had left her—it seemed, with reluctance—she found herself standing next to Jaelle, who had paused, breathless, after a fast, romping dance.

"I think Camilla was right," she said, laughing. "There are men who find scars irresistible on a woman! I have never been so popular!"

"I had half expected to find that Amazons were not allowed to take any notice of men—after Camilla warned me so sternly not even to look at them!" Magda could laugh about this memory now.

"Oh, this is only when there is work to be done, or the men are such as might consider a glance some sort of—of invitation," said Jaelle. "There have been times when I worked with men and they took no more notice of me than of another workman. We learn not to cause trouble—you will learn it, in the Guild-house—so that an Amazon can travel alone in a band of a dozen men, and will be accepted as one of them. But I also know how to behave when I want them to accept me as a woman—at Midwinter Festival, for instance! Or midsummer, when the dances—in Thendara, for instance—go on all night, and extend into the gardens! And you know the old proverb: 'What is done under the four moons need not be remembered when they have set. . . .' Although for my part I have never had any taste for waiting forty days after, to see if I would bear a child in the spring—"

She broke off, saying gently, "I am sorry—it is like talking with Rohana; I forget sometimes that she has been trained to the politenesses of women's speech. I did not mean to shock you, sister!"

Magda had not, of course, been shocked at the words; but she realized that she did not know Jaelle at all, in this madcap mood. And she herself had been brought up to observe the fairly straitlaced sexual taboos of the mountain women. This had been confusing to her during her off-world training and had tended to throw her, more and more, into the company of Peter; he respected them, to some degree shared them.

Jaelle said, "In any case, no one cares much what happens at such festivals; even dom Gabriel will turn a blind eye to whatever happens in the galleries and dark corners, or when the fires burn low. . . . Usually the old people go off to bed early and leave the young people to do as they please." She leaned close to Magda, and whispered, her eyes glowing with mischief, "There is a saying that you never master a language completely till you have learned to make love in it! I saw Darrill looking at you—I am sure he would be happy to teach you."

Magda felt her cheeks flaming, and Jaelle gave her a gentle pat on the shoulder. "I should not tease you, sister. Someday you will know how to take our jests, too. Here is Piedro, come to dance with you at last!"

Instead he took Magda lightly by the elbow, and said, "I want to talk to you for a minute." He guided her toward the refreshment table, dipped himself up some wine from the great cut-crystal bowl there. He said in an undertone, "What did Darrill say to you?"

"Only that he recognized me," she said, "and asked if dom Gabriel knew who I was."

"He asked me the same," said Peter. "I told him that since Lady Rohana knew who I was, I was quite sure dom Gabriel knew it also." He hesitated, about to fill her glass.

"No, I've had enough. I'm feeling a little dizzy," and she nibbled on a bit of cake instead.

Peter said, almost jealously, "I saw you dancing with Darrill. You certainly seem to be enjoying yourself!"

"I am. Aren't you? I've never had a chance to do this kind of thing before! And I've missed it!"

"It never occurred to me you would want to," Peter said. "I have gone to the Midsummer Festivals in Thendara these last three years; if I had thought of it I could have taken you. But"—he hesitated—"at the public festivals—not the ones in private houses like this, where everything is very decorous—but the public dances, where all comers mingle, the party sometimes gets a little wild. Dancing till dawn, pairing off in the gardens and all that; I didn't think you'd want to come."

Magda suddenly felt a violent resentment; he felt it was suitable to go himself, even if the party got a little . . . *wild.* Yet he had decided, without consulting her, that that kind of entertainment was not suitable for *her!* She said dryly, "You might have let me decide it for myself."

He raised his hand to touch the nape of her neck again; a suggestive touch, arousing memories she had tried to forget. He whispered, "I was jealous, darling."

She felt a sudden, almost completely irrational anger. How dared he make that decision for her? Had he felt free, then, to take a casual sweetheart for himself at these festivals—a privilege he felt himself justified in denying to her, as if he were her father or guardian?

He was still bending close to her, fondling her neck; she could feel his warm breath. He was a little drunk; not much. Like herself, he had been taught to take great care with alcohol or other mind-altering drugs, and he knew and watched his own limits carefully. He was a good agent, she thought, a gifted agent, and felt the old fondness surge through her, so that she did not move away when he put his arm around her and drew her into the shadow of the draperies at one side. He bent his head, murmured to her.

She tensed in his arms and said sharply, "Speak *casta;* have you forgotten where we are?"

He brought his lips down on hers and kissed her. "It's good to be alive!" he said violently. "It's midwinter-night—and I *knew* I was going to die. I *knew* there was no hope of rescue. Oh, Magda, Magda, Magda . . ." His voice faded out. He kissed her, hard enough to hurt. "And I'm alive, and you're here, and we're together again."

At first she did not protest, thinking it was a mere surge of gratitude, awareness of life instead of death; but his embrace grew quickly more demanding, more personal.

"Do you have any idea how much I want you, *need* you, how damnably I've missed you?"

Gently she tried to put a little space between herself and his demanding caresses, but he whispered against her throat, "You feel it, too, I know you do! You want me as much as I want you, or you'd never have come so far for me."

Against her will she felt herself responding; but a cold rational voice was saying in the back of her mind: *Now that you are free of him, do you truly want to start the whole miserable thing over again?* The excitement of the festival, a few drinks, the general atmosphere of license and the straitlaced rules relaxed for once, the fact that he'd been alone a long time and wanted a woman—that's what it was and that's all it was. She wouldn't be fooled into thinking it was more than that. Gently, but inexorably, she removed his hands from her.

"I'm sorry, Peter."

"Mag, Mag, I need you so. Don't you know we belong together?"

"I'm sorry, truly I am," she said with a sigh. "Until a little while ago, I thought so, too. But now I just don't feel guilty about you anymore. Now I'm just sorry I can't give you what you want."

"Is there someone else? That Darrill—"

"No, no. Nothing like that. Don't be foolish, Peter. I haven't seen him since I was nine years old!"

There had never been anyone else. Until now she would have sworn there never could be.

"Mag, you know there can never be anyone else, not for either of us, not on this world."

That, she thought, was partly true; they had shared the Darkovan childhood, the isolation from their peers, which had kept them from finding satisfactory mates elsewhere; drawn together by the knowledge that they were the only ones available for one another. Now she resented this; and resented, even more, how much he took it for granted.

"No, Peter. Whatever you're asking—no."

"I want you," he said, as if in pain. "I want you for always. I want to marry you again. And I want you now. Magda, Magda, come with me now! Our rooms are together, it's as if it had been intended—"

She said quietly, "You know I am not free to marry. Now."

"Oh, that! This Amazon game you are playing—"

"It's not a game." The very softness with which she spoke accentuated the finality of the words.

His voice was bitter. "Have you cut off your womanhood with your hair?"

"No," she said. "I don't think so. But I don't think womanhood means I have to go to bed with you just because you're lonely"—she had begun to use a ruder word—"and want a woman."

He touched her softly, intensely, and she hated her own arousal. He said, in triumph, "You want me, too. You know you do!"

"If I do," she said, suddenly angry, "that is *my* affair and not yours, unless *I* choose to make it so! Oh, God, Peter, why can't you understand? Do you want me just to be *kind* to you?"

He said, trying to hold her, "I'd settle for that," but she wrenched herself free.

"But I won't, and that's final! Peter, let me go. Jaelle is watching us!"

She moved away; only a few inches, but with such finality she might as well have been on one of the moons. Seeing the angry flush of offended pride lying along his cheekbones, she felt almost regretful; but nothing kinder would ever have made him believe her. He swallowed hard, and turned away; she watched him go toward Jaelle, saw the girl hold out her hand, with none of the shyness now she had shown earlier this evening. Peter took the slender fingers in his own, and although Magda could not hear what they said, she saw them move away together.

She watched them circle the dance floor, with a certain sadness. She was really free of Peter now. And suddenly, with her new dimension of awareness, she knew what she had done.

She had seen it, as they left Sain Scarp. Perhaps it was only chemistry, perhaps it was something more; but it had been immediate and unmistakable. Jaelle's weakness and collapse had misdirected Peter's response into protective kindness, self-effacing chivalry.

But it had been there, all the time, behind the kindness and the gentle, impersonal protectiveness. She had seen it again, when Jaelle had clung to Peter in her delirium. And now, feeling almost humiliated, she knew why Peter had come to her tonight; and it was not because he found her irresistible.

Peter was, first of all, a Terran agent; and he knew the rules. And one of them, a major one, was this: never, never—*never*—get seriously and deeply involved with any native woman on any planet where you're assigned. Casual liaisons were condoned, if not approved (every spaceport in the Empire had a red-light district), but anything more serious was forbidden.

And whatever it was between Peter and Jaelle, it was very real, and it was serious. Peter had been trying, a desperate last-ditch attempt, to protect himself against this involvement which could be so disastrous to the rules under which he lived. Magda was safe, Magda was one of his own. And yet . . . not quite.

He's like me; his sexuality somehow got to be Darkovan, just as mine did. He doesn't react to other women. But I'm near enough so that somehow he can be content with me. As I was with him. For a while.

If Magda had come with him, tonight, he could have resisted his own powerful, and dangerous, desire for Jaelle. But Magda had driven him away, with a blow to his masculine pride; and Peter had gone straight to Jaelle to heal that wound.

Now, with sudden dread, Magda found herself worrying about them both. Peter could risk his career for Jaelle. And Jaelle—what would she risk? She was no girl of the spaceport bars, but a woman of the Comyn, and, if Magda was any judge, deeply in love.

Irritably, Magda tried to dismiss the whole matter from her mind. It was definitely not her affair. Jaelle was no child; she was only a year or two younger than Magda herself, and, judging by the way she had been talking earlier, quite sophisticated enough to take care of herself. As for endangering Peter's career, Jaelle was not free to marry.

But even while she stood and watched a group of men dancing with torches, an ancient sword-dance, she wondered where in the lowering shadows Peter and Jaelle had gone. . . .

Somehow, the savor had gone from the evening. At midnight or thereabouts, dom Gabriel, Rohana and Lady Alida, with most of the older people, said good night and withdrew, hospitably bidding their younger guests to remain and enjoy themselves as late as they chose.

Darrill sought Magda out again, and urged her to accompany him into one of the long galleries where, he said, there were some very fine ancient murals. From the way he touched her, and spoke, Magda was perfectly sure that he had no more interest in the murals than she did herself. She made some tactful excuse, and when he had gone away, she wondered why she had not taken up the challenge. Peter and Jaelle had long since disappeared and not returned; she wondered what gallery *they* were exploring. From what Jaelle had said, Magda knew it was not regarded as particularly reprehensible to share a good deal of casual kissing—or more, if she wished—on midwinter-night.

Sooner or later, now that I'm free of Peter, I must find out how I react to other men. . . .

Then, angry with herself, she thought, *Damn it, before I complicate my life with another man, I want to know more about myself! I want to know what I am to myself, not always have to see myself through a man's eyes!*

A strange man came and asked her to dance again; she pleaded extreme fatigue, left the Great Hall and went up to the room she shared with Jaelle. Jaelle had not returned. Magda took off her beautiful gown, readied herself for bed and lay down. She expected to lie awake, worrying about Peter and Jaelle; instead she fell at once into a heavy sleep.

Hours later, she woke to see Jaelle standing in the doorway, barefoot, her face flushed, her short hair tousled. Her eyes were very bright. She came across the room and sat on Magda's bed.

Magda said lightly, "I didn't expect you back until later."

Magda could smell the girl's sweet heavy breath, and knew she had been drinking; was not sober now.

Jaelle said, "Oh, don't be angry with me, sister. I didn't want this to happen, I know how you feel."

"Angry?" Magda sat up and put her arms around Jaelle. "Darling"— the word she used was *breda*—"what right have I to be angry? Do you think—" Abruptly, it dawned on her just what Jaelle *did* think. "Do you think I'm *jealous?*"

Jaelle said with a nervous giggle, "This kind of thing is easier at midsummer when there are gardens. We have spent most of the night in the long galleries." Her teeth were chattering, whether with cold or nervous excitement Magda could not tell. "I—I should have gone with him as he asked me." She looked at the connecting door into Peter's room. "But— but I wanted to be sure, I don't like deciding things in a hurry and," she added after a moment, looking at Magda in appeal, "I did not want to—to tread on the hem of your garment."

Incongruously Magda realized that she was still making mental notes about the curious idiom. She hugged the trembling girl tight, and said, "Jaelle, anything between Peter Haldane and me was a long, long time ago." As she said it, she knew that it was really true. "Do you love him, *breda?*"

"I don't know," Jaelle said. "I'm not sure. I've never felt like this before."

Magda found herself wondering if Jaelle were a virgin. From her flippant jokes, and sophisticated comments, she had not thought so; but could an experienced woman be so uncertain? As if Jaelle had picked up the thought directly from her mind—and by now Magda was almost ready to believe that—Jaelle said in a low voice, looking down, "It's foolish, isn't it? I've come near to it many times. Before I took the oath, when Kindra saw that I liked to—to laugh with men and to flirt with them, she told me that before I bound myself, I should take a lover, test myself that way; she said that it might someday seem hard to me that I was bound by law never to marry. But somehow there was never anyone I could—could trust that much."

She added defensively, "So it never came to more than laughter or foolishness. Nor did I ever leave any man wounded by my teasing, or heart-scalded. But now"—she looked and sounded forlorn—"I have no more laughter. I think I am more afraid now, when I—when I love him, when I want him, than when I was a girl and the very thought of giving myself to any man seemed frightening, an open door to bondage and slavery. . . . I don't know myself anymore!" Her voice was shaking and she was very close to tears. "I don't know what I want! Oh, Margali, Margali —sister, what shall I do?"

Magda felt wrung, helpless. *What can I say to her?* She could understand that to Jaelle, brought up as she had been among women close-bound to one another by oath, it seemed completely natural to turn to another woman for comfort or counsel. *I am bound to treat every woman as my mother, sister, daughter . . . but I've always lived by such different laws . . . God help me, I don't know what to say to her!* If one of her own friends in the Terran Zone—Bethany, for instance—had come to her with such a question, Magda could have turned it off with a casual or even a crude joke. But she could not do that to Jaelle.

What would Rohana have said to her? Finally, in a voice shaking as much as Jaelle's, she said, "Darling, I can't advise you. I don't know if anyone could. You must do what you feel is right." Then, to her own surprise, she found herself whispering the words of the oath of the Free Amazons: "I swear I will give myself to no man save in my own time and season and of my own free will. . . ."

There was a moment of silence, then Jaelle whispered as if to herself, "In my own time and season," and smiled, tightening her arms around Magda; and Magda knew that somehow, by instinct, she had hit on precisely the right thing to say. She felt Jaelle's lips against her cheek for a moment; then, without a word, Jaelle pressed her hand, and went, on noiseless feet, to the connecting door, which closed a moment later behind her. She did not return.

Chapter Fourteen

Day after day the snow fell, pouring from gray skies as if it had forgotten how to stop. Then, ten days after midwinter, Magda was awakened by Jaelle, sitting on her bed.

"Wake up, sister, the sun is shining!"

Magda ran to the window. The sky was filled with thick, low, puffy clouds through which erratic sunshine spilled; in the courtyard below, pathways were being cleared by bundled men with long shovels; and horses, their breath streaming in the cold, were being brought around for departing guests.

Magda dressed hastily in her traveling garments, not at all sorry to resume them. Every day their stay was prolonged meant another chance of revealing who they were.

Jaelle began slowly to dress. Since midwinter, she had spent her nights at Peter's side, although she had been careful not to be found there in the morning by dom Gabriel's servants. When Magda teased her gently about what seemed like hypocrisy, she had said, "I do not care a *sekal's* worth what dom Gabriel thinks of me; he is not my guardian and I owe no man any account of my acts. I care still less what his servants think of me. The servants know, of course; they always know such things. But if no one of them sees me there, then there will be no one whose business it is to inform dom Gabriel. And although he probably knows, too—he is not a fool, and he has seen us looking at one another—if his servants told him in so many words, he would feel compelled to ask Rohana to reprimand me for putting the women of the Comyn to shame by sharing a commoner's bed. And for his peace of mind Rohana would feel she had to come and scold me, even though she and I agreed together when I was sixteen that she was not my guardian and no longer the keeper of my conscience. And she would try not to offend me because she knows that I am a grown woman and by law the mistress of my own acts, and I would try not to be rude to her because I love her. And when we had all forced ourselves to say all these things, I would still go on sleeping with Peter whenever I chose; so it seems to me wiser not to start all that in motion."

That reasoning seemed complicated to Magda, but she had to admit that it probably saved trouble for all of them. It was even possible that dom Gabriel, if it were brought directly to his notice, might feel compelled to call Peter personally to account. By the Amazon oath, Jaelle had declared her independence of his guardianship, but Magda had heard from Jaelle that some men still refused to recognize the Amazon Charter.

Peter joined them in the hallway; he took Jaelle's hand in his as they went down the corridor, and Magda, watching, thought that the trip back to Thendara, with just the three of them, was likely to be awkward in more ways than one. She did not grudge Jaelle a single moment of her happiness —and that they were happy, no one who saw them together could possibly doubt—but it *was* going to be awkward, and she, Magda, would bear most of the awkwardness!

The immediate family of Ardais, with a bare handful of the house-party guests, and estate officials, usually had their meals in a small breakfast room away from the Great Hall. As they came in they heard a burst of laughter. Dom Kyril was telling a funny story, which was one of the commonest midwinter pastimes, at this season when all outdoor work came to a dead stop.

". . . And everybody had to carry around a little torch to thaw out what he said before he could be heard; and this man made quite a bit of money by gathering up all the frozen speeches in a barrow, and carting them around to their owners. Only he wasn't quite as careful as he should have been, to make sure that they were delivered to the right owners, and when the spring-thaw came, and all the words thawed out again, there was a tremendous amount of trouble. The mule-driver thawed out what he had yelled at his team, and found he had the words of an old lady talking to her pet birds; and the young mother scolding her little children got the mule-driver's, and the children cried half the day; and the young wife telling her husband she was to bear his first son, got what the Free Amazon said to the man who—" He broke off and turned a full red as Jaelle giggled. "My apologies, cousin!"

Jaelle said dryly, "Kinsman, I heard all the jokes there are about Free Amazons, before I had turned fifteen; and most of them I heard in the Guild-house from my sisters. I would share them with you, but most of them would shock your delicate male sensibilities." It was the turn of the others to laugh. "Finish your story, kinsman; this is one I have not heard."

Kyril tried to take up where he had left off. "The aristocratic lady entertaining her guests was delivered the chatter of the men from the lowest tavern in the village, while the Keeper instructing her youngest novice found herself hearing what the Dry-Towner bellowed at his minion.
. . ."

"Enough," dom Gabriel said, with a glance at Lady Alida. "It seems to me this is a tale for the barracks, son, not for your mother's breakfast table." He glanced up to greet the newcomers, his eyebrows raising in question as he saw the women in Amazon clothing.

Jaelle said, "Uncle, with your leave, we will ride for Thendara today; it is a long journey at this season, and my sister has duties in the Guild-house."

"Impossible," Lord Gabriel said. "This is only the snow-break, my girl; tomorrow at this hour it will be snowing harder than ever. This storm will last another ten days at the least; only the guests who live within a few hours' ride are departing today. You would be well advised to remain until the spring-thaw, at least."

"You are more than kind, Lord Ardais," said Peter, "but we could not so long trespass on hospitality."

"You couldn't possibly travel more than a day's ride before the snow blocked you again," dom Gabriel said. "It seems to me nonsense, to spend the rest of the blizzard in a tent or travel-shelter when you could stay here in comfort."

Magda and Peter knew he was right. And indeed, the weather in the Hellers at this season was proverbial; from midwinter to spring-thaw, only the mad or the desperate ventured more than an hour's ride from their own firesides.

Toward afternoon the day darkened again, and the next morning the windows were a flurry of white snow, with the wind howling around the towers of Ardais like a banshee hard on the heels of its prey. And at breakfast dom Gabriel said triumphantly, "You see? You had better stay till spring-thaw, all of you!"

Afterward, Lady Alida drew Magda aside and said, "We should arrange for your testing, *mestra,* today; it should not be much longer delayed."

Magda was seized by such panic that she felt it must be perceptible to the *leronis.* As soon as she could get away she went in search of Lady Rohana, and found her in her private sitting room, working on the accounts of the estate. At first this might have surprised Magda; now she knew that every thread in the running of Ardais was spun through Lady Rohana's slender six-fingered hands.

"Forgive me for disturbing you, my Lady; may I speak to you alone for a moment?"

Rohana motioned her inside and dismissed the lady companion without whom, it seemed, she could not move half a dozen steps. "Certainly; this can wait till spring-thaw, if need be. What troubles you, child?"

Magda felt an overwhelming sense of presumption; she had come to a Comyn lady to complain about one of the lady's own caste! She said hesitantly, "The Lady Alida is determined to have me tested for *laran,* and I am afraid that if she explores my mind that way it may cause trouble for all of us."

Rohana looked grave. *This is my fault; I should have sent the Terrans away.* She said, "We were both surprised to find you in the rapport when we were working in the matrix. Have you been trained in these powers among your own people?"

Magda shook her head. "Among us, there are not too many who even believe that such powers exist, Lady. Those who believe in them, or claim to be able to use them, are thought ignorant, superstitious, credulous."

"I had heard that." Rohana knew that had been one of Lorill Hastur's reasons for the ban on too much mingling with the Terrans. *They do not believe in these powers; once convinced, they would be greedy to know all about them, and exploit them.*

Rohana said, "Belief or not, you seem to have this kind of *laran,* child. How came you by it?"

"I do not know, Lady. All my life I have been able to use hunches, but I believed it was simply that I had a talent for adding up things which were subliminal—just a little below the conscious levels of perception. And there have been times when my dreams were not—not nonsense, but told me things I did not consciously know; so I have learned to take heed of them."

Rohana leaned her chin thoughtfully on her hands. This meant they must reevaluate most of what they had learned about the Terrans. "Lorill is committed to a belief that Terrans and Darkovans are different races of beings, and that the Terrans are inferior; and he uses their lack of *laran* as proof."

Magda said, "My Lady, I am not supposed to tell this outside the Terran Zone, either; but the Lord Hastur is mistaken. This is not a belief, but a fact that can be proved; Terran and Darkovan are one race. It is known to us beyond question that Darkover was settled by Terrans long ago, by one of what we call the Lost Ships. In an age before the faster-than-light ships that we have now, there were ships that were sent out from Terra—it was not an Empire then—and some of them were lost and never heard of again. There is evidence from your languages that it was settled by a ship whose very name I could give you, and the names of those aboard. It is most likely that this knowledge was lost to you centuries ago, Lady—probably to keep the survivors from pining too much for their lost homeland—but your people are truly Terrans."

"Then psi gifts—you have them, too?"

"It is rumored that once they were more common than now; now they are very rare, and there was a time in our history when people used to pretend them, or feign them with clever devices and machinery, so they fell into disrepute and their use was considered charlatanry. But there seems evidence that once they were known."

Rohana nodded. "There was a time in the history of the Comyn," she said, "when we did selective breeding to fix these gifts in our racial heritage; it was a time of great tyranny, and not a time we are very proud to remember. It led to its own downfall, and we of the Comyn are still suffering the aftermath; not only in the distrust the common people have for us, but in that our fertility was lowered by inbreeding; and the gifts are linked to some dangerous recessive traits. But they are powerful, and when misused can be very dangerous. Which brings me to you, child. Normally, psi gifts waken in adolescence; when they waken later there are sometimes dangerous upsets and upheavals. Have you felt any strange sensations, any unexplained sickness without physical cause, any sense of being outside of your body and unable to get back, any wild emotional upheavals?"

"No, nothing like that," Magda said. Then she remembered the moment of altered perspective during the healing, but that had passed off quickly and of itself.

Rohana asked her a number of searching questions about her dreams and "hunches," and finally said, when Magda felt wrung out by the questioning, "It seems to me that your talents are slight, and that you have compensated for them very well. You could, if you wished, probably learn the use of *laran* with ease, and it would be interesting to see what use a Terran could make of this training. I would like to have the teaching of you; but it seems it would make more trouble than it is worth. You are committed elsewhere; and I have already gone against Lorill's will as much as seems wise. Yet," she added, almost wistfully, "if you demand this training, I could not refuse it to anyone with *laran;* and by law, birth and parentage cannot be used to refuse it to you."

Magda said firmly, "I think I have quite enough trouble without that!"

Rohana touched her wrist very lightly, that feather-touch Magda was beginning to guess was peculiar to telepaths among their own. "So be it, dear child. But if you ever have trouble with *laran*, you must promise to come to me."

She sat looking intently at Magda for a moment. "If Lorill is wrong—if it can be proved that what he believes about your people is wrong—I do not need to tell you what it will mean for both your world and mine."

To Magda, with her heightened sensitivity, the force of what she had always called "hunch" raising her perceptions, it seemed at this moment that she caught the very image in Rohana's mind: a great barricaded door, slowly swinging open between two locked-away worlds, two peoples; opening to give a bright and sunlit view. Magda thought, *We should be one people, not two . . . I would do anything for that.* . . .

Rohana said, slowly, more as if she were thinking aloud than speaking, and yet Magda knew she was meant to share the woman's thoughts, "Does it not seem to you, Margali, that there is a design of some sort in this? That of all the Terrans on our world, it should be your friend, who could be so easily mistaken for my son, who should be taken by Rumal di Scarp? I myself, in a quick look, can still be deceived, and must look at their fingers and hands to be certain, until one of them speaks. Does it not seem fantastic to you that of all the Amazons of Darkover, you should fall into Jaelle's hands, and that the two of you should be so tested that you have become sworn friends as well?"

Magda felt uneasy. She said, "Coincidence, Lady."

"One coincidence, perhaps. Two, maybe. But so many, like beads strung on a necklace? No, this is more than coincidence, my friend; or if it is coincidence, then coincidence itself is only another word for a design intended by whatever force it is that shapes the fates of man." She smiled, and seemed to come back to the practical world, saying, "Now I must ask something of you, child. Will you take care in what you say to your friends, and to your superiors in the Terran Zone, at least until I have had a chance to speak with Lorill?"

"Indeed I will," Magda said, smiling a little at the thought of Montray's face if she should ever try to tell him about the matrix operation that had healed Jaelle's wound within a few minutes, or that Lady Rohana had said that she herself had *laran.* If this was ever to be brought up between Darkovan and Terran, she was quite willing it should be someone other than herself who should do it—and she hoped there would be a more receptive audience than Russell Montray!

Rohana rose, and said, "Go now, Margali. I must think this over and decide what to do."

Magda hesitated just a moment. "But what shall I tell Lady Alida?"

"Don't worry about her. I will tell her that I have tested you myself," Rohana said, and her smile was droll. "Don't you realize that is what I have been doing?"

The blizzard lasted for another ten days—almost exactly as dom Gabriel had predicted—and when the weather finally cleared, the roads and passes lay blocked with drifts so deep that the three guests at Ardais were readily persuaded to remain for a few more days. Yet Magda had begun to brace herself, mentally, for their departure, and for whatever lay ahead. She could not return to her old life inside the Terran Zone, venturing outside it only in disguise; she knew the disguise had become her truest self. But what she could do instead—that she did not know either.

She found herself thinking again and again of what Rohana had said about a design in the chain of coincidences that had brought them together; even in the peculiar pattern that had drawn Peter and Jaelle together as lovers. If the Empire was to remain on Darkover indefinitely, sooner or later there would be—as on all planets inhabited by different groups of humans—entanglements, romances, liaisons, and eventually marriages, even children who belonged to both worlds. And someone had to be the first.

Of course, one day Darkover would be an Empire planet. It was inevitable. The Empire did not conquer; but once the contacted planet saw the pattern of the Galactic Empire, and what it could mean to be part of it, the rulers always asked to be affiliated. When that time came, Terran and Darkovan would all be Empire citizens, and such affairs and romances would concern no one but the two people involved, and perhaps their families. But now it could cause only complications.

Magda hoped their departure would not be too long delayed. Jaelle and Peter were beginning to be a little less careful, and Magda wondered what the end would be. Again and again, seeing them together, she felt the small, indefinable pricklings of "hunch"—or precognition. *Sooner or later, this meant danger. . . .* Yet how could she speak to Jaelle, warn her, without the younger girl thinking that she was jealous, or grudged her the happiness she had found with her lover? Still less was it possible to remonstrate with Peter. So she only watched them with growing disquiet and anxiety.

In anticipation of their imminent departure she began to sort and put together her possessions; Jaelle found her occupied by this, and suggested that most of their traveling clothes were in need of repair, and that they might profitably spend the day in putting them in order. Magda was surprised to find that Jaelle was an expert needlewoman; somehow this had seemed too feminine an art for an Amazon. Magda herself, accustomed to the readily replaceable, cheap synthetics of the Terran Zone, had never mastered the art; had, in fact, been taught to scorn it as being a pointless way of passing time for women who had no useful work to do.

When she said this to Jaelle, the younger woman laughed. "And so it is, much of the time! Last night in the hall, when Rohana invited us to join her women at the tapestry they were making for the hall chair cushions, I thought I should go mad! I love to embroider," she added, "but how Rohana can endure it, I cannot imagine! I myself should go mad, to sit there night after night, surrounded by those fools of sewing-women . . . stitch, stitch, stitch, gossip, gossip, gossip! Rohana runs the whole estate of Ardais, and does it better than dom Gabriel could do, and she sits in Council and gives advice to Hastur, yet there she sits among those foolish girls, and chatters with them as if she had never had a thought in her head more serious than whether to embroider the next cushion with a rainfish or a starflower! As if it mattered to anyone's backside what was embroidered on a cushion, as long as it was well stuffed!" But even as she spoke, she was setting small neat stitches in the torn fingers of her glove.

Magda, watching her, thought that it made good sense to learn an art of this kind, on a world like Darkover, where warm and durable clothing was a necessity of life. She said ruefully, looking at the mess she had made of the torn tunic, "I am even less skillful with a needle than a sword!"

Jaelle laughed. "My skill with a dagger is incidental," she said. "I told you I was no fighter, but for my first year or two among the Amazons I used to work at Kindra's side. She was my foster-mother and had been a mercenary soldier. And when there was peace in the Domains, she hired herself out as a bodyguard to escort travelers through the Kilghard Hills and the Hellers, and protect them against bandits, catmen and what-have-you. For a few years I worked with her; but I did not really like it, and gradually I discovered my real skill."

"What is that, Jaelle?" Magda remembered Rohana saying that the Amazons worked at any honest trade; but she was curious to know which of them Jaelle had made her own.

"I am a travel-organizer," Jaelle said. "People who intend to travel in the hills come and consult me. I can tell them precisely how many pack animals they will need for supplies for any number of men, for the length of their trip, and where to hire or buy them, and where to hire drivers for them, and precisely how much equipment they must buy—or I can buy it for them, on commission. Then I can advise them about how much of the different kinds of food they must buy to keep the men healthy, and provide them with guides and bodyguards, tell them what roads to take, how long the journey will last at the specific season of the year, what passes might be closed or what rivers in flood, and anything else they might wish to know. It is not a business to make anyone rich, but I make a good living at it. Some people only wish for an hour or two of advice, and I give it to them for a fee; others put all the preparations for the trip in my hands, and I do everything from buying pack saddles to choosing meals and equipment they can use at midwinter in the high passes."

"Tell me," Magda said hesitantly. "From what I have seen of Thendara —are there many men willing to turn such responsibility over to a woman?"

"More than you might think," Jaelle said. "Rafaella, who started this business, told me that in the first year or two, her business was almost limited to providing escort service for ladies whose kinsmen had no leisure to escort them and would not trust them to strange men. Amazon body-guards for women were much in demand because they knew the ladies would arrive unraped! But as it became known that the caravans we orga-nized could take quicker routes, and arrive without running out of fodder, or having to live on porridge-powder for the last four or five days, the ladies themselves began to insist that we be allowed to make plans for their husbands' business journeyings, and so it has grown to a point where we have as much business as we can do."

"It still seems a strange business for a woman—here," Magda said. "I have grown used to thinking that a woman's life on Darkover was always so limited. Oh, *damn* this thing!" She broke off, sucking the finger she had pricked with an incautious stitch.

Jaelle laughed, saying, "Don't bother; give it to one of Rohana's sewing-women. They will be glad to have something to do, and it will give them pleasure to think there is something, *anything* they can do better than a Free Amazon."

Jaelle, Magda thought, was a puzzle; she was devoted to her sisters in the Guild of Free Amazons—and yet she could be so contemptuous of other women! She said, "Do you really think all women would be happier as Amazons, Jaelle?"

Jaelle put her mended glove back with its mate and began to sort out some small things at the bottom of her saddlebag. She said, not looking up, "No, I don't. I used to think so, when I was younger. And I do truly look forward to a day on our world when all women will have the freedoms that we—the Guild—have seized and declared for ourselves; when they will have them by law, and not by revolt and renunciation. But I know now that there are many women who could not be happy living my kind of life." She sat in the windowseat, her legs folded up under her chin, her short hair tousled; she looked like an adolescent girl. She had a bit of ribbon in her hand and was absentmindedly twisting it about her wrists as she spoke. "Rohana's women. They think of nothing but marriage; they are shocked and troubled at the idea of any other life than they live. It seems dreadful to them, to think of hiring themselves out, as men do, at any work for which they have the strength and skills, instead of serving for a time as waiting-women in one of the Great Houses, and then going home, as Lanilla is doing at winter's end, to a marriage arranged by their families. I asked her what her husband was like and she said she did not know, and asked me, 'Does it matter?' It was enough for her that she would have a home of her own, and a husband. Did you ever want to marry, Margali?"

Magda reminded her softly, "I *was* married."

"But only for a time—"

"I did not know when I married that it was only for a time," Magda said, with a twinge of the old pain. They had made so many plans for permanence!

"Tell me: if you had had a child, would you have stayed with him? Do you think it can be a bond between you?"

"My mother found it so," Magda said slowly. "She followed my father to four different worlds; then we came here, and I was born, and she always seemed content."

"Content only to make a home for him? Is that your way, in the Empire?"

"She was a musician," Magda said. "She played on several instruments, and she wrote many songs. She translated many of the mountain songs into the Empire's standard language; and she wrote music for some poems written in *casta*. But my father was always the center of her life; after he died, she seemed to lose all joy in living, and seldom touched her music again; and she did not live very long."

"Rohana married dom Gabriel when she had seen him only twice," Jaelle said reflectively. "To me that seemed frightful, to be given to a man I barely knew, to lie with him, to bear his children. It seemed no better than slavery or rape made lawful! But when I said as much to Rohana, she laughed at me, and said that any man and woman, with health and good-will, can live together in kindness and make a good life for one another. She said she thought herself lucky that he was decent and kindly and eager to please her; not a drunkard or a gambler or a lover of men, as so many of the Ardais are. To me, that seemed like a man, who has received a cudgeling, rejoicing that he had not been horsewhipped as well. . . ." She was still absently twisting the ribbon around her wrists, looping and uncoiling it. "And now he is truly the center of her life. I cannot understand it, though I find I like him better as I grow older. But there are times, too, when it seems to me that Rohana has as much freedom as any of us, that she does as she wishes and has given up little. . . ."

She drew the loop of ribbon into a tight coil around her wrists, began to coil the loose end around her other arm. She said, "Margali, did you want a child at all? Why did you not have one? You are not barren, are you, *breda?*"

"I did not want a child at once," Magda said. "We were traveling together; I did not want anything to separate us." It had been a bitter quarrel; she looked away from Jaelle, unwilling even now to relive that painful moment.

Jaelle reached out to touch her hand lightly, saying, "I did not mean to pry."

Magda shook her head. "Afterward, when we agreed to part, I was glad I had no child, to remind me always. . . ." *But would we have separated, then?* The touch of Jaelle's hand suddenly heightened the awareness, the contact, and she found herself thinking, *Is she pregnant? Does she think she is, does she want to be?* But all she sensed from the touch of Jaelle's fingertips was . . . loneliness, fear. *I thought Jaelle was so happy.*

Magda knew that from this touch she could use her awakened ESP—what Rohana had called *laran*—to find out if Jaelle were pregnant. The thought suddenly frightened her. She did not want to pry that way, to use this new skill to intrude. She left go of Jaelle's hand as if the narrow fingers had burned her, and found her hand caught in the ribbon Jaelle had been winding and unwinding about her wrists. Caught off guard, she demanded, "What in the world are you *doing* with that thing?"

Jaelle stared down at it, in sudden shock. She wrenched it loose, and flung the ribbon across the room, with a look of horror and loathing. As if, Magda thought, she had found a poisonous snake coiling about her wrists!

"Jaelle! What's wrong, sister?" The affectionate term came readily to her tongue now; but Jaelle's moment of vulnerability had vanished again behind a barricade of flippancy.

She said, "Old habits! A puppy you don't housebreak almost before his eyes are open will still be wetting the floor when he's an old dog. I've had this habit since I was a little girl; Kindra told me that it was just a nervous habit, and that I'd outgrow it. But I haven't, see?"

Magda knew there was more to it than that, but she knew she could not ask questions; knew it with that indefinable inner knowledge she was beginning to trust. Instead she asked something she knew to be safer.

"Jaelle, are you pregnant?"

Jaelle's green eyes met hers, just a flash, and then looked away. She said, and sounded almost desolate, "I don't know. It's too soon to tell." Quickly she jumped off the windowseat, barricading herself again. "Come on, let's find one of those silly women of Rohana's and ask her if she can mend your outfit, and make her happy by thinking she is superior to a Free Amazon!"

Watching the girl as she bundled Magda's torn traveling clothes together, Magda thought, *She's so young and vulnerable! If Peter breaks her heart, I think I'll want to kill him!*

What was going to happen to Jaelle? For that matter—if this involvement was serious and lasting, as Magda was beginning to guess—what would happen to Peter? Could he really sacrifice his career for a woman? And for one who was not, by oath, even free to marry?

It was easy to talk about the inevitability of liaisons, love affairs, even marriages between members of separate peoples on Empire worlds. Magda had thought of them as inevitable statistics, before this. But it was different —completely different—when you knew the people involved, and guessed what they meant in purely human and personal terms. No statistics could give you even a clue to that.

Is this my fault, too? By refusing Peter, did I bring this on both of them?

Chapter Fifteen

The winter drew on; the snow lay deep over Ardais. To Jaelle this was a precious interlude, a time separated from anything else in her life, before or after. For the first time since her thirteenth year, she lived surrounded by ordinary women; she wore women's clothes, shared in the life of the household, and spent her days with women who did not live by the terms of renunciation and freedom of the Amazon oath.

She had tasted this life—but briefly, and unwillingly—when she was fifteen. Rohana had insisted that she must know the life she was to renounce, before she made that renunciation irrevocable.

But I was too young, I could not see it clearly.

And now it is too late. All the smiths in Zandru's forges can't mend a broken egg, or put a hatched chick back into the shell. I can never, never be one of them, not now.

I do not think I want to be. But I am not sure, not now. . . .

And there was the Terran, her lover. . . .

Like any young woman in the grip of her first serious love affair, it seemed to her that he filled her whole sky. The Guild-house and the life there seemed very far away. She knew this was only an interlude, that it must end, but she tried to live entirely in the present, neither remembering the past nor thinking ahead to the future, but simply savoring each moment as it passed.

But there were times when she woke in the night, held close in her lover's arms, and realized that she no longer knew what she was doing, or who she was, or what lay ahead for either of them. None of the thousand uncertainties could be answered in words, or even asked; so she would turn to him in desperation, holding herself close to him, demanding the one thing she could be sure about, the one certainty they shared. She had ceased to be cautious. She no longer cared to conceal what was between them. She knew that sooner or later this would precipitate a crisis, but in some indefinable way she felt that even this would be a relief from the terrible uncertainty.

And then, one night, when she woke, she heard around the towers the soft dripping of rain and running of melting snow, and knew that the spring-thaw had begun. Now reality would close again over their enchanted isolation; and whether anything would remain, she could not even guess. She dared not even weep, for fear of waking him. She knew he would have only one comfort to offer, and now even that was no comfort at all, before the knowledge of the inevitable.

When I took the Amazon oath, I believed I had made it impossible for any man to enslave me. Yet here I lie, bound in chains of my own making! What can I do? Oh, merciful Goddess, what shall I do?

By the time the sun rose, red and dripping behind the fog-bank, she had fought her way to calm, and was able to discuss their impending departure serenely. "I must cut my hair; it has grown too long here."

Peter came and passed his hand through the silky strands, long enough now to touch her shoulder blades. "Must you? It is so lovely."

"Nothing in the oath binds me to it," she admitted. "It is custom, no more; to show, when we work with men, that we do not seek to entice them with feminine wiles."

He put his arms around her, and held her close. "Must we part, then, my precious? I know you are pledged not to marry, but—is there no way, no way at all that you can remain with me? I cannot bear to let you go. Do you truly want to leave me so soon?"

She said, through the pounding of her heart, "I can remain with you for a time as freemate, if you wish."

"Jaelle, beloved, do you have to ask if I wish it?" He held her so tightly that he hurt her, but she almost welcomed the pain.

She thought sadly, *Have I come to this?*

"Don't cut your hair," he begged, caressing the locks at the nape of her neck, and she smiled and sighed.

"I will not."

He did not know, and Jaelle would not tell him, that Free Amazons who elected to remain for a time as freemate to a lover did not cut their hair; by custom, close-cropped hair was a sign among them of commitment to solitude.

She was dressed and ready before him. Since they made a point of coming downstairs separately, she started down to the small breakfast room. The sun, flooding in brilliantly through the stone-arched windows, would at any other time have given her pleasure, after so many dark days. Now it only meant the end of an interlude that could never come again. She might remain with Peter, but never again in such complete isolation, mutual self-absorption; the outside world would intrude, with other work, other commitments, and she grieved for the end of their brief honeymoon.

A hand on her wrist detained her; at a quick glance she thought that Peter had hurried after her, and smiled, but the smile slid off as she realized that the hand had six fingers, and simultaneously she recognized the voice of her cousin Kyril. *So alike, so different.* . . .

"Alone, *chiya?* Have you quarreled with your commoner lover? I should make a reasonable substitute to console you, should I not? Or did you turn to him because you so much regretted refusing me, when we were younger?"

She picked his hand off her arm as she would have removed a crawling insect. She said, "Cousin, we will all be leaving here very soon. For Rohana's sake, let us try to remain friends, for this short time. I am sorry for all our quarrels when we were not much more than children; don't torment me by bringing them up now that we are grown."

Kyril pulled her against him, in a mockery of a kinsman's embrace, and laid his cheek roughly against hers. "Nothing is farther from my mind than quarreling with you now, Jaelle."

Shocked and angry, she removed herself from his arms. She said, almost in entreaty, "This is not worthy of you, Kyril. I am your kinswoman and your mother's guest. Don't force me to be rude to you!"

"And is *your* behavior so worthy?" he demanded, "when you put our whole family to shame with this bastard from nowhere?"

Jaelle struggled to keep her composure. "If he is truly a bastard of Ardais," she said, "then the shame is in the misbehavior of his parents, and no fault to him. You were born Comyn, and legitimate, through no virtue in yourself. And as for *my* behavior—for the last time, Kyril, I owe *you* no account of my actions, nor any man living!"

He gripped her by the arms, his fingers digging cruelly into the soft flesh there. Through the touch her untrained *laran* gift—which she could never control but which, in deep emotion, thrust itself on her involuntarily— made her aware of his frustration and anger, and desire. He wanted her, crudely, sexually, and in a kind of intense, man-to-woman hostility that she had never known since—incredulously, she identified it as what she had sometimes sensed, without understanding, between her father and his women. It turned her physically sick; she thrust him away without trying to conceal her disgust. Her voice was shaking.

"Kyril, I do not want to hurt you under your mother's roof, where I am a guest. But you have known since we were fifteen years old that no Free Amazon trained in self-defense can be—can be raped. Don't put your hands on me again, Kyril, or—or I will have to prove it to you again, as I did then."

She realized, in shame and self-disgust, that she was crying.

When we were both fifteen years old, Kyril probably meant no real harm; it was a game he was playing, a game of adolescent pride: a little kissing and fondling, just to prove himself a man and my master. But I would not play that game with him then, and I wounded his pride more than he could endure. And I made him an enemy, and he is still my enemy.

"You bastard bitch," he flung at her, and his face was very ugly; the more terrifying because it seemed such a cruel caricature of the face of her lover. "By what right do you play the whore with this stranger, and then turn away from my touch like any chaste lady? By what right do you refuse me what you so freely give him?"

"You *dare* talk of rights?" Her tears gave way to flaming anger. "Rights? I *choose* my lovers, Kyril—and by what right, then, do you complain that I have not chosen you? I would not have you when you were an arrogant boy of fifteen bullying his mother's fosterling, and I will not have you now when you have grown into"—she caught back the crude obscenity on her tongue—"into her unworthy son!" She turned her back on him, hurrying toward the breakfast room, knowing that he would never dare make this kind of scene before dom Gabriel. She was not overly fond of Rohana's husband, but she knew him for an upright man who would tolerate no offenses toward a woman and a guest at his own table.

But Kyril followed close on her heels, gripping her from behind, his fingers digging into the bruises he had made so painfully that Jaelle cried out. "How dare you talk of my mother and your respect for her? It has not kept you from behaving like a harlot under her roof! Does my father know how you have shamed our kin by flaunting yourself in this stranger's bed? If he does not, my girl, then I promise you he shall know at once, and then your precious lover shall account to the Lord Ardais himself for how he has dealt with his kinswoman!"

"I am not his ward; I am a Free Amazon, and by law I am mistress of my own actions," she said, and again, with that frightening *laran* awareness, sensed that he took pleasure—an active, *sexual* pleasure—in the pain of his hands bruising her arms, in her uncontrollable sobs. She fought hard to get herself under control again. She would not, she *would not* feed that sick thing in him that found pleasure in her suffering. She said, breathing hard, but her voice calm and steady, "What has Piedro done to you, Kyril, that you want to hurt him this way? Why are you doing this? I had thought you his friend!"

"This has nothing to do with Piedro," said Kyril, and he was breathing hard, too. "He is a man; but you damnable Amazon bitches, thinking yourselves free of all the rules for women, thinking that you can pretend yourselves chaste ladies and demand that we treat you like chaste ladies, and then playing the whore when it suits you, flaunting your lovers— Zandru whip me with scorpions, but I will teach you that you cannot treat men that way!"

She turned her back on him, wrenching herself free of his hands, and went swiftly into the breakfast room. She was shaking so violently that she had to steady herself for a moment against the doorframe. Her heart was pounding, and the bruises on her upper arms, where he had gripped her, ached and throbbed. Magda was already in her place; Jaelle went and slipped into a seat beside her, nervously smoothing her hair. Magda, instantly aware that something was wrong with her friend, reached out her hand below the table, taking Jaelle's hand in her own.

"Jaelle, what's wrong?" she whispered. "You've been crying. . . ."

Jaelle clung to her friend's hand, but she could not control her voice enough to answer. *Do all men hate us that way? Can it really be true that all men hate us so much?*

Kyril had come into the room behind her; he said, "Father—" with a defiant stare at Jaelle.

"Later, my son," said Rohana. "Your father is very much occupied."

And indeed dom Gabriel looked angry and upset, staring furiously at the factor who managed his estate. "No, damn it, man, I'll not have it!"

"Lord Ardais, a thief is a thief, whether he steals copper coins or *sarm-nuts!*"

"Avarra's mercy, man," dom Gabriel said irritably. "Are you seriously trying to tell me that I should hang a hungry man who steals a few bushels of nuts to feed his sons so they can grow up to be my loyal servants?"

"If they steal nuts in one season, dom Gabriel, they will steal the trees themselves in another!"

"Then mark the trees you have ready for felling, and let it be known that any man who touches a marked tree will get a good cudgeling; and turn a blind eye when they help themselves to the downwood. If they cart it away to burn at their hearth-fires, it won't be there to feed forest fire another year! That last burn cost us half a year's profit in resins! But no more hangings, hear me? Or you'll find yourself hanging there beside them!"

The man grumbled, "You might as well paint up a placard at the edge of your forests, Lord Ardais: *Open to every thief in the Hellers, come and help yourselves!*"

"Don't be a fool, Geremy," the Ardais lord said. "No man can own a forest! My fathers have managed the lumber for centuries, and because they were clever at manufacturing resin and paint, and trading with the Dry Towns for sulfur to make book-paper, we have grown rich from the forests we did not plant! But I grew rich with the aid of the men who live there, and they have a right to feed themselves with the fruit of the trees, and warm their poor homes with the wood from the trees! The Gods hate a greedy man; and when I grow so greedy that I think I own the trees themselves, and the fruits of the trees, and even the men who live among the trees, then it is only a matter of time before these men take the law into their own hands and teach me the lawful measure of a man's ambition!"

"Yes. But, my Lord—"

Jaelle looked at dom Gabriel and shivered slightly; his face was dark with wrath, and she could see that his hands were trembling. It reminded her, faintly but frighteningly, of what she had seen in Kyril. He shouted at the factor, "Not another word, damn it! If you want to work for a bandit, and grow rich, go ask Rumal di Scarp if he needs a *coridom!*"

"Well said, Gabriel," Rohana said softly, reaching over to touch his sleeve. "But calm yourself. No one is arguing with you; we are all, I think, in agreement on that." She stared at the factor. "Are you not Geremy?"

"Yes, my Lady, certainly!" the man almost stammered.

Jaelle thought, *Why does Rohana always try so hard to placate him? If he shouted like that at my table, I would give him shout for shout—yes, and blow for blow, too!*

Magda saw Peter slide into his seat—he had come in while dom Gabriel was talking—and as he met her eyes, she knew what he was thinking. It was an opportunity given few Terrans, to sit at table with one of the Comyn lords and hear him expound his decisions. She knew Peter was making mental notes for a report in Thendara; so in her own way was she. But would she ever deliver it?

The factor had moved to the question of how to mark trees for felling when the thaw had progressed a little further, and the scarcity of ax-heads and saws in recent years.

Gabriel turned to Peter. "You have lived in Thendara; what do you know of the *Terranan?*"

Peter froze, saw Lady Rohana raise watchful eyes to her husband, but the question was obviously innocent, so he answered, "As much as any man in the street knows."

"Can you verify a rumor for me? When they were here in the Hellers, back near Aldaran, I heard that they traded in metal from off-world; that the off-world metals were stronger than our native alloys, and would take a more durable edge. Is this true, or is it like the tales of men with wings for hands, and pots for breathing on their heads?"

"I have never seen any men with wings for hands, nor yet with pots for heads," Peter said truthfully, "but I lived as a child in Caer Donn, and I have seen the off-world metal. It is good solid stuff, and can be traded in bars for forging, and as finished tools, and the tools are probably better than what your smiths can make."

"Rohana, you sit in Council," said the Ardais lord querulously. "Maybe you can tell me why that donkey Lorill has prohibited such trade?"

Rohana said soothingly that she was certain that the ban on trade was only a temporary thing, that the Hastur lord only wished the Council to examine the consequences of their world becoming dependent on resources not native to this planet.

Kyril interrupted. "May I speak now? I have a serious complaint to make, about a breach of hospitality—and decency! This man from nowhere, this nobody, had abused our hospitality—"

Rohana's voice was sharp. "Kyril, I will not have your father worried with such trifles! If you have anything to say, then you may—"

"I was not speaking to you, Mother," said Kyril, staring angrily at her. "Let my father speak for himself; I am weary of hearing you reduce him to a nonentity in his own household! Father, do you rule this household, or does my mother?"

Dom Gabriel turned toward them, and his face was red with anger that made Jaelle tremble. "I will hear what you have to say," he said. "But I will not tolerate insolence to your mother, my son!"

Kyril said, thrusting out his chin, "My mother, too, has failed in her duty, since she has shown herself powerless—or unwilling—to keep order and decency beneath this roof! Or are you unaware that Jaelle has been seduced by this nobody who calls himself Piedro, and that she has shared his bed from midwinter-night?"

Jaelle tensed, clenching her fists with mingled rage and distress. She felt Magda's hand close gently over hers, and sensed the mingling of fright and dread in her friend, as dom Gabriel's flushed face, red with rage, turned toward Jaelle. His eyes were squinted close, his mouth contorted.

He shouted, "Is this true? Jaelle, what have you to say for yourself, my girl?"

She opened her mouth angrily. "Uncle, I am not your ward—" she began, and Rohana said in a low voice, almost agonized, "Jaelle, *please*—"

The desperate dread in Rohana's voice somehow got through to Jaelle; she said, more gently than she had intended, "All I can say to you is that I am very sorry to give you offense, sir. I would not willingly have done it." She bit her lip and looked down at the plate in front of her, her hands shaking as she buttered her bread, struggling not to say any more.

Rohana's quick, grateful look was reward enough, but it could not calm dom Gabriel now.

He bellowed, "Is this true? Have you made a scandal here in my house, with your love affairs?"

She swallowed hard and raised her eyes to meet his. She said clearly, "There will be no scandal, Uncle, unless you make it!"

Gabriel swung on Rohana, rising from his seat, turning angrily between Jaelle and Rohana. "What of this, my Lady? Did you know of this and say nothing? Did you permit your shameless ward to play the whore while she is under your care? What have you to say to this, Lady? Answer me! Answer me, Rohana," he bellowed.

Rohana had turned dead white. She said in a low voice, "Gabriel, Jaelle is not a child. She has taken the oath of the Free Amazons, and in law neither you nor I have any responsibility for anything she may do, under this roof or any other. I beg of you to calm yourself, to sit down and finish your breakfast."

"Don't you quote that filthy law to me," the man shouted incoherently, and his face was so dark and congested with fury that Magda wondered if he were about to suffer a stroke. "Jaelle is a woman of the Comyn! I forbade you to allow her to join these female scandals, and now do you see what you have done? A woman of our clan, seduced and betrayed—" He actually raised his arm as if to strike Rohana.

Jaelle, in horror, rose to her feet. "Uncle! Rohana is not to blame for anything I may have done! If you are going to shout and carry on like a madman, at least shout at me!" she said angrily. "I am a grown woman, and competent in law to manage my own affairs."

"Law, law, don't you talk to me about the law," Gabriel shouted, beside himself. "No woman alive is fit to manage her own affairs, and it doesn't matter what you—law—" He struggled to speak, as if his rage had swollen his throat completely shut, got out a few words of gibberish, then clenched his fists, swayed and came crashing down on the table, shattering crockery and chinaware, overturning a copper pot filled with some scalding hot drink that flooded the table, drenching the cloth. He struck his head hard, seemed to jerk violently on the rebound, and fell heavily to the floor, where he lay with his body arching backward, his heels drumming the floor in repeated, convulsive spasms.

Kyril, motionless with shock, suddenly leaned half across the table, running to lift him, but Rohana was already there, cradling the unconscious man's head against her knee.

"Let him lie till it is over," she said in a low, angry voice. "You have done enough for one morning. Go and call his man to help him to bed. Are you content, Kyril? Do you know now why I begged you not to provoke or trouble him? Do you honestly think"—she raised gray eyes, literally blazing with anger, to her son's—"that anything—*anything* goes on under this roof which I do not know, or permit?"

Jaelle felt a lump in her throat, obstructing speech. She had seen epileptic seizures before, but she had never before seen dom Gabriel in the grip of one. Now, looking at Rohana, kneeling and holding her husband's head, she realized exactly why Rohana spent so much of her life—foolishly, slavishly, she had often thought—in keeping dom Gabriel quiet and content, in averting his rage and calming his anger. Rohana's burden was far heavier than she thought.

Could I myself do so much for any man, however I loved him? And Rohana was given to him by her family, hardly knowing his name. Yet all these years she has managed it so that few outside the household even know his disability! She must have seen the warning signs, and tried to avoid any trouble. . . .

"Mother, I am sorry," Kyril begged. "I truly thought he should know of this."

Rohana swept him with a look of utter contempt. "Did you truly, my son? You cannot bear to think of any woman who does not obey you as if you were a God! And now you thought you had her at your mercy! How petty you are, Kyril! So to salve your wounded pride, and to revenge yourself against Jaelle, you have goaded your father into a fit; and he will be ill for days." She brushed aside his excuses without listening. "Go and call his body-servant, and help carry him to his bed, and no more talk. You have insulted our guests, and I will not forgive you soon for this!"

He went, glowering, and Jaelle came to Rohana's side. "Rohana, I am sorry—I did not realize—"

Rohana sighed and smiled at her. "Certainly not, child; you thought you were dealing with a rational man. You spoke more gently than I would have expected, and you said nothing that was not true. And I know that Kyril provoked you."

Her eyes rested for a moment on Jaelle's arms as if she could see the painful bruises there, and Jaelle thought, *Does she truly read my mind?*

When Kyril had helped to carry the unconscious man away, Rohana rose to her feet. She looked weary and worn.

"I know that you three"—her glance took in Peter and Magda, too—"were planning to leave today. Can you delay one more day? Today I must remain and make certain Gabriel is recovering as he should; tomorrow I can be ready to ride to Thendara with you."

"To come with us? Why?" Jaelle asked.

Rohana looked at Magda and said, "Because I have made a very important discovery; I must talk at once with Lorill Hastur. He is under a misconception which, if it is not corrected at once, can have the gravest consequences for both our worlds. So, if you will have my company on the road to Thendara, tomorrow morning I will be ready to ride with you."

Chapter Sixteen

It was raining when they reached the travel-shelter at sunset, and as the party began to dismount, Rohana said, "I had hoped to reach Thendara today, but I have no great liking for riding half the night. It will be tomorrow for certain."

"I shall be glad to get there," Magda said, but then she began to wonder. Just what awaited her in Thendara? Even this one night's respite was welcome.

As she was unsaddling her horse, Darrill, son of Darnak, came up behind her, lifting the heavy saddle from her hands. She smiled and relinquished it, and stood beside him as he began giving their horses fodder. He waited until most of Rohana's guardsmen had withdrawn—Lady Rohana, as wife of the Lord of Ardais, could not travel without a considerable escort—then asked in a low voice, "Will you be glad to get back to your own world, Margali?"

She said, troubled, "I am not sure it is my world anymore, Darrill. I am sworn to the Free Amazons."

"But surely . . . Piedro told me that was but a disguise, a way of allowing you to travel in safety."

"Piedro does not know anything about it," Magda said, with unexpected sharpness.

"I don't think I understand."

"I am not sure that I understand it myself," she said. "It is true that I took the oath as a means to an end; not really aware of what it meant. But later I chose, of my free will, to honor it, and I will do so, whatever happens."

Slowly, he nodded. "I can understand that. But what will the Terrans say?"

That, she thought, *is the question. Will I spend the rest of my life as a fugitive from the Empire's justice?* "I will try to get a leave of absence to honor my obligation to the Guild-house," she said. "And after that I think I could work more effectively for the Empire. It would allow me to do many things that an ordinary woman could not do here, otherwise."

He said, very low, "Margali, when I first met with you on midwinter-night, I was very impressed with your courage and spirit. It seemed to me that no woman of our people could have so much, and I thought it must be only that you were a stranger, a Terran. Now there are times when it seems to me that you are even more like a woman of our own people. You are not like anyone I have ever known before." He raised his eyes, and looked directly into hers, and for a moment Magda thought he would kiss her. Then he swallowed hard, recalled himself, and turned a little away. He said, "Forgive me; I must finish with the horses."

As he went about his work, Magda found herself thinking, *If I am not careful, he will be falling in love with me. And that is a complication I cannot allow now. I must be very careful.* The thought made her a little regretful. *I discovered at midwinter that I must find new ways of relating to my world; but before I complicate my life with another man, I must find out more about myself!*

It might be flattering to have young Darrill in love with her; but it would be a cruel thing to test her new awareness of men by capturing his interest and perhaps his heart, when she was not free, could not make any permanent or serious commitment to anyone. Jaelle had defended her flirting on the grounds that she had never left any man wounded or heart-scalded by her teasing. *I must be very careful to avoid that, too,* Magda thought.

Inside the travel-shelter, which was one of the largest, the guardsmen, and Peter among them, had made their fire at one end; Rohana with her ladies, and Magda and Jaelle, at the other. As usual, Rohana sent word that Peter should come and join them at their meal. When they had finished, she looked at Peter and Jaelle, close together, their hands linked in the shadows, and said to Magda, "In common humanity, I think we should leave them alone for a few minutes." She raised her voice slightly. "Come, my ladies, I think the time has come to visit the guardsmen at the other fire and see if they are content with their rations and their comfort."

Rohana's maid, a fat and sentimental old woman, looked back with an encouraging smile at Jaelle, as they went toward the other fire, and Jaelle felt herself blushing. Then she forgot the woman, as Peter drew her into his arms for a long, passionate kiss. She sank gratefully into his arms, blessing Rohana for even this moment or two alone with her lover; it would not be more than a few minutes, but while it lasted she could reassure herself. . . .

Finally he loosed her. "I am dizzy with wanting you! At least it will not be long; we reach Thendara tomorrow. Do you still love me, Jaelle?"

She looked up, laughing, into his face. "Can you doubt it?"

"But you avoid me."

"Avoid you? Of course not, love," she said, with a little flicker of laughter. "You certainly do not think I could lie with you in the presence of a half dozen guardsmen and all of Rohana's maids!"

He looked away, uneasy at her directness. "That is not what I meant," he protested, "but we could be together more often on the road; you could ride at my side, spend more time in my company! All during this trip you have treated me like someone you might have met at a public dancing-class, not like your lover!" He used the word in the inflection that made its nearest meaning "promised husband," and she smiled, pressing his hand.

"You are my beloved," she said in a whisper, "and soon we shall be together as much as you wish. But I am an Amazon, Piedro. I have not told you much about our laws and customs, but one of the things we are taught is that there is only one way in which women can travel among men without causing trouble and dissension. And that is by behaving as human beings; not as sexual creatures, women whose major business in life is to attract men to protect and care for them."

"Oh, come, surely Lady Rohana and her companions—"

"Rohana is the wife of their lord, a sacred trust they must safeguard with their lives. And her ladies are covered by her—her special charisma. But I am an Amazon and I have renounced my protected status as *Comynara*. And I am working among them; I organized this journey. So I must not come among them as a woman who is—is free to be desired. Can't you understand?" she begged. "If I spend much time with you, show myself as your lover"—she, too, used the word in the inflection meaning "promised wife," and he pressed her hand—"then I show myself to them as a woman. And they begin to think of me as a woman, and before long they begin to compete in small ways for my favor and attention, and to show themselves before me as men, and soon there is dissension among them all, and ill feeling. So I must be just another worker, one of themselves. They must feel at ease with me, not temper their speech to a woman's ears, or feel compelled to give me their lightest work."

She did not shade her words with the faintest reproof, but Peter recalled that a few days ago she had frowned at him for helping her, unasked, with a heavy load.

He said, "Are you trying to tell me that there is no work which is beyond your strength?"

"No, no indeed!"

"I should think not," said Peter indignantly, looking at the slender girl. "And what do you do, proud Amazon, when you find something beyond your strength?"

She smiled and said, "Precisely what you do among men, when you find something too heavy to lift, or a task needing four hands to accomplish it. You are not a tremendously strong man, I imagine; when a task demands more strength than you have in your arms, I suppose you simply say to one of the other men, 'Come here and help me lift this before I strain my guts!' Well, that is exactly what I do. If I have made it obvious that I do not shirk any work within my strength, then they will help me as they would help another man with a task too heavy for him, and not with any thought of a woman who must be sheltered!"

"I hope you do not always intend to treat me that way!" he said, and she laughed and raised her hand to touch his cheek lovingly.

"When we are alone, beloved, I shall be so fragile and demanding that you will sometimes think I am Lady Rohana herself, who is not by law permitted to move as much as a day's ride without her maid and her lady companion and half a dozen guards! But you must not expect me to be anything other than I am, my love." She stood on tiptoe, pulling his head down and kissed him quickly. "Enough for now. Rohana and her women are coming back, and tomorrow we will be in Thendara."

"And tomorrow night . . ." Peter said, smiling at her, and for a moment she held herself against him, not at all unwilling to let him know she shared his eagerness. Then, sighing, they moved apart as Rohana with her ladies returned to their fire.

They rode down into Thendara a little after noon. Rohana said as they came through the gates, "What will you do now? Jaelle, you must go to the Guild-house, I know, with Margali."

Magda felt a small clutch of fear. *It's here. There's no more delaying. Oh, God, I'm frightened!*

Certainly, within my lifetime, Darkover will be a part of the Empire, and it will make no difference. The usual time from first contact to affiliation is about fifty years, and that's almost half over. But will that come too late to do me any good? Must I be exiled from one world to the other?

She thought this, not knowing that Darkover was to prove unique in the history of the Empire, and that not only her own lifetime but many lifetimes would pass before Darkover and the Empire were reconciled. Just the same, the curious little flash of precognition iced her blood again, and she pulled her fur-trimmed riding-cloak—Rohana's midwinter gift—about her shoulders.

"This is idiotic!" Peter said, looking back to make certain they were out of earshot of Rohana's women and the guardsmen. "You can't possibly do that, Magda. Somehow or other, we've got to get you out of that nonsense of spending half a year in the Guild-house. I'm sure you'd find it interesting, but we can't possibly afford to lose our only resident female expert. Come back with me now to the HQ, and let the people there think of some way to get you out of it."

Magda said, in exasperation, "Peter, you don't understand. I am oath-bound, and I will honor my oath. I will try, after, to make it right with the Empire authorities; but the obligation must be met nevertheless!"

"Oh, that," he said in contempt. "You know as well as I do that an oath taken under duress is not valid!"

Jaelle looked at him in shock and dismay; and Magda, with that new, devastating sensitivity to thoughts, knew that Peter had just shocked Jaelle to speechlessness. *An oath is sacred. What kind of man could ignore it?* And if he had no awareness of what the oath meant to Magda, how could he possibly know what it meant to Jaelle?

Can he ever know, Jaelle thought with desolation, *that it is the very mainspring of my being?* It was only a moment, then her love began to make excuses for him; soon he would understand. She smiled gaily at Peter and said to Magda, "We shall have to teach him better than that, will we not, sister?"

Rohana interrupted, sensing the strain: "The best way is for you, all three of you, to be my guests at Comyn Castle tonight. There is room in the Ardais suite for a dozen or more; and you, Piedro, can send word to your Terran supervisor that tomorrow we will all meet with Lorill Hastur. Both of them will be eager to know how this affair has ended."

They agreed to that compromise, and an hour later were all settled in comfortable quarters in the Ardais suite. Magda was tired from the long journey, and lay down for a nap, but she knew that sleep was simply another way of avoiding, for a time, the unendurable conflicts. Tomorrow, at whatever cost, they must be faced.

Peter stood for a few moments at the door of the room the women shared. He said, hurt, "Jaelle, you are avoiding me again!"

"No, my love. In a day or two we shall declare ourselves as freemates, before witnesses," she promised, standing on tiptoe to kiss him with a passion that swept away his doubts. "But just now I am Rohana's guest in Comyn Castle and for her good name I must abide, under this roof, by her laws and rules of conduct rather than my own. But I love you. Never doubt it, promise me, Piedro, promise."

"I promise," he assured her, then, in surprise, bent to wipe the tears from her eyes. "My love, my darling, why are you crying?"

"I—I don't know," she stammered, and although he knew she was evading him, there was nothing he could say. "Even though I am a Free Amazon, Piedro, you must sometimes just let me be a woman, and not always reasonable. . . ."

When he had gone away, and Magda had fallen into an exhausted sleep, Jaelle wandered, restlessly, around the Ardais suite. At this time of year it was deserted; Rohana and her guests seemed to rattle around the empty rooms and corridors like a few pods on a tree stripped by a storm. At last Rohana sought her out.

"Come and sit with me for a little while, Jaelle. It may be a long time before we can spend time together like this; at Council season I have little leisure to enjoy your company, and it may be many years before you can pay me another visit at Ardais."

They sat before the fire that had been kindled in Rohana's room. For a time they said little, but at last Jaelle got out of her chair and came and sat on the hearth-rug beside her kinswoman. She laid her head for a moment on Rohana's knee; hesitantly, Rohana stroked the soft hair. As a girl Jaelle had never permitted caresses and Rohana had quickly learned not to offer them, but for once she seemed to invite them.

At last Jaelle said, "I did not tell you this, but you probably have guessed. Piedro has asked me to remain in Thendara as his freemate; and I have consented."

Rohana looked down at Jaelle with a distant sadness. *She loves him so much; and I know I cannot really understand.* Rohana herself had been given in marriage very young, had obediently married the man chosen by her family, without question, and had never been touched by this kind of passion. At last she asked, with a hesitant tenderness, "Have you ever regretted your oath, Jaelle?"

"Never before this, never for a moment," Jaelle said. Then, forcing the words out, "Just the same, I think you were right, years ago, when you said I was too young for such a choice."

That struck to Rohana's heart, almost with physical pain. *Merciful Goddess, I gave her freedom, the freedom that had been denied to me. Was I so wrong?* For a moment time slipped out of focus, past and present blending together, and it seemed to Rohana that it was again the last day of Jaelle's long visit to Castle Ardais, in her fifteenth year. Rohana had known Jaelle was not happy there: she detested Kyril and had no great liking for Rohana's younger son and daughter; she thought Gabriel a petty tyrant; she had chafed at the need to wear skirts even for riding; and on the last day of her visit she had come to Rohana like this and told her, defiantly, that she would take the Amazon oath on the very day she was legally free to do so.

Rohana had foreseen this, but had still been dismayed by the actuality. She felt Jaelle had as yet no idea what she was renouncing.

She had said: "Be very sure, Jaelle; very sure. This is no game, it is your whole life. Don't throw it away like this!" And then she had begged: "Jaelle, will you give me three years, more time, as you gave Kindra, to prove to you that my life is no less happy than hers?"

She knew Jaelle was remembering, too (Or did the girl's awakening *laran* share her thoughts?), when Jaelle said softly, "Three years seemed a lifetime then; longer than I could bear to wait. And—forgive me, Rohana —you wanted to prove your life was happy; and yet I knew *you* were not happy. So it seemed—hypocrisy."

Rohana bowed her head. No; she had not been happy then, but she thought she had concealed it more carefully from Jaelle. She had felt harried then, trapped by the life she led, after her brief taste of freedom. She had been much beset with her adolescent children, and with the three-year-old Valentine, who was at the most active and troublesome age. And at that time she had been pregnant again with a fourth child she did not want; that had been the price she paid for Gabriel's final forgiveness. And though she had not wanted the child, Rohana was too much a woman to bear a child for most of a year and see it die without anguish. So when it had been stillborn, she had grieved as bitterly as if she had longed for it. But she had carried the child, that year, in anger and desperate rebellion, feeling that perhaps she had paid too high a price for Gabriel's goodwill and peace in her home. Now, before Jaelle grown to womanhood, she bowed her head and said, almost inaudibly, "You were right; I was not happy then. Now I feel more guilty than ever that because of my unhappiness you rushed to take the Amazon oath."

Jaelle laid her cheek against Rohana's hand. "Don't blame yourself; I don't think it would have made any difference. Even Kindra said I was stubborn and headstrong; she, too, urged me to delay a little. Perhaps"— she smiled fleetingly—"I am my father's daughter, too, though I do not like to think so."

Never before this day had Jaelle spoken her father's name in Rohana's hearing. She had some idea of what it had cost Jaelle to say this. She was silent, asking after a long time, "Then you will stay with your Terran lover?"

"I—I think so."

But she is not sure. "Is it fair to any man, Jaelle, to give him so little of yourself as a freemate gives?"

"Rohana, I give him what he wants of me! The Terrans do not make their women slaves to their will!"

"Just the same—don't be angry, Jaelle—it seems to me that a freemate gives little more than a prostitute." She used the coarse word *grezalis*, knowing that on her decorous lips it would shock Jaelle into listening. "It seems to me that it is no marriage unless you commit yourself to a man for all times: good and bad, in happiness or misery. You know that when I was wed, Gabriel was nothing to me but a burden I had to bear, because I had been born Comyn, and the laws of my caste required me to marry within my clan and bear him children with *laran.*"

"And you can call *me* whore? When you were sold like a slave for your family's pride of position, and I choose to give myself freely to the man I love and desire?"

Rohana put out a hand to stop her. "Jaelle, Jaelle darling, I did not call you a whore, or anything like it! I said: this was how my marriage seemed at the beginning, a grave burden I must bear for my family's sake. Yet now Gabriel is the very center of the world we have built together. A freemate says to her lover, because of this storm of desire, I will remain with you while it suits my pleasure; but if we lose our happiness I will leave you, sacrificing the happiness we have had and the good times that may come in the future, all because of the unhappiness of a year or two. There is no obligation to remain together and work to turn the evil times into good again."

"How can you do that? Do you not live with constant regret for the years of unhappiness you had to share, with no possibility of escape?"

"Not really," Rohana said. "It has taken us a long time to outlive unhappiness, but we have forged a bond that will last till death. And beyond," she added, smiling, "if there is anything beyond."

"You say this bravely," said Jaelle, "but I think . . . oh, Rohana, I do not want to make you angry."

"The truth could not make me angry, Jaelle. Only remember, darling, that it is *your* truth, and not necessarily *my* truth."

"Then I think," said Jaelle, "that because it is too late for regrets, you tell yourself you have never had them. I think you simply would not give up your power and position as wife to the lord of the Domain of Ardais."

"Perhaps," said Rohana, unoffended, "a marriage is spun of many small threads. Gabriel is only a part of my life, but not a part I would willingly renounce now. I did not love him when we were wed, but it would rend my heart into a thousand fragments to be parted from him now."

Jaelle, remembering Rohana's face as she knelt beside the unconscious man, knew dimly that this was true; but it seemed to her that this was only slavery to an ideal, and nothing like the overwhelming passion that had caught her up, almost unwillingly, into Peter's life. She said, trembling, "That is not what I call love!"

"No, I suppose not, dear," said Rohana, taking the small cold hands in hers, "but it is real, and it has lasted."

"Then you think love—love as I know it—means nothing? It seems to me you think marriage can be made by any two, however they feel about one another, as if"—for the first time in a dozen years, Jaelle spoke her mother's name—"as if Melora and Jalak . . . as if my mother, even in rape and captivity, could have built lasting happiness."

"Even that, under some circumstances, darling. But I went consenting to my marriage, with my family's support and blessing; Melora was torn by force from all her kin. But even then; had Jalak and Melora chosen one another, had she run away with him of her own will, or even, afterward, had he loved and cherished her for herself, and not as a pawn to his evil pride, and a memento to his hatred of her folk of the Domains—even then, perhaps, she could have found some peace; not happiness, perhaps, but content."

"Even in chains?"

"Even so, my darling. Had Melora loved Jalak, and willed to please him, she would have known that the chains were a game he played for his pride before all men, and she would have worn them to play the game with him, willingly. . . . Jaelle, if your Amazons made up an army and marched to free the women of the Dry Towns from their chains, no doubt there are some who would hail you as their saviors; but there are others, I am sure, who would bid you turn around and march home again, and not meddle in their affairs. Would you not wear chains to please your lover, Jaelle?"

She said, "He would never ask," but dropped her eyes, remembering her play with the ribbon; the fantasy game she had played as a little girl in the Dry Towns. She said, angry at the memory, "Had you no pity for my mother?"

"Only the Gods know how much," Rohana said. "I risked the anger of Hastur, and came near to destroying what happiness I had found with Gabriel, to bring her away before she bore Jalak a son; and to set you free, because she said she would kill you rather than have you chained in Jalak's Great House. Do you not remember that?" Her eyes flamed with the beginning of anger.

Jaelle took her hand, and after a moment kissed it. Rohana said quietly, "Jaelle, many woman wear their chains as I wear the *catenas.*" She thrust out her arm, showing her the ceremonial marriage-bracelet, whose twin was locked on Gabriel's arm. "A token of something that would be locked upon my heart forever, even if I refused, as you will refuse, to wear the outward symbol."

Jaelle said softly, "The Amazon oath binds me not to marry *di catenas.* I never thought I would want to," and her head went down on Rohana's knees, the slender shoulders shaking with the violence of her sobs. "I don't, Rohana! I don't!"

Rohana thought, *Then why are you crying so?* But she did not say so, sensing, through the feel of the girl's head against her knees, the very real heartbreak. She only stroked Jaelle's soft hair, tenderly. At last she asked, "Are you pregnant, darling?"

"No—no. He has spared me that."

"And do you really want to be spared, my precious?"

Jaelle couldn't answer; she was unable to speak. At last Rohana asked, very gently, "Will you stay with him in sorrow as in joy, Jaelle?"

Jaelle raised her flushed face. "I feel now that I would," she said in anguish, "but how can I be sure? How can I know he will love me in the evil times that come to everyone? How can I even know what *I* will be then? And yet—it seems that it is worth even this. Did you never love anyone, Rohana? Did you never want to give up everything—everything, your pledged way of life, your honor, *everything* because you could not—could not part from—" She put her head down on Rohana's knees, and cried desperately again.

Rohana's heart ached for her, and for a long-healed wound that Jaelle's words had torn. *Yes, there was a time when I would have given up everything: my children, the life I had made for myself, Gabriel—yet the price seemed all too heavy to pay.* At last she said, faltering, "There is nothing in this world that is not bought for a price. Even Kindra; she never regretted her oath, but she grieved to the day of her death for the children she had abandoned. It seems to me that is the one flaw in the Amazon oath; you women who take it guard yourselves from the risks all women take willingly. Perhaps it is only that every woman must choose what risks she will bear."

Jaelle listened, and the words fell heavy on her heart. *I came too young to the Amazon oath; most women make these renunciations in grief, knowing that they are real privations. To me it seemed only that I renounced slavery and embraced freedom. I did not weep when I took the oath. I could never truly understand why so many women made the oath only with tears. . . .*

"You love Piedro. Will you stay with him?"

"I—I must, I cannot leave him now."

"Will you bear his children, darling?"

"If he—if he wants them."

"But your oath binds you to bear them only if *you* want them," Rohana said. "You must choose, and perhaps it is that which I feel so wrong; that you women claim the right to choose."

"I will never believe that," Jaelle flared at her. "A woman not free to choose is truly a slave."

"But even the freedom to choose does not always guarantee happiness," Rohana said, capturing the cold hands again and caressing them. "I have heard old Amazons lamenting their childlessness, when it was too late to change their minds. And I—" She swallowed hard, for she had never said this to any living being; not to Gabriel, not to Melora, not to Kindra, who for so long had shared her innermost thoughts. "I did not want children, Jaelle. Every time I knew myself pregnant, I wept and raged. You weep because you are not to bear a child, but I cried more when I knew I was. Once I flung a silver bowl at Gabriel's head, and I hit him, too, and I shrieked at him that I wished I had killed him and he could never do this to me again. I hated being pregnant, I hated having little children around to trouble me, I feared childbirth worse, I think, than you feared the sword that gave you this." With light fingers she traced the still-crimson scar across Jaelle's smooth cheek. "Had I been free to choose, I would never have borne a child. And yet now that the children are grown, and I see that they are a part of Gabriel and myself which will survive when we are gone—now, when it would have been too late to change my mind, I find I am glad that the laws of my caste forced me to bear them, and after all these years, I have forgotten—or forgiven—all the unhappiness."

Jaelle said hoarsely, not wanting to show how much this had moved her, "I think, again, that you know it is too late for regrets; so you tell yourself that you have none."

"I did not say that I had no regrets, Jaelle," said Rohana, very low, "only that everything in this world has its price, even such serenity as I have found after so many years of suffering."

"You truly believe that you have paid a price? I thought you told me now that you had everything a woman could desire!"

Rohana lowered her eyes. She swallowed hard, and for a moment she remembered a day, years ago, when she had looked into Kindra's gray eyes and known the price she would pay. She could not face Jaelle; she did not want to cry. She said, "Everything but freedom, Jaelle. I think that would have been too dearly bought. But I am not sure." Her voice broke. "Nothing in this world is sure but death and next winter's snow. Maybe I do not want to be sure. The price I have paid is my freedom. You have your freedom; you are oath-bound to take it even now when you no longer want it. But at what price, Jaelle?"

Chapter Seventeen

Magda woke at twilight, to see Jaelle sitting on the foot of her bed. She looked pale, as if she had been crying; but she was calm.

"Sister," she said, "I know that you took our oath unwillingly; in a sense it was forced from you. Normally that would not matter; but you are a Terran, and you took it without the knowledge of what it truly implied. Do you want to petition for release from your oath, Margali? If you do, I will speak for you before the Guild-mothers."

Magda knew that this would solve some of her deep inner conflicts; more, it would free her from the fear of Terran retribution, not directed toward herself alone, but toward those who had aided her to desert her original loyalties. She considered it for a moment, but then she was seized by revulsion. Go back to her life in the Terran Zone, and the narrow, sterile world she had lived there, circumscribed by the little work of importance that a woman could do? She realized now that even through her tears and terror when she had taken the oath, it had still seemed a major decision in her life; and more, a genuine decision. *Here is a way I can follow. This is what I want, whatever the price I must pay.*

I was not forced to abandon Peter to death. Jaelle saved me from paying this price. But sooner or later I knew there would be a day of reckoning; and now I will meet it, whatever it may be.

She used the formal Amazon phrase. "Oath-mother," she said, "I told you: I chose of my free will to honor my oath, and I will keep it, until death take me or the world end."

"Even if it makes trouble for you with your own people, Margali?"

She said what she had said to Darrill on the journey: "I am not so sure they are my own people anymore." Her voice was not quite steady. "I have renounced allegiance to—*to family, clan, warden or liege lord.*"

Jaelle took her hands; suddenly she leaned forward and kissed her, as she had done when she accepted her oath. She said, "Allegiance for allegiance, my sister. We are sworn. But I think you must face the fact—we must face it together—that it may make grave trouble for you."

"I know that," said Magda, and could not keep from trembling a little. "If it had not been for Lady Rohana, I think Peter would have insisted on taking me to the Terran Headquarters, even if he had to do so by force, and under arrest."

"A beautiful reward for your loyalty to him," Jaelle said angrily, "But for you, he would be dead in Sain Scarp this moment!"

Magda felt compelled to defend Peter's point of view. "He is a Terran agent," she said. "To him, I think, loyalty to the Empire transcends any loyalty to persons."

"That is not right," Jaelle said, troubled.

Magda thought, *It's not a point of view any Darkovan can understand; so in many ways Peter is worse off than I. He is Darkovan in so many ways, he can never live at peace within the Empire; but he will never be free to renounce those very things which would prevent him from being wholly at home in Darkover . . . and he will always be torn, an exile. . . .*

"Jaelle," she said, "you told me once that the Free Amazons were allowed to accept any lawful work. If the Terran authorities would give me a leave of absence to honor my obligation to the Guild-house for their training, then when I had completed it, would I be allowed to continue the work I have been doing for the Terrans?"

"Do you mean that you would spy on us?"

"No, of course not," Magda said; the very idea was repellent. "But to build a bridge between our worlds; to help my people better understand all the small ways of your society, your language, your laws and customs— even if I did nothing more than my old work, to keep our translators from unwittingly offending against your customs; and I think I could do more, much, much more."

"That would not violate your oath," Jaelle said. "By our Charter you may accept any lawful work anywhere. That means that as a sworn Amazon you may work for the Terrans—" She broke off, as if she had seen a blazing light, and said almost in a whisper. "And so can I."

"How would that be arranged, Jaelle?"

"However you wish," Jaelle said. "By our Charter's laws, you must pay a portion of your earnings to the Guild. We renounce family and home, but this means that we have the protection of home and family always. Whenever you are sick, pregnant, unable to work or in a strange city, you can always turn to the Guild-house or to any Amazons there, and find a home where you can be cared for. Your tithes go to maintain the Guild-houses, and you have always sisters and friends there, and you have a lawful right to them. You need never live within a Guild-house unless you choose, although if you choose to live there you are expected to help with the maintenance of the house, to take your turn at housekeeping or gardening or whatever needs to be done. But it is our true home, where we come as others come to their family homes, wherever else we may go."

Magda had known no family life since her father's death; she and Peter had never seriously tried to make a home together. The thought of having a true home, a Darkovan home, to which she could go not as a stranger or a guest, but as of right, gave her a sense of warmth she had not known for years.

Jaelle said, "We can go there in old age when we are past work, or have our children fostered there."

"You bear children, then?"

"If we wish," Jaelle said, and the memory of Rohana's words brought a fleeting sadness to her face. "Did you think we took Keeper's vows? Our daughters can be fostered in the Guild-house till they are grown, when they can choose for themselves whether to join the Guild or to marry. Our sons are usually given to their fathers to rear, after they are weaned, but if your child's father is unwilling, or you think him unfit to raise your child, or if you do not know who fathered your child—then you can arrange to have him fostered as you wish; though no boy over five years old may live in the Guild-house." She was thinking out loud; suddenly she came back to the present. "Well, you will learn all that during your Guild-house training, sister."

Was it possible that she could share her two worlds? It seemed almost too good to be true. Magda said, hesitating, "You know that Lorill Hastur has forbidden contact between the Terran Zone and his people. It is easy to defy him in the Hellers, Jaelle; but here in Thendara?"

"Yes, that is one of the gravest difficulties," Jaelle said, "but Rohana is pledged to speak to Lorill. Her heart dwells in two worlds, too, and I think it is larger than either of them. And I think it is time that the people of Darkover, not the Comyn lords alone, knew something of the Terrans, and what they can do for our world. You heard Gabriel speak about Lorill's ban on trade. Hastur's will is not the voice of God, even to the Comyn! Let us find out what some of the others think. Will you come with me now to the Guild-house, sister, and see what we can do to settle this, before we meet tomorrow with Lord Hastur—and with your Terrans? Then we will know where we stand."

Magda hesitated. Then, knowing this was the moment of choice, she nodded.

"Yes, I will."

The next morning, the Lady Rohana sat beside Lorill Hastur in the small Council chamber, awaiting the arrival of the Terran coordinator. Peter Haldane sat across from them, looking both apprehensive and angry. Rohana could not read this thoughts, but she did not have to. This morning, Magda and Jaelle had vanished, and she was certain they had taken refuge in Thendara Guild-house. But they had left a message saying they would appear before Hastur at the Council, and it was not Rohana's duty to explain further when they had not.

Hastur leaned over and asked her in an undertone, "This was the man taken by Sain Scarp? Is he truly identical to Kyril? The resemblance is extraordinary; are we dealing here with Cherillys' Law?"

Rohana laughed. "I have not remembered Cherillys' Law since I was a psi monitor in Dalereuth Tower with you and Melora and Leonie," she said, "But no, it is not that; the Terran has only five fingers on either hand."

"Still, a remarkable likeness, and it goes to bear out what you said about a single race; although it seems fantastic to believe that our people could have come from another star, or that we would ever have permitted ourselves to forget such an heritage. And you told me that the woman has *laran*. May I ask how you found that out? I gave orders that no Terran was to witness a matrix operation."

"Jaelle was dying," Rohana said, "and her sworn sister had a right to remain with her. I can only imagine—" She frowned, trying to think it out. "Alida has the Ardais Gift; she is a catalyst telepath, and contact with her may have awakened latent *laran* in this woman. But if it had not been there, Alida could not have roused it. The man—Haldane—was there, too, and he showed no sign of being aware of what was going on. But whatever the reason, this woman has *laran*, and it means we must revise some of our preconceived notions about Terrans." She said "our" preconceived notions, but she really meant "your"; Hastur knew it and scowled.

He said, "Here is the Terran official, and his interpreter."

Rohana had met Montray before, and had not been impressed; she wondered if she had picked up some shred of Magda's contempt for the man. This time he was accompanied by a young man who spoke *casta* as well as either Peter or Magda, which was as well as any native-born Darkovan. He introduced himself as Wade Montray, the coordinator's son, and politely made himself known to each of them, while his father went toward Peter, glowering.

"So there you are, Haldane! Do you have any idea how much trouble you've caused? And where is Miss Lorne? She should be here! In fact, both of you should have reported back to the HQ last night for orders!"

Peter said rather stiffly, "I have not been informed that any charges have been filed against us. It did not seem proper to give offense to the Lady Rohana when she invited us to remain as her guests. I am certain that Magda will be here at the proper time." He turned toward the door, with an audible sigh of relief. "In fact, she is here. And the young woman with her was instrumental in saving my life, Montray, so you be polite to her, damn it!"

"Nice-looking girl," Montray commented, and Peter stiffened up again. "Montray, you've been on Darkover how long—ten years? If you haven't learned yet that it's not proper to make comments about a woman's looks, I suggest you put in for transfer as fast as you can, or never stick your head out of the Terran Zone!"

Magda had come into the room with Jaelle and three strange women, and was quietly seating herself with them on the fourth side of the room. Hastur said sternly, "Jaelle, what is this? I gave you no authority to invite any outsiders to this conference!"

"I did not ask for it, my Lord." Jaelle spoke respectfully, but with none of the fear most outsiders displayed before a Comyn lord. "Lord Hastur, it seemed to me that our Guild is very deeply concerned in these matters that are under discussion this morning, and I therefore asked these representatives to come and state our position before you and before the Terrans."

Montray demanded, "What did she say?" and his son began quietly repeating Jaelle's words, as Jaelle went on.

"My Lord, my Lady and respected off-worlders," she added, turning to the Terrans. "I wish to present to you *mestra* Millea n'ha Camilla, Guildmother of Thendara House." Millea was a tall and bulky woman, conventionally dressed, and as feminine as Rohana herself, *"Mestra* Lauria n' Andrea, the head of the Independent Council of Craftswomen, and *Domna* Fiona n'ha Gorsali, Judge of the City Court of Arbitration."

Rohana thought, admiringly, *Oh, Jaelle, you are far more clever than I ever believed!* The women seating themselves in a dignified row across the room were no ordinary Amazons; they were three of the most powerful women in the city of Thendara. The Guild of Craftswomen had successfully fought for the right to be recognized among the city's businesses; *Domna* Fiona was the first woman ever to be appointed a judge in the history of Thendara. Hastur could not dismiss them as unimportant.

Jaelle said, "Will you grant us the right to hear your deliberations, nobles?"

Hastur looked a trifle annoyed, but nothing could ruffle his long discipline in diplomacy. He rose and bowed politely to the three women. "I will not welcome you to this Council, for you came uninvited," he said, "but this is no secret conclave to work tyrannies; no concerned citizen may be denied the right to hear, and in turn, be heard."

Montray said, his son translating, "We welcome the chance to be heard by any citizens of Thendara. Be welcome, ladies."

Hastur addressed himself to Montray. He said, "When you were last before us, we granted permission for your employee, Magdalen Lorne"— Magda, seated among the Amazons, noticed that he did not hesitate or stumble even slightly over her Terran name—"to venture into the hills and negotiate for the rescue of your employee, the man Haldane, held captive at Sain Scarp. As I now understand the matter, the Lorne woman encountered a band of Free Amazons under the command of Jaelle n'ha Melora, and was required, according to their custom and the laws of their Charter, to swear an oath of allegiance to their Guild. Is this an accurate account of the affair?"

The Guild-mother Millea said, "According to the reports we have had from our sisters, this is true."

Hastur said, "I do not quite understand the difficulty. It seems to me that this is a matter for private agreement among the parties concerned, or at least for the courts of arbitration."

Montray listened with an angry frown; he said something, and his son shook his head, refusing to translate it.

Hastur turned to Magda and said, "Miss Lorne, did you have these women brought here that you might petition, in the presence of all concerned, to be released from your oath?"

Magda's voice was low, but very clear. She said, "No, my Lord Hastur. I am willing to abide by the oath I swore, and to honor it till death. But I am not certain that the Terran authorities will allow me to do so. They may possibly hold that my oath is not valid, or that because of prior loyalties I had no right to swear it."

Montray said something again, and the young translator said, just audibly, "I told you so."

Rohana, watching, realized that Magda had done an exceptionally clever thing. In private, the Terran ambassador might state that he did not believe in the validity of a Darkovan oath. But if he said so, in the presence of Hastur and three Guild-mothers from Thendara, he destroyed the credibility of every Terran on Darkover for decades to come. And if he didn't know it, and judging by his expression he hadn't, he was finding it out in no uncertain terms, both from the young and expert translator, and from Peter Haldane! From the look of frustration on his face, Rohana could tell, even without need for a scrap of *laran,* that he was consigning all of them, especially Magda, to whatever his Terran equivalent was for the coldest of Zandru's hells!

Domna Fiona said, "The noble guest from Terra appears to find some difficulty in accepting the decision; may we hear it, with Lord Hastur's permission?"

Montray said, waiting for his son to translate, "The difficulty is this: Miss Lorne is extremely valuable to us. She is the only woman qualified to act as an expert on the Darkovan languages, and to advise us on women's customs and the laws governing social usage on Darkover. It seems to us that we cannot, for the moment, spare her to any other work, valuable as it may be, and highly as we may respect those who would welcome her among them."

Rohana knew perfectly well that the polite phrases had been added by the translator, and suspected that Montray's original had been more emphatic and much less courteous. She did not understand enough of the Terran language to be sure.

"If that is the only difficulty, it can easily be settled," *domna* Fiona said. From the voice, and something about the narrow body in the judicial robes, Rohana suspected the woman was an *emmasca;* but the robes were too bulky to be sure. "If your problem is a lack of adequate experts on women's customs and the languages, then I think we can offer assistance. Sister," and she turned to Jaelle, who stood up nervously.

Her eyes met Peter's briefly across the room. Jaelle said, "Say to the Terran official that if it is agreeable to your people, I will offer myself to take my sister's place in working for you. I speak both *casta* and *cahuenga* fluently, and I can read and write in these and in the language of the Dry Towns; and I think I can help you to fill in what gaps there are in your knowledge of the customs of Thendara. And I think there are others of my sisters who would be willing to do the same, to the limits of your needs. We have been told"—again, briefly, she met Peter's eyes—"that you Terrans have had trouble in finding workers for anything but simple manual labor, and that you have sought for them without success."

Montray said, "That would indeed be welcome." He bowed politely to Jaelle. "But we had heard it was the will of Hastur that the people of Thendara should not give us this kind of assistance."

The Amazon Lauria, head of the Guild of Craftswomen, said quietly, "The Lord Hastur speaks for the Comyn, and for their sworn followers and those who owe allegiance in the Domains. But the will, or the whim, of Hastur is not yet the law of this land. With all respect, Lord Hastur"— and she made a deep bow to the Comyn lord—"we do not accept the right of Comyn to lay commands upon the free women of Thendara as to what lawful work they may accept, or what their relations shall be with the men of the Empire from the stars . . . or with their women. By the will of Hastur, the only women who have been permitted to know the men of the Empire are the women in the bars and brothels near the spaceport. We do not believe this will give a true picture of our world to the men of the *Terranan.* So we have come here today to offer you our lawful services in fields more suitable for meaningful communication between our two worlds: as mapmakers, guides, translators or any suitable work at which the Terrans wish to employ Darkovan workers and experts. And in return, knowing that you of the Empire may have much to teach us, we ask that a group of our young women be placed as apprentices among your medical services and other scientific branches of your knowledge to allow us to learn from you. Is that agreeable to you, messire of Terra?"

Of course, it was agreeable, thought Magda, watching Montray's face; it was what they had hoped for from the beginning, what they had so obdurately been denied on Darkover. She had never realized—and blamed herself for her own insensitivity—that the women of Darkover would resent being judged, by the Terrans, only by the women their men met in the bars and brothels. She herself, with her knowledge of such respectable women as she could meet in the markets and public places of Thendara, had gone a little deeper—but not much.

It wasn't, of course, total cooperation. There weren't that many Free Amazons, and they were rarely in positions of such power as *domna* Fiona. (It was also the first she had heard of the Courts of Arbitration. *What a lot I have to learn,* she thought, *and what fun I'm going to have learning it!*)

And afterward she would work again for the Terrans, and be one of the first to come and go between the two worlds, helping them to find a way to one another. Two worlds: and she would belong to both! She looked across at Lady Rohana, and the lady smiled. Again Magda had the image of a great door swinging wide, both ways, an opened door between locked-away worlds. . . .

Jaelle was watching Lorill Hastur. He seemed not very pleased, but he capitulated with such good grace as he could. *The fact is, the Free Amazons just aren't important enough—or so Hastur thinks—that he can, with dignity, take any notice of what we do. But where we go, others will follow, for their own reasons.* She caught Peter's eyes across the room, and smiled; and it seemed that her heart stopped at his returning smile.

I have found an honorable way we can be together in his world!

Montray was answering Hastur's gracious words with a little speech about friendship and brotherhood, carefully using all the wrong inflections while his son Wade carefully straightened them out and made them into the proper ones.

How will Montray get along without me to write his speeches? Magda realized, lightheartedly, that she didn't give a damn. She had more interesting things to do.

When it had all been settled, and Hastur and Lady Rohana and Montray—his son at his elbow to keep him from any too offensive mistakes— were exchanging amenities, Peter and Jaelle and Magda met for a moment in the doorway of the Council chamber. Peter knew the custom of the Domains too well to touch Jaelle in public, but his quick glance at her was like an embrace. But he spoke to Magda, with raillery:

"So you've had your own way, Mag, and made us all look like fools— doing what no man could manage to do! Have you really such contempt for us all, then?"

"Contempt? Not really," Magda said, but she could not help flicking a quick look at Montray, which Peter caught. "But he, at least, hasn't done so well with Darkover so far."

Peter said, "Everyone knew you were doing the real work of the coordinator's office, Magda. It's just the way the breaks run, that you couldn't have the title, too. Maybe someday you can have the job."

She smiled without bitterness and said, "No, thanks. Why don't you try for it, Peter?" She felt the strange little prickles of the hunch running up and down her spine as she spoke. "You'll make a good coordinator—or the first Legate, someday. I have something better to do."

"You've already done miracles," he said, clasping her hands warmly, and she shook her head.

"It wasn't I. It was Jaelle—and the Guild-mothers."

He said under his breath to Jaelle, "You are wonderful! I never believed you could do it!"

Jaelle said quietly, "I think you do not believe that women can do many things, Piedro, in spite of what Margali has done for us both. But perhaps you will learn, someday. I believed, for a time, that women among your people were more free than mine. Now I know that there is really not so much difference between Terra and Darkover. My foster-mother told me, once, that it was better to wear chains than to believe you are free, and weight yourself with invisible chains." Then she smiled at him, a luminous smile. "But there is always hope, and I am committed to a day when we are part of the Empire from the stars, and when we are not all strangers and aliens, but all people are—are—" She hesitated, stumbled for a word, and Peter said, "Where all men are brothers?"

She smiled, caught Magda's eyes and said, "And sisters."

He said, "Well, politics can wait; you and I have other things to think of today! Magda, will you come with us when we declare ourselves before witnesses?"

"I cannot," she said, glancing at the Guild-mothers. "I am not really supposed to leave the Guild-house for half a year after I am sworn." Suddenly she held out her hands.

"Oh, Peter, wish me luck! Don't hold it against me!"

He gave her a brief, almost brotherly hug. "I do, Mag," he said, kissing her on the cheek. "Looks like you'll need luck with those old battle-axes! But it's what you want, so be happy, love."

She said, "Jaelle—" and impetuously Jaelle flung her arms around Magda, holding her tight. Magda whispered, "You be happy, too."

"I'll come and see you," Jaelle promised. "Thendara house is my home, too."

Peter said, "But you must promise not to turn her against me, Magda! Must I cope with all those mothers-in-law?"

Jaelle said, laughing, "No one could turn me against you. But you must learn someday not to speak so of my mothers and sisters!"

She's grown up, Magda thought. *I've always thought of her as a young girl. But she isn't. She's a woman. And she isn't infatuated anymore. She knows him for what he is. And she loves him anyway.*

He would never understand that there could be loyalties—certainly not loyalties between women—that could go deeper than love. But he would do his best for the world they all loved, and his best would be very good indeed. And for that, if nothing else, Magda knew she would always love him a little.

The Guild-mother Millea turned and beckoned to Magda to join them. Magda kissed Jaelle again, and said, "Be good to each other." Then, slowly, but without looking back, she went across the room to join the three women.

Jaelle, standing and watching her go, seemed to catch from her mind the image of a great, opening door, swinging wide on a sunlit world and a brilliantly lighted future.

THENDARA HOUSE

ACKNOWLEDGMENT

Shortly after I completed the novel *The Shattered Chain,* I began writing, for my own amusement, the story of Magda in the Amazon Guild House. At that time Jacqueline Lichtenberg and I were corresponding regularly and frequently, and she suggested that I should also write the story of Jaelle among the Terrans. I said I didn't feel qualified just then to do so, but that *she* could, if she wished. So, for the fun of it, we wrote about half a dozen chapters each, passing them back and forth between us and discussing them, with an eye to eventual professional collaboration. However, we were both busy with other projects, far from Darkover, and Jacqueline's career was taking off in a far different direction. Also, it turned out, we had quite different ideas about where the story was going, and before long we discovered that we were pulling in opposite directions, and, with suitable expressions of regret and mutual esteem, abandoned this particular collaboration; she went back to her own "Sime" and "Molt Brother" seria—if that is the plural of series—and I to write other Darkover and non-Darkover novels, feeling that the botched collaboration was not redeemable, and tossing it into my bottom file drawer with other projects on what I believed would be permanent "hold."

Years later, taking up this collaboration, although I have rewritten almost everything Jacqueline did on it—for our writing styles and themes are very different—I note that my concept of the character of Jaelle has nevertheless been broadened and strengthened by her input on the chapters in which she had the first touch. Although this is not a collaboration, I am still greatly indebted to Jacqueline for allowing me to see a character of my own through her eyes. As she has graciously acknowledged my part in what I consider her best book. *Unto Zeor, Forever,* so I must acknowledge her part in this book of mine.

MARION ZIMMER BRADLEY

PART ONE

CONFLICTING OATHS

PART TWO

SUNDERING

PART THREE

OUTGROWTH

Part One

Conflicting Oaths

Chapter One

Magdalen Lorne

Light feathers of snow were falling overhead; but toward the east there was a break in the clouds where the dull reddish light of Cottman IV—the sun of Darkover, called the Bloody Sun by the Terran Empire—could be seen dimly through cloud, like a great bloodshot eye.

Magdalen Lorne shivered a little as she walked slowly up the approach to the Terran HQ. She was in Darkovan dress, so she had to show her indent cards to the Spaceforce people at the gates; but one of them knew her by sight.

"It's all right, Miss Lorne. You'll have to go over to the new building, though."

"They finally finished the new quarters for Intelligence?"

The uniformed man nodded.

"That's right. And the new Chief came in from Alpha Centaurus the other day—have you met her yet?"

This was news to Magda. Darkover was a Closed Planet, Class B, which meant Terrans were—officially, at least—restricted to certain Treaty Zones and Trade Cities. There was no official Intelligence Service, except for a small office in Records and Communications, working directly out of the Coordinator's office.

It's about time they opened a branch of Intelligence here. They could do with a Department of Alien Anthropology, too. Then Magda wondered what it would mean to her own somewhat irregular status. She had been born on Darkover, in Caer Donn, where the Terrans had built their first spaceport before shifting to the new Empire Headquarters here in Thendara. She had been reared among Darkovans, before the new policy of standardization of

Spaceport buildings to Empire-normal yellow lights—a policy making little or no provision for the red sun of Darkover and the fierce cold of the climate. This, of course, made sense for Empire personnel stationed on ordinary Empire planets, who seldom stayed in one post more than a year or so and did not need to acclimatize themselves; but conditions on Darkover were, to say the least, unusual for an Empire planet.

Magda's parents had been linguists who had spent much of their lives in Caer Donn; she had grown up more Darkovan than Terran, one of only three or four people who spoke the language like a native and were capable of doing undercover research into customs and language. She had never been away from Darkover except for three years of schooling in the Empire's Intelligence School on Alpha Colony; then she had accepted a position in Communications as a matter of course. But what had been, to her superiors, only convenient disguise, fitting her for research and undercover work on the planet of her birth, had become to Magda her deepest self.

And it is to that Darkovan self, Margali, not Magda, that I must now be true. And not just Margali, but Margali n'ha Ysabet, Renunciate of the Comhi-Letzii, what the Terrans would call Free Amazon. That is what I am now and must be henceforth, men dia pre'zhiuro. . . . Magda whispered to herself the first words of the Renunciate's Oath, and shivered. It would not be easy. But as she had sworn, so would she do. To a Terran, an oath given under duress was not binding. *Darkovan, the Oath binds me without question, the very thought of escaping it dishonorable.*

She wrenched her thoughts from that endless loop in her mind. A *new section for Intelligence,* he had said, *and a new Chief.* Probably, Magda thought with a resigned shrug, someone who knew considerably less about the job than she did herself. She, and her ex-husband, Peter Haldane, had both been born here, were naturally bilingual, knew and accepted the customs as their own. But that was not the way the Empire did things.

The new Intelligence Office was in a tall skyscraper, still shining with newness, high above the Port. By the Terra-normal yellow lights, too bright for Magda's eyes, she saw a woman standing; a woman she knew, or had once known, very well.

Cholayna Ares was taller than Magda, brown-skinned, with white hair—Magda had never known whether it was prematurely grayed or whether it had always been naturally silver-white, for her face was, and had always been, unusually young. She smiled and reached out in a welcoming gesture, and Magda took her old teacher's hand.

"It's hard to imagine you'd give up the Training School," Magda said. "Certainly not to come here—"

"Oh, I didn't exactly give it up." Cholayna Ares laughed. "There was the usual sort of bureaucratic hassle—each group tried to get me on their side, and I said a plague on both their houses, and put in for transfer. So I wound up—here. Not a popular post, so no competition for getting it. I remembered that you came from here, and you liked it. Not many people have a chance of building the Intelligence Service up out of nothing on a Class B planet. And with you and Peter Haldane—didn't I hear once that you'd married him?"

"The marriage broke up last year," Magda said. "The usual sort of thing." She warded her former teacher's look of curious sympathy away with a hard shrug. "The only problem it created was that they didn't send us out in the field together any more."

"If there was no Intelligence Service here, what were you doing in the field?"

"We worked out of Communications," Magda said. "Language research; at one time they had me recording jokes and idioms from the marketplace, just a way of keeping up with language and current slang, so people who *did* have to go into the field wouldn't make stupid mistakes."

"And so, my first day on the job, you come up to greet me and make me feel welcome?" Cholayna asked. "Sit down—tell me all about this place. It's kind of you, Magda. I always knew you'd make a good career in Intelligence."

Magda lowered her eyes. "That wasn't the idea—I hadn't been told you were here." She decided the only way to get it said was to say it. "I came here to resign."

Cholayna's dark eyes showed the dismay she felt.

"Magda! You and I both know what the Service is like! Certainly they should have offered you this job, but I always thought we were friends, and that you'd be willing to stay on for a while, at least!"

Magda had never thought of that. But of course it was the impression Cholayna would get. She wished the new Head had been a complete stranger, or at least someone she disliked, not a woman she had always liked and respected.

"Oh, no, Cholayna! I give you my word, it has nothing to do with you! I didn't even know you were here, I was in the field till last night—" She found she was stammering in her eagerness to convince Cholayna of the truth. Cholayna frowned and gestured her to sit down.

"I think you'd better tell me all about it, Magda."

Uneasily, Magda sat down. "You weren't at the Council this morning. You didn't know. While I was in the field—I took the Oath of a Renunciate." At the bewildered look on her colleague's face she elaborated. "In the files they're called Free Amazons; they don't like the name. I am bound to spend half a year in the Guild House in Thendara for training, and after that—after that, I'm not sure what I intend to do, but I don't think it will be Intelligence."

"But what a wonderful opportunity, Magda," Cholayna said. "I wouldn't think of accepting your resignation! I'll put you on inactive status, if you like, for the half year, but think of the thesis you can get out of this! Your work is already regarded as the standard of excellence, you know—I did hear that much from the Legate," she added. "You probably know more about Darkovan customs than anyone working here. I also heard that the Medic division has agreed to train a group of Free Amazons —" she saw Magda's slight wince and amended—"What was it you called them—Renunciates? Sounds like an order of nuns, what do they renounce? Sounds like a strange place for you."

Magda smiled at the comparison. "I could quote the Oath for you. Mostly what they—we—renounce are the protections for women in the society, in exchange for certain freedoms." Even to her, it sounded like a woefully inadequate explanation, but how could she explain? "But I'm not doing this to write a thesis, you know, or to provide more information for Terran Intelligence. That's why I came to turn in my resignation."

"And that's why I'll refuse to accept it," said Cholayna.

"Do you think I am going to spy on my friends in the Guild House? Never!"

"I'm sorry you see it that way, Magda. I don't. The more we know about the different groups on any planet, the easier it is for us—and the easier it is for the planet we're on, because there's less chance of misunderstandings and trouble between the Empire and the locals—"

"Yes, yes, I learned all that in the Intelligence School," Magda said impatiently. "Standard party line, isn't it?"

"I wouldn't put it that way." There was something like carefully controlled anger in the older woman's voice.

"But I would, and I'm beginning to see how it can be misused," Magda said, and now she too was angry. "If you won't accept my resignation, Cholayna, I'll have to leave without it. Darkover is my home. And if the price of becoming a Renunciate is to give up my Empire citizenship, why, then—"

"Wait just a minute, Magda—please?" Cholayna held up her hand to interrupt the angry torrent of words. "And sit down again, won't you?" Magda realized that she had started to her feet; slowly she sank down again in the chair. Cholayna went to the console of the office wall and dialled herself a cup of coffee; brought another to Magda, balancing the hot cups in her palm, and sank down to a chair beside her.

"Magda, forget for a minute that I'm your superior officer won't you? I always thought we were friends. I didn't expect you'd walk away without any explanation at all."

I thought we were friends, too, Magda thought, sipping at the coffee. *But I know now I have never had any woman friends at all; I didn't know what friendship was. I was always trying so hard to be one of the boys that I never paid any attention to what other women did, or didn't do. Until I met Jaelle, and knew what it was to have a friend I'd fight for and die for if I must. Cholayna isn't my friend either, she's my superior and she's using friendship to make me do what she wants. Maybe she thinks that is being my friend, it's a Terran way of thinking. I'm just not one of them anymore. If I ever was.*

"Why don't you tell me the whole thing, Magda?" The kindly look in Cholayna's eyes Magda was confused again. *Maybe she really thinks of herself as my friend.*

She began at the beginning, telling Cholayna how Peter Haldane, her friend and partner, and for a time her husband, had been kidnapped by bandits who had mistaken him for Kyril Ardais, son of the Lady Rohana Ardais. Fearing to travel alone as a woman, Magda had been persuaded by Lady Rohana to disguise herself as a Free Amazon. When she had later encountered a band of genuine Renunciates, led by Jaelle n'ha Melora, the deception had been discovered.

"The penalty for a man who invaded them in women's clothes would have been death or castration," Magda explained. "For a woman, the penalty is only that the lie must become truth; a woman may not enjoy the freedoms of the Oath without first renouncing the safety and protection of the laws specially protecting women."

"An oath taken under duress—" Cholayna began but Magda shook her head.

"No. I was given free choice. They offered to escort me to a Guild House where one of the Elders would decide the special circumstances— whether I could simply be sworn to secrecy and released." She sighed, wearily wondering if it had been worth it. "That would have lost too much time; Peter was to be executed at Midwinter if not ransomed. I chose, quite freely, to take the Oath; but I took it with a lot of—of mental reservations. I felt just as you do now. Only between then and now I—I changed my mind."

She knew that sounded ridiculously inadequate. She went on, telling only a little of the cruel conflict in her mind, when she had intended to escape, leave her Oath, even if she must kill Jaelle, or leave her to be slaughtered by bandits; and how she had found herself fighting at the woman's side, saving her life. . . .

Cholayna listened to the story in silence, rising once to refill the coffee cups. Finally she said, "I can understand, to some extent, why you feel obligated."

"It's not only that," Magda said. "The Oath has become very real to me. I feel myself a Renunciate at heart—I think I would always have been one, had I known such a choice existed. Now—" How could she explain it? She drained the cold coffee from the cup and concluded helplessly, "It is something I *must* do."

Cholayna nodded. "I can see that. I don't know if there is a precedent. I've heard of men going over the wall, going native, on some of the Empire planets. I don't think I've ever heard of a woman doing that, though."

"I'm not exactly *going over the wall,*" Magda pointed out. "If I were, would I be here in your office, formally turning in my resignation?"

"Which I do not intend to accept," Cholayna said. "No, listen to me—I listened to you, didn't I? There's no precedent for this; I don't think there's any way to give up Empire citizenship for a sworn-in civil servant, and you made that choice when you accepted three years training in the Intelligence School—"

"I've done enough work to repay the Empire—"

Cholayna silenced her with a gesture. "Nobody questions that, Magda. I am perfectly willing to put you on inactive status, if you must have your six months—half year—how long is the Darkovan year anyhow? But something has come up which ties in very well with what you have told me."

She turned to her desk and took up a file of printouts.

"As it happens, I have a transcript of that Council here," she said, and Magda glanced at the printouts—the Council where Lord Hastur had been forced to accept the validity of a Terran's Oath and where the Guild Mothers had arranged that the Terrans should engage the services of the Renunciate Jaelle n'ha Melora to work in Magda's place in the Terran Headquarters, prior to the employment of a dozen Free Amazons. "—Oh, very well, Renunciates," Cholayna amended quickly, "to be trained in medical technology by our Medic Department, and possibly in other sciences and skills. With Jaelle working among us, and you in the Guild House, it seems to me that during this half year you will be especially qualified to determine personnel practices for Darkovan employees in the Empire, especially among women. We are prepared to put you on detached duty. Living among Darkovan women, you can find out which women could handle the culture shock of living among Terrans, as well as letting us know how we ought to treat them for the best communication between Terrans and Darkovans. You are the only person who is qualified to do this, actually living in a Guild House."

Finally Magda said, "If you already know all this, Cholayna, why did you have me tell it to you?"

"I only knew what you had said," Cholayna replied, "and what the Guild Mothers had said about you. I did not know how you felt about it. Because the student was the right kind of girl when I knew her, doesn't mean the woman who had become a trained Agent was the kind we could trust."

Somehow the words softened Magda's anger, as Cholayna went on. "Can't you see? This is for the good of your Renunciates, as well as for the Empire—to cushion them against the worst of culture shock when they come here? Even, if necessary, to know which Terrans we can trust to deal fairly with them? You know, and I knew before I had been here a tenday, that Russ Montray is no more fit to be Legate, when they get a Legation here, than I am to pilot a starship! He doesn't like the planet, and he doesn't understand the people worth a damn. And I can tell, from the way you speak, that you do."

Is she trying to flatter me, to get me to do what she wants? Or does she mean it? Magda knew, of course, that Montray was considerably less fit than she was herself. Yet on a planet like Darkover, with its strictured traditional roles for men and women, Magda knew she could never be a Legate, or hold any comparable post, because the Darkovans would never accept a woman in such a position. Cholayna herself could hold her post in Intelligence only because she would never come into direct contact with Darkovans, but only with her field Agents.

"Magda, I can tell from the way you're looking at me, that something about this bothers you—"

"I do not want to seem to spy on my sisters in the Guild House—"

"I never thought of asking that," Cholayna replied, "only that you create, for us, a set of rules for Terrans who must come into close contact with Darkovan women in general, particularly with Renunciates in the service or employ of the Empire. This will benefit us, certainly—but I would think it would benefit your—your Guild Sisters even more."

There seemed no way to refuse that. She would indeed be doing just the kind of service for Darkover, and the Guild House, which the Guild Mothers had said, at that Council, that they would welcome. She remembered what the Guild Mother Lauria had said:

"We have come here today to offer you our lawful services in fields suitable for better communication between our two worlds. As mapmakers, translators, guides, or any work for which the Terrans require workers and experts. And in return, knowing that you of the Empire have much to teach us, we ask that a group of our young women be placed as apprentices among your medical services, and taught those, and other scientific skills . . ."

And this had been a real breakthrough. Before this day, the men of the Empire had been able to judge the culture of Darkover only by the women they met in the Spaceport bars and the marketplace. When she had heard Mother Lauria say this, she had realized that she would be one of the first to come and go, building bridges between her new world and her old one. She bent her head in capitulation. She was still an Intelligence Agent, no matter how she might resent it.

"As for your resignation—forget it. That isn't the kind of thing you could do without a lot more thought than you've given it. Leave the doors open. Both ways." Cholayna reached out and patted Magda's hand, an unexpected gesture, and somehow it softened Magda's hostility.

"We need to know how we should treat these Renunciates when they are employed by the Terrans. What are their criteria for good behavior? What would offend or upset them? And while you are in the Guild House, we may ask you to make the final choice of which women we can accept, which women are qualified for Medic apprentices, women with open minds, flexible toward changing customs—"

Magda said patiently, "Do you really believe that most of them are unenlightened savages, Cholayna? May I remind you that for all its Closed B status, Darkover has a very complex and sophisticated culture—"

"With a pre-space, pre-industrial technological level," Cholayna said dryly. "I'm not doubting they have great poets and a fine musical tradition, or whatever else it takes to make you Communications people call a culture sophisticated. The Malgamins of Beta Hydri have a highly sophisticated culture too, but they embody ritual cannibalism and human sacrifice. If we are going to give these people our own highly sophisticated technology, we must have some notion of what they're going to do with it. I suppose you are familiar with Malthusian theories, and what happens to a culture when you start—for instance—saving the lives of children, in a culture where population control cannot proceed, for religious or other reasons, at an equal level? Remember the rabbits in Australia, or don't they teach that classic example of Anthropology 1-A any more?"

She had only the vaguest memory of the classic example, but knew what the theory involved. The expansion of population, taking the brakes off predators or increasing survival at birth, created exponential expansion and resultant chaos. Terrans had been widely criticized for denying medical knowledge to native populations for just that reason. Magda knew of the policy, and the hard necessities behind it.

"I think, when you've had time to go over it in your mind, you'll know why you have to cooperate with us, even for the sake of your own sisters in your—" she hesitated and groped for the word, "Guild House." She stood up and her voice was crisp.

"Good luck, Magda. While you're on detached duty you'll get two rises in pay, you know." The gesture put Magda back in the service, and she wondered dimly if she ought to salute.

And I didn't manage to do what I came to do, I didn't resign. I needed, so desperately, to be one thing or the other, not torn between them like this. The real me, the truest me, is Darkovan. Yet too much Terran to be true Darkovan . . .

She had never really belonged anywhere. Perhaps, in the Guild House, she would find out where she belonged—but only if the Terrans would let her alone.

She went out of the Intelligence office, briefly debated going to her old quarters to retrieve a few cherished possessions. No. They would be of no use to her in the Guild House, and would only proclaim her Terran. She hesitated again, thinking of Peter and Jaelle, who would be married this morning as freemates—the only marriage lawful for a Renunciate. Jaelle would want her at the wedding; and Peter, too, in token that she bore him no grudge because he now loved and desired Jaelle.

I do not want Peter. I am not jealous of Jaelle. As she told Cholayna Ares, the marriage had been broken before she had ever known Jaelle. And yet somehow she felt she could not endure their newlywed happiness.

She hurried toward the gate and went through, taking off her Terran HQ identity badge and dropping it into a trash can as she went.

Now she had burnt her bridges; she could not return without special arrangement, for she would not be admitted as an employee. On a Closed Status planet, there was no free access between Terran and Darkovan territory. What she had done had committed her, irrevocably, to the Guild-House and to Darkover.

She hurried through the streets until she saw the walled building, windowless and blind to the street, with the small sign on the door:

THENDARA HOUSE
GUILD OF RENUNCIATES.

She rang the small, concealed doorbell, and somewhere, a long way inside, she heard the sound of a bell.

Chapter Two

Jaelle n'ha Melora

Jaelle was dreaming. . . .

She was riding, under a strange ominous sky, like spilt blood on the sands of the Drylands. . . . Strange faces surrounded her, women unchained, unbound, the kind of women her father had mocked, yet her mother had once been one of them . . . her hands were chained, but with ribbon links which broke asunder, so that she did not know where to go, and somewhere her mother was screaming, and pain crashed through her mind . . .

No. It was a noise, a blaring, somehow *metallic* noise, and there was a glaring yellow light cutting through her eyelids. Then she was aware that Peter was nuzzling her shoulder as he leaned over her to cut off the blaring sound. Now she remembered; it was a signal, a rising bell like the ones she had heard on her one visit to the Guest house at Nevarsin monastery. But a sound so harsh and mechanical could not be compared with the mellow, tempered monastery chime. Her head ached, and she remembered the party last night in the Terran HQ Recreation area, meeting a few of Peter's friends. She had drunk more of the unaccustomed strong drinks than she intended, hoping she would be able to relax her shyness before all the strangers. Now the whole evening was only a blur of names she could not pronounce and faces not attached to names.

"Better hurry, sweetheart," Peter urged, "don't want to be late your first day on a new job, and I can't afford to—one bad black mark against me already."

Peter had left the shower running. Her back ached from the strange bed; she wasn't sure whether it had been too hard or too soft, but it hadn't felt right. She told herself that was ridiculous. She had slept in all kinds of strange places, and certainly a good, icy shower would wake her up and make her feel refreshed. To her surprise the water was warm, lulling rather than bracing, and she could not remember how to adjust it for cold. Anyhow, she was awake, and went to dress.

From somewhere Peter had produced an HQ uniform for her, and she struggled into it, the long shaped tights that made her feel uncomfortably as if her legs were bare, the ridiculously low and thin shoes, the short black tunic piped with blue. His own tunic was like it, only piped with red. He had told her what the different colors meant, but she had forgotten. The tunic was so tight she could not pull it over her head, and it took her some time to figure why they had put the long fastener in the back where she had trouble reaching it, instead of in the front where it would have been sensible. Why would anyone want a dress that tight, anyhow? Cut looser, and with the press-together seam in the front, it would have been an admirable dress for a woman if she was breast-feeding a child, but this way it seemed a waste of materials—cut a few inches looser, it would have slipped over her head without needing the fastening at all. It felt rough against her skin, since no under-tunic was provided, but at least it had warm knitted neck-folds and tight sleeves. She was frowning at herself in the mirror when he came up behind her, already dressed, and took her shoulders, looking at her in the mirror and then hugging her hard.

"You look marvelous in uniform," he said, "Once they see you, every man in the HQ will be envying me."

Jaelle cringed; this was exactly what she had been taught to avoid. The dress was cut immodestly close to the curve of her breast and her narrow waist. She felt troubled, but when he turned her around and held her close, she buried her face against him, and in his arms, all the tension seemed to flow out of her. She sighed and murmured, "I wish you didn't have to go—"

"Mmmmmm, I do too," he murmured, caressing her, burying his lips in her bare neck—then, abruptly, raised his eyes and stared at the chronometer on the wall.

"Ouch! Look at the time! I told you I didn't dare be late back, this first day," he said, and made for the door. She felt icy cold, in spite of the hot shower, as he mumbled, "Sorry, love, I'm late, but you can find the way down alone, can't you? I'll see you tonight." The door closed, and Jaelle stood alone. Still roused from his touch and his kiss, she realized that he had not even waited for the answer to his own question. She wasn't at all sure she could get down to the office where she had been told to report this morning, in the bewildering labyrinth of the HQ.

She stared blindly at the chronometer, trying to translate Terran time into the familiar hours of the day. It was, as nearly as she could reckon, not yet three hours after sunrise. She remembered a flippant comment of Magda's:

I don't think you'll like it much in the Terran Zone, the other woman had said. *Sometimes they even make love by the clock.*

But she, too, had duties this morning. She could not stand here, staring uneasily at her image in the mirror. Nor could she imagine going among strange men, Terrans, in this immodestly tight dress. Not even a prostitute would go out in such attire! With shaking hands, she unfastened it and got into her ordinary clothes. The uniform was not warm enough, either, for the late-spring weather outside; inside the buildings, heated to almost suffocating warmth, the uniform might be sufficient, but she had to go outdoors—she stared at the little map of the HQ Peter had left her, trying to puzzle out the confusing markings.

She found her way, shivering in the morning drizzle, to the main building and showed the pass Peter had given her. The Security man said, "Mrs. Haldane? You should have gone through the underground tunnel, in this weather," and she looked around, seeing, indeed, no one on the elaborate walks and ramps.

She managed to puzzle out the signs—Peter had given her a crash course in reading the most common signs, and she had been taught a little Standard, which was not really so very different from *casta*—she had been told once that they had descended from a common language group before Darkover was settled, that *casta* was similar to the most common Terran language. She felt reluctant to ask directions from any of the men and women moving around in the rabbit-warren buildings; they all seemed to look alike, in tights, tunics of varying colors and trim, low, thin sandals. She rode up and down a time or two in the elevator until she figured out how it worked. It was not complicated, once you could understand why anyone would *bother.* Did the Terrans suffer from a racial paralysis of the legs, or something, that they could not walk up and down stairs? She supposed it made sense when there were twenty or thirty floors to a building, but why build it so high? They had been given enough room on the spaceport HQ to build rationally!

There was nothing wrong with Peter's legs, at least, she thought smiling; perhaps Terrans were just trained to be lazy.

Outside the section Peter had marked on the map—it was marked, too, with one of those signs that spelled, she knew, the Terran word for COMMUNICATIONS—she presented herself before a man stationed there. She said, "My name is Jaelle n'ha Melora," and proffered her pass.

"Just go over there and present it to the screening device," he said indifferently. She slid the pass through the slot, and the glass screen began to blink with a strange beeping sound.

"What's the matter?" he asked.

She stared helplessly at the blinking, beeping screen. "I don't know—" she began, "they slid my pass back out at me—" and she picked it up, bewildered, from the slot.

He glanced at it and at the screen. He frowned and said "You're out of uniform, and the scanners don't recognize you from the picture—see? And the name you said doesn't match the name on the pass, Miss." She puzzled this out to an honorific, roughly equivalent to *damisela*. Should she correct him? He pointed patiently to the name on the pass and said "You have to repeat the name in the form it's on the pass. See? *Haldane, Mrs. Peter.* Try saying it like that."

She started to protest that her name was Jaelle, that it was forbidden by Oath to a Renunciate to take a man's name, but quickly stopped herself. It was none of his business and how could she explain it to a Terran anyhow? Meekly she repeated "Haldane, Mrs. Peter," before the screen, and the door slid back and let her in. She remembered that some of Peter's friends last night—not the best friends—had called her Mrs. Haldane and she had had to correct them. But that was Magda's name too, then?

She went into a huge light room with the omnipresent yellow glare. Along the wall were strange machines she did not recognize. A young woman rose from behind a narrow table to greet her.

"I'm Bethany Kane," she said. "You must be Jaelle." Her Cahuenga, the Trade City language, was barely intelligible, so that Jaelle hardly recognized her own name. Bethany led her to a table with glass panels and strange equipment. "Leave your things here and we'll go up and get started; I'm supposed to take you up to Basic and Medic."

Jaelle could tell it was a memorized speech—she had obviously brought no "things" to leave, and the young woman seemed to want to say more, but couldn't. On an impulse Jaelle replied in *casta,* "Magda mentioned her friend Bethany to me; you are she?"

Bethany said with a relieved smile "I didn't know you spoke the city language, Jaelle—is that how you pronounce it, Zhay-el-leh?"

Bethany was a slight woman, with medium brown hair, brown eyes— *like an animal's eyes,* Jaelle thought—and she looked pretty and rounded in the Terran uniform which seemed so immodestly cut. How could the woman display herself like that, in an office composed of men and women together? Perhaps, if only women were nearby, it would not seem so—so— Jaelle fumbled for the concept; so deliberately enticing. Yet these women worked with men on easy terms and no one seemed to notice. She filed that away for later thought as they passed the uniformed men at a succession of doors and Bethany, taking her scribbled pass, got them through various tunnels and elevators through what seemed to Jaelle like miles and miles of corridor. Her sandalled feet, accustomed to stoutly laced boots, were aching by the time they reached their goal. She put aside her theory that Terrans were lazy; with this much racing about, perhaps they needed their elevators and escalators.

The next hours were the most confusing of her life. There was a place with lights flashing and glaring into her eyes, and a moment later a small, laminated card slid out of a slot, with a picture Jaelle, for a moment, did not recognize as herself; a small serious-looking red-haired woman with slightly frightened eyes. Bethany saw her grimace at the picture and chuckled.

"Oh, we all look like that in ID pictures. As if we were being lined up and photographed for a prison sentence; something about the lights and the pose. You should see mine!" But, though Jaelle expected her to offer it, she did not, and she supposed it must be some form of figurative speech, social noise. Then an elderly gentleman, round and good-natured, who spoke excellent Darkovan, questioned her at length about her place of birth ("Shainsa? Where exactly is that?" and finally managed to get her to sketch a rough map of the road between the Dry Towns and Thendara) her age, the date of her birth, and asked her to pronounce her name again and again while he scribbled it down in precise markings which, he said, might help others to pronounce it very accurately; Jaelle wondered why he could not simply tell them, or use one of the omnipresent voice recorders—at one point she had been startled to hear her own voice coming from one of them. But she had known there would be many unfamiliar things. At one point he called her "Mrs. Haldane," and when she corrected him, smiled gently and said, "The custom of the country, my dear girl." He used the phrase, which in Darkovan could have become an offensive intimacy, in such a fatherly fashion that Jaelle was warmed instead of offended. "Remember, young woman, you're among Terran barbarians now and you have to allow us our tribal customs. It makes record-keeping simpler that way. You're sharing quarters with Haldane, aren't you? Well, there you are."

"Yes, but I am a Renunciate, and it is not the custom to bear the husband's name—"

"As I say, it's our custom," said the man. "Do you have any proverb which says, When in Rome, do as the Romans do?"

"Who were the Romans?"

"God knows; I don't. Some old territorial people, I imagine. One could translate; when living among barbarians, follow their customs as well as you can."

Jaelle thought it over, felt her face crinkling in a smile. "Yes; we say, When in Temora, eat fish."

"Temora, as I recall, being a seacoast town," he mused. Then he began tapping on the odd keyboard with remarkably nimble fingers—she hoped they wouldn't ask her to use any machine demanding that much dexterity —and silent lights streamed across a glass plate before him. There was a beep, and he raised his eyes at the series of letter-lights on the glass.

"I forgot. Get her prints, will you, Beth?"

"Finger or eye, or both?"

"Both, I think."

Bethany led Jaelle to another machine and guided her hand against a curious flat glass plate; it flared lights, and Bethany guided her face against another with a place for her chin to rest. She jerked back, startled, as lights hurt her eyes, and Beth said soothingly "No, hold your head still and keep your eyes open; we're taking retina prints for positive identification. Fingerprints can sometimes be faked, but eyeprints never."

It took two more tries before she could conquer the involuntary response, twitching back and her eyes squeezing shut. Finally they clipped a laminated card to her tunic, with her picture in one corner and the odd squiggles which were, they told her, coded prints. Bethany said, "You really have to wear the uniform, you know. Twice already today you tripped the monitors with an intruder-alert—they're programmed to ignore anyone wearing uniform, because of the codes inside the tunic patch." She guided Jaelle's fingers to examine a roughness as of metal between the thickness of her uniform neck's cloth; Jaelle thought it had been torn and repaired, but it was evidently intended that way.

"Fortunately, the man on the main gate saw your pass and warned us that you were out of uniform today. But wear it tomorrow, won't you, like a good girl? Makes everything so much simpler."

Simpler; to have everyone looking just alike, like so many painted toy soldiers from a box!

"I know you're working under Lorne," the man went on, "but she got away with it because, working in the Boss's office as much as she did, she could pull rank." Lorne, of course, was the name Magda used in the HQ, she knew, but none of the rest of it was intelligible except that for some strange reason, perhaps a superstitious ritual, she must wear the uniform to keep from touching off alarms within the building. It probably wasn't worth arguing about.

"It's all right for today, your first day," the man added, "but tomorrow, show up in uniform, all right? And wear the badge at all times. It identifies your department and your face."

Jaelle asked, "Why should I have to wear my face, when I am already wearing my face?"

"So that we can see that your badge matches your face, and no unauthorized person gets into Security areas," the man said, and Jaelle, who was already confused, decided it was not worthwhile to go on asking why should anyone want to go where they had no business? It wasn't as if there was anything interesting in here to see.

"Take her on up to Medic, Beth, we're finished with her," said the man. "Good luck, Mrs. Haldane—Jaelle, I mean. Where are they going to put her, Beth? They can't put her in the Boss's office. He tends to make—" the man hesitated, "rude remarks. About certain people's—backgrounds."

Jaelle wondered if the man thought she was deaf, or feebleminded; she had met Montray, and no one with a scrap of telepathic ability could possibly be in doubt that he disliked Darkover and all the Darkovans. But it was polite of the man to try and spare her feelings; the first politeness she had encountered from Terrans, who were often friendly, but seldom polite. Not, anyhow, as she understood it; they seemed to have different standards of courtesy. Only after they were in the hallway did she realize that while she had answered a great many questions about herself, no one had bothered to introduce him to her and she still did not know his name.

"Next stop, Medic," remarked Bethany, and Jaelle, who knew the Terran word by now, after the long debates about allowing Renunciates to become Medical technicians, protested, "But I'm not sick!"

"Just routine," said Bethany, an answer Jaelle had heard so often that day that she recognized it, though she did not yet know what it meant, as a ritual answer which was supposed to cut off discussion. Well, she had been told it was rude to inquire about the religious rituals of others, and Terrans must have some really strange ones.

They went up farther, this time, than ever before, and Jaelle, catching a random glance out a window, shivered involuntarily; they must be as high as they had been in the Pass of Scaravel, and she clung, feeling dizzy, to a handrail. Was this some form of testing her courage? Well, a woman who had faced blizzards in the Hellers and banshees in the mountain passes would not quail at mere height. Anyhow, Bethany seemed unconcerned.

There was a different kind of uniform on this floor, and since she was to participate in whatever curious ritual was being done this time, she did not complain when they took away her woolen and leather Amazon outfit and dressed her in a white tunic made of paper. The workers here all had the same sign on their tunics, an upright staff with what looked like two snakes coiled around it, and she wondered if work emblems replaced clan or family blazonings here. She waited on benches for peculiar processes, was touched or prodded with strange machines, and they pricked her finger with needles. She shrank back at this, and Bethany explained, "They wish to look at your blood under a—" she used a strange word, and at Jaelle's blank look, elaborated, "A special glass to see the cells in your blood—to see if it is healthy blood." They stuck a glass plate in her mouth, and draped her from breasts to knees with a metal-treated heavy cloth, then left her alone with the machine, which made a curious humming noise, at which she startled and jumped. The young technician, a girl about Jaelle's own age with curly fair hair, swore angrily, and again Bethany explained hastily that they were only taking a picture of her teeth to see if they had holes or damaged roots.

"They could ask me," Jaelle said crossly, but when they tried it again, she held her breath and stayed as still as she could. The technician looked at the plate with pictured teeth and said to Bethany that she had never seen anything like it.

"She says your teeth are perfect," Bethany translated, and Jaelle said, with a sense of injury, that she could have told them that in the first place.

Then there was a room filled with machines, and the technician in charge of them, a man who spoke somewhat better Darkovan than anyone except the man who had questioned her so long in the photographing place, said, "Go in behind those curtains, and take off all your clothes. Right down to the skin. Then come out that end, and walk directly down that line, along the painted white stripe. Understand?"

She looked at him in horror; a good third of the technicians manning the machines were, in fact, male.

"I can't," Jaelle said, clutching in panic at Bethany's arm. "Do you really mean I am to walk through all those machines, completely naked?"

"The machines won't hurt you," Bethany said. "They're the new computerized scanners; no X-rays, nothing harmful or mutagenic. I'll go first and show you, see?" She stuck her head out and said something in Terran to the technicians, and translated to Jaelle; "I told them I'd walk through first and show you that they wouldn't hurt you." She was stripping off her clothes, and Jaelle watched her, making mental notes—*So that's how you manage the back fastenings? Do the tights really tear as easily as that, that she is so careful not to get her fingernails into them?*

"Program the metal-detector for the fillings in my teeth, Roy. Last time it beeped at me and they kept walking me back and forth half the morning."

"Fillings, teeth, all right," said the man, making some adjustment to the machine. "That's nothing, we had Lucy from Comm up here the other day and we forgot to get records and didn't program it to ignore her IUD. And of course anyone with a pin in a hip or something really fouls it! Go on through, Beth." And as Bethany walked, stark naked, down the row of machines, Jaelle realized that they ignored her absolutely, as if she were male or fully clothed. But when Bethany came back and would have pushed her from the cubicle, she hung back still.

"I tell you, the machines won't hurt you; it's nothing but light."

"—But—they're men—"

"They're Medics," Bethany said. "You're nothing to them but a set of bones and organs; they'd be more thrilled by a Colles fracture than if you had the most wonderful set of tits in the universe. Go on—you're keeping them waiting!"

Jaelle didn't understand quite all of this, but she supposed Bethany was trying to tell her that the men—Medics?—were like monks or healer-priests, interested in nothing but their work. Bracing herself, she stepped out of the cubicle, but to her relief, no one raised an eye, whether male or female, but stayed bent over the machines. One of the women asked in faulty Darkovan, "Wear you any metal? Teeth, fittings, anything?"

Jaelle spread empty hands. "Where would I have it put?" she demanded, and the woman smiled. "Right. Walk so—that side—turn. Stop there. Raise one arm. The other." Jaelle felt like a tamed chervine doing tricks. "Now turn again—lower arm—see? Machine no hurt—"

When she was dressing again, she asked Bethany, "What did those machines *do?*"

"Pictures of your insides, I told you. Tells them you're healthy."

"And as I told *you,* I could have told them that already," said Jaelle. Except for one or two wounds in battle—during her first years as an Amazon, she had fought as a mercenary at Kindra's side—and a broken wrist when she had fallen from a horse at sixteen, she had always been perfectly healthy.

Then they took her and put her into a contoured lounge and pasted gooey flat plates to her head, and pushed her down in the chair. She must have fallen asleep, and when she woke up she had a splitting headache, not unlike the headache she had had when Lady Alida had forced her, at fifteen, to look into a matrix jewel.

"She's very resistant," said one man, as she woke up, and another man answered, "That's normal for the indigenous population. Not used to technological environment. Beth said she spooked at the fluoroscopy machines. Hey—pipe down, she's awake already. Can you understand us, Miss?"

"Yes, perfectly—oh, I see. A language-teaching machine." That was nothing; the Comyn could have done that with a matrix and a well-trained telepath.

"Head ache?" Without waiting for her answer, the Medic handed her a small paper cup with a spoonful or so of pale green liquid in the bottom. "Drink this."

She did. He took the cup from her, crushed it in his hand and tossed it into a waste collector. She watched in amazement as it turned into pale slime and flowed out the drain. One moment it had been a cup; then, the next instant, without transition, it was a bit of pale slimy stuff, deliberately discarded and destroyed. Yet it was not old, or outworn, the new crisp feel of it was still in her hand, the *reality* of it. She could still feel it, but the thing itself was gone. *Why?* A few minutes later, changing back into her own clothes, Bethany told her to throw her paper tunic into the same kind of collector. It confused her still, to see the things dissolve and flow down the drain and exist no longer. The man who had worked the language machine—she heard him call it a D-Alpha corticator, which left her no wiser than before—handed her a neat packet of disks.

"Here are your language lessons in Standard for the rest of the week," he said. "Tell your husband to show you how to use the sleep-learner, and you can go ahead on your own."

Another machine! This man had not been introduced to her either, but she was accustomed to rudeness by now, and was not surprised when Bethany told her to hurry or they would be late to lunch. She had been hurrying all morning, but Terrans were always in a hurry, driven by the chronometer faces she saw everywhere, and she supposed there were some good reasons to serve meals on time; it was rude to keep the cooks waiting. There were no cooks visible, only machines, and it confused her to have to press buttons to get food, but she did what Bethany did. The food was all unfamiliar anyhow, thick porridges and hot drinks and bland textured messes. Sticking a fork in one peculiarly colored red mess, she asked what it was, and Bethany shrugged.

"Ration for the day; some kind of synthetic carbo-protein, I imagine. Whatever it is, it's supposed to be good for you." She ate up her portion with appetite, though, and so Jaelle tried to choke some of it down.

"The food in the Main Cafeteria is better than this," Bethany said, "this is just a quick place to eat and run. I know this was a boring morning, but it's always like this on a new job."

Boring? Jaelle thought of the last job she had undertaken; with her partner Rafaella, organizing a trade caravan to Dalereuth. They had spent the first day talking to their employer, finding out what men he had and how many animals, inspecting pack-beasts and making up their loads, visiting harness-makers to have proper packs made up. While Rafi had gone off to organize the hiring of extra animals, Jaelle had questioned the men about their food preferences and gone to purchase supplies and arrange their delivery. Monotonous, perhaps, and hard work, but certainly not boring!

The food was too strange to eat much; she could not have gotten it down at all had she not been ravenous after her breakfastless morning. The textures were too smooth, the tastes too sweet or too salty, with one fiery bitterness that made her splutter. At least Bethany was trying to be friendly.

Searching her mind, she realized she was still angry about the moment when she had walked naked between the rows of machines. None of the men had been offensive, they had not noticed that she was female. But they should have noticed. Noticed; not looked at her offensively, but noticed that she *was* in fact female and would have feelings about displaying herself before strange men. Possibly they should have had the machines entirely staffed by women, just to indicate that they understood her natural feelings. She hated the idea that they considered her just a nothing, another machine that happened to be living and breathing, a machine no one would have noticed except that it was not wearing the proper uniform! *A lot of bones and organs,* Bethany had said. She felt depersonalized, as if by treating her like a machine they had made her into one.

"Don't try to eat that stuff if you don't like it," Bethany said, noticing her struggle with the food. "Sooner or later, you'll find out which things you like and which ones you don't, and you can get native food—oh, I'm sorry, I mean naturally cooked food, things more like what you're accustomed to eating—in quarters. Some people prefer synthetics, that's all— the Alphans, for instance, have religious objections to eating anything that's ever been alive or growing, so we have to provide complete synthetic diets for them, and it's cheaper and easier to package them for the staff up here. They're not so bad when you're used to them," she rattled on, while Jaelle blinked, thinking of a world where everybody ate this kind of thing, not for convenience or cheapness but because they had religious scruples about eating anything which had once contained life. She supposed it showed, after all, a very elevated ethical sense. Anyway, there was nothing she could do about it.

By now she was numb to shocks and flung her half-emptied plate into the ubiquitous disposal bins, watching it flow away into slime and swirl away down the drain. Small loss, she thought. Upstairs again, in one of the large windowless offices, she felt the unease of incipient claustrophobia—it was unsettling not to be sure whether she was on the fourth floor or the twenty-fourth. She told herself that she could not expect to have everything familiar, among Terrans, and that at least it was a new kind of experience. But the strange sounds and background machine noises scraped away at her nerves. Bethany located a desk for her.

"This is Lorne's place; even when she's here she doesn't use it much, she worked mostly in Montray's office upstairs, but when I heard you were coming in, I had it cleaned out and set up for you. You wouldn't want to work under Montray, he's a—" She used an idiom Jaelle did not understand, comparing him with some unfamiliar animal, but the disapproving tone conveyed her meaning perfectly well. She remembered what she had heard in the Medic office, too . . . Montray, then, was the one who could not be trusted to treat Darkovans with ordinary courtesy. How, she wondered, had this man come to be in a position of authority if his character faults were so extreme that even his own staff felt free to comment on them? She resolved to ask Peter; she literally did not know how to frame the question for Bethany's ears without implying all kinds of insulting things about Terrans in general.

Bethany was explaining, in rapid-fire, how to use the voice-scriber, the throat-mike, the clearing key for erasure, the way in which the words would print on the screen before her. "You don't have to speak out loud, just subvocalize." She struck a key, and said, "Here, like this—watch."

On the screen, printed in luminous pale letters, the words appeared: HERE, LIKE THIS—WATCH. Jaelle swallowed as she slowly spelled them out.

"Wouldn't it be simpler if I just told this to the person who needs to know this?"

Bethany shrugged. "I suppose it could be done that way, but we need it for records—then the next Director of Operations, and the one beyond him, will be able to get it in your own words, years from now."

"Why should anyone be interested, say, fifty years from now, when we are no longer here and Rumal di Scarp is dead?"

"Well, it goes into the record," said Bethany, sorely puzzled herself. *That word again.* "Even by next week, your memory will have distorted what happened. . . . you really should have been debriefed, as Magda should have been, right after it happened, though I understand why it wasn't possible—you all spent the winter snowed in at Ardais, didn't you? But we have to get all this into the record, as clearly as we can. Then other Heads of Departments, or even people on other Empire planets, will have access to the information, even a hundred years from now. It all goes into the permanent record."

But that, Jaelle thought, was impossible; for anyone to report anything with that kind of permanent, frozen, once-for-all objectivity. She said, choosing her words to try and convey her distress, "But the truth I tell now about what happened at Sain Scarp is not the truth I would have told then. And what I tell now will not be the truth fifty years from now. I will have to recall all of it, fifty years from now, to see what the truth is then, because the only truth then will be what we remember—and not just me, but what Margali—Magda remembers, and what Peter remembers, and even what Lady Rohana and Rumal di Scarp himself remembers."

Bethany shook her head, clearly not understanding what Jaelle was trying to convey. "I'm afraid that's too complicated for me. Just tell everything you can remember, and we'll worry about that kind of ultimate truth some other time—all right?"

"But whom am I reporting *to?*"

"Does it matter? Tell it just the way you'd tell it to anyone who asked you what happened out there; put in every little detail you can think of— someone else will be editing the text and if there's anything really irrelevant, she'll cut it out."

"But how do I know what to say if I don't know who I'm saying it to?" Jaelle asked, confused again. "I mean, if you asked me to tell you, I'd tell it one way, and if, say, the Comyn Council asked, I'd tell it another way—"

Bethany sighed, and Jaelle could feel her frustration. She said, "I guess my *casta* isn't as good as I thought. It sounded as if you were saying you'd tell two different stories to us and to your own people. That's not what you mean, is it?" At Jaelle's vigorous headshake, she nodded and said, "I didn't think so; you look fairly honest to me, and Magda said nice things about you; I couldn't imagine you being that two-faced. I'll tell you what; just tell the story into the scriber, as if you were telling it to one of your Guild people, Elders—what's the word—?"

"Guild Mothers?"

"I guess that's it. Tell it as if you were telling one of your Guild Mothers, why don't you?"

She clipped the throat-mike, with its black snakelike attachment, to the neckband of Jaelle's tunic. "That's another good reason for wearing uniform; the standard uniform for your sector has a pocket in the neckband for a scriber-microphone and you can just tuck it in instead of messing around with clips." She demonstrated on her own uniform tunic. Jaelle flinched a little at the thought of being hooked up to any machine, but she supposed she would get used to it. It wasn't dangerous and she was not the barbarian they seemed to think her. It was up to her not to panic like a fish in a tree!

"Now just talk into it softly, or even subvocalize; I won't stand over you, it would only make you nervous, but I'll be right over here at my desk if you need me for anything," she said, and went away. Jaelle sat still, trying to decide what to do first. She said half aloud, "I'm still not sure I know how to handle this thing—" and heard the small humming and rattling sound; luminous letters swam on the screen and she saw in the slightly unfamiliar letters of Standard, her words in Casta: "I'm still not sure I know. . . ."

Chagrined, she pressed the clearing key and saw the letters disappear into flashes of light, as her paper cup and dinnerplate had vanished into nothingness. *Is anything permanent here?* she wondered; yet Bethany had been speaking of making her report accessible for all time. It was a sobering thought.

She said slowly, "I don't know where to start . . ." and as the machine hummed again, she saw the words appear in light on the screen. But this time it did not trouble her. How many times, she wondered, had she started out a report to Kindra, or to one of the Guild Mothers, of some mission accomplished or failed, with those very words? As if she had been sitting in the great gathering-room in Thendara Guild House, with the Guild Mothers and her sisters waiting to be told of what she had done, she began in a composed, formal way:

"On a certain night about ten days before Midwinter, I was traveling north to Nevarsin Monastery. With me were a band of the *Comhii-Letzii*, with myself, Jaelle n'ha Melora, as elected leader, Gwennis n'ha Liriel, Sherna n'ha Lia, and Devra n'ha Rayna on their way to take the places of three of our sisters who had been living in Nevarsin to copy records there, and Camilla n'ha Kyria, my oath-sister, as escort and guard. Because of a severe oncoming storm, we camped in a travel-shelter situated half a day's journey north of Andalune Pass. We found the place already tenanted by a band of strange men, about twelve in number; but invoking the traditional neutrality of the travel-shelters, we greeted them politely and made our camp at the opposite end of the building. Shortly after dark, a woman traveling alone, and in the ordinary dress of a Renunciate, entered the building; she identified herself as from Temora Guild House and was welcomed to our fire. This woman I learned later to be Magdalen Lorne—" She struggled with Magda's Terran name and was quite sure that what appeared on the screen was not what Magda's name looked like in Terran letters. She had once seen it written. She must have mispronounced it so grossly that the machine could not compensate and was reduced to a phonetic transcription of what she had actually *said*. She hit the clearing key and, biting her lip, called Bethany to ask the proper spelling.

To her great relief Bethany showed no exasperation, no sense that she had asked anything terribly stupid; she matter-of-factly spelled it for her and went back to her own desk, and Jaelle went on.

"We did not know her to be Terran or an Agent of Intelligence. We simply made her welcome among us and shared food as was traditional when Renunciates meet on the trail. While we were all sleeping there was a disturbance—"

She went on, the words flowing smoothly now, telling how Magda had been attacked by one of the bandits, breaking the travel-shelter's law of neutrality; when the men had been evicted from the shelter, Magda, under questioning, had been exposed as an intruder, and as the law provided, had been required to take the Oath. The next day Jaelle had turned over her leadership of the group to Camilla n'ha Kyria, in order to escort her new oath-daughter to Neskaya Guild House; when the others had gone, she and Magda had been attacked by two of the returning bandits and had fought them, in an encounter where Jaelle had been severely wounded. Magda, wounded herself, had saved Jaelle's life; and although she could then have ridden away on her mission, had stayed to tend Jaelle's severe and life-threatening wound. Later, Jaelle had discovered Magda's true identity, and had gone with her to complete the ransom of Peter Haldane from Rumal di Scarp.

She went on from there, briefly sketching in the encounter with a banshee-bird in the Pass of Scaravel, the ransom exchange, and the subsequent trip—what she could remember of it, since her memory of that time was blurred by the fever in her wound, and she remembered little of the journey except that Peter had taken her on his saddle when she could no longer ride alone.

She said little about their stay in Castle Ardais, except that they had been treated with kindly courtesy by Lady Rohana and welcomed by Dom Gabriel with due and gracious hospitality, even though he did not approve of Renunciates. She mentioned very briefly that Rohana was her kinswoman, and had been her guardian in childhood; even more briefly, that she and Peter Haldane had agreed to marry, upon their return to Thendara, and had done so. If they wanted to know anything more than that, they would have to ask her. How did she know what they wanted to know, and what business of theirs was it, anyhow? She was willing to report the part she had played in Peter's ransom—she supposed he would be reporting that from his own perspective—but while she would have gladly told her Guild Mothers how she had come to know Peter well, how she had clung to him during her illness, the growing closeness between them, and how she had first shared his bed after the Midwinter-festival, she was not going to report all that to a faceless machine, for Terrans who did not know either of them.

Inside the windowless room she lost track of time, and only when she looked up and discovered that others were closing up their desks and stations did she realize that her stomach was reminding her fiercely of her sketchy and inedible lunch.

When she stepped from the building into the spaceport HQ plaza, it was past sunset, and fine drizzling rain was falling. In the central cafeteria, which was at least spacious and well-windowed, she felt less claustrophobic than in the shut-in office with its clutter of desks; but everyone looked so alike in uniform that she did not see Peter until he actually touched her on the shoulder.

"Jaelle! What are you doing out of uniform?" But before she could explain, he went on, "I heard that somebody had tripped the monitors all over the station, but I never dreamed it was you!"

She was astonished at the anger in his voice; she started to explain, but he was not listening.

"Let's get on line for dinner—there's always a crowd about this time."

The food looked and smelled better than the synthetics which were all that had been provided in the other building at lunch; some of it was almost familiar, roasted meats and local grains and vegetables. She was relieved to see that Peter's choices and her own were almost identical. Well, of course; he too had been brought up near Caer Donn and was used to Darkovan food. In every way that really mattered to her he was Darkovan, though his protective coloration was so good, here among the other Terrans. It was a disquieting thought; which one was the real Peter?

He explained, too, why she had had to thrust her identity badge into the slot before releasing the food. "We're entitled to a certain number of meals as an employee; extras are deducted from our pay. Let's find a quiet corner, shall we?"

There were no really quiet corners in the cafeteria, not as she understood the word, but they did find a table for two, and sat down together. Around them were laughing, talking workers, mostly in uniform or the white smocks with the emblem of Medic Services. There was a crew of what looked like road workers, still brushing snow from the heavy parkas they wore over their uniforms. It was not, she thought, so different from supper in the Guild House. She felt, for a moment, fiercely homesick. She thought of Magda, eating her first meal there. Then she looked across at Peter and smiled. No, she was here with Peter and it was where she wanted to be.

But he still looked angry. "Damn it, you've got to wear uniform while you're in the building, Jaelle."

She said stiffly, carefully, "It was explained to me that it creates a problem with the—the machinery. I will—try."

"What's the problem, Jaelle?"

She wondered if she could really make him understand. "It is—is immodest. It makes me look—too much woman."

Was he being deliberately obtuse? He smiled enticingly at her and said, "That's the good part of it, isn't it? Why don't you want to look like a woman?"

"That's not what I meant—" she began, crossly, then broke off. "Why does it matter to you, Piedro? It is my problem, and I must deal with it in my own way. If you wish, I will explain that it has nothing to do with you —that you asked me to, and I refused."

"You can't do that," he said, harried. "I'm working under Montray now, and I'm in enough trouble with him without having him think—" he stopped, but to Jaelle, surprisingly, it was as if he had spoken aloud what was in his mind; *think I can't manage my wife.*

That did make her angry. She said, between clenched teeth, "Why should you think that it reflects on you?"

"Damn it, woman," he burst out. "You're wearing my name! Everything you do reflects on me, whether you mean it to, or not! You're certainly intelligent enough to understand that!"

She stared at him in consternation, knowing that she would never understand. She wanted to get up and walk out of the cafeteria; she wanted to scream at him. She only stared at him, her hands shaking. But before she could move, a voice said behind her, "Peter? I was looking for you. And this must be Jaelle."

A tall, brown-skinned woman, with hair silvered white, picked up a chair and set it down at their table. "May I join you? I was talking to Magda this morning."

Peter's face changed so rapidly that Jaelle began to doubt the evidence of her senses. "Cholayna? I heard on the grapevine that you were here. Jaelle, this was the head of Intelligence school when Mag and I trained there; Cholayna Ares."

The woman had a tray of the synthetics Jaelle had refused at lunch, but she ignored the meat and steaming vegetables on their trays. "May I join you? Or am I breaking in on a private discussion?"

"Please do," Jaelle said. There was nothing she wanted less than to be alone with Peter in this mood. Cholayna put her tray on the table and slid into a seat.

"It's nice to see someone dressed properly for this climate. I understand Magda tried to set an example by wearing clothes that fit the weather here, but those half-headed half-brains in the department couldn't think of anything except their wretched machines. Who's running this show, anyway? Old Russell Montray?" She made a small sound of scorn. "I wish someone in Head Center would show some intelligence and transfer him back to a Space Station; he might manage that and do it quite well. He's not really stupid, you know, he simply has no patience with strange planets and alien customs. I thought the essence of being Coordinator on a Closed Planet was to understand the people and the native culture, so that when they got around to setting up a Legate they would know what kind of person to choose. But Montray seems to have made so many mistakes already that it will take a century or more to smooth out the troubles he has caused. I knew that before I had been on the job three days. Who sent him here? And whatever could they have been thinking?"

"Political pull, I expect," Peter said, "the wrong kind; not where he wanted the job and somebody with clout fixed it for him, but the kind where somebody wanted to get rid of him, pulled strings, and kicked him upstairs—and he wound up here. They may have thought it was isolated enough that he couldn't make much trouble. Typical bureaucratic thinking —let him go make trouble somewhere else."

"Particularly stupid," Cholayna confirmed with a nod. "This planet may not have a great deal of trade potential, but because of its location, it's an important transit point; in twenty or so years, this will be one of the major intersecting spaceports anywhere in the Galaxy. If this fellow Montray has already created trouble with the locals, as it seems, it could take centuries to repair the damage. I've made a start, I hope, by putting Magda on detached duty, to try and analyze how we ought to be treating Darkovans, in contrast to how we *are* treating them. I will want information from you too on that, Jaelle. As for you, Peter, you know you really ought to be working out of my office, not Montray's; I hope he isn't going to make it a status point to keep you there."

Peter muttered something Jaelle knew to be a polite noncommittal social noise, but once again her erratic *laran* carried his thoughts as if he had spoken them aloud.

Not fair, dammit, I spent five years setting things up so that when Darkover got an Intelligence service I'd be at its head, and now some damned woman *walks in and takes over. Bad enough playing second fiddle to Magda. . . .*

She lost the contact then, but she had heard enough to make her look at Peter in dread and dismay. She liked Cholayna, and thought she would like working with her, in spite of the strange color of the woman's skin and her unreadable dark eyes; but if Peter felt this way, what should she do?

Chapter Three

Magda

As the doors of Thendara Guild House swung shut behind her, Magda thought, with a strange, desperate intuition, *I must never look back. Whatever I was before this, I must leave it forever behind me, and look only ahead. . . .*

Around her a great hall arose, panelled in dark woods and hung with curtains which gave an effect of space and air and light. The snub-nosed young girl had opened the door for her, directed her across the hall and said "The Guild Mother Lauria is waiting for you." She looked curiously at Magda, but only shoved her through another door, where the Guild Mother, Lauria n'ha Andrea, head of the Independent Guild of Craftswomen in Thendara, and one of the most powerful women in the city, waited for her. Lauria was a tall, sturdy woman, her gray hair shorn close about her head, one ear bearing an earring with a carved ensign and a crimson stone. She rose and extended her hand to Magda.

"Welcome, my child. You have been told, I know, that this will be your only home for half a year; until two moons past midsummer-day. During this time you will be instructed in our ways, and while you have the freedom of house and garden, you may not step outside the wall nor into the street, except on Midsummer-Festival when all rules are suspended, or under the direct orders of your oath-mother or one of the Guild Mothers." She smiled at Magda and said, "You have shown us that you are willing to honor your oath, even though you took it unwilling; you will promise to keep this rule, will you not? You are a woman grown, and not a child."

"I will obey," said Magda, but it seemed a bleak prospect, half a year, through the long, bitter Darkovan winter, oath-bound not to step outside.

Well, she had wanted this, why should she complain at getting what she wanted?

"Mind you," Mother Lauria said, "this is within reason. Should the house take fire, or some other catastrophe occur, which all Gods forbid, use your own soundest judgment; you are not pledged to lunatic obedience! You are bound to the house only so that you will not be confused by daily meetings with women who live in ways you must learn not to imitate. Do you understand?"

"I think so." They used to call it *deprogramming;* women on Darkover are brainwashed by the social roles expected of them, till it is a miracle that any of them are free enough to rebel and join the Renunciates. She remembered hearing Jaelle say once, *Every Renunciate has her own story and every story is a tragedy.* In such a traditional society as Darkover, only the desperately rebelling would dare break away.

I have rebelled against my home world and my adopted world too . . . but she cut off that thought as self-pity and turned to the older woman, who beckoned her into a chair.

"I suppose you are hungry and weary? But you do not want to face everyone just now in the dining room for the noon meal, do you? I thought not . . ." and she touched a little bell. The snub-nosed girl who had let Magda inside, appeared in the door.

"Bring something from the dining room, for me and for our new sister," she said, and as the little girl went out—she could not, Magda thought, be more than thirteen—Mother Lauria gestured to a chair beside the fireplace —no fire was burning, at this time of year. "Sit down and let us talk awhile; there are decisions to be made."

At the far end of the office was a great wooden door with copper panels; the door was hacked about as if with an axe, and partially burnt. Magda stared at the battered relic, and Mother Lauria followed her eyes.

"It has been here for more than a hundred years," she said. "The wife of a wealthy merchant in Thendara ran away to us, because her husband had ill-used her in ways too gross to repeat, and had finally required her to sleep in the attic and to wait on her husband and his new concubine in her own bed. The woman took oath with us; but her husband hired an army of mercenaries and we were forced to fight; he swore he would raze this house over our heads. Rima—this was her name—offered to return to him; she said she would not be the cause of our deaths. But we were not fighting for her alone, but for the right to live without male sufferance. We fought three days—you can see the marks of the battle."

Magda shivered; the slashed, burnt door looked as if, at one point, an axe had chopped halfway through it.

"And you stood against them?"

"If we had not, neither you nor I should be here," said Lauria. "All Gods grant that one day we shall all enjoy our freedom as of right, without keeping it at sword's point; but until that day we are prepared to defend our rights with the sword. Now, tell me a little more about yourself. I have heard the story from Jaelle, of course. Your name is—" she stumbled over it. "Mak-ta-lin Lor-ran?" She made a wry face. "Will it suit you if you use Jaelle's name for you, Margali?"

"That *is* my name," Magda said. "The name my father and mother gave me; I was born in Caer Donn. I was never called Magda except in the Terran Zone."

"Margali, then. And I see you speak the language of the Hellers, and are fluent in *casta;* can you speak Cahuenga as well?"

"I can," Magda replied in that language, "though my accent is not good."

"Your accent is no worse than any other newcomer to the City. Jaelle has told me you can read and write; is this in Standard only, or in *casta?*"

"I can read and write *casta,"* she said. "For my father was an expert in languages, and he wrote the—" she hesitated, groping for a Darkovan way to explain a dictionary. "A compilation of your language for strangers and foreigners. And my mother was a musician, and made many transcriptions of folk songs and music of the Hellers."

Mother Lauria pushed a pen and a scrap of paper toward her. "Let me see you copy this," she said, and Magda looked at the scroll and began to copy the top line; she recognized the scroll as a poem her mother had set to music. She was not used to Darkovan pens, which were not as smooth as the ones she used for her own work. When she finished, Mother Lauria took the paper in her hand.

"A clumsy hand and girlish," she said severely, "but at least you are not illiterate; many women when they come to us can only spell out their names. You have not the making of a scribe, but I have seen worse."

Magda flushed at this harsh judgment; she felt bruised and offended; she had never been accused of clumsiness in her entire life.

"Let us see what we can do with you, then. You are no scribe. Can you sew? Embroider?"

"No, not even a little," said Magda, remembering her attempt to botch together her trail clothes at Ardais.

"Can you cook?"

"Only for the trail, when traveling."

"Can you weave, or do dyeing?"

"Not even a little."

"Do you know anything of plants and gardening?"

"Even less, I fear."

"Can you ride?"

"Oh, yes, certainly," Magda said, glad to arrive at something which she *could* do.

"Can you saddle your own horse, care for his tack, look after his feed and care? Good; I am afraid we will have to put you to work in the stables," said Mother Lauria. "Do you mind?"

"No, of course not," Magda said. But she had to confess ignorance again when the women asked if she knew anything of farriery, of metal-working and forging, of veterinary medicine, dairying, cheesemaking, animal husbandry or bootmaking, and she had to answer no to all of these things. Mother Lauria looked a little more approving when Magda said that she had been trained in both armed and unarmed combat; but she said thoughtfully "You have a good deal to learn," and Magda guessed that Mother Lauria was as relieved as she was herself when the fair-haired, snub-nosed girl reappeared with trays and jugs.

"Ah, here is our dinner. Set it down here, Doria."

The girl uncovered the tray; a bowl of some kind of baked grain with a sauce of vegetables, mugs of something which tasted like buttermilk, and some sliced fruit, preserved in honey or syrup. She gestured to Magda to help herself, and ate in silence for some time. Finally, as she folded her napkin, she asked, "How old are you?"

Magda assumed she meant Darkovan reckoning, and told her age; only later did she realized that Mother Lauria had been testing to see if she could reckon the difference between the relatively short Terran year and the much longer Darkovan.

"You have been married, Margali? Have you a child?"

Magda shook her head silently. That had been one of the main causes of tension between them, that she had not given Peter the son he wished for.

"Has that marriage been formally dissolved, as I gather you Terrans can do by mutual consent?"

Magda was surprised that Mother Lauria knew this much. "It has. Terran marriage is not quite like Freemate marriage, but it is nearer to that than to the Darkovan *catenas*. We agreed to separate more than a year ago."

"That is fortunate; if you had a child under the age of fifteen, you would be required to make arrangements for its care. We do not allow women to take refuge here if they have obligations outside which have not been met. I assume you have not an aged parent who is dependent on you?"

"No; my mother and father have been dead for many years."

"Have you another lover now?"

Silently Magda shook her head.

"Will it be a great hardship to you, to live without a lover? I suppose, since you and your husband have been separated for some time, you have grown accustomed to sleeping alone; but will it be very difficult for you? Or are you perhaps a lover of women?" She used the very polite term, and Magda was not offended—she supposed that any society composed only of women must attract a certain percentage of those who would rather die or renounce everything than marry. She found this line of questioning uncomfortably personal, but she had promised herself that she would answer everything as honestly as she could. "I do not think I shall find it unendurably painful," and only after she had spoken did she realize how sarcastic it sounded. Mother Lauria smiled and said, "I hope not; but especially during your housebound time, this can be a problem, as anyone but a child would know. Let me think—it is hard to remember what to ask you. Have you been taught methods to prevent the conception of an unwanted child?"

Magda was really shocked now; of course such teaching was routine at puberty for any Terran, male or female, but she had been brought up in Caer Donn and absorbed the Darkovan attitude which considered such things proper only for prostitutes. She said "Yes," but wondered what the older woman must think of her, confessing to such knowledge!

Mother Lauria nodded calmly. "Good. We have the women in the Towers to thank for that; women who work in the matrixes must not risk interrupting their term by an undesired pregnancy, yet it is not possible to require that they remain celibate, sometimes for many years. There is an ancient bond between the women of Neskaya Tower and the Guild of Renunciates, which goes back to the history of the Guild; we were formed, as you may know, in the days of Varzil the Good, from two separate houses of women; the Priestesses of Avarra, who were an order of Healer-priestesses trained in *laran,* and the Sisterhood of the Sword, who were, during the time of the Hundred Kingdoms and the Hastur Wars, a guild of woman soldiers and mercenaries. Some day you shall read this history, of course. The Priestesses of Avarra taught us many things which could be done by any women, including those who had no *laran,* though of course it is easier for those who do. Among the Renunciates, it is criminal to bear a child who is not wanted by mother and father, and for whom no happy home is waiting, so we require this instruction for all our women." She took pity on Magda's embarrassment and said, "Oh, my dear, I am sure you feel foolish, but I must deal with blushes, outraged modesty and outright refusal from women who swear they would rather forswear men entirely. But it is our law; every woman, even those who have never lain down with a man and never intend to do so, must know these things. They need never use them, but they may not remain ignorant. Twice in a tenday, at our house meetings, one of our midwives talks to the younger women.

Are you strong and healthy? Can you do a good day's work without tiring?"

"I've never done a great deal of manual work," Magda said, relieved at the change of subject, "but when I was traveling I could spend all day in the saddle when I must."

"Good; many women who live indoors, doing only women's work, grow sickly for lack of exercise, and we have not so much sunshine here that we can afford to be without it. You may laugh to see grown women playing games and skipping rope like children, but it is not only little girls who need to run about and exercise. I hope you are not too modest to swim when the weather permits?"

"No, I like to swim," Magda said, but wondered when, on frozen Darkover, the weather permitted!

"Are your monthly cycles regular? Do they give you much trouble?"

"Only when I was living offworld," Magda said; she had found them troublesome in the Empire Training School, adjusting to different gravity and light and circadian rhythms; she had been in and out of the Medic office all the time, while she was on the Alpha planet, and had been given hormone shots and various kinds of treatment. Back on Darkover, she had reverted to her usual good health. She explained that, and added, "Before I was sent on this mission—the one of Ardais—I was given treatment by Terran medics to supress ovulation and menstruation; it is fairly routine for women in the field. At Ardais Jaelle asked me about this—she thought I was pregnant."

"That treatment is something we would find priceless," said Mother Lauria. "I hope your Terrans will help us learn it; when women must work alongside men, or travel for a long time in bad weather, it would be a great convenience. Some women have been desperate enough to consider the neutering operation, which is very dangerous. We do have a few drugs which destroy fertility for a period of half a year or more, but they are too strong and dangerous: I do not recommend that any woman use them. But women who have a great deal of trouble with their cycles, or women who have no talent for celibacy and great ease in getting pregnant—well, we elders cannot forbid them that choice. Now there is a very important decision to be made, and you must make it, Margali."

Magda looked at her empty plate. "I will do what I can."

"You saw the little girl who brought in your dinner? Her name is Doria, and she is fifteen; she will take the oath at Midsummer. She has lived among us since she was born, but the law forbids us to instruct girls below legal age in our ways. So that you, and she, will be in training together. You are not of our world, Margali. Yes, I know you were born here, but your people are so different from ours that some things may be strange and hard to endure. I know so little of the Terrans that I cannot even guess what those things may be, but Jaelle came here at twelve from the Dry-Towns and she had many difficulties; and a few years ago we had a woman here from the rain forests far beyond the Hellers. She had courage toward us, and good will, but she was really ill with the shock of finding so many things new and strange. And most of these were little things which we all accepted as ordinary to life; we had never guessed how hard she would find it. We do not want you to suffer in that way, so there are two courses we can take, Margali."

The old woman looked sharply at Magda.

"We can tell all of your sisters here that you are Terran born, and all of us can be alert to help you in small things and make allowances for you. But like all choices, this one would have its price; there would be a barrier between you and your sisters from the beginning, and they might never wholly accept you as one of us. The alternative is to tell them only that you were born in Caer Donn, and let you struggle as best you can with the strangenesses. What do you want to do, Margali?"

I never realized what a snob I was, Magda thought. She had not expected them to understand culture shock, and here Mother Lauria was explaining it to her as if she were not very intelligent. "I will do what you command, my lady."

She had used the very formal *casta* word, *domna,* and Mother Lauria looked displeased.

"First of all, I am not *my lady,*" she said. "We do not free ourselves from the tyranny of titles imposed by men, only to set up another tyranny among ourselves. Call me Lauria, or Mother if you think I deserve it and you wish to. Give me such respect as you would have given your own mother after you were grown out of her command. And I cannot command you in this; it is you who must live by your decision. I cannot even counsel you properly; I know too little of your people and their ways. I am sure that some day, all of us will have to know you are Terran; do you think you can overcome that strangeness? You need not carry that handicap unless you choose; but they might make more allowances for you . . ."

Magda felt doubtful. Jaelle had known she was Terran, and it had certainly helped ease them through some difficulties. Yet, though she and Jaelle had come to love each other, there had been strangeness between them. She said hesitantly, "I will—I will defer to your advice, Lauria, but I think—at first—I would rather be one of you. I suppose all women have strange things to face when they come here."

Lauria nodded. "I think you have chosen rightly," she said. "It might have been easier the other way; but this very ease might have left unresolved some strangenesses you would never settle. And I suppose you do truly want to be one of us—that you are not merely studying us for your Terran records." She smiled as she said it, but Magda detected a faint lift, almost of question in her voice, as if even Mother Lauria doubted her sincerity. Well, she would simply have to prove herself.

Mother Lauria looked at an ancient clock, the kind with hands and some internal mechanism with a swinging pendulum. She rose to her feet.

"I have an appointment in the city," she said, and Magda remembered that this woman was the President of the Guild of Craftswomen. "Since you have no close friend in the house now, I have told the dormitory keepers to give you a room by yourself; later, if you make a friend and wish to share a room with her, there will be time enough to change." Magda was grateful for that; until this moment it had not occurred to her that she might have been thrust into a room filled with two or three other women, all of whom had known one another most of their lives.

Mother Lauria touched the little bell. "You are not afraid to sleep alone, are you? No, I suppose not, but there are women who come to us who have never been alone in their lives, nurses and nannies when they are small, maids and lady-companions when they are older; we have had women go into a screaming panic when they find themselves alone in the dark." She touched Magda's hair lightly and said, "I will see you tonight at dinner. Courage, Margali; live one day at a time, and remember nothing is ever as bad or as good as you think it will be. Now Doria will show you over the house."

Magda wondered, as Mother Lauria went away, *Do I really look that frightened?*

A few minutes later the young girl Doria came back.

"Mother says I am to show you around. Let's pick up the trays and dishes first and take them out to the kitchen."

The kitchen was deserted, except for a small dark-haired woman, drowsing as she waited for two huge bowlfuls of bread dough to rise. She raised her eyes sleepily as Doria introduced Magda to her.

"Margali, this is Irmelin—she is our housekeeper this half-year; we take turns helping her in the kitchen, but there are enough of us living here that no one needs to do kitchen duty more than once in a tenday. Irmelin, this is our new sister, Margali n'ha—what was it, Margali?"

"Ysabet," Magda said.

"I saw you last night," Irmelin said. "You came in with Jaelle—are you her lover?"

Mother Lauria had asked her this too. Reminding herself not to be angry—she was in another world now—she shook her head. "No—her oath-daughter, no more."

"Really?" Irmelin asked, obviously skeptical, but she only looked at the bread dough. "It won't have risen enough to knead for another hour—shall I help you show her around the house?"

"Mother Lauria told me to do it—you can stay in the kitchen and keep warm," Doria laughed. "We all know that is why you volunteered to keep house this term, so you could sit by the fire like a cat." Irmelin only chuckled, and Doria added, "Do you need anything from the greenhouse for supper, fresh vegetables, anything? Margali has no duties yet, she can help me fetch it."

"You might ask if there are any melons ripe," Irmelin said. "I think we are all tired of stewed fruit and want something fresh." Irmelin yawned and looked drowsily at the bread dough again, and Doria went out, fanning herself vigorously with her apron, pulling Magda after her.

"Phew, I hate the kitchen on baking days, it's too hot to breathe! But Irmelin makes good bread—it's surprising how many women can't make bread that's fit to eat. Remind me to tell you sometime about the time when Jaelle took her turn as housekeeper, and Gwennis and Rafaella threatened to dump her out naked in the next blizzard if she didn't get someone else to make the bread—" Doria chattered on, still fanning herself. It was certainly not too hot in the drafty corridor between kitchen and the long dining room where she had sat last night, a stranger, hiding in Jaelle's shadow. And now it was her home for half a year, at least. There were long tables which would, Magda supposed, seat forty or fifty women, piled at one end, stacks of plates and bowls, covered with towels, awaiting the evening. Behind the dining hall was a greenhouse—the inevitable feature of most homes in Thendara—with solar collectors, and a woman wearing a huge overall wrap, kneeling in the dirt and patting soil around the roots of some plant Magda did not recognize. She was a big woman, with curly, almost frizzy straw-colored hair, her fingers grubby with soil.

"Rezi, this is Margali n'ha Ysabet, Jaelle's oath-daughter. Irmelin asked me if there was any fresh fruit for tonight."

"Not tonight or tomorrow," said Rezi, "but perhaps after that; I have a few berries for Byrna—"

"Why should Byrna have them when there are not enough for us all?" demanded Doria, and Rezi chuckled. Her accent was coarse and country; she looked like one of the peasant women Magda had seen in the Kilghard hills, working in field or byre.

"Marisela ordered it; when you're pregnant you'll get the first berries too," Rezi said, laughing.

Doria giggled and said, "I'll make do with stewed fruit!"

They went on through the greenhouse, into the stable where half a dozen horses were kept with several empty stalls; a barn behind, clean and whitewashed with a pleasant smell of hay, held about half a dozen milk animals, and a small dairy where, Doria informed her, they made all their own butter and cheese. Shining wooden molds, well-scrubbed, hung on the wall, but again, the place was deserted. A winter garden, with scattered straw banking some buried root vegetables, looked bleak and chilly. Magda was shivering; Doria said, surprised, "Are you cold?" She herself had not even bothered to pull her shawl about her shoulders. "I thought you were from Caer Donn; it doesn't seem cold at all, not to me. But we can go inside," she agreed, and led the way through a huge room which she called the armory—there were weapons hanging on the walls—but which looked to Magda more like a gymnasium, with mats on the floors and a sign reading, in very evenly printed *casta: Leave your shoes neatly at the side; someone could fall over them.* There was a small changing room at the side, with towels and odd garments hanging on hooks, which reminded Magda of the Recreation Building in Unmarried Women's Headquarters. Behind it was a larger room filled, to Magda's amazement, with steam, and hidden in the steam, a pool of apparently hot water. She had heard that there were many private houses in Thendara located over hot springs, but this was the first time she had seen it. Another sign read *Please be courteous to other women; wash your feet before entering pool.*

"This was built only four or five years ago," said Doria. "One of our rich patrons had it built in the house; before that, we had only the tubs on the dormitory floors! It's very good after unarmed-combat lessons, to soak out the bruises! Rafi and Camilla are wonderful teachers, but they are rough on anyone they suspect of slacking! I've had lessons since I was eight years old, but Rafi is my oath-mother *and* my foster-mother, and she doesn't like to teach me. Come, let's go upstairs," she added, and they went along another corridor to the stairs. "Here is the nursery at the top of the landing—there is no one in it now except Felicia's little boy, and he will leave us in another moon; no male child over five may live in the Guild House. But Byrna will have a baby in another month," she said, opening the door to the room, where a small boy was playing with some toy horses on a rug before the fire, and a young woman, sewing on something, sat in an armchair.

"How are you today, Byrna? This is Margali n'ha Ysabet, she is new—"

"I saw her last night at supper," Byrna said, while Magda wondered if every woman in the house had noticed her. She rose restlessly, pacing the room. "I'm tired of dragging around like this, but Marisela said it would be at least another tenday, perhaps a whole moon. Where is Jaelle? I had hardly a minute to speak with her last night!"

Magda realized again how popular her friend must be. "She is working in the Terran Trade City."

Byrna made a face. "Among the *Terranan?* I thought that was against the Guild House laws!" The tone of her voice made Magda realize how wise she had been to conceal her identity. She knew in general terms of the prejudice against Terrans but had never encountered it at close range before. Byrna asked, "What is your House, sister?" and Magda replied, "This one, I suppose—I am here for half a year training—"

"Well, I hope you will be happy here," Byrna said. "I'll try to help make you welcome when this is over—" she patted her bulging belly.

Doria jeered. "Maybe *next* Midsummer you'll sleep alone!"

"Damn right," said Byrna, and Magda mentally filed that away with what Mother Lauria had told her about contraceptives. "Where is she going to sleep, Doria? In your room?"

Doria giggled. "There are five of us in there already. Mother Lauria said she's to have Sherna's room while Sherna's in Nevarsin." She led Magda along the hallway, pushing open the door of a room with half a dozen beds. She said "We got permission this year for all of us to share—Mother Millea said we could all room together if we promised to be quiet so others could have their sleep. We have a lot of fun. Here are the baths—" she pushed a door, showing a room with tubs and sinks, "and here is where you put your laundry, and here is the sewing room, if anything needs mending and you can't do it yourself. And this is Sherna's room—yours now; she and Gwennis shared it for two years, then Gwennis moved in with her friend—" She gave the word the inflection which made it also mean *lover*. Well, that must be commonplace enough, Irmelin had asked it about her, casually, and gone on to make a comment about the bread dough!

Doria pointed to a bundle on the bed. "Mother Lauria arranged with the sewing room to find you some spare clothes—nightgowns, undertunics, and a set of work clothes if you have to work in the garden or stable. I think most of them were Byrna's—she is so pregnant now that she can't wear any of her clothes, but by the time she has her baby and needs them back, you'll have made your own."

Well, thought Magda, looking at the clothes on the bed, they were sparing no pains to make her feel welcome; they had even included a comb and hairbrush, and some extra wool socks, as well as a warm fleecy thing she presumed was a bathrobe; it was fur-lined and looked luxurious. The room was simply furnished with a narrow bed, a small carved-wood chest, and a low bench with a bootjack.

Doria stood watching her. "You know that you and I are to take training together? But you are so much older than I—how did you come to the Amazons?"

Magda told as much of the truth as she could. She said "A kinsman of mine was held to ransom by the bandit Rumal di Scarp; there was no one but I to ransom him, so I went alone, and wore Amazon dress to protect myself on the road; when I met with Jaelle's band on the road I was discovered and forced to take the oath."

Doria's eyes widened. "But I heard—was that *you?* It is like a romance! But I heard that Jaelle's oath-daughter had been sent to Neskaya! Camilla told us, when she came back after escorting Sherna and Devra to Nevarsin, and bringing Maruca and Viviana home—that must be why Irmelin thought you were Jaelle's lover, that you had come here on purpose to be with Jaelle! But Jaelle is working now in the Terran Zone, isn't she?"

Magda decided she had answered enough questions. "How did you come to the Amazons so young, Doria?"

"I was fostered here," Doria answered. "Rafaella's sister is my mother —you know Rafaella, don't you? Jaelle's partner—"

"I have not yet met her; but Jaelle has told me about her."

"Rafaella is a kinswoman of Jaelle's foster-mother Kindra. Rafi bore three children, but they were all boys. The third time, she and her sister were pregnant at the same time—and the father of Rafi's child was my father, you see? So when Rafi had another boy, my mother wanted a son, so they traded the children for fosterage; Rafaella's baby was brought up as my mother's son and my father's—which of course he *is*—and Rafaella took me, when I was not three days old, and nursed me and everything, here in the Guild House. I am really Doria n'ha Graciela, but I call myself Doria n'ha Rafaella, because Rafi is the only mother I ever really knew."

Magda was furiously making mental notes. She knew that sisters frequently shared a lover or even a husband, and that fosterage was common, but this arrangement still seemed bizarre to her.

"But I am standing here chattering instead of telling you what you ought to know. Some years we each look after our own rooms, but this year in House meeting we chose to have two women from our corridor sweep the floors every day and mop them every tenday. You must keep your boots and sandals in your chest, it is hard on the sweepers to have to sweep around and over them, so anything lying on the floor, they will pick up and throw in a big barrel in the hall and you will have to hunt for them. Do you play the harp or the ryll or the lute? Too bad; Rafi has been wishing for another musician in the house. Byrna sings well, but now she is short of breath all the time—I thought when I grew up to have no ear for music that Rafi would disown me! She has—" Doria broke off as a bell in the lower part of the house began to ring.

"Oh, merciful Goddess!"

"What is that, Doria? Not the dinner-bell already?"

"No" whispered Doria, "That bell is rung only when some woman comes to take refuge with us; sometimes it does not ring twice in a year, and now we have two newcomers in one day? Come, we must go down at once!"

She pulled Magda hastily toward the stairs and they ran down together. Magda, hurrying behind her, felt a curious little prickle which she had come to know as premonition; *this is something very important to me. . . .* but dismissed it, as anxiety born of Doria's excitement, and the stress of so many new things happening to her. Irmelin stood in the hallway, with Mother Lauria, and between them a frail-looking woman, bundled in heavy shawls and cumbered with heavy skirts. She stood swaying, clutching at the railing as if she were about to faint.

Mother Lauria looked about the women gathering quickly in the hall; many of the women Magda had seen last night at dinner, but she did not know their names. Then she turned to the fainting newcomer. "What do you ask here?" Somehow, Magda felt, the words had the force of ritual. "Have you come to seek refuge?"

The woman whispered faintly "Yes."

"Do you ask only shelter, my sister? Or is your will to take the oath of a Renunciate?"

"The oath—" the woman whispered. She swayed, and Mother Lauria gestured to her to sit down.

"You are ill; you need answer no questions at present, my sister." She looked around at the women in the hallway, and her glance singled out Magda and Doria where they stood at the foot of the stairs.

"You two are new-come among us; you three will be together in training, should this woman take oath, so I choose you as her oath-sisters, and —" She looked around, evidently searching for someone. At last she beckoned.

"Camilla n'ha Kyria," she said, and Magda saw, with a curious sense of inevitability, the tall, thin *emmasca* who had witnessed her oath to Jaelle. "Camilla, you three take her away, cut her hair, make her ready to take the oath if she is able."

Camilla came and put her arm around the strange woman, supporting the frail, swaying body. "Come with me, sister," she said, "Here, lean on me—" she spoke in the impersonal inflection, but her voice was kind. She suddenly saw Magda, and her face lighted. "Margali! Oath-sister, is it you? I thought you had gone to Neskaya! You must tell me all about it," she said, "but later; for now we must help this woman. Here—" she gestured, "put your arm under hers; she cannot walk—"

Magda put her arm around the apparently fainting woman, but the woman flinched and cried out, in a weak voice, drawing away from the touch. Camilla led her into a little room near Mother Lauria's office, and lowered her into a soft chair.

"Have you been ill-used?" she asked, and took away the shawl, then cried out in dismay.

The woman's dress—expensively cut, of richly dyed woolen cloth trimmed in fur—was cut to ribbons, and the blood had soaked through, turning the cloth to clotted black through which crimson still oozed.

Camilla whispered, "Avarra protect us! Who has done this to you?" But she did not wait for an answer. "Doria, run to the kitchen, bring wine and hot water and fresh towels! Then see if Marisela is in the house, or if she has gone out into the city to deliver a child somewhere. Margali, come here, help me get these things off her!"

Magda came, helping Camilla get off the cut and slashed tunic, gown, underlinen; they were all finely cut and embroidered with copper threads; she wore an expensive copper-filigree butterfly clasp in her fair hair. Magda stood by, helping and holding things, as Camilla bared the woman to the waist, sponged the dreadful cuts; what could possibly have inflicted them? The woman endured their ministrations without crying out, though they must have been hurting terribly; when they had done, Camilla put a light shift on her, tying the drawstrings loosely around her neck, and covered her with a warm robe. Doria came back, troubled, reporting that Marisela was not in the house.

"Then find Mother Millea," Camilla ordered, "and Domna Fiona. She is a judge in the City Court, and we must make a sworn statement about this woman's condition, so that we may legally give her shelter. She is not strong enough to take the oath; we must put her to bed, and have her nursed—"

The woman struggled upright. "No," she whispered, "I want to take the oath—to be here by right, not by charity—"

Magda whispered, more to herself than to anyone else, "But what has happened to her! What could have inflicted such wounds—"

Camilla's face was like stone. "She has been beaten like an animal," the *emmasca* said. "I have scars much like those. Child—" she bent over the woman lying in the chair, "I know what it is to be ill-used. Margali—you will find scissors in the drawer of the table." And as Magda put them into her hand, Camilla asked, "What is your name?"

"Keitha—" the word was only a whisper.

"Keitha, the laws require that you must show your intent by cutting a single lock of your hair; if you have the strength to do this, I will do the rest for you."

"Give me—the scissors." She sounded resolute, but her fingers hardly had strength to grasp them. She struggled to get them into her hands. She grabbed a lock of her hair, which had been arranged in two braids, and fumbled to cut it; struggled hard with the scissors, but had not the strength to cut through the braid. She gestured, whispering "Please—"

At the gesture Camilla unraveled the braid, and Keitha snipped fiercely, chopping off two ragged handfuls of hair. "There!" she said wildly, tears starting from her eyes. "Now—let me take the oath—"

Camilla held a cup of wine to her lips. "As soon as you are strong enough, sister."

"No! *Now* . . ." Keitha insisted; then her hands released the scissors, which slitherd softly to the floor, and she fell back, unconscious, into Camilla's arms.

Mother Lauria said quietly, "Take her upstairs," and Magda, following Camilla's soft command, helped Camilla to carry the unconscious woman up the stairway and into an empty room.

Chapter Four

The waterhole lay dark, oozing black mud and darker shadows; but behind the rocks, the crimson sun was rising. She was old enough to know what was happening on the other side of the fire, she was twelve years old, and in Shainsa a girl of twelve was old enough to be chained, old enough to be near at hand in the birthing rooms. But these women with unchained hands, these Amazons, they had sent her away as if she was only a child herself. Beyond the fire, in the growing sunrise, she could hear her mother's voice, feel the pain thrusting through her own body like knives, see the carrion birds circling lower and lower as the sun rose; and now the sunlight was like the blood poured out on the sands, like the stabbing feel of knives and her mother's anguish, pouring through her body and her mind . . .

Jaelle! Jaelle, it was worth it all, you are free, you are free. . . . but her hands were chained, and she was struggling, screaming, crying out. . . .

"Hush, love, hush . . ." and Peter was patiently untangling her flailing hands from the bedclothes, cradling her in his arms. "It's only a nightmare, it's all right—"

Only another nightmare. Another. God above, she's been having them every night. I don't know what to do for her.

Jaelle squirmed away from him, not quite sure why, only knowing that she did not want to be too close just now. She sought his face, frowning, troubled, for the hostility she could not find in his gentle voice.

"Kyril—" she muttered. "No. For a moment I thought you—you were my cousin Kyril—"

He laughed softly. "That would give anybody nightmares, I guess. Here, count my fingers. Only five." He pressed his hand against hers and she smiled faintly at the old joke between them. He was so like her cousin, Kyril Ardais, save for the six-fingered hands Kyril had inherited from his mother, Lady Rohana.

Kyril's hands, fumbling about her all that summer, until she had finally, sobbing with wrath and humiliation, had to use on him the Amazon training which made a trained Renunciate almost impossible to dominate. A Renunciate, they used to say, can be killed, but never raped.

For Rohana's sake she had not wanted to hurt him. . . .

"Honey, are you all right?" Peter asked. "Should I go and get a Medic? You've been having these nightmares every night . . . how long is it now? Ten days, eleven?"

She tried to focus on his words. They seemed to have some strange echo that ached in the palms of her hands, reverberated in her sinuses. The edges of the room seemed to be outlined with fuzzy lights, swelling up and shrinking and swelling again to loom over her. Her eyes hurt, and she jumped up with a wavering surge of nausea, dashing for the bath. The retching spasms shattered the last remnants of dream; she could not remember now what she had been dreaming, except for a curious taste and smell of blood in her mouth. She swallowed the flat sickly water from the shower, trying in vain to rinse it away, and Peter, troubled, went into the refreshment console and dialled her some kind of cool drink. He held it to her lips.

"I *am* going to take you to a Medic tomorrow, love," he said, watching her finish the drink, which bubbled and stung her lips; when she put it away he shook his head.

"Finish it, it will settle your stomach. Better?" He examined the headset on the pillow; somehow she had torn it loose in the dream. "There must be something wrong with the language program they gave you, or the D-alpha is out of synch—that can mess up your balance centers," he mused, holding it. "Or maybe it just stirred up something in your subconscious. Take it up to Medic tomorrow, and ask them to adjust it on the EEG file they have for you." He might, she thought distantly, just as well have been speaking in some language from another Galaxy; she didn't know what he was talking about and didn't care. He held the earpiece to his temple, shrugged. "It sounds all right to me, but I'm no expert. Come on back to bed, sweetheart."

"Oh no," she said, without thinking, "I'm not sleeping under that damned thing again!"

"But, love, it's just a machine," he said, "even if it is out of adjustment, it won't really hurt you. Baby, don't be unreasonable," he added, his arm around her shoulders, "You're not some ignorant native, from out in—oh, the Dry Towns—to get all shaky, just at a piece of machinery, are you?"

He pulled her down on the pillow. "None of us could get along without the sleep-learner tapes."

They lay down again, but Jaelle only dozed fitfully, trying to hear the soft words of the sleeplearner consciously, so that she would not sink again into the morass of nightmare. They had become constant; maybe there was something wrong with the machine? But the nightmares, she remembered, had started before she had brought home the tapes for the machine Piedro called a D-alpha corticator. She would have liked to blame it all on the machine, but she was afraid that was not possible.

Some time before the alarm was due to ring, he woke sleepily, moved it so it would not interrupt them, and began softly caressing her. Still more than half asleep, she yielded herself to this comfort which had become so central to her life and being; she let herself rise with him, as if flying above the world, soaring without gravity or bonds; held tightly in his arms, she shared the delight he knew in possessing her, binding her close with his passion. She had never been closer to him; she reached out blindly to be closer still, closer, seeking that last unknown which would actually merge them into one another's mind and flesh. . . .

My flesh. My woman. My son, immortality. . . . mine, mine, mine. . . .

It was not words. It was not feeling alone. It lay deeper than that, further into the base of the mind, at the very depths and foundation of the masculine self. Jaelle did not have the education to speak in the language of the Towers, about the layers of conscious and unconscious mind, masculine and feminine polarity; she could only sense it directly, deep in nerves long denied such awareness. She only knew that what was happening was making things come alive in her body and mind that were not sexual at all, and were quite at variance with what was going on. And some isolated, uncommitted fragment of herself rebelled, in words from the Amazon Oath:

I will give myself only in my own time and season. . . . I will never earn my bread as the object of any man's lust . . . I swear I will bear no child to any man for house or heritage, clan or inheritance, pride or posterity. . . .

Or pride. . . . or pride. . . . or pride. . . .

And at the very moment when she was ready to rip herself from his arms, tear herself away from what had once been the greatest delight in the world, something within her body, deep in a part not subject to conscious will, told her, *no, not now, nothing will happen . . .*

She did not move or draw away from him; she simply lay quietly, not responding, yet too well bred to rouse a man and leave him unsatisfied. But whatever had been binding them together had withdrawn; he was still holding her, caressing her, but slowly, the desire in him ebbed as her own had done, and he lay looking at her, baffled and dismayed. She felt herself hurting inside at the trouble in his eyes.

"Oh, Piedro, I'm sorry!" she cried, at the very moment he released her, murmuring "Jaelle, I'm sorry—"

She drew a long breath, burying her head in his bare shoulder. "It wasn't your fault. I guess it's just not—not the right time."

"And you were already feeling rotten, with all the nightmares," he said, generously ready to make for her the excuses she could not offer for herself; she knew it, and pain stabbed at her again. He got up, and went to fetch a couple of self-heating containers. "Look what I got for us; I know a fellow on the kitchen staff. Coffee; just what you need at this hour." He pulled the tab for hers, and handed it to her, steaming. It was hot, anyhow, and the taste didn't seem to matter. As she sipped it, he nuzzled her neck.

"You're so beautiful. I love your hair when it's this long. Don't ever cut it again, all right?"

She smiled and patted his cheek, still rough where he had not yet shaved. "How would you feel if I asked you to wear a beard?"

"Oh, come *on,*" he said, appalled, "You wouldn't do that, would you?"

She laughed softly. "I only meant I wouldn't ask it, love, it's your face. And it's *my* hair."

"Oh, hell!" He rolled away from her, looking stubborn. "Don't I have any rights, woman?"

"Rights? In *my* hair?" It touched the same raw nerve that the moment of deep seeing into his pride had touched; she set her lips and pushed the coffee away. She looked deliberately at the clock face and asked "Do you want to shower first?"

He rolled out and headed toward the bath, while she sat holding her head, trying to focus her eyes on the coffee containers and the wisps of steam that still leaked from them.

The room seemed to be pulsing, getting smaller and larger, higher now, then pressing down on her head. *Something,* she thought, *is wrong with me.* Peter, coming from the shower, saw her bending over, holding her head, fighting the compelling sickness to which she refused to give way.

"Honey, are you all right?" And then, with a smile of concerned pleasure, "Jaelle, you don't suppose—are you pregnant?"

No. It was like a message from deep within her body. She snapped. "Of course not," and went to dress. But he hovered near, saying "You can't be sure—hadn't you better check with the Medic anyhow?" and she thought, *how am I so sure?*

I refuse to be sick today, I simply won't give in to it.

She said, "I have a report to finish," and got out of bed. As she forced herself to move, the dizziness receded, and the world became solid again.

She was accustomed, by now, to the Terran uniform, the long tights which were astonishingly warm for such thin material, the close-cut tunic. Peter, smelling of soap and the fresh uniform cloth, came to hug her, murmur something reassuring, and dash off.

He wasn't like this at Ardais, she thought fuzzily, and put that away in her mind to think about when it would be less disturbing.

She had long finished the reporting of her trip to Ardais and was working now in Magda's old office in Communications, doing work she considered pointless, upgrading a standard dictionary—that was what Bethany called it—of Darkovan idioms. At least she wasn't working with the damnable sleep-learner-tapes, though she imagined that the work would be transferred eventually to such a tape.

I wonder if the sleep-learner—what did Peter call it, D-alpha corticator—is what's giving me these nightmares? Even he suggested that was a possibility! I'm never going to use it again—I'll sleep on the floor if I have to!

But she worked on conscientiously, upgrading outdated idioms and slang popular in her own childhood, recalling commonplace terms and vulgar language more common than the extremely polite ones. Well, this dictionary had been compiled—she remembered—by Magda's father, years ago in Caer Donn. No one would have used vulgar idiom in front of a learned scholar who was, moreover, an alien. But there were phrases she knew that she would blush to include on a language program to be used before men; furthermore, she was a little doubtful if these particular idioms were ever used among women, except in the Guild Houses.

The fact is, she thought, and wondered why it depressed her, *I do not really know how ordinary women talk, except for Lady Rohana. I went so young to the Guild House as Kindra's fosterling!*

Well, she would do what she could, as well as she could, and that was all they could rationally expect of her. She was not fully aware that she was stiff with resentment at the unaccustomed uniform, the collar-tab which held the throat-microphone so that she was, for all practical purposes, wired into their machines, the tights which made her legs feel naked. Nakedness would not have bothered her at all, inside the Guild House with her sisters, but in an office where men came through now and again—though, admittedly, not very often—she felt exposed, and tried to pretend that her desk and consoles could conceal her from them. Once a man walked past her desk—not anyone she knew, an anonymous technician who had come to do something mysterious at Bethany's terminal, pulling out wires and odd-looking slats and peculiar things.

So that's Haldane's Darkovan squaw. Lucky man. What legs. . . .

She looked up and gave the man a blistering glare before she realized that he had said nothing aloud. Her face burning, she lowered her eyes and pretended that he wasn't there at all. All her life she had been plagued with this intermittent *laran* that came and went with no control, forcing itself into her consciousness when she had no wish or will to know what was in another's mind, and often as not, failing her when it would have been priceless. An unwelcome thought intruded on her now, but it was one of her own:

Was I truly reading Peter's mind this morning, is that how he sees me?

No. I was sick, hallucinating. I promised him I'd see the Medic. I'd better go now and arrange it. When the technician had gone, she asked Bethany:

"How do I arrange to see someone in Medic?"

"Just go up there, on your meal break, or after work," Bethany told her. "Someone will make time to see you. What's the matter? Sick?"

"I'm not sure," Jaelle said, "Maybe it's the—the corticator; Peter said it could give me nightmares like that."

Bethany nodded without interest. "If it's not adjusted properly it can do that. Don't bother Medic with it; take the unit up to Psych and they'll adjust it. But if the headaches or nightmares keep up, you probably ought to see a Medic. Or if you're pregnant or something like that."

"Oh, no," said Jaelle promptly, then wondered, *how did she know, why was she so sure?* Maybe she had better check out the Medic after all. She would go on her meal break—she wasn't hungry and the kind of food she could get at the cafeteria at lunchtime wasn't the kind she would regret missing.

But shortly before the time when they left their desks for the meal, there was a curious beeping noise from her desk console. She stared, wondering if she had broken something, if she would have to summon back that technician who had looked at her so offensively.

"Bethany—"

"Answer your page call, Jaelle—" she saw that Jaelle did not understand, and said, "My fault, I forgot to show you. Push that button there— that round white thing that's blinking."

Wondering why they called it a button—it would certainly be hard to sew it on a coat or tunic—Jaelle gingerly touched the pulsing light.

"Mrs. Haldane?" The voice was unfamiliar and quite formal. "Cholayna Ares, Intelligence. Could you come up to my office? Perhaps you would be willing to have lunch with me; I would like to talk with you."

Jaelle already knew enough about Terran speech patterns to know that the words, framed as a polite request, were actually a command, and that there was no question of refusal. She was in Magda's place; the woman she had met last night in Peter's company was Magda's superior officer—at least that was one way of describing it—and therefore Jaelle's as well. She said, trying to tailor her words to Terran forms of politeness, "I should be pleased; I'll be there at once."

"Thank you," said Cholayna's voice, and the light blinked off.

Bethany raised her eyebrows.

"Wonder what *she* wants? I'd surely like to know how she wangled this post out of Head Center! Intelligence, for heaven's sake, when she couldn't go into the field anywhere on this planet! Of course, all she has to do is sit in her office and boss everybody around like a spider in the middle of her web, but an Intelligence officer ought to be able to blend into the scenery, and she'll never be able to do that here! Of course, Head Center may have forgotten what a freak this planet is, and I'll bet anything Cholayna didn't know when she put in for transfer here—"

"I don't think I quite understand," Jaelle said, wondering if she ought to be offended, "Why is this planet such a freak?"

"It's one of the half-dozen or so Empire planets which were settled entirely by a homogeneous group, colonists from one ethnic area," Bethany said. "And though there may have been a few blacks, orientals or what have you on the original ship's crew, genetic drift and interbreeding lost those traits a thousand years before the Empire rediscovered you. A planet with 100 percent white population is rarer than a hen hatched out with teeth!"

Jaelle thought about that for a moment. Yes, she had noticed Cholayna's bark-brown skin and bright brown eyes, but she had simply believed that perhaps the woman had nonhuman blood; there were tales in the mountain of crossbreeds with trailmen or even catmen now and then, though the *kyrri* and *cralmacs* did not, of course, interbreed with humans. "But in the Ages of Chaos," she added, explaining this, "humans were often artificially interbred with *cralmacs;* I simply thought she was only part human, that's all."

"Don't let Cholayna hear you say that," Bethany said, with a shocked grimace. "In the Empire, calling someone half-human is the dirtiest—not the second dirtiest—thing you can say to them, believe me."

Jaelle started to express her shock—what disgusting prejudice!—but then she remembered that among ignorant peoples, even here, there were certain prejudices against nonhumans, and there was no accounting for custom and taboo. *Don't try to buy fish in the Dry Towns.* She held her peace, wondering why, with the vaunted Empire medical technology, they had not discovered or rediscovered this technique and why they did not make use of it.

She said "I had better go up to the Intelligence Office. No, thank you, I can find the way myself."

Cholayna made Jaelle comfortable in a soft chair, and ordered up lunch for her from the console, which seemed to have more choices than the lunch cafeteria.

"I haven't had much chance to talk to anyone Darkovan," she said frankly, "and I know that on this planet I won't be able to do field work; so I have to depend on my field agents. I'm here to organize an Intelligence department, not to work in it. I'll have to depend on you, and on anyone else here who knows the planet and grew up in the field. I didn't want to lose Magda Lorne, but I wasn't given the choice. I want to feel I can rely on you, Mrs. Haldane, as I would have relied on Magda. I hope we can be friends."

Jaelle put a fork into her food before replying. She had never known a woman who was neither the property of some man, nor yet a Renunciate. At last she said, "If you want to be my friend, you can start by not calling me *Mrs. Haldane.* Peter and I are not married *di catenas* and the Renunciate's Oath forbids that I shall wear any man's name—though I can't seem to make Records understand that."

"I'll try and have it fixed," Cholayna said, and Jaelle could see the woman's lively brown eyes absorbing the information. "What should I call you, then?"

"I am Jaelle n'ha Melora. Should we truly come to be friends, my sisters in the Guild House call me *Shaya.*"

"Jaelle, then, for the moment," said Cholayna, and Jaelle noted with appreciation that she did not hurry to use the intimate name. "I was Magda's friend as well as her teacher, I think. And there is a good deal you can do for us here; I am sure you know that we have agreed to train a group of young women in Medic; perhaps you can make it easier for them among us. You are the first, you know."

Jaelle smiled. "But I am not, of course. Two of my Guild sisters worked on the Spaceport when you were building it."

Cholayna said, surprised, "Our employment rolls show no sign of Darkovan women employed—"

Jaelle laughed. "They were both *emmasca*—neutered; you probably thought them men, and of course they would have taken men's names. They wished to see what your people were like, who had come from beyond the stars," Jaelle said. She forbore to add that what they had told, in the Guild House, had been the subject of many jokes, some vulgar.

Cholayna laughed softly. "I should have known that while we were studying you, you would be studying us in return. I will not ask you what you thought of us. Neither of us knows the other well enough for that, not yet."

Jaelle was pleasantly surprised. This was truly the first Empire subject she had met who did not jump to unjustified conclusions about Darkovan culture. Perhaps Cholayna was the first truly educated Terran she had met, except for Magda, who was more Darkovan than Terran.

"Are you sure you have had enough to eat? More coffee? You are sure?" Cholayna asked, and at Jaelle's refusal, shoved the dishes into the disposal unit, and took up a cassette from her desk. Jaelle recognized her own writing on the label; it was the report she had made up about Peter's ransom and their winter at Ardais. One with Peter's familiar label was beside it.

"I see from this," she said, "that you were born in the Dry Towns, and lived there until you were almost twelve years old."

Jaelle wondered suddenly if the lunch she had eaten had contained something poisonous to her; her stomach heaved, reminding her that she had intended to go and see the Medic. She said curtly, "I left Shainsa when I was twelve and have never returned. I know very little of the Dry Towns: I have even forgotten the dialect of Shainsa and speak it like any stranger."

Cholayna looked at her silently for a long moment. Then she said, "Twelve years is long enough. At twelve, a child is formed—socially, sexually, the personality is fully created and cannot really be changed thereafter. You are far more a product of the Dry Towns than you are, for instance, a product of the Renunciate's Guild House."

Jaelle caught her breath, not knowing whether the flooding emotion was rage, dismay or simple disbelief. She found herself actually on her feet, every muscle tensed.

"How dare you?" she almost spat the words at Cholayna, "You have no right to say that!"

Cholayna blinked, but did not give ground before the flood of fury. "Jaelle, my dear, I wasn't speaking of you personally, of course; I was simply restating one of the best established facts of human psychology; if you took it as a personal attack, I am sorry. Whether we like it or not, it's a fact; the earliest impressions made on our minds are the lasting ones. Why should it trouble you so much to think that you might be basically a product of Dry-Town culture? Remember, I know very little about it, and there is very little about it in the HQ files; I must rely on you to tell me. What did I say to make you so angry?"

Jaelle drew a long breath and discovered that her jaw was aching behind her clenched teeth. At last she said "I—I did not mean to attack you personally, either. I—" and she had to stop again and swallow and unclench her teeth; if she had been wearing a dagger, she realized, she would have drawn it, and perhaps, before she thought, used it, too. *Why did I explode like that?* The rage slowly drained from her, leaving bewilderment behind.

"You must be mistaken, in this case at least. If I were a product of the Dry Towns, I should be a—a chattel, as women are there; chained, some man's property; a woman unchained is a scandal—she must bear the mark of some man's ownership. I swore the Renunciate's oath as soon as I was old enough, and I have—have forgotten—everything I have done since I left the Dry Towns has been a way of—"

She stopped, her voice trailing into silence, completing in her mind, *a way of proving to myself that I would never wear chains for any man. . . . Kindra said once to me that most women, and most men too, believe themselves free and weight themselves with invisible chains . . .*

Cholayna brushed her hand absently over her silver-white hair. "If everything you have done since you left the Dry Towns has been a way of proving that you were not one of them, then, whether you live by their precepts or no, they have formed everything you have done. If they had left no influence on you, you would have chosen your way without thinking whether it was their way or the reverse—wouldn't you?"

Jaelle muttered "I suppose so." She was still carefully breathing, forcing herself to relax, to unclench her fists.

Cholayna added, casually, "I know little of the Renunciates, either. You spoke of the Oath, and so did Magda, but I know nothing of it. Is it a secret, or can you tell me what a Renunciate, a Free Amazon, swears?"

Jaelle said tiredly. "The oath is not secret. I will gladly tell you." She began "From this day henceforth I swear—"

"Wait—" Cholayna lifted a hand. "May I turn on a recording device for the records?"

There was that word again! But what was the point in arguing? It was, perhaps, the only way to make the Guild House comprehensible to an outsider. She said, "Certainly," and waited.

"From this day I renounce the right to marry save as a freemate; no man shall bind me *di catenas* and I will dwell in no man's house as a *barragana,*" she began, and steadily recited the Oath from beginning to end. How could Cholayna believe that she, if she were truly, as the woman said, a product formed by the Dry-Town culture, without hope of change in personality or sexuality or will, could have freely chosen the Oath? Ridiculous, on the face of it!

Cholayna listened quietly, nodding once or twice at some provision or other.

"This is, of course, not strange to me," she said, "for in the Empire, and particularly on the Alpha planet where I grew up, it was taken for granted that women had these rights and responsibilities; although we also admit," she said with a faint smile, "that the father of a child also has rights and responsibilities in determining care and upbringing. Some day, if you wish,

I should like to discuss this with you at length. Also, I can see why it was that the Free Amazons—forgive me, the Renunciates—were the first Darkovan women to seek to learn from the Terrans. I have two things to ask of you. The first is that you should visit Magda in the Guild House and talk with her about choosing suitable women as candidates for Medic training—or whatever else seems suitable."

"That will be my pleasure," Jaelle said formally, but her mind ran counterpoint, *If she thinks I will help to persuade our women to act as Intelligence spies, she may think again.*

"Jaelle, what was your work among the—the Renunciates? What sort of work do they do?"

"Any honest work," Jaelle said, "Among us there are bakers, cheesemakers, midwives—oh, yes, we train midwives especially in the Guild House in Arilinn—herb sellers, confectioners, mercenary soldiers—" Abruptly she stopped, realizing where this line of questioning was leading.

"No, we are not all soldiers, Cholayna, nor mercenaries, nor swordwomen; if I had to gain my porridge with the sword, I should have starved long ago. The outsiders think always of the more *visible* Free Amazons, the ones who hire out as soldiers and mercenaries. There was a time, long ago, when there was a Sisterhood of the Sword—in the Ages of Chaos—it was dissolved when the Guild, the Comhi-letzii, were formed. The Sisterhood were mercenaries and soldiers, then. You asked what I did? I am a travel-organizer; we provide escort for ladies traveling alone, at least that was how it started, because we could chaperone as well as guide and protect. Later, men also came to us, so that we could tell them how many pack-beasts to hire, what food to buy for them, and how much they would need for the journey—we also act as guides through the worst country and the mountain passes." She smiled a little, forgetting her anger. "They say now that an Amazon guide will go where no man in the Hellers will dare to set his foot."

"That would be invaluable to us," Cholayna said quietly. "Mapping and Exploring can always use guides and personnel who can tell them how to outfit themselves for the weather and the terrain. Lives have been lost for lack of that knowledge. If the Renunciates will consent to work for us, we will be truly grateful." She paused a moment. "I wish, too, that you would consent to talk with one of our agents about what you remember of the Dry Towns, however simple. I am not asking that you should spy upon your own people," she added shrewdly, "only that you should help to prevent misunderstandings—to tell us what your people think *our* people should know about your world, forms of courtesy, ways to avoid giving offense by ignorance—"

"Yes, of course," said Jaelle. She could not remember now why she felt so angry at the very thought of talking about the Dry Towns. She was an employee of the Empire, so employed with the consent of her Guild Mothers, and as such she should obey every lawful command of her employer.

"For instance, we have an agent—his name is Raymon Kadarin—who is willing to go into the Dry Towns and send back some information from there. I want you to meet him, to see if you think he could go into the Dry Towns without being immediately spotted as a spy. What we know of the Domains—" she broke off as a light began to blink on her desk with repetitive insistence.

"I told those fellows not to disturb us," Cholayna said, frowning slightly, "Just let me get rid of them, Jaelle, and we'll go on. Yes?" she snapped, pressing the blinking stud.

"The Chief's on a rampage," said the disembodied voice. "He's looking all over for that Darkovan—you know, Haldane's girl? Finally Beth said she was in your office, and he made a scene. Can you send her down here double-quick and calm him down?"

Jaelle felt herself clench tight with wrath. She was not *Haldane's girl,* she was not a *girl* at all, she was a woman and an Empire employee in her own right, and if they wanted her, they could have the courtesy to ask for her properly by name! She started to blurt out some of this, then saw Cholayna was frowning, and sensed that the woman was almost equally angry.

"Jaelle n'ha Melora is in my office, and I have not yet finished my conference," said Cholayna coldly. "If Montray wishes to speak with her, he may request her to come to his office when I have finished."

Jaelle had met the Legate at the Council and had not liked him. She knew that Magda, too, had small respect for the man who had been her immediate superior; that he knew far less of Darkover than Magda herself, or any of half a dozen agents who worked under him. Peter, too, had said something like that; *Granted, the man's a career diplomat, not an Intelligence Agent, but he ought to know something about the world where he's stationed!*

Cholayna pushed the button and it went dark. "That will hold him for a little while, but I can't guarantee that he won't send for you right away. I've done my best." She smiled at Jaelle, in a sudden, conspiratorial way, and Jaelle realized she liked this woman, she had one friend here, at least.

"Now, how would you like to record what you know of the Dry Towns?" Cholayna asked. "You can put it into a tape for Records, or you can talk directly to the Agent . . ."

I'd rather not do either, Jaelle thought. She hated talking on tape, but she had not learned to relate to the men she found here in the Headquarters. The thought of talking to a strange Terran Agent, to any Terran man without at least the tacit protection of Peter's presence, frightened her. Yet the words of the Amazon Oath tormented her, *I shall appeal to no man as of right, for protection.* . . . what, she thought distractedly, has *happened* to me, since I have come to live here as Piedro's freemate?

Cholayna was still expectantly looking at her and Jaelle realized that she had not answered. She stammered, "I'd—I'd like to think about it a little, before I make up my mind."

What I really want, she thought, is to talk mostly to the women. I feel safe and comfortable with Cholayna, even with Bethany. I feel secure relating to Darkovan men, even those who detest everything the Free Amazons stand for, because I know how to disarm their suspicions, to work among them as one of themselves. She did not think she could learn to do that with Terran men, and she didn't really want to try.

And then she felt ashamed of herself. She was a grown woman, a Renunciate, she should not expect to hide behind Cholayna or even behind Piedro. She said almost aggressively, "I'll talk to the Agent," and stared at the floor, uncomfortably conscious that Cholayna was looking at her with sympathy.

I'm a big girl now, I don't need to be protected or mothered . . . she told herself, wishing she could feel the truth of that.

The light on Cholayna's desk blinked again, and she said to it, irritably stabbing with one polished nail at the button, "What now?"

"Mr. Montray to see you," answered the voice, and Cholayna raised her eyebrow.

"The moutain cannot fly to the birds, therefore each of the birds must fly to the mountain," she said wryly. "That is an old proverb on my planet, Jaelle. I'm afraid I'll have to let him in. You can go, if you'd rather."

Jaelle shook her head "I shall have to meet him sometime," she said, bracing herself for the graying, disapproving Montray. The man who entered, however, was a stranger, at least twenty years younger than the Legate Jaelle remembered.

"You were expecting my father?" he asked at Cholayna's look of surprise. "I'm Wade Montray, and Father send me up to look the girl over and see what use we could make of her—" He broke off, looked around at Jaelle and grinned apologetically.

"I did not know you were still here; I don't mean to be rude. I believe I saw you at the Council, but we weren't formally introduced."

Now she remembered; he, at least, spoke the language flawlessly and had interrupted some of his father's more tactless and unsuitable comments. "Yes, I remember seeing you, Mr. Montray—"

"Wade," he said, "but I know that isn't easy to say in your language.

I'm usually called Monty, miss—" again he broke off. "I am sorry; I don't know the polite address for a Renunciate—"

"I am Jaelle n'ha Melora. If you do not feel ready to use my name, you may say *mestra*. But if we are to work together and I am to call you Monty, I should be Jaelle."

He nodded, repeating the name carefully. "May I take her down to the Old Man's office, Cholayna? Or do you still need her up here? If you do, I'll try and smooth it over a little." He hesitated and said, "Look, he really doesn't mean any harm. It's just—well, he's been running everything, Intelligence, and Communications, Linguistics, all that stuff out of his office, and all of a sudden he doesn't know where his authority leaves off and yours begins, so he's feeling a little raw around the edges."

Cholayna nodded. She looked a little grim. "I can see that it would be hard for him. Technically of course I am not responsible to any planetary Coordinator, but only to Head Center. I'll try not to—to step on his feet, unless he gets in the way too much—I mean, in the way of Empire Intelligence. Jaelle, please feel free to call on me for help any time. And ask Peter to come in and see me sometime tomorrow, will you?" Cholayna turned her attention back to the lights blinking on her console, and Jaelle turned to the door with young Montray. *Monty,* she reminded herself, to distinguish him from his father.

"Your command of the language is excellent," she said, as they went down the hall. "How—"

He grinned at her disarmingly.

"How do I speak the language so well when Father still needs an interpreter? I came here before I was ten years old, and I've always been good at languages. The old man kept expecting, every year, that he'd be shipped out next year to a place he liked better, and so he never bothered with the language. I was shipped offworld for a proper Empire education when I was fourteen, but I liked it here and couldn't wait to come back. Sorry, I didn't mean to bore you with my personal problems. We can take this elevator."

The sickening drop was less frightening now; her legs were almost steady under her as they stepped out. In Montray's office, the plump, balding official was seated near a window looking out over the spaceport.

"I asked you to come down here, Mrs. Haldane," he said, in *casta* so poor and stumbling that Jaelle decided it would not be the least use to correct him about her name, "because I have a special assignment for you. My colleague here, Alessandro Li." A tall man, standing beside his desk, turned and bowed to Jaelle.

"He has been sent here as a Special Representative of the Senate at Head Center, with diplomatic status, to investigate whether Cottman Four shall retain its Closed World status or be reclassified, and to make recommendations about a Legation here. Sandro, this is the first Native Darkovan woman in Intelligence; she is married to Peter Haldane—"

"I know Haldane's background in Intelligence," the man interrupted. "Alien anthropology specialist; excellent field operative." His *casta* was better than Montray's, though not perfect. He turned and bowed slightly to Jaelle. "It is a pleasure to meet you, *domna.*"

Jaelle forbore, for a moment, to correct him. Alessandro Li was a tall man, hatchet-jawed, with steel-gray eyes under protruding eyebrows, the whole face shadowed by bushy dark hair and made—to Jaelle's eyes— ridiculous by a foppishly trimmed moustache.

"Do you think you can fit him to travel incognito in the Hellers and the Kilghard Hills, *mestra?*" Montray asked.

The first thought that came to her mind was an absurd, *not with that moustache,* but she bit it back; after all, the man was new to her world and even from traveling between mountains and Domains she knew that the small things, dress and culture patterns and body language, varied so enormously that their significance could not be taken for granted. She saw, however, a gleam of amusement in Monty's eye and knew that his first thought had been the same as hers. So she studied Alessandro Li for a moment without speaking. At last she said, "He could pass in the Hellers, up around MacAran country; some of them are dark and—and bony, like that. He would have to wear his hair longer, and either shave clean or wear a fuller beard. And he would have to be properly dressed, of course. And there is no way that he could pass until he has more training in the language."

"I wouldn't know about that," said the elder Montray with unexpected humility. "Languages aren't my strong point; that's why I miss Magda; she was my best interpreter. Wasted, of course, as an interpreter; she was the best undercover agent we had. But you think he could, eventually, pass?"

Alessandro Li was trying to meet her eyes; Jaelle colored and dropped her own. There was no way he could know—yet—that this was rude in their society, but Monty spoke up.

"To start with, Sandro," he said, "you don't try to make eye contact with a strange woman, not here in the Domains, unless you think she's a prostitute trying to pick you up. If Jaelle's husband were here, he could call challenge on you for looking at her like that. Call it your first lesson in cross-cultural courtesy here on Darkover."

"Oh, right," the man said promptly, and dropped his eyes. "No offense meant, miss—excuse me—*mestra,* is that right?"

"None taken," she said just as promptly, "but this is the kind of thing I mean. Piedro could help him more than I, of course. And it wouldn't be easy. It would be simpler to prepare—" she gestured toward Monty, who laughed and said, "I'd like to work in the field, of course. But as for sending Sandro out in the field—well, it seems to me that it would make more sense to let the actual fieldwork be done by our trained operatives, the ones who can go out and never be spotted as Terran because in everything that counts they *are* Darkovan; Haldane, Lorne—Cargill, Kadarin, even myself. Then we could report to Sandro and he could make his final decision from that."

Russell Montray leaned his chin on his hands and thought about that for a moment. Finally he said, "There's only one problem with that. Haldane, Lorne, Kadarin—the ones who can really pass in the field—they *are* Darkovan, for all intents and purposes. Yes, they've taken a Service oath, and I'm not questioning their loyalty, but it's natural that they'd think in terms of what's best for Darkover, not necessarily what's best for *us.* No offense meant, Jaelle—" he mispronounced her name, but at least he wasn't calling her *Mrs. Haldane* and she could tell that he meant to be friendly—"but Haldane married Darkovan—and now Magda has pledged to spend half a year in that Free Amazon women's commune or whatever it is. And we don't want the decisions made by someone who's gone native on us; the investigation must be supervised by an objective observer, not prejudiced in favor of the Darkovan view of everything. Do you understand?"

Jaelle stared out the huge window that overlooked the spaceport. One of the Big Ships was there, a ground crew crawling over it, servicing the spaceborne monster which had come here, not because it cared to come to Cottman Four, Darkover, but simply because Darkover was a convenient way station on the way to somewhere else. The quick retort on her tongue, that Sandro Li would be equally prejudiced in favor of the Empire's view, would not mean anything to Russell Montray.

From this height, the service crew around the ship looked tiny as so many scorpion-ants. No wonder this was why the elder Montray thought of the Darkovan view as something distant, irrelevant. He did not know Darkovans personally, he did not wish to know them, they were something other than human, forever set apart. What was it Bethany had said? The filthiest insult, in Empire language, was to call someone half-human.

"I am going to assign you to Sandro Li, to work with him, to be personally responsible for him," he said. "It's your job to work with him on languages, to get him ready for fieldwork, and I'll hold you responsible if anything happens to him."

He had used the words, *personally responsible,* which would have made it a matter of honor and pride to defend him to the death. For a moment

Jaelle's hand, automatically, sought for a knife that was not hanging at her belt; the gesture, arrested, made her feel foolish. She said in a low voice, "On my honor by my oath, I will hold myself responsible for him."

But Monty had seen the gesture. He said, "We're not asking you to be his bodyguard, Jaelle. You weren't hired as a knife fighter. What my father means is—you're to accompany him if he goes off base, make certain he doesn't get into any avoidable trouble, avoid any incidents; train him to get along in the Trade City without getting himself into trouble. Understand?"

She nodded. "First of all," she said, "you must have a Darkovan name. Alessandro is near enough to a name used in the Kilghard Hills, but no one would call a man *Sandro;* it is too much like that of *Zandru.* Zandru is Lord of Choices, good or evil, and of the Nine Hells."

"Equivalent of the devil," Monty put in, and Alessandro Li raised his bushy eyebrows. "What would a child named Alessandro be called, then?"

"Probably—Aleki," Jaelle hazarded, and he pronounced it after her, stumbling, "Ah—lee—kye, is that right?"

She nodded. "And he should—" she hesitated, but these *Terranan* would not know the difference, and why should she hesitate? "Monty, get him to a barber; a Darkovan-trained one. And get rid of that moustache, first thing. Piedro can help to find him proper clothes."

Alessandro Li—*Aleki,* she reminded herself—gently touched the maligned moustache; a little regretfully, she thought. "So begins my transformation into a Darkovan," he said, at last, with a shrug. "All in the day's work, I suppose. Where do I find a barber, Monty?"

The transformation was remarkable; Jaelle had not thought it could make so much difference. His face was transformed entirely by the absence of the moustache which had been its strongest feature, and the barber had trimmed the eyebrows, too, giving the whole countenance an entirely different look. Jaelle was curious about the barber who could effect this kind of change—what did he think? Had she supervised a change which would enable this man to spy on her people?

Who are my people? And why? I have never belonged in the Domains, any more than I belonged, as a child, in the Dry Towns. I have never belonged anywhere except among my sisters in the Guild House, and now I have forsworn that. . . . and she broke off, shocked at herself. She had not forsworn anything. It was her right to take a freemate, as she chose, and to accept any lawful employment. She was building a bridge between two worlds, as her friend and sister Magda was doing, as her beloved Piedro was trying to do. Why must the interests of Terran and Darkovan conflict? Could they not be working at what was best for both?

Aleki was looking at her, awaiting her approval. He had been dressed in the fur-and-leather clothing which any sensible man, traveling in the Venza mountains near Thendara, would wear, and the Terran sandals had been replaced by thick boots.

"No one would think you Terran," she said, and then, confronted with an apparently Darkovan man, was conscious of the immodestly revealing Terran uniform. That was the difference; he took it for granted, a Darkovan would not. To cover her confusion she said quickly, "You don't smell right; Piedro—Peter would be able to advise you about that better than I."

"Haldane? I am eager to meet him," Aleki said. "I know of his work; wasn't he the first Terran to travel to the seacoast, Temora and Dalereuth? Or was that Magda?"

"They were married at that time," Jaelle said, "I believe they share the work and the credit. And if you wish to meet Piedro, nothing is easier; will you join us for dinner?"

"A pleasure; would you object if Monty joined us too?"

"Not at all." Actually, Jaelle was relieved; Monty's presence made the whole affair simply the business of Intelligence.

Peter was waiting for them inside the entrance to the main cafeteria; he recognized Monty at once, and the two men shook hands. Monty introduced Alessandro Li, repeating also the Darkovan name *Aleki* which he had been given.

"A pleasure, Haldane. I know your work. I had hoped to meet Magda as well," Aleki said.

"Well, that could be arranged; she is still in Thendara," Peter said. "Are men allowed to visit the Guild House, Jaelle?"

"Of course; though they are not allowed to go beyond the Strangers Room," Jaelle said, and she could see Aleki filing away this information in his mind.

"I'll find us a table where we can talk," Aleki said, moving away, as Peter and Monty went with Jaelle toward the food console dispensers.

Behind them someone said, low but clearly audible, "That's Haldane's girl; he picked her up in Thendara. She's gorgeous, at least now he's got her in civilized clothes. Back in the mountains, I hear, they still wear animal skins. What legs! Lucky man—I've heard all kinds of stories about Darkovan marriage—"

"I heard a girl and all her sisters share the man," said another voice, "Reckon this one has any sisters? Or maybe Haldane's into—"

At the first syllable Peter had stiffened, going silent, and now, as the words trailed off into obscene speculation, he whirled, grabbing the man by his shirt front.

"Watch your filthy tongue, you bastard," he growled. But Jaelle, adrenalin spurting inside her brain, pushed Peter angrily away.

"This is *my* fight!" She gave Peter another hard shove, so that he reeled and half fell into Monty's arms, then, her hands stiffening into weapons, caught the man across the throat; he fell as if he had been struck with a hammer. A deftly aimed kick stretched the first speaker, moaning and clutching himself, on the floor. Jaelle, her mouth trembling, and her breath coming in little catching half-sobs, turned back to Peter.

Then black-uniformed Spaceforce guards were there, dragging them apart; Jaelle tightened, but the man only pushed her away, almost respectfully, with his arm; Peter put his arm around her, but she straightened, resentfully. The words of the oath. . . . *defend myself by force if I am attacked . . . turn to no man as of right for protection* were beating in her pulse like little hammers inside her head.

The Spaceforce man said mildly, "Disturbing the peace in a public place; shall I give each of you a citation? Can't you go work out in the gymnasium? The cafeteria isn't the spot for martial arts."

Peter snarled, "The filthy bastards were running off at the mouth about my wife!"

"Hard words break no bones," said the Spaceforce man. "Anyhow, it looks as if the lady can take care of herself." His eyes rested a moment on Jaelle, and she could almost *hear* his thoughts, but all he said was "I don't know what Darkovan customs are, ma'am, and I don't want to know, but our customs here include, no brawling in public places. You're a stranger, so I won't cite you this time, but no more fighting in here, all right? Haldane, you ought to teach your lady to behave herself in public." He turned away; his partner picked up the man Jaelle had slammed to the ground, who was shaking his head and ruefully fingering his throat. The other was still moaning; he grabbed the offered arm of the Spaceforce man and said, "Can you help me up to Medic?" He groaned again, staggering as he walked. The first man, with the bruised throat, gulped again and came toward Jaelle; she tensed, but he only husked, "Serves me right; me and my big mouth. I got to hand it to you, lady, you fight like a man," and went to his own table.

Aleki beckoned to them from a table for four in the corner. Peter nodded and went toward the food line. Jaelle was shaking, now that the crisis was over. She chose the first foods she came to, at random, and went back to the table, but when she put a forkful into her mouth she could not swallow.

"I have heard that the Renunciates were fighting women," Aleki said quietly. "Are you trained with a sword as well?"

She said, and knew her voice was small and shaking, "I can handle a knife. I—" her throat closed; she touched the healed scar on her cheek. She was still pulsing with fury.

Animal skins! When one of the prized trade items was the luxurious marl-fur from the Hellers, when the supple tanned and dyed leathers from the Kilghard Hills brought almost their weight in copper!

Monty said, "I have seen fighting like that in the Intelligence School; women as well as men are trained to defend themselves. But I had not expected to find it on Darkover—"

"No, most women are trained only to turn to the nearest male for protection!" Jaelle heard the note of contempt in her voice only after she had spoken, and saw the hurt reflected in Peter's face. He said, sliding into his seat, "They were insulting me, not you, Jaelle. Didn't it ever occur to you that I was the one being insulted?"

"On *my* behalf," she said stiffly.

"All that happened was, you made it worse," he said, setting his chin in the sulky line she dreaded. "Did you hear those men—*teach your lady to behave in public?* That's what you've got to do, Jaelle—learn how to behave in public! I don't care what you do or say when we're alone, but in public it reflects on me if you behave as if you were just out of some wild village in the Hellers!"

"Reflects on *you*—" she broke off. He sounded, it occurred to her, rather as Dom Gabriel had sounded when he spoke of the Free Amazons; as if it insulted the men of her family that a woman should learn to defend herself, rather than relying on her menfolk.

He was brought up as a Darkovan, she thought. *I thought, as a Terran, he would understand; Terran women are more independent . . .* and with a queer little sickening lurch inside her, Jaelle thought of what Cholayna had said that day; that the personality was formed by the age of seven and could not be much changed thereafter.

Had she been so swift to fight—when, actually, it *was* Peter being insulted—because she could not bear the thought that perhaps, within herself, there was a woman of the Dry Towns who wished to be chained, as symbol that she was lawfully the property of some man? Had she lashed out with her fists to silence that voice, not the casual obscenities of the two men? Was Peter, inside himself, a man of the Hellers who felt his wife should turn to him in all ways for protection and care? Could either of them ever escape the doom of their upbringing?

Of course we can, she told herself angrily. Otherwise no woman could ever become a Renunciate; and the Renunciates are all women who have renounced their birthright and overcome the chains put on them in childhood by their upbringing. I too shall overcome. . . .

Several of Peter's friends, who had seen the controversy, made a point of coming over to say something friendly. Evidently the men who had made the rude remarks were not generally liked, and though not many people had heard what remarks started the fight, they disapproved on principle of that kind of rudeness. They lingered on in the cafeteria, drinking and eating and talking, until it took on some of the characteristics of an impromptu party, and finally the kitchen staff had to turn them all out.

But outside, Jaelle turned away invitations to come up to various rooms in quarters and continue the partying. She felt exhausted. She had intended to see the Medic that day, but she had not done so. Peter was still silent and sullen, and she dreaded the reproach that would come into his eyes when they were alone. Had she truly wounded his pride so much?

And should it matter to her—as an Amazon—if she had?

She turned to him as soon as they were alone. "I'm sorry—" she said, but he was already speaking. "Jaelle, I didn't mean to be so—" and as they heard each other, they laughed and fell into one another's arms.

"You're wonderful," he whispered. "I love you so much! I know how hard this is for you—" and again, reassured, she felt that she was sheltering in his love, that it was a rock to cling to in this strange and alien place.

But that night, after they had made love till they were exhausted, and she had fallen asleep in his arms, she roused up shrieking from a dream in which her half-forgotten father, Jalak of the Great House in Shainsa, came with chains for her hands, saying she was far past the age where she should have been wearing them, and when she begged Peter to help her, he stood back and held her while the bracelets were slipped lovingly over her wrists.

Chapter Five

Magda sat at supper in the dining hall of Thendara Guild House, looking back over her fourth full day as a Renunciate. The first day they had asked her to stay with Keitha, who was feverish and ill from the aftermath of the beating she had received; the next day she had been set to help Irmelin in the kitchen. She had been incredibly clumsy about sweeping, and peeling vegetables for supper, but Irmelin had merely made a few grumpy remarks about fine ladies who didn't ever get their hands dirty. She had been gentle and good-natured about showing her how to wield the ungainly mops and brooms, and to slice vegetables without cutting herself. She found herself helplessly resenting the waiting on table, and dishwashing afterward; why had no one ever invented the simplest labor-saving devices to save women from these dehumanizing tasks?

Today had been worse; she had been sent to work in the stables. She did not mind feeding, watering or even exercising the horses, for in the big paddock the sun was bright overhead and the air fresh and clear, but the heavy barn-shovels were worse than kitchen mops, and the smell of manure was sickening. This, she told herself angrily, is why they had an Industrial Revolution on Terra; somebody got sick and tired of shoveling horse manure!

Her partner in this work was called Rafaella; she remembered that Rafaella was Jaelle's partner in their travel-counseling business, and had hoped to find her friendly, but Rafaella had had little to say to her. At the end of the day Magda was exhausted; she had never done manual work before, and she was glad to wash off the dirt and grime; but even though she washed her hair, she fancied that the stable smell still clung to it. The smell of the soap was harsh after the perfumed cosmetics of the Terran Zone. She lingered in the hot pool, trying to soak away fatigue, until Doria and another group of very young girls came in, and there was a lot of noisy and cheerful horseplay, running around naked and climbing in and out of the tubs and playfully squabbling over the soap. The noise they made finally drove her out of the pool room entirely, and only later did she admit to herself that she was jealous of the fun they were all having together.

Now, hungry after her day in the barn, she still found the food hard to get down; it was some kind of meat, or more likely, entrails, stewed with coarse-ground meal, and flavored with a highly spiced sauce; the bread was dark, coarse and unleavened, and there was some stewed fruit in honey which might have been tolerable if it had been chilled, but which was served warm. She was accustomed to Darkovan foods, and liked most of them, but by unlucky chance, the foods tonight were all new to her and distasteful; she nibbled at buttered bread, pushed the stew around on her plate, and longed, angrily and hopelessly, for a good cup of coffee. She had been trained, in Intelligence, to eat any kind of alien food without protest or visible distaste, and usually she managed it, but tonight she felt exhausted and let down. Could she really endure a half year here, among these strange women and in these uncomfortable conditions?

She sat in her place next to Doria; across the table was the elderly *emmasca,* Camilla, who had witnessed her oath, and beyond her was the new woman, Keitha. Today she looked better, with some color in her cheeks, and her bright hair, roughly hacked off for the oath-taking, had been neatly trimmed around her neck. She was wearing Amazon clothing which looked shabby and much-worn; probably from the same castoff-box as Magda's own. She still seemed shy and lost and ate little.

Camilla's gaunt face was kind with concern.

"But you are eating nothing, Margali—don't you like the tripe stew?"

"Oh, is that what it is?" Magda took another forkful and wished she hadn't. "It's very good," she lied, "but I'm not very hungry tonight." She took another piece of bread and buttered it. At least she *could* eat the bread, and with the warm stewed fruit on it, it wasn't too bad.

Mother Lauria rapped with a glass for silence. "Training Session tonight," she said. "It is compulsory for all new sisters and for everyone who has been oath-bound for less than three years, and everyone, of course, is welcome. The Sisterhood is meeting in the Music Room tonight, so Training Session will be in the armory."

There was a loud and audible groan. "Everybody remember to bring your extra shawls," somebody grumbled, "It's freezing down there!"

"We'll put the mats down for you to sit on," Rafaella said. "And a little cold won't hurt you! It keeps you alert so you won't go to sleep, as you might otherwise after a heavy supper!"

Magda whispered to Doria as they left the dining room, "What is the Sisterhood?"

"It's a secret society," Doria whispered back, "It links the Guild Houses together, that's all I really know about it, and most of the women who belong to it are healers or midwives; Marisela belongs. They're sworn to secrecy about it and they never tell."

Camilla came and linked her arm through Magda's as they went downstairs toward the armory. "I thought Jaelle was taking you to Neskaya. Why are you here? I heard that Jaelle was back for a night or two, but I had no chance to speak to her; I saw the scar on her cheek, though. What happened?"

"She and I were attacked by bandits," Magda said. "We spent the winter at Ardais; she was too ill to travel. Then we came here to Thendara—"

"Well, it is not surprising, that she should want her oath-daughter in her own house," said Camilla. She drew Magda after her into the Armory, where women were dragging the mats into a close circle. Camilla tossed Magda a blanket.

"You are cold, I can see, even with your shawl; wrap up in this," she said.

Mother Lauria said, "My sisters, all of you have seen the new ones among us; it is many years since we have had as many as three to be trained together. You all know Doria; Rafaella has done what each of us hopes to do some day, brought a grown daughter or fosterling to take the Oath from her hands. Now it is time for you to know Margali n'ha Ysabet, who took the Oath at the hands of Jaelle n'ha Melora last winter, and Keitha n'ha Casilda, who took oath from Camilla n'ha Kyria here in this house four days ago. Camilla, you are oath-mother to one of these and oath-sister to the other; will you lead us in the first round tonight?"

"With pleasure," said Camilla, "Doria, you have not yet taken oath, though you have lived among us all your life. Why do you want to take the Renunciate's Oath?"

Doria smiled and said confidently, "Because I was brought up among you; it is my home, and will please my foster mother."

Rafaella said quickly, "That is not a good reason. Doria, did I ever ask or require of you, as a condition of my love, that you should become an Amazon?"

Doria blinked, confused, but she said, "No but I knew you wished—"

"But what was *your* reason?" asked Camilla, "Yours, not Rafi's."

"Because—well, really, because—I have lived here all my life, and I wanted to be really one of you—not just a fosterling here—but a real Amazon—"

Irmelin asked, "Were you afraid that if you did not take the Oath you would have nowhere to go?"

"That's not fair," Doria said shakily, but Irmelin insisted. "Tell me. If we refused to take your oath, what would you do?"

"But you aren't going to do that, are you?" Doria protested, "I've lived here all my life, I've just *expected* to take the Oath when I was fifteen—" She looked shocked and afraid.

"Just tell us," Irmelin said, "If we refuse you the oath, where will you go? What will you do?"

"I suppose—I don't know—back to my birth-mother, I suppose, if she will have me—I don't know, I don't know, I don't *know,*" Doria cried, and burst into tears. Camilla shrugged, and turned to Keitha.

"You. Why did you come here, Keitha?"

"Because my husband beat and ill-treated me, and I could bear no more —and I had heard a woman could take refuge here—"

"How long had you been married?" Magda recognized the speaker as the heavily pregnant Byrna.

"Seven years."

"And had your husband beaten you before this?"

"Y—yes," Keitha said shakily.

Byrna made a wry face. "If you had endured his beatings before this, why did you suddenly choose to endure no more? Why did you not try to arrange your life in such a way that you need not endure his beatings and abuse, rather than running away?"

"I—I tried—"

"And so, when your feminine wiles could not soften his heart, you ran away because you had failed as a wife?" asked a woman whose name Magda did not know, "Do you think we are a refuge for any woman who cannot manage her husband?"

Keitha lifted blazing gray eyes and said, "You *did* take me in! Why did you not ask me all of this *before* I took Oath then?"

There was an odd little murmur around the circle, and Magda recognized it, with surprise, as approval. Camilla nodded as if Keitha had scored a point, and asked her, "What form of marriage did you have? Freemate, or *catenas?*"

"We were married *di catenas,*" Keitha confessed. Magda remembered; this was the most formal kind of marriage, where the *catenas* or marriage-bracelets were locked on the arms of both parties, and the marriage was difficult to dissolve in law.

"Then you were oath-bound," said Camilla. "What do you think of the proverb which says that one who is false to her first oath will be false to her second?"

Keitha stared rebelliously at Camilla. Her eyes were reddened and a tear was trickling from the corner of one eye, but she said clearly, "I think it nonsense; for your proverb I offer you another; an oath broken by one does not thereafter bind the other. My husband vowed when we were bound by the *catenas* that he would care for me and cherish me; but I had nothing from him but abuse and vile language and of late, beatings till I feared for my life. He had violated his oath many times; at last I chose to consider that, in breaking it, he had released me from observing it." She swallowed hard and wiped her eyes with the back of her hand, but she stared defiantly at the women, and Camilla, at last, nodded.

"So be it. Margali, tell us why you wished to become an Amazon?"

Magda was suddenly grateful that she had been the third one interrogated; she realized that the point of the procedure was to put the questioned one on the defensive, and force her to justify herself. She said clearly, "I did not, at first, wish to become an Amazon; I was forced to take the oath since I had been found wearing Amazon—Renunciate garb and impersonating one of you."

"And what were you doing running around in Amazon garments?" asked Rafaella.

Magda said, "I knew that no man would molest a Free Amazon; I did not want to create a scandal or expose myself to insult while traveling alone."

"Tell us," said Rafaella, "Did you feel it right to take advantage, unearned, of an immunity which other women had won at the point of their knives, and earned by years of renunciation?"

The hostility in her voice made Magda cringe, but she kept her own words steady.

"I knew too little of your ways to consider whether it was right or wrong. Lady Rohana made the suggestion—that I travel as a Free Amazon—but I myself will take responsibility for what happened."

"And why did you later abide your oath?" asked a woman Magda did not know. "Since you have taken it under what were really false pretenses, why did you not petition the Guild Mothers to have it set aside?"

Magda glanced at Mother Lauria, impassive, wrapped in heavy shawl and cloak, across the circle. Surely she would say something? But she did not meet Magda's eyes. Magda drew a breath, trying to form her words in such a way that they would convey her meaning without revealing what she had sworn never to reveal while she was in the Guild House. She could not explain that she felt this the best way to serve her two worlds, building a bridge between Terran and Darkovan; and that somehow she must free herself from the fetters of custom which prevented women from doing anything very important on Darkover. Finally she said, "I felt it wrong to break an oath I had sworn. And since I had no commitment elsewhere—"

That was not really true. She had sworn the Service oath. Yet in this way she could better serve as a Terran agent, and serve, too, the world she had chosen as her own.

"Commitment!" One of the women pounced on that at once. "Do you think we are simply a place for idle women who have nothing else to do? Why do you think you have anything to give us, in return for the protection of the Guild House and your sisters?"

"I am not sure," Magda said, struggling to keep her calm, "but maybe you can help me to find out what I have to give."

Camilla said, "That is a good answer," but her words were almost drowned out by Rafaella's hostile voice:

"Don't you think we have anything better to do than to teach ignorant women what they want out of life?"

Magda felt anger stirring in her, and was glad. If she was angry enough, perhaps she would not cry. "No, I don't," she said sharply, "If you did, you would be doing it, not sitting here trying to make us angry!"

There was an outburst of laughter all around the circle, and small sounds of approval. I was right, Magda thought, that *is* what they are trying to do; probably because Darkovan women are taught to be so submissive. They want us to *think,* question our own motives, defend them. The one thing they do not want us to do is to sit here meekly and accept what we are told.

Mother Lauria said "Keitha brought jewels and tried to make a gift of them to the House. Do you know why they were refused, Keitha?"

"No, I don't," said the fair-haired woman. She moved restlessly where she sat; Magda wondered if her back was still raw with the dreadful wounds of her beating. "I could understand why you refused, if they had been my husband's gifts to me. But they were a part of my dower property from my own mother; why am I not free to give them to you? Should I give them to my husband? And I have—" suddenly her voice wobbled, though she tried to hold it steady, "I have—now—no daughter to whom I might give them."

Mother Lauria said, "First, because no woman can buy a place here. I am sure you had no thought of it; but if we accepted gifts, there might some day be a difference made between the few women who can pay, and the many who can bring nothing. Early in our history, we asked women to bring a dowry if they were able; and we were accused of luring rich women to us, for the sake of their dowries. Also, none of us is perfect; if we allowed such gifts we might be lured into accepting some woman not fit for the life, out of greed for her riches. So it is our first rule; no woman may bring anything to us when she enters here except the clothing she stands in, the skill of her hands, and the furnishing of her brain and mind." She smiled and added, "That, and a more precious gift; her unknown self, that part of herself which she has never learned to use . . ."

She went on, but Magda did not hear; suddenly it was as if a voice had whispered in her mind:

Sisters, join hands and let us stand together before the Goddess. . . .

Before Magda's eyes a vision suddenly appeared, as clearly as if the circle of women seated on the armory mats had vanished; it bore the form of a woman, but taller than womankind; clothed in the gray and starry robes of the night, gems sparkling in her dark hair, and her face seemed to look upon Magda with divine compassion and tenderness. *My daughters, what do you seek . . . ?*

In confusion, Magda wondered, is this some new test they have arranged for us? But across the circle she could still hear Mother Lauria saying to Byrna, "You may be excused if you are weary, child," and Byrna, shifting her weight uncomfortably, replying, "No, please—this is the only chance I get to be with all of you!"

Magda could still see, faintly, the shimmering form—but was it inside her mind, a vision, or was it real, standing before her in the circle? She blinked and it was gone. Had it ever been there? Magda wondered if she were going mad. Next, she thought grimly, I shall be hearing voices telling me I am to be the new women's Messiah!

Rafaella had evidently been asked to lead the next round of questioning, and Magda shrank inside. Rafaella had been consistently unfriendly. She had heard only half or less of the question;

". . . teach you to be women, and independent, rather than mere chattels of men?"

Keitha answered hesitantly "Maybe,—as cadets are taught in the Castle Guard, to use weapons, bear arms, protect ourselves? That is the way in which boys are taught to be men—"

She braced herself for instant refutation, looking scared, but Rafaella only said mildly "But we want you to be women, Keitha, not men; why should we train you as boys are trained?"

"Because—because men are more self-sufficient, and women are meek because they have not been taught these things—"

"No," said Rafaella, "Although all Amazons must learn to defend themselves if they are attacked, there are women among us who have never held a sword in their hands; Marisela, for instance. Doria, what do you think?"

Doria suggested "Maybe—to learn a trade and get our own living, so we need not depend on any man to feed and clothe us?"

"You need not be an Amazon for that," said a woman Magda had heard called Constanza. "I sell cheese in the market, when we make more than we can eat, and there I see many women who earn their own living; they work as maids or servants, or they do washing, or work at leather-crafts. Some do so because they have shiftless or drunken husbands, and they must support their little children alone; and I know a woman who works as a maker of wooden dishes because her husband lost a leg riding mountain trails. Yet she defers to him in everything, as he sits in his wheeled chair at the back of their stall. That alone is not the answer."

Rafaella asked, "Margali, what do you think?"

Magda hesitated; she was sure nothing she would say could be the right answer, that this part of Training Session was only to make the newcomers unsure, to dispel their early and ignorant prejudices. She looked around the circle of women, as if she might find an answer written in one of the faces. Two of the women, she saw, were seated under a single blanket wrapped round them both, their hands enlaced, and as she looked, one of the women turned to the other and they exchanged a long kiss. She had never seen public lovemaking between women before, and it startled her.

Rafaella was still awaiting her answer. Magda said uncertainly, "I don't know. Perhaps you will tell us."

"We are not asking what you *know,* but what you *think*—if you know how to think," Rafaella said waspishly.

Thus urged, she tried to put some of her inarticulate thoughts into words.

"Perhaps—by getting us out of women's clothing, stop using the women's language—because these affect the way we think, the words we use, the way we walk and talk and dress—" she fumbled, "because we have been taught to behave in certain ways and you will teach us different —better—ways of behaving—"

And then she was unsure, remembering Jaelle's love of finery, and the way in which, talking to Dom Gabriel or to Lady Rohana, Jaelle's language had been as proper as the Lady's own.

"You are all right in a way," said Camilla, "and you are all wrong. Yes, you will all learn to protect yourselves, by force if you cannot do so by reason or persuasion; but this in itself will not make you the equals of men. Even now, a day is coming here in Thendara when every little matter need not be put to the sword, but will be decided more rationally. For now, we accept the world as men have made it because there is no other world available, but our goal is not to make women as aggressive as men, but to survive—merely to survive—until a saner day comes. Yes, you will all learn a way to earn a living, but being independent of a husband is not enough to free you of dependence; even a rich woman who marries a poor man, so that they live upon her bounty, considers herself, by custom, bound to serve and obey her husband. Yes, you will learn to wear women's clothes by choice and not from necessity, and to speak as you wish, not to keep your words and your minds in bonds for fear of being thought unmannerly or unwomanly. But none of these is the most important thing. Mother Lauria, will you tell them the most important thing they will learn?"

Mother Lauria leaned forward a little, to emphasize what she was saying.

"Nothing you will learn is of the slightest importance, save for this: you will learn to change the way you think about yourselves, and about other women."

The difference is **in** *the way you think about yourselves.* . . . Magda thought soberly that the Guild Mother was right. Magda herself had grown up to take it for granted that she would earn her own living, had gone to the Empire Intelligence school on Alpha, had been taught to defend herself in both armed and unarmed combat. And in the Terran Zone she had had no special restrictions of dress or language.

Yet I am as much a slave to custom and convention as any village girl in the Kilghard Hills. . . . Was it Lady Rohana who had spoken, once, about women who think themselves free and weight themselves with invisible chains?

Men too suffer in chains of custom and convention; perhaps the woman who most needs freedom is the hidden woman within every man. . . . Magda did not know where the thought had come from; it was not her own, it was as if someone had spoken it clearly within the room, and yet no one was speaking except Mother Lauria; but Magda lost track of what the Guild Mother was saying. She blinked, expecting to see again the form of the woman in gray and silver, the evening sky, divine compassion in her eyes . . . but no, there was no trace of it; her eyes opened on grayness in which strange faces moved, men and women, and before her in the gray waste a tall white tower gleamed . . . an *emmasca,* a woman who had been subjected to the neutering operation. "What am I then, a banshee?"

Before the angry look in the older woman's eyes, Magda said meekly, "I don't know; I thought—I had been told—that a neuter, an *emmasca,* was made so because she refused to think of herself as a woman."

Camilla reached for Magda's hand and gave it a little squeeze. Her voice was still stern, admonishing, but she gave Magda a secret smile as she said, "Why, that is true; I began by refusing to accept myself as a woman. Womanhood had been made so hideous to me, so hateful, that I was willing to accept mutilation rather than see myself as a female. Some day, perhaps, you will know why. But that is not important now. What is important is that here, in the Guild House, I learned to think of myself as a woman, and to be proud of it—to rejoice in my womanhood, even though—even though there is, in this *emmasca* body of mine, very little that is female."

She was still holding Magda's hand. Self-consciously, the younger woman drew it away. Camilla turned to Doria and asked "What do *you* think is the difference between men and women?"

Doria said defiantly, very determined not to be caught out again, "I say there is no difference at all!"

This answer provoked a perfect storm of jeers and laughter, with a few obscene remarks, about the politest of which was "When did you father your first child, Doria?"

"You just said the physical difference wasn't important," protested Doria, "Camilla cut Margali to pieces for saying the difference was a physical one, and if the physical one makes no difference—"

Quickly a voice—a man's or woman's, Magda could not tell—said, "There is an intruder; someone has strayed here, perhaps in a dream! Lock your barriers!"

And suddenly the grayness was gone, and Camilla snapped, "Margali, have you gone to sleep here among us? I asked you a question!"

Magda blinked, in disorientation, wondering if she was going mad. She said "I am sorry; my mind was—was wandering." *It was indeed,* she thought, *but wandering where?* "I am afraid I did not hear what you asked me, oath-sister."

"What, do you think, is the most important difference between men and women?"

Magda did not know whether Keitha or Doria had answered this question; she had no idea how long her mind had been drifting in the gray wasteland. The faces she had seen there, the image of the woman who must, she realized, be a thought form of the Goddess Avarra, were still half-lingering in her mind. She said, trying to gather her scattered thoughts, "I think it is only a woman's body that makes the difference." This was the enlightened Terran answer, and Magda was quite sure that it was the right one; that the only difference was the limited physical one. "Women are subject to pregnancy and menstruation, they are somewhat smaller and slighter as a general rule, they do not suffer so much from cold, their—" she stopped; it was doubtful if they would understand what she meant if she said their center of gravity was lower. "Their bodies are different, and that is the main difference."

"Rubbish," Camilla said harshly. She made a gesture indicating her spare, sexless body, arms muscled like a man's.

"I never said—nor did Camilla say—that the difference was not important," said Mother Lauria, "and it would take someone far more stupid than you, to believe that there is no difference. The difference is there, and not insignificant. Keitha, have you any idea?"

Keitha said slowly, "Maybe the difference is in the way they think. The way they—and we—are taught to think. Men think of women as property, and women think—" she frowned, and said as if discovering something, "I don't know what women think. I don't even know what I think."

Mother Lauria smiled. She said, "You have come very close to it. Perhaps the most important difference between men and women is in the way society thinks about them; the different things that are expected of them. But there is no really right answer, Keitha. You, and Margali and Doria too, you have all said a part of the truth." Stiffly she rose to her feet. "I think it is enough for tonight. And I heard the bell in the hall telling us that the Sisterhood have finished. I told the girls in the kitchen to bring us some cakes and something to drink. But let us go into the Music Room for that—it *is* getting a little chilly in here."

A little chilly—that struck Magda as a masterpiece of understatement; her own fingers were blue with cold, and she felt that the cold of the stone floor seeped up through her legs and buttocks, even through the thick mat. Hugging the blanket round her, she rose and went after the others.

She was hungry after the supper she had not been able to eat; the cakes were short and crisp, decorated with nuts and dried fruit, and she ate several of them hungrily, and drank a huge mug of the hot spiced cider they had brought for those women who did not drink wine. Her mind was still full of the discussion; a form, she knew, of simple therapy, forcing people to think, to protest, to break up old habits of thought. But she hoped all the sessions would not be like this. She felt intensely uncomfortable, her mind still picking over the questions and the many answers that had been given. Why had she chosen to be an Amazon? What is the difference between men and women? She was still testing and re-formulating answers, things she might have said, and that, she supposed, was the reason for the discussion. She heard one of the women say to another "It's an intelligent group," and the listener reply skeptically, "I'm not so sure of that."

"Oh, they'll learn," the first replied, "We did."

Doria's eyes were still red when Magda joined her. "I certainly made a fool of myself, didn't I?"

"Oh, that's what they intended you to feel," Magda said lightly. "Cheer up, you didn't sound any sillier than I did."

"But I grew up here, I *should* have known better," said Doria, threatening to dissolve into tears again. One of the younger girls—Magda recognized her as one of Doria's roommates—came and wound her arms around Doria, saying comforting things to her, and led her away. Magda raised her eyes and found Keitha looking at her with a faint ironic smile.

"Trial by fire," Keitha murmured, "Do you think we survived, fellow victim?"

Magda laughed. "Considering that their whole objective was to put us on the defensive, I think so," she said. "It's likely to get worse before it gets better."

"Are all the sessions like that, I wonder?" Keitha asked aloud, and a woman who had not been present at the session—she had been introduced to Magda as Marisela, the house midwife and healer—came up and smiled at them both. She said "No, of course not; the next session I will conduct, at which time I will instruct you all in the female mysteries, supposing that some of you may have had mothers who were too shy to speak of such things to their daughters."

"At least I will not be so completely ignorant at that," Keitha said, "I have delivered children on my husband's estates, and I was thought to have some skill as a midwife."

"Oh indeed?" said Marisela, interested. She was a pretty woman, dressed, not in the Amazon boots and breeches, but in ordinary women's clothes, a tartan skirt and shawl, over a full-sleeved tunic and bodice. "Then there will be no question of teaching you a trade; perhaps they will send you to Arilinn Guild House when your half-year is finished, to learn the midwife's art and some of the special skills which the women in the Towers have taught us. If you have even a trace of *laran,* it will be very welcome. What about you, Margali? Have you any of the skills of a healer or midwife?"

"None," confessed Magda. "I can bind a wound on the trail, or bandage a cut or scratch, but nothing more." But as Marisela drew Keitha away, and the two sat down to talk together, Magda thought of the word she had used. *Laran,* the Darkovan term embracing telepathy, clairvoyance, and all the psychic arts. Rohana had tested her, during the winter she spent at Ardais, and told her that she herself had some trace of it.

Was that how she had come to see the curious visions she had seen? Had she been, unwittingly, spying on the meeting of the Sisterhood, with the *laran* she did not really understand and did not know how to control? It seemed, for a moment, that around Marisela's slender shoulders she could almost see the gray mantle of Avarra. . . . she wrenched her thoughts back to the music room and began inspecting some of the instruments. Some were familiar; her mother, who had spent her life studying

Darkovan folk music, had played several of them. She recognized some
rryls, both a small hand-held one and another tall one played standing
before it; they were something like harps. Other instruments she would
have classified as lutes, dulcimers and guitars, though there were no reed
or brass instruments visible. There were a few others so alien she could not
even imagine how they would be played.

"Do you play an instrument, Margali?" Rafaella asked, almost in a
friendly way.

"I am sorry; I did not inherit even a little of my mother's gift for
music," she said. "I love to listen, but I have no talent."

The couple who had been embracing under the blanket in the armory
were snuggled together in a corner now, the taller girl leaning on her
friend's shoulder, the other's hand just barely touching her breast. Magda
turned her eyes away, feeling uncomfortable. In public, like this? Well, it
was, after all, their home, and they were young, not more than sixteen or
so. Caresses as simple as this, exchanged in public by young people—if
they had been boy and girl, instead of two young girls—would not have
turned an eyebrow in the Terran Zone. Suddenly, with intense loneliness,
she wished she were there.

She wondered if Jaelle were wishing the same thing. *Everything that
seems so strange to me here,* she thought, *is dear and familiar to her.* She
wondered if Jaelle felt equally alienated from everything she knew.

"Are you feeling homesick, Margali?" asked Camilla, behind her, and
put her arm around Margali's waist.

"A little, maybe," Magda said.

"Don't be angry with me for speaking to you so roughly, oath-sister; it is
part of the training, to make you think." She followed Magda's eyes to the
girls embracing in the corner.

"Thank the Goddess for that! Janetta has been moping so since Gwennis
left, I was beginning to be afraid she would throw herself out the window!
At least, now, she seems to be comforted."

Magda did not know what to say. Fortunately, before she had to answer,
Doria grabbed her elbow.

"Come and help me take the cups back to the kitchen, Margali, and put
away the cakes that are left over. Irmelin is sulking because we did not eat
them all up—do you want another one?"

Magda laughed and took another of the crisp little cookies. She helped
Doria and Keitha gather up plates and cups, brush crumbs from the table
and throw them into the fireplace. Rafaella was running her hands over
the surface of the large *rryl* and Byrna called out "Sing for us, Rafi! We
haven't had music for a long time!"

"Not tonight," Rafaella said. "I am too hoarse, after eating all those cakes! Another time; and besides, it is late, and I have to work tomorrow!" She covered the harp and went out of the room. Doria and Magda took the rest of the cups to the kitchen, and turned up the stairs. Just ahead of them, she saw Janetta and her friend, still clinging to one another, so mutually absorbed that they stumbled on the stairs and had to steady each other. Byrna behind Magda, sighed, watching them go off, arms still round one another, toward their room.

"Heigh-ho; there are two who will not sleep alone tonight," she said as the door closed behind them, "I almost envy them." Another deep sigh as she clasped her hands over the weight of her child. "What a she-donkey I am—what would I do with a lover now if I had one? I am so tired of this—"

With a clumsy impulse to comfort, Magda hugged her. "But you're not really alone, you have your baby—"

"I'm just so *tired,* I want it to be *over,*" said Byrna, and her voice caught in a sob, "I can't *stand* dragging around like this any longer—"

"There, there, don't cry—it won't be long now," Magda said, patting her shoulder gently. She led the sobbing woman to her own room, helped her off with her shoes—for Byrna was now so clumsy in the waist that she could not reach her feet—helped her into her nightgown and tucked her into bed. She kissed her on the forehead, but did not know what to say. Finally she said, "It can't be good for your baby, to cry like this. Think of how good you'll feel when it is all over," and as she looked up, she saw Marisela on the doorstep.

"How are you feeling, Byrna? No signs yet?" she asked, and Magda, feeling superfluous, went away. Some of the women were still clustered in the hall; they exchanged goodnights, and went toward their own rooms, but Camilla lingered a moment.

"Are you lonely, oath-sister?" she asked gently, in an undertone. "Would you come tonight and share my bed?"

Magda was stiff with astonishment; for a moment she did not believe what she was hearing. It took an effort not to pull away from Camilla's hand. She reminded herself that she was in a strange place and it was for her to adapt to *their* customs, not the other way round, Camilla had certainly meant no offense. She tried to turn it off lightly by a laugh.

"No, thank you, I think not." *I've had some weird proposals, but this* . . . Camilla's touch was not unpleasant, but Magda wished she could free herself from it without distressing the other woman or sounding unfriendly.

Camilla murmured "No? But I have not yet been welcomed back among you, oath-sister—" Her fingertips were just lightly touching Magda, but Magda was very aware of the touch and it embarrassed her. She was aware that some of the women still in the hallway were looking at them; but she was anxious to keep from offending Camilla, who had done nothing offensive by her own codes. She tried gently to free herself from the other's touch and murmured very softly "I am not a lover of women, Camilla. But I thank you and I am glad to be your friend."

The other woman laughed, unoffended. "Is that all?" she said, and, smiling, released Magda. "I thought you might be lonely, that is all; and we are oath-bound, and there is no other close to you in this house, with Jaelle away from us." She leaned forward and kissed Magda gently. "We are all lonely and unhappy when first we come here, however glad we are not to be where we were before. It will pass, *breda.*" She used the intimate inflection, which could make the word mean *darling* or *beloved,* and that embarrassed Magda more than the kiss. "Good night; sleep well, my dear."

Alone in her own bed, she thought about the evening. She knew intellectually that the raising of unanswered, and unanswerable questions, the deliberate arousing of emotions never fully faced, was taking its toll. She could not sleep, but lay awake, restlessly going over and over the questions and the many answers in her mind. Doria's tears, the two young girls embracing, Byrna's outburst, Camilla's kiss on her lips—all spun together in fatigued, almost feverish images. What was she doing here among all these women? She was a free woman, a Terran, a trained agent, she need not wrestle with all these questions so important to the women enslaved by Darkover's barbarian society.

Invisible chains. . . . it was as if a voice had whispered it in her mind. Where was Jaelle now? Lying in Peter's arms, in the Terran Zone. Mother Lauria had asked if she would find it too difficult to live without a lover. No, *that* was not what she wanted . . .

And then, abruptly, the image of the Goddess Avarra drifted before her eyes again, her compassionate face, her hands outstretched as if to touch Magda's. Through all the unanswered questions and the turmoil in her heart, Magda suddenly felt a great peace and contentment washing outward through her mind.

She slept, still pondering; what is the difference between man and woman? What makes a *Comhi-letziis?* She slept, and in her dream she knew the answer, but when she woke she had forgotten it again.

Chapter Six

"Yes, certainly, you could pass within the Dry Towns as a native," Jaelle said, studying the face of the tall, thin man before her, his beaked nose, high forehead, the shock of silver-gilt hair above it, "Fair hair is not common in the Domains, but most Dry-Towners are light-haired and pale-skinned. Your main problem would be the—the interlocking of customs and family relationships. You would have to have a very good story to cover what you were doing; it would be safer to pose as a man of the Domains, a trader."

The man Kadarin nodded thoughtfully. He spoke the language, she thought, flawlessly. She could not guess his origin. "Perhaps you should travel with me, and keep me informed about customs—?"

She shook her head. Never, she thought, never. "I would have to wear chains and pretend to be your property," she said, "and the Amazon oath forbids it. Surely there must be men among your Empire Intelligence—" she only heard the sarcastic tone in her voice after she had spoken, "or even women who are capable of that."

"I'll manage," he said, "but I wish you could tell me more. Cholayna Ares said you had actually lived there till you were twelve—"

"Behind the walls of the Great House of Shainsa," she reminded him, "guarded night and day by women-guards; I went beyond the walls only twice at a festival. And all I knew has been wrung out of me anyhow, by your damned D-alpha corticator or whatever you call it!"

Under light hypnosis, she had dredged up memories she had not even known she had. Playing with Jalak's other daughters, twining ribbons about their arms, pretending they were old enough to be chained like women. The sight of a would-be intruder into the women's quarters, his back flayed to ribbons, staked over a nest of scorpion-ants, and the sound of his screams; she could not have been more than three years old when her nurse had inadvertently let her see that, and until the session with the corticator she had wholly forgotten. Jalak, listlessly petting his favorites in the Great Hall at dinner. Her mother, in golden chains, holding her on her lap. Being punished for trying, with one of the boy-children of the house, to steal a glimpse out through the walls. . . .

She shoved them all away, slamming her mind shut; that was over, over, except in nightmares!

And her mother's death on the sand of the desert, her life bleeding away . . .

"I can tell you no more," she said curtly, "Dress yourself as a trader new to the Dry-Towns, speak softly and challenge no man's *kihar,* and you will come safe away. A foreigner may do in ignorance what one of their own would be killed for attempting."

Kadarin shrugged. "It seems I have no choice," he said, "I thank you, *domna.* And in return for all my questions, may I ask you one thing more, a personal question?"

"Certainly you may ask," she said, "but I cannot promise you an answer."

"What is a lady of the *Comyn,* with all the marks of that caste, doing among the Renunciates?"

The word *Comyn* dropped into the silence of the room, quiet and inoffensive, was, for Jaelle, weighted heavily with painful memory. She said, "I am not Comyn," and left it at that.

"*Nedestro,* then, of some great house?" he probed, but she shut her lips and shook her head. Not for worlds would she have told him that her mother had been Melora Aillard, bearing all the *laran* of that house, Tower-trained; kidnapped into the Dry Towns, married to Jalak of Shainsa . . . rescued by Free Amazons, only to die bearing Jalak's son, in the lonely deserts outside of Carthon. Yet before his steel-gray eyes she wondered if perhaps he had enough *laran* to read it in her mind.

Laran! The Terranan had something worse than *laran,* with their damned corticator which could stir up all the forgotten nightmares in the brain! She was told they had a strong psychic probe, too, but she had refused to submit to that. If she would not have a properly trained *leronis* meddling with her mind, when they would have sent her to a Tower, why should she submit to the crudely mechanical machines of these *Terranan?* She was relieved to see the man Kadarin rise and take leave of her with a courtly bow. Where had he come from, she wondered, what was his race of origin? He was not like anyone she had ever seen before.

She put the thought aside; she was to spend the rest of the morning working with Alessandro—Aleki, she reminded herself of his Darkovan name—preparing him by speaking of the background of the Domains, and elementary forms of courteous address among them.

They had been working for several days, in one of the smaller offices in the new Intelligence department, sometimes with the presence of the younger Montray—Monty—and sometimes alone together. Jaelle did not object to this; Aleki's manner was completely impersonal; he never seemed to regard her as a woman, but simply as a colleague. Jaelle, nervous and suspicious at first, now felt almost friendly toward him.

Aleki's first business had been to read through everything about Darkovan society which had been gathered by agents working in the field. Much of it was signed by Magda Lorne or by Peter Haldane, a fact which made it especially interesting to Jaelle; how much they had discovered about her world! Today she found him running through the account she herself had made of her trip into the Hellers, and comparing it with Magda's account and Peter's. As she came in he pushed it all aside and greeted her.

"But I do have some questions to ask you," he said. "Before we begin, are you thirsty? May I get you something? It may be a long session—I have a lot to say. Coffee? Fruit juice?"

She accepted the fruit juice, and took a seat at the table across from him. He fussed with the console, fetching some sort of hot drink for himself, and brought it, steaming, to the table.

"All three reports I have here, as well as some of the others," he said, "speak of wintering in Castle Ardais—am I saying it right?"

"Are-dayze," she corrected him gently, and he repeated it.

"How is it that you, a Free Amazon—and I understand they are not very highly regarded in the society—were accepted as a guest at Castle Ardais, with Haldane and Lorne, and no questions asked? Is hospitality so open in the mountains as it is on Darkover?"

This man is very intelligent; I must not underestimate him. "Lord Ardais would indeed shelter anyone homeless in his Domain," she said, "but I was welcomed as kinfolk there; Lady Rohana is—is a kinswoman of my mother."

"And you are related, then, to Comyn . . . for I understand the Ardais are of the Comyn? I do not entirely understand how it is that the Comyn rule all the Domains," he said. She could almost feel his curiosity, a palpable presence, and cursed the unwanted *laran* which thrust itself upon her, not controlled or desired.

"Nowhere in these Records," Aleki said, "is there any indication of how the society of Darkover took on such a feudal cast, or why the hierarchy called Comyn rose to power. Of course, what we know of Darkovan history is far from complete—"

"Most of us know little more," Jaelle said carefully. "What records we *do* have of the origin of Darkovan society are lost in what we call the Ages of Chaos. At that time—" she hesitated, knowing she should not speak—it was the will of the Hasturs that no Darkovan should speak to the *Terranan* —of the heyday of the Towers and of the old matrix technology which had all but destroyed their world.

"About the earliest time of which we have much history," she said, "is about five hundred, seven hundred years ago, when all these lands—" she touched the map he had copied, lying on the desk, "were divided up into a hundred or more little kingdoms."

"It seems a small country to be divided up into a hundred kingdoms," Aleki commented, and she nodded.

"You must understand, many of the kingdoms were very small; they used to say that a lesser king could stand on a hilltop and look out over his whole kingdom, unless a resin-tree had grown up that season to hide a half of it," she told him. "There is a children's game called 'king of the mountain'—is it played on your world?—where one child scrambles to the top of a hill and the others try to push him off, and whoever succeeds is king— until someone else pushes him off in his turn. It seems some of the smaller kingdoms were much like that. I know the names of only a few of them— Carcosa, Asturias, Hammerfell. About the time of the signing of the Compact—surely you know the Compact?" she broke off to ask him.

"Isn't that the law in the Domains that no weapon may be used which does not bring the user within arm's reach of death?"

"That's right," she said, "It reduced wars to the minimum; and, as I said, about the time of the signing of Compact, there were a series of wars called the Hastur Wars, and slowly, one by one, the Hasturs conquered all these lands; then they broke them up again into what we call the Seven Domains, each ruled over by one of the Great Houses of the Hastur-kin; the Comyn. The Domain of Hastur rules over the Hastur lands to the east, the Domain of Elhalyn over Hali and the western hills, the Altons rule over Armida and Mariposa, and so forth and so on. . . ."

"I can see the Domains outlined on the map," said Aleki. "What I want to know is how they came to power, and why the common people should obey them so unquestioningly. If you are a kinswoman of Lady Rohana, as you say, then you are evidently akin to Comyn and must know something of their history and power."

"I know no more than anyone knows," Jaelle evaded, "and through all this land there are very few who have not some trace of Comyn blood. Even I, and I am, as you pointed out, no more than a simple Renunciate."

She had begun to feel that this was some sort of testing, like a Training Session before she had taken the Oath. Again, all her hidden conflicts and loyalties were being brought out and explored. He persisted:

"I still do not understand why the common people should so unquestioningly do the will of the Hasturs."

"Do you people in the Empire not obey your governors and rulers?"

"But our rulers are chosen from among ourselves," he answered. "Though we still call ourselves 'Empire,' we are an Empire without an Emperor, and structured like a Confederation—do you know these terms? We offered Darkover full membership, with autonomous government and representation in our Senate by members chosen by themselves. Almost all planets which we occupy are more than happy to be members of a star-spanning Empire, rather than remaining isolated barbarians bound to their own solitary worlds. Yet Darkover has not joined the Empire, and we do not know why; we do not know whether it is truly the will of the Darkovan people or only the will of the Hasturs and of the Comyn."

For the first time she sensed that he was being wholly honest, and that he was puzzled. After a moment she asked him quietly, "Was Darkover given a choice? Or did you simply come here, establish yourselves, and *then* offer us membership in your Empire?"

"Darkover—Cottman IV—*is* an Empire colony," Alessandro Li said quietly. "You were colonized from Terra, many years ago. When we came here, we knew that; you had lost your history—perhaps within those Ages of Chaos of which you speak. The Comyn have chosen not to make this fact known to your people, so that you people may reclaim your heritage. Normally, local planets are pleased to have the resources of a star-spanning civilization."

It was a temptation to repeat the arguments she had heard, against the Empire and against the *Terranan,* but how could she speak for Comyn? And if she did, Aleki might badger her for more detail than she felt able to give. She realized that this long explanation had been given in order to draw her out, to get her to speak unguardedly, and she withdrew carefully from the offered gambit.

"I personally see no reason for making Darkover just another of the worlds of the Empire," she said. "But I am not privy to the mind of Hastur. The Hasturs have probably gone into the matter much further than I, and I for one am content to let them judge these matters."

"Wouldn't you prefer to have a voice in the decision yourself?" he asked her curiously, "rather than mindlessly obeying the will of a ruling caste?"

"I do not *mindlessly obey* the will of any man, be he Hastur, husband or God," she flashed back at him. "But the Comyn have studied this subject and I have not had the opportunity to know all sides of the matter as they have. Piedro has explained your system of representative democracy to me, and it seems only a way for the decisions to be placed in the hands of those unfit to make them. Would you rather listen to the voices of a thousand—or a million—fools, or to the voice of a single wise man well trained in these matters?"

"I do not automatically assume that a thousand, or a million, of the common people must be fools, or that one who speaks for the ruling class must be wise," he retorted swiftly. "And if the thousand, or the million, are fools, is it not the business of the wise to instruct them, rather than letting them remain ignorant?"

"You are making an assumption I do not accept," replied Jaelle, "which is that instructing a fool will make him a wise man. There is a proverb which says—a donkey may be schooled for a hundred years, and only learn to bray louder."

"But you are not a donkey. Why do you assume that your fellow commoners are not competent to learn as well as you?"

"I am not ignorant," she said, "but I cannot see as far as the Comyn. I have no *laran,* and even if I learned as much as I am capable of learning, I cannot read the minds and hearts of men, nor see past and future as they can do. It is this which gives them the strength to rule, and the wisdom which persuades the head-blind to accept their wisdom."

"*Laran,*" he said quickly, "what is *laran?*" And Jaelle realized a moment too late that he had led her into this debate, just for this reason—that she might speak, unguarded. She cursed the pride that had led her to enjoy sharpening her wits on this *Terranan.*

"Laran?" she repeated blandly, as if she hardly remembered what she had said. But he had, of course, one of those forever-be-damned *records,* the words she spoke had been recorded on to one of their wretched devices and he could listen over and over to what she had said, analyze it, know what she had betrayed.

"*Laran.* I know what the word means, of course—psychic power, which most Terrans consider superstition. And your people believe that the Hasturs have it?"

She hesitated just a moment too late before answering; she should have said quickly that yes, the common people superstitiously believed in the powers of the Comyn. But now it was Alessandro Li who backed away, courteously.

"I think we have done enough for one day, Jaelle. We would not want to be late for the Legate's reception tonight."

"Certainly not, since you're the Guest of Honor," she answered, and at his startled look cursed herself again; worse and worse; she remembered that she had not been told this, that Piedro had not known.

"How did you know that? Are you psychic yourself?" he asked. She said, "Oh, no, when there is an—an important guest such as yourself, it doesn't take *laran* to guess that the Legate will honor him at a reception." She stood up quickly. "I'm afraid my mind was wandering a bit."

"I hope I have not tired you; I'm afraid I am a very demanding taskmaster," he said in apology, "but we'll break this up for today; you can go and make yourself beautiful for the reception. I am looking forward to knowing your husband better. I know his work in records, of course, he must be quite an exceptional man, to have attracted so competent a wife."

She ordered herself not to blush at the compliment, resisting the impulse to tug at the immodestly short skirt. Years of Guild-House training should have made her immune to this kind of thing. She stood up, remembering the sharp teaching of the Guild Mothers, *your body language says more than your words, if you behave like a woman and a victim, you will be treated as one; try to stand and move like a man when you are working among men.* She said in her most businesslike manner "I am sure Piedro will be honored," and strode away.

She should warn Piedro; this man was sharp, he could put together small hints in an uncanny way. He might lead Piedro to talk too much. How could she blame her husband, when she had done the same thing? But she had made the mistake of underestimating Li; Piedro at least would be forewarned.

How much does Piedro know? Goddess! I wish I could talk to Magda! she thought.

At one of the high windows overlooking the spaceport, she paused, casting an eye at the great, declining, bloodshot eye of the sun. Perhaps she had time to go through the streets of Thendara to the Guild House, talk with her oath-daughter. . . . but no. There was this accursed reception to get through, and Piedro had warned her this morning that all the invited personnel were expected to be at their finest; he had suggested that she visit the personal-services department and have her hair done.

She shrugged and decided to do exactly that. She had been curious about it anyhow; it was a ritual which all of the women here at HQ seemed to undergo at frequent intervals, and she knew that Peter would be pleased if she went to considerable lengths to make herself beautiful for him. And in the last few days she had been working so hard in Aleki's office that she had seen Peter only when he was asleep, or nearly so.

The personal-services area was on the cafeteria floor, painted in a rosy pink color which made Jaelle, raised under a red sun, feel comfortable and soothed. She had begun to think of this time among the Terrans as an adventure, something to relate with pride to the young Renunciate novices when she was old and housebound.

She punched her ID card into the first machine, and a sign flashed: TAKE A SEAT AND RELAX, YOU WILL BE ATTENDED SOON. She read the afterimage of the words—sign reading was an exercise in reading swiftly. To Jaelle it was gone before she could focus her eyes. She took one of the gently contoured pink chairs, and waited, thinking over the last days. Time! Alessandro Li was fiendishly aware of time, even more than average Terrans, who were all clockbound to an incredible degree. She had heard gossip among the women in Communications; Bethany said that under normal circumstances, an official on his level would have done nothing, not even requisitioning an office to work in, until after the official reception; but he had begun work immediately, and had kept her with him most of these days. She felt wrung dry, as if he had actually pressed her and squeezed out all the juices of her knowledge; and this was only a beginning. There was so much tension in the awakening memories—for she had told him, and Kadarin, things she did not know that she knew or remembered—that even when she returned to their apartment she would lie awake, aching, her mind racing, too tired to sleep, hardly closing her eyes until it was time to get up. Time! Time! She lived at the mercy of a clock face, time to work, time to eat, time to make love, time, always time!

At home, she had been able to call an attendant whenever she needed something she could not do for herself; even in the Guild House, where none was servant to another, women did for each other these sisterly services. It was never hard to find some sister who would help you to lace your dress, curl your hair or cut it, lend cosmetics or clothing. Here everything was done by machines, it seemed. At length another sign flashed, YOU MAY GO IN NOW, and she took her courage in her hands and went into the pink room; and stopped cold in the doorway.

Rack that tilted every which way, chairs that tilted and turned to the tables, clamps to hold the head, straps to hold the victim in place. . . . the darkness reeled around her for a moment and she had literally to hold to the door. For a moment she was a child again, back in the insane years before her real life had begun, a child who had secretly crept to the door of a hidden room to steal a glance, not knowing it was her father's torture chamber. . . .

Mother! Mother! For a moment she wanted to run, shrieking, as she had done then, to hide her head in her mother's lap—

Then, abruptly, it was just another room, a Terran room filled with machinery, that did with metal fingers what flesh and blood could have done better. She could even make out, now, robot machines for cutting hair, for curling it, for soothing cosmetics . . . perfumed sprays. The room smelled and looked calm and soothing, but Jaelle could not force herself to step inside; finally she managed to free her feet, which seemed, as they had seemed then, rooted to the ground. She fled down the corridor, through the cafeteria, out the heavy doors and across the hard paving, forgetting to use the underground tunnel, never seeing the Terran eyes that turned to watch her fleeing form, stare at her. She threw herself, gasping, on her bed and buried her face in the pillows, glad beyond belief that Piedro was not there to demand explanation of her curious behavior. Had she disgraced him again? She no longer knew or cared.

It seemed only moments later—had she slept for a few minutes, an hour?—when the door chimed softly. A visitor at this hour? Or had Piedro forgotten his key-card again? Keys and locked doors, for her, belonged to matrix laboratories, dungeons—torture chambers!

Braced to welcome Peter, she was amazed to find Bethany Kane standing in her door.

"Jaelle, honey—are you all right? I saw you running across the court as if the devil was after you! Listen, is that bigwig from the Senate bothering you? He has no right to do that! I dropped in, but his secretary said you'd gone down to get your hair done—can I come in? People are sleeping on this corridor and I don't want to wake them up." She came in, as Jaelle gestured, then suddenly took in Jaelle's disheveled appearance.

"What's the matter? Not going to the reception? I was going down to have my hair done, too, I thought we could go together—"

Bethany went and stood before Jaelle's dressing-table, running her fingers through her own hair. "I'm a mess, and Montray will expect everyone on the staff to look their best. Do you have some extra curlers? Or are you going down to the beauty shop—?"

She was looking expectantly at Jaelle, and Jaelle said woodenly, "I did go down. But I—I decided not to go in."

"Honey, was somebody down there nasty to you? If they were, you ought to put them on report. They're there to wait on people, and if anybody made a single nasty remark—"

"Oh, no." Jaelle smiled faintly. "I didn't see any people down there at all—I thought it was all done by machines!"

Bethany chuckled. "Well, most of it is, but there *are* people there to make sure the machines do what they're expected to do," she said. "You've let your hair grow lately, haven't you? What are you going to do with it tonight?"

Jaelle shrugged. "It's not long enough to braid; what is there to do with it?"

Bethany surveyed her with consternation. "You're not going like *that*, are you? Honey, Peter would *die!* Here, sit down, let me see what I can do. Why, you've never even used the cosmetic console in the dressing room, have you? Show me what dress you're going to wear, and I'll figure out something."

Bethany managed, in the next twenty minutes, to show her several features of the bath and dressing table that she had not known existed. She was creamed, curled, elaborately made up, her hair elegantly fluffed into reddish-gold curls. For a little while it felt as if Bethany was indeed one of her Guild-sisters, and she was readying herself for Festival in the streets of Thendara at Midsummer. It was certainly easier than the strange, terrifying room full of machinery would have been, and at last she surveyed herself in the mirror with a certain pleasure; the new Jaelle who looked out at her would hardly have been recognized by the Guild-sisters. Bethany's deft fingers had arranged her hair into a soft halo, deftly accented her high cheekbones and the green glint of her eyes, softened her freckles to a gilt blur, and done something to her eyes so that they looked deep-set and mysterious.

"You look marvelous," Bethany said. "You're going to be the hit of the reception! I didn't realize you were a beauty, Jaelle!"

Somehow she felt disloyal to the Guild House. Dressing and preening herself like this, for a group of *Terranan?* Well, she rationalized, it was part of the job, to look her best—even Bethany had said so. Impulsively she hugged her.

"Thank you, Beth," she said, and Bethany yipped, "Look at the time! I've got to get down and change my own dress, or I'll be late! Anyhow, Peter will be coming in pretty soon—"

Bethany had hardly gone when he came in, breathless.

"Sweetheart, you look wonderful—you've done something to your hair, haven't you? I came to pick up my dress outfit—I'll have to dress over there. Do you know what they've had me doing, the last three days?"

"No, I don't," she said, "You've hardly seen me, you haven't told me anything."

"Don't nag, love, I'm in a real hurry. They've had me crawling around in the dust of the old Records section, trying to clear space for a new model corticator programmer. The place is filled up with old file boxes and *books,* for God's sake, I didn't know we still had any, and look at the dust!" He held out filthy hands. "I haven't seen the light of day this week! I should be getting hazard pay, all the germs in there—anyhow, Montray wants me in his office in ten minutes." He flung the suit over his arm. "Where are my dress shoes?"

"In the closet, I suppose." She was pleased that Peter had noticed the pains she had taken with her appearance, but he had so quickly taken it for granted.

"Well, for heaven's sake, *get* them for me, will you? I'm late, and I've got to do something about this damned beard—" he vanished into the bath, and Jaelle, fuming, went to pull out his shoes. She had performed many jobs in her life, but that of valet was new, and she didn't see why she had to perform as his body-servant; if he needed that kind of personal servant, why didn't he hire one for himself? Inside the bath Peter bellowed out a gutter curse and something metal crashed against the wall. He stormed out, raging.

"Jaelle! I hear so much about how great you are down in the office, keeping the desks stocked and doing all the little chores Mag used to do, and now I find you've let me run out of depilatory! Hellfire, girl, do you think I can go to the Legate's reception looking like a spaceport tramp?" He rubbed his beard. "Now somehow I've got to make time to hit the barbershop! Here, give me those!" He grabbed the shoes she was holding. "Don't be late to the reception, hear me?" And he was gone, without a word, without a kiss, without really looking at her at all.

Jaelle sank down, shaking, the ache inside her so enormous and empty that she could hardly breathe. Somehow, the slam of the door behind him had broken something in her, a self she had created here, the reflection of herself in Piedro's eyes. As it broke, she felt her teeth clench, the soft beauty Bethany had painted on her face suddenly vanishing into the cold, tough-minded Amazon Kindra had trained.

She was tempted not to go to the reception at all. But it was part of her job. . . . *obey any lawful command of my employer* . . . and Magda would have turned herself out stunningly because, if Magda had been doing the work she was doing, Magda would have seen herself as the appointed assistant of the Guest of Honor and known she must do him credit.

The cafeteria level had been rearranged into a gala banqueting hall, already filling with brilliant uniforms, costumes from a dozen different worlds. There was a bar at one end, dispensing drinks which looked delicious, brightly colored and cool. Waiters were carrying trays of little tidbits, and the cafeteria tables had been moved, combined into formal patterns, draped with linen and adorned with flowers. Real flowers. Well, thanks to Lady Rohana, she knew how to behave at a formal banquet. A man she knew slightly from Communications offered her a drink from the bar and she accepted it, saying a few formal words of small talk without hearing herself. She looked around for Peter, but he had not yet appeared. She thought of him in the clutches of the curious beauty-shop machines, having his hair and beard attended to, and cringed.

"Jaelle?" It was Wade Montray, bowing to her. "You look very beautiful tonight." She accepted the compliment as the social noise it was, hardly personal at all. "Sandro Li is looking for you. See—over there by the head table, next to the Legate."

She made her way through the crowd toward him, brushing aside greetings. Crowds had never bothered her before this, and certainly this was not as crowded as Midsummer in Thendara, but for some reason she felt strange, taut, and it seemed to her that too many people were looking at her, *there's that Darkovan girl, the one Haldane married, some sort of Darkovan nobility, no I heard she was a free Amazon, a soldier, a fighter, look at the knife scar on her cheek. . . .*

Aleki bowed to her. He was wearing some sort of formal clothing strange to her, dark-red, with gold lace and decorations on his breast; she supposed it was suggestive of his Imperial rank. He was very unlike the informally dressed man she knew from the office.

"I told you to make yourself beautiful for tonight, but I did not realize that you would dazzle us all," he said, smiling at her, and for a moment it seemed that he was ready to seize her, to grasp at her . . . no; he was smiling courteously, he had not touched her, why was she so intensely, painfully aware that he desired her, that he had not touched a woman for a long time and that he wanted her? The Amazon in Jaelle cringed, but he had said nothing, his manner was perfectly correct, why was she so open to him just now? She felt as if the room were full of a ringing silence.

His voice seemed to reverberate from very far away. For an instant it seemed that the few sips she had had of her drink were nauseating her and that she would disgrace herself by vomiting here before the whole assembly. She grabbed at vanishing self-control and said as calmly as she could, "I didn't hear you, sir. It's a little noisy in here."

He looked around cheerfully. "We *are* a noisy crowd tonight, aren't we? I asked if you could hunt up Peter Haldane for me."

She had had no chance to warn Peter against this man, who was so alert to find out what she had no wish to let him know about Darkover. Her eyes searched the crowd for Peter's familiar shape, and she braced herself to cross the crowded room through the onslaught of mental voices.

How do the Comyn who have full laran, *like Lady Rohana, ever manage to appear anywhere in a crowd?* For the first time in her life, she wished she had had some of the training given routinely to the telepaths of the Comyn, to control her *laran. . . .* but then, it had never seemed to her that she had enough *laran* to be worth training! She moved through the crowd, carefully keeping her face blank, she would not stare about her in panic like a mushroom-farmer in the big city for his first Festival!

She knew Peter would be wearing gray, the steel-gray which was so becoming to his red hair and gray-green eyes. She looked through the crowd and finally saw a red head. She made her way to his side and touched his arm.

"Alessandro Li wishes to speak with you," she said formally.

"Let's not keep him waiting, then," he said, and took her arm. She pulled upright, bracing herself.

"I can walk by myself," she said stiffly.

"Honey, are you still mad at me? Let's not fight, not here at a party!"

She drew a long breath. She said, "Piedro, listen to me, please. Li is very curious about the Comyn; he's determined to find out what lies behind it. For three days he has been after me with his questions; don't underestimate him. I did. And I don't know what he wants, but I am not sure it is good for Darkover. I may have told him too much already; be careful what you say to him."

Peter grimaced. He said "I can't afford to play games with an Imperial bigwig. I've got to cooperate. Montray—the Coordinator, not Monty, Monty's a decent sort—old Montray just threatened me—he wants to send me offworld."

"Peter!" Suddenly she forgot her quarrel with him, at the shocking thought that she might somehow lose him. "What? Why?"

"They've located a planet something like Darkover—feudal setup, low technology, all that—and he says with my experience here, I'd be a good one to send there. Personally, I think he's afraid I'll have his job if I stay here; I know twice as much, ten times as much, about Darkover as he does and he's afraid somebody will find it out. And if I can convince Sandro Li that I'm really needed here to unravel this mystery—do you see?" He swung around and caught her wrist. "Jaelle, I'm fighting for my life, as much as you were when you and Mag met the banshee on the trail. Won't you back me up? I want to stay on Darkover—with you. Help me, don't fight me, beloved!"

People slid by, on either side of them. In this crowd, so filled with voices she did not really hear, voices that penetrated her mind brutally, she could not think clearly. She swallowed hard and said "Come along; just—just be careful what you say, or even what you hint, or he'll get it out of me."

Li greeted Peter with great cordiality, indicating, as people began to move toward the banquet tables, that Peter and Jaelle were to be seated near him at the head table.

She was aware, at least partly from the subliminal chatter of telepathic sound, that the Terrans here in Thendara Spaceport regarded Li much as the common people of Thendara would have regarded the Heir to Hastur; here to judge them, in authority over them. Peter was talking to Li with all the charm of which he was capable, emphasizing to the Imperial investigator that he knew more about Darkover than any other man working here.

She could tell that Aleki was impressed. She also realized what neither Montray nor Peter had bothered to tell her; that on Li's report depended, not only the future status of Darkover in the Empire, but the future of the Terran installation. He had the power to withdraw the Empire entirely, except for a few officials to tend the spaceport; or to increase the HQ staff until it was a full colony administration; he could open the world to trade, or close it completely.

The fate of Darkover in relation to the Empire is in this man's hands. Even the Hasturs have little to say about it. This is too much of a responsibility for me! It is too great a responsibility for anyone!

At one point in the dinner, when the main course had been finished and they were lingering over sweets and tiny, delicious glasses of variously-scented and colored cordials, Aleki said, "In your work I have found frequent mention of Miss Lorne's work. Why is she not on the station? Is she on leave offworld? I found her name on the *inactive* roster."

Cholayna Ares, tall and elegant in low-cut draperies of fire-red which accented her smooth dark skin and frost-white hair, leaned across to them and said, "She is on detached duty in Thendara, Sandro; she is in the Renunciate Guild House."

"I am extremely eager to meet her," Li said. "Do you suppose that I could request her to come in for an interview?"

"I doubt it," Jaelle said, "she is serving her housebound time among the Amazons; she is not allowed to leave the House for that period—"

"But that is barbarous!" Li said. "To imprison an Empire citizen—"

"Hardly imprisonment," Jaelle said calmly, "since it is voluntary."

Peter leaned forward. He had, Jaelle suspected, drunk a little too much. He said "I can tell you anything Magda could tell you, Sandro. Most of the places she went, she managed to go while she was under my protection. You don't realize yet how many doors are closed, here, to any woman. Magda's a fine agent; If she'd been born a man, she'd be the Legate by now! But here on Darkover, no woman could be accepted that way. And now she's gone over the wall, gone native. I can fill in most of Magda's reports for you."

"Can you really?" Li's face was sharp, and intent.

"I can and I will." Peter reached for another drink.

"I'll take you up on that," Sandro Li said, and turned to listen to the speaker at the head of the table.

An hour later, Jaelle faced Peter across the small room they shared. She knew he had drunk too much; his face was flushed, his speech incoherent, but he was not so drunk he could disclaim responsibility for what he had done.

"Peter, don't you realize? That man is out to destroy Darkover—the Darkover we know—to turn it into another Terran colony! And you're helping him!"

"I think you're exaggerating. In any case, what does it matter? He's only here to investigate how well the HQ is doing its job on Darkover. I owe him cooperation; so do you and so does Magda. If it weren't for men like him, there would be *no* Empire."

"Would that be such a misfortune?"

He took her shoulders and turned her toward him. She permitted it, not sure why she didn't kick him away.

"There's no reason Darkover can't accept what's good about the Empire while keeping what's good in its own way of life. It's not wrong to hate ignorance and poverty. Look, *chiya,* I was born on Darkover, it's my home too, I love it—I want to stay here, be part of it." He bent to kiss her, burying his face in her scented hair. "I was fighting—I *am* fighting—for the right to stay here, as any man would fight for his land, his home, his wife. I do it with words instead of a sword, that's all. But I *am* Darkovan. You heard what Cholayna said when she heard about our wedding?"

She had heard; somehow it had nested in her heart, almost with pain. Cholayna had said; *with your red hair and Peter's, what beautiful children you will have.*

"I want a son," he whispered, "as much as any man of the Hellers would want a son. A son to live here on Darkover, our world. . . . Jaelle, Jaelle . . ."

He picked her up and carried her to the bed. She allowed it, even enjoyed his touch; he laid her down, whisked away the filmy green of her dress, flinging it unheeded to the floor. As he drew her into his arms once again he was wholly open to her. She could feel it in him, like an eternal and unhealed wound, Magda's refusal to give him the child he desired. His body possessed hers but it was she who possessed his mind, he was at her mercy . . .

. . . *and suddenly she knew him as Magda had known him, he really believed that he could treat her as valet, comrade-in-arms, personal servant, breeding-anima, and somehow repay it all just with the ardor of his lovemaking* . . . the rage that boiled up in her then cut off thought; she twisted aside, a knee, a shoulder, both arms stabbing up, and he rolled helplessly aside, shocked and vulnerable. She sprang up, crouching into a defensive posture, and he lay stunned, staring at her in absolute disbelief.

"Sweetheart—what's wrong?"

"Next time, *ask* me if I feel like making love!" The confusion and outrage on his face felt good to her. "Next time I might even agree to bear you a child. But ask. Don't—don't take!" She felt she could not endure to look at him. He thought he had only to caress her and she was enslaved to his will!

He was sitting on the bed, drunk and miserable. "Jaelle, what did I do wrong? Tell me!"

She did not know. What did happen to love? Now she only wanted to hurt him, to lash out at him, to jeer at his vulnerability! She said, low and hard-faced, "Don't ever—*ever*—take me for granted, *Terranan!*" and slammed the door of the bath behind her, turning on the water full force. She stood under the shower and cried, cried till she felt empty and helpless as she had left Peter there. When she came out of the shower he was asleep, a bottle empty on the floor beside him; he reeked of the cheap Darkovan wine from the port. She threw the bottle down the disposal chute, pulled her cloak from the closet and fell asleep on the floor by the bed.

She woke late, and he was gone; she had not even heard him leave. And she was glad.

Chapter Seven

Someone was calling Magda's name, in her sleep, from very far away. "Margali—Margali!"

It was dark in the room; outside it was snowing hard. Camilla, wrapped in a thick furred gown, was standing by her side. Magda sat up and asked, "What is it? I'm not on kitchen duty, Camilla." There was no particular hour to get up; but for the convenience of women who worked in the city, an early hot breakfast was served, and the women on kitchen duty were roused early to cook and serve it. Anyone sleeping through this breakfast had to rummage in the pantry for cold bread, or go hungry until dinner.

"I'm sorry to wake you at this hour, *breda*, but Byrna is in labor and should not be left alone; will you come and sit with her for a time?"

Magda got out of bed, huddling her thick nightgown round her, her feet cringing at the touch of the stone floor. "Where is the midwife?"

"It always happens this way—babies come in clusters! Marisela has slept in the house these last ten days, but tonight of all nights she was called out to the other end of the city. But it is Byrna's first child, and there is no great hurry. You will have time to wash your face and dress."

Magda went down the hall to the community bath and splashed her face with cold water; she flinched at its cold bite, knowing that if she stayed here a hundred years she would never, never get used to this. It had never seemed to occur to anyone that anyone would want a warm bath in the morning, so in the morning there was no hot water—it was as simple as that. Magda supposed that when you were doing hard manual work it made sense to wash off the day's grime in the evening—she still remembered her tenday in the stables, and how welcome a hot bath had been then. But it was one of those cultural differences that really hurt.

"What time is it?" she asked Camilla, as they went down the corridor.

"Just after midnight. We have taken her upstairs, so she can make as much noise as she likes, and not fear waking anyone who needs sleep. Rafaella is upstairs with her now, but Rafi is pledged to leave at sunrise and she must have a little sleep."

In the fourth-floor room, a fire had been lighted, and Byrna was walking back and forth in front of the fire, wrapped in thick shawls over her chemise. She turned and said "Thank you for coming to stay with me, Margali—I'm sorry to get you up like this—"

"It's all right," said Magda, taking her hands awkwardly. "How are you feeling?"

"It doesn't hurt as much as I thought it would, not yet," Byrna said, "It's like a bad case of cramps, and it sort of comes and goes; between times I feel fine."

"And it won't even hurt that much, if you remember what Marisela told you, and breathe into it," Rafaella said, coming to put her arm around Byrna's waist. "I've had four, and I know." She gave Byrna a hug, and went to the door with Magda. She said, "Do you know how to handle this early stage?"

Magda shook her head. Rafaella always made her feel stupid and incompetent. "I've never been with a woman in labor before."

Rafaella raised her eyebrows. "At your age? Where, in Avarra's name, were you brought up? Well, all you can do at this stage is to keep her cheerful, remind her to relax if she starts to tense up. The most she can do, at this stage, is not to interfere with what's going on inside. Let her drink as much water as she wants, or tea—" she added, indicating a kettle boiling over the fireplace on its long arm, "and if she feels faint, put a spoonful of honey in it. Don't worry if she vomits, some women do. The important thing is just to be with her, reassure her."

Magda faltered. "What if the—the baby comes before the midwife gets here?"

Rafaella stared at her in puzzlement. "Well, so what? If it comes all by itself, that's the best thing that could happen. They do sometimes come like that, no pain, no fuss. If it does, just wrap it in anything handy—don't cut the cord—just lay it on top of her and go and yell for somebody who knows what to do; any of the Guild Mothers would know." She added impatiently, "There's nothing to handling a baby that comes by itself; it's when they *don't* that you need help! Camilla will be in and out; if Byrna starts wanting to push, tell Camilla to go and get somebody in a hurry, but I don't think that will happen for hours yet. And for heaven's sake, calm down, you'll frighten Byrna if you're this nervous! If there were anybody else, I'd never leave her to you, of all people! But how was I to know anyone your age would be so ignorant?" Rafaella went and hugged Byrna again, said, "Have a nice little Amazon for the house, won't you?" and went away with Camilla, leaving Magda alone with Byrna. They looked at each other rather helplessly; then Byrna said "Oh—it's starting again," and grabbed Magda around the waist, leaning heavily on her, breathing hard and panting softly. When it was over she drew a long, gasping breath and said *"That* one really hurt!"

"Well," said Magda, "maybe that means it won't be as long as you think."

"I want to rest for a while." Byrna dropped down on the mattress which had been laid on the floor, covered with clean, but ragged sheets. She sighed restlessly.

"My oath-mother promised to be here for the birth, but I have heard there are floods in the Kilghard Hills, and she could not travel." She blinked tears from her eyes. "I'm so lonely here, with no oath-sisters in the House—everyone's been so kind to me, but it's not like having my oath-sisters here."

Those who witness you oath are your family. . . . Magda remembered the swift growth of her own bond with Jaelle, and that Camilla had treated her with unusual friendliness. "Byrna, we are all your sisters, bound by the oath—every one of us here."

"I know. I know." But Byrna blinked tears away and her hands clenched into fists. She closed her eyes, shifted her weight again and seemed to fall asleep for a moment. Magda rose and mended the fire, tiptoed back and sat beside the apparently sleeping Byrna.

After a long time Byrna stirred and twisted restlessly. "Even when I'm breathing the way Marisela told me, it hurts. It hurts so much, and Marisela promised it wouldn't . . ."

Magda tried to remember random things she had read. "Just breathe quietly; try to feel as if you were floating," she said, and Byrna was quiet again, resting. After a time she hoisted herself up wearily and began to walk, leaning on Magda. "They said it would go faster if I could stay on my feet."

Later, Camilla came back, carrying a cradle in her arms. "How are you feeling, Byrna? Look, here is a cradle for your little one; I found it in the storeroom, and an embroidered blanket; I made this one myself, fifteen years ago, for Rafaella's last baby. Doria slept under it. And now she is an Amazon herself!"

"It looks like new," Byrna said, caressing the woolly fabric, and Camilla laughed. "No baby uses it for very long. How do you feel?"

"Awful," Byrna said, "and it seems to be taking a long time."

Camilla felt about her body. "You're coming along well enough. It may not be as long as we think. Try to walk some more, if you can."

She disappeared again, and the time seemed to stretch out. Byrna walked and Magda held her upright, holding her when the contractions seized her; later she lay down to rest, or slept a little, moaning. After three or fours hours, gray light began to steal through the window.

"Look," Magda said, "it's morning. The sun will be up soon." Byrna did not answer, and Magda thought she had dozed again, but then she heard the woman whimper softly. "What's the matter? Is it very bad? Lie back and relax, Byrna—"

"Lie back, Byrna, don't make a fuss, Byrna, relax, Byrna," the woman mimicked savagely, sitting up on the bed. "Don't I know it all? You don't really give a damn," Byrna flung at her, and started to cry, "There's nobody here who cares, and I'm so miserable—" She sobbed, curling herself up, holding herself, and Magda was dismayed. She felt she was breaking all the rules—surely nothing like this would ever have been allowed in Medic HQ in the Terran Zone—but she sat down on the edge of the mattress beside Byrna, laying a tentative hand on the shaking shoulders. "That's not true, Byrna. I'm really sorry your oath-mother isn't with you, but I'll try to help you all I can, really I will. And it will be over sooner than you think."

Byrna flung her arms around Magda and burst into agonized, passionate crying. Magda patted her, helplessly.

"Is it so bad? Don't cry, they say the worse it is, the sooner it is to being over." It was one of the few things she could remember from the midwives' lecture a few days ago. "If you feel so bad now, then this is the worst, you'll feel better soon when you start to bear down. But please, lie down again—try to relax—"

"It isn't the pain," Byrna said distractedly, "I could stand that, it isn't that—" she clung to Magda, moaning. Magda held her, letting Byrna clutch at her hands with bone-crushing force. She could *feel* the deep, racking shudders that passed through Byrna, and it reminded her of that moment under the matrix, when Lady Alida had gone deep into the cell-structure of the wound on Jaelle's face and Magda had found herself sharing it. *Laran. Must I feel everything she feels?*

But the paroxysm passed and Magda wondered if she had merely imagined it. She persuaded Byrna to lie back on the pillows, sponged the sweat from her face, and persuaded her to sip a little tea with honey. Tears were still rolling down Byrna's face, and to distract her Magda asked, "Do you want a boy or a girl?"

"A girl, of course—I was there when Felicia had to give up her son, since no male may live in a Renunciate house after he is five. She said he would soon be a stranger to her, yet she did not want to leave the House and her sisters, and hire a nurse to keep him when she was at work, and face all the dangers of a woman living alone in the City—I think if I bear a son I will give him up at once, before it tears my heart to let him go. Felicia wanted a son, she said she did not want to be troubled with fifteen years tied down to rearing a girl, but now that Rael is gone she is moping like a chervine that has lost her calf. I will not be that foolish, I will give him up at once."

"Who is your child's father, Byrna? Or would you rather not tell—"

"His name is Errol, and he is a cousin of mine. His wife has no son, and she said she would welcome a child of his to foster—" and then Byrna began to cry harder than ever. Magda, alarmed, asked, *"Breda,* what is it?"

Byrna wept "I can't stand it, I can't stand it—"

"The pains? Sister, shall I go and call Camilla, or one of the Guild Mothers? Keitha has had children, too, she might know—"

"No, no, not the pain—" she sobbed till her whole body shook. "Only—only—I am oath-breaker, forsworn—"

"Byrna, don't—this is no time—"

"It's true, true! That is why I wanted my oath-mother here, to confess to her, to have her forgiveness—" Her body convulsed again and Magda was sure she was making it worse with her violent crying.

"The oath—" she wrenched out, twisting and writhing, "I am sworn . . . *bear no child save in my own time and season. . . .* I have been taught, I know there are ways of preventing the conception of a child I did not want—but it was Midsummer, and I—I wanted to please Errol, so I lay with him even though I was *raiva,* ripe for conception, and not—not protected—but I was lonely, and he wanted me—we have been lovers for many years; at one time we had spoken of marriage, but I was—at that time I wanted to be independent, to do only my own will, so I chose the Guild-House, and went away to Dalereuth, and then, when I came back to Thendara, I found that he was married, and unhappy. And it seemed—oh, I hardly know how to tell you, so *right* somehow, with the music, and the dancing, and a—a starlit night with all the moons above us, and yet—I knew it was wrong, to risk this, to risk it—and so I am forsworn, forsworn—"

Magda was confused, not aware of the particular ethical point involved. She remembered how, at Midwinter Festival at Ardais, she had come near to surrendering herself to Peter, just because the old habit of love for him was so strong, and he had wanted her so much. But she could have done so, thanks to Terran medicine, without this kind of risk. *She* had been properly protected against conception . . . and she remembered what Mother Lauria had said on her first day in the house, that this training would be beyond price to the Renunciates. It was a sin that they did not have proper contraceptives, so that women need not take this kind of risk, bear unwanted children . . . and suffer this kind of guilt.

She held Byrna till her sobbing quieted a little, and said gently, "It is too late for regrets of that kind, *breda*. Done is done. Now you must just think of your baby." What a foolish thing to say, she thought, as she mouthed the phrases; what else had Byrna been thinking about for all these months?

Obediently Byrna lay down; and then a look of surprise came over her face. She began to gasp deeply, to breathe in a new way, gulping in deep breaths and letting them out in a harsh, straining groan. Magda admonished her to relax, but Byrna seemed not to hear, gasping out between the heavy groans "Something's happening—it doesn't hurt as much now—"

Oh, God, Magda thought, she's beginning to bear down, I've got to go and call somebody who knows what to do—

Byrna gasped "I need to—to *hold* something—" and grabbed at Magda's hands, straining, hauling, her face reddening with the effort. Magda tried to brace herself against panic.

"O-o-h," Byrna groaned, but curiously it was not a sound of pain; only of tremendous effort; Magda could almost feel it in her own body and it was a curiously satisfying sensation—what the hell was happening to her? More to the point, what was happening to Byrna?

Byrna clutched her hands and let out a long howling cry, more a grunt than a scream. "It's coming," she yelled, "I can *feel* it, it's coming, it's coming *now*—" She gulped air again and gave herself over to the groaning, straining effort. Magda tried to wrest her hands away.

"Let me go and call somebody, Byrna—"

"No, no, don't leave me—" Byrna grunted the words out and went into a long shriek; Magda could not free herself. Maybe someone would hear Byrna yelling, but she could not get free without hurting her, maybe she should run and call somebody—but Byrna was tugging at her hands, crying out, that hard yell ending in gasping grunts.

Oh, Camilla, why don't you come back—!

The door burst open and Keitha was in the room. She said briskly, "I heard her, and I've delivered enough babies to know what that kind of yell means. Here, let me—" she drew the shawl and chemise back. "Get behind her, Margali, hold her up—yes, like that, hold her up, that's right." Magda obeyed, numbly, not knowing what was going on; Byrna was sitting half-upright, her legs spread, Magda behind her, gripping her around the waist. Byrna arched her body, strained, howling aloud, as Keitha braced her knees upright. She said swiftly, "No time to call anybody, no time to wait—I can manage."

Byrna gasped and yelled again, her body arching with effort. She was babbling, but Magda could not understand the words. Keitha knelt before her, and out of the corner of her eye Magda saw something red, slick, wet, streaked with blood. Byrna's harsh gasps and cries were blood-curdling; Keitha murmured something reassuring, and then Magda saw the wet, wriggling body of the child as Keitha lifted it, gently, tilted it head downward. There was a faint mewing wail, then the newborn baby began to scream indignation at leaving his warm nest. His. Magda could see the tiny folded genitals against the little body. Byrna relaxed against Magda, held out her arms.

"Let me hold him," she whispered. "Oh, Keitha, give him to me."

"He's beautiful," Keitha said, smiling, and laid the naked child on Byrna's belly. He wriggled toward the breast, and Byrna guided him gently; Magda suddenly wanted to cry, she wasn't sure why.

I didn't want a child, she thought, any more than Byrna did. Yet she's so happy with it now. He's so beautiful, she thought, looking blissfully at the baby against Byrna's body, and I could have had Peter's child, and I would have been as happy as that—she felt her breath catch in a sob.

"Margali," said Keitha, "Go and call Mother Millea. I would go myself, but I can manage the afterbirth, if I must, and you can't."

But Magda had not reached the door before Camilla came in, and beside her, heavily wrapped in outdoor cloak and hood, was Marisela, who looked at them and laughed as she took off her mantle.

"So you have cheated me out of a birth-gift, Keitha? Well, I have been up all night delivering twins; both born backward and I thought the mother would bleed to death. But they are both alive, and so is their mother, and they were both sons, so the father—" she made a wry face, "forced a double fee on me. So I am glad the hard part is already over." She went quickly and washed her hands in the basin near the fire, then came and said, "Let me see. Well, you managed that nicely, Keitha; she is not torn, even though it came so fast? Well, he is not very big. Here, little man," she said, taking up the baby and handling him in her expert fingers, turning him over, checking the cord, the stumpy little toes and fingers, putting a finger in his mouth to see if he sucked at it, swiftly inspecting nose, ears, the back of his pudgy neck, "Well, what a fine little fellow you are, every finger and toe where it should be." She laid him down again at Byrna's breast. "How do you feel, Byrna?"

"Tired," the woman said blissfully, "and sleepy. And hungry. Isn't he *beautiful*, Marisela?"

"He is indeed," said Marisela. She was a small, competent-looking woman, her hair cropped in Amazon fashion, but she wore women's clothing. She said, "I will send one of your friends down to get you some hot milk with honey; you are not bleeding much, but I will put something in it anyway, and then you will sleep for a while. And when you wake up, you shall have as big a breakfast as you want to eat," She looked at Magda and said, "You are the new one, aren't you? I forget your name—"

"Margali n'ha Ysabet," Magda said.

"I am sorry; I spend so much of my time out of the house I sometimes do not remember you all. I remembered you, though, Keitha," she said, touching Keitha's cropped golden head, "Did I not deliver your daughter? She must be a big girl by now."

Keitha's face crumpled. She said, shaking, "She—she died just before Midwinter, of the fever—"

"Ah, Goddess, I am sorry!" Marisela exclaimed.

"I—I begged my husband to send for you, who know so much of healing, but he would not—would not let a Renunciate under his roof—"

"Ah, I am sorry, but I might have been as helpless as they," said Marisela gently, "I am skilled, but against some fevers there is no help. But now you are here, and some day, Keitha, we must talk. For the moment, I am grateful to you for doing so well with Byrna's baby. I must finish this," she added, holding her dripping hands well away from her, exactly as Magda had seen Medics do in the Terran HQ, and bent over Byrna to check the afterbirth. "Camilla, will you wrap up Byrna's little man?"

Magda watched Camilla's long, callused fingers, tender on the child; Camilla held the baby, crooning, for a moment against her meager breast. How can a neuter, a woman who has no female hormones—and besides that, she must be fifty at least—appear so motherly? How, in any case, did a neuter, an *emmasca,* think of herself, of children? Magda could not even guess. She had always believed that this kind of motherly feeling was a matter of hormones, no more than that.

"Margali," Marisela said, "Go down to the kitchen, and heat some milk; put honey in it, and bring it up here for Byrna, to have with her medicine, before she sleeps."

Magda went downstairs, feeling weary; now she must stir up the banked fire and heat some milk! To her aching relief, however, Irmelin was already there, quietly moving around the huge stove. Rafaella was there too, dressed for riding, eating a bowl of hot porridge at the table.

"So Byrna's had her baby? And now Marisela wants some hot milk and honey for her," Irmelin said, kindly. "You sit down there by Rafi and have some tea; made myself some when I came down, it's poured out there. So Byrna's had her baby—what was it? Boy or girl?"

"A boy," Magda said, drinking the hot tea gratefully as Irmelin put the milk to heat.

Rafaella swore, slamming her fist on the table. "Hellfire! Poor brat, and she'll have to give him up—Zandru's hells, how well I remember that! There ought to be a better—hellfire!" She slammed out, leaving her porridge-bowl knocked over, spilling milk and runny porridge over the table. Magda stared after her, wondering what was the matter.

Irmelin watched her, sighing, but she came and mopped up the milk without speaking. She said curtly, "Drink your tea, Margali, and take this up to Byrna," and her eyes were distant, her lips set. Magda sipped at the sweet milky tea, longing almost passionately for a strong cup of black coffee. Her head was aching, and she felt exhausted. She took the milk upstairs.

The baby, wrapped in blanket and kimono, was lying in Byrna's arms; Byrna had been washed, her hair combed and braided, and she was lying with her eyes closed and peaceful.

"Let me put him in the cradle while you drink your milk, *breda*," Camilla said, holding the cup to her lips, but Byrna clung to the baby. "No, I want to keep him, please, please—"

Marisela told them to go and get some breakfast, saying she would stay with Byrna for a few hours, to make sure she did not begin bleeding, and Camilla sighed as they went down the stairs.

"Poor little thing," she said, "I hope Ferrika will come here in time to comfort her before she yields up her child—I am troubled about her." She put her arm around Magda, and said, "You are weary, too—had you never delivered a child before?"

"Never," said Magda. "Had you?"

"Oh, yes—I could have managed, had Keitha not been there. Rafaella's second son was born like that, and long before she looked for it; she had not counted her time properly and did not know she was within forty days of labor." She began to laugh. "We were riding together near Neskaya Guild House: we had been on fire-watch. She barely had time to get her breeches off; the child was born into my hands as I bent to see if she was truly in labor. We wrapped it in my tunic and she rode home beside me!" The tall *emmasca* chuckled. "I have heard that Dry-Town women ride till the very day they are delivered, but this equalled anything I had ever heard!"

The smell of breakfast cooking rose up the stairs, but Camilla did not turn toward the dining-room; instead she pulled the house-door open. The street was empty and dark, snow still falling heavily, though the light was stronger. Magda felt lost in the world of thick snowflakes, lost, very alien in this strange world. She felt that if by chance she should look in a mirror she would not recognize herself. Camilla heard her sigh, and tightened her arm around Magda's shoulder.

"You are weary of being housebound, I can imagine; but dark and dismal as the days are now, it would be worse to be shut up inside in the full summer. The time will pass before you know it. Look, there is blood on your tunic, and on your wrist," she added, picking up Magda's hand. "We have an old saying in the hills where I was brought up; if blood is spilt on you before breakfast, you will shed blood before nightfall. Are your courses due?"

For a moment Magda did not quite understand the phrase, which Camilla had spoken in the *cahuenga* vernacular; Camilla repeated the question in *casta* and Magda shook her head.

"Oh, no, not nearly." The snowflakes, whirling up from the street, felt cold on her cheeks. Camilla looked at her, troubled.

"But you have been here more than forty days and you have not had them—*breda,* are you pregnant?"

Damn it, was everybody watching her so closely as *that?* She said in exasperation "Damnation, no!"

"But how can you possibly be sure—" Camilla's face changed. "Margali! Have you taken a fertility-destroyer?"

Again, for a moment, Magda did not understand; when she did she thought that was probably the nearest equivalent to the Terran medical treatment which had suppressed menstruation and female function. She nodded; it saved argument.

"Don't you know those drugs can *kill* you, child? Why do you girls do it?" Camilla broke off and sighed. "I of all people have no right to lecture you, being what I am . . . and beyond that danger forever. It has been so long, so long since I can even remember what it was like to be driven by those hungers and needs. But at times—when I think of Byrna's face when she looked at her child—I wonder." The deep sigh seemed to rack her whole body; but her lips were pressed tight together, and she stared impassively at the falling snow. Magda had wondered before; what could drive a woman to the illegal and often fatal neutering operation on Darkover; it would not have been simple even for Terran medicine, yet she had seen more than one *emmasca* in her travels. She did not speak her question aloud, but at her side Camilla stiffened and looked away from her, staring into the whirling snowflakes, and Magda wondered if the woman could really read her mind.

Camilla said at last, "Only my oath-mother, Kindra, knows all; it is something of which I do not often speak, as you may imagine, but you are my sister and should know the truth. I—" she stopped again for a moment, and Magda protested, "I did not ask—you do not need to tell me anything, Camilla—"

She does read my mind! How? Magda remembered, with a curious sting of apprehension, how at Ardais she had stood by as Lady Rohana and the *leronis* Alida worked with the matrix to heal Jaelle's wound, and how she had found herself within the matrix, working with *laran.*

Camilla said, "Once I— bore another name, and my family was not unknown in the Kilghard Hills. My mother said," she added, her voice flat and detached, "that there was Hastur blood in my veins; which means probably that I was festival-born, and not the daughter of my father. I was destined for a great marriage, or for the Tower, a *leronis.* My father's freehold was attacked one day by bandits; they slew many of my father's sworn men, and me they carried away, with some of his cattle, to be a plaything for them. You can imagine, I suppose, how they used me," she said, still in that flat, detached voice. "I was not yet fourteen years old, and mercifully I have forgotten much."

"Oh, Camilla!" Magda's arms tightened around the older woman's spare body.

"I was ransomed, and rescued, at last," Camilla went on, rigid in Magda's arms, "My family was concerned, I think, mostly that I was spoilt for a grand marriage. And a *leronis* must be—" she paused, considering and turning over words, almost visibly, "untouched. I was not yet old enough even to know that I was with child by one of the—animals who had stolen me. I remember no more; my mind was darkened. I am told I laid hands on my life." Her eyes were distant, looking inward on horror; at last she gave herself a little shake and her voice was alive again.

"It mattered no further to my family what became of me. I was healed, but I knew I could never again endure the touch of any man without— horror. The Lady of Arilinn it was, Leonie Hastur, sanctioned it, that I should be made *emmasca;* and so it was done. For many years I lived among men, as a man, and refused to admit even to myself that I was a woman. But at last I came to the Guild House; and there I found, again, that womanhood was—was possible for me." She smiled down at Magda. "It was half a lifetime ago; sometimes for years together I remember nothing of that old life, or who I was then. We should go and sleep; only when I am weary do I talk such morbid rubbish."

Magda was still speechless, horror-stricken, not only by Camilla's story, but by the frozen calm with which she told it. Camilla smiled again at her and said "My oath-mother Kindra said once to me that every woman who comes to the Guild House has her own story and every story is a tragedy, one which would hardly be believed if it was played in a theatre by actors! When I saw Keitha's scars—I too was once beaten like an animal, and bear scars like hers on my body; so the story is fresh in my mind, and raw again."

Magda protested, "Surely that is not true of all Renunciates, though? They cannot be all tragedies! Surely some women simply come here because they like the life, or choose it for themselves—Jaelle, she told me, grew up in the Guild House, foster-daughter to Kindra—"

"Ask Jaelle, sometime, about her mother's death," said Camilla. "She was born in Shainsa; but it is her story, not mine, and I have no right to tell it."

Magda laughed uneasily. "My story is no tragedy," she said, trying to speak lightly. "It is more like a comedy—or a farce!"

"Ah, sister," Camilla said, "that is the true horror of all our stories, that some men, hearing them, would think them almost funny." But there was no mirth in her voice. "You should go to breakfast. I will give no lesson in swordplay today." She held out her arms and gave the younger woman a quick, warm hug. "Go and sleep, *chiya.*"

Magda would have rather stayed; she did not want to be alone. But she went obediently up to her room and to bed. An hour or two later she found herself awake, and unable to sleep again; she went to the kitchen and found herself some cold food; afterward, at loose ends—for the Guild Mothers had excused her from any duties today—she went into the library and read, for a time, the history of the Free Amazons. It crossed her mind that she should make careful notes, to file all this in the Terran records one day, but she did not want to think about that just yet. Later in the day Mother Lauria found her and asked her to take hall duty, the lightest of the assigned tasks inside the house. This meant only that she should go to the greenhouse and find flowers and leaves there for the decorations, which were beginning to fade, and afterward, stay in the hall and let anybody in or out, or answer the door if anyone came to the House on business.

Magda was learning simple stitches, but she still disliked sewing; she brought down a cord belt she was braiding, and sat working at the intricate knots.

Two or three times she got up to let someone in, and once brought a message to Marisela, which she gave at the door of the room where Byrna was sleeping, the baby tucked in beside her. She was half asleep, in the gray light of the hallway, when suddenly there was a loud and shocking banging on the door.

Madga jumped up and pulled the heavy door open. A huge burly man, expensively dressed, stood on the doorstep: he glowered at Magda and said, using the derogatory mode, "I wish to see the woman who is in charge of this place." But the inflection he used made it obvious that his meaning was, "Get me the bitch who is in charge of this rotten dump."

Magda noticed that there were two men behind him, as large as himself, both heavily armed with sword and dagger. She said, in a polite mode which was a reproof to him, "I will ask if one of the Guild Mothers is free to speak with you, messire. May I state your business?"

"Damn right," growled the man, "Tell the old bitch I've come for my wife and I want her right now and no arguments."

Magda shut the door in his face and went quickly to the Guild Mother's sanctuary.

"How white you are!" Mother Lauria exclaimed. "What's wrong, child?"

Magda explained. She said "I think it must be Keitha's husband," meanwhile glancing at the huge, copper-sheathed door commemorating the battle which had claimed their right to a woman who had, like Keitha, taken refuge here generations ago.

Mother Lauria followed her eyes.

"Let us hope it does not come to that, my child. But run down quickly to the armory, and tell Rafaella—no, Rafi is away with a caravan to the north. Tell Camilla to arm herself quickly, and come. I wish Jaelle were here, but there is no time to send for her. You arm yourself, too, Margali; Jaelle told me that you fought with bandits when she was wounded near Sain Scarp."

Magda, her heart pounding, ran down to the armory and quickly armed herself with the long knife the Amazons did not call a sword—though Magda could not see the difference. Camilla, arming herself, looked grim.

"Nothing like this has happened for ten years and more—that we should have to defend the house by force of arms as if we were still in the Ages of Chaos!" She looked doubtfully at Magda. "And you are all but untried—"

Magda was all too aware of this. Her heart pounded as they hurried along the stairs, side by side. Mother Lauria was waiting for them in the hall. There was a furious banging, on the door, and Mother Lauria opened it again.

The man on the doorstep began to bluster. "Are you the woman in charge of this place?"

Mother Lauria said quietly "I have been chosen by my sisters to speak in their name. May I ask to whom I have the honor of speaking?" She spoke with the extreme courtesy of a noblewoman addressing the crudest peasant.

The man snarled, "I am Shann MacShann, and I want my wife, not a lot of talk. You filthy bitches lured her away from me, and I want her sent out to me this minute!"

"No woman is allowed to come to us except of her free will," said

Mother Lauria, "If your wife came here it was because she wished to renounce her marriage for cause. No woman within these walls is wife to you."

"Don't you chop logic with me, you—" The man spat out a gutter insult. "You bring my wife out here to me, or I'll come in there and take her!"

Magda's hand tightened on her knife, but the Guild Mother's voice was calm. "By the rules of this place, no man may ever pass our walls except by special invitation; and I am afraid I really have nothing more to say to you, sir. If the woman who was once your wife wishes to speak with you, she may send you a message and settle any business left unsettled between you, but until she wishes to do so—"

"Look, that wife of mine, she gets mad at me sometimes, once she ran away to her mother and stayed almost forty days, but she come cryin' back to me again. How do I know you're not holding her there and she wanting to come back?"

"Just why would we do a thing like that?" asked Mother Lauria mildly.

"You think I don't know what goes on in places like this?"

"Yes," said Mother Lauria, "I think you do not know at all."

"Keitha, she's too much a woman to get along without a man!" Shann blustered, "You send her out here right now!"

"I'm really afraid, you know," said the Guild Mother with great composure, "that you are going to have to accept my word: Keitha n'ha Casilda has expressed no desire to return to you. If you wish to hear from her own lips, we allow visitors on the night of High Moon, and you are welcome to come, unweaponed, alone or with members of your immediate family, and speak to her either alone or in our presence, as she herself wishes. But at this hour and on this day no man may enter here unless he has business here, and you, sir, assuredly have none. I ask you now to take yourself and your men away from here, and not to create a commotion on our doorstep."

"I tell you, I'm coming in and get my wife," Shann shouted, whipped out his sword and started up the steps. Camilla and Magda, long knives drawn, quickly stepped forward and blocked the way.

"You think I'm not a match for a pair of girls?" He whipped the sword down, but Camilla, moving swiftly as a striking snake, caught his blade with hers and struck it from his hand. He missed his footing on the stairs and stumbled, almost falling. He shouted to his men "Come on! Let's get in there!"

Magda braced herself for another attack. The white light of the snow in the street, the two huge men slowly advancing, Camilla at her shoulder, the knife-scars on her face white and drawn. For Magda the scant few seconds it took for the men to mount the first step seemed to last an eternity.

Then the men were on them and Magda felt herself thrusting, twisting the steel; the man's sword clanged, whipped sideways, slashed quickly back, and Magda felt a line of fire slice along her leg.

It didn't hurt, not yet, but while she blocked the next stroke—skills learned in Intelligence training, years ago, were coming back rapidly— what she mostly felt was shock.

You get this kind of training, it's routine, but you don't expect to have to use it, not really. You find you can do it, her thoughts raced, *but you don't believe it, not while you're doing it, not even while you're bleeding.* Her mind lagged behind but her body was fighting, driving the men back, down the steps. One slipped in the snow and Magda felt the sword go in under his breastbone before she fully knew it, felt the body sliding back off the blade, pulled by its own dead weight. She brought her knife up to guard against the next man; did not realize that Shann had gone down, bleeding, under Camilla's sword; that Camilla had said, to the third man, "Had enough?"

Magda did not hear: she was going after the third man in a flurry of sword-strokes, forcing him back and down the steps. Her blood sounded loud in her own ears and there was a blurry haze, blood-colored, before her eyes. A voice inside her seemed to be screaming, *Kill them, kill them all!* All of her rage against the Darkovan men who had kept her from the work and the world she wanted, her terror of the bandits who had disarmed her and shown her her own weakness—it was almost a sensual frenzy, letting the sword move almost without volition, until she heard someone shouting her name. By now the sound meant nothing. She saw the man before her slip, stumble to his knees. Then another sword struck hers down; she whirled to face her attacker and in the moment before she struck, she saw Camilla's face; it made her pause, just a moment, and her sword went flying with a violence that knocked her hand numb.

"No, Margali! No! He surrendered, didn't you see him raise his sword in surrender?" Camilla's hand bit into her wrist, a cruel grip that paralyzed her fingers.

Magda came up to her senses, shaking; she looked, in consternation, at the man she had killed, and Shann next to him, groaning in his blood at the foot of the stairs. The third man had backed off and was staring in dismay at a wound in his forearm, from which fresh blood welled up.

Camilla said furiously "You have disgraced your knife!" She pushed Magda down, hard, on the steps, and went down the stairs to the wounded man.

"I most humbly beg your pardon, sir. She is new to fighting, and untried; she did not see your gesture of surrender."

The wounded man said, "I thought you women were going to kill us all, surrender or no! And this is no quarrel of mine, *mestra!*"

Camilla said, "I have honorably sold the service of my blade for thirty years, comrade. My companion is young. Believe me, we will so deal with her that she will not so disgrace her blade again. But are you not Shann's sworn man?"

The mercenary spat. "Sworn man to that one? Zendru's hells, no! I'm a paid sword, no more. It's no business of mine to lose my life for the likes of him!"

"Let me see your wound," Camilla said, "You shall have indemnity, believe me. We have no quarrel with you."

"And I have no quarrel with you, and no blood-feud, *mestra.* Between ourselves, I'd say that if his wife left him he'd given her cause four times over, but my sword is for hire, so I fought while he fought. But he is no kin or sworn comrade." Awkwardly, with his unwounded hand, he thrust the sword back into its sheath, and pointed to Shann. "I'll go find his housefolk and his paxmen to haul him home; he's nothing to me, but when I fight at a man's side, I don't leave him to bleed to death in the street." He looked regretfully at the man Magda had killed. "Now *he* was a pal of mine; we've been hiring out our swords together for twelve years come midsummer."

Camilla said gravely, "Who grudges his blood to a blade had better earn his living behind the plow."

The man sighed, made the *cristoforo* sign of prayer. "Aye, he's laid his burdens now on the Bearer of the World's Wrongs. Peace to him, *mestra.*" He looked at his wounded arm. "But it goes hard to have blood shed after surrender!"

Mother Lauria came down the steps. "You shall have whatever indemnity a judge names as fair. Camilla, take him to the Stranger's Room and bind up his wound."

Camilla turned angry eyes on Magda. She said, with savage contempt, "Get inside, you, before you disgrace us further!"

Puzzled, feeling betrayed, Magda managed to stumble inside. The wound in her thigh, which she had hardly felt at the time, began to throb as if it had been burned with fire.

She had fought for the house. She had done her best—had the man truly surrendered before she struck him?

In the mountains I disgraced myself because I was afraid to fight, then when I fight I disgrace the Guild House. . . . She felt sobs choking her, and braced herself against them; if she let herself cry now she would break into hysterical crying and never be able to stop. . . .

"*Breda—*" said a soft, troubled voice, and Keitha's pale, tear-stained face looked into hers. "Oh, how cruel she is! You fought for us, you are hurt too—and she cares more for that soldier's wound than yours! And you have shed your blood for us! Come, let me, at least, look after your hurt—"

Magda let herself lean heavily on Keitha as they went up the stairs. Keitha went on, indignant, "I saw it all—how can Camilla be so unjust? So the man had surrendered—what of that? I wish you had killed them all—"

Magda's leg had begun to hurt so badly that she felt dizzy. Blood was dripping on the floor. Keitha drew her inside the bathroom on their floor, pushed her down on a little wooden bathing stool and gently pulled off the slashed breeches. The cut was deep, blood still welling up slowly from the bottom. Magda clung to the stool, suddenly afraid of falling, while Keitha sponged the wound with icy water. While she was working on it, Mother Lauria came slowly up the stairs and stepped inside.

She looked coldly at the two women. "How badly are you hurt, Margali?"

Magda set her teeth. "I don't know enough about wounds to know how bad it is. It hurts."

Lauria came and examined the slash herself. "It is a clean wound and it will heal; but painful. Did you get it from a surrendered man fighting for his life?"

Magda said clearly, "I did not; it was the first man, the one I killed, and I was fighting myself for my life, since I suppose he would not have stopped at killing me."

"Well, that's something," Mother Lauria said.

"How can you blame her so!" Keitha cried. "She fought to defend us, she is hurt and bleeding, yet you let Camilla bully her and call her harsh names, then you come and bully her further, before her wound is even bandaged—"

The Guild Mother's face was stern. "To kill a surrendered man is *murder,*" she said. "If Camilla had not struck down her sword, she could have killed a defenseless man and brought blood-feud on us. As it is, we are fortunate that he was only hired mercenary; had he been one of Mac-Shann's sworn men, they would be bound to avenge him! Thendara House would have had to answer challenge after challenge, and it could have destroyed us! Fortunately, his wound is not disabling, and Camilla has been a hired mercenary herself and knows their codes of honor. She is dressing his wound in the Stranger's Room, and she hopes he will accept a cash indemnity for the wound so shamefully given."

Magda lowered her head, accepting the guilt. Yes, she had lost control, she was to blame. She remembered Cholayna Ares, in Intelligence school, warning them. *Never lose control, never lose your temper; never kill unless you wish to kill.* To keep her fear at bay, she had clung to her anger, and it had disgraced her. She sat trembling, feeling that Mother Lauria's anger was a tangible thing, a sort of red glow around the woman. And then she wondered if she were going mad.

Lauria turned on Keitha in angry scorn.

"And you, you have not even inquired whether he who was your husband is alive or dead! Are we to be assassins for your grudge?"

Keitha said furiously, "I care nothing, truly, whether he lives or dies! Am I to return good for evil like a *cristoforo?* I have renounced him forever!"

"Not true," said Mother Lauria. "If you had truly renounced him, you would not fear to know whether he lived or died, and could tend, like Camilla, the wounds of a fallen foe without hatred."

"She had not suffered at his hands—" Keitha began.

"What do you know of what Camilla has suffered at the hands of men?" Mother Lauria demanded, and Magda remembered what Camilla had told her . . . had it been only this morning? It seemed so very long ago. Mother Lauria sighed.

"Well, Margali's wound still bleeds; fortunately, Marisela is still in the house, though I hate to wake her like this when she was up all night. Margali, do you realize what you have done?"

Magda was still fighting the urge to hysterical crying.

"I didn't know—I did not see that he had surrendered—"

"When you take sword in hand it is your business to know," said Mother Lauria grimly. "There is no excuse in this world, or the next, for striking down a surrendered man. Name your oath-mother!"

It had the force of a ritual demand; Mother Lauria knew perfectly well what the answer was.

"Jaelle n'ha Melora."

"You have disgraced her too," Mother Lauria said, "and when you are well again, she shall deal with you!" She went away, and Magda sat sobbing on the bench. Her leg hurt fiercely, but in her distress she hardly felt it.

"Well, what have we here?" asked Marisela cheerfully, as she came in, and Magda looked up, frightened; would Marisela too think it her duty to scold and browbeat her? She deserved it, whatever they might say or not say. And they would hold Jaelle responsible, and that was the worst!

But Marisela only knelt to examine the cut with gentle, experienced hands. "Nasty, but it will heal; the muscle is not much damaged. I will have to stitch this. Can you help me get her to her room, Keitha? It will be easier to do it there, and afterward, I fear, she will not be in much shape for walking, poor little rabbit." She stroked Magda's cheek and added, "This is a miserable thing to happen when you first take sword in our defense. Help her to her room, Keitha, while I fetch my things."

It was a nightmare of pain and effort, but somehow Keitha got her to her room and into her bed. Magda felt a twinge of fear through the pain, when Marisela came in—in the Terran Zone, she knew, a cut this deep would be sewn under anesthetic! Marisela sponged it with some icy stuff that numbed it slightly, then quickly and skillfully put in several stitches; Magda was by now so unstrung that she could not be brave, but disgraced herself again, she felt, by sobbing like a child. Keitha hugged and comforted her, and Marisela held some kind of fiery cordial to her lips; it made her head swim. Afterward Marisela kissed her on the forehead, said, "I'm sorry I had to hurt you so, *breda,*" and went away. Keitha sat beside her, holding her hand.

"I don't care what they say! To me it is no disgrace! They should not bully you that way!"

But now it was over, and the hysteria subsiding, Magda knew what Camilla meant. She had disgraced her steel.

I can't do anything right, she thought. I was a failure in the Terran Zone, a failure as a wife—I couldn't even give Peter the son he wanted—now I have failed here too, disgraced Jaelle, disgraced Camilla who taught me—I have failed here too, she thought.

Keitha held her, whispering, "Don't cry, Margali." She turned Magda's head between her hands and kissed her; and to Magda's dismay and horror, she felt no impulse to push the kiss away; instead her awareness was strange, intense, frighteningly sexual; she felt herself returning it, pulling Keitha closer, even though, in that sudden overwhelming awareness, she knew Keitha had not meant it that way, had meant only to comfort her as she would have kissed her own child, that Keitha would have been horrified if she had had any idea how Margali had interpreted her gesture. She could feel Keitha's compassion and kindness as a warm flood of soft colors wrapping her, just as she had felt Mother Lauria's rage, a red halo surrounding her and lashing out to strike . . .

What was in that stuff Marisela gave me, anyhow? I am drunk, drugged, I am going mad . . . was this why she had failed with Peter, was it this Camilla had read in her the other night, was this what she really wished for when her defenses were down? Had Peter been right, when he accused her of being half in love with Jaelle herself, and jealous of him?

But she was too exhausted to be afraid. She let herself float, remembering the moment at Ardais when she had been *inside* the matrix. The bed was floating, it was like being far out in space, swirls of light tracing themselves round and round inside her eyes, faster and faster. For a moment she was back there at Ardais, with Lady Rohana looking up at her, troubled, and saying, *If you have trouble with* laran *you must promise to tell me at once.* But how could she, Magda wondered, when Rohana was *there* and she was *here?* It seemed that Keitha was calling to her from very far away, but she thought, Keitha is my friend, I do not want to upset or frighten her as I was frightened of Camilla that night, so she hid herself and did not answer. And then there was another face in the darkness, a beautiful woman's face, pale, surrounded in a cloud of pale reddish-golden hair, and all blue as if she saw it through the color of a pale blue fire, and at the last, yet another face; round, calm, practical, a woman's face under close-cropped greying hair, an Amazon, saying quietly, *We must do something for her, she belongs to us and she does not know it yet.*

A Terranan?

She is neither the first nor the last to claim a heritage in an unknown world.

And then the world went away and did not return.

Part Two

Sundering

Chapter One

It was snowing. The world outside the high HQ tower, beyond the windows of Cholayna Ares's office, was lost in a flurry of white, and Jaelle, looking out into it, wished she were outside in the snow, not in here, in the yellow light, where no hint of natural weather ever penetrated.

Peter saw her look out wistfully into the storm, and pressed her hand. Since the night of Alessandro Li's reception, he had been gentle, apologetic, tender with her; she could not hold on to her anger, and in the past weeks he had tried, again, to be the man she had loved at once in Sain Scarp, had clung to at Ardais. He had tried, conscientiously tried, in spite of his Terran upbringing, to remember her independence, never to take her for granted. She had begun to hope again; perhaps, perhaps, even if they had lost what first drew them together, they could grow into something stronger and better than before. *That first intense sexual glow, I should have understood, I could never expect that to last forever, but now that I am no longer a delayed adolescent in the grip of her first infatuation, perhaps Piedro and I can find something more mature, more genuine. It was not all his fault, either. I have been selfish and childish.*

He said gently, "I'd like to be out there, too, walking in the snow," and for a moment, so great was their attunement, she wondered if perhaps he too had rudimentary *laran;* many, perhaps most, Terrans did. As they grew closer, perhaps it would develop and she could have with him the kind of understanding she craved.

Cholayna smiled at them both and said with a glimmer of irony, "If you two lovebirds can spare me a moment—" and Peter let go of Jaelle's hand and she saw the self-conscious color creeping up his face. Cholayna said,

"Oh, don't apologize. I wish I could give you both a year's leave so you could go off for a proper honeymoon, but conditions really don't allow it. By now, Magda should have had plenty of time to decide if there are any women in the Thendara Guild House who would be suitable for Medic technicians, and perhaps others we could use here in different employment. What's the possibility that she could come here to talk about it, Jaelle?"

"Absolutely zero," Jaelle replied promptly. "I told you; she is in her housebound half-year for training, and during that time she cannot leave the house except at the direct command of a Guild Mother."

Cholayna frowned a little and said, "I understood you were her superior; can't you send for her and order it?"

"I suppose I could," Jaelle said slowly, "but I would not do that to her. It would set her apart from the others and she could never recover, if she is really to be one of them."

"I think you're being overconscientious," Peter said. "The decision to use Free Amazons—excuse me, Renunciates—in Terran employment is an important one for both our worlds and it should be implemented as soon as humanly possible, before we lose the momentum of that decision."

"Just the same, we don't want to disturb Magda's cover," said Cholayna, "If she has gone among them as one of them we don't want to single her out in any way. Jaelle, could you go there and talk privately to her?"

Jaelle was suddenly overcome with a flood of homesickness. To visit the Guild House, to be one with her sisters again! "I'd be glad to do that, and I can talk to Mother Lauria about it, too."

"The only thing wrong with that," Peter said wryly, "is that I can't come with you, can I?"

"Not to the Guild House, I'm afraid," she said, but smiled, thinking that one day before long they would surely walk in the snow together, through the city she loved. He loved it too, he had spent years living as a Darkovan in her world. Why had she begun to think of him as a Terran and alien? Somehow she must help him, as well as herself, to recapture the Darkovan Piedro she had loved.

"I want to talk a little about the kind of woman we need here," said Cholayna. "Above all, they must be flexible, capable of learning new ways of thinking, doing, capable of adjusting to alien conditions. In fact—" she smiled at Jaelle and it was like a warm touch of the woman's hand, "like you, Jaelle; capable of surviving culture shock."

"Ah," Peter said, "but there aren't any more like Jaelle. When they made her, they broke the mold."

"I don't think I'm as unique as all that," she said, smiling, but already her mind was running over the women she knew in the Guild House.

There might be others she did not know as well, suited to training among the Terrans. Rafaella would never make a Medic technician, but she might be useful as a mountain guide, would certainly be valuable to the Terrans for her knowledge of travel in the hills and the Hellers. Marisela—Jaelle frowned for a moment, thinking of the midwife's skill and the adaptability which allowed her to work in the city with women who despised the ordinary Free Amazon. Marisela, certainly, would benefit by this kind of training, but could they spare her in the Guild House? She shrugged it off, deciding that she would talk it over with Mother Lauria, and raised her eyes to meet Cholayna's smile.

"Where were you?" she asked, smiling, and Jaelle laughed and apologized. "Thinking over the women in the Guild House."

Cholayna laughed and dismissed her. "Well, go and talk it over with your Guild Mothers. Some day, perhaps—would it be possible for me to visit a Guild House?"

"I don't know why not," Jaelle said, responding again to the woman's spontaneous friendliness. "I think Mother Lauria would like you very much. I wish you could have known my oath-mother, Kindra." They were, she decided as she went down to her quarters, very much alike in many ways. Although Cholayna had grown up in a world where no one had made it difficult for her to learn and grow, and she had come to her strength, not by revolt and renunciation, as an Amazon must do, but simply by choosing this work. . . .

And then Jaelle was shocked at herself. Was she criticizing her own world, in favor of the *Terranan?* Had a few tendays here corrupted her so much?

Corrupted? Is it corruption, then, to love Peter or to appreciate his world? She slammed the door of her quarters and tore off her uniform with shaking hands. It was, indeed, time to revisit her home!

She got into her embroidered linen undertunic, heavy drawers and the thick woollen breeches and overtunic; sat down to lace her boots. Swearing, she ran her hand through her long thick hair. Time, and more than time, to have it cut. No, damnation, why should she? She was living as Peter's freemate—*which the terms of her Oath permitted her to do,* she reminded herself severely. Yet the thought persisted; what would Rafaella say, or Camilla, when she appeared in the Guild House with long hair instead of the distinctive Renunciate cut which proclaimed her independence of any man? Oh, damn them all! She fingered a pair of scissors, looked reflectively in the mirror, remembering Peter's hands caressing her hair. She actually set the scissors to her neckline, then swore again, angrily, and flung them down. It was her own hair and her own life, and if she wished to please her beloved freemate that too was her privilege. Yet the sting of guilt remained.

If it was snowing outside, she should have creams to protect her face against the wind and chill. She rummaged in the drawer, appreciating the soft perfumed Terran cosmetics; the perfume was a little stronger, the texture somewhat smoother, than those she could have bought in the market or the ones that some of the women made in the Guild House when funds were short for a time. As she was smoothing the stuff on her face, she encountered the small calculating device of beads which she used to keep track of her women's cycles by the movement of the moons; the beads colored like the four moons, violet, peacock-blue, pale green and white. She slid down a violet bead, for she had noted that Liriel's disc was full, and stopped, staring at the beads. She should have pulled down a red bead for bleeding, at least a tenday ago. She had been so disrupted by the dreadful fight with Peter, and the distress accompanying it, and after it, her exacting work with Cholayna and Aleki, that she had simply pulled down the beads mechanically every day without noticing.

Was it simply the disruption of the cycles which, she had been warned, might come with living by artificial yellow light? Or was it possible that she might have become pregnant, that Peter, in the ecstatic reunion which had followed their quarrel, had managed to make her pregnant?

She could not help a deep-based flicker of pleasure at the thought, immediately followed by doubt and dread. Did she really want this? Did she want to be at the mercy of some small parasite within her body, sickness, distortion, the appalling ordeal of birth which had killed her own mother? For a second her mind flickered the terror of a nightmare. . . . *red spilling into the parched sand of a waterhole, sunrise and blood* . . . and a sharp stab of pain in her hands told her that without knowing it she had clenched her fist so tightly that her nails dug into the palm. Nonsense, what was she thinking, this mixture of old nightmares?

Peter would be so pleased when she told him! For a moment she anticipated the delight that would spread over his face, the tenderness and pride that would light his eyes.

Pride. The words of the oath reverberated in her mind, *Bear a child only in my own time and season; bear no child for any man's heritage or position.* . . . Oh, nonsense, she told herself. Peter was not Comyn, even though he looked so much like Kyril, he had none of the particular pride in heritage which was so much a part of Comyn life. The sneaking thought remained, *Rohana too will be pleased, that I have chosen to bear a child for the Aillard Domain,* and she slammed that thought shut, too. Not for Aillard. Not for Peter. For myself, because we love each other and this is the surest confirmation of our love! *For myself, damn it!*

But she slammed the drawer shut on the beads, almost with guilt, when she heard Peter's step.

"Jaelle? Love, I thought you were going to the Guild House—"

"I am just going," she said, and tried not to look guiltily at the drawer. *If he were telepathic like Kyril, he would know without being told, without even seeing the beads.* She had once explained the device to him, but he had never paid much attention to it, though he admitted he had seen them for sale in the market and wondered if they were a kind of abacus. He had shown her how an abacus worked, telling her it was the most ancient Terran variety of calculator.

"Surely you won't go in this blizzard, Jaelle—"

"You've been in the Terran Zone too long, if you call this little flurry of snow a blizzard," she said gaily. She wanted to get out into the bracing cold of the weather, not skulk here in the debilitating artificial heat of the HQ buildings.

"Let me go with you," he said, pulling on his outdoor boots and jacket. She hesitated.

"Love, in Amazon clothing I should not walk through the streets of the city with you this way, and it will expose you, too, to comment and gossip —" and at his blank look she elaborated, "You are still in uniform."

"Oh. That. I can change," he offered, but she shook her head.

"I would rather not. Do you really mind, Peter? I'd rather be alone now. If I come to the Guild House in the company of a Terran—or of any man —there will be talk which will make my mission harder."

He sighed. "As you wish," he said, pulling her close and kissing her. The kiss lingered suggestively.

"Wouldn't you rather stay here where it's nice and warm?"

The thought was tempting. Had she fallen into the Terran way of making love by the clock, with no room for emotional spontaneity? But, firmly, she disengaged herself from his arms.

"I'm working, darling. I really do have to go. As you're fond of reminding me about Montray, Cholayna's my boss."

He let her go almost too promptly. "You'll be back before dark?"

"I might spend the night in the Guild House," she said. "It's not the sort of thing I can do in an hour or so." She laughed at his crestfallen look.

"Piedro, love, it's not the end of the world, to sleep apart for a single night!"

"I suppose not," he grumbled, "but I'll miss you."

She softened. "I'll miss you too," she whispered into his neck, hugging him close again, "but there are going to be times when you're out in the field, and I'll have to stay alone. We might as well get used to it now."

But the hurt look in his eyes followed her down the stairs, out into the chill of the base, past the Spaceforce guards which separated the HQ from the Trade City. Feeling the welcome cold of snow on her cheeks, she still wished she had softened their parting with her good news.

But there would be time enough for that.

It would be better, Magda thought, if someone would call her names. Anything would be better than this endless, reproachful silence, this careful courtesy.

"Are you quite ready, Margali?" Rafaella asked. "Will you work with Doria and Keitha? I think they need more practice in falling."

Magda nodded. The big room called the Armory was filled with the white light of the snow outside, for the windowshades had been rolled back to let in maximum light. Mats were unrolled on the floor, and a dozen women were doing beginning exercises in stretching and bending, in preparation for the lesson in unarmed combat which Rafaella was about to give.

Magda remembered her third day in the house, when she had had her first lesson under Rafaella. After several days of struggling with unfamiliar tasks, baking bread, trying to learn to milk dairy animals, struggling with heavy barn brooms and shovels, it had been a great relief to come upon something she could actually do. She had been thoroughly trained in unarmed-combat skills in the Intelligence schools on Alpha, and she was eager to show Rafaella that she was not a complete idiot.

She had been prepared—then—to like Rafaella, knowing the slight, dark woman was Jaelle's partner in their travel-counseling business. Also, on her first evening in the House she had heard Rafaella singing to the harp. Magda's own mother had been a notable musician, the first Terran to transcribe many of the Darkovan folk ballads, and to make the historical connections between Darkovan and Terran music. Magda was no musician herself—she had a good sense of pitch, but no singing voice—but she admired the talent in others. She had been ready not only to like, but to admire Rafaella.

But Rafaella had been, from the first, persistently unfriendly, and when, in that first lesson, it became apparent that Rafaella expected her to be completely stupid, as clumsy as the housebred Keitha, Magda had summoned all her knowledge of Terran *judo* and Alphan *vaidokan*. When she had twice thrown Rafaella on her back, the older woman had stopped the lesson and frowned at her.

"Where in Zandru's hells did you learn all that?"

Too late Magda realized what she had done. She had learned it on a planet half a Galaxy away, from a Terran-Arcturian woman who had trained both her and Peter in self-defense; but she was in honor bound to Mother Lauria not to say so.

"I learned it—when I was a very young woman," she said. "A long way from here."

"Yes, I remember, you were born in the Hellers near Caer Donn," said Rafaella. "But did your father permit such learning?"

"He was dead by that time," said Magda truthfully, "and there was no other who had a right to object to it."

Rafaella looked at her skeptically. "I cannot imagine any man but a husband teaching such things to a woman," she said, and Magda said, again truthfully, "My freemate had no objections."

Quite without intending it, Magda remembered a time early in their marriage—before the growing competitiveness that had destroyed it—when she and Peter had worked together in unarmed combat techniques. Rafaella scowled at her.

"Well," she said, "it is certain that I can teach you nothing more; rather, you have much to teach us all. I hope you will help me, and the rest of us as well, to learn some of those holds. I suppose it is a technique known in the mountains." And so Magda had become a second teacher of the lessons in unarmed combat. It was not as easy as she thought it would be; she had learned the techniques to use them, not to teach them, and she had spent considerable time working alone, trying to figure out how she did things. But it had given her some much needed self-esteem, and she had even, a little, managed to disarm Rafaella's unfriendliness. Until the day when she had fought for the house and disgraced them. Camilla had managed to disarm the man's anger, and they had escaped blood-feud at their door, but they had had to pay a heavy cash indemnity which the house could ill afford. Magda had been kept in bed almost a tenday after the wound, and had just been allowed up.

"Are you able to work this way?" Rafaella asked. "You do not want to break the wound open and start the bleeding again."

"Marisela said I should exercise it carefully," she said, "or it would grow stiff."

Rafaella shrugged and turned her back. "You know best," she said, and went to the corner where she was trying to induce Keitha—without much success—to relax and fall perfectly limp on one of the mats.

Byrna, wearing an old pair of trousers too large for her, wrapped twice about her waist, touched Magda's shoulder. She said "Don't be upset; Rafi is like that. She's cross because she's been teaching unarmed-combat here in the House for the last twelve years, and now you come here, a newcomer, and you are better at it than she is. She's jealous, can't you tell?"

Magda was not sure, but she said firmly, "Shall we get started?" and began to do the ballet-like stretching exercises which preceded a workout. Her leg hurt, and she stopped, rolled up her trousers and looked at it. It was firmly scabbed over; she knew the pain was only the stretching of muscles gone soft while she had been in bed.

"Me too," said Byrna, groaning, "Marisela warned me to exercise all the time I was pregnant, and I was too lazy, and now every muscle shrieks at me!" She winced as her arm jostled her full breasts. "And I will have to go upstairs in half an hour and feed the little one! But I suppose I should get a little exercise, so I will get back into condition somehow."

"Come over here and work with me, Byrna," said Rafaella, "I have had the experience of working out while I was nursing a hungry suckling, and I can show you how to recover your muscles quickly. And you, Margali," she added formally, "will you do me the favor of working with Keitha for a time?"

Magda thought; of course; *as soon as I begin talking with someone who is really friendly to me*—for since the night when Byrna's child was born, she had grown to know and like the other woman very much—*Rafaella calls her away, and I am alone again.* Keitha obediently came to her, moving stiffly, and Magda said, "Try to make your whole body soft and limp, Keitha. Until you stop being afraid of hurting yourself, you will always be tense, and then you *will* hurt yourself." Keitha, she thought uncharitably, was as stiff as a barn broom; when Magda urged her to fall over, she stiffened and went down, putting out an arm to try to break her fall.

"No, no," Magda urged. "Try to *roll* as you fall. Limp—like this," she said, demonstrating, falling relaxed and unhurt on the mat, and Keitha, though she tried bravely to imitate Magda, could not repress a cry of pain.

"Ow!" She rubbed her bruised shoulders and hip. Magda was tempted to lose patience with her, but she said only "Watch how Doria does it." She looked up as some of the other women approached, asking, "Do you want to work with us?"

The other women said, with perfect politeness, "No, thank you," and went to the far end of the room, pointedly ignoring them.

Keitha is friendly, and Byrna, and Doria. For the others, I don't exist, Magda thought, and shrugged, turning back to Doria. The one thing she had not wanted was to get into direct competition with Rafaella; but somehow she had managed that too.

"Keitha, I won't let you hurt yourself," she said, trying to encourage the woman to relax. "Look, like this—" and again she let herself go limp, landing easily. After two or three more tries, Keitha, though still stiff, had lost some of the terrified rigidity which had made every fall a painful ordeal. Well a lifetime of decorous, ladylike movement was not easy to overcome.

Byrna and Doria were practicing holds together; Doria tripped and fell clumsily, and as she picked herself up, Magda, watching, realized something which she had not noticed, even in herself, until she noticed it in Doria.

"It is not so much a matter of *movement* as of *breath,*" she said. "Try and visualize the center of your body *here,* and try to breathe from it." She pointed at the center of her abdomen. "This point here, your center of gravity, really doesn't move; your body moves around it. That is why methods of self-defense designed for men are not really so suitable for women; a woman's center of gravity is lower, because of a man's bony structure."

"But some women are built almost like men," Doria protested, "Rafi— she's so tall and thin—" and she looked at her foster-mother, who stopped work and listened. Magda felt self-conscious as she said, "It is not so much a matter of male or female as a matter of different bone structure; everyone must learn precisely where her own—or his own, for a man—where the particular balance point is for the body, and learn to move around it. Part of it can be done through what we call centering, in the—" she stopped and gulped; she had been about to use the Old Terran word *dojo,* still used in the Alpha Colony for a martial-arts school—"in the place where I studied," she hastily amended. "You can learn this *centering* through breathing and meditation, and through physical practice, learning to move your body around this absolute physical point, wherever it is. I am taller and heavier than you are; it would be different for me than for you, and different yet for Rafaella, or Camilla"—she looked around the room to see if the old *emmasca* was there. She was, but she was busy at relining the grip on a knife hilt, and seemingly paying no attention to the lesson. Rafaella, however, had stopped working with her group and had moved closer to listen, and Magda felt, again, the self-consciousness as she finished, hunting for the right words—it was not easy to find equivalents for the Terran style of martial arts and translate them into Darkovan; she had to use the language of Darkovan dancing, for there was no other. "It is a kind of balance; you find a place where your center is motionless and your body moves *around* it, balancing on that spot."

"She is right," Camilla said, raising her head. "This I had to learn for myself, when I studied swordplay among men; it may be one reason I am better with a sword than many men. They did not notice, thinking me a man, and it is true that I am very tall and thin, but my center is still lower than a man's of my height; I had to learn to compensate for that, and the constant practice to match myself against men gave me more skill than many of them." She came and touched Doria's shoulder. "You are very thin, and your hips still very narrow—I do not think you are quite full grown yet; your balance will change as you grow, but once you have learned how to find your center, you will know how to recognize the changes."

Some of the women were moving and balancing curiously, trying to test for themselves whether what Magda said was true. Keitha said scornfully, "It sounds like that old mystical theory—that the center of a woman's body is in her womb!"

Rafaella chuckled. "Nothing mystical about it. That's exactly where it is." Keitha made a gesture of revulsion, and Rafaella added, "Ask Byrna if her balance did not change when she was pregnant?"

"Indeed it did," Byrna said, "and I still have not recovered my old balance, having carried the child so long!"

Rafaella said directly to Keitha, "Why do you think a child is carried just *there?* Because it is exactly where the body is balanced and can best take the weight of a child." She looked Keitha over with an experienced eye. "I should imagine you would carry very low—am I right?"

Keitha said sullenly, "Yes. What of it?"

"That is your trouble in movement," Rafaella said. "You are trying to brace your body from the small of your back, as a man does and you should bring your weight forward—try to stand like this," she added, readjusting Keitha with a careful hand. She looked at Magda with momentary camaraderie. "You are so tall I would judge that you carry very high, don't you?"

"I don't know," Magda said, "I have never been pregnant."

"No? Well, when you are, I am sure you will notice the change in balance," Rafaella said. "Keitha, if you bring your weight forward—look how Margali stands—you will balance more easily." She moved away, and Magda said, "Doria, will you try with me? I want to show them—"

Doria turned to her, taking the braced stance for practice, and Rafaella reached out and moved her roughly into position.

"Not that way, stupid thing," she said. "How dull you are, Doria!"

Magda drew a deep breath, and said, carefully, "Rafaella, I think Doria would do better if you were not constantly standing over her and correcting her. She is doing well enough."

"She is *my* daughter," Rafaella flared, "and it is not enough for her to do *well enough!* That is all very well for outsiders—" she looked scornfully at Keitha, "who have never been taught to believe in themselves and have to learn here what every girl should learn before she is ten years old! But Doria was brought up among us, and there is no excuse for her to be so stupid and clumsy!"

Doria was struggling with tears again, and Magda bit her lip; Rafaella was so anxious for the girl to excel that she kept Doria constantly on the edge of hysteria. "Rafaella, forgive me, but it was you who asked me to teach Doria, and I believe it is for me to say when she is doing well or not—"

"It is for you to say *nothing!*" Rafaella snapped. "You ignorant hill-woman, it is not even sure that they will let you stay among us, after what you have done!"

Magda fought twin impulses; to turn on her heel and walk out of the Armory, to slap Rafaella harder than she had ever hit anything in her life. She felt again the terrifying surge of fury which had overcome her when she had fought for the house; she knew with her last grip on sanity that if she struck Rafaella now, with the skills she had learned in Alpha's Intelligence School, she would kill the woman with her bare hands. Shaking, her hands gripped into fists, she walked a little away from them.

Camilla said peacefully, "Rafaella, at Doria's age a girl can learn better from a stranger than from her mother—"

Rafaella put her arm around Doria and murmured, "Darling, I only want to be proud of you here in our own Guild House, that is all. It is only for your own good—" and Doria burst into tears and clung to Rafaella.

At that moment the door opened and Mother Lauria looked in to the Armory. Her eyes widened at the scene—Doria sobbing in Rafaella's arms, Magda with her back to them all, the rest staring—but she said only, "Is Margali here? You have a visitor in the Stranger's Room; I am sorry to call you from your lesson—"

"Oh, *she* has nothing to learn from any of *us,*" Rafaella said, but Mother Lauria ignored the sarcasm.

She beckoned Magda to the door. "There is a Terran, a man, who has come and asked for you by the name you are known here."

Magda's throat tightened; who could it be but Peter? And why would he come? Had something happened to Jaelle? "What is his name? What does he want?"

Lauria said disdainfully "I cannot remember his barbarian name. You need not meet him unless you wish; I can have the girls send him away."

"No, I had better go and see what he wants. Thank you, Mother." Magda was grateful that the Guild Mother had come herself to give this message; it was not usual for her to put herself out this way for anyone, rather than sending a message.

"Please yourself," Mother Lauria said, and went away. Magda was suddenly conscious of her hot, flushed face, her sweat-soaked tunic, her hair straggling in damp wisps about her face. She went into the room behind the armory, washed her face in cold water, stripped off the sweaty tunic and put on the fresh one she had learned to keep there after a lesson. She laced her overtunic and was combing her hair neatly back when Rafaella came in.

She said scornfully, "Are you readying yourself to meet a lover?"

"No," said Magda, struggling for composure against the rage that kept threatening to get out of hand again, "but I have a guest in the Stranger's Room and I do not want him to think that a Free Amazon must be a filthy slattern from a dung-heap, either!"

"Why are you so concerned with what a man would think of you? Is it so important to you that men must notice your beauty, your desirability?" Rafaella asked with a curl of her lip, and Magda held herself by force from answering, walking past Rafaella in silence. Some day, she thought, some day I will slap that look off her face, it would be worth whatever they did to me for it! She went down the hall to the little room at the front of the house that they called the Stranger's Room. She was still shaking with anger, ready to fling defiance in Peter's face—how dared he break in upon her here?

But seated on one of the narrow chairs, she saw a complete stranger. She had seen him somewhere before, but he was certainly no one she knew well; and she fancied he looked with surprise and disdain at her tunic and breeches, her cropped hair. She said curtly, "May I ask your business here?"

"My name is Wade Montray," he said, "And you are Magdalen Lorne —Margali, as they call you here?" He spoke Darkovan, she noticed, and very good Darkovan at that. Language tapes, the ones she and Peter had made, no doubt. He tiptoed quietly to the door, and looked into the hall. "Nobody listening, and I doubt if they have the technology to bug a room, but you can't be too careful."

Magda said frigidly, "I doubt if anyone here would trouble to intrude on a private conversation, being sufficiently busy with their own affairs. If we have to talk, by all means talk freely." Yes, she had met this man, he was the Coordinator's son, like herself, brought up on Darkovan. She felt immense distaste for the suspicion in his voice; had she really once been a part of the vast paranoia of the Intelligence Service?

"I wanted to be careful not to blow your cover here, Miss Lorne. Jaelle Haldane will be down here in a few days to talk with you, so Cholayna says, and I really ought to leave it to her. But she has her job and I have mine. I have to travel into the Hellers this winter, and I understand you were there last season. Your report's full of intriguing gaps, and I need to know more about what you know of that ruling caste—Comyn, is it? And you spent the winter at Castle Ardais as the Lady Rohana's guest; there's a lot you could tell us."

"There is nothing to tell, really, except what I put in my report," Magda said cautiously. "I do not suppose you are interested in the menu for

Midwinter-Festival feast, the names of the men with whom I danced at the Festival Ball, or the depth of snow on the day after Festival."

"Look, I'm interested in everything—absolutely everything," said Wade Montray. "Your previous reports have been very full; I'm curious to know why you filed such a sketchy one about this mission!"

"I went on leave," Magda evaded, "and I did file a report with Cholayna Ares; check with her."

"I understand, but under the circumstances, I'd appreciate it if you'd come down to the HQ and file a fuller report," said Montray. "Haldane does good work, but I don't think he has quite the grasp of the situation that you do."

He was trying to butter her up now; she recognized it with distaste. The Training sessions had made her very aware of the techniques which men used to get on the favorable side of a woman, and she was angry at the familiar condescension. "I remind you I am on leave, and that this is my first leave of absence in six years; you have no right to interrupt it."

"Oh, I'll see that you get extra pay for breaking into your vacation time," Montray said, and Magda was resentful suddenly at the Terran idea that her wishes could be set aside by an offer of extra pay! Were all the Terrans as mercenary as that?

"I am sorry, I would rather not. What would you do if I had gone offplanet, as I would have had every right to do? Why should you assume I am required to be accessible?"

"Oh, come on," he said, and she noted that his smile was singularly sweet, "It couldn't hurt you that much to come down on a free afternoon and fill in the gaps for me, could it? For that matter, we could get you a special bonus if you would keep a log while you're here and file a full report on whatever happens in the Guild House, we don't have a lot of data on the Free Amazons—excuse me, Renunciates, I did remember that —and if we're going to be employing them for Medic and Tech training, we need all the help we can get."

"I absolutely refuse," she said angrily, and he changed his tack.

"Have it your own way," he said. "I didn't mean to upset you. You're certainly entitled to spend your leave in peace and quiet, if you want to."

Peace and quiet! That's the last thing I would find here, especially now! Against her will she smiled at the thought, not knowing that the smile transformed her face and made a mockery of her annoyance. Seeing it, he was encouraged.

"Look, Miss Lorne, off the record—all right? I don't want to break into your leave, but why not come out of here, where we can talk without worrying about who might overhear us; we can have a quiet drink somewhere in the Trade City, and you can fill me in on what I need to know. I have a scriber with me; I can just put it into Records, or if you like, I'll keep it off the record, for my ears only. No trouble, no fuss, and then I'll leave you in peace. How about it?"

Unexpectedly, she was tempted. To go away from here, out of the perpetual atmosphere of distrust and hostility, to slip back into her familiar Terran self; even the thought of a drink, or of some Terran coffee, was intolerably tempting. She sighed, regretfully.

"I'm really sorry, I wish I could," she said, smiling, "but it's quite impossible, Mr. Montray." She had slipped into speaking Terran Standard, and suddenly realized it.

"Mr. Montray is my father," he said, grinning, "I'm Monty. And why is it so impossible?"

"In the first place, even if I could go, it wouldn't do for a Renunciate to be seen sitting around in a bar with a Terran in uniform." Quite against her will, she realized that she was smiling; her eyes twinkled with amusement. "And I couldn't go; I'm pledged to remain here in the house until Midsummer, and I can't leave without permission of the Guild Mothers."

"And you put up with it? A free citizen of Terra? Imprisoned?"

"No, no," she said. "It's part of the training system, that's all. And you yourself said you didn't want to blow my cover. If I, a probationary Renunciate, went off with a Terran—well, you can imagine what they would say."

Damn what they say; but I gave my word, and I'll keep it or die trying.

He took it philosophically, and rose. "If you can't, you can't; but I warn you, I'll come back at Midsummer," he said, "and I'll get the report somehow." He held out his hand; suddenly homesick for a familiar gesture, Magda took it. She watched him go, thinking with some regret that he was a familiar voice from a world she had renounced—and now, paradoxically, found that she missed.

She returned to the Armory, but the lesson had ended; a few of the women were soaking in the hot tub, but Rafaella was among them, and Magda, though her hurt leg was aching and she would have enjoyed the heat of the tub, decided against joining them. She decided to take advantage of the privilege still allowed her, and go up and lie down. For the first time she was beginning to doubt her ability to endure for the half year of housebound training.

She liked the women here, most of the time. She even liked Rafaella, or would if the woman would let her, and she liked Camilla and Doria and Keitha, very much. But it was the little things, the cold baths, the food, the stupid insistence on manual work, and now the constant friction, since that fight when she had lost her temper. She couldn't really understand how they felt about it; the man had, after all, been attacking the House. Even if she had killed him, he would have deserved it.

Could anyone, ever, completely renounce their world? Had she been a fool to try? Should she simply give it up, tell Mother Lauria it was too much for her, petition to have her Oath, her forced Oath, set aside after all? Maybe she would not have to make that decision; maybe, when they came to review the dreadful thing she had supposedly done, they would expel her from the Guild House and that would relieve her of the choice. *And how would I face Jaelle, then?*

There was no regular noon-meal served in the Guild House; anyone who was hungry at mid-day went down to the kitchen to find cold bread or meat, and after a time Magda, who was used still to the Terran mealtimes, and liked a light snack at noon, went down to the kitchen. She poured out a mug of the bark-tea which always simmered in the kettle over the banked fire—it wasn't coffee, but it was hot and the kitchen was cold, and her hands curved around the hot mug with comfort—and sliced bread from a cut loaf, spreading it with butter and soft cheese from a crock. It was too much trouble to slice the cold meat in the cool-room, and it was too cold in there anyhow. She sat nibbling, wondering where Irmelin was. The bread for supper was rising at one end of the table in a huge bowl, puffing up under a clean towel. She was brushing up the crumbs and rinsing her mug—one of the strictest rules, that anyone coming to the kitchen for food must leave it as clean as they found it—when Irmelin stuck her head in the door.

"Oh, Margali? You weren't in your room. I hoped you would be here," she said. "Will you take hall-duty? Byrna is nursing the baby."

Magda shrugged. "Certainly," she said, and started for the hall, but Irmelin held her back, the chubby woman's face alive with curiosity.

"Are you not Jaelle n'ha Melora's oath-daughter?"

"Yes, I am," Magda said, and Irmelin nodded. "I thought so; she is here to see Mother Lauria, and they have been closeted in her office for hours—" Her eyes widened, and she added, "I suppose Mother Lauria sent for her to discuss what they're going to do about you! I hope they let you stay, Margali! I think Camilla was too hard on you—we can't all know the honor code of mercenary soldiers, and I don't know why we should!"

With her very kindness she had managed, again, to destroy Magda's peace of mind. Was it so serious that they would send for Jaelle from the Terran Zone? But Irmelin added fussily, "Go, now, sit in the hall to let people in, I have to knead down the bread and get it into the pans for tonight's dinner, and if Shaya will be here I want to make some spicebread."

Magda sat in the hall, listlessly plaiting the belt, and remembering against her will the last time she had worked on it. When the doorbell rang again she was braced for trouble, and when she found a man, in the green and black uniform of a Guardsman, on the doorstep, she set her chin aggressively.

"What do you want?"

"Is Byrna within?"

"You can see her in the Stranger's Room, if you wish," Magda said.

"Oh, I am glad she is up again," the young man said.

"May I tell her who is asking for her?"

"My name is Errol," he said, "and I am the father of her son." He was a very large, very young man, his cheeks still downy with the first shadow of beard. "My sister has just had a baby and she has offered to nurse this one with her own, so I came to take him away."

So soon. He is only a tenday old. Oh, poor Byrna. Her distressed look must have reached the very young man, for he said uncertainly "Well, she *told* me she didn't want to keep him, so I thought the sooner I took him off her hands, the better it would be for her."

"I will go and tell her." She showed the young man into the Stranger's Room, and hesitated, wondering what to do now; but the doorbell rang again and fortunately, Marisela stood on the steps.

"What shall I do, Marisela? The father of Byrna's baby is in there—" she pointed, "and wants to take him away—"

Marisela sighed; but she only said, "Better now than later. I will tell her, Margali; go back to the hall, child."

Magda obeyed; and after a considerable time she saw Errol coming from the Stranger's Room, carrying a thickly wrapped bundle in his arms, with the clumsiness of a man not accustomed to handling babies. Marisela, at his side, was talking attentively to him, and she left Marisela to let him out; it struck her that probably, at this moment, Byrna was in need of some sympathetic company. If anyone came to the door, they could just knock until Irmelin, in the kitchen, heard them and could leave her bread-rolls long enough to let them in!

She found Byrna in her room, flung across her bed, crying bitterly. Magda didn't speak; she only sat down beside Byrna and took her hand. Byrna raised her tear-blurred face, and flung herself, sobbing, into Magda's arms. Magda hugged her, not trying to talk. She had had half a dozen things ready to say; but none of them seemed worth the trouble.

They shouldn't have let him take the baby. It's too soon. Everything we know tells us that at this stage, Byrna needs her baby as much as he needs her! It's cruel, it's not right . . . and through the woman's trembling in her arms, it seemed that somehow she could *feel* the vast pain and despair.

She said nothing, just held Byrna and let her cry herself into exhaustion, then laid her gently down on her pillow.

"He's too little," Byrna sobbed, "he needs me, he really needs me—but I promised, I didn't know when I promised how much it would hurt—"

There was nothing Magda could say; she was relieved when the door opened and Marisela came in, Felicia at her side. "I hoped someone would come to stay with her. Merciful Avarra, how I wish Ferrika had come back!" She bent over Byrna, said gently, "I have something to make you sleep, *breda.*"

Byrna could not speak. Her eyes were swollen nearly shut with crying, her face blotched and crimson. Marisela held her head as she sipped the cup at her lips, laid her down. "You will sleep after a little."

Felicia knelt at Byrna's side, took her hands and said, "Sister, I know. I really do, remember?"

Byrna said, her voice hoarse and ghastly, "But you had your little boy for five years, five whole years, and mine is still so little, only a baby—"

"And it was that much harder for me," Felicia said gently. Her big gray eyes filled with tears as she said, "You did right, Byrna, and I only wish I had had the courage to do the same, to give him up at once to the woman he will call mother. I kept him here for my own comfort, and then when he was five years old, he had to go among strangers, where everything is different and they will expect him already to know how to be what they call a little man—" she swallowed hard. "I took him to my brother's house —he cried so, and I had to tear his hands away and leave him, and they had to hold him, and I could hear him all the way down the street, screaming 'Mother, Mother—' " Her voice held endless pain. "It is so much better—to let him go now, when all he will know is love and kindness and a warm breast—and if his foster mother has nursed him herself she will love him so much more and be gentler with him."

"Yes, yes, but I want him, I want him—" Byrna sobbed, and clung to Felicia; Felicia was crying now, too, and Marisela drew Magda gently out of the room.

"Felicia can help her now more than anyone else."

Magda said, "I should think she would make it worse—isn't it cruel for them both?"

Marisela put her arm round Magda and said gently, "No, *chiya,* it is what they both need; grief unspoken turns to poison. Byrna must mourn for her child, even though it is like death. And she can help Felicia, too; Felicia has not been able to cry for her son, and now they can weep together and be eased by knowing the other truly understands. Otherwise they will both sicken with the first sickness that comes near them, and Byrna, at least, could die. Give the Goddess her due, child, even when her due is grief. You have never borne a child, or you would know." She kissed Magda's cheek and said gently, "Some day you too will be able to weep and be healed of your grief."

Magda watched Marisela go down the stairs, staring after her in amazement. She supposed Marisela was right—she had come to respect the woman, she knew as much as most Medics, in her own way, and she supposed she had a good grip of the psychology of the matter; everyone knew that stress could cause psychosomatic illness, though she was surprised that Marisela would think of it. But certainly Marisela was wrong about *her*, she had no particular sorrows, she had nothing to cry about! Anger, yes, enough to burst with it. Especially lately. Resentment. But grief? She had nothing to cry about, she had not cried more than three times in her adult life. Oh, yes, she had cried when she had been hurt and Marisela had stitched up her leg without anesthetic, but that was different. The idea that she might have some unknown and hidden grief for which she should be healed, struck her as the most fantastic thing she had ever heard.

There was the sound of a mellow chime; the bell warning women who had come in from working in the city that dinner would be served in an hour and that they should finish bathing, changing their garments. Magda went upstairs, still frowning. She passed Byrna's closed door, hoping that the woman was sleeping.

I was sad, but not enough to cry about it, when I realized that Peter had not managed to make me pregnant; and then, when we separated, I was glad not to be burdened with a child. And especially now—what would I do here with a child? I could now be in Byrna's predicament. The idea is ridiculous. Marisela could use some sensible Terran training, both in medicine and psychology.

As she stripped off her clothes to change for dinner, she sighed at the thought of confronting Rafaella again at the meal, or meeting the unspoken resentment of the others. But there was nothing she could do about it, and she would not hide in her room and let them know that it bothered her. She was a Terran; and even more than that, she was a Renunciate, and she would somehow manage enough strength to get through this time.

Chapter Two

Inside Mother Lauria's office the women heard the chime, and Mother Lauria sighed. "I must go, Jaelle; it has been good to have this talk with you. You will spend the night in the House, won't you? It does not matter which women you and I think are qualified, I cannot require of any woman that she leave her sisters and take employment among the Terrans. She herself must wish to go."

"But we cannot let any woman go who wishes," Jaelle insisted, "They must be the right ones—we do not wish them to fail and the Terrans think us silly women, think the women of the Darkover are all fools and children who hide behind the safety of home. And they should not be lovers of women, for that is a thing the Terrans despise. I would like to consult with Magda about it—"

"The very last one. She is new to us—"

"She has been among you three moons; as long as I have been among the Terrans."

"But the women in the House do not know she is Terran; they would wonder why I consulted with a newcomer, instead of a veteran who has been among us for years. I might as well ask Doria!"

"You could do worse; children's eyes see clearly," Jaelle said. "I am sure Doria knows our faults and weaknesses as well as I do myself. But before we make any decisions I would like to speak privately, at least, with Magda. I can see that you would not want to call her out from the rest and consult with her—" Jaelle felt troubled; she had not known Magda had chosen to be anonymous here. But Mother Lauria had risen, firmly, and interview was over.

Jaelle went and washed her hands in the downstairs scullery. Her home, she realized, and for the first time since she was eleven, she had no designated place here! She went into the dining hall, and after a moment, there was a cry of "Jaelle!" and she was caught enthusiastically in Rafaella's arms.

Jaelle returned the hug and laughed gaily at her partner's surprise. "You didn't expect to see me, did you? How is the business?"

"As well as can be expected, when you have been away so long," Rafaella returned, half teasing, but with a note of real resentment. "To work among the *Terranan!* How could you?"

"I am not the first, and shall not be the last," Jaelle said quietly. "You will hear about that in House meeting. And you have left the House to live with a freemate, more than once, have you not?"

"But with a *Terranan!*" Rafaella's vivacious face grimaced in fastidious distaste. "I would as soon couple with a *cralmac!*"

Jaelle laughed. "I have never lain down with a *cralmac,*" she said, "and know nothing about their bed manners, though in the mountains I once knew a woman who said she slept every night between her two female *cralmacs* for warmth, so they cannot be as disgusting as all that! But, seriously, Rafi, the Terrans are men like other men, no more different from us than hillmen from lowlanders; differing from us only in language and customs, no more. They are far more like to us than the *chieri,* and there is the blood of the Ancient Folk in all the Hastur kin. I had not thought to hear you, of all people, repeating superstitious nonsense about the Terrans, as if they had horns and tails!"

Perhaps, she thought, it is no miracle that Magda chose to be anonymous here, if this nonsense about the Terrans is common to the women here! I thought the sisters of my own Guild House had better sense! But she let it pass—she had no wish to quarrel with her friend and partner.

"But tell me about the work and how it goes, Rafi. You could take someone else into partnership for a time, you know, while I am away, or even permanently—there is enough work for three, most years. And how is my baby, Doria?"

"Your *baby* is in her Housebound time, and will take the Oath at Midsummer," Rafaella returned dryly. "If she can manage to be admitted—she is at the very worst stage in growing up—every time I say a word to her, she bursts into tears! I am really ashamed of her. The business? Well, I have had to turn down two caravans, but we are doing well enough. There is a new maker of saddles—"

"Can you find somewhere else to talk?" asked a tall, slender woman, hair gleaming faint gold, a long apron pinned over her trousers. Rafaella took her friend's shoulder and shoved her along so that the woman cou set plates and bowls along the long table. "Our sister Keitha, she came to us at the same time as your oath-sister Margali," Rafaella said, and turned to introduce Jaelle. Women were streaming into the hall now, singly and in little groups, standing about and talking, finding seats, amid clattering dishes. There was a good smell of hot bread fresh from the oven, and Jaelle sniffed, appreciatively.

"Real food! I'm starved!"

"What's the matter, don't the Terrans feed you? You've certainly gained weight," Rafaella said, raising her eyebrows. "Or is there another reason for that, Shaya?"

Jaelle smiled at the pet name, given her in this house when she was younger than Doria, but drew a little away from Rafi; she didn't want to talk about that yet.

And yet if I had a child, I could keep it and raise it myself with Peter's help, I would not need to face the fact that it might be a son whom I must give up when he was five years old. I have always felt that Amazons should not have children; there are enough unwanted girls whom we can take into our homes and our hearts, as Kindra took me.

But I was not unwanted. Mother—mother loved me, I think, though I cannot remember her at all. Sometimes, in the dreams I have been having under those damned machines, I think I remember her a little. And Rohana would gladly have fostered me. Yet I chose to come here . . .

Magda, coming into the dining hall, felt a sudden wave of dismay and distress, and stopped hesitantly on the threshold. What was happening to her? She was having peculiar small hallucinations all the time now. Was she losing her mind? She looked around the room, saw Rafaella by the fireplace, talking to a woman in a blue dress; but not an Amazon, for the woman's hair was long and coppery-red, curling at the tips. Then the woman laughed and turned her head toward the door, and Magda froze; Jaelle!

She was sure she had not made a sound, but Jaelle turned as if Magda had called her name, her face filled with delighted surprise.

"What is it, Jaelle, what's happened, why are you here?" Were they, in fact, discussing her crime? She had been told that the matter must be taken up with her oath-mother. But Jaelle said gaily, "I am not housebound, *breda;* I would have come before, but this was my first chance—I have been very busy, as you can imagine."

Magda searched her friend's eyes; there was more in them than a casual visit. The whites of the eyes seemed bloodshot, but she knew how rarely Jaelle cried. *Perhaps*—a nagging, intrusive thought, *Peter doesn't let her get much sleep.* She dropped the thought as if it had burned her. *You'd think I was jealous!*

"Mother Lauria and I have been discussing the women who can be chosen to learn Terran medicine, but I want to talk with you about that. Not here, though." The chiming of the supper bell interrupted them; Mother Lauria came in and took her seat, and Jaelle sniffed with delight.

"I am so tired of food that comes out of machines! Real bread, fresh baked—and tripe stew, if I'm not mistaken. Wonderful! Here, let's sit here," Jaelle said, seizing her hand, responding to Camilla's beckoning hand, bending to give Camilla a quick hug and kiss. "Well, Aunt, you look hearty and well, did Nevarsin's climate agree with you? Come sit by me, Margali, let's eat and you tell me everything they've been doing to you around here!"

Magda laughed. "That would take more than an evening!"

"*Breda*—" Jaelle said, startled, as if actually seeing her for the first time. "*Chiya,* what have they been doing to you here? You *have* lost weight," she scolded, "The housebound season is hellish for everyone, I know, but you mustn't let it affect you this way!" Then Jaelle took Magda in a close embrace, long and hard and deliberate.

Magda could not see the tears Jaelle hid against her shoulder, though she sensed that Jaelle was clinging to her as if for comfort. But she also saw Janetta's knowing smirk, and sensed that all eyes were on them. She pulled back a little.

"Don't, Jaelle!" She could not conceal her unease; the room seemed suddenly full of a ringing silence, as if all the noises of dishes and silverware were echoing in a vast, vaulted chamber from many miles away.

Jaelle withdrew, frowning. She asked, almost formally, "Have I wronged you somehow, oath-daughter?"

"Oh, no," Magda said, shocked; lowering her voice, she murmured, "It's only—I didn't want—I mean, everyone in the Guild House already believes I am your lover . . ." her voice trailed off. She was half expecting Jaelle to reply sensibly, "What does that matter?"

However, Jaelle only murmured, "I see," and sat down as if nothing had happened. But her look sent a chill through Magda; it was the same look Jaelle had given her that first night, when Jaelle had rescued her from the bandits bent on rape; icy, detached, verging on contempt. The next moment, though, it was gone and Magda was wondering if she had imagined it, as Camilla and young Doria were hugging and kissing Jaelle and trading around so they could all sit together around the corner of the table.

Jaelle said over Doria's head, "This is my baby, Margali; she was no more than three when I came here as a fosterling, and she has always been my pet and plaything—and now look at her, all grown up and ready for the Oath! I'm so proud of you, *chiya!*"

Doria glanced at Magda with a tiny shared grin, and Magda thought, *she hasn't seen us shaking all over at Training Sessions or she wouldn't be so proud of us! Thank heaven there won't be one tonight; I couldn't stand it, in front of Jaelle!* Or, she wondered, was there? Tripe stew usually appeared on the nights of Training Sessions or the almost equally frightening house meetings. She had never lost her distaste for tripe stew; as the dish passed, she shook her head, passing it to Jaelle. Jaelle stared.

"Really? It's my favorite and I'm starved for it! Well, the less there is for you, the more for the rest of us!" She helped herself liberally. "Sisters, you'll never appreciate the food here until you have to try to eat what the Terrans call food!" She was exaggerating, almost a burlesque.

"You can have my share, and welcome," Magda said, trying to hide her bitterness. Here was Jaelle, *home,* feasting and laughing and enjoying herself as if she'd been locked in solitary confinement on bread and water. While in the Terran Zone Jaelle had fifteen choices at every meal, and didn't even have to help cook them, music from several different planets, all the books ever written, rounds of parties and visiting among Base personnel—as Peter's wife she would be required to attend most of the official functions—sports, swimming (and in an indoor, properly heated pool at that), and all kinds of games and recreation. *And here I am, struggling with stable brooms, and in disgrace at that . . . and fed on tripe stew, dammit!*

Magda found a bowl of something which tasted faintly like baked yams or pumpkin—and helped herself. Then someone passed her the leftover dish, filled with some mixture of grain baked with cheese and reheated in milk. "I saved this *just for you,* Margali." Magda gritted her teeth, knowing that this was intended as a subtle insult; most of the women considered the stuff barely fit to eat even when it was served fresh, but it made its appearance on the table, because it was cheap, all too often since the House had been let in for the enormous cash indemnity by the man Magda had wounded. She told herself not to be hypersensitive—everyone knew how much she disliked the tripe stew—and helped herself without comment. But just last night, the girl who had "saved" it for her had made, just too loud, a comment about how their food budget had suffered, and why.

She was buttering herself a piece of bread when Jaelle said quietly, "You don't have to eat that *reish,* Margali!"

The word she had used meant literally, stable-sweepings; horseshit. Magda took a spoonful.

"Never mind, I like it, really, better than the tripe stew."

"You couldn't! Listen, *breda,* you're my oath-daughter, you don't have to take that kind of treatment from anybody! Not in my own house!" Now it seemed that, from the light touch of Jaelle's hand on her wrist, the woman's own rage flowed into Magda, she was filled with fury, *how dared they treat her that way!* A grain of sanity insisted in Magda that it was all very silly, she really liked the grain-and-cheese dish as well as anything else they served here, but through her own sanity she felt Jaelle's fury, a slight to her oath-daughter was a slight to Jaelle as well. Jaelle took the dish in her hand, and stood over the woman who had handed it to Magda.

"That's very generous of you, Cloris, but knowing how much you like it, we couldn't possibly deprive you of it!" Jaelle said, eyes flashing, and dumped the whole soggy mess on Cloris's plate. Magda knew—and Cloris did, too—that she had come very close to dumping it on Cloris's cropped curls. "A present—from *my oath-daughter!*" She put enough emphasis on the words that Cloris bent her head, color rising in her round cheeks, and put a fork into the mess, choking down a spoonful. Jaelle stood over her, triumphant, for a moment, then came back to her seat, where Magda was pretending to eat the baked-pumpkin stuff, and picked up her own fork.

Slowly, the tension in the room dissolved. Camilla and Doria were asking a hundred questions about the Terran Zone; they spoke a rapid-fire Cahuenga that Magda could hardly follow, but she did sense Jaelle's anger melting away as she talked on, and after a time it was the old Jaelle, merrily regaling her friends with larger-than-life adventures in faraway places; all the little foibles of the Terrans grew and seemed hysterical.

Magda felt a stab of resentment. Jaelle wasn't telling them anything she couldn't have told them, yet she was honor bound, oath-bound, to say nothing about it. She had made the wrong decision. If they had known she was Terran, they might have accepted her differences and blamed her less, they would have excused her blunder in the sword-fight as unfamiliarity with custom, not dishonorable negligence. She had been so proud of her own ability to pass as a Darkovan; Peter had warned her once that it would destroy her! Magda blinked back tears of self-pity, and pushed the food around listlessly on her plate. Jaelle had forgotten her, and the only two people in the house who really liked her, Doria and Camilla, were so wrapped up in Jaelle that neither of them had a word to say to her. The hall, which was large and drafty, seemed colder than ever; there was a cold draft blowing on the back of her neck where her hair used to be, she'd probably have a cold tomorrow, and these people didn't have a decent antiviral drug in the house!

She rose quietly and slipped toward the door. No one would know or care that she was gone. But as she paused on the threshold, Mother Lauria rose in her place.

"Before you all go off to your evening tasks or to rest," she said, "Jaelle will be leaving at first light tomorrow; so there will be a few minutes in the music room, if you wish to greet her, before house meeting. Remember, the meeting is obligatory for everyone tonight." Her eyes locked for a moment with Magda's, and Magda felt the old tightness in her throat.

House meetings were somewhat less disturbing than the training sessions, whose very purpose, of course, was to upset and humiliate the probationers, breaking old patterns—to teach us, Keitha had said once, to be women, not girls or ladies. Keitha usually came away from them in tears, but Magda had not yet been reduced to tears, though she usually lay awake for hours afterward turning over all the things she knew she should have said, or suffered racking nightmares. The meetings, by contrast, were usually routine affairs—the last one had taken up two hours complaining that the women who cleaned the third floor did not keep the baths stocked with towels or menstrual supplies! But Magda knew that in this meeting, her Oath was to be called into question. Rafaella had all but told her so this afternoon in the Armory. She knew she would never be able to face the psychological assault troops, and remembered Marisela's words, with dismay. Are they never going to be satisfied until they can get me to break down and cry in front of them all, was that what they were waiting for? Magda shoved the curtain aside and fled, running up the wide stairway, taking the steps three at a time; half sobbing, she stumbled, slid down a couple of steps, scrambled up, and gained the upper hallway, locking herself into the second-story bath by the simple expedient of blocking the door with a stool. She felt nausea rising, the very walls seemed to bulge outward around her, blurring before her aching eyes.

Jaelle found her there, sitting on the floor, clutching a towel over her eyes, swaying back and forth, unable even to cry. *"Chiya,"* said Jaelle, kneeling on the floor beside her, "What is it? What have we done?"

Magda let the towel drop and for a moment it seemed that Jaelle's words, her very presence, held the bulging walls in place, forced the words into solidity. *Of course, she is Comyn, a catalyst telepath, an Ardais,* she thought, and irritably wondered what the words meant and where they had come from. She was battling the impulse to throw herself into Jaelle's arms, cling there and cry herself senseless, to enfold the other woman within herself, cling to her strength. . . . then inside her, a spark of defiance flared. Jaelle had the strength to face the Terran Zone's culture shock, to make jokes about it at supper, then come up and offer solace to Magda because *she* couldn't! She could not display weakness—not before Jaelle, of all people. She bit her lip, tasting blood in her mouth as she fought for control.

Jaelle, seeing the unfocused eyes, the beads of sweat filming Magda's brow under the clinging curls, thought quite logically that Magda was simply afraid; she knew her Oath would be challenged tonight, and, knowing what the Oath had cost Magda, she ached for her friend. But Jaelle had been a soldier before anything else. Kindra and Camilla had schooled her to hard stoicism, reinforcing the rigid strength of a desert-born woman, and the last months had been, for her, the hardest fight of her life! And Magda was not facing the machines and dehumanizing life of the Terran Zone, she was here surrounded by the love and concern of all the Guild House sisters!

She said, with a sting of harshness meant to be as bracing as the first touch of cold water in the morning, "Margali n'ha Ysabet, listen to me!" Magda's Amazon name rang out like the clash of a sword. "Are you a woman, or a whimpering girl? Would you disgrace your oath-mother in our own House?"

Magda's rising pride grabbed that and held on to it, *I can do anything she can do, anything any Darkovan woman can do!* It gave her the strength to pull herself to her feet, and say through set teeth, "Jaelle n'ha Melora, I will not disgrace you!"

Jaelle knew, with the knowledge which she could never control, but which, from time to time, thrust itself on her undesired, that the spiteful tone was armor against total nervous disintegration; all the same, the cold tone hurt. She said icily, "Downstairs in the music room, before the clock strikes again," turned her back and added, with chilly detachment, "You had better wash your face first." She turned and went, fighting the awareness that what she really wanted to do was put Magda into a hot bath, rub her back until the tension went out of her, then tuck her up comfortably in bed and comfort her, as she would have done for Doria when the child had gotten into one of the inevitable fights that faced an Amazon fosterling in the Thendara streets from the street girls—and boys.

But Margali is a woman; my oath-daughter, but she is not a child, I must not treat her like one!

Left alone, Magda had an insane impulse to change into Terran uniform and confront them on that basis, fling their damned oath into their faces and storm out before they could throw her out. *If I had a uniform in the building, I might,* she thought, then was glad she had not, knowing she would regret it all her life. Magda was Darkovan enough to guard the integrity of her given oath with her very life; yet a traitorous part of her self persisted, as she washed her swollen mouth, in knowing that she might be going back in the morning to the Terran Zone with Jaelle—or without her. Either way, it would not be her fault, she would not have given up. All the tension, which had been building to impossible heights since the sword fight, would be over. Painful as the breaking would be, it could not help but be better.

In the music room, Jaelle and several others were clustered around Rafaella, begging her to sing.

"Rafi, I have had no music since I went to the Terran Zone; nobody plays there, nobody sings, the music comes out of little metal screens, and is only sound to mask the sound of machines, not real music at all. . . . sing something, Rafi, sing 'The Ballad of Hastur and Cassilda. . . .' "

"We should be here all night, and Mother Lauria has called us for House Meeting," Rafaella protested, but she took up the small *rryl* which looked to Magda like a cross between a guitar and a zither, and began softly tightening the pegs, bending her ear close as she tuned the instrument. Then she sat down, holding it across her lap, and began to sing softly, a ballad Magda had heard in Caer Donn as a child. Her mother had told her it was immeasurably old, perhaps even of Terran origin.

> When the day wears away,
> Sad I wander by the water,
> Where a man, born of sun,
> Wooed the *chieri* daughter;
> Ah, but there is something wanting,
> Ah, but I am weary,
> Come, my fair and bonny love,
> Come from the hills to cheer me . . .

And a curious, haunting refrain in a language Magda did not know; she would like to ask Rafaella where she had learned the song, what was the language of the ancient refrain, to check it against the Terran language banks. . . . but she held aloof. Surely Jaelle had confided in her best friend how she had found Magda in the bathroom having hysterics, they were all waiting for her, the last to arrive . . . yet the old song recalled her childhood, her mother, who had always worn Darkovan clothes for warmth in the frigid hills of the Hellers, wrapped in a tartan shawl; the very sound of the *rryl* was like the one her mother had played, and Magda had tried for a time to learn the chords;

> Why should I sit and sigh,
> All alone and weary. . . .

The soft arpeggios of the accompaniment died; Mother Lauria came up behind Magda and laid a warm, dry hand on her shoulder. Magda turned, and the old woman said softly, "Courage, Margali." But the kindness in her voice was blurred in Magda's ears. Magda only thought, does she think I am going to disgrace them all by breaking down? Damn her anyhow! Mother Lauria read the defiance in her face, and sighed, but she only propelled Magda into the center of the group, where the women were finding seats, on chairs and benches and on the floor on cushions.

Rafaella put the *rryl* carefully into its case and sat down cross-legged beside Jaelle, as silence fell on them all. Mother Lauria said, "Shall we begin? I will take the meeting myself, tonight."

They brought an armchair for the Guild Mother and placed it at the center, and Magda felt a renewed stab of misgiving. Usually the Guild Mothers or elders presiding over the meeting sat on the floor, informally, like everyone else. Normally there were house meetings only every forty days, and the trainees were not allowed to speak at all in them; they were gripe sessions, or serious discussions of house finances, policies, visiting hours and work assignments.

Magda wondered if she was building up nightmares out of nothing. After all, the woman was old and had a lame knee; she was the oldest of the Guild Mothers and her knee would not let her sit on the floor for a long meeting!

Lauria opened soberly, "The House has been alive with talk and gossip for more than a tenday. That is not the way to handle troubles, with talk and secret slander! Tonight we must talk of violence, and other things; but first let us have this trouble in our House spoken openly, not whispered in corners like naughty children talking smut! Rafaella, you have had the most to say, let us hear your grudge openly!"

"Margali," said Rafaella, turning to look at her, and Magda felt all the eyes of the women turning to follow, "She has disgraced us; she has brought a heavy indemnity upon us, she has dishonored her steel, and she does not even seem to realize the gravity of what she had done."

"That's not true," Magda cried out. "What makes you think I don't realize it? But what would you have me do? Weep night and day?"

Mother Lauria said, "Margali—" but Jaelle had already silenced Magda with a hand on her shoulder. "Hush, *chiya*. Let us handle this."

A girl called Dika—Magda did not know her full name—said, "See, even now she has not learned manners! And it's common knowledge that her oath was irregular, taken on the trail! She should have been questioned in a Guild House before she was ever allowed to come among us!"

"And she sits there brazen, not caring," Janetta said, and Magda suddenly realized—distantly, intellectually—what they meant. It was a cultural reaction she was lacking. Yes, she spoke the language, had learned it as a child—but she had been separated from the Darkovans who were native to her at an early age, she did not have the right body language, the right subtle signals to show her very real remorse and guilt; they were expecting a reaction she did not know how to give, and that was why they were so hostile all the time. All, that was, except Mother Lauria, who knew she could not be expected to react quite as she should, and knew why. She understood her guilt, in their framework, but she didn't know how to show them that she knew it!

This has always been my curse; too much Darkovan to be Terran, too much Darkovan ever to be happy in the Terran Zone . . . I came to the Amazons to find my own freedom to be what I really am, but I don't know what that is, and how can I find it if I do not know what it is I must find here?

Mother Lauria said, "There has been too much gossip and too little truth about the irregularity of Margali's oath. Jaelle, she took the oath at your hands, and Camilla, you witnessed it; let us hear the truth from your lips, before us all."

Magda listened while they told the story, mentioning that she had been traveling under safe-conduct from Lady Rohana Ardais; there were small murmurs all round the room at this, for Lady Rohana was a much-loved and respected patron of the Thendara Guild House. Camilla told how they had administered the oath under threat, as the Amazon charter required, and why. Mother Lauria heard her out in silence, then asked formally, "Tell us, Margali, did you take the oath unwillingly?"

Mother Lauria knew that perfectly well; she had been at the Council where it had been discussed in full. She gulped down her misgivings, and said, hearing her voice thin and childish under the high ceiling, "At first— yes. It was something I had to do, before I could be free to keep my pledge to my kinsman. I was afraid I would have to make promises I could not, in conscience, keep." Should she tell them, here, that she was Terran and that by Terran law an oath under duress was invalid? No; there was enough trouble here between Terran and Darkovan without her adding to that old quarrel. "But as Jaelle said the oath to me, I—I seemed to find the words of the oath engraved somewhere upon my heart—believe me, the oath is now at the very center of my being . . ." Her throat tightened and for a moment she felt again that she could cry.

Jaelle's hand was on Magda's shoulder, reassuring. "Have I not told this company how Margali fought for me, when she could have held her hand, and my death would have freed her from all obligation? She abandoned the mission which meant so much to her because she would not leave me wounded, to freeze or die alone. She brought me across the Pass of Scaravel, under attack by banshees, and later brought the three of us to Castle Ardais under little more than the strength of her own will." Jaelle fingered the narrow red scar on her cheek and said vehemently, "No woman here has an oath-daughter more faithful under trial!"

"But," said Rafaella, "Camilla has told us how she first failed to defend herself against a gang of drunken bandits. And did she not kill that one who wounded you in a fever of bloodlust and revenge, rather than disciplined self-defense? I submit that she is unstable and unfit to bear steel, and that she has proved it again in this house, not a tenday past."

Jaelle said angrily, "Rafi, who among us comes to this house fit to bear a sword? Why do we have training sessions, if not to teach us what we do not know? Would you send Keitha, or Doria, to defend this house at sword's point?"

"Doria would never have struck a defenseless man who had surrendered his weapon," Rafaella began angrily, but Mother Lauria motioned her to quiet.

"What Doria would have done is not at issue. But you have raised a fair question; if Margali has learned nothing among us in her time here—"

"But," said Magda, pulling away from Jaelle's restraining hands, "I have learned—truly! I know what I did was wrong—"

"Margali," said Mother Lauria, "you will be silent until you are spoken to."

Magda sank back, biting her lip, and Mother Lauria continued, "Margali's oath has been formally called into question; and therefore three of you, other than her oath-mother, must speak for her; and they must be from those who have been oath-bound for at least five years."

Magda felt curious calm settling over her. At least, this was the end. She had done her best; but mentally she was already returning the borrowed clothing to the sewing room, gathering her few possessions, and walking out into the ice-glazed streets of Thendara, wholly alone for the first time in her life. *I have done the best I can. But Cholayna will have her triumph; she refused to accept my resignation. Did she know I would fail?*

But Camilla said angrily, "If you are going to call Margali's Oath into question, question mine too! I was angry, yes, furious enough to beat her senseless, but what she did was my fault, and not her own; I put her beside me to defend the House, because I knew she was a skilled fighter—and I thought, in the haste of the moment, that this was enough. I had forgotten that her skill with a knife outstripped her training; I forgot that, facing men for the first time in many moons, she might well go berserk with all the repressed rage we have been systematically raking up inside her mind in the training sessions."

She turned to Rafaella and said seriously, "Few of us come here with any knowledge of fighting; we learn it here, only AFTER we have learned to discipline our emotions. If I had had to face men in the middle of my own training here—I who had lived among men as a mercenary soldier—I would have killed them all, I think. I don't know where Margali came by her skill at fighting, but she has much to teach us as well as to learn from us—you yourself have seen that, Rafi, this very day you had her helping you to teach unarmed combat! She has many skills, though she is not yet fit to use them anywhere outside our training hall. I forgot how she had come to us and how she had behaved outside; it is my business to know such things, and when I had gotten over being angry with her, I realized it was my fault and not hers, and I will take full personal responsibility—" she used the formal phrase—"for the mistake which exposed her weakness."

She came and stood beside Magda; then dropped down behind her on the floor, and Magda saw the stern pride in her face. At that moment, any resentment she had ever felt against the old *emmasca* for her harshness, her threatened beatings, dissolved, never to return. The word "personal responsibility" was the one used in the most serious matters of honor, and Camilla had engaged hers in this matter.

She is my oath-sister, and she takes that sisterhood seriously—more seriously than I do myself! Magda said spontaneously, "Camilla, no! My hand struck the blow of disgrace! I should have known better, I take responsibility for it—"

"You will be silent, Margali," Mother Lauria said harshly, "I will not say this again. One more word without leave, and I will send you from the room to await the decision elsewhere! One has spoken. Two more are required."

Marisela said in her sweet reedy voice, "I will speak for Margali. Have you not heard from this how much Margali has learned? She does not shirk responsibility, even when another has offered to assume it for her— even if she spoke out of turn, her intentions were good. Margali cannot be held to blame that she failed a test which should never have been laid on her. Yet we have, all of us, silently been holding her to blame for a tenday and more—and which of us could withstand so much disapproval from her sisters for so long, in the midst of her housebound time and thrust, evening after evening, into the training sessions and all their weight of distress—and still come down among us, composed and quiet, and ready to shoulder all blame?"

She looked earnestly round the circle. "Sisters, we have all been where Margali is now—feeling like fumbling children, all our old certainties lost, and with nothing yet to put in their place. Look at her—she sits there not knowing whether we will throw her into the street to fend for herself, or make her way alone back wherever she came from—yet this is the woman who, laboring under all we have laid on her in the last days, still found it in her heart to go, unasked, to comfort Byrna. None of us here—not one, not even those of us who have borne children and had to give them up—could find a moment for our sister, because she is from another House. I speak for Margali, sisters; this woman is truly one of us and I, for one, do not challenge her oath."

There was a long silence. At last Mother Lauria said in that curiously ritual way, "Two have spoken, but a third is wanted."

And the silence was prolonged, until Magda felt her legs gather under her to take her from the room as sentence was pronounced. Whether or not they threw her out, she would not stay under this roof to Midsummer if all of them felt her dishonored.

Rafaella stirred, and Magda braced herself to listen to Rafaella's gloating, her accusations. Instead Rafaella said, slowly, "In simple justice—I must speak for her myself."

For a moment Magda did not understand the words, as if the words had been in the alien language of the song Rafaella had sung.

"She fought to defend us; not wisely, perhaps, but without hesitation; she took up the sword knowing she could have died here on our doorstep, and who will fight for an oath she does not, in fact, believe and honor? She fought, perhaps, with hatred when she should have fought with discipline, but I do not think she is incapable of learning discipline, in time. More than this, I know that Byrna would have spoken for Margali if she were able to be here—I call Marisela to witness for that. Margali has given generously to all of us, including my daughter, in training hall—in a time when she needs all her strength for her own learning. Not many of us could have done this during our own training time—I know I could not."

"Nor I," said Camilla roughly.

"It is usually not required of us. We have required of Margali more than most of us have to give; perhaps instead of blaming her because she has not done perfectly, we should give her credit that she has not done worse under such heavy demands. And more than this. She has made me see something to which I have been blind—" Rafaella stared at the floor, her slender musician's hands twisting restlessly. She said at last, "She has made me see that I have been unfair to Doria, as well as to her. I am not Kindra; *she* managed to foster Jaelle in this house and still put her through her housebound time here without favoritism—and without demanding more of her than Jaelle could give. Margali has made me see that I cannot do this with Doria. I think Doria should be sent to another Guild House for her housebound training and for her Oath." Magda saw her swallow hard, and she dashed her hand across her eyes, but then she raised her head and stared tearlessly at Mother Lauria. "I speak for Margali, and I ask, when you have considered this, that you send Doria away. I am not fit to train her; I am too eager that she should—should honor my pride, rather than her own good."

Mother Lauria looked up at Magda. She said quietly, "Three have spoken. Margali's oath shall stand. As for Doria—I have thought of this myself, Rafaella, but I had hoped it could be avoided. She is a child of this house—"

"I don't want to go away," Doria cried. "This is my home, and Rafi is my mother—"

"But I am not," Rafaella said harshly, "You were born to my sister; so I thought I could be—impersonal with you. But I cannot; I—in my pride, I have asked too much of you. You know that an Amazon who has a birth-daughter in her own House must send her elsewhere for her training—"

Mother Lauria held up her hand. "One thing at a time! Doria, you know you must be silent here unless asked to speak! Rafi, we will talk of this later; for the moment, we have not done with Margali. Three have spoken for her, and by the laws of the Renunciates, her oath must stand. But we cannot have the house torn with dissension. I will have no more gossip and silent slander; if there is anything to be said against Margali, say it here and now, and thereafter be silent, or say it before her face."

Mother Millea said, "I have no objection to allowing Margali to stay among us. I do not dislike her. But the truth is, she did bring indemnity and disgrace upon us, and I do not think she fully understands all the laws of our Charter. If Jaelle were living here, it would be Jaelle's responsibility to instruct her oath-daughter in these things. Since she is not, we might consider extending the housebound time, so that she may complete her training—"

Oh, no, Magda thought, *I couldn't take it. . . .*

Mother Lauria said, "There is precedent for that, too; the housebound period may be extended another half year if a woman has not sufficiently learned our ways to be trusted in the outside world. Still, I am reluctant to do this with a woman Margali's age. If she were a girl of fifteen, I would certainly demand it, but surely there is a better way than this."

Camilla said, "It is pure chance that it was Jaelle and not I who took her oath; we were both present. I will volunteer to instruct her myself, as Jaelle might do."

"And I," said Marisela, and Mother Lauria nodded. She said "If any of you has an unspoken grudge against Margali, speak it now, or be silent hereafter for all time."

Magda, glancing hesitantly around the circle, seemed to hear unspoken fragments of thought. Marisela said quietly, "I can tell that your grudges are too petty to speak, in the light of this—is it true? I think Margali is an extraordinary woman, and one day we will all be proud to claim her as one of us."

Janetta, one of the younger women who had not been allowed to speak for Margali—and Magda had not expected it, for Janetta was the lover of

Cloris, who had created the crisis over the leftover dish at supper—said thoughtfully, "I think some of us have forgotten what it was like to go through training. Rafi is right; I couldn't have done it, but it wasn't asked of me. But I think maybe we expected too much of her, because she was Jaelle's oath-daughter."

The third of the Guild Mothers, who had sat silent through the entire proceeding—Magda remembered hearing that she was a judge in the Court of Arbitration, and wondered if that was why she had taken no part in the affair—said in her rusty old voice, "I think there is a lesson for all of us in the way we have been behaving; none of us is more than flesh and blood, and we must not ask more of a sister than we would be willing to endure for ourselves. That is true of Rafaella and Doria as well as Margali."

Rafaella had been leaning against Jaelle's shoulder; she turned around and held out her hand to Magda. She said, "Janetta is right; I had forgotten, and I was angry with you this afternoon because you made me see what I was doing to Doria. I—I don't want to lose her. But for her own good, I see now that I must leave her training to others. Will you forgive me?"

Magda took the hand Rafaella gave her, feeling embarrassed. "I ought to have put it more tactfully. I was rude—"

"We were both rude," said Rafaella, smiling. "Ask Camilla sometime what I am capable of—" she raised her face, laughing, to the old *emmasca*. "When we were both in training together, we drew our knives on one another! We could both have been sent away for that!"

"What did they do to you?" Magda asked, and Camilla chuckled, pressing Rafaella's shoulder.

"Handcuffed us together for ten days. For the first days we did nothing but fight and scream at each other—then we discovered we could do nothing without the other's help, and so we became friends. They do not do that any more, not in this House—"

"But then, we have not had any two trainees draw knives on one another since then," Mother Lauria said, smiling as she overheard them. "But we have not yet learned all we can from this affair. It is still painful to speak of it; but we must speak of it *because* it is painful. Keitha, your oath has not been called into question, you are not here on trial, but tell us, Keitha, why, after Margali had wounded the surrendered swordsman, you were heard to declare that we should have killed them all?"

Magda had to admire the old woman's skill as a psychologist. She felt the pressure lifted from her shoulders, yet she did not feel Keitha was being attacked in her stead; only challenged, as usual during training sessions.

Keitha took time to frame a reply, knowing it would be torn to shreds before the words were well out of her mouth. Finally she said, "He had no right to follow me here—he would have killed some of you, killed Camilla certainly, dragged me back unwilling, raped me—by the Goddess," she burst out, and Magda could see that she was trembling, "I wished then that I had Margali's skill with a sword, so that I could have killed him myself and not put my oath-sisters to the trouble!"

"But," Camilla said gently, "the men with him were only hired swords, and they followed the code of the sword; when he was himself felled, they surrendered at once. What is your quarrel with them, oath-daughter?"

"A man who hires out his sword to such an immoral purpose—does he not then forfeit protection? If not of men's laws, at least of ours?"

Rezi said angrily, "I think Keitha is right! Those men who fought alongside her husband agreed to what he was doing, they would have served their own wives the same—how do they deserve to be treated better than he?"

Camilla's soft voice—so feminine, Magda suddenly realized, in spite of her lean angular body and abrupt manners—came quietly out of the dimness in the shadow of the room. "Surely, if men see that we women cannot abide by civilized rules of behavior, they will turn all the more quickly against us?"

"Civilized rules! *Their* rules!" Janetta sounded furious, but Mother Lauria ignored her.

"Keitha, was it those men you hated? Or was it all men you wished to see punished in them?"

"It is Shann I hate," she said in a low voice, "I want to see him dead before me—I wake from dreams of killing him! Is there no one here who has ever hated a man?"

"I think there is no one here who has not," said Rafaella, but Mother Lauria went on as if she had not heard. "Hate can be a shackle stronger than love. While you hate, you are still bound to him."

Camilla said quietly, "Hate can lead you, if you cannot harm the one yourself, to turn upon yourself. I sacrificed my very womanhood so that no man could ever desire me again. It was hate cost me this."

Magda remembered the grim story Camilla had told, and wondered how the old woman's voice could sound so calm. Keitha flared, "And is that such a price? You don't know what you have been spared!"

Camilla's voice was hard. "And you don't know what you are talking about, oath-daughter."

"Is that not why you became a mercenary? To kill men in revenge for the choice they cost you?" Keitha asked.

Jaelle said into the silence, "I have known Camilla since my twelfth year; never have I known her to kill any man needless, or for revenge."

"I fight often at the sides of men," Camilla said, "and I have learned to call them comrades and companions. I hate no man living; I have learned to blame no man for the evil done by another. I have fought, yes, and killed, but I can admire, and respect, and even, yes, sometimes, love where love is due."

"But, you," Keitha said, "*you* are not a woman anymore."

Camilla shrugged slightly. "You think not?" she said, and Magda wondered if she only fancied the pain in the woman's eyes.

And behind her it seemed that Jaelle had spoken aloud, then Magda realized with dismay that somehow she was reading Jaelle's thoughts, that no one except herself could hear; *Camilla was no less foster mother to me than Kindra—perhaps more, since she had no child and knew she would have none. I love Camilla, but it is so different from the way I love Piedro. I love him . . . sometimes . . . at other times I cannot imagine why I ever even liked him. Never, never could I turn against one of my sisters that way. . . .*

And Magda was thinking, in a desperate attempt to distance the subject by intellectualizing it, they talked a lot about the differences between men and women, but none of their answers ever satisfied her. She could get pregnant and Peter could not, that was the only difference she could see in the world of the Terrans, they did not share the most dangerous of vulnerabilities. And then somehow she felt as if her whole sense of values had done a flipflop, he had been dependent on her, and now on Jaelle, to give him the son he so desperately desired . . . before, she had always seen herself as taking all the risks, but now Jaelle could bear him a son, if she would, *if she would.* . . . now he was at Jaelle's mercy as he had been at hers; she saw it almost with a flash of pity. Poor Peter. And then, in a flash, *was Jaelle pregnant?* Then the sudden linkage broke and slammed shut and Magda was alone in her mind again, confused, not knowing which were her thoughts and which came from elsewhere. She had missed some of what Camilla was saying.

"I have gone to some lengths to prove myself the equal, or more, of any man, but I am past that now; I can admit my own womanhood and I need not prove it to you. Why does it distress you to think of me as a woman, Keitha?"

Keitha cried out, "I cannot understand you! You are free of the burden none of us can endure, and yet you choose to be woman, you *insist* upon it . . . does not even neutering free you?"

Camilla's face was very serious now. "It is not the freedom you think it, oath-daughter," she said, holding out her hand to Keitha, but Keitha ignored it.

"It is easy for you to be sentimental about womanhood," Keitha cried, tears running angrily down her face, "You have nothing more to lose, you are free from the desire of men and from their cruelty, you can be a man among men or a woman among women as you choose, and have it all your own way—"

"Does it seem so to you, child?" Camilla took Keith's hand gently in hers, but the younger woman wrenched it away in angry revulsion. Camilla's face twisted a little, as if in pain.

"Can I really be a woman among women? You are not the first who has refused to accept me as one of you, though it does not often happen in my own house. Perhaps men are a little kinder; they accept me as a comrade even when they know I have nothing to offer them as a woman, they defend my back and offer their lives for mine by the code of the sword. My sisters here could do no more. Yet I am all too aware that I am not one of them."

Keitha, savage in aroused hatred, said viciously, "Yet you sit here and dare to boast of your comradeship with our tormentors and oppressors!"

"I was not boasting," Camilla said quietly, "but it is true that I have come to know men as few women have the chance to know them. I no longer want to kill them all for the vileness of a few."

"But doesn't everyone here have a tale to tell, of men worth nothing but our hate? I am filled with it—I will never be free of it—I want to kill them, to go on killing them, but I would be more merciful than they, I could kill them cleanly with the sword where they kill and torture, enslaving the body and the soul—I will never be free of it until I have struck down a man and seen him die—"

"Is that why you came here, Keitha?" asked Marisela gently, "to learn to kill men?"

Mother Lauria said "A man? And any man will do?"

"Are they not all the same in their treatment of women?" Keitha demanded.

Mother Lauria looked round the circle. "Here sits one," she said, and her eyes came to rest on Jaelle, "who has said the same thing so many times that their sound is a permanent echo within this room; yet she has taken a freemate and dwells with him outside the Guild House. Jaelle, can you talk to Keitha about men, and whether they are all the same?"

Magda could feel Jaelle's agitation, like a living presence, though Jaelle was silent and did not move. Finally she said "I do not know what to say, Mother, I would prefer not to speak yet—"

"Is that because you need it, perhaps, more than the rest of us? You know the rules; none of us may spare ourselves, nor ask our sisters to speak of what we will not share—"

But Jaelle looked steadily down at the rug, and Mother Lauria shrugged. "Doria?"

The girl giggled nervously. She said, "I have never known any man well enough to love him—or hate him either. What can I say?" She turned to Jaelle and said, "You were the last woman I would ever expect to take a freemate! You had said so often that you wanted nothing of men—"

Mother Lauria looked at Jaelle so long and intently that the younger woman said, "Don't—I will speak." But then she was silent for a long time, so long that Magda actually turned to look at her, to see if she was still physically present there. At last she said, "Men—are all the same— just as, in a way, women are all the same. Each man is different, yet they all have something in common which makes them different from women, I don't know what it is—"

There was a round of giggles and laughs all round the circle, and the tension slackened a little, but Jaelle said, distracted, "I don't think that was what I meant. I have lain with only this one man. I like it—I suppose he is not much different from Keitha's husband—better mannered, perhaps; they have laws in the Terran Zone, no man may lay violent hands on his wife, no more freely than on any other citizen. But I would have to ask some woman who has had many lovers whether they are all the same in this way—"

Rafaella said with a faint laugh, "It is a common illusion of young women that men are all different from one another," but then she said into the laughter from the rest, "No, seriously; no man is like another, but they are not so different, either."

"In the Terran Zone, a woman is not her freemate's property, not in law," Jaelle said, "but there is something in a man which seems to drive him to *possess* . . . I never knew this existed before." She shook her head, and her hair, the color of a new-minted copper coin, cascaded around her shoulders and her face, gleaming in the firelight. "In intimacy—the mind —it is raw—I don't know—" she said half aloud, running her fingers through her hair, shaking it into place with a gesture of pride and defiance.

And suddenly it seemed Jaelle was at one end of the room and all her sisters were at the far end; Magda knew it had never been there before between Jaelle and her sisters, but it was there, a gulf wider than the abysses between the stars; she thought, *I could get up now and proclaim myself a Terran and I would be less alien than Jaelle at this moment.* Jaelle was far away, alien, alone, with nothing save her pride and her flaming hair and the word, *Comyn,* which echoed softly in Magda's mind, echoed from all over the room. *Comyn.* The very word was like a solid wall which separated Jaelle from the only family she had ever known.

They had known of her blood, of course, knew that Lady Rohana was her close kinswoman; but never in all these years had Jaelle spoken any word or given any hint that she cared for her Comyn blood; her red hair seemed no more than an accident of birth. Now it was in the room with them, and Magda, looking at the faces which were suddenly those of strangers—and she knew that she saw them through Jaelle's eyes—sensed fear; a wary fear reserved for gods, not men; for Comyn, aliens, outsiders, rulers. . . .

For this moment, Jaelle was an outsider, not a cherished sister, and they all knew it. Trying to break that frightening silence, Magda turned and took Jaelle's hand in her own. She said, "I think it is a game they like to play with us; possession. They like to think they own us; they know they do not and it makes them insecure. Women do not—do not suffer so much from separation as men do. Perhaps we should not blame them so much for trying to pretend they own us. It is their nature. Thay have nothing else."

"Their nature!" Felicia spoke from the shadows, her eyes still swollen, her voice husky. "Are we not to blame them for possessiveness, when I have seen my son torn from me, sobbing, screaming my name—" she turned on Lauria, in shaking anger. "Their nature! Does their nature demand that they shall have command of the world, of their women and their sons, that they and they alone have a right to immortality through their children? What kind of world have they built, where a woman must give up her sons, to be taught to fight and kill as a sign of manliness, never to weep, never to show fear, to instill into his nature the need to *possess.* . . . to possess his women and his children, to make him into the kind of man from which I fled—is it not in my nature, too, to desire my sons? And I am denied this here among you—" She put her face in her hands and began to cry again, heartbrokenly.

Janetta flared, "Would you have your sons grow up among us, then, to turn on us and try to possess us when they are grown?"

Rafaella snarled, "There should be a better way than to return them to that very world, to be made into the kind of men we hate! Perhaps, if they were reared among us they would be different—"

"They would still grow to be *men,*" Janetta cried, "and they do not belong here in the Guild House!"

Mother Lauria raised her hands, trying to impose silence, but the clamor grew. Magda was thinking, almost in despair, not knowing whether the thoughts were hers or another's, *We give up our sons because that is all men want of us, perhaps what they are trying to do here is hopeless and unnatural. . . .*

Jaelle said into a sudden silence, "I have thought—sometimes—I would like to have a child. I have—have thought some of you foolish for allowing yourselves to become pregnant." She folded her hands in her lap to keep from wringing them. "But how do you know? The Oath says—we must bear children only in our own time and season. But how do you—how do you *know* whether it is your own wish, or—or only a wish to please *him?*"

"If you had borne two or three children," Keitha said with great bitterness, "you would know."

"Would you?" Rafaella asked, and Magda felt the confusion and dismay, Rafaella had borne sons and given them up, and she was torn apart with Felicia's misery . . . *how do I know all this?*

Cloris said, "Do we not spend all our time here learning to know our own minds and our own wishes from what men expect of us?"

"No," Jaelle said. "There's no way for ordinary minds to know, they can teach that only in the Towers—oh, there's no talking to you, you don't even have *laran,* how can you know?" And suddenly Magda realized again that Jaelle had not said this aloud, that she had flung no more at Cloris than a strangled "No—" and stopped, shaking. Marisela leaned over and took Jaelle's hand, a firm clasp that silenced the red-haired woman. Magda too was held silent, hardly hearing what Mother Lauria was saying:

"You have given us another important thing to consider; how do we know when we do our own will, or the will of another whose approval is important to us?" She went on talking, but Magda was no longer listening, and heard only snatches of the rest of the training session. One of the women said ". . . if we all chose never to bear children, and if all women were as we were, then should we be as extinct as the *chieri,* the desire of a woman to bear is as inborn as the desire of a man to engender," and Janetta said in protest, "That is not a true desire from within us, it is a desire we have been told we must have! I have never known a man, I never shall; I do not feel it is right that a Renunciate should renounce men and their world and their property, and continue to lie with men, to love them, to bear them children for whom we must take these wretched compromises! If we have given up men's rule, cannot we give up the power over men which comes from lying with them?"

Marisela asked gently, "Would you have us all lovers of women, Janetta, as some men say we are?"

"And why not? At least I will never bear a child to be snatched away into the world I have renounced and made into the kind of man I hate!"

"Yet I would not want to live in a house without children," someone said. "Life would be worse without such as Doria, and Jaelle who was fostered among us—and the house is empty—" Magda could feel Felicia's awful grief for her child, and Marisela's memory of Byrna's baby. . . .

Mother Lauria said gently, "The wish for children is after all a natural desire, and cannot be dismissed as something born of man's pride alone. That can be destroyed quickly enough by ill treatment, sometimes even in men it can be destroyed. There are men with no desire for women, and I think that sad, too. This is part of what we share with men, too; the wish for children, our immortality, companions for our old age, or even, like our little Doria, little ones to cherish and care for and watch them growing to womanhood among us—"

"And for that selfish desire," Janetta argued, "you would bear a child into a world which enslaves women and corrupts men to go on enslaving them?"

Magda found a curious picture floating in her mind; a woman, beautiful, queenly . . . chained, hung about with heavy chains that hindered her, weighed her down . . . the image shattered; was she hallucinating again?

". . . but you had a choice, Felicia; you could have kept your son, by living outside the House, or even with your son's father."

"It seemed I could not bear either choice," Felicia said, shaking, "I could not bear to leave my sisters. Yet no woman can teach a man to live as a man. A man who could live by our code would be an effeminate, never at ease anywhere—I would not condemn my son to such a fate."

"Yet if we despise the way men live," said Mother Lauria, "Is it right to allow them to bring up our sons to be more of that kind of men?"

Keitha said, "I would prefer a man to be effeminate rather than to be masculine at the cost of all decency and consideration."

Mother Lauria said quietly, "Some day, perhaps, there may be another answer for us. But the world will go as it will, not as you or I will have it. May the Goddess grant that some changes come in our lifetime; yet we, who are changing the world, will always suffer for it. I do not think your suffering is wasted—nor Keitha's, nor Camilla's, nor Byrna's—every one of us is suffering to show the men of the Domains that perhaps we would rather suffer than live by their rules. And yet if men and women are to live forever barricaded from another, how then shall the human race go on?"

Marisela said slyly, "Perhaps as they say the Terrans do it—with machines," and the room broke up into an uproar of laughter; even Mother Lauria laughed. Only Magda did not laugh; she was not intending to tell Mother Lauria about the worlds where that was actually the normal procedure. The women began unwinding stiffened legs, rubbing cold hands over the fire; they clustered in small groups, talking softly, while some of the others went to the kitchen, bringing back a huge kettle of hot cider and plates of cakes and sweets. Magda dipped up a cup of the hot, spicy drink and stood by the fire, separated from the others. Camilla, Rafaella and Jaelle were clustered near the fire; the moment of alienation Magda had seen, when Jaelle seemed suddenly apart from all of them, was gone as if it had never been. Magda wondered if she had imagined it. Mother Lauria came, leading Doria by the hand, and gestured Rafaella away, and Jaelle, looking up, signalled Magda to join them. She took up a plate of the crisp little fried cakes which always made their appearance on these nights, and went over to Jaelle.

"Where is Camilla?"

"She went to speak with Keitha," Jaelle said. "That is a bad situation, Margali; Camilla is her oath-mother, there should not be so much hostility between them."

"I cannot imagine what has caused it," said Mother Lauria, joining them, with Rafaella and Doria at her side. "I thought you would like to know, we have settled it that Doria shall go to Neskaya for her training—"

Fine, Magda thought, *one more friend gone!* Doria hugged Magda shyly.

"I'll miss you, Margali, and Keitha,—I don't want to go away," she said tearfully. "This is my home, but—but—"

"But everyone leaves her home for training, and you may not be different," Jaelle said, "Remember, Kindra made me spend half a year with Lady Rohana at Ardais, so that I might know for certain what the life was, that I was renouncing—so that no one could say I had renounced it without a clear idea of the choice I was making. At least you, Doria, are going to another Guild House. I know many of the women in Neskaya—you will find many friends there, and they are all your sisters, after all."

Behind her, Magda heard Rafaella ask, "But what can Keitha possibly have against Camilla? Surely not just that she is an *emmasca,* neutered—she could not possibly be as cruel or bigoted as that, could she?"

"I do not think it is only that," said Jaelle. "Camilla is a lover of women; she has been kind and affectionate with Keitha, and possibly Keitha has misunderstood her affection—"

Magda's face burned, though rationally she knew the words were not directed at her, neither woman knew anything about the moment when she had kissed Keitha, in her delirium after being wounded—how could they? And she was sure Camilla had not told either of them of the encounter where she herself had rebuffed Camilla.

"Keitha is a *cristoforo,* " said Rafaella, "and they are as bad as the Terrans on that subject. But Camilla is not the type to press her wishes where she is rebuffed, even gently. Certainly Keitha does not think of Camilla as a danger to her, does she? Margali, you know her as well as anyone here, what does she think?"

"I don't know what Keitha thinks," Magda said, "I don't even know what I think myself. But if Keitha cannot see that Camilla is a good and honorable woman, then it is certainly her loss."

"But there cannot be hostility between a woman and her oath-mother," said Rafaella, "it is un-natural and wrong. Something must be done about it!" She hovered with her hand over the plate of sweet cakes, then shook her head, laughing. "I have eaten too many already, I am as greedy as if I were four months pregnant! Jaelle, are you spending the night in the house? You surely can't go back through the streets of Thendara at this hour, can you? And listen," she added, pausing, and they could hear the violence of sleet against the windows, the wind that hurled itself incessantly around the corners of the houses in the street.

"I like hearing it," said Jaelle, though Magda shivered. "In the Terran Zone, we are so insulated from the weather, we never know whether it is snowing or the sun is shining—"

"If you are staying, would you like to sleep in my room? They moved Marisela out because she had to come in and out so often, a midwife's sleep is like a farmer's at calving season! And Devra is still in Nevarsin, so there is plenty of room there—"

"Yes, and perhaps we can have a few minutes to talk about the business," Jaelle said. "I think you may need to take a partner, after all, for the next year or two—"

"Jaelle! Are you pregnant, then? I would like to meet that freemate of yours, if he could change your mind about something like that," Rafaella said, teasing, but Jaelle shook her head. She said, "It's too soon to be sure, Rafi. Believe me, you would be the first one I would confide in, but of course there is always the possibility. In any case I will be with the Terrans for at least a year, I have given my word. There is also—"

"There is also the matter of which women to send to learn their medical techniques," Mother Lauria said, "and I will try to consult you about that, Rafaella, before we make the final decisions. Perhaps when she finishes her housebound time in Neskaya, Doria might like to go; I was thinking of sending her to Arilinn, for midwife's training. She has clever hands and she is good with animals, she might be good at that too. But not tonight," she added, looking around the room, where only a few small groups of women remained, the others having scattered. Three or four were settled down in a corner by the hearth, drinking wine, as if they had decided to make a night of it; two others were absorbed in some kind of card game; Irmelin with two of her helpers was gathering up the used plates and mugs. Mother Lauria said, "I had hoped to bring this up in the meeting, but it went otherwise and I did not want to keep you all too late. Margali, will you and your oath-mother come for a moment to my office before you go upstairs?"

Magda had to admire the deft way Mother Lauria had singled the two of them out—*you and your oath-mother*—as if it had only to do with Magda's challenged oath. Rafaella gave Jaelle a goodnight kiss. "You had better sleep with Margali tonight; you and I always spend half the night talking, and I am sleepy." She punctuated the words with an enormous yawn. "We can talk business at breakfast. But don't stay away so long next time, love—the Terrans can't be keeping you as busy as all that, can they?"

Jaelle hugged her goodnight. "Sometime I'll tell you all about Terran clocks!"

In Mother Lauria's office, the Guild Mother said, "You have had a chance to see us and to remember our strengths, Jaelle—have you any suggestions?"

Jaelle's smile wavered. Magda thought she looked very tired. She said, "Only negative ones; I do not think Janetta would suit the Terrans—or the other way around."

Mother Lauria nodded. "It is a pity," she said. "Since Janni is clever and learns quickly, I am sure the Terrans would find her excellent at their —*technology.*" She used the Terran word; there was no equivalent one in *casta.* "I think Keitha, too, would be valuable, and such learning valuable to her; Marisela is already taking her along on maternity calls—Keitha is a skillful midwife already, and with Terran training too, she could take Marisela's place here when Mari is away on Sisterhood business."

"I have never understood the Sisterhood," complained Jaelle.

The old Guild Mother smiled faintly. "Nor do I; nor does anyone who is not sworn to them, Shaya. But they go far, far back into the history of the Renunciates; some say they were the original Renunciates. Be that as it may—I do not think Keitha is yet able enough to control herself around strange men." She sighed. "We should be thinking which of our best women we wish to send for the Terran training, not only which ones are able to survive among them! It is one of the strengths of our training, that it makes us hard and inflexible, and yet that is a weakness too . . . no society which is not open to new things can grow and change as we need to do. Kindra used to say that we should learn from everything which came into our lives."

Magda said hesitantly, "Perhaps we should simply describe what the Terrans want in House meeting, and ask which women would like to volunteer—and perhaps let one of the Terran women come here so that the —the Guild Sisters can see that Terran women are not so different." Cholayna Ares, she thought, she would understand the Amazons and the Guild House, and the Renunciates would respect her strength and integrity. Yet Cholayna's brown skin might arouse their xenophobia. She told herself she was being silly; certainly these women could learn to respect a woman of a different ethnic group!

"That might be arranged. I myself would like to meet with some of these Terran women, Margali. Among other things—" her smile was kind. "I think it might help me understand you better. Sooner or later there must be meetings of this kind."

Jaelle said "Perhaps—perhaps you could come and visit the HQ, Mother? And perhaps—" she made the suggestion hesitantly—"invite some of them to dinner in the Guild House and let them speak in House meeting about what they offer, and what they ask?"

Magda was glad the suggestion had come from Jaelle instead of herself; though she smiled at the thought of a regular Empire Recruiting agent here in the Guild House. Well, why not? There were women here capable of profiting by Terran education; she could, for instance, see Rafaella as a starship captain!

"I will think about it, and that is all I can say at the moment," Mother Lauria said, "though I would gladly visit there. And now I must send you both to bed."

Dismissed, Jaelle looked at her hesitantly. "You don't mind, do you? She took it for granted that as your oath-mother I would prefer to stay in your room—"

"All right by me," Magda said, remembering the many nights she and Jaelle had spent together on the trail. Alone in their room, Magda asked, "And Peter, is he well?"

"Oh, yes, very well." Jaelle had lapsed into a brooding silence, which Magda was reluctant to disturb. She found Jaelle a nightgown; it was far too long, and Jaelle looked like a child dressed in her mother's clothes. She sat on the edge of the bed, saying, "This reminds me of when I first came here. There were no children in the house, and Kindra could find nothing to fit me; I learned to sew by cutting everything down to my own size!"

"How old were you when you first came here, Jaelle?"

"Oh, eleven, thirteen—something like that, I don't remember much."

"Where were you born?" she asked. Jaelle frowned and said curtly, "Shainsa. Or so I'm told; I don't remember a thing about it. Your Terrans have already been after me to allow them to hypnotize me with one of their machines and tell them every little thing I remember. But I don't want to remember—that's why I forgot it in the first place."

"I don't even know where Shainsa is. Isn't it one of the Dry Towns?"

"Yes. In the desert beyond Carthon," said Jaelle, clipping off her words in distaste. "I didn't have time to bathe before supper; I think I'll try and find a free tub."

She went off to the the common bath, and Magda, chilly even in the long warm nightgown, crawled into bed under the extra blankets she had managed to cadge. Her feet felt like ice; she tucked them alternately behind her knees, wondering why no one on Darkover had ever invented a hot-water bottle. *Maybe I could be a public benefactor and re-invent the warming pan,* she thought fuzzily, wondered why Jaelle was taking so long —had she fallen asleep in the tub? She did not wake when Jaelle came back in the dark, crawling over her to the wall side of the bed, to lie there fighting sleep until the familiar night sounds of the House, and the familiar scent of the mattress stuffed with sweetgrass lulled her into the deepest sleep she had known since she went to the Terran Zone.

Magda dreamed. She was downstairs in the training hall—or was it the great ballroom at Ardais where she had danced, at Midwinter? Lady Rohana was there too, but with her hair cut short like an Amazon's; and Peter was there as well, but they had to cross the pass of Scaravel before the snows began, and he kept trying to urge her to leave the ballroom with him. But now Peter belonged to Jaelle and had no right to try to persuade her this way. Finally she went out with him on to the balcony, but the balcony had become the causeway leading to the bandit stronghold of Sain Scarp, and Rumal di Scarp was there, so she drew her knife and defended the steps of the house against him, her sword moving as if by its own volition, defending Peter from his attack, and she went on, and on, disregarding his surrendering gesture, even though she knew that she would disgrace herself as an Amazon; but she didn't stop, she went on slashing and striking until he lay dead at her feet in a pool of blood. The blowing snow in the pass turned to a stinging sandstorm, and beneath the shadow of a great rock she saw the pool of blood, crimsoning the desert in the light of the rising sun, and she was screaming, screaming—

With a rush and a gasp, she woke, realizing that she was kneeling bolt upright in bed, the covers flung on the floor, and it was Jaelle who was screaming . . . no, she was no longer sure there had been any screams at all, except in the dream whose fragments were even now fading to the shocking memory of blood on desert sand. The room was filled with pale light from the snow outside, reflecting the small green moon.

"Damn dream," said Jaelle, gasping. "I'm sorry, *chiya.* I've been having nightmares—want me to sleep on the floor?"

Magda shook her head. "I was having a nightmare too—it's my fault as much as yours. I always have nightmares after the training sessions."

"You too? I used to lie awake after session for hours because I was so afraid of the nightmares I got. What was yours?"

Magda groped at vanishing fragments of nightmare. "Sain Scarp. Fighting someone. A pool of blood—I'm not sure," she said, though, with eidetic terror she could see Peter's face at the center of the pool of blood.

"I was dreaming about—I think it was my mother," said Jaelle, off guard for a moment. "Awake I can't even remember her face—I was so young when she died. But I have nightmares about her. I know she died in the desert, but that's all I've ever been able to remember." Yet Magda could see the nightmare in her mind. Clear, the blood spreading on the sand, frozen horror that would not let her move. Deliberately, to break the paralysis, she leaned over and tugged the blankets.

"Aren't you too hot with all these?" Jaelle asked.

"Hot? God, no, I'm freezing," Magda said, crawling gratefully under the blankets again. She wished for hot coffee or something like it. "Lady Rohana was there too, only she was dressed like an Amazon, or there were Amazons there too, I don't remember . . . somebody was bleeding to death—no, it's gone. What's the matter, Jaelle?"

"Nothing, only I'm cold after all," Jaelle said, her teeth chattering. "It's so hot in Quarters, I've gotten used to it. Here, let's try and keep each other warm." She pulled Magda close, and the other woman's body warmth was like an anchor, welcome, somehow solidifying the wavering edges of the light.

"Peter never had any patience with dreams," Magda said, finding the image floating in her mind without knowing why, "He always said no one was interested in them but Psych and Medic—if I just had to talk about my dreams, I ought to go down and find a psych-tech who would at least have a professional interest in them. Does he do that to you?"

Jaelle shook her head. "I didn't know the machines could give you nightmares, until he told me."

"But a properly adjusted corticator shouldn't bother you so much," Magda said, concerned. "You should make sure they have it properly adjusted to your alpha rhythms, of course. Who are you working with?"

"I can't remember all their names. There are so many—"

"You ought to have an office to yourself, at least," Magda said. "I spent years getting out of that madhouse down in the Coordinator's office; you mean, after all the time I put in getting out of that mob scene, you let them put you back there? Jaelle, as a special resident expert in languages, you deserve a private office—you have to fight for your privileges, especially being a woman, or they'll walk all over you!"

Jaelle drew a deep breath of relief; so her loathing of the crowded office with the jammed, claustrophobic desks was not simply a sign of personal failure, as Peter often seemed to think; Magda hated it too.

"You're a special expert, not a routine clerk," Magda reminded her. "Insist on what's due you. They'll expect it and respect you for it." She thumped her pillow into a more comfortable position. "One thing I really miss here is a clock with a luminous dial. I never know what *time* it is!"

And that was one of the things Jaelle appreciated most; being free of the tyranny of the continual emphasis on time. She supposed it was one of the cultural differences that went deepest. She only said "I don't think I'd ever miss it," and snuggled under the quilt. Magda buried her face in the pillow, and Jaelle moved into the warmth of her body.

After a time they began to dream again. They were in some kind of tower, at the very top of a tower, and she and Magda were standing at opposite ends of a circle; somehow Magda seemed to look out from her own eyes and from Jaelle's too, holding up, in their arms, a glittering rainbow-colored arch, like a glittering geodesic dome . . . the word *geodesic* came into Jaelle's head, alien, but she was not really curious about what it meant nor did she wonder from what odd experience Magda had become aware of its meaning. The dome was transparent but very strong, it would protect those below who were working—it was very important work but what they were doing neither of them could quite see, though Marisela seemed to be down there working, and there was a pleasant-looking man in his forties, wearing the green and gold of the Ridenow Domain, who looked up at Jaelle and suddenly met her eyes, and for a long minute they looked at one another, so that Jaelle knew that if she ever met this man in real life she would recognize him at once. He said softly, *Are you here out of time, or astray in a dream, chiya?* and she had no answer for him. And there was another Amazon there, her face round and snub-nosed—Jaelle had seen her somewhere but could not remember her name. Something was growing under their hands, and Magda felt very proud of what they were doing. Someone said in her hearing, *Everyone of us here has had to outgrow at least one life,* and Magda heard someone repeating a fragment of poetry—she knew it was very old:

> He who lives more lives than one,
> More deaths than one must die . . .

and she said fretfully, "It's bad enough to have to die once, isn't it?"

"Oh, there's nothing to dying," Marisela said, "I've done it a few hundred times. You'll get used to it."

Magda seemed to be talking to a tall man with fair hair whose face Jaelle could not see. He reminded her a little of Alessandro Li but he wasn't, and he picked up Magda bodily and carried her across a sudden, blazing strip of fire . . . Jaelle felt the fire sear Magda's feet, and tried to run to her, but the dome was slipping through her fingers. And then she was in Peter's arms, and he was holding her down, only it was not Peter, it was her cousin Kyril Ardais, and she heard herself say fretfully that she should have counted his fingers before going to bed with him. Only somehow it was not Kyril either, it was one of the bandits who had attacked them, and Magda was in Peter's arms . . . no, Magda knew it was not rape, she knew she had gone willingly into Peter's arms only now when she had left him she knew that in a very real sense he had been using her all that time, dominating her because he knew she was his superior in their shared work, and now Jaelle was going to have his child, but they were alone, trying to climb down the cliffside of a mountain, ice-steps hewed into the side of the mountain, and she was looking for Lady Rohana, because Jaelle was pregnant by one of the bandits and she was going to die in childbirth unless she could bring Lady Rohana to her in time. She was dying, she was bleeding to death on the sands of the desert, there was a blizzard with sand that cut like blowing snow in their faces, and Jaelle was lying on the sand bleeding, and yet as she twisted and screamed in childbirth, it was somehow Magda's child she was trying to bear, the child Magda should have borne Peter but she had left Jaelle to it. . . .

And they woke again in each other's arms, clutching each other tightly, the heavy blankets and quilts kicked off them. Magda pulled away, reaching for the blanket, but Jaelle held her.

"Oh, the Gods be thanked, I am here safe, here with you, *breda,*" she said, gasping, holding Magda tight, "I was so frightened, so frightened—" and she pulled Magda down close to her. "What were you dreaming this time?" And she held Magda tightly and kissed her.

Magda felt the kiss and for a moment it blended into the magical way in which she had shared Jaelle's thoughts in the dream. Then, shocked and shaking, she pulled away. What had this place done to her? She felt weak and drained and the early snow-reflected light at the window sent knives through her head. Jaelle looked up at her and the laughter died in concern. "It's all right, Margali," she said in a whisper. "There's nothing to be afraid of, you're here with me, *bredhya.*" She tried to pull Magda down again into the comfort of her arms. But Magda pulled free, stumbling, her dressing robe dragging on the floor behind her. The floor felt unsteady, bulging and rippling under her feet, and when she got into the bath and splashed her face with icy water it seemed to burn her skin without clearing her vision or cooling her fever.

Irmelin was there under the icy shower; the very sight made Magda shiver. She looked surprised to see Magda.

"Awake so early? You are not on kitchen duty, are you? Or helping Rezi with the milking?" She moved aside, and said, "I'm finished here," and picked up her towel. She stopped a moment, concerned, watching Magda clinging to the basin. "Are you ill, Margali?"

Magda thought, Yes, something is wrong with me, but she only shook her head.

"There is blood on your nightgown," said the plump, smiling woman. "If you take out the stain now with cold water, you will be doing a kindness to the women who are working in the laundry this moon."

"Blood?" Magda was still in a stupor of horror from the dream; she started to say, *but I'm not even pregnant.* She caught herself—how foolish! She bent to look; it was true. The heavy nightgown was spotted with blood.

Well, that explained part of the dream, anyhow; explicitly sexual dreams had always heralded the onset of her menstruation. The treatment she had been given in the Terran zone, to suppress the cycles of ovulation, must have worn off. She had not been expecting it. Peter had always laughed at the sexual dreams she had at that time, saying that if she had been equally passionate earlier in her cycle, he might have been able to make her pregnant—she cut the thought off, angry at herself for remembering. She went to the cupboard where supplies were kept, and Irmelin, watching her, said, "You really do look unwell, Margali. If I were you I would ask Marisela for some of the herb medicines she keeps for such things, and then go back to bed and try to sleep."

She did not want to disturb Marisela's rest, but it was a temptation; to go back to bed, to huddle there and complain of sickness, to put it all aside. And the thing which made her feel sickest was that she wanted nothing more than to go back to Jaelle, let the woman comfort her, find the same kind of rapport she had had with Keitha after the fight, when Marisela's drug had worn down her defenses, and this time follow it as far as it would lead. But she could not face Jaelle, she could not face anyone with this thing, whatever it was; she was helpless, unprotected . . . she felt entangled, enmeshed in conflicting loyalties like spiderwebs. Her hands shook as she washed out her nightgown.

I am jealous of Jaelle. Not because she has Peter, but because Peter has her, now . . . he accused me of this once and I would not believe it.

She went back to the room, hurrying into her clothes. Jaelle sat up and watched her, troubled.

"Oath-daughter," she said. "What have I done? What are you worrying about? Did you think—" and she stopped, not able to follow Magda's troubled thoughts; the erratic *laran* she could never command had deserted her again, and she did not know what Magda was worrying about, she only knew the other woman was desperately troubled, and could not imagine why. Why would Magda not accept her comfort? Magda put on her shoes and clattered down the stairs, running; when Jaelle followed, some time later, Magda was neither at breakfast in the dining room, nor anywhere else in the house, and when she asked if anyone had seen her,

Rafaella said, puzzled, that Margali had volunteered to help with the milking in the barn.

And suddenly Jaelle was angry. *If she would rather do hard work in the barn than face me and have this out together, so be it.* She sat down by Rafaella and dipped up a dish of porridge, flooding it with milk and shaking her head when Rafi passed her the honey jar.

"Very well," she said. "Let's talk about the business, for I should be back at the Headquarters by the third hour after sunrise."

Chapter Three

Jaelle was sure, now, that she was pregnant, though there was as yet no trace of the early-morning sickness. And that brought back a memory from the Guild House, years ago. It had been before Kindra died. Marisela had said, in one of the first midwives' lectures Jaelle had been allowed to attend after her body had matured, that morning sickness was at least in part because the body and mind were in disagreement; one or the other, mind or body, rejecting the child when the other wished for it. And she would not have been surprised if this sickness had come in her confusion.

She had not yet told Peter. Part of her confused mind wondered if she was being spiteful. He wanted a son so very much. Did she take malicious pleasure in denying him the knowledge that would mean so much to him? No, she was sure it was not that.

In my heart what I want is for him to know without being told. To read it in my heart and mind as even Kyril, much as I despise him, would know. And this made her guilty again, that she so much wanted—no, *needed*— Peter to be what he was not. Yet she had rejected, with so much determination, her Comyn heritage. Rejected it again and again, the first time when, as a child, she had asked for fostering in the Amazon house rather than remaining with Rohana; Rohana had loved her mother and would have gladly fostered Melora's daughter. She had rejected it again, when at fifteen she had chosen to take the Oath rather than to honor the training of a Comyn daughter, to be trained in *laran* in a Tower, and then to marry a Comyn son as they decreed. They had not wanted her to renounce her heritage. She stood too near the head of the Aillard Domain—Jaelle was not sure how near; she had not wanted to know.

The Oath was specific; bear no child for any man's house or heritage, clan or inheritance, pride or posterity. As she had asked in the Guild House: how did she know whether she wanted a child for herself, or because Peter so much wanted it? And what of a woman's heritage? Did she not wish to bear a daughter for the Guild House, or for her mother's inheritance?

And why should she think so much about it now? Since she was already pregnant, there was not very much she could do about it. She had deliberately neglected the contraceptive precautions that the Terran Medics had carefully explained to her. A child had chosen her, even if she had not really chosen the child.

Yet, when she walked that morning into Cholayna's office, it struck her that she would very much like to confide in Cholayna.

Yet—confide in a stranger, when she had not even told the father of her child? Was this only the habit of turning to another woman for comfort or validation? She remembered that she had sought reassurance, almost permission, of Magda, before she shared Peter's bed, and had rationalized it by telling herself that she wished to be sure her friend would not feel jealous, because Peter had once been Magda's husband.

But Cholayna was her employer, not her friend or oath-sister!

"Jaelle," Cholayna said, "I am to talk this morning with one of the Renunciates, a—Guild Mother?" She hesitated, stumbling a little, on the title. "Her name is Lauria n'ha Andrea—did I pronounce that right? And I want you present as interpreter."

"It will be my pleasure," Jaelle said formally, thinking that Mother Lauria had lost no time. "But you speak the language so well I do not think you truly need an interpreter."

Cholayna said with her quick smile, "I may pronounce the words properly, but I need someone to be sure I use all of them properly. Do you know what I mean by *semantics?* Not the meaning of the words, but the meaning of the meanings and the way different people use the same words to mean different things."

Jaelle repeated that she would be honored, and Cholayna started to speak into her communicator. "Ask the Darkovan lady—" and stopped herself. "No, wait. Jaelle, would you be kind enough to escort her into my office yourself? She is known to you."

Jaelle went to obey, thinking that Cholayna had an intuitive grasp of the right gesture, the personal touch, which would make her invaluable in dealing with Darkovans. Russell Montray did not have that intuitive sense. Yet Peter would have had it, or Magda, and she thought Monty would know, or be capable of learning it. And it was her personal responsibility to be sure that Alessandro Li learned it.

Mother Lauria was in the waiting room, her hands composedly clasped in her lap, her clear blue eyes moving around the room, studying every detail.

"What a pleasant place to work, Jaelle, though I suppose the yellow lights must be a little difficult to tolerate at first." As they went into the inner office, she asked, "Is it proper courtesy to bow to your employer, as we would do to one of our own, or to clasp her hand, as Camilla has told me the Terrans do in greeting?"

Jaelle smiled, for Cholayna had asked her the same sort of question. "For the moment, a bow will do," she said. "She is well trained in our courtesy and knows that we do not offer our hand unless it is a sincere offer of friendship."

But as the two women bowed to one another, Jaelle suspected that beyond the courtesy there was, at once, a sincere liking for one another, tempered with mutual respect, as Cholayna welcomed Mother Lauria, urging her to a comfortable seat, offering her refreshment. "Can I offer you fruit juice or coffee?"

"I would like to try your Terran coffee; I have smelled it in the Trade City," said Mother Lauria, and as Cholayna dialled her a cup from the refreshment console, sniffed the cup appreciatively. "Thank you. An interesting mechanism; I would like to know how this arrived here. I still remember, when I was told that messages came over wires, looking up to watch for the papers to come swinging along the wire. It was not till much later that I realized that what traveled over the wire were electrical pulses. And yet the idea was logical to me at that time, though I know better now." She took a sip of the coffee, and Cholayna briefly explained the refreshment console, that the essence of the drink was kept in stock there and immediately mixed and reconstituted with hot or cold water as the computerized combination required.

Mother Lauria nodded, understanding. "And the yellow lights, they are normal for your home star?"

"For the majority of the suns in the Empire," Cholayna qualified. "It is rare for a sun to have as much red and orange light as the sun of your world, and many of the people who work here will not be here long enough to make it worth the trouble of adapting to a different light pattern. But if it is more comfortable for you, I can adjust the lights here to what you would consider normal." She touched a control, and the lights dimmed to a familiar reddish color. At Jaelle's look of surprise, she smiled.

"It's new; I had it done just the other day. It could have been installed all over the HQ if anyone had had the imagination to think of it. It occurred to me that if we are to have Darkovan women working in Medic, some compromise will have to be made between what is comfortable for natives to this planet, and career employees accustomed to a brighter sun.

I, for instance, come from one of the more brilliant worlds, and I can hardly see in this light, so I must have a work area tasklighted for my own eyes. But this is restful when I am not reading." She added, "I imagine that your eyesight is comparatively much better. On the contrary, I suppose you have less tolerance to ultraviolet—if you had sun reflecting off snow, for instance, you would need to be much more careful to guard against snowblindness."

"I have heard women who travel in the Hellers say that this is a problem for them," Mother Lauria confirmed, "and I am sure you know that one of the major items of Terran trade here is sunglasses."

"While I can tolerate desert sunlight on my own world without any kind of eye protection," Cholayna said, smiling, "and people from dimmer suns must safeguard themselves very carefully against sunburn or retinal burns; Magda told me that in her first week on Alpha she was nearly blinded. I have noticed that the normal lights in here are difficult for Jaelle to tolerate."

"I did not think you had noticed," Jaelle confessed. "I have tried not to show discomfort."

"But that is foolish," Cholayna said. "Your eyesight is valuable to us. There is no reason your quarters should not be wired for red light—Peter too was brought up on Darkover and would appreciate it, I am certain. It is only necessary to speak to my technicians. My own skin tones, too, are an adaptation by my people to a more brilliant sun," she added.

"That, I should think, would be one of the difficulties our people would have should they take to traveling in space."

"You are quite right," Cholayna confirmed, "and if your women work among our medical technicians, we must make some kind of accommodation, for our lights, which are even brighter in Medic than up here, may make them uncomfortable or even damage their eyes. For instance," she added to Jaelle, "I have noticed that whenever you have been in Medic, even though you have not complained, you seem to develop headaches."

It had not occurred to Jaelle before, but now she did realize it; that at least a part of her intense reluctance to go down to the Medic floors was an unconscious distaste for the more brilliant lights down there!

"This is one of the reasons I came here," Mother Lauria confessed, "I wished to see for myself the conditions under which our women, when they come to you for teaching, will be expected to work."

"It would not be difficult at all to arrange a tour of the Medical facility for you," Cholayna said. "I can ask one of the Medic aides to show you around the hospital, or it can be arranged for a day when the new trainees can come with you. We have a standard orientation program in the Empire for planetary natives being given training. There are so few Darkovan employees now that it has not yet been done, and I am afraid that Jaelle, and a few of our others, have simply had to handle the cultural changes as best they can. But of course once we begin to have a number of them, such a program will have to be implemented at once—" She stopped, glanced at Mother Lauria and then at Jaelle.

Jaelle said promptly, "I do not quite understand 'orientation program' myself, Cholayna, and I am sure Mother Lauria does not."

Cholayna explained, and Mother Lauria instantly comprehended.

"It is like Training Session for newcomers to the Renunciates; even though they have not changed worlds, it is so different a life that they must be taught how to adapt," she said. "I think it would be best, then, Cholayna—" Jaelle noticed that Mother Lauria used the Empire woman's given name easily, which she herself had not yet learned to do— "if you came to visit us in the Guild House and spoke to our young women. Then you could arrange the tour and orientation procedures. And it might be possible to arrange a similar program," she added after a moment, "for Terran, or Empire, women who, like Magda, are to be sent into the hills and back country of our world, so that they will know how to behave, and —" her eyes twinkled—"not run the risks Margali, Miss Lor-ran, had to undergo."

Cholayna chuckled too. "That had occurred to me, of course. We would be very grateful to you, Lauria. It is not even a question of spying, but all of our women who work in such things as Mapping and Exploring occasionally have to take refuge, because of bad weather or something of the sort, in the outlands, and it is better if they know how to behave and do not outrage local opinions of how a lady should comport herself."

When Mother Lauria rose to go, they had arranged that in a tenday Cholayna should come to dine at the house, that Jaelle would accompany her, and that afterward she should talk with Marisela and other women who had had some basic training in medical techniques. Later she would address the whole Guild House in House Meeting, and discuss the women to be given training. As Jaelle conducted her outside, Mother Lauria said, "I like her, Jaelle. I had expected a woman from another world to be more alien."

"I feared you would think her strange, and perhaps feel reserve or dislike, because she is so very alien," Jaelle said, and Mother Lauria shrugged.

"The colors of her skin and hair? I have traveled in the Dry Towns, child; I know their coloring and the bleaching of their hair are an adaptation to the desert; it is not strange to me that a woman from a brighter sun should have a different skin color. Beneath that skin she is a woman like ourselves. A roan horse and a black can travel equally far in a day's journey, and I am not fool enough to judge her by the way the skin of her foremothers has adapted to protect her against the sun of her childhood. I was impressed, too, by the practicality of her clothing, for an active woman who must work among men."

Jaelle looked down self-consciously at her close-fitting Terran uniform. "That is strange, I still feel this clothing is not modest."

"But you were born and reared in the Dry Towns," Mother Lauria said, smiling, "and all your childhood you knew that a woman's garb was to make it easier for a man to see and admire her body. Beneath the Amazon, you are still a woman of the desert, Jaelle, as we are all the daughters of our childhood. I was born in the Kilghard Hills, I knew that a woman's clothing was to keep her from the free movement of a man's work. I admire your employer's uniform, and what you are wearing, because they so admirably allow free movement, without false modesty. I am rebelling against one kind of restriction in women's clothing, and you against one that is quite other."

Jaelle bit her lip and was silent. This was so much like what Cholayna had once said to her that she was beginning to wonder if it was really true. "I thought I had forgotten everything from the Dry Towns."

Lauria shook her head.

"Never. Not in your lifetime. You were almost a grown woman when you left there. You can choose not to remember, as no doubt you have done; but not to remember should be choice, not failure."

To return to the outdoors, they had to pass through the hallway outside the Communications office, the "madhouse" as Magda had called it. As they passed, Bethany came out and almost stumbled into Jaelle.

"Oh, Jaelle! I was coming up to Intelligence to look for you—you're needed in Montray's office, the Coordinator, that is. Something about a Mapping and Exploring plane down in the Kilghard Hills, and field people in to talk to the M & E people up here; Piedro's there too, and they want you right away."

"I will go as soon as I have escorted Mother Lauria to the gates," Jaelle said in *casta,* which she knew Bethany spoke well, and introduced the woman to Margali. Mother Lauria greeted her kindly and added, "I wished to add; we would welcome some of your associates when you come to visit the Guild House. It is not right that women should be separated by language and customs. That is the kind of difference that matters more to men."

Jaelle thanked her, but really she couldn't see Bethany in a Guild House, even as a visitor. She called over her shoulder to Bethany "Talk to Cholayna on the intercom; tell her I'll go right down to Mapping and Exploring."

"Right," Bethany replied, and Jaelle, frowning, went down the escalators with Mother Lauria. The old woman, frowning, said, "I can well see that ordinary women in ordinary skirts would be endangered on a device like this! Truly, your uniforms are more sensible. But, Shaya, my dear, if you are wanted you must go at once to your work; I am neither so old nor so crippled that I cannot find my way out, even from this labyrinth!"

Jaelle gave the old woman an affectionate hug for goodbye. "It is only that I am reluctant to say goodbye to you—I miss all of you more than I thought I would," she confessed.

"Then the remedy is simple, you must come back to us more often," Mother Lauria said. Jaelle stood at the foot of the stairs, watching the small, sturdy, determined woman walk away through the uniformed people on the base. She was so much herself, Jaelle thought, and here everyone seemed all alike, as if they had put on the same face with their uniforms. Yet, as she stood watching Mother Lauria, she felt, suddenly, a little dizzy at the realization. . . .

Every one of the Terrans here on this base, space workers around the big ships out there, technicians down in Medic or up in Mapping or Communications, the port workers who looked like thronging ants from the view station high above the Port where Peter had taken her one day to watch one of the ships taking off, the men and women who repaired machines or kept track of traffic on computer monitor screens, the Spaceforce men who guarded the port gates or kept order in the big buildings, even those who supervised laundry or cleaning machines or cleaned tables in the cafeteria —every one of these many people, more here on this small base than in the city of Thendara, every one of them was like Mother Lauria, a separate person with feelings and different ideas of his or her own, and perhaps if she knew and understood them as well as she knew Peter or Mother Lauria or Cholayna, she would understand that person and like or dislike him or her for what he was, not just as a "Terranan." But of course, why have I never thought of this before? She stood without moving on the escalator until a uniformed Spaceforce woman in black leathers, hurrying down the escalator, pushed her gently aside as she ran.

Jaelle looked after her. She thought, *she is a fighting woman, she would appreciate knowing about us, the Amazons, how do I seek her out and make friends with her? What kind of training would make a woman choose that life among the Terrans?* She watched the leather-clad woman out of sight, and suddenly she knew that this woman was someone she would like, wished that she could follow her on her work. . . . and at that moment it seemed that she heard an enormous babble of voices, disjoined fragments of thought, here, there, from the woman in leather, from the guard standing quiet at the gates, even though she could not see him it seemed that she looked through his eyes as he let Mother Lauria out of the gates, and at the same time she heard Piedro demanding to know where she was, she should hurry . . . he was up in the Coordinator's office, pacing, and for the first time she saw Piedro through Russ Montray's eyes, envy for the younger man's freedom of movement, he had the work he wanted on the planet he wanted, and I am stuck here on this frozen lump of a world hanging over a desk . . . what the Coordinator wanted, she suddenly knew, was shining in her mind then, a glowing world of water and rainbows shining, and little shimmering gliders skimming over the water, and he saw his own son choosing a world where dressing like an animal in fur was real, and she looked down through strange eyes into the glare of a welding arc on some unimaginable part from the inside of one of the spaceships, and worked the arc with skilled fingers, knowing that the part was a Joffrey coil and that metal fatigue would cause it to part in some strange stress . . . all this flared and blazed through her mind in a single instant, too much for any one to tolerate at once, and the stress from high in a Tower above the port where a woman's hand hesitated over a communications device, bring the ship down now, or wait, no, half a second more, and someone scalding himself with a kettle of boiling soup up in the kitchen . . .

Then it all overloaded and Jaelle slid to the surface of the stair, collapsed and fell down half a dozen steps, jarring, unconscious, to the ground. Dimly she heard voices, concerned questions, someone pulling at her identification badge to see who she was, for the first time she understood through the eyes of the technician what the badges were for, and she saw someone hurrying down from Medic, and the immediate jangle of thoughts here, has she broken that wrist? She landed pretty hard . . .

No! No! It's too much!—Jaelle tried to scream but her voice was only a whimper, her hands went up to cover her ears but it was not sound and there was no way to shut it out. Then she overloaded and as she slid down into welcome unconsciousness she wondered what a fetal position was and why it should surprise them.

Piedro's face wavered above her as she opened her eyes. A Medic pulled him away. "Just a minute. Mrs. Haldane, do you know where you are?"

She blinked and decided she did. "Medic—Section Eight, right?" Too late she realized that he had called her Mrs. Haldane and she had decided not to answer to that name.

"Do you remember what happened?"

She took a tiny mental peek at it, and decided she did not want to talk about it—*blazing stars, the battering of ten thousand thoughts, a Medic stitching up a torn eyelid, arclight flare, murder in an angry mind*—she slammed the doors of her mind on panic and confusion. "I think I must have fainted. I forgot to eat breakfast this morning."

"That would explain it," the Medic said. "Nothing much wrong, Haldane, if she wants to go back to work it's all right—if she feels like it. If not, I'll write her a half-day clearance."

"God, I was scared," Peter said, squeezing her hand, "when Spaceforce called that they'd found you unconscious on the stairway—you shouldn't go around skipping meals, love."

"I was late," she evaded, and inside, irritation flared, *it doesn't matter to him except that it made him late for that meeting with the Coordinator! He didn't even think about what every Darkovan man would be eager to know about his wife.* And then she was confused, when he had made it clear that he cared about having a child she was angry and now when he seemed not to care she was angry again! She leaned on his shoulder, for a moment, but at the touch it came flooding back again and she straightened and drew away. He misinterpreted the gesture.

"Still feeling faint, love? We'd better stop by the cafeteria and feed you." She demurred—they were already late in the Coordinator's office—but he insisted on taking her down to the dining building and getting her a quick meal. She didn't want it, but thought, *it serves me right for lying,* and forced the stuff down, hoping it wouldn't come right up again. He had gone to great pains to fetch her things, from the limited lunch selection of synthetics, that he had seen her eat, and she was touched, but again she found herself carefully evading his fingertips, and after a moment she realized why.

Do I really think that if I touch him he will be able to read my mind? Where did I get that idea?

Or is is that I do not want to know for certain that he cannot?

Still, it seemed his instinct had been right. The food seemed somehow to block the enormous overload of sensation and reduce it to manageable proportions. Had she been under less tension, she might have enjoyed the visit to the Coordinator's office, high above the port with a vast view reaching from the Venza Mountains high above the city, and the Comyn Castle, at one edge of the sky, and at the other, a vast expanse stretching halfway to the plains of Valeron, dim and blue at the edge of an indistinguishable horizon. The Coordinator was there, with his son and Cholayna Ares and many people Jaelle did not know, admiring the view.

Alessandro Li was speaking of it as they came in: "Grand view you have up here, Russ!"

The Coordinator turned his back on it, shrugging. "Not my type of scenery and the sun's the wrong color," he said. "Can't see worth a damn." *I should imagine the natives would go blind.* It was a moment before Jaelle realized that he had not said that aloud. Damn it, if she was going to be hearing both what people would say and what they did *not* say, it was going to be an uneasy conference! It also occurred to her that he had been here quite long enough for his eyes to be as well adapted to the light as Magda's or Piedro's except that he had so carefully insulated himself from that light. She tried, as she found she could, to draw within herself and avoid the contact, and the effort turned her pale.

"We might as well get down to business," Montray said, "Some of our field men came in last night with a report of a downed plane out in the Kilghard Hills. I think they've finally found Mattingly and Carr."

"Remember, I'm new here," Li said, "Who are Mattingly and Carr?"

It was Wade Montray, Monty, who answered.

"Mapping and Exploring," he said. "About three, four years ago. Plane went down in the Kilghard Hills somewhere in a freak storm, and although we sent our airsearch people, we never saw a sign of it; we imagined it must have been buried in the snow somewhere in the wild country. Now some of our field people have spotted it—"

"I can show you exactly where," said one of the men, and unrolled a huge sheet of paper with markings on it which Jaelle did not understand, but his words told her it was intended for a map, a sort of aerial picture of the Kilghard Hills—or, rather, a symbolic representation of the Hills as they might look from high above. He pointed. "We have to get back the downed plane before the locals start salvage work—"

"Why would they do a thing like that?" someone asked.

It was Peter who answered.

"This is a metal-poor planet," he said, "the metal of the hull would make anyone who found it rich. Not that we'd normally begrudge the salvage. But the plane's instrumentation—we don't want them knowing what kind of surveillance we've been running on them."

Li asked "They have no aircraft at all?"

"None to speak of. They do use gliders in the mountains, mostly as a recreational item, though I heard once that they were used for messages and fast relay in firefighting. As I said, we don't want them to know how closely we've been studying their countryside outside the Trade Zone— treaty restricts where we can and can't go, though they aren't stupid and they must know we have some field people out. But I think we ought to hear whatever it was they said," Peter added, and the man from Mapping and Exploring nodded. "Bring the people in."

Cholayna said, "This is the sort of thing I am beginning to hope we can do openly with the new Darkovan employees. If their surveying techniques are primitive, they might find it useful, and good for trade relations as well."

"You'd think so," the Coordinator grumbled, "but they don't seem to have invented it in all the years they've been here. If ever there was an example of a planet regressing to the primitive—"

"I'm not so sure," Cholayna dissented, but Alessandro Li said quietly, "Let's hear the report first. We can argue about cultural acceptance later."

The men who came in were apparently ordinary Darkovans, but they spoke flawless Terran, and Jaelle, curious about who they might be, without any attempt to reach for the information, found the awareness she needed. They were all the sons of Terran spaceport personnel from the old days at Caer Donn, mostly by Darkovan women of the lowest class from the spaceport bars and wineshops; they had been given Terran education, then sent back into fieldwork from Intelligence. Cholayna was thinking that this was all wrong, but that nothing could be done as long as the families of Darkovan women were adamant in rejecting the children of such mixtures. With irritation Jaelle switched off the knowledge and tried to follow what was going on.

The men had snapshots, too, which were passed around, and when they came to Jaelle she said, "I know this area. I have traveled near it—" and pointed to the peculiar configuration of one of the hills, like a falcon's beak. "It is not too far from Armida—the Great House of Alton," she added at a curious look from Cholayna. "Rafaella and I have escorted caravans past there."

"Do you know the people at—what was it, Armida?" asked Li, and she shook her head ruefully.

"No indeed! I saw the old *Dom* Esteban, before he was lamed, once in the City, and once when I was a young girl I rode to Arilinn City and saw Lady Callista, who was Keeper there, riding out with a hawk. But know them? No indeed. They are the highest of Comyn nobility, folk of the Hastur-kind—" She chuckled. "To them, a Renunciate would be among the lowest of the low!"

"Yet you do have relatives among them," Piedro said, "Lady Rohana at Ardais was hospitable to all of us for your sake, Jaelle."

Li's eyes were sharp on her, but Jaelle only said, "Oh, Rohana is a rare soul—she has no prejudice against Free Amazons and other low forms of life! Besides, my mother was her first cousin and I think they had been lovers when they were young girls in the Tower. Some of them are my kinfolk, but I assure you," she added, laughing, "none of them would be proud to claim the relationship!"

"However that may be," Russ Montray said dryly, "You do believe that you could find the place where this picture was taken, Mrs. Haldane?"

She took the rough aerial photograph and studied it.

"Unless a blizzard should cover it again," she said, "which is not at all unlikely. But it is a difficult place to get into. I cannot imagine how a plane could have fallen so far. But then I do not understand how your planes stay up, so perhaps it is not surprising that I do not understand it when they do not. But we do not have to worry about finding it," she added, "They will bring it to us."

Russ Montray scowled at her and asked, "What did you say?"

Russ Montray jerked his head toward her, in sharp disapproval. "What was that you said?" he demanded, and Jaelle felt again that fuzzy consternation, she had spoken out of a certainty that even now was ebbing away like the tides.

Montray said, his lips pressed together tightly in scorn, "I don't know where you got your information, Mrs. Haldane, but the facts are, shortly after we received this news from our men in the field, we had a message from the—" he frowned, fumbled; Monty filled in for him quickly.

"From one of the aides of the Regent, Lord Hastur, in the City. They also have located our plane and they have offered to retrieve the bodies of the men in return for a share of the salvage in the metal."

Jaelle pressed her hand against her head. This was absurd, she never got headaches! Well, she had never been pregnant before either; she supposed it was natural enough.

The Coordinator said, "I think we should tell them, hands off! It's our ship and our metal and what the hell do these Darkovans think they are anyhow? Just another Terran colony like any other—"

"I venture to remind you," Peter said softly, "of the Bentigne Agreement, that a Lost Colony which established its own culture is not subject to automatic attachment by parent stock in the absence of cultural continuity. And in the case of Darkover there is less cultural continuity than in any other planet I studied in the Intelligence School."

Monty said, "It seems a fair enough arrangement. Mounting a full-scale salvage operation into the Kilghard Hills would be expensive—even if we could get permission to do it, which isn't by any means certain—"

"It's our plane," his father insisted. "We certainly have a right to recover it, and we don't want the natives mucking around with the machinery—they'd probably be dumb enough to melt it down for the metal!"

"The operation would belong to Intelligence," Cholayna said quietly, "though certainly the Coordinator's office has some interest in the matter. What's the problem, Russ? Didn't you bother to get permission for the Mapping and Exploring Flights, and are you afraid you'll have to answer for illegal surveillance outside the Trade Zone?"

Typical Montray trick, Jaelle found herself picking up the thought, and realized her arm was linked with Peter's and she was once again reading his thoughts. Certainly Russell Montray was incompetent, if even his own subordinates felt this way about him! *Possibly the whole history of the Empire on Darkover has been bungled because some damned bureaucrat wanted to get rid of Russ Montray and pushed him out here.* It was hard to believe that a civilization spanning the stars could have made a mistake as petty as this—wouldn't a stellar empire make mistakes only on the grand scale?

"Whatever the case may be," Montray said, frowning, "we have been summoned to speak with the Regent, and you, Mrs. Haldane, are familiar with their protocol; you are our choice for interpreter. Can you be ready to go in an hour?" His chilly eyes rested on her, but it was over her head that he spoke to Cholayna Ares. "I'm trusting you to find the leak in Intelligence Services; Mrs. Haldane shouldn't have found out about it before I saw fit to release it. You ought to check your people, Ares."

"I'll let you go in a few minutes to be ready for the trip into the City," Cholayna said. "I wish I could go with you; perhaps some day I'll have a chance." Jaelle heard; *some day when this planet isn't quite so xenophobic; visiting the Guild House will be a good start.* "But before you go, Jaelle, just how *did* you hear about the envoy from the Hasturs? I know I didn't leak it to you—couldn't, I didn't know it myself. You're on good terms with Sandro—Aleki, I mean. I won't let it get back to him, but was he talking when he shouldn't?"

Jaelle shook her head. "Peter didn't know either," she said. "That's the truth, Cholayna, I don't know where I picked it up. Somewhere—someone in that room knew and I must have read it in his mind and thought it was something everybody knew. I don't know how I did it. . . ."

Cholayna laid a light hand on her arm. "I believe you, Jaelle. I've heard something about the ESP that's common on this planet. The earliest reports spoke of it, then everything closed down. I've suspected before this that you were psychic. Don't worry about Montray. I'll smooth him down." Jaelle read in the woman's mind an uncomplimentary epithet she did not understand. "Go and get ready for the trip, and be sure to dress warmly; it's a beautiful day, but my own ESP, such as it is, tells me there's a storm coming up."

But she did not even glance toward the window, and Jaelle was sure she was not speaking of bad weather.

Jaelle was ready, even eager, for the trip into the City, but Peter spoilt her enthusiasm at once; he was furious when he saw she was wearing Darkovan clothing.

"What are you trying to do to me, dammit?"

She realized now she would never understand him. "What has it to do with you? We are going over to my side of the wall this time! And you should know how our people—" she said *our* people deliberately, trying to remind him, "react to Terran uniform; not even a prostitute would dress this way in Thendara. Why, Magda was intelligent enough to know that—" she stopped herself before she said something unforgivable.

He scowled at her and said, "You are going as an employee of the Empire and of the HQ—" but he stopped there, jerked his head forward and said, sullenly, "Let's go."

At least he knew he could no longer make arbitrary demands of her which she would obey without protest, simply out of a desire to please him. And she had yielded so far, she wore uniform around the HQ, understanding that in a sense it made her invisible, not singled out everywhere as *that Darkovan woman Haldane married*. But she would not wear it in her own city.

Outdoors the weather was so mild and pleasant that she felt even Peter must toss off his sullen mood; one of those wonderful days in early spring when, although snow is still only a cloud-flicker away, the soft air seemed to hold all the beauty of summer. It was a delight to walk the cobbled streets of the City, away from the sounds of machinery and the bland characterless music that was supposed to mask the sound and never did. Peter himself, and Li, and Monty, and even the Coordinator, whose intolerance of cold weather was a joke all over the HQ, had come out wearing light summer uniform. She slipped her arm through Peter's, unable to endure a barrier between them on this lovely day.

"Piedro! Would it really please you to have me dress as if I were a shameless woman? I know it is custom in the HQ, but would you really display me in this way before all the strangers in the street? Even if Cholayna visits the Guild House, I shall supply her with proper clothing!"

He stopped then, and thought it over for a minute. Then he said quietly, "It's not fair to you, and I know it. I shouldn't blame you. But especially right now, while Li is here examining the status of the colony—they're saying I wrecked my career; I could have been the first Legate here. I don't see why it should make any difference, especially as you are adapting so well to life in the HQ, and there's really no question of conflict of interests. But I felt it might be better, just now, not to—not to ram it down their throats, that I'd married across the wall."

He stopped, and Jaelle felt as if he had slapped her. But it was nothing she had done. He had married her knowing who and what she was, and what it might do to his career. Now if he was having second thoughts, she should not blame herself for them. She had never guessed at this kind of ambition which would be willing to build on a lie! She stared straight ahead, blinking back tears she would not shed. All her pleasure in the beauty of the day had gone. Now, in the afternoon sky, there was as yet no trace of the late-afternoon fog preceding nightly sleet or rain. Jaelle's life often depended, traveling in the hills, on her ability to judge weather conditions for a whole caravan, and she felt a little uneasy prickle down her spine.

There's a storm coming. Maybe Cholayna did mean weather after all.

The Terran escort left them at the formal outer gates of the Comyn Castle, where a very young cadet, unshaven fuzz downy on his cheek, very stiff in his shiny new uniform, informed them self-consciously that the Lord Hastur had sent an honor guard to escort the guests. Peter replied politely, in flawless *casta,* but Jaelle wondered if he knew what was perfectly clear to *her,* that the guard was not to do them honor but to keep these clumsy intruders out of places where they were not wanted.

They were guided into a room Jaelle had never seen before, but she guessed at once that it was the Regent's presence chamber. She had never thought they would be allowed to see Prince Aran, not even to pay their respects; had supposed they would be fobbed off with some minor functionary, but it seemed that the Hastur would deal with them himself. So it was serious. Prince Aran Elhalyn, like all the princes of the Comyn, held purely ceremonial and ornamental functions; the real power of the Council lay in the hands of the Hasturs.

Guarded by two more of the youthful cadets in green and black uniform, some unidentifiable metal fragments were laid out on a polished table. The Terrans began to drift over to examine them, when one of the young cadets cleared his throat hesitantly, and Jaelle tugged urgently at Peter's arm. He spoke in an undertone to Coordinator Montray, who turned as, between two more of the Guards, a slender, pale-haired man, not much over thirty, came into the room. He wore elegant blue and silver, the colors of the Hasturs, and his manner was quiet and unassuming; yet Jaelle could see how much in awe of him all the Guardsmen were.

He said, "I am Danvan Hastur, and my father, the Regent, has been unexpectedly called away on family business; he sent me to make you welcome; please forgive him, it is not intended to slight you that I am sent in his place." He bowed to the strangers, and Peter translated this for the Terrans.

The Coordinator said, "Haldane, say whatever is suitable about the honor he does us, and tell him as diplomatically as you can that the sooner we get down to business, the sooner he can get back to family matters or whatever they are."

Jaelle stood listening quietly while Peter translated in his perfect *casta;* the young Hastur listened with a bland smile, but Jaelle, nevertheless, had the feeling that he understood what Montray had really meant.

When the formalities had been concluded, Hastur gestured them toward the table. "These are the bits of the fallen aircraft which contain identifying numbers or letters, which of course our people could not read. Everything else, I am assured, is only bare metal, and you must realize that these people, although they are very poor, are very honest; in returning these materials, they are renouncing what would to them be a fortune. It would be generous of you to reward them in some way."

Montray said, "In our culture people don't expect rewards for common honesty—no, don't translate that," he added with a wry face. "Their sense of duty is probably different from ours. If I live here a thousand years, and it seems I'm going to, I'll never understand a world where honesty isn't taken for granted as duty, and rewards kept for something unusual."

Aleki said cynically, "Oh, come, Montray, you can't be *that* naïve. Matter of relativity. Suppose somebody left a hill of diamonds lying around and told you to guard this heap of worthless rocks? That's the whole history of Terran civilization—taking valuable things that the natives never thought were valuable, and trading them for worthless junk. How do you think we got the plutonium on Alpha?"

"It *was* worthless to them, with their current level of civilization—or lack of it," argued Montray, "but we can talk ethics some other time, if you don't mind. Right now, tell him we appreciate the courtesy, and make a note to send the farmers or whoever found this stuff, some kind of reward."

Jaelle, remembering a conversation at Ardais, volunteered quietly, "A few good metal tools—spades, hammers, axes—would be the most welcome reward possible."

"Thank you, Jaelle. Make a note of that, Monty," Aleki said, "and Haldane, start getting the data on those fragments before they're moved."

Peter went with Jaelle to read off the numbers and record them on his pocket scriber.

"Flight recorder, tapes intact," Peter said. "We can find out why the plane crashed, though I suppose, in the Kilghard Hills, bad weather and crosswinds are as far as we have to look." He sorted through the neatly packaged fragments. "Only three ident disks? Mattingly. Reiber. Stanforth. There is a Carr listed in the records. His disk must still be out there in the wreck. How many bodies did they find?"

Jaelle translated the question, and Danvan Hastur shook his head. "I fear I have no idea. You must question the men, who said they are willing to guide you to the wreckage. But they told me that they buried the bodies decently. The plane was, you understand, at the very bottom of a nearly inaccessible ravine; they felt that transporting the men out would have been unnecessary labor, since nothing could now be done for them."

Jaelle paused with a piece of metal in her hand, a picture suddenly clear in her mind, *a plane crashed on a high ledge, perched there precariously for moments, then when a single figure made its way outside, the sudden precipitous crash into the irrecoverable depths . . .* she clutched at the edge of the table, dizzied, wondering at the vertigo when had suddenly overcome her.

"One of the men survived the crash?" she blurted. "What happened to him?"

Hastur's pale eyes met hers and Jaelle realized she had spoken in her own language. "How did you know there was a survivor, *mestra?* Have you *laran?*"

She blundered, "I held this—and I saw him, plunging out of the plane, on to the ledge, when it fell—"

Peter turned to look at her, startled, and she realized she had drawn all eyes to herself. Hastur ignored the other Terrans. "It is true there was a survivor of the crash; he is living at Armida. I have a message from the Lord Damon, Regent of Armida for the Lord Valdir, who is still legally a child, that the man Carr is in his employ. He was asked if he wished to send a message to his kin, and declined, saying he had no living relatives and the Terrans had no doubt presumed him dead for many years."

"That can't be allowed," said Coordinator Montray when this was translated to him, "he must return and regularize his status."

Monty said under his breath to his father, "No, sir, that was what that business was all about last year. Private contracts between Terran citizens and Darkovan employers are legitimate, if we want to be able to hold contracted Darkovans to their terms of employment." He asked Lord Hastur, "Tell me only this, sir, who is the patron of the man Carr?"

"The Lord Damon Ridenow himself," said Hastur, and Monty's eyebrows went up. "That settles *that,* father. The rule says that if a Darkovan of substance makes himself personally responsible for the Terran employee, it's legal, and there's nothing we can do about it. Lord Domenic out at Aldaran asked for a dozen Terran experts in aircraft design—he wants to try and get helicopters or some form of VTOL aircraft working out there. Lorill Hastur has half a dozen hydroponics experts working with solar technology out on the Plains of Arilinn. If Lord Armida wants to keep this Carr working for him, all we can do it put it into records that he's alive and well somewhere in the Domains, and leave it at that."

They ended the session by bundling up the logged thirty pounds or so of assorted debris to be returned to the city for study. Lord Hastur stated, "I am willing to mount a salvage operation, complete with guides to take you there, when weather permits. But I think we must meet soon and discuss the rules under which your overflights for Mapping and Exploring are permitted."

The Coordinator said, "With respect, sir, we do not accept your jurisdiction over our flights. You are making no use of your airspace whatever and there is no traffic problem. We intend to continue all necessary mapping flights, and, while we are grateful for your cooperation, it should be abundantly clear that we ask this cooperation as a favor, we do not admit that we are required to do so. Our position is unchanged; Darkover is an Empire colony and while we will not interfere with the self-determination of your people, we do not admit that these overflights come under your jurisdiction to protest."

Hastur's face went pale with anger. "About that, sir, you must speak with my father, with Prince Aran and with the Comyn Council; you are invited to appear before us at Midsummer, if you wish, and present your case. And now, I fear, duty calls me elsewhere. May I offer you help in having these things transported to the Terran Zone? And it would be welcome if you would speak with the people who brought these things and make arrangements to sell them the metal for adequate compensation or to have it transported." He arose and departed, followed by his escort, and the Terrans were left alone.

"Cool customer," said Aleki, "I'd give a lot to know why everybody is so damned deferential to these Comyn—Jaelle," he added, "aren't you related to some of them?"

"Only distantly," she lied, eager to get away from them and suddenly unwilling to remain there any longer.

"What about that damned metal? It's no good to us, but we don't want to disturb the local economy by leaving it out there to start what amounts to a gold rush, either. We've got the important part here—" Li gestured to the identification disks, flight recording box, the fragments which identified the particular aircraft. "Should we waive the rest of it out there? Haldane, Monty, you know local conditions; what do you recommend?"

Peter said, "The Regent of Alton has the reputation for being a reasonable and honorable man. Granted, I've never met him personally, but he has that reputation. I suggest we send someone to discuss it with him; after all, it's on his land."

"Good idea," the Coordinator said, "and at the same time we can find out about this man Carr. What the hell, if he wants to take some job over the wall, nobody's stopping him, and after all, he didn't come in to collect his severance pay!" He laughed uproariously, and Jaelle could not help but see the grimace of the other Terrans behind his back. Did anyone take this man seriously?

"But we've got to make sure," the Coordinator went on, "that they're not holding this man Carr out there to squeeze out everything they want to know about the Terrans. Brainwash him. We might wind up having to send someone out to rescue him!"

Peter said in his dryest tone, "Somehow I cannot imagine the Regent of Alton would be guilty of anything so dishonorable."

"Look here, whose side are you on anyhow?" demanded Montray. "You always take all these native bastards right at face value and if they're as simple as all that, how come they're not doing what all the other natives on uncivilized planets do when the Empire lands on their world—coming up and begging for a piece of the action? Something's going on out there that we don't know about and I've got a gut feeling that those bastards you call *Comyn* have something to do with it!"

Monty said, and his tone would have frozen liquid hydrogen, "However that may be, sir, I suggest you keep your voice down. We are, after all, in *their* territory and if there is anyone here who speaks even a little Terran standard, you have just insulted their highest nobility. We can discuss what Haldane is to do when we are safely behind the walls of the HQ again."

Jaelle said in a tone almost as stiff as Monty's, "If you question your safety, I venture to remind you that the word of a Hastur is proverbial, and Lord Danvan has assured us of our safety. Nevertheless, I suggest that we should be gone from here before we give him cause to regret his courtesy!"

"Let's load up that stuff, then," Li commanded. "We can give it to Spaceforce when we get down to the gates; until then, Monty, Haldane, you're able-bodied, can you divide it up between you? Careful with that recorder box, I'll take that," he added, and tucked it into a uniform pocket. "I'll turn it over to Flight Operations personally, though I don't suppose it will tell us anything except bad weather. All right, let's get going."

One of the cadets remaining cleared his throat self-consciously and said to Jaelle, "*Mestra,* will you kindly inform the *Terranan* captain, or officer —I don't know his proper designation, acquit me of deliberate failure in courtesy—that the Lord Hastur has required us to give any assistance desired in transporting your property through the gates and to the City. They need not burden themselves like animals; we are here to assist them."

Jaelle relayed the information; the Coordinator said, "I'll bet they'd like to get their hands on it, wouldn't they?" but quickly, before that could sink in, Peter said, "Thank you, friends," to the cadets in the most courteous inflection, then added, "Monty, let him take it, Li, hand him the Flight box; it will come to no harm, and when someone of Lord Danvan's rank offers a courtesy it should be accepted gracefully."

"Who the hell do you think you are, Haldane?" growled the Coordinator, but Aleki said under his breath, "He's the resident expert on protocol, sir, he has the right to override you on matters of this kind; dammit, don't make an issue of it!"

Russell Montray sullenly gave up the Recorder box to the leader of the cadets, and they went out toward the gates.

As they passed through the corridor outside the Presence Chamber, Peter said in a low voice, "Against the wall, everybody. Someone's coming through and by their look I would say they were high placed in the Comyn. Let them pass and for God's sake act respectful!"

Jaelle could almost hear the Coordinator's snarl that they were Terrans and they didn't bow down to feudal lords from any damned pre-space culture, but he did not speak aloud and they moved against the wall in varying attitudes of courtesy, grudged or real. The man in the lead was somewhat like the young Hastur-lord who had spoken with them, though his hair was gray through the silvery blond, and the others were crowded behind him. Then there was a cry of recognition.

"Jaelle! My dear child!" And in a moment Jaelle was in Lady Rohana's arms.

Lady Rohana Ardais seemed to have shrunk; she was smaller, more frail. There was more gray in her dark-red hair than Jaelle remembered.

"My dear, I looked for you in the Guild House, but I did not find you there, and the Guild Mother was not there to tell me where you could be found! Blessed be Avarra who guided me to this meeting, child!"

Lorill Hastur took Jaelle briefly into a kinsman's embrace. She was surprised by that, as if it had happened to someone else. Surely he could see that she was a Renunciate, that she had among other things renounced what status she might ever have had in Comyn.

"I met you once as a child," he said, and touched the feathery edges of her short hair, "It is almost all I remember about you; how lovely your hair was, and what a pity that the Renunciates should sacrifice it."

She dropped him a confused curtsy and for the first time in her life the dress of a Renunciate seemed awkward.

"But who are all these people, my child, and how is it that you come among them?"

Danvan Hastur, behind his father, said quietly, "They are the Terran embassies who have come to speak about the downed aircraft on Armida lands, sir."

Jaelle pushed Peter forward and said shyly, "This man, Lord Hastur, is my freemate. He was born in Caer Donn and has lived among Darkovans most of his life."

"Rohana spoke of him," said Lorill Hastur, "and I remember that he was among those who helped to formulate the concept of making *medical technology* available to our people through the employment of Renunciates in the Trade City." He nodded courteously to Peter. "Rohana, if you would like to speak with your foster daughter, I can spare you for a time from our counsels," and passed on.

"Do stay and talk with me," Rohana said, clinging to Jaelle's arm, "There are so many things we have to say."

Jaelle looked hesitatingly at Peter. He said, "It's very kind of you, Lady Rohana, but my duties—"

"Stay if you want to," Montray said, but as the great door swung open before them, wind lashed through the room, and he shrank back. Jaelle realized that she should have expected this—why had she not been sensitive to the very unseasonable weather? This was the sudden late-spring blizzard that could sweep across from the pass unseen until it struck full force, blanketing the city in white-out within minutes and without warning. Once Jaelle had been caught out in it at Midsummer-Festival itself. "Zandru's kiss," she said aloud, then explained to Montray, hesitating. "I fear we must seek hospitality here—we cannot go out in this. My Lord Hastur—"

He turned back to her and nodded. He said to one of the waiting cadets, "Conduct the Terran dignitaries to guest quarters, if you will," and Monty thanked him with flawless courtesy. Russell Montray had the good sense to keep quiet.

"And you, Jaelle, and your freemate," Rohana said, "you will of course be my guests tonight." She smiled gaily. "I did not know that the weather would be so favorable for my wishes!"

But as the Terrans were conducted away to guest suites, Peter watched uneasily; and when he and Jaelle were together in the luxurious guest rooms in the Ardais part of Comyn Castle, he said restlessly, "I don't feel right about this, Jaelle. I don't think Montray knows enough of Darkovan protocol, and I should be there with him."

"Monty will get along all right," said Jaelle, "and I've been working every day with Aleki; if he doesn't know enough to keep the old man out of trouble, he's not as good as I think he is."

"That's the point," Peter almost snarled. "You really don't understand all this, do you? You never have. I need to be there, Jaelle—not tucked away somewhere in the lap of luxury while somebody else reaps the reward. I want old Montray's job, it's just as simple as that, and if I'm not there, this newcomer, this Sandro Li, is going to step in and take over by being on the spot, and where am I? Out in the cold, good for a field agent, but never considered for top administration!"

Jaelle was, for a moment, speechless with shock. The idea that anyone would actually scheme for one of the tiresome administrative jobs, the kind of thing forced upon the Comyn by birth and the inescapable inherited requirements of nobility, struck her with such shock that for a moment Peter seemed a stranger to her.

"Then of course you must go at once," she said when she could speak at all. "We cannot let you be passed over in your *ambition.*" She used the stinging derogatory inflection as one would speak of a toady office-seeker, sniffing around for bribes and preferment, but he seemed not to understand that she had insulted him, and Jaelle stood wondering why she had ever been able to endure his presence at all. He was not the man she had loved at Ardais, he was not anyone. He was a dirty little manipulating office-seeker, caring only for preferment and his work, why had she never seen it before?

"I knew you'd understand. After all, it's to your benefit too, if I make good at this job," Peter said, smiling—*of course, he is content now that he has his own way*—and dropped a quick kiss on her forehead before she could bend to escape it. She stood silent in the middle of the big room, not even taking off her outer garments, tears stinging her eyes. She had made so many excuses not to see him for what he was. And now she was trapped, she was bearing his child.

Melora—my mother—must have felt like this in the Dry Towns. She must always have believed that somewhere there was rescue, and that her kindred would ransom her. And then she knew I was to be born and that no matter what should happen, rescue or no, the world would never be the same.

I am bound for my term of employment, and when Peter knows about the child he will never let me go.

. . . bear children only in my own time and season, at my own will and never for any man's place or pride, clan or heritage. . . . the words of the oath rang in her mind, and she knew she was forsworn. She had known it in the Amazon Guild House that night when they spoke of children, and now there was no escaping the knowledge; she had been blind to it then, but now it was clear to her. . . .

The servant at the doorway had stood unmoving, but now she came and gently took Jaelle's cloak from her, laying it aside, and asked in a soft deferential way if she could bring the lady any refreshment. Jaelle had spent so many years, first in the Guild House where no woman was servant to another, and then among the Terrans where service was not personal at all, that she felt awkward as the woman took her cloak. She murmured thanks and declined refreshment, wanting only to be alone, to come to terms with the new and unwelcome knowledge thrust on her.

But the woman persisted: "If you are sufficiently refreshed, the Lady Rohana wishes you to attend her in her private sitting-room."

That was the last thing Jaelle wanted. But she had come to Comyn Castle of her free will and now she was, like any other woman of the

Domains, subject to Comyn. Rohana was her kinswoman; more, she was a patron and benefactor of the Guild House and there was absolutely no way to refuse her polite request. She could have stalled, said she was too tired for speech, delayed by asking for food or drink which Rohana would have been bound by hospitality to give her. But why did she not want to talk with Rohana, who had never showed her anything but the greatest kindness?

In the little sitting-room, which was the identical twin of the room at Ardais where Rohana went over her estate accounts with her steward, and saw Dom Gabriel's clients and petitioners, Rohana was waiting for her.

"Come here, my dear child," she said, and from habit Jaelle started to take her place on the little footstool at Rohana's knee; then realized what she was doing and withdrew, taking an upright chair across the room from her kinswoman. Rohana saw what she was doing, and sighed.

"I sought you at the Guild House," she said, "but the Elder in charge could tell me only that you were working among the Terrans, and I did not know how to look for you there. I came to Thendara at least partly for your sake, Jaelle, on Comyn business—"

Jaelle heard her own voice sounding as harsh as a stranger's.

"I have no business with the Comyn. I renounced all that when I took oath, Rohana."

Rohana held up her hand. She said, as if Jaelle were a disruptive adolescent still fourteen years old, "You have not heard what I came to say. You are interrupting me, *chiya.*" The reproof was given gently, but it was a reproof, and Jaelle colored, remembering that by her own choice, she was not Rohana's equal in the Comyn, but a subject and a citizen and very much Rohana's inferior. She murmured a ritual formula.

"Your pardon, Lady."

"Oh, Jaelle—" Rohana began, then composed herself again.

"I do not suppose, behind the walls of the Terran spaceport, that you have heard. Dom Gabriel is dead, Jaelle."

Now Jaelle saw what she had not seen, the dark dress of mourning, the swollen eyes, still red-rimmed with weeping. *She mourns him, though she was given to him unwilling, and he used her ill for most of his wretched life.* She had not loved the dead man; yet she remembered jesting with Magda at Midwinter-Festival.

Oh, anything belonging to Rohana he will treat with courtesy . . . puppies, poor relations, even Free Amazons. He had never been knowingly unkind to her. "Oh, Rohana, I am truly sorry!"

"It is better so," Rohana said calmly, "he had been ill for many moons; he would have hated to be disabled or helpless. A tenday ago he fell in a fit, and none of the medicines we had could restore him; he had thirty seizures between midnight and dawn, and Lady Alida said that if he woke again he would probably never know me again, nor the children, nor who he was nor where. I was, in a dreadful way, relieved when his heart failed." She closed her eyes for a moment and Jaelle saw her swallow, but she said calmly, "The Dark Lady indeed showed mercy."

This was so true that Jaelle had nothing to say except, "I am truly sorry for your grief, Rohana. He was always kind to me in his own way." Then she recalled that Rohana's oldest son was five-and-twenty; while Gabriel lived, Rohana had been Regent for her ailing husband, but now she was subject to her own son, who would succeed his father. "And now Kyril is Lord of Ardais."

"He feels himself quite ready to be Lord of the Domain," said Rohana. "I wish this had come when he was older—or else when he was much younger and still willing to be ruled by me."

Jaelle could honestly mourn for Dom Gabriel, at least a little; but she had never had anything but dislike and contempt for her cousin Kyril and Rohana knew it. "I rejoice I am not born an Ardais and therefore at his command."

"As do I," Rohana said wryly. "His first act as Warden was to arrange a marriage between his sister Lori and Valdir, Lord Armida. Valdir is not yet fifteen, nor Lori either, but that did not stop Kyril; he wanted that Alton alliance. He has never forgiven me that I did not interfere a few years ago, when Lady Callista of Arilinn left the Arilinn Tower, to get her for his wife. I had hoped Lori would marry your brother Valentine, Jaelle—my daughter to marry back into the Domain of my birth. But of course your father and Valentine's was a Dry-Town man, and so Kyril has already forbidden the marriage—he is now Valentine's guardian."

Jaelle had seen her brother Valentine fewer than a dozen times in her life; he had been born when her mother died and she had not wanted to remember. Dom Gabriel would never have been unkind to a child, but Kyril had detested his young cousins; Jaelle had escaped to the Guild House, but for Valentine there had been no escape till his tenth year, when he was sent to Nevarsin monastery.

"Valentine and Valdir are *bredin;* when Valdir marries, Valentine will go with him as his paxman, and no doubt Valdir will find him a good marriage somewhere," Rohana said. "You need not fear for him."

"I hardly know him," said Jaelle, "but I am glad he will be out of reach of Kyril's malice. But Lori, how does she feel about making a marriage with a kinsman she hardly knows?"

"Oh, she thinks him charming," said Rohana, "All the Altons are brilliant, and I think Valdir likely to be one of the best of them. You do know that the last Heir, young Domenic, was killed in Thendara, in a swordplay-accident, a few years ago, and the Domain is under a Regent, Lord Damon Ridenow, who married Domenic's sister Ellemir. But Valdir will be fifteen this summer, and assume his place as Warden of the Domain—"

"I know," Jaelle said, and felt a curious prickle in her mind which dismayed and annoyed her. Why had the affairs of the Altons been brought to her mind just now? The downed plane on Alton lands. Peter, saying that the Regent of Alton was an honorable man. Somehow it made her think of the curious dream she had shared with Magda; there had been someone in Ridenow colors, green and gold. . . . what had the affairs of the Comyn to do with her?

Rohana sat up straight and Jaelle could see that she was angry. Had Rohana read her mind? She did not know that she was virtually broadcasting her annoyance and displeasure, and that Rohana, whose *laran* was fully trained and under control, was as annoyed by her undisciplined mind as Jaelle would have been angered by one of the young girls making a noisy disturbance in the Guild House when the House was supposed to be quiet.

"I am sorry the affairs of the Comyn are so tiresome to you," she said dryly, "but you must bear with me while I rehearse them to you, since you are, after all, deeply involved in them—"

"When I took the Oath of the Renunciates—"

"When you were permitted to take that Oath because of my intercession," Rohana reminded her coldly, "You were allowed to take the Oath, and renounce your place in the succession of the Aillard Domain through your mother, Melora, only because I certified to them—not quite truthfully, I now fear, though I did not know it then—that you had no usable or accessible *laran*. But though you can renounce your own heritage, you cannot renounce it for your unborn daughter."

"I have no daughter, born or unborn—" Jaelle began, but Rohana met her eyes.

"You still lie to yourself, Jaelle? Or will you have the insolence to lie to me, and deny that you are carrying a daughter by your Terran lover?"

Jaelle opened her mouth, and closed it again, knowing that she had nothing to say. She had known, and barricaded her mind from the knowledge. Rohana went on, quietly.

"When I was born, there were many daughters in the Aillard succession. That was more years ago than I like to remember, and time has not been kind to our Domain. My mother, Lady Liane, married a man who took her name and rank, rather than she taking his." The Aillard, alone among the Comyn, traced descent through the female line, mother to eldest daughter. "My mother had two younger sisters; her youngest was your mother's mother, Jaelle. Melora and I were cousins and *bredini;* we were fostered together in Dalereuth Tower. I left there to marry Gabriel;

Rohana was kidnapped by Dry-Town bandits and bore Jalak of Shainsa two children. You and your brother Valentine."

Jaelle said, her mouth suddenly dry, "Why do you tell me what I have always known?"

"Because my eldest sister, Sabrina, had no daughters, but only sons. My sister Marelie married into the Elhalyn Domain and for better or for worse, her sons and daughters belong to that Domain and are not Aillards. I wished Gabriel to renounce his father-right in Lori, but he would not, and in later years he was too ill for me to persuade him; so that Lori was reared, not for the Heirship of a Domain, but for marriage. But you have not married, Jaelle; you are still an Aillard; in fact, you have taken vows which mean that any daughter you bear is *yours,* not your husband's. Your daughter, Jaelle, will be Heir to Aillard, whether you like it or not. And she will inherit the powers of the Domain."

"No! I will not allow it—"

"You cannot stop it," Rohana said, "Such is the law. We have been watching you since Melora died. Obviously, Sabrina was not pleased to see Melora replace her—"

"Especially since the father of Melora's child was a Dry-Town bandit," Jaelle said dryly.

"Nevertheless, Sabrina is now past childbearing; so she cannot bear a daughter. Melora had an older sister—"

"Did *she* have children for the Domain?"

"We thought that she would do so," said Rohana, "She bore a *nedestro* daughter to Lorill Hastur; festival-gotten, so we had her married off for convenience to a small-holder. That girl would now be—God help us, how the years pass!—she would be past forty. I saw her once when she was young; she was very beautiful, and she was destined for a Tower."

"Why can she not be Heir to the Domain? Or are the Hasturs jealous of their daughters?"

Rohana shook her head. "Before she was fifteen, she was stolen by bandits; she was ransomed, but she ran away again—perhaps she had a lover among them—and we never heard anything else of her. Though Leonie of Arilinn told us not to look for her—either she was dead or something had happened to her which meant she could never return to her people. I am sure she is dead now. So the succession passes to you, Jaelle, for better or for worse; and if not to you, to your daughter. This is why I brought you here; to tell you this."

Jaelle realized that, without knowing it, she had crossed her hands over her belly, as if to protect the child within, the child she had never thought of except as a tie to bind her to marriage and to Peter. But this was worse than child to a Terran, if she must bear a child to Comyn, to be servant and master alike. Comyn. She *would* not. She was sworn to bear no child for place or position, house or heritage—

"And as Regent for your unborn child, who is Heir to Aillard, you must take a seat on the council," Rohana said, "although Lady Sabrina is still Regent by name. Unless you wish to make Sabrina your daughter's Guardian," she added icily. "Then you may continue to pursue your own wishes as a Renunciate and neglect your duty. But you must give birth to your daughter and place her properly in the hands of Comyn, to be brought up as her birthright dictates."

"She is half Terran," said Jaelle rebelliously.

"You still do not understand, do you, Jaelle?" Rohana said. "This is not the first time that the female line of the Aillard has died out; but it must not do so again. We have been unfortunate now for three generations. Your duty to the Comyn—"

"Don't talk to me about my duty to the Comyn," Jaelle said, stifled. "In all the years of my life what have they ever done for me?"

"I do not ask for you," Rohana said coldly. "You renounced that life before you were old enough to know what it means. Life demands of everyone that they make promises before they are old enough to abide by them; *honor* is abiding by these pledges even when it becomes difficult."

Jaelle had been thinking something like this . . . *had she forsworn her oath to the Renunciates when it became difficult? . . .* and she lowered her eyes. Rohana said again, more gently, "You made your own choice. But you cannot make that choice for your daughter. I know enough of the Renunciates to know that even a Guild Mother cannot make that choice for her daughter, even if the girl was born under the Guild-House roof. Your daughter must be reared knowing her duty to Comyn, that she is Heir to Aillard, and you must know what it is that is demanded of her. I ask you, Jaelle, to take a seat in Council this summer, when Kyril is installed as Warden of Ardais and when your daughter is chosen for Aillard."

"What is the alternative?" asked Jaelle.

"I hope you will not force us to think of alternatives, Jaelle. Only if the child dies, or you die in childbirth, would that be a viable option."

I am not a slave and I do not want my daughter enslaved. I want to live for myself, not for that arrogant caste which rejected my mother and abandoned her to slavery, then rejected me because I was my father's daughter as well as my mother's. She said aloud, "The Comyn would have none of me because of my Dry-Town blood. Now you say they will overlook it in my daughter, and her Terran blood as well?"

"At that time," said Rohana quietly, "they had a choice. There were other heirs to Aillard. Since that time there have been deaths. Death gives a woman no choice, either, and she is a harder task-mistress than the Comyn. Necessity does not consult convenience, Jaelle."

And the dead women, Jaelle thought, had been Rohana's kinswomen.

Blood, spreading on sand, dark shadows of the waterhole, pain splitting her forehead. . . . somehow she managed to force the picture out of consciousness again. Rohana watched her narrowly but said nothing, and Jaelle was grateful. Somehow she feared that Rohana must look right into her mind, see her dawning *laran,* reach out to take her from her refuge among the Renunciates . . . *no refuge. I have abandoned them too. Where does duty send me? Duty to whom? To Comyn, to the Terrans my employers, to Peter my freemate, to my sisters in the Guild House? There is no escape from conflicting oaths . . . no more than from birth or death. . . .*

She said, "Kindra used to tell me, nothing is inevitable but death and next winter's snow. There must be another answer even for this."

"Ah, Jaelle," said Rohana, gently, leaning forward to stroke the younger woman's soft hair, "Life is not as simple as that. I do not demand any choice from you now. I did not ask you here to bully you. Go away and think about it, darling. Ask Peter what he thinks—she is his daughter too, and whatever the Renunciates may think about it, he has some rights over his child. You need not decide now. Even when the child is born, I only ask that you should not close too many doors too soon. Leave her a choice, too. Your mother risked, and lost her life, so that you might have a choice, so that you would not grow up in chains. That, I suppose, made me soft with you, so that I did not insist on bringing you up strictly by the laws of a Comyn daughter; Melora was given no choice, I was given no choice. . . ."

Jaelle looked sharply at Rohana, but then realized that Rohana had not spoken of herself, she had said aloud only, *Melora was given no choice.* She repeated it now, "Melora was given no choice, and she had died to give you choice, so I would not force anything upon you. You have had many years of freedom; is it not time, now, to do something for someone besides yourself?"

Maybe she is right, maybe she is right . . . maybe I owe something to those who came before me, those who will come after me . . . Rafaella tried to choose for Doria, and it is not working, Doria has had to be sent away . . .

She bowed her head and said "I will think about it. But surely you did not travel this long road from Ardais only to argue with me about the destiny of my daughter . . ."

Rohana seized on this so eagerly that Jaelle knew Rohana, too, must have been troubled by their quarrel. "Not only for that, of course," she said, "but to bury Gabriel, and to hear Kyril installed as Warden for the Domain. . . . There will be a special session of Council called; the Hasturs are already traveling here from Carcosa, and Prince Aran with his wife and daughter. Word has been sent through the Domains—but I do not suppose all this is of the slightest interest to you, child. Go and rest; you will need your sleep. I will ask them to send you some supper, something light, and you can rest well and in the morning go home, or stay here and talk with me again, just as you choose. I will send you more precise details about when the Council is to meet, and you really should try to be present for your daughter, and to meet the other members of the Domain —you do know, child, that you have family members other than myself and Kyril, you should know them!"

"I am no more eager to know them than they have been to know me all these long years since Mother died," Jaelle said, but she said it gently; she realized she was just as unwilling to hurt Rohana's feelings as ever.

The guest suite where she had been taken was quiet and empty, and Jaelle ate some of the soup and roast bird which Rohana had sent to her. She supposed that Peter was dining with the Terran group in the faraway guest suite where they had been sent, and almost wished she were with them. But she was not sufficiently familiar with Comyn Castle to try and find her way there. She drowsed on a soft chair, hardly aware of how comforting it felt to be among familiar things. No, not familiar, she had never known luxurious surroundings like this, since she was old enough to remember she had known only the tidy, comfortable, but completely non-luxurious surroundings of the Guild House. Luxuries like these might have been hers all the time if she had chosen to remain with Comyn rather than honoring her Renunciate oath, and why was she thinking of that now? After a time she fell asleep, to be wakened by Peter coming in very late.

"I'm sorry I woke you, love," he said. "I would have come back sooner, I wouldn't have wanted to leave you alone here, but I knew you were with Lady Rohana and she'd look after you. I felt obligated to take care of them."

"Of course you had to," she said warmly. It was one of the things she loved about him, his sense of duty. *Did that mean she had none of her own?* She shied away from this question.

"Have you had dinner? Rohana sent me in all kinds of lovely food, and I could hardly eat any of it," she said, "There's all kinds of cakes and cold fowl and wine there on the side table—"

"I ate something with the others," he said. "They don't appreciate good food, except Monty. Sandro Li—what is it you call him, Aleki?—wouldn't touch any of it, he said he didn't trust natural foods, they weren't as safe and couldn't be as nourishing as the kind scientifically computed for vitamin and mineral content. Makes me want to be out in the field again." He took up a leg of fowl in one hand and a slice of some kind of nut pastry in the other and came toward her, gnawing hungrily on the bone. "I come to stay in a place like this, I realize how—how alien the Terran Zone really is. Poor girl, you've been at your wits' end there, haven't you? Maybe in a few weeks when this Carr business is all settled we can get away for a few weeks, make a trip into the back country, the mountains—Dalereuth maybe, I have always loved the seacoast and you haven't been there at all, have you? Leave everything behind us and just make the trip down through the mountains by road—just the two of us, get back to each other again. Hey, hey—" he came and bent over her, dropping the roast meat in a clumsy haste to take her in his arms, "You're crying, Jaelle—I've been a beast, haven't I, getting all tied up in worrying about business and promotion and all that nonsense and never remembering what's really important! It takes something like this to remind me that there are other things in life. I'm sorry I was so nasty to you earlier. It would serve me right if you hated me after all that, but I don't know what I would do without you, Jaelle, I love you so much. . . . I need you—"

She buried her face into his neck, sobbing. Why had they grown so far apart? And he did not even know any of this, did not know about Dom Gabriel's death, or the demands Rohana had made, or their child—

"Listen, Peter," she said earnestly, reaching up to pull his face against hers, "you do know that Rohana is my kinswoman, and she had so many things to tell me, so much I cannot decide it all alone." In a rush, she told him everything, but as she had hoped, he paid little heed to what Rohana had said about her child being Heir to the Aillard Domain.

"The important thing," he said, holding her close, "the one that's important, that's our baby, Jaelle. We've had a lot of trouble, but now it's all going to be worthwhile, now we have someone other than ourselves to think about." He kissed her so tenderly she wondered why she had ever doubted him.

"That comes first, Jaelle. Just you, and me—and the baby."

Chapter Four

Magda was beginning to feel restless, almost claustrophobic; the women were friendlier, even Rafaella, but she was so tired of being indoors; sometimes she would step into the garden just to breathe the air of freedom. Even, she thought wryly, if the air of freedom smells a little too much of the stables!

She was still wearing castoffs from the box of outworn clothing, but tradition demanded that she must make herself a full set of clothing before the end of her housebound half year. She understood, after a fashion, why this was so—women of the upper classes, coming to the Renunciates, were accustomed to wearing clothing made only by the labor of servants and others, and it was necessary that they should know the cost of their labor. Keitha, on the other hand, enjoyed a chance to sit and sew and was now covering the neck and sleeves of her new undertunic, with daintily embroidered butterflies. Magda envied the ease with which she did it.

"Oh, this is restful for me," Keitha said. "At any moment Marisela may summon me out to attend a confinement, so I will rest and embroider while I can—"

"It is not restful for me," Magda said, biting her lip as she stabbed her finger again with the needle. "I would rather muck out barns than sew a single seam!"

"That is obvious from your work," said Keitha, examining the stitches with a critical eye. "What was your mother thinking of!"

"She was a musician," Magda said, "and I do not think she could sew any better than I can; she was always busy with her lute, or with her translations." Elizabeth Lorne had played nine instruments, and had collected over three hundred mountain folk-songs of Darkover. Magda, who had little musical talent, had not been close to her mother, though in these last months she had been more and more aware of how like her mother she was, absorbed in her work, craving something to do for herself. She wondered, now when it was too late to know, what her mother's marriage had really been like. She had surely not let herself be consumed in David Lorne's career among the Terrans but had always done her own work. . . .

"My mother said I must never ask a servant to do anything for me that I could not do for myself," Keitha said. "Otherwise a lady is slave to her own servants. Now I am grateful for it, though I do not like to work with horses. But Marisela says I must learn to attend to my own horses and saddle and tack, because a midwife is required to go by law to any woman within a day's journey who has need of her, and farther if she can. And Marisela says I may not always have serving men or women to look after my animals for me."

Magda smiled a little; *Marisela says* had become the most important words in Keitha's vocabulary. Magda had begun to suspect that one of the main points of Amazon training was to regress women to their adolescence, so that they could grow up again in a way that would not make them subservient to fathers, brothers, the men who ruled most Darkovan households. If it took them back to the stage of having crushes on other women, well, that was not a crime either, though it was surprising to see it in Keitha, who had been brought up as a *cristoforo* and had made some unkind remarks about lovers of women in the Guild House.

She pricked her finger again with the needle, swore as she tried to tie off a short end of thread. Camilla was not the only woman who had made such an offer to Magda, but she had always smiled and refused in such a way, she hoped, as not to give offense. It had been harder to refuse Camilla, who had been her friend when she so desperately needed friends.

But I am not a lesbian, I have no interest in other women . . . and that brought her mind back to that unsettling episode with Jaelle. Well, that had been a dream, a shared nightmare, it had no real significance. But as she struggled with her thread, trying to poke the end through the eye of the needle, she remembered the night it had been brought up in training session. . . .

. . . Cloris and Janetta had claimed that any Renunciate who had love affairs with men was a traitor to her Renunciate Oath. "It is men who oppress us and try to enslave us, like Keitha's husband who beat her and tried to bring her back by hired mercenary soldiers. . . . how can a free woman love men who live like that and would drag us back to them?"

"But all men are not like that," Rafaella had insisted, "The fathers of my sons are not like that, they are content to leave me free. They might like it better if I would dwell with them and keep their house, but they allow my right to do as I will."

And Keitha had cried out, at white heat, "We leave our husbands and come here for refuge, thinking ourselves safe from pursuit, and then we find we are not safe from our sisters either! Here in this house, no later than yesterday, one of my sisters made—made an unlawful request of me—"

Mother Millea said in her gentle, neutral voice, "I suppose you mean by that, Keitha, that someone asked you to go to bed with her. Who styled that request unlawful? Or did she not leave you free to refuse if you would?"

"I call it unlawful," Keitha cried, and Rezi said, laughing, "You called it something worse than that, didn't you? I confess that I am the vicious criminal involved, and she fled from me as if she thought I would rape her then and there, without even the courtesy to look me in the face and tell me, no thank you!"

Keitha was red as fire, tears dripping down her face. "I would not have named you," she said angrily, "but you boast of it?"

"I will not let you make me ashamed of it," Rezi said. "Among men, if two young boys swear to be friends all their lives and allow no woman to come between them, even if they marry and have children later, none denies their right to place their friendship first among all things! *Donas amizu!*" she said scornfully. "All the writers of songs have nothing but honor for a man who places his *bredu* higher than wife and children, but if two women so pledge one another, it is taken for granted that when the girl grows to womanhood, her oath means only . . . *I will be loyal to you until my duty to my husband and my children comes first!* My love and loyalty are all to my sisters, and I will not waste love on a man, who can never return it!"

Magda thought, confused, *but all men are not like that, Rafaella is right,* and lost track of what was being said. Now she thought, *I wonder if Keitha is intellectually honest enough to recognize what is happening between her and Marisela, or if Marisela will ever make her aware of it?*

Janetta put her head in at the door and said, "Margali, Keitha, Mother Lauria wants you both down in the hall."

Magda gratefully bundled her sewing into an untidy ball and thrust it into the wooden cubbyhole bearing her name. Keitha stopped to fold her work more neatly, but Magda heard her steps behind her on the stairs and they ran down side by side.

Camilla was there, dressed for riding, and Rafaella and Felicia, with a little group of women Magda did not know; but on their sleeves they bore the red slashmark of Neskaya Guild House.

"Margali, Keitha, are you weary of being housebound? Are you willing to put yourself in some danger? There is fire in the Kilghard Hills, on Alton lands; the Guild women are not required by law to go, but we are permitted to share this obligation, when all able-bodied men are required to go. There is no law which says you *must* go," she repeated carefully, "but you may go if you will."

"I will go," Magda said, and Keitha added more timidly, "I would be glad to go, but I do not know what use I should be."

"Leave that to us," said one of the strange women, "if you cannot fight the fire, you can help around the camp, but we can use every willing pair of hands."

Mother Lauria looked at them one after the other, then said, "Good; I will send you, then." Magda realized that they had in effect been ordered to go; the housebound time required that they remain indoors unless specifically ordered to go by a Guild Mother.

"You must learn to bear yourself properly among men, and to work with them as one of themselves, not with a woman's special privilege. You are in the charge of Camilla and Rafaella; you are to obey them implicitly, and to speak to no one, and especially to no man, without their permission. Is that understood? Good; go and dress yourselves for riding, and wear your warmest clothes and cloaks, and strongest boots. Fetch clean linen for four days, and be down here before the clock strikes again."

As she made ready to ride, and rolled her clean underlinen in the small canvas bag Rafaella had given her, Magda was shaking with excitement. She was a little frightened, too; but, she reminded herself, she was stronger than many men required by law to meet this obligation. *And I am a Renunciate.*

As they saddled their horses, Rafaella said quietly to Keitha and Magda, "Some of the men with whom we will travel will try to lure you into conversation; or they will make rude and suggestive remarks. Whatever they say to you, you may not reply to them, not a single word; pretend if you wish that you are deaf and dumb. If they lay hands upon you, you may defend yourself, but you must accustom yourself to the fact that they resent us, and learn to live with it, since there's no helping it."

The detachment of men waiting at the City gates was an ill-assorted crew. At their head were three dozen young Guardsmen in uniform, commanded by a smart young officer not yet out of his teens.

"Valentine Aillard, *para servirte, mestra,*" he said, giving Rafaella a cool and courteous nod. "Your women are welcome; we can use every pair of hands. Have you rations and tools?"

"They are on our pack-animals there," Rafaella said, and gestured to the women to fall into line. The polite young officer had evidently made it clear to his Guardsmen how they were to behave, for, though the Guardsmen looked at them with some curiosity, there were no overt signs of resentment. It was otherwise with the other men, traveling to the fire-lines with the guardsmen but all too obviously not under military discipline. There were soft whistles, coos intended to attract attention, and leers; and as they took their place in the line, a murmured obscene phrase or two. Magda ignored them; Keitha was as red as a bellflower. She drew her hood over her head, and Magda thought she was crying under its shelter. The women from Neskaya House, all of whom were in their forties or older, rode by the men without a glance their way, while Camilla—Magda remembered that at one time she had been a mercenary soldier—rode ahead with the Guardsmen, chatting casually with them.

Keitha whispered, "Why is she allowed to speak with them when we are not?"

"Probably because they do not yet trust us to know how to behave," Magda whispered back. "Do you *want* to talk with them?"

"No," Keitha whispered vehemently. "But it seems to me strange that she will talk and be friendly with the same men who are treating us so badly."

That had occurred to Magda too, but she supposed Camilla, who had been a Renunciate for many years, had managed somehow to make the distinction between men who accepted her as one of themselves and those who treated her as a woman to be cajoled. In any case Camilla was a law to herself.

All afternoon they rode, and well into the night; finally the officer at the head of the column called a halt and they camped in a meadow; the Amazons cooked over their own fire, and later laid their blankets in a circle. Rafaella said, "Keitha, you will sleep with me, and Margali, you with Camilla. Whenever we are among men this way, we always sleep two and two; just to make it abundantly clear to any men that we are not seeking company. And if anyone does get the wrong idea, you can protect one another."

Magda could see the sense in this, although she was sure that the men around the other fire, if they did not get the idea that the women wanted their company, were sure to get another idea which might be almost equally mistaken. She reminded herself sternly that it was none of their business what the men thought. Still, it made her self-conscious when she spread her blankets with Camilla's.

Rafaella asked one of the women from Neskaya, "Where is my daughter? I had hoped to see Doria with you."

"I told her she could come if she wished," the woman said, "and she was as eager to get out of the house as any of us; but it was the first day of her cycles, and hard work and hard riding at such a time are no pleasure; I could see she was really feeling ill, so I did not try to persuade her to go."

Rafaella said angrily, "I do not like to think of my daughter shirking! I have ridden and worked hard when I was seven moons pregnant, and she let that stop her?"

The other woman shrugged. She said, "There is no law to say that all women must react alike to their bodies; because you do not mind hard work, would you force it on her? I am sure, if the fire was near and we really needed every available hand, she would have been right beside us— she does not strike me as lazy or slothful. There were enough of us who were willing and even eager to come. Don't worry over her, Rafi; she is out of your hands now. If she really shows any sign of slacking—and so far I have seen no sign of it—let the Neskaya Guild Mothers deal with her."

Rafaella sighed and said, "I suppose you are right," and was silent. After a time the other woman said gently, "I think perhaps the children of Renunciates have a harder time than those who come to us from the outside world. We expect so much more of them, don't we?" and Magda saw the strange woman stroke Rafaella's hair gently. "I have a daughter who chose to leave the Guild and marry. She is happy, she has two children, and her husband treats her as well as even I could wish, but I still feel I failed with her. At least your daughter has taken oath, my sister, and is no man's servant or slave."

Camilla murmured into Magda's ear, "And if I had said that to Rafaella, she would have slapped me. I am glad that someone else thought to do so." She stood up and called the women around the fire. "Before we sleep," she said, "Annelys will give you some instructions in firefighting." Annelys was the woman from Neskaya Guild House; she gathered the women around their fire and gave them some rudimentary instructions about the theory of firefighting, what to do under various conditions, elementary safety precautions; although she emphasized that most of them would be put to doing ordinary manual work on the fire line and would not need to know what was going on, but only obey instructions precisely. Around the other fire, Magda could hear one of the young officers telling the men almost the same things; his voice was mostly a sound with no words distinguishable but now and then a chance silence or a gust of wind their way would bring them a few words.

"If it were only the Guardsmen," Camilla murmured—she was sitting between Magda and Rafaella—"we would all work together and camp together too. But some of these men are riffraff and we do not trust them.

After a time you will learn which men can be trusted and which cannot. Always err on the side of caution. You should know that."

Annelys heard her and said, "I am not so sure that any men can be trusted completely. They are not when I am in charge of any work details of Renunciates, believe me, Camilla."

Camilla shrugged. "Maybe I am more trusting than you. Or perhaps it is only that I have nothing more to lose, and any man who lays a hand on me will draw back a bleeding stump—and knows it perfectly well!"

Annelys yawned. "Well, today was a long hard day, and tomorrow will be longer and harder still. Let us sleep, my sisters," she said, and bent to cover the fire. Magda was tired and sore from riding, and the ground was hard beneath the thin blankets, but even as she told herself that she could not possibly sleep under such conditions, she drifted off. She woke once in the night, seeing the campfire like a sullen red eye, still smoldering; Camilla had moved close to her, and Magda put her arms around the woman, glad of the warmth, for she was cold. Camilla murmured something drowsy, shifted her weight in her sleep, and Magda snuggled close; Camilla kissed her lightly and Magda felt her drift off into deep sleep again.

But Magda felt troubled. As she had done all too often in the last few weeks, she found herself examining her thoughts closely.

Jaelle. Exactly what had happened between them? They had wakened in one another's arms, out of a shared dream, the *laran* she had not known she possessed . . . and Jaelle had pulled her down and kissed her, not the casual light kiss she could have taken for granted, the offhand sleepy kiss Camilla had just given her, but a real kiss, the kiss of lovers, with an intensely sensual awareness which frightened Magda. Like many women whose experience has been entirely conventional, she found it hard even to imagine that she could respond to such a thing. Jaelle had not been angry . . . but Magda had run away. Now, close to Camilla, she tried again to test her own feelings. Camilla, too, had once asked this of her, and Magda had refused her but she no longer knew why.

Is this what I want, then, is this why my marriage failed, because at heart I am a lover of women . . . ? She felt troubled, alien to herself. Finally, telling herself firmly that hard work awaited her tomorrow, she managed to drift off into uneasy dreams.

Before noon the next day they began to smell and hear the fire, a roaring, a dull acridness in the air, lurid red against the sky. Along the hillside a row of grimy forms, men and boys, stretched out with hoes and rakes, scraping a firebreak in the soil; when they reached the camp, they found others felling trees within the firebreak.

Magda and Felicia were put to scraping firebreak-lines with the men; Keitha, they judged, was not strong enough to work on the lines, so they sent her to the fire-camp where women were cooking and hauling water. Camilla was sent to the tree-felling party with Annelys and some of the others.

Magda could not, where she was working, even see the fire, but she could hear it; the grubby hoe in her hands scraped blisters, even through her gloves, and her back began to ache before she had been at the work for an hour, but she kept on. After an hour or so, some men brought a pail of water along, and she straightened and drank in her turn. The man beside her on the line looked at her for the first time, her smudged face and filthy hands, the rough riding clothes, and said, "Zandru's hells, it's a girl! What are you doing here, *mestra?*"

"The same thing you are doing, man—fighting a fire," Magda said before she remembered that she had been ordered not to speak to any man, good or bad, and lowered her head, draining the cup and returning it to the old man who was carrying the water bucket. The old man said, "What is a nice girl like you doing out here among all the men, girlie? Shouldn't you be back at the camp, where my wife and daughters are?" But Magda shoved the cup into his hand and picked up her hoe, bending to grub away at the line, and after a time the man, grumbling, moved on to offer his cup to the next man.

No one had bothered to explain to Magda what they were doing, but Annelys's explanation had told her a little, and she supposed that the idea was to scrape away everything burnable beyond a certain distance, so the line was barren of anything which could support the fire. At dusk they were relieved by another party, Magda was almost too weary to stand; her hands were blistered and her back felt as if it would never stop hurting. Down in the camp there was a place to wash hands and face, and the women passed them big bowls of bean soup which had been simmering all day over the cookfires within the ring. Magda wished there was a place to bathe, but they were all in the same predicament, grubby and sweating and smelling of smoke. Magda started off toward the latrine, but one of the Amazons from another Guild House grabbed her and reminded her that they always went two by two, for protection, and though Magda felt self-conscious about going to the rough latrines before the other woman, when she saw the faces of some of the men outside she was glad.

Barbarian. Among the Terrans I could work among the men and no one would touch me unless I invited it! Yet a thousand years of different customs set them apart. The ordinary women, protected by their long skirts and the caps on their braided hair, walked where they wished alone, and no one would dare to touch them because they were known to be the property of some man who would avenge any rudeness offered to his possessions. The Free Amazons belonged only to themselves and therefore they were any man's for the taking. . . . *Barbarian,* Magda thought again. But the Terrans had their own faults. . . .

When the Amazons had spread their bedrolls, again two by two, at their own end of the camp, Keitha, who had joined them, whispered "The women were worse than the men. They stared at me as if I were something with a thousand legs which they had found in their porridge bowl, and one of them asked why I was not home caring for my children. And when I told them—"

"Never mind," said Rafaella gently. "We have all heard it. We have had time to get used to it, that is all, and you will too. Remember to be proud of what you are and what you have done; if they do not understand, that is their worry and not yours. We have all done well for the Domains today; go to sleep, love, and don't let anyone make you think less of yourself for doing what you think right." Magda was surprised at the kindness in Rafi's voice; in general she had little patience with Keitha's timidity.

Camilla murmured, "It's true, though, the men are not nearly so bad as the women. Once the men get it through their heads that we work to the limits of our strength and want no special privileges, they accept us. The women never do. They feel that by working beside men, we endanger their privileged status; how can they convince their husbands that they are fragile and delicate when we are there to give them the lie? Keitha thought she was going to easier work than ours because she is not strong—"

"Do you accuse me of shirking?" Keitha blazed.

"Never, oath-daughter; your work is suited to your strength as ours to what *we* can; but it is just as well you should have encountered this. I would a thousand times rather work amid the hostility of men, than of women. Your trial is far more severe than ours. No woman thinks me a danger when I work beside her husband—" she added grimly, and Magda, looking at the scarred and haggard old *emmasca,* knew Camilla's scars burned as deep inwardly as outwardly, "but you are young and pretty, you could have a man, a husband, a lover whenever you chose. They will forgive me for renouncing what they think I could never get even if I wished for it. But they will never forgive you, and you may as well know it now as later."

The next morning was damp and dripping. "Let us pray that it will smother the fire," Camilla said grimly as she drew on her boots. "Margali, child, let me see your hands." She drew a harsh breath as she examined the blisters. "Here; put on some of this cream, it will harden the skin a little," she said, and made Magda smear her hands with it before she drew on her gloves. They stood in line with the men for breakfast, bowls of thick grainy porridge, cooked with onions and other herbs. There were buckets of beer and pails of a hot grain drink. There were more comments from the men, but Magda kept her eyes down and pretended not to hear. Camilla, on the other hand, laughed and jested with the men; many of them knew and evidently respected her. She told Magda that she had served alongside them in the last border war.

As she took up her place beside Felicia on the fire-lines, a man called softly, "Hey, pretty things, what are you doing with that old battle-ax? What did they do, get hold of you before you knew what you were missing? Come over here with us and we'll show you a good time—"

Magda ignored the comments, staring straight ahead. She had a hoe which was too short for her, and stopped to trade hoes with Felicia, who was not as tall as she was. While they were settling into place again, a man ran down the slope.

He was small and slender, with dark-red hair, wearing a cloak of orange and green. "The fire's jumped the break up that way," he shouted, "Don't go up there! Get back and move the men, move up the carts, we've got to bring the camp back down—"

There was a stir in the ranks of men. "It's Lord Damon," they heard someone say, and the men hastened to do as they were told. Magda was set to piling up food supplies and blankets on a wagon, and as she handed them up to Felicia, she could see the man they had called Lord Damon, talking in low worried tones with the line bosses, drawing maps on the ground with a long stick. Someone handed him a mug of beer; he took a sip or two, rinsed his mouth and spat on the ground, coughing, then drained the cup and asked for another. His clothes, though fine, were filthy and rumpled as if he had slept in them on the ground like the others. His voice was hoarse with fatigue and smoke.

"Stop gawking," Camilla told her harshly, "Go over to that other wagon and lead the horses away; carefully, now, don't let them bolt!"

Magda started down the slope, her hand on the bridle of the near horse. The animals, smelling of fire, snorted and reared in the harness, balking and neighing, and finally Magda unknotted her sash to tie over her mount's eyes; but the animal smelled the smoke in the cloth and reared, shying away. Magda called to Keitha to bring her apron and tied it around the animal's head. Now it came peacefully as Magda urged it along with soft words.

Lord Damon came down a little way toward them. "A good thought," he said. "Stay to the right of the dry watercourse there, as you lead them down, and set up camp there—" he pointed, "in the shade of that grove of featherpod trees where the men have been felling them. Make a firebreak around the camp, at least three spans wide. Go with them—" he pointed out half a dozen women who followed the wagon down, and after a time, another wagon lumbered along. The blindfolded horses came quietly to Magda's touch on the rein, as she urged them along step by step.

"So there, good fellow, come along, that's right—"

At the indicated spot the women began off-loading the wagons, piling bowls and kettles and blankets into the arms of waiting helpers. Magda worked hard, pulling down loads of blankets.

"Here," she said, piling a final armload into a woman's hands, "these are ours, from the Guild House; could I trouble you to set them down over there?"

The woman glared at her and let the blankets drop deliberately from her arms into dead leaves and brambles. "Take them yourself," she said. "I am no servant to you filthy *lemvirizi—*"

Magda gasped at the foulness of the word. "Sister, what have we done to deserve this? We are here helping your people to fight the fire—"

The woman glared at her, twisting her face. "The Gods send forest fire to punish us for our sins, because we tolerate such as you among us; a sign that the very ground itself cries out against such filth as you. I am no sister to any of your kind!" She turned her back on Magda and strode away, and Magda, shaking all over, bent to pick up the fallen blankets. Tears stung her eyes; she tripped over a loose stick on the ground and almost let them fall again.

"Let me help you, sister," said a soft voice, and Magda looked up at a strange woman; her hair was cropped like an Amazon's, and she wore a Renunciate's earring, but she wore ordinary women's dress, skirt and tunic. She took a part of Magda's load, but Magda stood silent, staring. She knew the woman, she had seen her, heard her voice somewhere . . .

"Are you one of us, Sister?"

"I am Ferrika n'ha Fiona," said the woman. "Pay no heed to these ignorant women, we will teach them better some day. I am midwife at Armida," she added, over her shoulder, as she dumped the load of blankets where Magda had asked and bent to straighten them, but someone called out, "Where is the healer-woman? They are bringing three men down with burns!" and Ferrika said swiftly, "I will speak with you later," and hurried away, her tartan skirts trailing in the dust. Breeches, Magda thought, really made much more sense out here, if the woman was a Renunciate why didn't she dress like one?

Later she was sent to clear away brambles, a hard dirty job that snagged her clothing and tore her gauntlets. A new firebreak was being built and it seemed so far from the fire that Magda asked in dismay, "Do they really think it will come down here?"

In answer the woman pointed. "Look."

Magda drew a breath as she saw that the fire had topped a hill to the right of them and was burning across where their camp had been last night, little tongues of flame racing down across bramble and underbrush. Here and there a resin-tree would take fire and shoot up like a flaming torch, sparks flying hundreds of feet in the air.

"Everybody to the lines down there," a man shouted. "Women, too, all of you, from the camp! If there aren't enough shovels, grub it up with hoes, rakes, bare hands if you have to, we're working against time!"

Magda worked where they sent her, back bent, trying not to look up or listen to the fire. The smoke hurt her throat and the dust from the fire-break made it hard to breathe; Magda pulled her tunic up over her mouth and tried to breathe through it as some of the men did, wishing for a moment that she had a woman's kerchief. Some of the villager women were working beside her in the lines, their skirts tucked up to their knees, but still caught on dead branches and tore on briars; and Magda thought that her own Amazon breeches were more modest as well as more comfortable, and wondered why she was thinking then about that? They were hauling at brush and brambles now so that the men could get at the trees to fell them, and around her she heard fragments of snatched, breath-less conversation—felling these trees was a sacrifice of good timberland but anything was better than letting the countryside burn! A man touched her on the shoulder—the noise made it difficult to hear connected words—and beckoned her to one end of a two-man saw; she was quite sure he had no idea she was a woman, for she did not see any of the other Amazons doing such work, but she went without comment.

As the young boys carrying water came down the line, she saw the man she had seen this morning, the one they had called Lord Damon, riding along the bare patch. She supposed he was in charge of the whole opera-tion, a kind of engineer.

"No good," he said vehemently to someone Magda could not see. "They've got to pull out up there and let it burn; it's gone anyhow, and the best we can do is put all our men down here on this side. That way we can hold the line and keep it from burning over toward Syrtis—there are five villages down there, man!" He looked down to where the workers were straightening their backs for a moment, drinking as the buckets were passed; he saw Magda and gestured to her.

"You led the horses this morning, didn't you, lad? Good thinking. I need someone with his wits about him to carry a message to the men on the other side of that ridge up there. Give your end of the saw to that man there—" he pointed—"and come here."

She remembered that she had been ordered not to speak to any man; but that could hardly apply to listening to orders given by the man who was bossing the job! He was hardly looking at her; his eyes were troubled, surveying the distant roar and swirl of smoke and fire.

"Go up along that ridge there, and you'll come to a gang of men working under a big man, fair as a Dry-Towner; ask for Dom Ann'dra if you can't find him. Tell him he must pull out all the men along that ridge and let it burn out, it's hopeless. Tell him I need all the men he has down here on the east side, to keep it from burning over toward Syrtis. Have you got that?"

Magda repeated the message, pitching her voice as low as she could. "And who shall I say sent the message, *vai dom?*"

He looked straight at her for the first time. "Oh, you're not one of my men, are you? You're one of the group they sent out from Thendara, right? Tell him Lord Damon sent word. Run along, now."

Magda went off as quickly as she could through the heavy tangled underbrush. As she climbed the slope she could see the fire on the other hill they had left that morning, burning down relentlessly toward the new firebreak; where they had breakfasted was all afire now, but there was a long stretch of clean firebreak between the workers and the fire. The stench was horrible, with overtones of roasting meat, and Magda thought of the animals trapped in the fire. As she caught sight of the gang of men, she saw, with them, a gaunt, familiar figure in gray tunic and heavy trousers; Camilla. Magda recognized her only by the low Amazon boots; Camilla had tied a sweat-rag over her face, for the dust and heat were terrible. She was the only worker on the line who had not stripped to the waist.

Magda would have spoken to her, but her message was too imperative; she went along the line, looking for a tall fair-haired man. But the smoke was thicker here, rising from the other slope, so she could hardly see; she asked a man hastily "Where is *Dom* Ann'dra? A message from Lord Damon—"

The man coughed and pointed through a thick haze of smoke, and Magda plunged into it; behind her someone shouted but she could not distinguish the words. Now she saw, indistinctly, a tall man in a broad-brimmed hat, fair-skinned and well over six feet tall.

"*Dom* Ann'dra?" she called, and the man turned. "I gave orders no one should follow here—"

"A message from Lord Damon," she said quickly, coming up to him, coughed for a moment, then quickly repeated her message. Her eyes were streaming with the smoke. The tall man, Ann'dra, swore angrily.

"He's right, of course, but I'd hoped we could save the pastures up here; horses will go hungry this summer! All right, go down as fast as you can, and tell him I'll have everyone down there in half an hour, got that?"

Magda nodded, coughing too hard to speak; his face, blackened with smoke, took on a look of concern.

"You should get out of the smoke as fast as you can, lad. Come this way —" he motioned her along, back toward the workers, taking the hat from his head and waving it in great sweeps.

"Pull back, men, pull back, Lord Damon needs us below—Raimon, Edric, all of you, grab the tools and get down—" he shouted, abruptly his voice took on a new sound of warning.

"Hi! Look out there, drop everything and *run*—breakthrough over there!" Magda stared in horror as a wall of flame leaped from nowhere and came roaring up the little gully she had crossed on her way up here. The thick, choking smoke was suddenly sweeping all around her, and when she started to run she was overwhelmed by coughing, stumbled and fell. Then she was picked up in strong arms and carried to clearer air; *Dom* Ann'dra set her down after a minute and stared at her.

"God almighty," he said but he had spoken in Terran! While Magda stared at him he shook his head and said in the mountain tongue, "Sorry— I mean, we've got to make a run for it; have you something you can tie over your face?" Magda ripped at her undertunic; it was no time to think about modesty! The smoke was so thick no one could see anyhow.

"Good," he said tersely, and took her hand. "Don't be scared, I won't let go of you, but you've got to trust me; you might get a bit scorched, but better that than roasted for the devil's supper! Hang on, now!" Holding hands, they ran directly toward what looked like the center of the fire. Magda felt a blast of heat, smelled her hair singeing and searing pain in the soles of her feet; she heard herself screaming, but she ran on, her hand held tight in the big man's grip. Then they were through the flame and out of the smoke, coughing and choking and gasping. Her eyes were streaming; suddenly the world went dark and she slid to the ground.

"Ferrika!" she heard *Dom* Ann'dra bellowing, "Is the healer-woman in the lines? Well, get *somebody* up here, and make it fast! We've got to get this youngster down fast, he risked his life to get through—" and Magda felt herself lifted up; he scooped her up, arms beneath shoulders and knees, as if she had been a child. Then he drew a quick breath, staring down at her in consternation and said in a whisper, "Good God, it's a girl!"

She said in a shaky whisper "Don't—I am all right—put me down—"

He shook his head. Only then did she realize that he was still speaking Terran. "Put you down, *hell,* your boots are burned half off your feet. And who are you?"

"I am a Free Amazon from Thendara—"

"Yeah," he said in an undertone, staring skeptically, "that's what you say. Now who in the hell *are* you? Intelligence?" His eyes flared at her like steel filings in flame, out of the blackened, grimed mess that was his face. "Whoever you are, you've got guts enough for three, girl. Those boots aren't going to be good for much."

Ferrika, the Renunciate Magda had seen briefly in camp, came hurrying toward him; at her side was Camilla.

"Vai dom, the Amazon from Thendara says the messenger is one of hers and she will take her to her sisters—" She stopped and cried out with compassion as she saw Magda's burnt boots, the raw blistering of her flesh that showed through. "Sister, let me take you where we can care for those feet—"

Ann'dra nodded. "Look after her; I've got to get these men down to Lord Damon, and you people get off the ridge as fast as you can. I need to find out what Damon needs, and do it right away!"

Ferrika and Camilla made a chair of their arms to carry Magda. Now she could feel terrible pain in the soles of her feet, but she followed *Dom* Ann'dra with her eyes.

Intelligence, huh? And he had spoken Terran, too. Yet Damon seemed to know and accept him as one of them. What was going on here? She was coughing and choking, her eyes were streaming and her chest hurt; she realized that Ferrika and Camilla had set her down on a blanket. Rafaella appeared from somewhere with a stoneware mug of cold water, holding it to Magda's mouth. Camilla said, "I saw the fire sweep around you, Margali, and I thought you had been killed. . . ."

Rafaella's voice was tart. "I notice she managed to fall where there was a handsome man to carry her to safety."

"Let her alone, Rafi, can't you see she's hurt?" Camilla snapped, "Should she have stayed there to burn? I am not sure I would have had the courage to run through the fire like that, even if the Hastur Lord himself, let alone *Dom* Ann'dra, held my hand!"

"Who is *Dom* Ann'dra?" Magda asked, coughing.

"Brother-in-law to the Regent; he married the Lady Ellemir's twin sister," Ferrika said, and glanced up at the burning ridge, scowling. "What are the *leroni* about, up there? I heard—" and she broke off abruptly. "Sister, let us dress those feet of yours. And you, Camilla," she added sharply, "no more work on the lines for you. There is *livani* tea in the kettle, it is good against the smoke; get yourself a cup quickly, and bring some here for your sister—" She looked into Magda's eyes, puzzled. "I do not know your name," she said, "but surely I have seen you before—"

"You helped me with our blankets this morning," Magda began, but Ferrika shook her head.

"No, before that," she said, and abruptly Magda knew where she had seen the snubbed nose, the freckled, round face and green eyes, before this.

The night of her first Training Session, when her mind had drifted to the Sisterhood . . . and she knew that Ferrika recognized her, too, and was staring at her in puzzlement. She said something in a strange language, but Magda only shook her head, not understanding. Ferrika looked more perplexed than before, but she only said, "Drink this, it will clear your throat."

Magda sipped at the hot, sour drink; she made a wry face at the taste, but it did soothe her smoke-rasped throat and somehow it made her nose stop streaming. Camilla, too, was sipping the stuff; she wiped her smoke-blackened forehead with her torn sleeve.

"Let me see those feet. Are you hurt anywhere else?"

Camilla knelt anxiously beside them. Magda's forehead was singed a little, her eyebrows burnt and some of her hair singed, but the burn was not serious. Camilla held her hand while Ferrika gently cut away the ruined boots, scowling.

"These soft-leather things—you can see why they are not suitable for work on the lines!" Ferrika scolded. They had burnt through quickly, and the last remnants had to be picked away from the burned flesh with tweezers; Magda flinched, but did not cry out.

"A bad burn," Ferrika said, "You will do no walking for a day or two. It may be deeper than it looks." But to Magda's surprise, she did not touch the burn, only held her hand over the flesh, two or three inches away, first one foot, then the other. When she sighed and straightened, she looked relieved. Magda thought of Lady Rohana, concentrated and serious but not touching Jaelle's dreadful wound. *Laran?*

"Not as bad as I thought," Ferrika said, "but not superficial either; skin, but no serious burning into the muscle. With proper boots you would not have been hurt at all. I must bandage them, and she must be carried; she must not walk on those feet at all."

Tears were streaming down Magda's face. She thought it must be the aftermath of the smoke. "I came to help and I am a burden—"

"You are honorably wounded," Camilla said gruffly. "We will care for you."

Ferrika was rummaging in her case of medicines. It looked very like the one Marisela carried. "Bathe her face with this lotion, Camilla, while I dress her feet. But she must not walk on the bandages, either, and we must find her a pair of boots from some old man in the campsite, who can go barefoot without trouble."

"I had forgotten," Magda said with a sharp catch of breath, "I had a message for the Lord Damon—"

"Give it to one of the women, then," said Ferrika, "for you are not going anywhere on those feet."

Magda repeated the message to Rafaella, who nodded and hurried away. She lay back, closing her eyes and trying to ignore the pain as Ferrika smeared her feet with some sharp-smelling herb salve, and wound them in thick loose bandages. Camilla gently sponged her face with the cooling lotion.

"Poor child, when I saw the smoke close round you I was sure you were dead—I thought I had lost you, Margali—" she repeated hoarsely, holding Magda close against her. Magda realized, shocked, that the older woman was almost crying. Camilla rarely showed emotion. But Ferrika straightened up and said, "I must get back to the lines; others need my skill," and Camilla rose.

"I too must get back to the lines—"

"You stay here," Ferrika commanded, and Camilla looked angrily at her.

"What do you think me?"

"I think you too old for this work; you should never have come out," said Ferrika. "You will be more use in the camp among the women."

"I would rather work among the cows!" Camilla said scornfully, and went before Ferrika could say anything more. Ferrika sighed, looking after the elderly *emmasca* as she strode away.

"I should have known better; always Camilla must be stronger than anyone, man or woman! Stay here and rest, Margali," she commanded, and went. Magda lay back on the blanket; her feet hurt less than they had, but the pain was still enough to make her tremble. After a time it subsided to a dull ache; she lay on the blankets, alone except for a woman who was tending the fires at the back, and an old man who lay on one of the blankets, covered up warmly and breathing raucously; when the woman came to look at her Magda cringed, remembering the scorn and contempt one of the women had shown, but the strange woman only said, "You must call out to me if you need anything; more tea?" Magda felt fiercely thirsty and sipped another cup of the hot sour herb drink.

"I heard that someone had been burned, but I thought it was one of the messenger boys," she said. She moved her head indicating the old man on the blanket. "Gaffer Kanzel was overcome by the smoke this morning, but he'll do well enough with rest; what's his son thinking of, to let the old man come? I must go and tend to the supper—you're one of the Renunciates from Thendara, no?"

Magda nodded and the woman said, "I have a sister in Neskaya Guild House; I'll trade work, one of your sisters is at the next fire, so she can come and be close to you." She went off and after a minute Keitha came up to her.

"I heard someone had been burned, but I did not know it was you,"

Keitha said, bending over her. "That was a nice woman who sent me here; she says she has a sister who is one of us. And I heard there are Renunciates among the healer-women who are helping here, too—"

"One of them bandaged my feet."

"I have a fire to tend, and stew to keep from burning," Keitha said, "but I will come and bring you drinks—she said you must drink as much as you possibly can. Do your feet pain you much, Margali?"

"I'll live," Magda said, "but they hurt, yes. But go and do your work, don't worry about me."

Reluctantly, Keitha went back to the fire, and Magda lay on her blanket, trying to get into a comfortable position on the hard ground. After a time she fell into an uneasy drowse, waking when the sky was crimson with sunset. Keitha came to give her more of the hot herb-tea and a plate of stew, but Magda could hardly swallow, though Camilla came and skillfully propped her up, and would have fed her with a spoon if Magda had let her.

"No, no, I am not hungry, I can't swallow," she said, "I am only thirsty, very thirsty—"

"That is good; you must drink as much as you can, even if you cannot eat," said Ferrika, standing over them, and they looked up to see the slight, dark aristocrat who had been called Lord Damon.

"Mestra," he said to Magda, "I am sorry for your injuries; I sent you into danger, not even knowing you were a woman."

She said, "I am a Renunciate," proudly, at the same moment that Ferrika protested, "You know better than that!"

She spoke without the slightest hint of deference and Lord Damon grinned at her. He looked tired and disheveled; he was chewing on a strip of smoked meat, half-heartedly, as if he were too tired to sit down and eat properly. His face was still grimed with smoke, but Magda noted that his hands were scrubbed clean, as he set the meat aside and said, "Let me look at your wounds, mestra; I too have something of the healer's arts."

And after a whole day fighting fire on the lines he still must go around the camp and see who is wounded . . . well, what would you expect of Damon? For a moment Magda thought someone had spoken the words aloud, but she realized that she had heard them as she was beginning to hear unspoken thoughts. She saw Lord Damon's face contract slightly as he unwrapped the bandages, and knew, without being told, that he felt, physically, the pain he caused her for a moment. *Perhaps he is too tired to shut it out.* Then it was gone, and he said quietly, "Painful, I am sure, but not really dangerous. But be careful not to let the bandages get wet or dirty; otherwise the burns will become infected; do you understand that this is important? You must not try to be brave and walk on them, you must let your sisters carry you everywhere; and drink as much as you can, even if it means you must let them carry you to the latrines every hour or two; the burns create poisons in your body and you must rid yourself of them." His manner was as courteous and impersonal as a Terran Medic's, and Magda was astonished.

He straightened to go. "Carry my compliments to the Guild-Mothers in Thendara and tell them that again I have cause to be grateful to the Sisterhood."

Rafaella bowed deeply. "You honor us, *vai dom.*"

"It is you who honor us," Damon said, and touched Ferrika lightly on the shoulder. "I will leave you with your sisters for the moment; you know how to get in touch with me if you need me," he said and walked away. Ferrika went to look at one of the women who had scalded her hand on a stew kettle, and from across the circle of the camp Magda heard her ordering others who had inhaled smoke to drink more of the tea which was kept boiling on great kettles over the cookfires.

"He doesn't treat her like a servant," Keitha said, and there was the faintest hint of criticism in her voice. One of the strange women said, "Maybe she isn't."

"You do not know Ferrika," said Camilla coldly, "if you are hinting that she is his concubine. She is a Renunciate."

"Maybe," Magda said, "she's just his friend." The others gave her skeptical looks, but what Magda had sensed between the Comyn aristocrat— what were the Comyn anyhow?—and the Renunciate was an easy acceptance, a kind of equality she had not yet seen given by any man to a woman on Darkover.

Someone called from another fire *"Mestra'in,* we have heard that there is a minstrel among you; will it please you to come and play and sing for us? We have worked hard for our music!"

Rafaella rummaged in the packs they had slung across their horses. Magda had not known that she had brought her small *rryl.* "I will play for you with pleasure, but my throat is too thick with smoke to do anything but croak; anyone who still has breath to sing, may sing!"

She went toward the fire. Camilla explained, "A new crew of men has been sent out from Neskaya, and they are on the lines; so there is some leisure in the camp tonight; though all of us may be called out if there is another turn for the worse like this afternoon!"

Magda lay silent, listening to the *rryl's* sound. One or two of the Renunciates had gone to listen to the music, though Camilla stayed near Magda in case she should want anything. Magda shut her eyes and tried to sleep; the older woman had been working hard all day, too hard, and Magda was worried about her. Magda knew it would be no use to try and urge her to work less tomorrow.

But silence had fallen over the camp, and Rafaella had come back to the fire and spread her blankets beside Keitha's, when there was a stir and a flare of torches and the sound of riders. From a distance Magda heard the voice of Damon Ridenow, as she had heard it when he came to their fires, and other voices; then at the center of the camp there was a bustle of sound and several riders were sliding down from their horses. Magda sat up and looked at them; men and women in long bright cloaks, some in the blue and silver of Hastur, others in the same green and black of the cadets of the City Guard. Camilla sat up and said, "Altons of Armida, yes—"

"The *leronyn* from the Tower," someone said.

"Now, perhaps someone will have this fire under control—" another voice said somewhere, "If they have gathered the clouds they can bring rain to drown the fires. . . ."

Magda sat upright to watch. She saw the tall man they had called Ann'dra, and Lord Damon, and a slender woman whose hair blazed like brilliant copper under the blue and silver hood. She looked round quickly and came toward the fire where the Renunciates were camped together.

She said in a clear voice, speaking the pure *casta* of Nevarsin and Arilinn, "Where is the Renunciate who was wounded on the lines today?"

Magda cleared her throat and said, "It is I, but I am better—"

She came and stood by Magda's blankets. At her side was a somewhat taller woman, in a green and black cape; Magda could see that she was pregnant, though she carried it well, almost with careless ease.

The smaller woman in blue said, "I am Hilary Castamir-Syrtis, and it was our land you risked your life to save, as Ann'dra has told us. We owe you a debt, *mestra*. Will you undo the bandages?" she said to Camilla, and the old woman began to untie and unfasten them.

Lady Hilary knelt beside her, and as Ferrika had done earlier, passed the palm of her hand two or three inches above the soles of Magda's feet. "What is your name, *mestra?*"

"Margali n'ha Ysabet," she said.

"Trust me; I will not hurt you," she said, and touched a leather thong about her throat. Magda remembered Rohana's gesture, when Jaelle had been so terribly wounded in Castle Ardais, and it seemed suddenly to Magda that through the layers of leather and silk she could see the blue shimmer of a matrix stone. Lady Hilary closed her eyes for a moment and it seemed to Magda that she could feel a blue shimmer. Abruptly her feet felt as if they had been seared afresh with fire; she gasped with the pain, but it passed quickly and the blue haze was gone.

"Your feet will be healed now, *mestra*, I think you will have little trouble; but the new skin is very tender and you must be very, very careful not to walk on them for a day or two, or break the skin and allow them to become infected. I have other injuries to heal, or I would stay and speak with you; I too have reason to be grateful to the Renunciates. I wish you a good night," she said, and went away, at her side the woman in the green cloak, who had not spoken a word.

Magda looked, by the firelight, at her feet. As she had half expected— she had seen this healing from Lady Rohana when Jaelle was wounded— there was no sign of bleeding nor blackening where fire had seared and bare ground and brambles had torn. Her feet were covered with a layer of grayish scarring with patches, between the scars, of pink thin baby skin, very tender and painful when she touched it with a tentative finger. But it had been healed.

One of the women said scornfully, "They are no proper Comyn, and not a proper Tower. Do you know what they call them in Arilinn? Forbidden Tower . . . they work under the ban of Arilinn! They even say—" she lowered her voice as if whispering delicious scandal, and Magda did not hear what she said, but she heard small shocked exclamations.

Camilla said clearly, "What good are the Towers to those of us outside the Comyn? Except for these, who will come out of their walls to help and to heal."

"I don't care what you say," one of the men at the next fire said, "it's not right for a *leronis* to go about the countryside with common folk! And both the Lady Hilary and the Lady Callista were thrown out of Arilinn Tower by the old Sorceress and she wouldn't do that without good reason. They'd ought to live quietly at home if they couldn't live decent in the Tower—riding all around the countryside putting out fires and healing the common folk—" he spat, and the sound was eloquent. "We're doing all right with the fire, we don't need their sorcery to come and put it out for us!"

"I say nothing against the Lady Leonie," Camilla said quietly. "Once she was kind to me when I greatly needed kindness. But perhaps the Lady knows little, cloistered as a sacred virgin within her Tower in Arilinn, of the needs of those who must live in the world, and do not know how, or would be too much in awe of them, to seek them out for help or healing."

"I've even heard—my sister is a steward's helper at Armida—that they're teaching the common folk *laran,*" said one woman with scorn. "If it can be taught to the likes of us, what good is it? The Comyn are descended from the Gods! Why should they come and meddle in our lives?"

Camilla said scornfully, "I cannot talk to such ignorance."

"They're like you Renunciates," said the woman with a concentrated spite. "Won't stay in your place, won't marry and have children, no wonder you want the Hastur kinfolk to come out of *their* proper place too! Want to turn the world upside down, all you folk, make the masters servants and the servants masters! The old ways were good enough for my father and they're good enough for my husband and me! No men of your own, so you want to come out here brazen in your breeches, trying to show off your legs and get them away from us . . . well, *mestra,* I'm telling you, *my* husband wouldn't touch you with a hayfork, and if he did I'd scalp him! And if I see you waggling your tits at him I'll scratch out your eyes!"

Camilla chuckled. "If all men but your husband vanished from the earth, dame, I would sleep with the house-dog. You are heartily welcome to your husband's attentions for all I care to contest them."

"You Amazons are all filthy lovers of women—"

"Hold!" said an authoritative voice. "No brawling in the camp; fire-truce holds here, too!" It was Ferrika's voice, and the strange woman moved away in the dark. Ferrika said, "Go to sleep, my sisters; 'the man who argues with the braying of the donkey or the barking of his dog will win no cases before the high courts.' "

Silence settled around the Amazons fire, but Camilla still seemed ruffled as she drew off her boots to sleep.

"I have met with the old *leronis* of Arilinn—I do not say where, but it was when I was very young," she said in a low voice to Magda. "She healed me when I had much need of healing, mind and body—I told you some of this. But the folk of Arilinn know nothing of the needs of common people. If what befell me had happened to a commoner maiden, the Lady would have shrugged and told my folk to marry me off to whatever man would have damaged goods. Because I was one of her own, she had pity on me—" abruptly she broke off. "What has come to me that I babble like this?"

Magda pressed her hand in the darkness. "Whatever you say to me I will never repeat, I promise you, sister."

"That woman called me lover of women as if it were the worst insult she could imagine," Camilla said. "I am not ashamed to hear it spoken, . . . except when I am among women who use it as the worst abuse they can imagine—"

"You are my friend, Camilla, I do not care what you are."

"I think you know I would like to be more than your friend," Camilla said. "I should not say this when you are hurt, but you know I love you. . . . and I would dearly love to make love to you; but I am not a man, and my friendship does not depend on it. It is for you to choose . . ." her voice trailed away. Magda felt deeply troubled.

Was this what she wanted then, was this why she had run away from

Jaelle—the old children's taunt: *only truth hurts.* Living among women, certainly it was not surprising . . . maybe it was indeed what she wanted; her marriage with Peter had caught on the snag of independence and competitiveness, she had not been content to think of him as husband and lover. Nor had she felt impelled to seek another lover, or to turn to any man. She thought, with deep disquiet, maybe it is a woman I want, I don't know, I do love Camilla, but I never thought of that. . . .

Maybe I ought to take Camilla as a lover, it would make her happy and it wouldn't hurt me, and at least then I would know if that is truly what I want. But do I want to find out? She said gently to Camilla, "We will talk about this when we are back in Thendara, I promise you," and felt warmed by the comforting touch of the older woman.

She lay with her head against Camilla's shoulder, and at last she knew that the older woman was asleep. But she could not sleep. The pain in her feet had all but subsided, but the healing skin itched with maddening intensity, and she knew she must not scratch it. How had Lady Hilary done that? And now she was reading thoughts again. . . .

She listened to the quiet noises of the camp, to the faraway sound that she knew was the roaring of the fire. Could it jump a firebreak as it had done before and suddenly blaze among them, roaring and destroying? They slept here, and others worked along the fire-lines. . . .

After a little it seemed as if she slept, but she was still conscious of her chilled body, feet itching furiously, as she seemed to look down on the camp from a greyish height; she saw herself lying curled up against Camilla, the other women snuggled close for the warmth, the dying cookfires carefully safeguarded inside rings of stone; then she saw the brilliantly colored cloaks of the men and women, the tall man called Ann'dra, Lady Hilary in her blue cloak with the blazing hair, the dark, diffident Lord Damon, the silent woman who had been pointed out to her as Lady Callista, and they were somehow joined like dancers around a blue blaze like the matrix Hilary had used to heal her feet. . . . they were weaving in a colorful dance weaving in and out and at the same time they knelt motionless and fixed on the matrix . . . Ferrika reached for Magda and drew her into the dance, and then they were dancing among clouds, she was helping Hilary to scoop up the clouds and roll them through the sky to where the fire raged below. . . . they felt damp and soft and palpable, like bread dough, under her hands when she punched them down. It felt as if she squeezed them between her fingers and the moisture came oozing out, they grew softer and softer and more pliable, and then rain was trickling from the clouds, trickling down and then pouring, and then flooding. . . .

Magda woke sharply to the drops splashing on her face. At her side Camilla sat up sharply and cried out, "It's raining!" And all over the fields, the men in the camp sent up a great cheer. No fire could stand against this hard, soaking rain.

And I was part of it, she said to herself, confused, and then dismissed the thought. No doubt she had felt the first drops and the whole dream had come out of that. Some of the women were hurrying to pull their blankets into the shelter of the trees, the wagons; Camilla hauled out a waterproof tarpaulin from their pack and spread it over her blankets and Magda's, beckoning Rafaella and Keitha into the shelter, like a small improvised tent. The rain kept pouring down and there were groans of discomfort and cold mixed with the cheering, but better, they all admitted, to be cold and wet than burning up, and this meant crops and livestock and trees would be saved.

Good luck, Magda wondered, weather wisdom, or had the Comyn aristocrats with their matrixes created the rain? She had no reason to think the latter except for her bizarre dream.

Or had it been a dream at all? Unlikely that they could have aroused the storm. But on the other hand, it was even more unlikely that Lady Hilary could have healed her burnt feet without even touching her.

Who was she to set limits to other people's powers? A long rumble of thunder drowned out thought and she clung to Camilla, her feet icy in the cold, while someone grumbled, "Damn it, couldn't they have managed rain without downpours and lightning?"

Some people, thought Magda drowsily, were never satisfied.

Chapter Five

There was still no morning-sickness but Jaelle did feel strange and queasy, and had gotten into the habit of lying in bed while Peter shaved and showered and readied himself for work; only when he had kissed her good-bye and gone did she rise and find herself a snack somewhere in their rooms—it was simpler than braving the strange smells of the cafeteria in the early morning.

This morning, by the time she reached Cholayna's office, Monty and Aleki were there, rummaging in files and pulling out printouts.

"There's a fire," Cholayna said. "On Alton lands; I went out with the helicopter. I can't believe they're fighting it by hand!"

"We have been doing it for centuries, long before the Terrans came here," Jaelle said stiffly, "and will be doing it when they are gone."

Peter came in, and Jaelle realized he was dressed for the field; leather breeches, woolly tunic, surcoat and cloak lined with rabbithorn fur, high boots. She envied him. "Ready, Monty? Now remember, Aleki, you're a mute, deaf and dumb; there's no way you could pass yourself off as Darkovan yet with your accent, but it'll give you a chance to observe."

Cholayna thrust a cartridge into the terminal and a fuzzy picture wobbled across the screen; billowing smoke, long lines of men and women scraping bare lines with hoes and rakes and crude tools, some men on horseback directing movement of lines.

"No earth-moving equipment, no tractors, no sprayer planes! We sent out an offer of help—seems like they could use us to spray the flames with foam. But since we heard about that crashed plane in the Kilghards out near Armida, the natives have been nervous about their overflights,"

Monty said. "Look, there are three villages down that line, you can see them—" He pointed as the picture of the lines of men and women was briefly overlaid by a picture from the weather satellite. Jaelle wondered, not for the first time, if anyone had bothered to tell the Domains about the spy-eye of the satellite in the sky.

Sometimes Renunciates went out on the firelines; Magda was house-bound, and need not go, though Camilla and Rafaella always went. *If she was in danger, I'd know.*

"Go and check out Aleki's costume, Jaelle, you know better than I do what he ought to need," said Cholayna. "Peter had Monty all ready even before I got the report, and they were going alone, but Aleki pulled rank on them and said he was going, whatever they said." She smiled a little ruefully. "Even if it means leaving you with what he ought to be doing while he's out on the lines!"

"Don't talk as if I was saddling her with the whole department's work," Alessandro Li said defensively. "Language reports, and I want her to check out the satellite printouts and mark the general layout of the Dry Towns. Next week I'll take her on an overflight, if she wants to go—you haven't been up in one of our planes yet?"

"Hell, I'd have taken her if I'd thought she'd want to go," Peter said, "But some other time, all right, Aleki? The horses are ready right outside the gates in the Old Town . . ."

Jaelle was studying the wallscreen, heavy smoke and ashes sweeping over the hills, a blackened swathe left behind. She knew that country, she had ridden through it; every few years, the resin-trees caught and they grew so quickly that new fires came down. Cholayna was frowning and saying something about the destruction of vital watershed.

"Trouble is, there's no rain in sight at all," Peter said. "The people at Armida should be warned about the satellite picture; the winds are going to sweep across from Syrtis, and Armida itself could go up in flames. Jaelle—"

She wrenched herself away from the picture, so vivid it seemed she could smell the smoke, the acrid smell of ash and the crash of fire. She turned Aleki round, scowled.

"Those boots aren't right. They'll think you're a woman in disguise, or an effeminate, Peter, he's got to have proper boots."

"In hell's name," Aleki protested, "I saw the regulation issue for the field, and I can't walk in the damn things! Do I have to be some striding macho bully, stomping around all over everything? Are the men all as insecure as that?"

"I'm not interested in their psychology," said Peter dryly, "Custom of the country, and all that; those boots would mark you what they call a sandal-wearer anywhere outside the city, and wouldn't look too good even indoors. Go down to Field Issue and get some proper ones. You take him down, Jaelle."

She went down and found him a pair of boots, helped him to haul them on, grumbling all the way. She readjusted the knot of his scarf and warned him again to be deaf and dumb. "Your first trip into the field, you're going to feel very much as I did my first day here," she said. "But it's only a beginning."

On the roof of the copter landing, Peter was arguing with Monty. "If they come in like this, costumes or no, they'll know we're Terrans right away. I think we should ride with that crew down there." He pointed at a group of men saddling up in a street near the HQ.

"They need able-bodied men to fight fire," Monty said. "I don't think they would care whether we were Terrans or *cralmacs* provided we could carry a hoe, and if we go in the copter we can get there sooner and do more work without tiring ourselves out by riding in. The important thing is to help them fight the damned fire! It might even be good public relations, if they knew that the Terran Empire sent able-bodied men to help them—"

"I'd like to remind you both," said Alessandro Li, "that we are still working for Intelligence; this isn't a humanitarian mission. Haldane, who are those people getting ready to ride?"

Peter had a strong pair of binoculars tucked in his belt; he raised them and looked down into the street. "Second call-up; the first one, only volunteers went, but this party is evidently taking out all the men they can find, there are old men and little boys no older than twelve in that lineup— I went out one year. And there are three or four Comyn, with a few dozen Guardsmen, and at least one *leronis*."

"You mean the lady draped in red?" Monty asked, and Peter nodded.

"Comyn again! Damn it, I wish I knew what made the whole countryside jump like frogs whenever they nod their heads!" Aleki said, "but the ones who know won't tell. One of these days, Jaelle, we're going to have a long talk about that, aren't we? Let's get the horses and go. Forget the copter. I don't want anything marking us as Terrans. Intelligence, remember."

Jaelle said swiftly, "I am going too. I have fought before this on the firelines—and I need not keep the camp with the women; I am a Renunciate and I can do a man's work."

"Commendable spirit in your lady," said Alessandro Li dryly, "but tell her to stay at home, Haldane, she's more use to us here for language and liaison. If she wants to be helpful, let her get on good terms with what's-her-name, Lady Rohana."

"I need to go. And Magda must be there, if they are calling out all the able-bodied—"

"Able-bodied men," said Monty firmly. "You know as well as I do that they haven't reached the point of calling out women, Jaelle."

Peter interrupted as she opened her mouth to answer, "You are not going out there, Jaelle. There's a full-fledged forest fire raging out there, and you—"

"I have probably fought more fires than you have," she said angrily. "I went first into the lines when I was fourteen—"

"Forget it," said Cholayna. "We don't have time to wait while you get medical clearance—"

"Medical clearance? To go into my own countryside?"

"Right," Peter said. "You're here in Magda's job, and one of the first rules is that nobody—nobody—goes into the field without clearance." The two men were striding toward the elevator; Jaelle said quietly, stepping in after them. "You forget. I am a Darkovan citizen. I am not subject to those regulations—"

"That's what you think." Peter stabbed roughly at a ground-level button. "When we were married, I applied for Empire citizenship for you, so our kids would have it. Besides, by your own Oath, you are here to abide by the terms of your employment. That's one of them. The matter, sweetheart, is closed." He leaned over and kissed the tip of her nose. "See you when we get back, love." He walked quickly away.

Some day, she thought angrily, he was going to throw their marriage, and her Empire citizenship, up at her once too often. She toyed with the notion of going into the hateful surroundings of Medic and getting the damned clearance, to spite them all. They could hardly prevent her . . .

. . . but then they would have her registered as pregnant, and something told her that this one thing she ought to keep from them. For some reason she did not want that on the Terran records. She asked herself if she was only spiting Peter—he would surely want his coming child registered. She started to go, then something inside her said, cold and clear, *No.*

Rationalizing this, she thought of her last visit to Medic, the machines which looked inside and through her, the feeling of being completely depersonalized, her body a machine among other machines, violated. If they knew she was pregnant, it would be worse. She had some days off coming —Peter had explained that to her; she went up to the office and asked Cholayna for the day off to visit the Guild House.

As she had half expected, Cholayna asked if she might come along. Jaelle went up and dressed quickly, feeling relieved as she slid into her Amazon clothing; leather breeches for riding—they were tight in the waist, she would have to borrow a pair from Rafaella to wear till the baby was born—and proper boots. When she joined Cholayna at the gates, the woman was wearing a heavy weatherproof down jacket which would have been wonderful for the Hellers in winter, but made Jaelle wonder how Cholayna avoided suffocating in it today—it was really not that cold.

"But I was born on a really hot world," Cholayna said, shivering even in the heavy clothes, and looking in dismay and disbelief at Jaelle's light tunic, over which she wore only the lightest of riding cloaks.

"But it's almost summer," Jaelle said, and Cholayna chuckled.

"Not to me, it isn't."

But Cholayna kept pace with Jaelle, even in the high-heeled sandals in which Jaelle could not have taken four steps without breaking her ankles. Walking beside Cholayna, Jaelle felt like a young girl again, the Amazon fosterling; there had been a time when Kindra had taken employment as a guard for warehouses about the city. When she made her morning rounds, she had sometimes taken her foster daughter with her; it was then that they had had some of their best times together, mother and daughter. It was those months that had made Jaelle an Amazon.

She could have confided in Kindra as she could not in Rohana. Once she had conceived a child, Rohana could not see her, Jaelle, at all, but only the potential mother of a child for the Aillard Domain.

But surely there would be someone in the Guild House that she could talk to.

They were walking through the marketplace and she saw rounded eyes, curious glances at Cholayna's dark skin. But one would have thought Cholayna had never experienced anything but these shocked or hostile glances; she strode along blithely in her uniform and Jaelle envied the woman her confidence.

I was like that once, when I walked with Kindra and the townspeople stared and jeered at the Renunciates. What has happened to me?

Only on the very steps of the Guild House did Cholayna hesitate for a moment and ask, "Should I have worn makeup, Jaelle? I could have painted my skin so that I looked like anyone else. I do not want to embarrass you in your own home. . . ."

Jaelle liked Cholayna more for asking, but she shook her head defiantly. Renunciates themselves were different, if they could not accept Cholayna's differences so much the worse for them!

And indeed, when Irmelin answered the door, she stared for a moment at Cholayna, but quickly collected herself to welcome Jaelle with a hug.

"I know Mother Lauria will want to see you," she said to Cholayna, and showed the Terran woman directly toward the Guild-mother's office. But to Jaelle's inquiries she told her that Rafaella, Camilla and Margali were all out on the fire lines, they had been gone from the house for several days now.

All of my oath-sisters. There is no one here I can talk to. She supposed Marisela had gone with the others, but Irmelin told her that the woman was in the house, and guessed, of course, why Jaelle wished to see her.

"You're expecting a baby, Jaelle? Why, how nice for you!" Jaelle supposed she should have expected that; she said all the appropriate things, and let Irmelin bring her into the kitchen and sit her down with a cup of hot bark-tea and a piece of fresh buttered bread from the ovens, as if Jaelle were again the twelve-year-old fosterling who had been everybody's pet in the Guild House.

"I'll fetch down Marisela to you, there's no reason for you to be running up and down all the stairs—"

"Irmi, it will be four moons before running up and down stairs would bother me," Jaelle protested, but just the same, Irmelin's fussing comforted her. At least someone cared; she sat dripping tears into her tea. After a time Marisela came into the kitchen, dipped herself up a cup of tea and sat down, letting it steam in front of her. She smiled at Jaelle, that smile which seldom reached her mouth but only twinkled behind her eyes.

"Well, you look healthy enough, Shaya, is there some reason I should have come down to you?"

"Oh, Marisa, I'm sorry, I *told* Irmelin—"

"No, sister, it's all right, I slept through breakfast and am glad to have some company, with everyone out on the fire lines."

"Can I get you something?" Marisela started to shake her head, then looked sharply at Jaelle and said, "Yes. I would like some bread, sliced very thin, please, and honey instead of butter." And Jaelle, busying herself with cutting the bread with the proper knife, and finding the honey crock and spoon and spreading it, found that she no longer wanted to dissolve into tears. She wondered why Marisela was smiling as she sat down again, sliding the plate of bread and honey toward her. The older woman asked, "How far?"

Jaelle counted mentally and told her, and Marisela nodded.

"So that is why you were asking all those soul-searching questions about not knowing our own minds and how to tell whether we are pleasing ourselves or someone else," Marisela said. It was not a question and not sympathetic, and Jaelle felt as if Marisela had flung cold water over her, but she realized she was not entitled to ask for sympathy. No one had bidden her lie with Peter, nor marry him, and she could have made certain she did not get with child. She blinked fiercely, but she no longer wanted to cry. Done was done.

So she told Marisela, making a good, funny story of it, all about the

Terran Medic machinery which had inspected her inside and out, and Marisela laughed with her.

"I think we can all agree that you do not need such care as that. You are young and healthy; only if you should begin vomiting, or show any sign of bleeding. Take care what you eat, drink much milk or beer but little wine, get as much fruit and fresh food as you can, and tell the Terrans, if they should ask, that you have seen your own medical adviser. You should come back to the House to bear your child, but the Terrans may not allow it—they think what we know of medical practice is limited and barbarian, and I must admit that to a certain extent they are right and I am not altogether sorry for it. Just the same, two days ago I lost a mother and her child and I would have given all I own for some access to your Terrans' skills—"

"Well," Jaelle said, "Cholayna is in there arranging ways for you to have such help," but Marisela shook her head.

"Ah, no, my dear, it is not as simple as that. It sounds like a perfectly simple thing, and a thing that is all good, that I should be able to save mothers alive to care for their children, and save their children alive so that no mother may weep because half the little children she bears do not live past weaning. But it is not such a good thing as all that."

"Do you dare to say it is a bad thing?"

"Aye, and I do say so," Marisela said, and at Jaelle's indignant stare, she said, "I want to speak with your friend anyway. Shall we go and talk with Mother Lauria? Finish your tea, it is good for you."

Jaelle had grown up thinking of Mother Lauria's office as a sacrosanct place, not to be breached except in emergencies, but Marisela simply knocked and went in, and Mother Lauria smiled at her.

"I was going to send for you, Marisela. Cholayna—" she struggled a little with the name. "Is that how you say it?"

"Near enough," said Cholayna and nodded in a friendly way to Marisela. "So you are the house Medic, as we would say it. It is you who should choose women to be instructed in Medical techniques, or you yourself may come and learn them with the younger women—"

"I should be interested," Marisela said, "and knowledge is always a good thing, but will you teach them only to use their medical sciences or will you teach them when they should not use them?"

"I do not understand," Cholayna said. "The business of a Medic is to save lives, and Mother Lauria was just telling me how you had had to let a woman die because you could not save her or her child. We can teach you ways to save most of them. . . ."

"So that every mother will have a dozen living children?" said Marisela, "and then, how shall they be fed?"

"I am sure you know that we have knowledge of contraceptive techniques," Cholayna said. "So that a woman can put her strength into bearing only one or two children and not spend all her life in bearing them and watching them die."

Marisela nodded. "If the two she does bear are the strongest and best, and we could be sure of that," she said, "but suppose the two who survive are the weakest, and so their children will be weaker yet? Ten, twenty generations down the road, we will be a people of weaklings, kept alive only by sophisticated medical techniques and thus dependent on your technology. If a woman is saved alive when her pelvis is too small, then perhaps her daughters will live to bear more children with this defect, and once again, we are dependent upon more and more medical help to keep them alive in childbirth. Believe me, it hurts my heart to watch women and children die. But when a child is born, for instance, blue and unable to breathe because he has a hole inside his heart . . ."

"That can be repaired," Cholayna said. "Many of our people are living who would have died here at birth . . ."

"And his children will multiply those defects," said Marisela. "Oh, believe me, on the cases where something has gone wrong in the womb and the child is lacking strength, perhaps we should save that child alive, but if it is a defect he will pass to his own sons? Better that one should die now than that a hundred weaklings should sap the strength of our people. And it is like a lottery—the first two children are not always the brightest, the strongest, the best; so often a great leader or genius will be born seventh, or tenth, or even twentieth among the children of his family."

Cholayna said stiffly, "I am afraid I do not like playing God and deciding that women must suffer that way."

"Is it not playing God to decree that they shall *not* so suffer?" Marisela asked. "We once had a breeding program here where we chose to tinker with our genes, to create the perfect people and the perfect race. We bred *laran* into our people and we are still suffering for it. Perhaps when the Goddess decrees that some must die at birth, She is being cruel to be kind."

"I still feel we should not reject the gift of the Terrans when they wish to teach our people their arts," Mother Lauria said, and Marisela nodded.

"Oh, I am sure you are right. But I pray all the Gods that we have the wisdom to know where to end it. There is no virtue in saving some lives which will be a burden to everyone in the household, everyone in the village, everyone in the world. I—I do not want to play God in deciding who must live and who must die, so I leave it to the mercy of the Goddess. If I in my small self have the power to decide that this one must live and this one must die, I can only say, my business is saving lives, I will save alive all I can. That way lies chaos. Perhaps it is better not to have that power."

"I cannot agree that anything which diminishes a woman's power can be right," said Cholayna, and Marisela sighed.

"In theory surely you are right. But sometimes it is a terrible temptation to take the short view and do the immediately humane thing, instead of what might be best for all of humankind over the centuries."

Jaelle asked angrily, "Do you mean you would let people die if you could possibly save them?"

"Alas, no," said Marisela. "I would not, and perhaps that is why I fear that power so much. I hunger for all your knowledge, so that I need never see a woman bleed and die, or a baby struggle to breathe; I hate to lose the fight with that Dark Lady who stands beside every woman at this hour, contending with me for Her due. But my business is to save life when I can, as I said, and I will, I suppose, in the end, stick to my business of saving lives. The Dark Lady is a very ancient and friendly adversary, and she can care for her own."

Cholayna looked at her with interest. She said, "That is a point of view often debated at Head Center. I had not expected to hear it in this House—"

"From a native midwife, or would you call me a witch doctor or sorceress?" asked Marisela, and they smiled at each other in the friendliest way.

But Jaelle was restless as the conversation went far afield into complicated matters of ethics, and was relieved when Cholayna rose to go. Cholayna said, "You may stay as long as you wish, Jaelle, you are certainly entitled to a holiday," but she went for her cloak, telling the older women that she had some work to do. She could surely find some work in Monty's office, since he, and Aleki, had left so much undone when they went to the fire lines.

But, restless and alone that night in the Quarters which seemed so much too big for her, with Peter away, she could not rest. The Guild House now seemed as unfriendly as the Terran Zone. And her main reason in going there had failed; she had wanted to see Magda, and Magda had been away on the fire lines, and Marisela and Mother Lauria, friendly as they were, were not really involved in her problems. There was no reason they should be.

She had wanted, no, needed to see Magda and make friends again with her. Would it be better to pretend that nothing had happened, or to insist that they talk frankly about it? Perhaps it meant nothing. After all, Magda had had a tremendous load on mind and spirit; all the pressures of the housebound time, hostility because of the fight and the indemnity, the fear of being dismissed from the Guild House, the pressures of the training sessions and the endless nightmares . . . was it any wonder Magda had no extra strength to deal with Jaelle's troubles?

Yet it was more than that. Jaelle searched in her mind and found only a confused image of herself picking Kyril's hand off her arm as if it were a crawling bug; intrusive, unpleasantly suggestive of an unwanted intimacy. Yes, and before supper when she had hugged and kissed Magda, the other woman had drawn away uneasily. *Everyone already thinks I am your lover. We should talk about that; between oath-sisters there should be no such barrier.*

It was taken for granted in the Guild House, but after the usual adolescent experiments, she had never thought about it. For a time when she had first set up the business with Rafaella—they had been lovers, for a time, but it had seemed no more than a way of cementing deep friendship, and Rafaella was at heart far more interested in men; after a few weeks it had simmered down into affection, had in fact never been much more. She had taken it for granted as part of their bonding; had, she now realized, felt that she and Magda should have shared this gesture of trust, of love and openness to one another. But if it was not the custom among Magda's people, as it certainly was not among, for instance, the *cristoforos,* why did she feel so rejected? Was she afraid Magda would come to despise her, and if she could lose Magda's friendship over a thing as simple as that, was her friendship worth having?

She held endless conversations inside her own mind, but once or twice when it seemed she could almost see Magda's face . . . *I shall be reaching her with* laran *if I do not take care.* . . . she tried, in a panic, to slam her mind shut. Now she regretted she had never accepted Rohana's offer, no, her plea, that she should go, even briefly, to a Tower to have her *laran* trained. Now it was too late. Was it too late? And then she would find herself crying again.

She had completely ceased to use the corticator tapes; but she realized that the Language department did not know it, they were complimenting her daily about her growing command of the language.

One evening, when she came into her rooms, she found Peter there, stripping off mud-crusted shirt and trousers.

"No, don't kiss me yet, sweetheart, for God's sake wait until I get out of these things and shower; to put it bluntly, I stink," he said. She sniffed. He certainly did. She supposed her senses had been sharpened by constant access to the level of sanitation in the Terran Zone, where the slightest stain was instantly scrubbed away and disposable clothing was the norm. He thrust his toward the disposal, then wrinkled his nose, bagged them and shoved them into a closet.

"I guess I'd better take them down to be cleaned; they're field clothes and a little grime will make them more authentic," he said, with a wry grin. "How's junior?" He patted her still-flat tummy as he headed for the shower, and she heard his voice trailing off, mostly something about how good it was to be back where he could get hot water and civilization.

The Empire people think civilization and plumbing are the same thing. They are neurotic about smells and dirt, she thought. He should have kissed me, at least! She lay down on the bed, feeling bruised. He hadn't asked about her, only the baby. She felt angry at herself for feeling that way; he was tired, just off the trail, and she was certainly being too sensitive, but like Rohana, once she was pregnant she was not herself, only a sort of walking nest for the damned baby! She buried her face in the pillow. Not an honest feather in it, some damned synthetic stuff. She took a long breath and she smelled again the aseptic, the *Terran* smell of it. It was only the smell. She would not cry. She *would* not.

She could go now, she didn't have to stay here. In half an hour's walk she could be in the Guild House. But she was sworn; she was legitimately employed to fill Magda's place in the Terran HQ. Magda had not violated her pledge to the Guild House, under stresses far worse than this; she must at least match Magda's courage.

Would they even *want* her in the Guild House, swelling daily with a Terran's baby like any drab from the spaceport bars? She could tell herself it was different as much as she wished, but she had wanted Peter, she had wanted to lie with him and now there was a child coming, a child who would never be at home in either world. She was crying now, she did not hear Peter come out of the shower, and when he tried to embrace her she fought and cried hysterically until in the end he had to call a Medic. She spent the rest of the night down on the Hospital floor, drugged into unconscious sleep. There was nowhere else to go.

Part Three

Outgrowth

Chapter One

Although Magda's household time would not end till forty days after Midsummer, custom freed the Renunciate novices for the day itself, and Magda came down to breakfast to hear the women discussing their plans for the holiday. Keitha and Magda had been told they might go where they wished during day and the night following; but must be back within the House by dawn.

"What are your plans, Keitha?"

"A midwife cannot make many plans. But before Doria left for Neskaya, she asked me to go this day and see her birth-mother. The woman will not come and see her daughter here, but Rafi says she often asks if Doria is well and content."

"That she does," Rafaella said, sliding down her bowl for porridge. "I think she is afraid Doria will try and make Amazons of her other daughters, but I do not think any of Graciela's other girls have sense enough to take the Oath. She has not seen Doria ten times in the five years before this, but the day Doria was fifteen she began plying her with gifts and offering to find her a husband. Nothing would please her more than to have Doria repudiate her fosterage here and marry the first oaf who offered for her. I do not think she will be glad to see either of us, but whether or no, we will take her Doria's gifts and greetings. And I shall see my youngest son, whom I have not seen in half a year."

Magda remembered that Doria's mother had given her up when she was born, in return for Rafaella's son.

"I too was promised I might see my son," Felicia said, "but I do not know if I can bear it yet, or whether it might be cruel to him. . . ."

"Rafi, you are wanted in the stable," said Janetta, poking her head into the dining hall.

"Well, what is it?" said Rafaella impatiently, "Does one of the horses wish to give me Midsummer greetings?"

"A man who says it is business," Janetta told her, and Rafaella grumbled, threw down her fork and, still munching on a piece of the excellent nut cake which had made its appearance on the table in lieu of ordinary bread and butter, went off toward the stable. Two minutes later Janetta came back and said, "Margali, Rafi wants you too."

Magda had not finished her breakfast, but she was pleased enough at the disappearance of Rafaella's hostility that she went at once; she had tried enough to reassure Rafaella that she would fill Jaelle's place in their business as much as she could, and it was worth being disturbed even at the holiday breakfast. She said, "Save me a piece—" she hesitated; she could hardly call it coffee cake, which would have been the Terran word, and no one had mentioned what they called it; she pointed and Keitha laughed. "I'll guard it with my life!"

Rafaella was talking to a tall man shrouded in a thick cape; he was at the head of a string of horses, among them a few of the fine Armida-bred blacks. Several, too, were the shaggy ponies of the Hellers.

"Margali, I am sorry to ask you to work at Festival, but I did not expect these ponies for another tenday—"

"I too am sorry to disturb you on holiday, *mestra,* but I was in the City now," said the man, and Margali suddenly recognized his voice; he was the big fair-haired man who had carried her out of the fire lines, *Dom* Ann'dra. *The Terran!* But he was talking about the ponies in an accent better than her own.

"I could not find the ten you wanted, but I have seven here; they are strong and already immune to the hoof-rot, and all have been broken to halter and pack."

Rafaella was going to one after another, examining teeth, patting soft muzzles. "They are good ones," she said, "but why are you in the City so late in the season, *Dom* Ann'dra? Is your lady traveling with you? And the Lord Damon, will he be in the City for Council Season?"

"No, I am traveling all but alone this year, but since I was coming this way, I was able to escort Ferrika to you." He held out his hand to help down a woman in a heavy traveling mantle who was seated on one of the horses. Over Rafaella's shoulder, as he turned, he recognized Magda and said, "Oh, it is you—I was concerned about you, *mestra;* did your feet heal properly?"

"Oh, yes, quite well," Magda said. "Only my boots were burnt beyond repair: my feet are fine."

Rafaella and Ferrika hugged one another and Rafaella said, "I had hoped you could come earlier in the season, Ferrika—"

The small snub-nosed woman smiled and said, "I too wished to come; but there was need of my services at Armida."

"More children on the estates? Or one of your ladies?"

Ferrika shook her head. She looked grieved. "The Lady Ellemir miscarried a child earlier this year; and her sister stayed to nurse her,—Lady Callista will not take her seat in Council this season—"

"I wonder, then, that you would leave your lady," Rafaella said, but Ann'dra interrupted. "Ferrika is not servant to us, but friend; and Ellemir is well again. But none of us have any heart for merrymaking this year, and there is little to be accomplished at Midsummer, so I came to do what business I must and pay my respects to the Lords of the Council; then I shall be off home again, probably at dawn, I was sorry to disturb your festival, but I did not wish to stable the beasts in a public compound when they could be in their new home."

"I am grateful to you," Rafaella said. "It takes a tenday or so to quiet them after the long trip; they are far better here in their own stable. Ferrika, *breda,* don't stand out here, go inside and greet your sisters, breakfast is on the table!"

"And holiday nut cake? Marvelous," Ferrika said, and went into the house. Rafaella handed a pony's lead to Magda and said, "Will you take this one into that box-stall down there?"

When she came back Rafaella was writing, propped against the wall. She handed the paper to *Dom* Ann'dra.

"Take this to my patron, *Dom* Ann'dra, and she will arrange to have you paid; the horses are for her, I understand. May the Goddess grant that Lady Ellemir is well again soon."

"Amen to that. Shall I bring the other ponies when I come again?"

"Or sooner, if you have a messenger you can trust," said Rafaella. "And I need a good saddle-horse for an oath-gift to my daughter at Neskaya Guild House; is one available?"

"Not a good hand-broken horse for a lady, no; we always have too many orders for those." *Dom* Ann'dra said. "I could not promise you one of those for more than two years. But I can let you have a good halter-broken filly if you would like to train it yourself."

"I will not have the time; but Doria should break her own horse anyhow," Rafaella said. "Send it to Neskaya Guild House for Doria n'ha Rafaella."

Dom Ann'dra scribbled something on the papers he held. "I'll send a man there with it within a tenday," he said. He looked past Rafaella again at Magda curiously, and she almost heard, *What is she doing here?* Well, she thought, I certainly would like to know what *he* is doing here! No doubt he was on field assignment, had probably been so for years; if she went to the Terran Zone she might be able to look him up in Records; Cholayna or Kadarin would certainly know. She helped Rafaella stable and feed the new ponies. When she went back to the hall the porridge was cold, but Irmelin had brought fresh bread and opened a new jar of some kind of conserve, and a second nut-cake which vanished as swiftly as the first.

Ferrika was sitting at Marisela's feet, her head in the woman's lap.

". . . so tragic . . . so many of the noble ladies do not really want children and cannot wait to turn them over to wet nurse and foster mother. But the Lady Ellemir is one of those who, as soon as their arms are empty, already hungers for another babe at her breast. Four years ago, when the Lady Callista could not suckle her child—though I think myself it was more that she did not wish to—Ellemir nursed Hilary along with her own Domenic."

"Was she long in labor this time?"

"Not long, they had hardly time to summon me from the steward's wife," Ferrika said, "but all the more tragic because this time it was almost a matter of a few more days; if she could have carried the child even another tenday it might have lived. A girl, and born alive too, but we could not get her to breathe, her poor little lungs would not open, for all we could do. It was just a little too early. Once I really thought she would breathe and cry . . . a little mewing sound . . ." Ferrika buried her head in Marisela's lap and the older woman patted her hair.

"Perhaps it is just as well; once or twice I have done what seemed a miracle and saved one alive when it seemed hopeless, but then they grow up crippled or partly paralyzed and cannot speak—it was the mercy of the Goddess."

"Tell that to Lady Ellemir!" retorted Ferrika, blinking back her tears. "A girl, it was, perfectly formed, with red hair, and she had *laran* too, she had been real to them for three times forty days . . . I thought they would all go mad with grief. Lord Damon has not left my lady alone for a moment, day or night."

"But think; even with *laran,* if the poor babe had grown up sickly . . . better an easy death and a return to the Goddess, who may send her forth again when the appointed time comes for her to live . . ."

"I know that, really," Ferrika said, "but it was so hard to endure their grief. They had already named her . . ."

"I know, *breda.* But you are here with us, and you must stay until you are refreshed and cheerful again. You have had no holiday for a year and this has been hard on you, too, hasn't it, *chiya?* Come, you must meet our sister Keitha, she works with me, and next year we will send her to the Arilinn College of Midwives. Also she will have Terran training, which will help her perhaps to save some of the ones who might die for no good reason. I want you two to know and love each other as sisters."

As Ferrika embraced Keitha, behind them Camilla said, "How will you spend your holiday, Margali?"

But before she could answer, Rezi, who was on hall-duty, pushed her way quickly through to the fireside.

"Marisela, Rimal the Harp-maker is at the door, his wife is in labor—"

"Oh, no!" Magda said, "On your holiday, Marisela," but the midwife was rising with a good-natured smile. Keitha asked "Will you need me, *breda?*"

"I think so; it is twins and her first confinement," she said, and Keitha made a rueful face and went for her cloak. Marisela chuckled. "Like the beast-surgeon and the farmer, we have chosen a profession where we know no holidays except that the Goddess sends. Finish your breakfast, Keitha, there is no such hurry as all that! Rezi, fetch him some tea and cake in the Strangers Room and tell him we will be with him as soon as we can." Nevertheless she was heading for the supply cabinet where she kept her midwife's bag, and shortly afterward they heard the door shut behind her. Camilla chuckled.

"Who would be a midwife!"

"Not I," said Magda, reflecting that this was one thing which did not change from Terran to Darkovan; no Medic could ever count on a free holiday, especially in maternity work!

"And what will you do with your holiday, since by good fortune you have not chosen to become a midwife?"

"I am still not sure. Go to the market, certainly, and buy some new boots," Magda said, regarding the ancient and tattered sandals.

"And I," said Mother Lauria, "will stay in the house and write up the year's records, and enjoy an empty house with no one to trouble me! Perhaps I will go to the public dance in Thendara tonight, to listen to the musicians."

"I will certainly go," said Rafaella, "for they have asked me to be there to take a turn at playing for the dancers. And you, Margali?"

"I think so." She had always wanted to attend the public Festival dances in Thendara's main square, but she had not felt she could go alone, and Peter had never been willing to take her. She knew they became rowdy at times, but, as a Renunciate she could take care of herself.

Rezi came in from the hall again, bearing a basket of flowers.

"For you, Rafi," she said, and the women began to laugh and cheer.

"You have a lover so tenacious, Rafi?"

Rezi said, "The lad who brought them is not fifteen, and he asked for his mother," and Rafaella, laughing, hurried out to the hall, snatching up a piece of the festival cake.

"Boys that age are always hungry! Just like girls," she added over her shoulder, laughing.

Magda found herself remembering Midsummer, a year ago. She and Peter had still been married then. She had already known that the marriage was ending, but he had sent her the customary basket of fruit and flowers. It had been the final reconciliation before the quarrel that had smashed the marriage beyond repair. She wondered if he had sent Jaelle flowers this morning. She missed Peter. She was so tired of spending all her time with women!

"And what will you do today?" Camilla asked.

"I think I shall simply walk in the city and enjoy the knowledge that I am free to go wherever I wish," she said, realizing suddenly that she really had no place she wished to go. "But I will certainly buy new boots. And you?"

Camilla shrugged. "There is a Festival supper in the House for everyone who has no place else to dine; I have promised to help cook it, since Irmelin wishes to spend the day with her mother—she is old and blind now and Irmi fears every time she sees her may be the last. But you young ones always want to go out; enjoy yourself, *breda*. And there is a women's dance tonight; I may go to that, for I love to dance and I do not like dancing with men."

Magda thought she might return to the Terran zone for a visit. But she really had no friends there now. No doubt Peter and Jaelle had plans for this holiday already.

She was coming down with her jacket and the remnants of the burnt boots—it might shorten the wait for a new pair—when Camilla called.

"Margali, a man came asking for you; I sent him into the Stranger's Room. He has a strange accent—perhaps he is one of your kin from beyond the Hellers?"

A slight, dark man, faintly familiar, rose from a chair as she entered. He spoke her Darkovan name with a good accent, though it was not the accent of Thendara. The Terran. Montray's son—what was his name—

"Monty," he said, reminding her. She looked at him appraisingly.

"Where did you get those clothes?"

"Not right?"

"They'll pass in a crowd. But the boots are too well made for a tunic as cheap as that one; anyone who could afford boots as good as that could afford to have had his tunic embroidered, not just trimmed with colored threads. And the undertunic is too coarse."

"Haldane okayed them," Monty said. "I wore them on the fire lines; and he didn't do with me what he did with Li—he ordered Li to pretend to be deaf and dumb, so I thought I'd pass. . . ."

"Why have you come here?" she asked sharply.

"Jaelle happened to let it drop that you're free to go out today. May I escort you—I see you're dressed to go out—for a little way, have a few minutes conversation with you?"

Well, if this man was in Intelligence there was no reason to offend him because she thought his father a fool.

"You can show me where you bought those boots; they're good and I need a pair made," she said, "and we can talk on the way to the market. Don't talk in front of the women in the hall, they might spot your accent as wrong."

He bowed. It was not really a bad imitation of the proper bow of a Darkovan servant facing a woman of high rank; he wasn't stupid, or unobservant, he simply hadn't had the training she and Peter had had. Or—presumably he was a graduate of the same Intelligence school on Alpha—he hadn't had the experience. She guessed he was four or five years younger than herself. He followed her at the proper one step behind, through the hallway, and not until they were out of sight of the Guild House did he come up to walk beside her.

"The Karazin market?"

"I think so," he said, "and if I'm going to walk with you I ought to carry that package, hadn't I?"

She handed him the rolled bundle, but it burst open, and he stared in consternation at the charred soles, and scorched uppers.

"How the devil did you do that?"

"I was caught in one of the break-throughs, where the fire jumped a break."

"I heard there were Renunciates there. Were you hurt?"

"Superficial burns on my feet; they're healed now."

"That explains Jaelle—"

"Jaelle? Did she go into the fire lines? Oh, I wish I'd seen her—"

"She didn't go; Peter told me she's pregnant," Monty said. "She couldn't have gotten Medical clearance, though she wanted to come and even made noises about it."

Magda said a proper "How nice," but inside she felt a curious sinking cold. So Jaelle would give Peter the son he wanted so much.

"We can go down here and get your feet measured for boots," he said, "and then we can sit and talk awhile—it's not forbidden to sit and talk to me in a public place, is it?"

Magda shrugged. "Not at Festival, certainly. It's not commonplace, but at Festival we do as we please." And if they saw her sitting in a public place with a man, they could hardly think. . . . She cut that thought off in the middle, defiant; let them think what they wished. Again in the person of a mute servant, he handed her package while she arranged with a cobbler to have the soles replaced and bargained for a new pair—he had none to fit her, but if she could return in three hours he would have the soles patched on the old ones and they would serve till the new were ready.

Magda paid for the work, grateful for the money she had earned helping Rafaella; even after paying her tithes to the house, she had enough for the mended boots and for the new pair. Anyway, she had some back pay in the Terran Zone, banked there, and she should arrange to convert some of it to Darkovan money; she had not needed much in the Guild House but that was more good luck than good management. Food and clothing were available in return for the help she gave in maintaining the House, and now that Rafaella had accepted her in Jaelle's place and given her work she could do there—sorting loads, packaging travel-food into separate day rations—she had begun to pay her share. When she had finished at the bootstall she walked down the street and Monty caught up again with her.

"Now where can I talk to you?"

"What is this all about?"

"You know that perfectly well," he said, exasperated. "I need a report from you—I told you that when I came there before. We're going to have eight of them down in Medic—Cholayna told me the other day. We need to know more about what makes them tick. You're the only expert we have on Darkovan women."

"Ask Jaelle," Magda said, and he laughed.

"I'm afraid she's a little too prickly for me. In a society like this one, I can see how women who *had* gotten out of it would be a little bit on the defensive—what I can't imagine is how she came to marry Haldane. Can you explain it?"

"Since I think you know that he and I were married once, I suppose that question is purely rhetorical."

"No," Monty said, suddenly serious. "Not at all. Working in the field and seeing the different way men treat women in the Darkovan culture has caused me to re-examine some of my own values. I wonder, sometimes, if perhaps women really prefer a culture where they're looked after. Cared about. Cherished and protected. We make such a big thing of equality, but the women here seem happy enough. Oh, there are exceptions, but seriously, Magda—" he had spoken her Terran name, but she did not correct him, since no one was near enough to hear, "it seems to make sense, to give women supremacy in their own sphere, and not bring them into direct competition; let them have one place where they can be really superior, and keep it separate. Lots of societies work that way. . . . hell, you had anthropology and sociology of culture on Alpha, you know what I'm talking about."

"I don't like the assumptions behind that kind of culture," Magda said sharply. "Why should everything be divided up into what women do and what men do?"

"Well why *shouldn't* they? It happens anyway; it's just that some societies admit it, and others try to pretend it doesn't exist. *Most* women are less competitive, less athletic—why should a society be based on the exceptions? I don't see anything wrong with a man spending his life in, for instance, dress, but I wouldn't force all men to wear dresses, for instance, so that the few who want to won't feel conspicuous. I remember one nursery school I was in where they wouldn't let the boys play with trucks and spaceships because they said we shouldn't get stereotyped. There were a couple of little girls there who really wanted to play dolls and the nurses kept shoving them at the spaceships and trying to get them to play football."

"So you'd give the girls the dolls and the boys the spaceships, and leave it at that?"

Monty shrugged. "Why not, as long as the girls who want the spaceships and toy trucks get a chance to try them out now and then? But I never got up the slightest interest in playing dolls, no matter how many they shoved into my little hands. At least on Darkover they would have taken it for granted that since I was a boy, I had a right to act like one."

Magda chuckled. "Well, I never had to fight for my chance at a doll *or* a toy truck. I usually spent my time with paints and listening to my mother play the harp. And dancing. Remember I grew up in Caer Donn."

"I envy you," he said seriously. "A wonderful chance, to grow up in the world you really live in . . . you know my father. He has lived thirty years on Darkover and still can't tolerate the light of the red sun because he lives all the time under Terran-style lights."

"Don't envy me, Monty," she said, matching his seriousness. "It's not an enviable option, to grow up never knowing where you belong, not—not knowing the recognition signals. I was never really Darkovan, and my young friends knew it. And I knew it, Oh, God, I knew it! And when I went to the Terrans it was worse . . . how the devil did I get into all this?"

He smiled. He had, she realized, a nice smile. "I admit I led you into it," he said, "I wanted to hear what made *you* tick. You're *the* expert, you know, on Darkovan culture and language. That doesn't surprise me, I don't think any man has the power of observation about details that a good woman can have."

"I'm glad you admit us to that competence," she said dryly. "I wondered if perhaps you thought my proper sphere of influence was judging suitable clothing."

"Well, that's one of them," he said equably, "and you're living proof that a woman can pass better than a man."

"Well, in a Guild House, anyway," she said, losing the impulse to argue with him.

"Look, you keep saying you want better understanding between Darkover and the Empire. Start contributing to it, then. Help me understand."

That sounded reasonable. While she was thinking it over, he said, "You have two or three hours to kill, anyhow, while your boots are getting ready. We won't make it a formal report. Just come back to HQ with me, and we can have a drink in my quarters while you put some basic reports on file for me. And show me how to access your other reports, or how to get clearance to work with them, okay? Good God, girl, don't you even know your work is posted as *the* standard of excellence not only here, but all over the Empire? Even when I was still on Alpha I heard about Lorne's work on Cottman Four, and I was hoping I'd be put on assignment with you!"

Flattery, Magda thought; *he's trying to get what he wants. That's all.* But after the discouragement and self-doubt of the last weeks it touched something so deep in her that she could not help feeling warmed and satisfied by the words.

"All right. If I can have a few minutes to get down to the credit transfer department . . ."

"All the time you want," he said amiably, having made his point.

Going in through the Spaceforce-guarded gate, it felt like the times she had come back with Peter from a field assignment, still in field clothes, but ready to take off her Darkovan *persona* and return to her true self. *I believed then that it was my true self and the Darkovan Margali only a mask. What is the truth?* She was no longer sure.

His quarters were in Unmarried Personnel, not too far from her own old rooms; he found her a seat, asked what she would have to drink.

"Coffee," she said without a moment's hesitation, "if you had to ask me what one thing I missed most, that would be it . . . that, and a hot shower in the morning."

He went to dial it from the console. "Pretty primitive in the Guild House?"

"Oh, no," she said, flicked again on the raw by that assumption. "They have hot baths, hot tubs to soak in, everything . . . it's just that they have a different lifestyle and a different set of priorities. Some things you have to be brought up to; they take it for granted that a nice cold bath is just what you need to wake up in the morning, and hot water is a nighttime indulgence. And I've had to adapt." She laughed, turning the coffee cup between her hands. "I never realized how Terran I was until I *had* to be Darkovan 28 hours a day, ten days a week." She sipped the coffee; it still tasted good to her, despite the sudden strangeness; she wondered if the caffeine in it, now that she was unaccustomed to it, would give her some unexpected high.

"Well, now. What do you need to know? Languages? That's simple—sleep with the corticator tape for at least seven days. Too many people here try to cheat—they can get along after one or two days so they never go back, and that takes time; I grew up on the language, of course, in fact I probably made the tapes you're using, but when I learned the Dry-Town language I slept with it for two full tendays. You have to know it, not on the surface, but where it counts, down in your guts. There was some excuse when we didn't *have* the tapes in full, but now we do. Program the subconscious all the way, not just the superficial language course. You have clearance to use a Braniff-Alpha level corticator, don't you?"

"I've always been nervous about it. I don't like the idea of anything mucking around with my very nerve synapses!"

"It's the only way you can get it on the same level you'd have gotten it when you were a child," she said. "And it's better than being deaf and dumb!"

"That's for sure," Monty laughed. "Now can you put in a report on the Free Amazons—oh, pardon me, Renunciates—"

She corrected his pronunciation slightly, knowing it was temporizing. But a dozen of her sisters would be working here in Medic. She was, in a sense, doing this for the Guild. Monty found her a scribing machine, and Magda sat down to her work.

"The name Guild of Free Amazons, commonly used by Terrans and in the Empire," she began, "is a romantic misconception, based on a Terran legend of a tribe of independent women. The true name of the Guild in their language could be better translated as the Order of Oath-Bound Renunciates," and went on from there, explaining what she knew about the history and original charter of the Amazon movement, which had begun formally in Thendara only about 300 years ago, and for almost half of that time had been a highly secret movement, operating underground, with only a single concealed Guild House which operated almost like a cloistered convent; only recently, in the last hundred years, had the Amazons begun to operate openly and build other Houses of Refuge.

She heard, for a while, Monty moving around the quarters, then lost consciousness of him as she went on making her report; she translated the text of the oath and explained some of its more obscure provisions, mentioned some of the taboos and courtesies of the Amazons among themselves and those observed by the common people toward them, including the incredible hostility toward Free Amazons found among the commoner women in the Kilghard Hills. But when it came to speaking of the common accusation that they were haters of men and lovers of women, she found it difficult to keep the detachment of the trained anthropologist. She welcomed, in a sense, the ability to recapture her Terran self, to remain an outsider; but when she began to speak of this she hesitated, played back what she had said, then wiped the last ten minutes and substituted some vague generalities about relationships of the Amazons with men on the fire lines. Monty came in again while she was finishing this up, and said, "Now I understand how your boots got in such a mess. Tell me—you were out in the edge of the Kilghard Hills, then, as the fire was coming down toward Thendara?"

Magda nodded. He said, "I ordered us up some lunch; dictating is hungry work and your throat must be dry, at least." He set a tray in front of her, and she smelled it appreciatively. *Terran food . . .* she told herself defensively that she had been brought up on Darkovan foods and liked them but that she was enjoying the change, it was nice to have something different. She had forgotten the completely different textures of synthetic foods, and tasted them exploringly.

He drew up a chair, digging into his own meal, looking appreciatively at the pile of narrow spindles she had piled up. "That's *marvelous,"* he said fervently, "You'll get a footnote in history or something, and I won't deny that I'll get a footnote to the footnote for talking you into it!"

She chuckled, shoving aside a tube of apple-flavored synthetic. The stuff, she decided, was as bland and flavorless as she remembered it. "You ought to have a footnote on your own. Or aren't you planning to follow in the Old Man's footsteps?"

Monty's laugh created sudden intimacy between them. "You know, and I know, that my father is no more fit to be Coordinator on a planet like Darkover than that donkey in one of your folk tales—Duran, was it?"

"Durraman," she said. "The one who starved to death between two bales of hay because he couldn't decide which one to bite into first . . ."

"Seriously, it's not his fault, Magda; he wanted to command a space station, it was what he was trained for; he got in with the wrong political crowd," Monty said. "My good fortune, of course, this was my world from the moment I could decide. . . . more coffee?"

She shook her head, pushing the tray away. "That *was* good," she admitted, "for a change, anyway."

He glanced at his chronometer, which kept Empire time. "You don't need to hurry; your boots won't be ready for another hour," he said, "but I hate to ask you to do any more dictating; you've done a heroic job already. I can't thank you enough, but you'll find a bonus on your credit when you get back . . . by the way, when *are* you coming back? The Old Man was talking about a special liaison post created just for you. . . ."

"Forty days more to fulfill my obligation to the Guild House; after that, I'm not sure. I might apply to change citizenship—"

"Oh, don't do that," he said quickly. "Empire citizenship is too valuable for that; Haldane put through for citizenship for Jaelle, so their kid will be born a full citizen. Be as Darkovan as you like, but hang on to your citizenship. Just in case."

Yes, that was the Terran way. Defend against all contingencies, never make a full commitment without leaving a way of escape. Cover yourself. She glanced again at her timepiece. "I should run up to Intelligence HQ, now they've got one, and check in with Cholayna—"

"She's off duty," Monty said, "and I happen to know she went to the Meditation Center and put through a notice not to be disturbed for at least eighteen hours. I suspect she's in an isolation tank or something—she belongs to one of those queer Alphan religions. Very odd lady, though it's good to have someone really competent in Intelligence. Only one drawback; she can't do her own fieldwork. So we have to depend on you. Could I ask a personal favor, Magda?"

"You can always ask," she said, smiling, and suddenly knew that in a sense she was flirting with him, letting the personal part of their communication take over momentarily from the business one, as a way of flattering him . . . was this worthy of an Amazon? It was the Terran way. She had never noticed it before, but now she knew she was doing it, and heard the harsh voice of Rafaella, *is it so important to you that a man must consider you beautiful?* Rafaella certainly was not the one to talk, she had three sons by three different fathers. . . . at least Camilla, who was a lover of women, was consistent! But through all her doubts it was reassuring, that she could still attract attention, not only professionally, but as a woman.

"You know how to pass as a native. Haldane can do the same thing. I will take the Braniff-Alpha corticators—I will believe it is safe if *you* say so —but can you tell me what I am doing wrong, so that in the Old Town I can pass as a native, as you and Haldane and Cargill do?"

"Why not ask them? They are men and would know what is necessary for a man. . . ."

"No," he said. "I'd trust a woman to spot a man and a man to spot a woman, any day. For instance I think I'd spot you even if you wore Darkovan clothes . . . I mean, when you weren't off guard, as you are here; I think I'd read you in the market, for instance. You don't walk *quite* like them—no, it's your eyes; you don't keep them down, not in quite the same way. You—" he groped for words, "you keep them down but I can tell you're doing it deliberately, not automatically. Is that just being a Renunciate?"

"Maybe, in part. Though you're right; I always had some trouble with that. You get into your Darkovan outfit and I'll tell you what you're doing wrong. And while you're doing it, I need to get down to credit transfer . . . oh, damn, I can't go into HQ in this outfit, I'll set off every alarm in the place!"

"One of the women in my office is about your size, and she lives just down the hall; let me go borrow a spare uniform for you."

She acquiesced, warning him not to tell anyone who it was for. She did not want, on her day off, to be flooded with old acquaintances eager to know all the details of her curious field assignment. When he came back with it he stood aside and let her change in his sleeping quarters. She was surprised at how naked she felt in the narrow tunic and tights, after months of the loose, unrevealing Amazon dress. She was conscious of her cropped hair—short even for a Terran, but she brushed it into a fairly smart coiffure, and Monty had thoughtfully asked for a few cosmetics as well so that she could make up properly. As she stepped out he whistled admiringly.

"In that outfit you were wearing, I didn't realize what a smasher you were!"

Again she laughed, realizing how far she had come from such compliments. It felt familiar and strange at once to walk down the HQ halls, knowing that the uniform made her invisible, just another employee with a right to be there. It was different and somehow comforting to drop her individual identity and slip into anonymity.

Soon she would be out of seclusion. Would they want her back here? If so, then she must acknowledge to all her sisters that she was Terran; would they hate her for it? When she got back, Monty was in Darkovan clothing again and she applied herself to critical study.

"Your hair is too short. To look really right, you would have to let it grow down at least to *here.*" She brushed a fingertip along his neckline. "Now walk for me . . ." and she watched him seriously. Finally she said, frowning, "I know what it is. You walk too—too lightly, unencumbered. Darkovan men . . . all of them, except beggars and cripples. . . . grow up wearing a sword, and even when they're not wearing it, they're wearing it, if you know what I mean. Here," she said, picking up the Amazon knife she had laid aside. "Belt this on—try walking with it. It's not a sword, of course—"

"It sure looks like one."

"Legally it's not," Magda said.

"By law and charter no Amazon may wear a sword."

"What *is* the difference?" Monty asked, studying the blade. It did, Magda realized, look very much like what any Terran would call a sword. "About three inches," she admitted dryly, and they laughed together as he belted it on.

"No, you are leaning to one side to compensate. And keep your wrist a little back so you won't be knocking against the hilt; remember when you first started wearing a wrist-radio and had to learn not to bang it into things? Wrist back—lower—so it won't get in the way but you could draw it at once if you had to. You have to psych yourself into it; you grew up wearing it, you started wearing and training with it when you were about eight, you never went out without it, you would feel as naked if it wasn't there as if you forgot to put your pants on in the morning."

"Good God," Monty exclaimed. "I knew the culture was aggressive, but do they really start their youngsters at eight?"

"The valley men. In the mountains the kids start carrying daggers almost as soon as they can walk, and using them, too. It's just part of the realities of their world; there are plenty of things bigger than they are, out there. And until you can feel that down in your guts, not just know it intellectually, you'll never have more than a superficial understanding of what it's like to be a man on Darkover. Their women are less protected than our men—there were women on the fire lines and they weren't all Renunciates, either!" After a minute she suggested, "You should get yourself a sword and wear it all the time around your quarters in here."

"How in the world do I sit down in the thing?"

"That's the point," Magda said. "Wear it for six weeks, and you'll know. You'll be able to sit down with it and get up with it and walk with it and work with it and run with it, and slide into a seat in a tavern without bashing the next guy with it."

He followed that, nodded slowly. "Haldane did all that?"

"Damn right, and more; his father actually let him work out with an arms-master with the other boys his age in the village where we grew up. In Empire uniform, he told me once, he feels undressed. We both do." She glanced self-consciously at her long legs in the thin tights. "And I have to change back before I leave." She headed in to the inner room to take off her uniform, adding, "Also, dance as much as you can. Men here start learning it when they're about five. Like everybody else."

"I did hear that," Monty said. "The old proverb—get three Darkovans together and they hold a dance. I did some work in ballet as well as martial arts before I came back here. . . . studied gravity-dancing on Alpha."

"That explains it," she said. "How you manage to pass at all; you don't walk quite like the average Terran who has no notion of how to move. I noticed that you were graceful. Most Darkovans think Terrans are incredibly clumsy. Dance—they say—is one of the very few wholly human activities; most things are also done by animals, but there's a saying: *only men laugh, only men dance, only men weep.*"

"I've noticed that," he said, "the way both men and women move, gracefully. . . . you move like them," he added, "like a feather. . . ."

She was suddenly self-conscious about the way he was looking at her. "I must go and change," she said. "Not even a whore would go out on the streets like this."

He did not look away. "I cannot decide which way I like you better. Darkovan women are so modest, so—" he hesitated, searching for a word, "so womanly. It makes me more conscious of myself as a man. Yet in your Amazon clothing you seem to be trying to negate all that, to be distant. And in uniform—you are very beautiful, Magda," he said, and came over to her. He turned her slowly round and kissed her. "I have been wanting to do that since I first set eyes on you that day in the Guild House when you were so angry with me. And now when I know you are not some sort of shrew or spitfire but a beautiful woman—and, and, so many things, a colleague and a friend and a woman too—" he stopped talking and kissed her again.

She said after a minute, softly, "Am I really so intimidating?"

"Not now. Don't go and change, Magda, stay with me here awhile . . ." and he drew her against him. Letting him kiss her again, she felt again the curious ambivalence. She liked him. She did not want him to be attracted to her this way. Yet it was reassuring, to know that even through her defenses, she was still desirable—he kissed her bare neck, and she drew away, troubled.

"No," she said in a low voice, "Monty, no. I came here with you for work, not for—not for this."

He did not move away. "It is not true what they say—that the Amazons are haters of men and lovers of women, is it?"

And that is what they say, and now I am wondering is it true? One of the women said it once in Training Session . . . that a woman who gives her love to men is traitor to other women, that men are always trying to reduce us only to something they can, or cannot, have as a sexual conquest, because it means they do not have to take us seriously. He was talking about how my work is the standard of excellence here . . . does he need to seduce me simply to prove that for all that, I am no more than a woman to be taken?

Nevertheless she let him draw her down on the couch, gave herself over to his kisses. She was uneasily conscious of her own response.

I don't want to. I have lived alone and celibate for more than a year, I should be eager. He's a very nice person, but I really don't want to. What's wrong with me? I should never have let it go this far. If she were going to stop him she should have done it swiftly and decisively when he made the first move, she had let him think she wanted it too. It would be cheap and small-minded to stop him now.

It's not as if I were a virgin, for heaven's sake!

After a time he whispered "This is foolish, Magda, kissing like children, with all our clothes on—we're both rational grown-up people. You do want me too, don't you?"

Do I? Do I not? Or do I simply want to reassure myself that I am still capable of reacting to a man, that I have not become an alien sexless thing —like Camilla—why am I thinking now of Camilla? That frightened her. She looked up at him and smiled.

"Of course I do," she said clearly, "but I never go to bed with a man before I know his first name."

He laughed down at her with relief and pleasure. His eyes were dark and shining, his face flushed. "Oh, that's all right then," he said, accenting the absurdity, "I don't use it because there's no Darkovan equivalent. That doesn't bother my father but it does bother me, I don't like having a name no one can pronounce, so I'm Monty. My name is Wade. I really ought to take a Darkovan given name for myself, I just haven't made up my mind yet. Isn't that ridiculous? But if that's all it takes—" He leaned down to her, laughing, and she smiled and let him draw her down again to the couch.

When she was dressing again, before his mirror, he came and touched her face gently.

"You are so lovely," he said in a soft voice, "but in those clothes you look so hard and strange. I hate to see you hide yourself in them, even now that I know it is a lie, that you are not really like that."

She said, laying her hand lightly on his arm, "No, Monty. It's not a lie. It is—it is *part* of what I am. Can you understand?"

"No," he said, "Never. But I'll try. Shall we have that drink now?" He was trying to accept her lightness but she liked him a little better now that she knew it was not entirely casual with him.

It was not casual with me either. I liked him and he is a friend, even if it meant no more than that. Is it wrong to wish to give pleasure to a friend, even if he is a man? She sat beside him, drinking, knowing that he needed somehow to stay close to her through this strangeness. She wished she could make him understand that it was strange to her too.

To give myself only in my own time and season . . . the words of the

Oath rang in her head. *But I don't know what that means anymore. Was I using him for my own needs . . . not sexual needs, but the need of demonstrating to myself that I could still attract a man? Is that what the Oath means, to use men for our needs instead of letting them use us for theirs? Don't we both have needs?*

"It's hard," he said, fumbling, "to get involved or not to get involved. I —I don't want to get married. And yet I just can't get that interested in, in the kind of women I might find in the red-light district. I played around a little because—because—this isn't going to make sense—in a way they were Darkover to me. The only part of it I could have. The real world is a billion light-years away from those girls, and I know it, yet I can—*could* have them, at least in a limited sense, and I couldn't have the rest. Do you understand what I'm saying? And, oh, hell, it suddenly occurred to me, this woman knows, I can level with her. . . . you know, I really *didn't* invite you up here to seduce you, it never crossed my mind—"

"Never mind, Monty. Things happen. As you said, we're both grown up." She sipped from his glass and patted his hand. How absurd that she should be the one to reassure him!

"Perhaps you can show me where to find a sword? I'd like to try that thing you told me about," he said, and she nodded.

"Of course. Although, really, Peter would know more about it. He really knows weapons, and I'm no judge, though I've been taught a little, a very little really, about using them. Peter really *is* an expert."

"All right, I'll ask him, though I really don't know him that well. Actually I know his wife a little better; we work together a lot. Jaelle. You know her, don't you, she's your friend?"

"My oath-mother in the Guild. It's a very special relationship," Magda said, and wondered why the thought filled her with such pain. What had come between them, that they were no longer close friends as they once had been? She did not want to think about that.

"She's a nice little thing," Monty said, "and she seems so isolated here, out of her depth. Oh, competent—very competent. But she looks so sad. She must really be crazy in love with that man, to have left her world for him. A woman who would do that for a man—oh, hell," he broke off, as the door-chime made its discreet announcing burp, "I'll see who that is and try to get rid of them, shall I?"

"Not on my account, Monty, I really have to go and get my boots," she said, as he went to the door.

"Oh, come in, Li. You know Lorne from Intelligence?"

"Cholayna's filled me full of stories about her," Alessandro Li said, bending over her hand. Magda picked up her knife and began to belt it on, fancying that Alessandro Li's eyes followed her. She flushed, knowing it was foolish. He could not possibly know what had happened between them and probably would not care if he did. She said, "Ask Peter about it, Monty. He can get you a good one, and I understand buying swords is a specialized business—you have to know what you are doing, and on a metal-poor planet like this, they are not cheap! But it's a lifetime investment."

"Thinking of taking up swordplay, Monty?"

"No, but I'll never be able to pass in the field until I learn to handle them, or at least to look as if I knew how," Monty said.

"Not the kind of thing that would attract me," Li said offhand. "I really do know your work, Miss Lorne, it's a pleasure to meet you. Jaelle gave me the Darkovan name of *Aleki,* by the way."

She nodded. "Living here, it's a good idea to have one, to learn to answer to it and think of it as *your* name, an automatic reflex."

"That's what's wrong with Father," Monty said suddenly, "he can't think of himself as having anything to do with this world. After—how long? Eleven, thirteen, years, he still feels like an alien."

"Well, after all," Aleki said, "he *is* alien. It's not healthy—useful for our work, maybe, but not healthy—to get to thinking of one's self as belonging to an alien world. I don't think it's ever right to lose sight of the fact that it's a pretense, a mask. . . . to let the mask become real. Granted, when we appoint a Legate here, he should be a man who feels real concern for the natives, and can identify with them. But he should be a career Empire man first and foremost. Take Haldane, for instance. He's smart, he knows this planet backward and forward, and he's got a mind like the proverbial steel trap. When he's a bit older—of course I don't have to tell either of you that it's going to depend in part on my report whether they set up a Legate in here or not, and when. Haldane's sharp and ambitious—couple of bad spots in his record, but he's young yet, and he's learning. What about it, Miss Lorne? Do you think Peter Haldane would make a good Legate, or are you the right one to ask? You were married to him once, weren't you?"

"I don't know if I am the right person to ask or not," she said, "I like him, but I'm not blind to his faults, if that's what you mean. Of course he'd do better as Coordinator than Russ Montray. Who wouldn't?" But she glanced apologetically at Monty. "Anyone would. *I* would."

"You could have a shot at Coordinator if it were most worlds, but not on Darkover," Aleki said. "It's just one of those things; this society won't accept a woman in the job. If you want a Coordinator's job somewhere else, Lorne, I can put you up for it. Not here, though. But you were telling me what you thought about Haldane—"

"I'm not sure the mistakes he's made are reversible," she said slowly, almost with apology, "or whether they mean a flaw in his imagination. But he's committed to Darkover and wants to stay here."

"I don't know," Aleki demurred, "in a key position like this, you want a man who's unquestionably loyal to Empire, who puts Empire first and the particular planet second—"

Magda shook her head. "If it was up to me," she said, "I'd want a man who thought of the planet first—just to counterbalance all those bureaucrats who are going to put the Empire first; a Legate ought to be a spokesman for the planet itself."

"That's a job for their Senators and other key men in Empire government," Aleki said, "though it's true that they do sometimes think of a Legate as a man to speak up for the world in question. Different theories of how to appoint people, that's all. That's why, even if the Darkovans would accept a woman in the job, you wouldn't make it higher than Coordinator; your service record shows you have a tendency to go native—think from a planetary, not an Empire point of view, and a Legate can't be provincial, planet-minded. Haldane, at least, seems to be working hard to develop a larger point of view." He accepted the drink Monty poured for him. "Oh, thanks."

"No more for me," Magda said, "A Renunciate can't go around the streets drunk, not even at Festival! More coffee, though; that's wonderful."

Monty indicated the pile of spindles on the table beside the couch. He said, "Miss Lorne came in on her day off and added to our files on the Renunciates."

"And now I am off to spend the rest of the day with the women from the Guild House—"

"Don't go yet," Aleki said, "I've been wanting to have a talk with you ever since Jaelle mentioned you. I looked up everything about you in Records. While I was out on the fire lines, I saw some women from Neskaya Guild House—"

"We were there from Thendara, too," Magda said, "but I didn't see you."

"You wouldn't have noticed me if you did," Alessandro Li said, goodnaturedly. "I was supposed to be deaf and dumb, and a servant."

Monty chuckled. "That's just what Magda told me I had better be, walking through the streets this morning!"

"You were in the Kilghard Hills," Aleki said. "Do you know anything about—" he hesitated over the word, "the Comyn?"

"All I know is in my report from Ardais," Magda said, conscious that she was evading him, and he scowled. "Not enough. Somehow I think the Comyn, whoever or whatever they are, are the key to this whole crazy planet. You know how it is; normally they come to us, begging to join with the Empire—eager for technology, all the benefits of a star-spanning Empire, but these people think their own little frozen ball of mud is the center of the whole damn universe!"

"You can't blame them for that," Magda said. "Doesn't everyone?"

"Not a question of blame. But Darkover is an anomaly and I'd like to know why. I can't ask Jaelle much about the Comyn—I gather she's related to some of them. We don't have any men in the field—we heard a rumor around the Trade City, a few years ago, of some kind of power struggle in the Comyn. Had to do with something they call the Towers, some kind of rebellion led by a man called Lord Damon Ridenow—and when I went out fighting fire, there he was bossing the whole job."

"Well, you ought to know what's going on out there, then," said Magda, "You've got one of the best men in the field I ever met. I'd never have spotted him, but we were trapped together behind the fire, and I heard him swearing in Terran." And then she was struck with doubt; had she heard him or had she picked it up with that special extra sense she seemed to be developing?

"Best man in the field? What the devil are you talking about?" Aleki demanded, "We don't have *any* men on Alton lands. The only field Intelligence man we have that's really good is Kadarin, and he and Cargill are out in the Dry Towns. Who are you talking about?"

"They call him *Dom* Ann'dra," Magda began, and broke off at the sudden fierce look of triumph on Aleki's face.

"I knew it. I knew it, damn it, for all their talk about contracts and this man being in the legitimate employ of Lord Damon! He's managed to get himself so well in there because he has no known ties with Intelligence—and there's some talk that the Darkovan nobility use psi powers, so we couldn't ever plant an undercover Intelligence man on them! They'd read him, read his mind, but this one, somehow they managed to do a *real* undercover operation; crash his plane out there, have him listed as dead, and now you say this Ann'dra—hell, I *saw* the man, running all over as Lord Damon's special sidekick, and I never spotted him myself as Intelligence!"

"I don't think it's like that at all," Magda said, remembering the man she had met in the stables that morning. This man was one of them, no longer torn between two conflicting worlds; he had found a home. "The Empire has him listed as dead. Maybe he wants it that way."

But Aleki was not listening. "I've got to find out what he knows. Just now, when we're making really crucial decisions about Darkover, he could be the key to the whole thing."

Conflicting Oaths. As much as the Renunciate Oath meant to her, she was in a sense sworn here too. She was Terran, though she did not want to be, and the thought terrified her. She rose decisively.

"I really have to go, Monty." As he rose to escort her, she shook her head. "No, no, I was finding my way around this place when you were still studying for the Service entrance exams!"

She could see that hurt him. Was he so conscious of himself as novice and of her as expert? *He doesn't deserve anything but good from me. I used him and I despise myself for it, and now I'm trying to make him feel small. What a bitch I am!* She let him put his arm round her.

"Are you going to the Festival Ball in Comyn Castle?"

"A Renunciate? My *dear!*" She had to laugh. "The people in the castle don't know we exist; they'd invite you people first!"

"Well, that is exactly what they have done," Monty began, and Aleki said, "As it happens I will be there myself; I came here to tell Monty, and that was one reason I was pleased to find you here, Miss Lorne." He handed Monty a sheet of elegant parchment.

"As you can see, it requests the Coordinator, with chosen members of his staff and suite, to attend the Ball as a gesture of good will between Terrans and Darkovers," he said, "and people who have lived here a long time, know how to behave properly, dance well and so forth—such as you, Miss Lorne."

"As a matter of fact, I did know," Monty said. "The old man mentioned it. But what with one thing and another, I never got to mention it to you, Magda." His grin struck her as oddly boyish and vulnerable, a side of him she had never seen, hiding behind the hard masks Empire men wore. Peter had shown her this side too, and she wondered if all men had it, even Darkover men like Dom Gabriel or Kyril Ardais, hiding behind the imposed roles of their society. *Men are as much trapped in their social roles as women. Aren't they?* But they at least had the benefits of those roles; it was easier to play the role of master than of slave!

Her first impulse was to refuse at once. A Renunciate at Festival Ball, and as part of the Terran delegation? If anyone who had seen her at the Guild House was there, her careful cover of half a year would go up in smoke.

But they would have to know who she was, sooner or later. She *was* Terran; why pretend she was not? And it might just be the first chance any Terran woman had ever had or would ever have—to attend Festival Ball in Comyn Castle!

"You can fill me in on everything I need to know," Aleki said, "and keep me from making any real social blunders . . ."

"And my father will be leading the delegation," said Monty, "You owe it to all of us to come and keep him from doing something disgraceful."

"Oh, surely Jaelle—or Peter—"

"I'm not sure Jaelle likes me," Aleki said, "She's civil enough, but I get the feeling somehow that she's fighting me. Haldane resents me, and I don't blame him. His career's here on this world, and I come and then I go but still he knows my report can make or break him. There's no way he's ever going to like me. I'd like to go with someone who's not hostile to me."

She sighed and nodded. "When you put it that way, of course."

"Do you have anything to wear? Or shall I have them requisition something for you?"

"I can do better than that. At Midwinter, Lady Rohana gave me a gown —I wondered when I'd ever have a chance to wear it again."

"Shall I fetch you from the Guild House?" Monty asked, and she laughed merrily.

"Heavens, no! I can imagine the talk that would cause! I love my sisters, but they have one trait I despise in women—they gossip! I don't grudge them their fun—but I don't want to be part of it either. I'll meet you in the street near the castle."

She gave Aleki her hand; Monty insisted on taking her to the door. *I like him better as a colleague than a lover. I would rather be his friend than his mistress.* Reluctantly, she let him take a farewell kiss; she did not want to hurt him.

Walking back through the streets, she remembered that Jaelle had once accused her of being too protective toward men. *Probably true,* she thought, *I'm stronger than most of the men I know, and they're so damned easy to hurt. The Amazons say it's wrong to hurt a woman; why is it right to hurt a man?*

Or have so many of them suffered so much at the hands of men—Camilla, for instance—that they no longer believe men can be hurt at all, but are always superior and invulnerable?

She could feel for Monty—alone and friendless on a strange world— because she remembered when she had been alone on the Alpha colony for training, a stranger from a pioneer world, an exotic, a difficult conquest, there were so many men who had wanted to seduce her because she was alien and different; not because of who or what she was. She had been so lonely. She was lonely now . . .

Men are so weak. Or do I surround myself with men who are weak, because the strong ones would challenge me too much?

There was no one on hall duty, but Rezi came, her hands floury from the kitchen, to let her in.

"Some of our sisters from Bellarmes Guild House are here for Festival, and you will be going to the women's dance tonight, won't you? Camilla said she was going with you."

Magda thought she really would have preferred the women's dance to the dance in the public square of Thendara, but she shook her head. "I am sorry; I am promised elsewhere. I did not think Camilla would have involved me in her plans without asking."

Rezi made a rueful gesture. "Very well; but do not come and weep in my lap if Camilla is angry with you!"

Magda flared, "I am not Camilla's property nor is she mine!"

Rezi laughed and shook her head. "You and Camilla must settle your lovers' quarrels without me."

Magda went up the stairs frowning. It had never occurred to her that Camilla might expect, or feel she had a right to expect her company at Midsummer. *I should have known. Oath-sisters are family.* If it came to that, she thought she would rather be with Camilla, or even with Rezin whom she really did not know well or like much, than with Monty and Aleki and the whole damned Terran delegation! But she had given her word, and it was important to her work.

She spread her holiday gown on the bed to air; she had showered in the Terran HQ, so she set about brushing up her short hair; while she was at it, Camilla came into the room and stopped short in delighted amazement.

"How pretty you look, *breda!* But that gown is too fine for the women's dance; our sisters from Bellarmes have been on the road for days and have only traveling-wear, and many of the women will be poor widows and the like who would live with us in the Amazon house if they could, but they have children or aging parents they must care for. Festival gowns like that would make them feel very shabby, so we usually do not dress up at all for the women's dances. Besides, dresses like that are only to attract men!"

"Oh, Camilla, I am sorry! But I cannot go to with you to the women's dance, I am expected elsewhere . . ."

Camilla's low voice was filled with ripples of amusement. "And no doubt you have been invited to Comyn Castle and Lord Hastur himself will lead you out to dance!"

Magda began weakly to giggle. "I don't know about Lord Hastur," she began, "but the truth is, Camilla . . . oh, you'll never believe this!" She broke off; she could hardly tell Camilla about the Terrans and Alessandro Li's insistence that it was her duty to come.

Fortunately Camilla assumed at once that she had had the invitation through Jaelle, who was her oath-mother; and an invitation from Comyn amounted, after all, to a royal command.

"How splendid! You must tell me all about it afterward, *breda.* You have no jewels, but I have a necklace of firestones I can lend you; it is just the color to look beautiful with that dress," she said, and went to fetch it. When Camilla brought it, Magda stared at the precious jewels.

"Camilla, it's too much, I can't take that—"

"Why not? What is mine is yours," Camilla said simply, "and it is for sure I shall never dance at Comyn Castle with the Hasturs! It was my mother's; I saw her only once after—" she hesitated, "after what I told you; but when she died, it was sent to me by a messenger. I never wear jewelry; but there is no reason it should lie forever in a box and not be displayed on the throat of a beautiful woman for once." She put it round Magda's neck, and Magda said impulsively, "You are beautiful to me, Camilla!"

Camilla laughed. "I did not know you suffered also from poor eyesight with all your other troubles," she said, but she smiled at Magda, and caught her close in a quick embrace. "The Comyn ball ends at midnight," she said, "and we will go on in the public square till dawn. Come and join us afterward."

Magda said impulsively, "I would really rather stay with you. I only wish I could."

I would. This isn't a pleasure for me, it's going back on duty. Camilla's worth any ten of them, and more fun to be with!

Camilla's face lighted. She said, "Really?" and caught Magda closer still. She held Magda tight, her face buried in Magda's hair. She whispered "Margali, Margali . . . you know I love you . . ." and could not go on. After a minute, when her voice was steady again, she said, "You are not, like Keitha, a *cristoforo*. . . . it does not horrify you . . ." and broke off again.

I should have expected this. I have been backing away from it since I came to this house. I discovered this day that it was not a man I wanted. I did not want Peter, and Monty was no better. I should have known all along. . . .

I gave myself to Monty and I did not care for him. And Camilla is my sister, my closest friend here, she has cared for me and stood by me when I was in disgrace, whenever I was alone here and needed a friend, there she stood, asking for nothing, offering me love and devotion. In the name of the Goddess herself, how can I blind myself to the truth, how can I give myself to Monty who is nothing to me, and refuse Camilla this? She kissed Camilla's soft greying curls, raised the woman's face and kissed her on the lips. Camilla smiled at her, breathless, and Magda said hesitantly, "I—I don't know—no, I am not a *cristoforo*, the idea does not—does not trouble me in that way, but I—I don't know, I never thought about it—" she fell silent, fumbling for words.

Never thought about it, that I could love my friends, instead of responding to men who are after all alien to me. . . . she knew that it was more than this, she was not certain, but if she could try to make Monty happy, when he was nothing to her, she was willing—even eager—to turn to Camilla.

"But I don't know—I have never—"

Camilla stopped her confused words with a kiss; but then, taking Magda's face between her hands, she looked at her seriously.

"Do you mean this? Even when you were a young girl, you had no *bredhya . . . ?"*

Numbly, Magda shook her head. *Never. I had no woman friend, not even an ordinary friend, not a lover, till I came to the Guild House. I did not even know that I wanted a woman for a friend until I discovered myself risking my life for Jaelle.*

It almost seemed to her that Camilla could read her thoughts a little.

"It's all right, love," she said in a whisper. "Love is a simple thing, a very simple thing . . . come and let me show you how simple."

Chapter Two

There was nothing inside the HQ to distinguish Midsummer from Midwinter. The light was the same—no windows to throw back the heavy winter draperies, no smell of baking in the air, none of the street sounds of merrymaking. But when Peter came in, she managed to find a smile for him.

From behind his back, rather self-consciously, he produced one of the baskets of fruit and flowers that vendors sold at this season in the streets. She was touched; he must have gone into the Old Town for it.

"From Midwinter to Midsummer; we have been together half a year, Jaelle. Who could forget that? And when Midwinter comes again, we shall be a family of three." He caught her close in his arms, kissing her, and she felt a flood of warmth for him. He had remembered. But it was not, quite, the old warmth. That was gone forever, and there was only emptiness where it had been. As she nibbled on a piece of the fruit, and went to find something to put the flowers in water, she wondered if this was why Renunciates vowed never to marry *di catenas;* because that first feeling went away so swiftly . . . he came up behind her, holding her familiarly and whispering in her ear.

"You must find your finest outfit," he murmured, "for dancing tonight, even if you don't do much dancing in your condition—"

"I don't really want to go to the public dance in the square," she demurred. "It's always so crowded, and there are riffraff—sometimes an Amazon will get into fights with men who want to prove something—"

"Nonsense," Peter said. "I'll be with you; do you think I would let any man lay hands on my wife? Yes, yes, I know, you're strong, your Oath says you can protect yourself, but if you think I'd let a pregnant woman fight . . . anyhow, there's no question of the public dance," he added. "It's a famous first for Darkover, darling, and I'm sure you had something to do with it. An invitation has come from Comyn Council for Montray and a delegation from the Terran Headquarters; and of course they specified you and I should make one couple, since you are Darkovan and I have worked so often in the field that I know manners, language, protocol for such things. They are trying to cement good relations by asking certain hand-picked members of the staff—"

"That would certainly leave out Russ Montray," Jaelle said, noting that her tone was acid. Peter shook his head.

"Unfortunately the Coordinator can't be left out, but an unofficial word came that I'm supposed to stick to his elbow and make sure he doesn't do anything too ghastly. And of course Monty will be there. But you're assigned to stick tight to Cholayna, since she's never been in the field and never will, and she's the only woman here with rank suitable for the Coordinator. I wish we could manage to get Magda from the Guild House but I don't suppose they'd let her go. Between us we're hoping to keep the Old Man out of trouble."

Jaelle still cringed at the disrespect in his voice. If the man was so incompetent, they should remove him from office, or at least make sure he was a figurehead without power; as Comyn Council had done with several recent kings, and she supposed they had done with *Dom* Gabriel—everyone knew Rohana had been the real power behind Ardais, for many years.

Peter directed her eyes to the invitation. "Look, we were specially requested—" and he pointed. "Mr. and Mrs. Peter Haldane. . . ."

Men dia pre'zhiuro . . . never be known again by the name of father, husband or lover . . . "Peter," she said, her voice dangerously quiet, "I am not Mrs. Peter Haldane. I am Jaelle n'ha Melora. I will not say this to you again."

He flinched, but protested. "I know that, love. But the Terrans do not understand, and why does it matter what they call you? It is a legal formality, no more. They probably looked at your name on the payroll lists—don't blame *me* for it."

She let the paper drop with a curious sense of finality. *My whole identity gone. Not Jaelle n'ha Melora. Not even Jaelle, daughter of Jalak. Just an attachment of Peter Haldane, wife, mother of his child. . . . I am no one. Not here. Peter is right. It doesn't matter.*

She saw him relax. "I was sure you'd be reasonable," he said. "That's my good girl." Clearly without speech she heard him say, *I knew you'd see it my way.* "What are you going to wear? You can't go in uniform, or in Amazon breeches. . . ."

"I suppose I shall wear the green gown Rohana gave me at Midwinter," she said, trying to recapture the excitement of their first dance together, but he did not even remember; he shook his head and said "That's been seen; for this you should have something new and special."

"I have dresses at home in the Guild House, but my own clothes would not fit me now." She looked ruefully at her thickening waist. "But Rafaella and I have always worn one another's clothes, and she is heavier than I; her dresses will fit me perfectly now, and she would be glad to lend me one."

How she had twitted Rafaella when her waist had thickened and she could not wear Jaelle's clothes!

"I can't let you borrow somebody else's used clothes!"

"Piedro, don't be absurd, what are sisters for?"

"My wife does not have to *borrow* clothes, or wear an old, worn dress!"

"Piedro," she said, reasonably, "Rafaella dresses very well, she never wears a Festival gown more than once or twice, and no one here has seen any of them, they might as well be new." It seemed that Piedro was two men again, her lover, and this crazy Terran with his absurd prejudices and notions, standing between her and her beloved Piedro. "Be reasonable, Piedro. Where in Thendara would we find a dressmaker who would make us a gown on Festival itself? I must either wear my old green gown—though I cannot think of a gown I have worn but once as *old*—borrow one from Rafaella—or wear my old breeches," she finished, laughing. "There is no other choice!"

"I hadn't thought of that. It *is* short notice, isn't it?" He frowned, then his eyes lit up. "I know, we'll go down to Costuming and get them to make up something; it isn't a holiday here. Let me have the green gown—we'll have it copied in some other fabric; do you like blue?"

That took the rest of the day, with barely a moment to snatch a bite of dinner before it was time to get dressed. It seemed to Jaelle that she was always at something in haste—food, hello-good-bye, a shower, piece of paper with important message, a piece of clothing, a minute for lovemaking. She was getting heartily sick of it, but it wouldn't do to be too late; by the time the dress was sent up by messenger, carefully wrapped in plastic sheeting, she was saving seconds, and looking wistfully at the comfortable trail leathers as she brushed out the curls in her hair. As the yards and yards of skirt spilled from the box, Jaelle gasped; it was exquisite, low-cut, trimmed with marl-fur and embroideries. Then, looking more closely, she realized it was not spider-silk, nor fur . . . there was not an inch of honest thread in it. Just chemicals, all artificial, like all Terran clothing. Darkovan made, it would have cost a season's income from a good-sized estate, but it was a sham, a fraud.

"Peter, I can't wear this!"

But he was in the shower and could not hear, and by the time he had turned off the water, she knew she could not refuse. He had spent a week's pay on having it made up so quickly; he could have requisitioned it from Costume as a work expense and turned it back for recycling afterward, but he knew her aversion to recycling things and had paid for it and arranged for her to keep it as a Midsummer-gift.

Yet how could she wear this artificial gown? She would look like a Terran masquerading as Darkovan. . . . *well, that is what I am. Mrs. Peter Haldane. Part of the Terran delegation.* As she struggled with the hooks, she wrinkled her nose; it didn't smell right. She rummaged in her drawer, bringing out the small silken sachet packet Magda had given her. Her first sewing project, Magda had told her, apologizing for the crooked stitches; the uneven straggling stitchery reminded Jaelle suddenly of Camilla, her first year in the Guild House, teaching a small bewildered Drytown child to sew.

I always thought I would grow up in chains. I had forgotten that. She remembered her first year in the house; maturity had come upon her. In the Guild House it was a happy celebration, admitting her to the company of women, where in Shainsa it would have meant she would be ceremonially chained. *Yet here I am again in chains . . .* and she was horrified at herself. Kindra had said it so often; it was better to wear chains in truth than to weight yourself with invisible chains and pretend that you are free. *Oh, mother, mother, I wish I could talk to you. . . . I cannot even remember my own mother's face. Only Kindra's . . .*

"What are you doing, *chiya?*" Peter asked, coming out of the shower, naked, and starting to get into his breeches. She showed him the sachet and he nodded.

"I've seen Magda do that; she used to buy all her clothes in the old Town when she could—she said the stuff from Costume never smelled right—and she never took off a dress without rubbing the seams with sweet spice, and she taught me to do it too." She caught the familiar scent of incense from his cloak as he slung it about his shoulders.

"That's what's wrong with Aleki," Jaelle said abruptly. "His clothes come from Costume; he doesn't smell right in them."

"Right; I knew there was something and I couldn't put my finger on it," Peter said. "I'll mention it to him, shall I? Might come better from a man —you look lovely, *preciosa.* Let's go."

In the walk across the marketplace, though a few members of the delegation complained about the rough cobblestone and holiday footwear, Jaelle began to believe that it was Midsummer; the familiar smells and sounds, the Festival crowds. Even through the lights which blazed in the

Old Town she could see the four moons, all nearing full together. Their invitation was accepted at the doorway and she heard musicians already playing. A few professional dancers were already giving displays of dancing, while the guests drifted around the floor, greeting friends; then the first general dance began and Jaelle let Peter swing her out on the floor. The new dress felt lighter than a dress of honest fabric; she felt as if she were floating, as if tensions she had not known she had were dissolving.

She had never before danced in Comyn Castle at Festival. She had renounced this heritage, had spent her life among the Renunciates and their simpler Festival celebrations. Yet she might come here again and again, if she did as Rohana asked, and took a Council seat. *And it would please Peter so* . . . in shock, she realized that she was actually considering it, and the shock was followed by a sharp wave of dizziness, almost but not quite nausea.

"*Chiya,* what's the matter?"

She smiled at him, faintly. "Its a nuisance, being pregnant. I need air—"

"Sit here—by the open door. I'll get you a drink," he said, and she sighed with relief as she let herself collapse there. "I don't really want—" she began, but he was already gone, hurrying toward the buffet table.

She was near the balcony doors; and it was very warm. She went out on the balcony, leaning against the stone rail, breathing in the night fog. The multicolored moonlight turned the fog to pearly rainbows. She could smell the heavy scent of flowers, and the soft chirring of insects. It was so pleasant, after weeks of sterile indoor smells and yellow harsh Terran lights. She sat still on the bench. Soon she must go inside or Peter would worry when he could not find her. But it felt so good to sit here and breathe in all the smells of the summer. Momentarily, she dozed, then snapped awake, hearing a voice she could not reconcile with the smells of the Castle garden. Alessandro Li; an angry whisper in Standard.

"I told you he would be here! What luck!"

"Alessandro—Aleki—hasn't Jaelle been able to teach you anything? He is the son-in-law of Lord Alton; you simply cannot approach him and start asking impertinent questions about the private business of the Domain—" It was Magda! What was Magda doing here?

"You don't understand, Magda. This man is the key to everything I was sent here to find out about Darkover. Carr knows—"

"This man is *Dom* Ann'dra Lanart, and that is what you must deal with," Magda said sharply. "I don't know if he's Carr or not—"

"Well, I do; personnel pictures. And who else would he be? You said yourself he was Terran!"

"Pictures be damned," Magda said, and then Jaelle heard Monty's voice.

"He may or he may not be the one you are looking for, Sandro. But you can't approach him here, and that's all there is to it. Dance with him, Magda; that's what we're here for, not to make trouble."

"I'm hardly going to make trouble," Aleki said, but Jaelle could hear that he was angry. "I simply must talk to him; why don't you help me find a way to do it, instead of being so damned stubborn?"

"You are hardly the one to talk about being damned stubborn," Magda said angrily, "Once and for all, get it out of your head, and stop thinking like a damned Terran, with your mind on business even at a Festival ball!"

"Magdalen Lorne!" That was the voice of the elder Montray, being heavily jocular, "Is that any way to talk to your superior, and at a party too? You look smashing. Monty, why didn't you tell me you'd hunted her up and talked her into coming? I might have pulled rank on you, son, and grabbed her for my escort myself!"

"Cholayna," Magda said, and Jaelle could hear the relief in her voice, "How charming you look. Are you here with the coordinator?"

Cholayna's gentle, neutral voice said, "Not nearly so many stares as I had expected. I don't know whether it is simply good manners, or whether they just expect that Terrans will look freakish."

"If they're so narrow-minded they'd stare at you because your skin color is different," Alessandro Li said, "then to hell with them all. They're just a bunch of ignorant natives after all. Hullo, Haldane, where's your lovely lady?"

"She felt a little faint," Peter said. "I left her by the doors while I went to get her something cool to drink."

Jaelle, knowing this was her cue, picked herself up and went back inside the balcony doors. "I went out for a breath of air. It was very warm in there." She accepted the glass Peter put in her hand and sipped. It was the pale mountain wine, and it made her think of their first dance, at Midwinter. She wondered if Peter remembered. Magda was wearing the rust-colored gown she had worn at Midwinter, with a superb necklace of fire-stones; Jaelle went to examine this.

"Did Camilla lend you this? It is exquisite," she said. "I have seen it among her treasures; she let me wear it at the party in the Guild House when I took my oath. . . ." and as she mentioned Camilla's name, she saw something she could not identify; trouble, unease . . . *fear?* What was troubling Magda? She could still see it, as an uneasy haze, when Monty came and demanded a dance, and as they moved away, she saw the way Monty's hand glided to Magda's bare neck, the way he hovered over her, an intensity almost sexual . . . *what is the matter with me, why am I seeing things like this? It can hardly be a side effect of pregnancy; at least it's not one I ever heard about!*

"We've got to think of a way to get that girl back," said Alessandro Li, "No offense, Haldane, but she's worth any ten other employees in Intelligence; the girl's a genius, we can't let her waste herself in the field like this! She deserves a holiday, certainly, but we can't take the chance she'll go over the wall! That seems to be what happened to Carr; he certainly isn't listed as being on detached or undercover status! Yet every damn time I spotted Carr and tried to move in on him tactfully, Magda would drag me off for another dance."

"But Magda is right," Jaelle said gently. "Even if this Carr is someone you wish to know, there is a right and a wrong way to make someone's acquaintance. Even at Midsummer, you cannot possibly walk up to *Dom* Ann'dra Lanart and say, 'Hi, Andy, what's new?' " Savagely, she mimicked the Terran's accent, and Peter cringed.

"I don't know why not," Montray said. "I wouldn't be that crude, of course, but surely I could speak to an old employee—not that he was ever in my department—and request him to do me the courtesy of coming in to straighten out his legal status. There are standards of manners among Terrans too—even if you do not think so, Mrs. Haldane. I am sorry we have made such a bad impression on you." And as Magda and Monty returned, the Coordinator touched Magda on the shoulder.

"Miss Lorne. I would like to remind you that both Alessandro Li and myself outrank you very much; and I am going to make it an official order. Find us a way to communicate with the man Carr, and do it before we leave here."

She said icily, "May I remind you that at the moment I am officially on leave, and that I am here as a favor?"

"You are here officially under my orders, like every Terran on this planet," said Montray grimly, "and that includes Andrew Carr. I don't know why we are handling this man with gloves; he is, after all, a citizen of the Empire . ."

"Once and for all, he is *not,*" Magda said, "I took the trouble to check his legal status. He is carried on the rolls as *dead,* and legal death, carries legal termination of citizenship . . . and legally, termination of citizen's privileges carries also freedom from citizen's duties . . ."

"If you are going to argue legalities," said Montray, "he is a year away from being legally dead; he is *presumed* dead for one more year; after another year he may be legally dead. There is a difference."

"No," Peter said. "On the Darkovan side a man is who he says he is, unless he has committed a crime."

"That's rubbish and you know it," Montray said. "You've spent too much time in the Darkovan sector and you are going native. And you,

Miss Lorne, are going to obey orders or you can be shipped offplanet—it's as simple as that."

Magda said, trapped and furious, "If you want a scandal which will insure that we are not only the first Terran delegation invited here, but also the last, you let those orders stand! In a specific matter involving protocol in the field—and you can't deny that we are in the field—a resident expert has a legal right to override even a direct order from a Legate, if said order would damage the reputation and credit of the Terran Empire. And, take it from me, this one would."

Sobered, he stared at her, and Jaelle knew Magda was right. But would either of them back down? At last Li said heavily "What's the proper protocol for approaching him, then?"

"An introduction must be made by a mutual acquaintance," Magda said, "and the one of higher rank must initiate the introduction. The Regent of Alton is not here this year—I have heard that his lady is ill—and *Dom* Ann'dra is here as his personal delegate."

"Can't you see," Cholayna said gently, "that is exactly why we must talk to him before he disappears again. Any Terran who can work himself so strongly into the hierarchy of a Domain—I am not the expert you are, Magda, but I know it is extraordinary."

She said slowly, "If he is a member of the household of the Regent of Alton, your best choice would be to send a man in the field to Armida, and ask for a private interview with *Dom* Ann'dra—not with Andrew Carr— and make certain that the interview was private; *then* broach your business. Treat him as if he were a field agent whose cover you were reluctant to disturb."

"I hardly have time for that—" Alessandro Li said, but old Montray sighed. "You're right, at that. I guess I'm getting too old for this job, Lorne. And I'm used to having you as my right hand."

"We can arrange that," Cholayna said, "but it will take time. . . ."

"We have plenty of that," Monty said, "Carr—Dom Ann'dra, I mean— isn't going to run away. He's evidently well established there and highly visible." He touched Magda's hand and moved closer to her. "And if we stand here arguing all night, the Darkovans will surely think we are plotting against them. I suggest we dance. May I—"

Jaelle, watching them closely, saw again the tension between them; but the elder Montray moved in. "Rank has its privileges," he said with heavy-handed jocularity. "My turn for a dance, Magda. I wouldn't step out on this floor with anyone else, but you know how to make me look acceptable."

Peter, also reminded of duty, said to Cholayna, "Would you like to dance?" and left Jaelle talking to Alessandro Li, who promptly asked her for a dance.

"Do you mind if I don't? I'm still a little short of breath," she said. She stood fanning herself, watching the dancers. The music came to an end; her eyes went to where Cholayna and Peter had come to halt, near the buffet.

"Who is the lady who came to speak to Haldane?" Aleki asked suddenly, and Jaelle saw, with surprise, that Lady Rohana had left the line of dowagers and approached Peter and Cholayna.

"She is my kinswoman—my mother's foster-sister," said Jaelle, "Lady Rohana Ardais—"

"And the man beside her?"

"Her son. My cousin Kyril. Yes, I know of the resemblance," she said, and indeed it was stronger than ever; Peter in his Terran dress uniform, his cropped red hair bright in the room, and Dom Kyril, his hair slightly longer, curling about his earlobes; Dom Kyril bowed stiffly and she saw him say something polite to Cholayna, and all at once it seemed that the space between them in the room melted as if she was standing by Peter's side, and Rohana spoke beside her ear.

Is Jaelle here tonight, Piedro? I was hoping to speak with her about taking her seat in Council—she did tell you that she is now expected to attend Council as one of the few remaining in direct succession to the Aillard Domain, I suppose?

Jaelle felt herself turn white. She had not wanted Peter to know that; she had carefully not spoken of it. The room around her suddenly went fuzzy and dim and Magda was suddenly holding her arm.

"What is it, *breda?* Are you still feeling faint? Perhaps you should not have come to anything as crowded as this," Magda said solicitously. "Please, sit down again, we'll sit here for a little while and talk. I wouldn't think Peter would have dragged you here tonight if you weren't feeling well, as strongly as he feels about having a child. . . ."

Jaelle, through Magda's touch on her shoulder, could feel the other woman's thoughts, the sharp regret, *you are doing what I could not manage to do, giving him that child* . . . "How did you know? Did Marisela tell you?"

Magda shook her head. "No; she did not mention it. Were you in the Guild House?"

"While you were on the fire lines, *breda;* I was worried about you," Jaelle said.

"It was not she who told me, it was Monty; I was in the Terran HQ today, making a report," Magda said, and told Jaelle how Monty had come to the Guild House, and how she had happened to be invited. She left out a certain private half-hour, but Jaelle, with that frightening new awareness, picked it up anyhow, and was shocked. She didn't want to know. Why had Magda told her this? But Magda *hadn't.* She had picked it up from the other woman's mind. *Laran* again. To ward away her uneasiness she said flippantly, "Just like a Terran; working all day even at Midsummer!"

Magda lowered her voice and said, "We'd better speak Darkovan."

"I thought we were," Jaelle said. "Is it normal, Margali, to be so confused? Those machines—I never know, any more, which language I am speaking. . . ."

"That could be one of the side effects of the corticator," Magda began, and stopped, as if frozen; to cover it, she took a couple of wine glasses from a servant circulating with a full tray.

"There is *Dom* Ann'dra," she said, and Jaelle, following her eyes, saw a small group of men in the colors of the Alton Domain, with a tall man, fair as a Dry-Towner, at their center. Was Magda seriously trying to tell her that this man was the renegade Terran who had supposedly gone down with the plane, and reappeared somewhere in Alton lands, in the service of the Alton Regent? Chewing her lip, Magda said, "I must speak with him, warn him. He said that he would be leaving the city at dawn . . ." and Jaelle no longer bothered to question how Magda knew. But as Magda started to move away from the bench Jaelle tugged at her hand.

"You were just lecturing them on protocol; how can you—"

"But I do know him," Magda said. "He saved my life on the fire lines. And he came to the Guild House this morning to bring Ferrika there. . . ."

"I do not know Ferrika at all," Jaelle said. "She took the oath at Neskaya, but is she not Marisela's oath-daughter? And yet she was traveling with this *Dom* Ann'dra, whoever he is—" Jaelle was frowning, confused, but Magda murmured, *"Breda—"* and Jaelle was touched, knowing Magda rarely used the word with that inflection, "—trust me. I promise I will explain later."

And she moved toward the man she had called *Dom* Ann'dra.

And then Jaelle saw something which made her realize why she could never be Magda's replacement, or even her equal, in the Terran Zone. As she moved into Ann'dra's visual field, Magda was a very proper and ladylike Darkovan woman, except for the short-cropped Amazon curls. Then, for perhaps a half a second, just as Ann'dra's eyes lighted on her, she became transformed into a Terran; it was as if Jaelle could see through the Darkovan lady, who might have been Comyn of the second rank, to the woman standing there, as if in the half-naked Terran uniform, a perfect representative of the Empire. And then again she was a correctly courteous Darkovan noblewoman, bowing to a Comyn noble and tacitly asking permission to approach him.

Dom Ann'dra bowed over Magda's hand. Jaelle was not close enough to hear any of what they were saying, though it was low-voiced and quick, but she was confused again, surely this man was a Comyn noble, how could anyone possibly believe him Terran? Then Magda was back at her side again, and they were drifting together toward the buffet table, and Jaelle found that she had one sharp impression in her mind of *Dom* Ann'dra, Comyn or Terran; a tall powerful man, fair-haired, not handsome, but with an impression of immense power and self-confidence. It reminded her of—she searched in her mind for impressions—of the time when she had been presented, as a child, to Lorill Hastur, Regent of Comyn. He had been a small, quiet man, soft-spoken, almost diffident—or perhaps that was only good manners. But nevertheless she had the impression, behind the courteous quiet facade, of almost awesome personal power, kept perfectly controlled. It was what she associated with Comyn. *Dom* Gabriel had never had it, but then, he had been, since she knew him, an invalid. But that a Terran should have it? Nonsense; it must be only a trick of his great height and enormously powerful frame. The buffet was all but deserted; Jaelle scooped up a cup of some fruit drink but when she put it to her lips it was too sweet and she set it aside almost untasted.

"Look," Magda said, "I think he is leaving." And indeed *Dom* Ann'dra and the man with him were bowing before Prince Aran Elhalyn as if taking formal leave.

"It doesn't make any difference, you know," Jaelle said abruptly. "That man could talk all day to Montray, or to Aleki, without giving anything away that he didn't want them to know."

Magda was filling a small dish at the buffet with an assortment of fruits in cream. It looked delicious, and Jaelle looked at the other colorful delicacies almost wistfully, wishing she could manage to feel hungry enough to try them.

Magda said, "Can't you see? That's why I had to keep them apart. No matter what he told Li, it would be wrong; what's the old proverb, it takes two for the truth, one to speak true and one to hear? Alessandro Li has made up his own mind about Carr; the truth is beyond him. What he wants is an excuse to have the Comyn declare Carr *persona non grata* so that Li could wring him out and find out everything he thinks Ann'dra can tell him about the Comyn. Then the Altons would have a grudge against the Terrans that would last for generations. And if Carr made up the lies Alessandro expects to hear he'd find some way to twist it . . ." Magda broke off, and Jaelle could almost hear her say, *I am disloyal, disloyal to my own people as I have been disloyal to everyone,* and her dismay stabbed with real pain at Jaelle.

She is my sister, and I cannot help her because I myself am so filled with confusion!

Magda gasped, "God above!" and abruptly she was thrusting through the crowd, muttering apologies. Jaelle, following slowly with her plate in hand, saw that Alessandro Li and Russell Montray, Peter hurrying behind them, were approaching Carr's party near the door. Peter caught at the Coordinator's shoulder, expostulating with him in a whisper, but Montray wrenched loose.

He walked up directly to Carr and said something in a low voice.

Jaelle could not hear what Dom Ann'dra said in reply; she saw only the frosty politeness in his voice. Montray said something loud and aggressive this time, and Dom Ann'dra's two bodyguards closed in, one on either side, clearly ready to protect their lord from this bumptious alien.

The tension was now plain enough to draw attention from onlookers, as Montray said, clearly enough for Jaelle to hear every word, "Look, I just need to talk to you for a few minutes; I'm sure you don't want to do it in front of everybody here, do you? But I'll do it that way if you leave me no alternative . . ."

Peter grabbed him urgently, physically hauling him backward, and Ann'dra's bodyguards closed in, their intent and threat unmistakable. Suddenly a little murmur ran through the crowd, and Aran Elhalyn, prince of the Domains, between his aide and young Danvan Hastur, came toward them, the crowd parting with little respectful murmurs to either side. Magda caught Alessandro Li by the shoulder and said something urgent in an undertone, and Li turned and bowed to the nobles. He was speaking Terran Standard and Magda, at his elbow—and Jaelle noticed, it was very clearly the *Terran* Magda again—translated in fluent *casta;*

"Majesty, your pardon is humbly beseeched; this matter will be attended in private; and we gravely regret any disturbance." Even before Magda finished speaking, Prince Aran waved a negligent hand, dismissing the matter, and turned away, and Alessandro Li said in a savage undertone, "Montray, damn it, one more word and I'll make damn sure you never get another post except punching buttons in a penal colony!"

Jaelle wondered how she could hear at this distance. It didn't matter. Peter came and guided her to the rest of the delegation. The music had surged up again and a group of cadets in black and green were dancing some kind of energetic dance with a lot of stamping and kicking; Prince Aran had withdrawn to watch them.

Dom Ann'dra and his party were gone. Peter shook his head and muttered "That tears it. Everybody knows what Montray is. Nobody has taken official notice of it before now—"

Russell Montray was muttering, "I am going to make an official appeal to Lord Hastur. That man is a Terran citizen and I demand the right to speak to him officially—"

"Let it alone sir," Monty said quietly, "before you get us all expelled from here. Haldane knows what he's talking about. And so does Magda—"

Montray turned on them both in a fury. "And I've had enough of both of those damned so-called experts, and their insubordination," he snarled, in a grim undertone. "I've put up with it, and knuckled under to the way you go around bootlicking the natives, just about long enough! Because you think you are rated *expert*, you think you can get away with anything! Well, I have heard enough and I mean enough! The minute I get back to HQ I am going to put through a formal request to have both of you transferred out, as far as I can, somewhere in the other end of the Galaxy, and I'll make damn sure neither of you ever gets clearance to get back! I still have that much authority, and I should have done it a long time ago! As for you, Lorne, I want you back on HQ and under orders tonight. Not tomorrow. Tonight."

"I am officially on leave," Magda began.

"Leave canceled," he snapped. "Recalled to active duty under orders under Section 16-4—"

"To hell with that," Magda said, and to Jaelle it seemed that visible, electrical sparks were flying from her eyes and creating a field of light all round her, "I resign. Cholayna, witness it. I'm sorry, it has nothing to do with you—"

"Magda," said Monty, putting his arm around her waist, "Honey, listen to me. Everybody calm down. Father—" he addressed the angry Montray, "this is neither the time nor the place—"

"I've calmed down and listened for the last time in my life; don't you think I know what everybody here thinks, that I'm just a figurehead and no one has to listen to me? Well, it's about time I stopped listening to that shit! This whole damned planetary administration has been mismanaged for forty years, we've been handling people with gloves and it's about time we made them realize that they can't face up to the Terran Empire that way. There's going to be a new deal around here. I am going to have some new Intelligence people here, people whose main loyalty is to the Empire, and I want a clean sweep of the people who have been mismanaging everything so badly! As for you, Haldane, I knew when you married a native woman that your judgment and loyalty had gone to hell, and I should have fired you right then. And I'm going to be rid of all of you if it's the last thing I do."

"It probably will be, sir," said Alessandro Li. "The way Darkover is being handled at Central is a matter of very high policy," but Montray was too angry to listen.

"Then, damn it, maybe I can get transferred out myself—which I've been trying to do for seven years!" He turned and strode away; Peter said, numbly, "Good God," and turned to Jaelle.

"Darling. Go back with Li and Monty, will you? I've got to get to him before he gets that request sent through Empire channels or we're all in the porridge pot. We can appeal, but by that time—"

Monty put a hand on Magda's arm. "Don't worry about the Old Man. He'll calm down. Haven't you ever seen him in a tantrum before?"

"I was dealing with his tantrums when you were doing entrance examinations for the Service," Magda said wearily, "but I've just dealt with the last one. I meant it, Monty. I resign. And I have to back inside the Guild House by sunrise—"

"I'll go with you and spend the night in the Guild House," Jaelle said, but Peter seized her shoulders.

"No, Jaelle! Don't fight me now, for the love of God! Go back to the Terran Zone and wait; I've never needed loyalty so much—what kind of wife are you, anyhow? For my sake, for the baby's sake—I'm fighting for all of us!"

The baby. I had forgotten. What can I do? I have no choice now. Alessandro Li said, "Let me escort you home, Jaelle," and she slumped against him. All she wanted was to run through the streets to the Guild House, run *home*—but it was not her home anymore. Why was she deceiving herself?

Peter had hurried away after the Montrays. She never remembered that walk back through the streets of Thendara, only that they were filled with gaiety, crowds laughing, drinking, dancing, tossing flowers. When she was in her quarters alone, she found small flowers caught in the folds of the imitation dress in which she had danced so gaily.

She found herself thinking, with a bitterness that astonished her, *I hope they do send him offworld, I hope I never have to see him again. Never think again of my failure. My failure? No, his; he loves no one, he thinks only of his own ambition and his own work . . .*

She told herself she was not being fair. Her needs and Peter's had been so different, they had really had no chance; but they had been blinded by passion. She had never known a man before. She had not been prepared for the all-encompassing pull of love—of sex, if she must be perfectly honest with herself. She had been ready for a love affair; and she had not been able to admit that it was no more than that. But they each had needs the other could not meet. He had needed—if he needed anything—a woman content to further his ambition, to be there when he needed her and patiently stand aside when he did not. He was not cruel or heartless; he was a kind and good man. But the magical togetherness and blending she imagined had never been there; or it had been there only a little while and she had imagined that it continued only because she had needed so much to feel it there.

If she had truly loved him, friendship and kindliness and shared goals could have come to take the place of that first blinding passion. They could have accepted this new level of closeness, enough to build a pleasant life together, as even Gabriel and Rohana had done. But Gabriel and Rohana, whose marriage had been arranged, had never been led to expect anything more, and had never been blinded by that first rush of passion. She and Peter had had nothing more, and when that was gone, nothing was left.

Nothing left—except Peter's child. Poor unwanted child, perhaps it would be better if it was never born. No, it was not unwanted; Peter wanted it. And she really had wanted it too, for a little while. Or perhaps it was her body, ready to exercise its natural function, which had wanted the child. *Any child. Not just Peter's.*

Now she could see why Magda and Peter had not stayed together. To Peter a woman was a necessary convenience, a background to his ego. Suddenly she felt sorry for him. He needed women, but he needed them to be all wrapped up in him in a way neither of them could be. She was sorry for the thing in Peter which attracted strong women to take care of him. She supposed it had been happening all his life, but when he had them he must weaken and destroy them because he feared their strength.

It did not matter now. It was over, as this Festival Night was over.

But I am sworn, for the legal term of my employment. Because Peter is false to what he has promised, must I be false too? She had at least known enough not to marry him *di catenas*. Freemate marriage could be dissolved at will; among the Terrans there were a few legal formalities. She was still responsible for Monty, and for Aleki. And after that disastrous near-meeting with *Dom* Ann'dra, or Andrew Carr, or whoever he was, who knew what either of them would do? By the Amazon oath she was not liable to any man. . . .

She had been with the Terrans too long. Now the Amazon Oath too seemed too constricting. She had taken the Oath when she was too young to know what it meant. But could she now forswear it because she had outgrown it? That was not the honorable way. Rohana had said, *honor is abiding by those oaths even when it is no longer convenient.* But Rohana, for her own purposes, would bind her to the greater slavery to Council and

Comyn; she could not trust Rohana completely, any more than she could trust the Terrans.

She did not want to wait for Peter to come in. Nor did she care how his confrontation with Coordinator Montray had come out. He had created the problem for himself and must now deal with it as best he could. He was perfectly competent in his own way, he did not need her help, and if she thought that he did, that was just one more symptom of what had gone wrong between them. There was such a deep sadness in her, because all the sweetness had gone awry. But Kindra had always said; *there is no use fretting after last winter's snow.* And the love they had shared was further away than that.

Quickly she dressed herself in uniform, checking the small communication device built into the collar. How quickly habits grew! She remembered how she had resented this. She would go down to the cafeteria and find something to eat, then go to Cholayna's office and try to work out some new arrangement. The Darkovan women who would soon be coming here to work in Medic would live outside the walls, and come here only to work, surely they would let her do the same. Part of her knew she would miss the conveniences of the Terran way of life.

She was fastening the final tab on her collar when she heard Peter's step. She could see, as he walked in, that he was very drunk. She shivered; once when Kyril was drunk he had tried to molest her and she had had to defend herself. To this day she hated drunkenness. But Peter only flung a surprisingly vicious curse at her.

"Peter, what's the matter? What did you find out from Montray? Where have you been?"

He looked her straight in the eye. "What the hell do you care?" he said, and pushed past her. She heard the shower running.

Part of her wanted to stay and have it out with him when he was sober. Another part did not care. She said "You're right, I don't," knowing he could not hear her over the running water, and went out.

Chapter Three

Magda moved slowly through the streets of the Old Town, Cholayna's words still in her ears; she had promised to wait, to think over her resignation when the older woman could come and talk to her in the Guild House but she wished she had not. She wished she could flee back to the company of her sisters in the Guild House and never return to the Terran world at all. The effort to confront old loyalties again had taken its toll of her.

After the half year free of the conflicts between men and women, even the most casual contacts between the sexes now seemed strange and abnormal to her; she found herself examining the least of them for nuances. Of course, that was what the housebound time was all about, to break old habits, to examine life rather than living mindlessly by old patterns laid down in childhood.

She had half promised to meet Camilla at the women's dance . . . was that where her loyalties now lay? Suddenly she was troubled again. She was a trained scientist, a skilled professional, what was she doing here, after a day spent in using the special skills she had trained for. Was she seriously thinking of giving it all up, going back to obey their silly damn rules, mucking out barns, asking permission to step outside the garden? She thought wearily that if she had a grain of sense she would go back to the HQ, put in for transfer—Montray had threatened her with it anyhow —and get right away from a world she desired and hated and of which she could never be a real part.

Would she really be able to give up the Renunciates? Seriously, now, without worrying about things like stables and bathrooms. She had discovered a kind of solidarity which she had never known, a world of women. If that world was small and petty in many ways, built on denial and restraint, by women who thought themselves free but were bound in a hundred small ways, what life was entirely free? And there were amazing freedoms in that life. In all her twenty-seven years she had never found a world so near to fulfilling all her dreams and needs; could she leave it because it was not perfect?

Who was the Terran philosopher who had written that since no man could be free, that man could be counted fortunate who could find a slavery to his liking? The Comhi' Letzii, the Sisterhood of the Unbound, had at least chosen for themselves.

As I choose. . . .

And there was Camilla to be considered, too . . . she had avoided thinking about Camilla, yet Camilla was one of the reasons, she knew, why she now wished to take flight.

Within a single day, in the sudden freedom of Midsummer, she had broken through her self-chosen isolation; first with Monty—and she was still not sure why she had done that, though it had seemed reasonable enough at the time—and then with Camilla. She had been astonished at herself—even now her mind shrank from confronting all the new things she had discovered about herself. But now she knew why she had fled, in panic, from Jaelle's touch.

I was not ready to know that. I am not ready now.

Even now she could not identify herself as a lover of women, she could never embrace all the narrowness of women like Rezi or Janetta, who considered only women to be fully human, and considered the slightest contact with a male, even father, brother or employer, as treason to their sisterhood. Even Camilla was not like that. But she could not look down on the Rezis and Janettas either, knowing what she knew. And they were her sisters too. She could turn her back on them only by turning her back on the Guild House forever.

And she could not do that. They had accepted her, given to her, a stranger, all the sisterhood and friendliness and love she had hardly known how to accept. But now the housebound time was nearly over. Camilla at least must know her real identity. To any or all of the others she could lie, but Camilla deserved honesty from her. Camilla must know the truth, even if her love turned to rejection and revulsion.

It was late; most of the revelry in the open streets had subsided, though in the public squares and gardens, she knew, the dancing and drinking and feasting would continue most of the night. Even now, in dark buildings and entry-ways, she could sense the warmth and sweetness of the night, where the four moons floated brilliantly overhead and couples enlaced, lovers for an hour or a lifetime, in search of somewhere to end the night together. Peter, she thought, this time without bitterness, and Jaelle. Magda turned her eyes away from the many couples and sighed. It seemed that all of Thendara was coupled this night, and only she was alone. She need not have been alone, Monty would have been happy, if, the troubles of this night ended, she had been waiting for him in his quarters. Then she need never face what was awaiting her in the Guild House, or at the women's dance . . .

I should have gone with Camilla anyhow. I never should have let Monty talk me into going to the damned Festival Ball. What is it to me, any more, what the relations are between the damned Comyn aristocracy, and the Empire?

Surely this was the street and the house where the women's dance was to be held? But the place was dark, locked, silent and forbidding, and Magda stared at it with dismay. *What do I do now?* Then she heard laughter and voices: down the street light flooded from the open doors of a wineshop whose clientele had spilled over into the street, and instruments were playing; against the light, shadowy forms were dancing in a ring-dance on the uneven cobbles.

It was very late. At one table a knot of Guardsmen were gathered, some of them with women; at another, two tables had been pushed together and Magda recognized many of the women. Mother Lauria was there, and Rafaella, but she got up and went to dance with one of the Guardsmen as Magda approached. Camilla was there with a glass in her hand, and Keitha and Marisela in their working clothes, with the white coifs all midwives wore in the city, tied around their hair. Keitha raised her glass and beckoned.

"Come and sit with us, Margali—it is lucky to be born under the four moons, and it seems that half the women in the city are eager to give their babes that luck! But any mother who has not dropped her burden by now is probably too drunk to go into labor this night—let us follow!"

Magda accepted a drink from the pitcher on the table, and one of the young Guardsmen at the farther table came over to them.

"Well met under the four moons, Margali! Do you remember me? We met in the winter past at Castle Ardais, and now I have taken employment here in the city—remember, we knew one another as children at Caer Donn, you had dancing lessons with my sisters—I am Darrell of Darnak; will you come and drink with me?"

She smiled, letting him bow over her hand. "I am sorry, but my sisters are waiting for me—"

He looked at her with comical disappointment. "All night I have traveled around the city looking for you. When you have greeted your friends and quenched your thirst, will you dance with me?"

Magda hesitated, glancing at Camilla, who said, "Dance if you like, child." She smiled up at Darrell, saying, "We are companions of the sword; may I offer you a drink?"

"I think I have already had too much to drink, but will you favor me with a dance, *mestra?*"

Camilla chuckled. "I do not dance with men, brother. But I am sure there are others in our company who would be pleased."

Marisela rose, laughing, and moved toward him. "I have been busy all this day, and have had small chance for merrymaking. But Festival Night must not pass without a dance or two. If my sister will introduce me—I cannot dance with a man whose name is unknown to me!"

Magda laughed and presented Darrell to Marisela who looked flushed, pretty, younger than she was in her blue gown; she pushed the white coif back so that her short copper-colored hair stood out in curls around her face. Darrell bowed and pulled her into the circle-dance that was forming in the street; Janetta pulled Mother Lauria into the circle, too, but Camilla shook her head as they gestured her and Magda to join them.

"You look tired, Margali," said Camilla, "but very pretty. How was the great ball? Were all the great folk of Comyn there? And the Lady Rohana? And Shaya, was she there with her freemate? What sort of man is he?"

"Yes, they were both there," Magda said, wondering how to answer Camilla's question; what could she say to Camilla about Peter Haldane? "But Jaelle looked very tired, I think—she is pregnant, you know."

"Little Jaelle, with a baby of her own!" Camilla said, diverted as Magda had hoped. "Only a season or two ago, it seemed, I cut her hair for her and gave her her first lessons with the knife. I suppose she will return to the House for the birth?"

Some of the partnerless Guardsmen had come up and asked the remaining Amazons to dance; it seemed that another, impromptu party was in the making. Some of the women danced together instead. But a few men remained alone at the table, with one woman—no, Magda realized suddenly, they were all men, what she had thought a woman was only a very slender, extremely young man, with delicate features, who had allowed his hair to grow considerably longer than most men; he had furthermore pinned it back in a way that suggested, though it did not actually imitate, a woman's coiffure. And in this last group, Magda noticed a few Terrans. One was actually wearing the black leathers of Spaceforce.

Of course. It made sense. At Festival, when all classes mingled without prejudice, it would make sense to certain men to get away from the Terran prejudice. *In Darkovan Society it would not matter so much that they are lovers of men. Or even that they are Terran. Outcasts do not look down on other outcasts.* She had seen one of the men on the spaceport that very day.

He had taken her ident pass. She thought vaguely that he should have gotten himself Darkovan clothing, not come down here in uniform. Who was she to criticize, who sat here beside a woman who was her lover?

Darrell, son of Darnak, had come back, and Marisela was thanking him for the dance. One of the more effeminate men had risen and said diffidently to Marisela, "I like to dance, but I have no sister and no woman friend. Will you honor me, *mestra?*"

Marisela smiled acceptance. Of course; even at Midsummer men did not dance together in Thendara, except in the all-men circle dances. She wondered why. Why shouldn't men dance together if they wanted to? Women could dance together, in fact it was considered the most suitable thing for women in strange places! She was sure the young man would rather have danced with his friend at the other table, than with Marisela. She had seen them holding hands. But they couldn't dance together. How strange, and how sad, that even on this most permissive of nights, men were still more trapped than women. She could wear, and as a Renunciate *did* wear, breeches in public. If this man wore skirts, and he looked as if he would feel and look better in them, he would be lynched. How sad, and how foolish, people were!

Camilla asked, "Will you dance with me, Margali?" and Magda hesitated. She would have liked to. But she could not get up and dance with Camilla in front of those heartbreaking men. Darrell bowed expectantly and Camilla gave her a little indulgent shove.

"Go and dance, child."

Reluctantly—she wished Camilla had forbidden her!—she moved away. It was a dance in couples. She hoped he would not speak of their shared childhood in Caer Donn, he had known her as the daughter of the Terran scholar Lorne, and she did not want that mentioned just yet. But it was obvious he had other things on his mind. He was a good dancer, but he held her just a fraction too close, and she would have refused a second dance, except that they were at the far side of the square and it would have seemed unkind. It was very warm; such unseasonable warmth in Thendara always predicted severe storm very soon. The smell of the air told her dawn was not far away. As the second dance ended she could see the musicians finishing their drinks and putting their instruments away. Darrell steered her into a darkened doorway and touched her lips. She did not protest, kisses at the end of a dance did not commit her to anything, but when he tried to embrace her, murmuring, "I do not want to end this night alone," she pushed him away.

"All around us, all men and women do honor to the loves of the Gods—"

No. This was too much. Already this Festival had brought her more than she wanted of such matters, and she would not, she simply would not give herself to him here in the open air as some of the women were doing, scarcely troubling to shelter themselves from the eyes of passersby as they took the license of this night. She hardly knew this man. "No," she said, pushing him away again. "No, I am honored, thank you, but no, really no—"

"But you must," he muttered, trying to nuzzle her bare neck; if she had known how drunk he was she would not have danced with him at all! His hands were hot and urgent on her bare neck and he was trying to fumble into her breast. She wished she were wearing her Amazon tunic instead of the Festival gown. She knew how to defend herself, but this man was a childhood friend and she really did not want to hurt him. She shoved him roughly away, but as his hands clung she followed it with a ringing slap which made him blink and stare at her stupidly.

"You aroused me and now you refuse me—"

She said in exasperation "I danced with you; you roused yourself! Don't talk like a fool, Darrell! Are you honestly trying to claim I deliberately roused you? Why, if that were so, every woman in Thendara must go veiled like a Dry-Towner!"

He hung his head, with a shamefaced grin.

"Ah, well—no harm in asking."

She was glad to return his smile. "None. Provided you only ask and do not try to snatch unwilling!"

"You cannot blame me for that," he said good-naturedly and bent to kiss her bare shoulder, but she moved out of reach; she was not trying to flirt with him! Damn it, after all those months of isolation and celibacy, suddenly men, handsome and eligible men at that, were literally crawling out of the trees! First Monty, now this perfectly nice young Guardsman— if it had not been for Camilla would she have agreed to go with him this night? She would never know. Camilla was there.

She could see against the shadow of one of the buildings, a woman in Amazon clothing—Rafaella, surely—standing in a man's arms, so violently embraced that it was almost a struggle; both were fully clothed but from their movements it was reasonably obvious what was happening. She turned away, embarrassed, and went back to the bench where the last of the women lingered.

Camilla yawned, covering her mouth with a narrow hand. "We must be away to the Guild House," she said. "The moons are setting, and you and Keitha, child, must be indoors by dawn."

She chuckled. "I could stay out as late as I wished—but by now my only desire is for my comfortable bed."

The owners of the wineshop were now unobtrusively removing every bench as soon as it was vacant, stacking them, eager to call it a night. The Guardsmen who had been dancing, finding their seats gone, wandered away down the street. The group of women were still sharing a final pitcher of wine. Rafaella came back to where Magda sat with Camilla and Keitha—Marisela was exchanging a final word with a young man, and ended by kissing him in a motherly way on the cheek, so Magda supposed he must be a nephew or something of that kind. Rafaella's face was flushed, her hair mussed, the laces of her tunic undone; she bent over Camilla and whispered to her, and Camilla reached up and patted her cheek.

"Enjoy yourself, *breda*. But take care."

Rafaella smiled—she was a little drunk too, Magda realized—and went away, arms enlaced with the man who had been holding her. Keitha's eyes were as wide as saucers. Janetta leaned over from the next bench and said, "Bold creature! Such indecent ways cast shame on all Renunciates; they will come to think us no better than harlots! I wish we were still in the ancient days when no Renunciate might lie with a man, or her sisters would cast her out!"

"Oh, hush," said Marisela, coming back to the table. "Then we were denounced as lovers of women, seducers of decent wives and daughters, luring their children astray because we had none of our own! All women cannot live as you do, Janetta, and no one has appointed you keeper of Rafi's conscience."

"At least she could do such things in decent privacy, not before half the city of Thendara," Janetta complained, and Marisela laughed, glancing around the all-but-deserted square.

"I think they are trying to get us to leave. But we have paid for the wine, and I for one will sit here and finish it." She raised her glass. "It is easy for you to talk, Janetta, you have never been tempted in that way, and for the love of Evanda spare me your next speech, the one about the woman who lies with a man being a traitor to her sisters, I have heard it all too often, and I believe it no more than I did when first I heard it. I care not whether you, or anyone else, lies down with men, women, or consenting *cralmacs*, so that I need not hear them argue about it when I am trying to sleep—or finish my drink!" She raised her glass and drank.

But I agree with Janetta now more than I ever did, Magda thought. *Yet here I sit beside a woman who has been my lover, and for whose sake I refused a man this night.* For that matter, Camilla had laughed and blessed Rafaella, and why not? She picked up her own glass, then heard a voice say, "Margali—" and looked up into the eyes of Peter Haldane.

He was wearing Darkovan clothing; no one but herself, surely, would have known him for the young Terran among the delegation at Festival ball in Comyn Castle this night.

Camilla said to Magda, "Finish your drink, child, I shall be back at once," and with Marisela and Mother Lauria, wandered away to the latrines at the back of the wineshop garden. Peter sank down across from Magda. She had never seen him so drunk.

She said in the language of Caer Donn, "Piedro, is this wise?"

"Wise be damned," he said. "I've been fighting for my life. Montray was so damned determined I'd be on that ship pulling out just about now for the Alpha Colony, up for discipline before Head Center Intelligence. I finally went over his head, got Alessandro Li to pull rank on him, and Cholayna—where the hell were you, Mag? It was your problem, too. And what were you up to with Monty?"

She said, "I'm sorry you were having trouble, Peter." She was not, definitely not going to discuss her relationship with Monty here, nor with him. "But it is all right, then?"

"Till he starts in on me again. God, I'd give ten years of my life to get that man shipped off Darkover; I swear, if I live, I'll do it. Even his own son knows—" he broke off. "But what are you doing here, Mag? In *this* place?" His horrified eyes fell on the last remaining table except for theirs, where a couple of the men were still drunkenly pawing one another and the effeminate who had danced with Marisela was asleep with his head on the table. Magda noted, with sadness and some pity, that he wore a woman's butterfly-clasp in his long hair.

"Maggie, don't you know what this place *is?*"

She shook her head. He told her. His outrage seemed misplaced.

"At least no one will trouble women alone here. And anyhow, *you're* here."

"Looking for you," he said. "They told me some women from the Guild House were still here drinking, dancing—wanted to talk to you," he said with drunken earnestness. He saw Camilla's drink on the table and absentmindedly picked it up and drank it. It seemed to thicken his speech immediately. "Need you," he said. "Need you to talk to Jaelle. You're her friend. My friend too. Good friends. Both need you, both of us. Need you to talk to her, tell her what it means. Be a good Terran wife. Back us up. She's having a baby," he informed Magda with drunken seriousness. "My baby, got to get her straightened out so she can help me instead of fighting me all the time. Got to get in good with all the higher-ups so we can bring up our baby here. My son. Only she won't help me the right way. She doesn't know how to handle Terran bureaucrats. You always handled old Montray just fine. Maggie, you talk to her, you tell her—"

She stared at him, not believing what she had heard him say.

"You," she said, "have got to be right out of your mind. Peter! You want me—*me?*—to talk to Jaelle, and tell her how you want her to act as your wife? I never heard such a thing in my life!"

"But you know the kind of trap I'm in, how I need it—"

"Handle it the way I did," she said sharply. "Tell them all to go to hell. If you want to let them push you around, don't come crying to me!"

He grabbed her hand, held it, staring into her eyes with drunken intensity.

"Never should have let you go," he said thickly. "Mistake of a lifetime. Nobody like you, Maggie. You—you got to be the best there is. Only now there's Jaelle. I love her, if only she'd settle down and put her weight behind me, do what she ought to do. And now there's our kid. My kid. F'the sake of that kid, I got to stick to her. Can't quit. Can't bring the kid up like some damned native, out in the outback of nowhere—wish *you'd* had our kid, Maggie, you'd have done it right . . . you got to help us, Mag. My friend. Jaelle's friend. Talk to her, Maggie."

"Peter," she said helplessly, "you're drunk; you don't know how outrageous that sounds. Go home, Peter, and sober up. Things will look different when you're sober, when you've had some sleep—"

"But you've got to *listen* to me!" He grabbed her, pulled her close to him. "I got to make you understand just what a bind I'm in—"

"*Bredhiya,*" said Camilla's gentle voice behind her, "is this man annoying you?"

Camilla, tall and somehow formidable, was towering over the slightly built Peter, who was swaying on his feet. Of course Camilla had spoken in the intimate mode which gave the words only one possible meaning. Camilla, too, was more than a little drunk. Peter looked at them both with horror and sudden dismay.

"Damn," he said, "now I understand. Never saw it before. No wonder you wouldn't stay with me, no wonder . . . and I thought you'd come here because you didn't understand. Of course you wouldn't be the one to talk to Jaelle. What the hell would you know about it?" He made a gesture of disgust and revulsion. "So *that* was why you left me, went into the Guild House. Of course you couldn't be a decent wife to me, to any man—"

She said angrily, "How dare you speak to me that way?"

"How dare *you* speak to any decent person? You?" He wrinkled his nose in wrath. "If I catch you anywhere near Jaelle," he said in drunken wrath, "I'll—I'll break your neck. You stay away from my wife, hear me, I don't want you corrupting her!"

Camilla, of course, had not understood a word of all this, but she could tell perfectly well that he was being offensive. She said, not knowing that

Peter could understand—he had, after all, been speaking the last few sentences in Terran Standard—*"Bredhiya,* shall I get rid of him for you?"

"You—" Peter snarled. It was a gutter insult, and Camilla's hand closed on her knife-hilt. It flashed.

"No!" Magda cried out. "He's drunk—he doesn't know—"

One of the men at the other table lurched over, closing his hand on Peter's shoulder. He said with thick earnestness, "No, no, no sense picking a fight here at Festival, brother, no sense talking to the likes of them." He gestured at Camilla and added, "I'm the one you came down here to find, brother. Come on over here with us, we're all friends over here." He put his arms around Peter, breathing heavy camaraderie, wine-laden, into his face. "C'mon, brother, it's late and I'm still all alone, come on, leave all them bitches out of it. Let them go off by themselves if they want to, who needs *them?*" he shoved his own tankard in Peter's face. "Drink up, little brother, drink up."

Peter could not push the man's hand away; he swallowed, coughed on the strong liquor, sank down at the other table, staring up in bewilderment at the man.

"Look, I didn' come down here lookin' for you—" he muttered.

"Aw, come on," said the man, staring down intensely into Peter's flushed face, "what else you come down here for? I know you Terrans, you can't find what you're lookin' for on *your* side of the wall, can you? None of our brothers over there, got to come down here in the city, we get a lot of you fellows. . . . I know all about it, here, have another drink—"

Oh, poor Peter! Magda thought, but somehow she could not resist an unholy glee. Camilla said in an undertone, gathering up their possessions, "Come along, Margali, it's better than a duel at this hour."

Magda stared in dismay at Peter, who had sunk down, semiconscious, too drunk even to express his anger. He slid down, slowly, under the table, and the man who had urged him to drink knelt over him.

"Ah," he urged drunkenly, "don't go passing out on me now, little brother, thats no way to treat a pal. . . ."

Magda did not know whether to laugh or cry, but Camilla urged her gently away. She could not help wondering what would happen to Peter when he woke up there . . . would he get back to the Terran Zone with his virtue intact?

Camilla put her arm around Magda's waist as they walked down the street. "I shall be glad to get home to our bed," she said, yawning, "I am sorry I am too drunk and weary to end the night as is fitting for Midsummer . . . that is no way to treat you at Festival, *bredhiya.* . . ."

Magda flushed, snuggling against Camilla's arm round her waist. Through all the aggravations of this evening she remembered the lovemaking of this afternoon, amazed at herself. In Camilla's arms she had discovered another whole new self, a Magda previously unknown to her. She remembered, with a wave of heat, how she had cried out to Camilla in surprise and wonder and delight. Body and mind were all alive with a sudden hunger to know that delight and that wonder again. Why had she never guessed?

"That Terranan . . . how did you come to know him?" Camilla demanded, suddenly suspicious.

"He is—Jaelle's freemate," Magda said, then fell silent before the dawning suspicion in Camilla's eyes; but the older woman said no more. The streets were already filled with greyish-pink light. At the door of the guild House she stopped, touched Camilla's hand.

"I swear you shall know everything some day, oath-sister," she said, using the word in the most intimate form. "Not now, Camilla, I beg you, give me a little time."

Camilla stopped in the street and put her arms around Magda, holding her close. "You are my sister, and my beloved," she said. "You are sworn to me and I to you. Tell me what you wish, whenever you wish, and in your own time, my precious. I trust you." She kissed Magda, and suddenly leaned forward and picked her up.

"Come love," she said, "we must be inside before the last moon sets, that is our law." She carried her up the steps and inside the house.

What a bitch I am, Magda thought. I've played hell with two men today—three if you count Peter—and now I'm using Camilla's love and devotion to give myself time—time to think what I can say to her.

But she was overcome with such a wave of fatigue that she could hardly stand on her feet. Without protest she let Camilla lead her up the stairs.

Toward morning, Magda began to dream. She was living in Married Personnel Quarters in the HQ skyscraper, but somehow all the showers and bath sections had been redesigned, and women from the Guild House were living in little doorless cubicles all along the corridors, so that she wandered in them for hours trying to find a place for a shower unobserved; and through all this she could not allow them to know that she was pregnant nor that she had had a mark tattooed on her back. She was not sure what it said, but it was something like the "Product of the Terran Empire" mark which went on goods imported to fully developed planets and prohibited on Class B Undeveloped ones like Darkover. She kept trying to find Jaelle in the confusing quarters, because Jaelle knew Terran writing and could read it to her. It had been done while she was asleep and somehow they had made a mistake while she slept, and tattooed Jaelle with the mark too. And she was pregnant, and she kept thinking how pleased Peter would be, but what would Jaelle think? If she could only find Peter, they could all straighten it out, but he was nowhere to be found in the miles and miles of tiled corridor, because all the Quarters had been redesigned for Darkovan living on the HQ base and he was out somewhere redesigning the Guild House for Terrans who wanted to explore living on Darkover in native style. "But that would make it no better than a hotel," she heard someone say querulously in her mind, and then she and Jaelle were trying to hold up the roof of the Guild House while Marisela and someone else whose face she could not see . . . was it the small freckled Amazon who had bandaged her feet on the fire lines? . . . could search through a long telescope for *Dom* Ann'dra Carr. Only, though she could see the ground lenses clearly, sparkling blue like Lady Rohana's matrix, the telescope was invisible and kept slipping out of their hands as if it had been greased with glycerine. Then someone was calling her, and Bethany from the Coordinator's office was saying, "Margali? Oh, I think she slept last night in Camilla's room. . . ." and she woke, to hear those very words spoken aloud, followed by a knock on the door.

"Margali? Margali? Camilla, is she there?"

Magda woke, blinking, grasping at absurd troubled remnants of the dream. Camilla, sitting up in bed, was swearing under her breath as she hunted for her stockings.

"What is it? Who wants me?"

"Mother Lauria, downstairs," said Irmelin. "There is a visitor and only you can talk to her, for some reason or other—a woman who has had some terrible skin disease and is all discolored, dark as a *cralmac*'s hide. . . ."

Cholayna, Magda thought, and jumped up, grabbing some clothes and running to splash her face with the icy water. *What in the devil can she want here? And is Jaelle with her?*

Jaelle was not; Cholayna had come alone, and was talking amiably with Mother Lauria in the Stranger's Room. When Magda came in, Mother Lauria said, "I will leave you alone for a moment; but I hope you will both join me in my office in a little while. Margali, you have not breakfasted; shall I send for tea and rolls in my office? Mestra, may I offer you breakfast?"

Cholayna smiled and nodded. "I had forgotten it was a holiday here and that some of you would still be sleeping," she said, as Mother Lauria went away, "and they told me they could not find you in your room, they thought for a minute that you were sleeping out; some of the women slept out of the House on Festival Night." Abruptly and with a flash of memory Magda remembered Rafaella with her hair mussed and her tunic open, showing her breasts, going off with the Guardsman. How was she better than that? She had spent yesterday morning in Monty's arms and this morning they had had to look for her in Camilla's bed. Nonsense; she was a grown woman, it was nothing to Cholayna where she spent her night, or with whom. Magda braced herself, remembering that she had resigned last night. She said bluntly, "Why have you come here? None of it is anything to do with me any more. No, I mean it this time, Cholayna, you can't talk me out of it the way you did when you first came here. What do I owe you now?"

"Not to me," Cholayna said, "but to your sisters, and perhaps to yourself. You have a very rare opportunity, Margali." She said the name in Darkovan, and Magda was astonished. But still distrustful.

"You tell me that, Cholayna? I have heard it all before, and it has brought me nothing but grief—always between two worlds and never at home in either—" Astonished, Magda discovered that her eyes were prickling as if she were about to cry, and she stopped herself, appalled, wondering, what on earth do I have to cry about? I'm *mad*, not unhappy! And then such a surge of misery flooded up within her that she clamped her teeth over the pain, knowing that if she shed a single tear she would cry and cry until she melted like Alice into a pool of tears. She said, tightly, against it, "Everyone who has told me that has wanted to use me one way or the other. When can I be simply myself, do what is good for myself and not for a hundred other people?"

"When you are in your grave," Cholayna said gently, "No one alive lives only for herself. We are all part of one another, one way or another, and anyone who does any action which is not for the common good is little more than a murderer."

"I am not interested in your religion!" Magda almost shouted.

"That is not religion." The other woman's dark face held an eerie calm. "Philosophy perhaps. It is a simple fact; no one can do anything without either helping or harming everyone with whom she has any contact of any kind. Only an animal does not take that into account." Her face softened. "You are very dear to me, Magda. I have never had children; I decided many years ago that they were not for me since I could not rear them among my own people and I would not bring them up haphazardly, crammed into the niches and crannies of a life roving around from world to world. I hoped I had found in you something that women find in their daughters—a sense of continuity—" She stopped, and Magda, ready to throw a rude or angry voice back into the woman's face, was silenced.

She thought, *if I betray Cholayna, then I am false to the real spirit of the Amazon Oath,* and wondered what in the world had brought that into her mind.

She asked sullenly, "What do you want of me, Cholayna?"

Cholayna reached for her hand, then sighed and did not touch her. "At the moment? Only to take no irrevocable decisions. I could have killed Montray; I am not sure it would not have been a good thing if I did, but alas, the habit of non-violence is too strong—and he is not even good to eat!" The joke was not a good one, but she laughed nervously anyway.

"If you feel you must go out of our reach for a time, at least help me to settle, with Lauria, which of your sisters shall work with the Headquarters, learning our ways for the benefit of both worlds."

Part of Magda was angry at Cholayna for presuming to use the special speech of the Amazons, for speaking about her sisters and her duty to them, but there was a curious feel in the room, as if Cholayna were not speaking only in words but somehow communicating with her on a deeper level. She knew things which the older woman had not told her, would never dream of telling her, had probably never told anyone alive, things of which Cholayna was not fully aware herself, and it terrified Magda to know this much about any human being. She thought, *she is wide open, without knowing clearly what she meant by the words, and so am I.* She sensed the weariness in the long, lean face and body, the pain from the alien sun, the sense that it was very dark here, the longing for the brighter warmth and light of her own world; Cholayna was living in what to her was an eerie half-light. She knew that Cholayna was potentially a lover of women, as much or more than Camilla, but because of the worlds where her life had been spent, it had never surfaced into her consciousness. But this was why she had spent her life in the teaching and training of younger women, in a half-formed hope that one day some one of them would give her, she hardly knew what herself, some returned warmth which she identified with the warmth of her own sun which had been so long denied her. And she did not clearly know this herself, and yet Magda knew it, and her scalp crinkled and icy fingers of dread ran down her back one by one, she did not know what this meant and could not guess. It was like the night she had wakened in Jaelle's arms and the other woman, drawn perhaps by that flooding awareness between them, had kissed her; only this time it could not be dismissed as a random sexual impulse, it was deeper than that. A thing of the spirit? Magda was not comfortable with such ideas and she suspected that Cholayna would be appalled by them.

Yet the emotion was there and she could neither identify nor restrain it. As for rebuffing it, it would have been as unthinkable to slap Camilla when she proffered her love and devotion. Magda lowered her head so that Cholayna would not see the tears in her eyes and said ungraciously, fighting whatever it was that was making her want to cry, "Well, I will do that, of course, I don't want to leave any loose ends. Mother Lauria is waiting for us."

In Mother Lauria's office the older woman had sent for breakfast; there was a platter of hot bread, smoking and sliced, another plate of the cold sliced Festival cake, raisins studded all through it, left over from the day before; and a huge steaming pitcher of the roasted-grain drink the Amazons drank in lieu of wine or beer. There was also a bowl of hard-boiled eggs and a dish of soft curd cheese. Impelled by a feeling she would never have considered until this morning, Magda said quickly, "You will not want to eat the eggs, Cholayna, since they once had life, but everything else you can eat freely."

"Thank you for warning me, Magda," said Cholayna imperturbably. "I do not expect the world to be arranged for my convenience; I have, perhaps, become too dependent on man-made foods. Perhaps the Alphan scruples are foolish anyway. It was a wise sage who said that it is not what goes into our mouths that defiles us, but what comes forth from them; lies and cruelty and hatred. . . ." She helped herself to the cheese, and took a piece of the cake, and Magda saw her turning it thoughtfully in her mouth.

"Have your people such a saying?" Mother Lauria asked. "Some women in this house make a point of eating only grains and fruits; yet their sage wrote that everything which shares this world with us has life, even to the rocks; and all things prey and feed upon one another and come at last to feed the lowest life of all. So that we should eat reverently of whatever comes to us, bearing in mind that some life was sacrificed that we might live and that one day we will feed life in our turn. Ah, well, another philosopher has written that the morning after Festival makes every drunkard a philosopher!"

She laughed and passed a jar of fruit conserve to Magda, who spread some on her bread, wishing she could explain her feelings in terms of a simple hangover!

"Well, we must decide," said Lauria briskly, finishing the tea in her mug. "I feel that Marisela should be the first."

"I agree, and I doubt not she will teach the Terrans as much as she learns from them," said Cholayna, "but can she be spared here?"

"Probably not, but she must have this chance all the same," said Mother Lauria. "Keitha can do her work, and later have her turn. I would like to send Janetta—Margali, are you as sleepy as that? Should I send you back to bed?"

"Oh, no," Magda said quickly. It had seemed to her for a moment that Marisela was standing in a corner of the office listening to their deliberations and at the same time she knew Marisela was upstairs in her bed, still half asleep, wondering how long she could enjoy this delicious sleep before someone came in search of a midwife and roused her. She was not alone in bed, and Magda recoiled, not wanting to know this about Marisela either.

She said hastily, "Janetta is too rigid, she could not, I think, accept Terran ways."

"She is more intelligent than you think her," Mother Lauria said. "There is little here to challenge her mind; I had hoped to send her to Arilinn, but she would never make a midwife, she's not sympthetic enough to women. She herself has decided she wishes for no children, having a certain distaste for the preliminaries. Yet there is no other training available to her; Nevarsin will not train female healer-priests. She is extremely clever, too clever for most of the things ordinary women, even Amazons, are able to do. She has no interest in soldiering, nor has she the physical strength for it. I think she would be very valuable to you; and what she learns would be priceless to us as well."

Magda still felt skeptical, and Mother Lauria continued "You do not know Janni's story. She came from a village where her mother was left widowed with seven children, and had no other skills to keep them, so she became a harlot. She tried to train Janetta to her trade before the girl was twelve. For a year or two Janni was too young and timid to resist; then she ran away to us."

Camilla had said it once; every Renunciate has her own story and every story is a tragedy. *How have I earned my place among them?*

"There is a young woman called Gwennis," Mother Lauria said. "She is at Nevarsin now, working with some scrolls in the keeping of the brothers —you do not know her, Margali—"

"I do not know her well enough to recommend her for this," Magda said, "but she is my oath-sister, after all—she was in the band led by Jaelle."

"I think she would be a good choice," Mother Lauria said. "The very fact that she volunteered for that work would perhaps make her good at this. And perhaps Byrna; she has an inquiring mind—not to mention that she is still pining for her child and this would be a blessing, give her something new to think about. Cholayna—" she used the Terran woman's name hesitantly, "have you any particular ideas about what age these women should be?"

"I do not think it matters," Cholayna said. "They should, perhaps, not be too young. Your people, I have heard, are trusted with responsibility at an earlier age than ours; but if the Empire people thought them mere children, they might not take them seriously enough, as independent adults. Not younger than twenty, I should think."

"So old?" Mother Lauria asked. Magda was remembering that Irmelin was one of the most bookish women in the House, spending most of her leisure hours in reading or sometimes in writing for Mother Lauria in her office, and suggested her name.

"I think she is too lazy, perhaps, too content with things as they are," Mother Lauria said. "Three years ago, perhaps, but not now. Though if she wishes it, once it is made clear to her how much work it is, she might be given a chance. Certainly she is intelligent enough, and does not shrink from hard work."

"What I would like," Cholayna said, "would be a chance to administer one of the specific intelligence tests to all of your women . . . we have some very good ones which are not culturally biased, measuring only the ability to think abstractly and to learn."

"That might be valuable to us as well," said Mother Lauria. "Certainly there are stupid women, just as there stupid men, but the most intelligent of women can be taught as a girl that seeming stupid is her most useful skill when she is among men, and most of them are clever enough to learn to do *that!* The ones who cannot learn that, or will not learn it, are often the ones who come to us. But sometimes we have women who are even afraid to try to learn to read, because they have been taught so well that it is beyond their skills! How, in Evanda's name, anyone can think that a woman who spins and weaves and grows food in her own greenhouse and supervises her servants, teaches her children, and manages all of a family's resources, can be called stupid, I will never know! It is as if we should call a farmer, who can manage crops and animals at all seasons of the year, stupid because he knows nothing of the philosophy of the ancient sages! Women come here thinking themselves stupid, and I do not know how to convince them otherwise. But perhaps, if your tests were presented as games, and I could convince them that there are different kinds of learning . . ."

"Well, certainly we have enough tests, and people to administer them," said Cholayna. "I am thinking of one of the technicians in the Psych department. She might be a good one to send here, not only for your sake but for her own—I think she could learn much from you. She is—" Cholayna hesitated; "I am not sure of your word—Magda, help me? One who has no sexual interest in men—"

"Menhiédris," said Magda, using the politest of many words; ruder ones were used every day in the Guild House but she was feeling sensitive on that subject just now.

"She would welcome knowing that there was a place in this culture which would not despise her," Cholayna said. "A good many of our cultures are—shall we say far from perfect? It would interest her to know how your society structures such things. She might feel at home among you, more than some others, if you think they could accept anyone from another world. As, perhaps, you have accepted Magda—Margali?"

Mother Lauria said rather stiffly, "I am glad you think there is something where we can teach as well as learn from you," and Cholayna smiled at her with disarming friendliness.

"Oh, you must not judge us by our worst and narrowest, Lauria. It is unfortunate that our Coordinator is a narrow-minded man, the worst rather than the best, a political appointee who has never wished to be here at all. But we have those among us who truly love the worlds where we are assigned, and wish to share them. Magda, for instance—"

Mother Lauria's face softened.

"Margali has been truly one of us," she said, "and if there are others of your people who are like her—or like yourself, Cholayna—we would welcome them as friends. And to be just, there are enough of our people who are narrow-minded, who judge your people by the men in the spaceport bars, not your scientists and your wiser men. There are even some who still think your people sky-devils . . . For their sake, I think, Margali, it is time to reveal the truth; who you are and where you came from, so that when they speak disparagingly of Terrans, those who know better may say to them, 'but look, Margali is one of them, and she has lived as a sister to us in this house for a whole year,' and show them that their prejudices are foolish . . . what do you say to that, Margali?"

Magda felt dismayed; surely not yet, surely she could not yet face the sudden shock and hostility with which at least a few would greet her . . . and even as the thought crossed her mind it seemed she could almost see the hostile faces, the rejection where there had been friendship, the awkwardness when they knew she had won friendship under false pretenses. . . .

Again Cholayna was taking it for granted that she would again agree to put herself on the line between the two cultures, that again she would choose to be in the vulnerable spot of liaison of her two worlds. How they would despise her when they knew! And Camilla, Camilla would surely hate her. . . .

I never allowed myself to be vulnerable to any man as I have been to Camilla; always before I have been guarded, trying always to be strong and in perfect possession of myself. With Camilla it is different, and I cannot bear that she should judge me harshly, it would be worse than when I lost Peter. One of the reasons he left, she thought, *was because I was too independent and could not surrender myself and my judgment, and now. . . .*

"Margali?" And suddenly Magda knew that she had lost track of the conversation, that both Mother Lauria and Cholayna were looking at her. She said at random, "What was that you said about Camilla? I am sorry, my mind was wandering," and then she was frightened. How had she known they were speaking about Camilla?

"Are you ill, Margali? You are as white as a shroud," Mother Lauria said, and Cholayna asked, smiling, if she had danced too late last night.

"No one is good for anything on the day after Festival," Lauria said. "This was the wrong time for this visit, perhaps, but you could not know that. All we said, Margali, was that Camilla is in the house and she probably knows the women better than I; when you have trained a girl in swordplay and self-defense, you know all her weaknesses. The same is true of Rafaella, but she slept out last night, Camilla said. Would you run upstairs and ask her to come down to us? Your legs are younger than mine."

Magda was glad to get out of the room, and on the stairs she stopped, gasping, holding herself together by sheer force of will. It was happening again, once again it seemed as if she were like a spider at the center of the web, twitching everywhere and feeling the threads move, upstairs to where Marisela was awake and singing as she splashed her face with the icy water . . . *someone is on the steps seeking a midwife, but how had Marisela known that? The same way that I know it?* Lady Rohana called it *laran* . . . *but she also said I had learned to barrier it, what has happened to my control?* She could feel Irmelin downstairs in the kitchen, she could hear Rezi and two other women cursing as they struggled with barn-shovels; the very dairy-animals sensed the disturbances of midsummer, or was it only that after dancing till very late the inflexible routine of caring for the animals did not fit well with a hangover? *Keitha . . . Keitha is more prejudiced even than I about lovers of women, I was not the only women to succumb to someone I loved at Midsummer. . . .*

"In Evanda's name, why are you blocking the staircase?" demanded a cross voice behind her, and Magda, shaking, drew herself upright to face Rafaella. She was still wearing her holiday gown, which looked strange in the morning glare, and her hair was mussed, her eyes reddened. It was obvious even to Magda how she had spent the night . . . *or am I reading minds again?*

She moved to one side, with a murmur of apology, but Rafaella stopped and looked at her, taking her brusquely by the arm.

"What in hell ails you? You look as if you were going into labor or something like that!"

"No, no, I'm quite well—Mother Lauria sent me on an errand—"

"Then go and do it," Rafaella said, not unkindly, "but you look as if you, not I, were the one who had spent a sleepless night and drunk too much. Well, I don't suppose we are the only ones; when you have done your errand, you had better spend the rest of the day in bed—preferably alone!" She laughed and went on up the stairs, and Magda, feeling her face flush with heat, managed to recover herself and go on up to Camilla's room. The older woman was awake and half dressed; she heard Rafaella on the stairs and put her head out into the hall.

"So you woke the dawn-birds, Rafi love—was it worth it?"

Rafaella rolled her eyes expressively, then chuckled. "How would you know if I told you? But oh, yes—for once in the year! Now I shall go and sleep!" She disappeared into her room, and Camilla chuckled softly as she turned to Magda.

"Did you come to find me? I supposed that Mother Lauria and the Terran woman would send for me sooner or later. . . ."

Is she doing it too? Magda felt brittle, raw-edged as if she would fly into pieces; one part of her was seized by Rafaella's much too clear surface memories of the night just past, he must have been quite a man, a memory of excitement, pleasant athletic competence, and she was furious with herself because the shared memory sent a flood of sexual heat through her own body, and now Camilla was reading her message before she delivered it. Did they all do it? It had never happened before, Camilla was redhaired, it was not impossible she had some Comyn blood; faded now, gingery sand-colored, but when she was a young girl she must have been bright redhead, *Tallo,* they said here, like Jaelle, but as she looked at Camilla it seemed that the gaunt scarred face slid off and what she saw was a lovely child, fourteen or fifteen, shining dark-red curls, a delicate arrogance, a sheltered child treated like a princess . . .

. . . *a lovely child, yes, small good it did me,* then a flood of confused memories tumbling one over the other, *a delicate child suddenly torn away from home into the hands of bandits, the roughest of men, repeated brutal violation, a plaything for the cruellest of them, from hand to hand like a whore, no, worse than a whore, not even a human being, beaten like an animal when I tried to escape . . . lashes ripping flesh from the bones.* . . . Magda had seen the scars on face and body. . . . *I cannot be reading all this,* but her own body was racked with the shame, horror, pain . . . and then a flood of denial, dread. . . .

"No," she managed to gasp, "Camilla, don't—" and again shame washed over her, how could she refuse even to remember when her friend had had to endure all this, when the memory alone was enough to make Magda retch. . . .

"Margali! *Bredhiya* . . ." Camilla caught her as she swayed, and the touch brought another flood of the unendurable, intolerable memories. . . .

Then, abruptly like a slamming door, they were cut off, and it was only the familiar Camilla again, saying gently, "I am sorry, I did not know you were—vulnerable to that."

"I think—I am going mad—" Magda choked. "I am—I keep reading people's minds—"

Camilla sighed. "I suppose—Jaelle has the Ardais Gift, a little; she is a catalyst telepath, and you are so close, she has perhaps awakened your own *laran*. And of course she does not know how strong it is; she has managed to barricade herself so well, she hardly knows she has *laran* at all. And of course I learned long ago to remain barriered, for months at a time I never even think of it; living among the head-blind, one does learn to keep barriers up. I promise you, my dear, I have never tried to read you, never—violated your privacy. A long time ago I made the decision to set all that aside. I have never turned back. This does not happen twice in five years. Forgive me, sister."

"I think—perhaps you should forgive me," Magda managed to murmur. The world was slowly coming back into normal focus, but it seemed that only the thinnest of veils guarded her from that unendurable wide-openness to everybody and everything.

"You have had no training," the older woman said, "and I when I was a girl—after—" she moved her hand, unwilling to speak, and Magda knew what she meant, after the ordeal of which Camilla had spoken only once, after what she had read. . . . *how can she live with such memories?*

"My family could never manage to forget," Camilla said quietly. "I had to learn, or die. But enough of that, love—now we must go down to Mother Lauria. Margali, are you all right?"

Magda managed to nod. Once again she felt a desperate wish to lean on the strength of the older woman. She could not endure what was happening to her, and despite Camilla's words she was not ready to admit that it was, in fact, happening.

She could hear excited voices at the door as she came downstairs, and Marisela's gentle voice soothing the tumult.

"Yes, yes, I understand, my little ones—no, truly, your Mammy isn't going to die, she is going to birth your little brother or sister, that is all. Yes, yes, I will hurry. Irmelin, take our little friends here into the kitchen and give them some bread and honey—things were too confused at home for breakfast this morning, were they not, girls? And you can look into the Guild House kitchen and see what it is like, you would like to have a look, wouldn't you?" She made a laughing gesture at the women on the staircase, then her eyes met Magda's and her face changed as abruptly as if she had been slapped.

"Ah, Goddess, I did not know—Margali, I know I must speak with you, and yet—" she pressed her hands, distracted, to her head. "I must hurry; in spite of what I said to the little girls, this is the woman's fifth child and there is not much time to spend." She came quickly to Magda and put her hands on her shoulders, looking into her eyes. Magda thought, *she knows what is happening to me. But that is not possible.*

"Promise me, little sister, that you will not do anything rash before you and I can sit down together like sisters and have a good talk, such as we have never had—I am at fault, I should have known better, but promise me, Margali—now I must go and get my bag. But wait, do you really need me as much as that? My duty to a sister comes first; shall I send Keitha to take care of this confinement and stay with you, *breda?*"

But already the overload of sensation and confusion was fading. *I am imagining things,* Magda thought, overtired, *I drank too much last night, and you can believe anything when you have a hangover.* "Of course not, Marisela, go along; look, the children are waiting for you." The little girls had appeared at the door to the kitchen, their faces and pinafores smeared with honey. Marisela still looked uncertain.

"Look after her, Camilla, just while I go up and arouse Keitha—"

"Pah!" Camilla wrinkled her nose with contempt. "You *leroni,* you think you have the answers to everything, don't you? I'll look after her. You attend to birthing babies, which is what you do best!" She laid an arm around Magda's shoulders, and Marisela sighed and turned to the little girls, grabbing up the black canvas sack in which she kept the tools of the midwife's trade.

"Come along, let us get back to your Mammy, my dears."

"Come along, love," Camilla said. "Mother Lauria is waiting," and Magda, pulling herself together, followed her into the office; but it seemed still that she could see the troubled blue eyes of the midwife resting on her back.

Yet inside the office it was as if a button had been pushed and her mind clicked over into another gear, all the way back to normal. Camilla was perfectly barriered . . . *she will not do that incredible thing to me, not as Marisela has done, she is so tightly barriered from years of habit, I do not think Camilla has even read me enough to know I am Terran. But perhaps I should have asked Marisela to stay, perhaps she can help me learn to shut all this out. . . .*

But no. It had never happened, Magda decided, looking from Cholayna's wise brown eyes to Camilla's level gray ones. She was simply imagining things. Camilla was listening to Cholayna's description of what they wanted, giving serious attention to it.

"Gwennis," Camilla said, "Margali, she was among your oath-sisters that night we witnessed your oath, but perhaps you would not remember her—it is a crime not to know your own oath-sisters. She would be good for this, the very fact that she was willing to go and learn at Nevarsin—"

"If she is Margali's oath-sister," Mother Lauria said, "I would not like to separate them again as soon as Gwennis has come back, by sending Gwennis to the Terran Zone, unless Margali is to go too," and Magda realized, and again it struck her with the difference, Mother Lauria really meant it just like that; her priorities were so different it was still impossible, even after half a year in the House, for Magda really to understand how her mind worked. She really thought it was more important that Magda and Gwennis should remain together, just because of the accident that they had both happened to run into one another that night in the travel-shelter where Magda had taken the Oath, than that Gwennis should have an opportunity to study under the Terrans! Suddenly Magda felt alienation again, *She was so different, here among these strangers,* and fought furiously to shut it out again. It was just a matter of making up her mind not to surrender to it. Camilla was looking at her expectantly, and she said, pulling herself together, "But I really know nothing about Gwennis; I met her only that one night." She knew Camilla, and Mother Lauria too, would be shocked if she confessed that of the women who had been there when she took her oath, she could remember only Jaelle and Camilla, and she could not even remember which had been Gwennis, and which the other women—Sherna, was it? Devra? She was not even sure of their names. Yet she was sworn to them.

They spent hours working in Mother Lauria's little office, but the afternoon sun had begun to grow dim in the room when Mother Lauria stretched and yawned.

"Well, I think we have the proper group—if only the women we have chosen are pleased; if they all refuse then we will have to start again—"

"But they will not all refuse, certainly," said Camilla. "One or two of them might, which is why we have chosen ten instead of five or six. And you, of course, will want to talk to them—Cholayna," she added, rather shyly. Magda was pleased to see that they liked one another. *But still Cholayna has not mentioned that I am Terran. How will Camilla feel when she knows that? Will she hate me? I love her, I do not want to leave her,* and then Magda realized she must be tireder than she thought; she was seeing pictures again, herself riding away from Camilla, the older woman's sad face . . . when would they meet again, if ever? This was nonsense; she would not leave Camilla, not now. Not for a long time, she hoped, though she was still not sure there would be any kind of permanent commitment.

At one moment, during the long love-play before they slept this morning, Camilla had stopped for a moment, looked at her with heartbreaking intensity. "Margali, I would swear an oath with you; you know that?" and Magda had laughed and kissed her, but inside she thought; *No. I am not yet ready for this. Not yet, if ever.* Something inside had warned her not to say anything rash.

Just like a Terran. Keep control all the time, never just let anything happen . . .

"I think we are all too tired to go on much longer," Mother Lauria said, "and we have done as much as we can before we bring it up in House meeting, which will be in four days. You can come then and talk to us, Cholayna, and meet these women face to face, and ask them for their own opinions. So—" she rose, briskly, though Magda could see the lines of weariness in the old woman's face. "Cholayna, will you stay and eat dinner in the House? Our women may as well begin to get used to you as our friend."

"It would please me," Cholayna temporized, "but perhaps we should go a bit more slowly, until they know who I am and why I am here. Once I have been introduced in your House Meeting, and they have a chance to decide for themselves whether they wish to make friends—"

"You are right," Mother Lauria said, "then I shall expect you on the evening of that night; you will dine in the House with us before the meeting?"

"I should be honored," she said. It seemed to Magda that she was a little fearful.

"Remember, Mother Lauria, that Cholayna does not eat meat, or any food which has once had life."

"That can be arranged, easily enough," Mother Lauria said, and Cholayna smiled with relief as she went into the hallway to find her outer coat, a thick fur thing covering her uniform, which was more adapted to the heated corridors of the Headquarters.

Janetta was on Hall-duty; Mother Lauria introduced her to the Terran woman. Janetta's face lighted—she had been suggested, Magda remembered, for this kind of learning, and evidently Mother Lauria had mentioned it to her.

"Janetta will escort you back through the city," Mother Lauria said. "No, really, Cholayna, it is growing late, and if you lost yourself—there are some quarters where a Terran would not be safe, and some where a woman would have trouble, and you are both. I am sure that you, like Margali, can protect yourself, perfectly well, but it would be easier if you had no need to do so; I am sure she has told you that one of the first laws of a Renunciate is that it is better to avoid a situation causing trouble than to get out of it once it has happened."

"I should be honored," said Janetta with quiet formality. She laid a hand for a moment on her knife. "Nothing will happen while she is in my care, Mother."

"But this is ridiculous," Cholayna said, laughing, "Do you really think I need an armed escort?" No, Magda realized, she had not said it, once again she had heard Cholayna *thinking* those words, then realizing that they would have been offensive, a rebuff of something that was very serious to Janetta; aloud Cholayna said only, "Thank you, Janetta; it is very kind of you, and kind of you, Lauria, to arrange it." The two women stood looking at one another for a moment, then Lauria suddenly laughed and hugged her.

"All Amazons are sisters, and the Goddess grant, one day I may truly welcome you as one of us; till then, you are welcome among us as a kinswoman, Cholayna," she said, and Cholayna, hugging her in return, said seriously, "May it be so, indeed."

Magda, watching, knew she had witnessed something very important, more important than anything Montray had babbled about diplomatic relationships, in its own way just as important as that invitation from Comyn Castle to bring a Terran delegation to Festival ball. *Now indeed I have done the work which I came here to do,* she caught herself thinking, but she shook Cholayna's hand and heard the woman saying that she would see her in a few days from now.

"I like her," Camilla said, as they stood in the hallway watching Janetta escort her down the walk, "as I never thought I would like any woman from another world. Kindra—who was my Oath-mother as well as Jaelle's —used to say that a day would come when we would find we had much to learn from the Terrans, and every year I grow more convinced of how wise she was. You knew the Terrans when you were in Caer Donn as a child, did you not, Margali? I could see that you knew one another well." She yawned. "Well, we have spent the whole day at this, but I do not think it was wasted. I had meant to go out for a ride today, I am weary of being housebound, and I thought I might get leave to take you out with me. But it is too late now to ride, I think—look, the night's rain is beginning; Janni will be soaked before she returns!"

"Oh, she won't melt," Mother Lauria laughed. "She is used to being out in all weathers. . . . Margali, how tired you look, my dear! Take her upstairs and put her back to bed, Camilla, and we will send you both up some supper. You won't mind that, will you, my girls?" She winked at them kindly, and Magda thought, abashed, *She knows we are lovers; well, of course, she probably takes it for granted that any woman coming to the house will experiment before the Housebound time is past. Even Keitha, who was so scornful . . .* and she remembered how she had sensed, this morning, that Marisela was not alone . . . well, their work had thrown them together, as with Magda and Camilla, only perhaps she was more open to it than the *cristoforo* Keitha—

"And where is Marisela?" Mother Lauria asked, so appropriately that for a moment Magda wondered if the Guild-Mother, too, was reading her mind. "I knew she went out on a case this morning; it must have been unusually difficult, poor girl, she will be half dead when she comes home; I think I will make her go up and have supper in bed too! These things always happen, for some reason, the day after Festival—is Keitha still here to look after her when she comes in?"

"No indeed," said Irmelin, who was on hall-duty. "I saw her go out with her midwife's bag; a man came for her, and since Marisela was not yet back, she went out with him—"

"She should not go about the city alone," said Mother Lauria, troubled, "Legally she is housebound still; but worse than that, her husband might still try to revenge himself on her, or to catch her outside alone, so that he could get her home and imprison her . . ."

"She knew that," said Irmelin, "but I think this man had spoken in her presence to Marisela; Keitha knew him and said she could not let a woman suffer when there was need of her skill. I think she believes her work as midwife may even be more important than her Renunciate's Oath—"

"There is nothing in either to negate the other," said Camilla, "yet I am her Oath-mother and I worry about her; I should go to the man's house and make certain she is all right, perhaps escort her home to be sure she is safe. Marisela would never forgive me if I let anything happen to her. . . ."

"That would be a good idea," said Mother Lauria, relieved, "Irmelin, did she leave word where she was going?"

"To the Street of the Nine Horseshoes," said Irmelin, and Camilla pulled down a cloak from the ones hanging in the hallway.

"Shall I take Margali with me, Mother?"

"Indeed not," said Mother Lauria severely. "It is bad enough for one novice to go out into the streets on the night after Festival, which Keitha should not have done without asking leave; though I can see how it would seem natural to her to rush off to deliver a child. But not both of them. If you don't wish to go alone, take Rafaella or someone, but not Margali."

Camilla bowed somewhat ironically to the Guild Mother and went out, saying, "I will be back as soon as I know she is safe—"

"No, no, wait and escort her home," said Mother Lauria, "though I am sorry to send you out when you are so tired. But Margali is a big girl and can put herself to bed for once!" She chuckled, and Magda felt herself blushing. She said, "Don't be silly, I am not as tired as all that; I will go and see if they can use any help in the dining room putting supper on the table, since Keitha is not here."

"You mustn't mind," said Irmelin while they were putting on their aprons and taking down crockery bowls. "It is always so, they like to tease the women who have become lovers—after a few days they will take you for granted, as they do Cloris and Janetta, but if you and Camilla quarrel and stop sharing a bed they will tease you again for a few days, that is all; you heard how they teased Rafi when she went home for the night with a man—and speaking of Rafaella, did I not hear her on the stairs just now?"

"No, she went out hours ago, when you were all in Mother's office," said Rezi, "She said she had a caravan to take out, Shaya had sent for her from the Terran Zone. I had all kinds of questions to ask her, but she had no time for any of them, and Margali—"

"Never mind," said Mother Lauria hastily. "Go after Camilla; take your knife and go swiftly. If it is truly a trap that Keitha has walked into—"

Rezi's face changed. She said, "By the Goddess, I never thought of that! And Keitha is out alone—the Street of the Nine Horseshoes, you said?" She was drawing on her cloak as she spoke. "I'll catch up to Camilla before the end of the street."

The door banged behind her, and Mother Lauria said, "We need not wait dinner. I am sure there is nothing worth waiting for anyhow; the night after Festival there will be nothing on the table but leftovers."

"Well, there is half a roast rabbithorn," Irmelin said, "and plenty of the gravy and stuffing. And if anyone does not want leftovers there is plenty of good bread and cheese, and after Festival it would do anyone good to fast for a day or two anyhow." The women moved around, finding seats.

Magda was glad Camilla had not gone alone; the woman was not young and they had had a couple of sleepless nights. Yet she wished she could be the one to fight at Camilla's back, if fighting was needed; she envied Rezi, who was sent matter-of-factly to defend her sister. She took up a piece of cheese and nibbled it absentmindedly.

She should have gone with Camilla. Mother Lauria was wrong. Camilla was her oath-sister and her lover; it was her personal responsibility to fight beside her; and Keitha was her oath-sister as well, so that it was her personal responsibility to protect Keitha too. She should have argued Mother Lauria into realizing that it was an obligation of honor.

I have been Terran all this day and now I am thinking like a Darkovan again. . . .

There was a stir in the hallway and loud shouts, and three women came into the dining hall, their outdoor cloaks soaked.

"Ah, how it rains! As if it were trying to make up for good weather on Festival night, like always," they cried. "Well, we are back, everybody—"

"Sherna! Gwennis! Devra!" exclaimed Mother Lauria, coming forward to embrace them, and then everyone was up from the table to hug the newcomers, to help them off with their coats, to ask a thousand questions. It was the tall quiet one, Devra, who recognized Magda first and hugged her.

"Margali! I had heard you were going to Neskaya, but of course Jaelle would have wished to bring you to her own House—where is Jaelle n'ha Melora?"

"Oh, she has taken a freemate, and is living in the Terran zone—"

"Jaelle? A freemate? Now will I truly believe that Durraman's donkey can fly," said Gwennis, laughing boisterously. "She would be the last woman in the world, I had thought, ever to give herself over to a man—she has been with Rafaella too much, that is all, Rafi has corrupted her—"

They all crowded to the table, teasing and joking. Sherna demanded, "Where is Camilla?"

"She and Rezi went off—there was some worry about one of our novices," Mother Lauria said, "A fear her husband might try to find her again outside the house; so they went to escort her home." And then the three of them had to be told all about the fight with Keitha's husband and his hired mercenaries, about how Keitha had apprenticed to Marisela and later become her lover, rapid-fire gossip and shared memories and allusions which Magda could hardly follow. They told, too, how Magda had fought for the House and been wounded—by now, Magda realized in surprise, they were not angry with her over the indemnity, but proud of her for defending them so well.

"Cloris, fetch a couple of bottles of the good wine from the cellar," Mother Lauria said. "We will drink to the return of our sisters."

"We have more to drink to than that," said Rezi, coming in, with Keitha and Camilla, all very pale. "As you thought, Mother, it was a trap. Oh, yes, there was a woman in childbirth, but while Keitha was there in the house someone had sent word to Shann MacShann. We found him in the street outside, ready to waylay Keitha when the child was born and she was done with her work."

Keitha looked pale but peaceful, though Magda could see that she had been crying. "I should have been terrified, if my sisters had not been there. As it was, I told him that I should die before I ever came back to him, and laid my hand on my knife, saying that I would turn it either on myself or him, as he chose. So he took himself off, swearing and cursing me and vowing I should wait forever for the return of my dowry; and I told him to keep it for the boys when they were grown. I do not think he will trouble me again. He said at the last, as if it would make me wish to come back, that now he had found a decent woman who would not run away, so if I ever changed my mind—" she smiled faintly, "it was too late. I think he was shocked when I wished him happiness with her. I did not tell him how sorry I was for her, whoever she is."

Camilla hugged Keitha and said "We are all proud of you, *breda*. So now we can drink to his downfall as well. And you will really have something to tell Marisela when she comes back," she added with a sly grin, and Keitha blushed crimson.

The wine was brought and poured, and they all drank, laughing and toasting each other.

"So now we are all here from that night in the travel-shelter except Jaelle," said Sherna, coming over and hugging Camilla and Magda together, "Where is Shaya? Is she out with Rafaella on her travel-business? Did not one of you say she had taken a freemate, of all things?"

"Ah, Goddess! How stupid I am," exclaimed Rezi. "Jaelle was here, and asking for you, Margali—it was hours ago! But you were closeted with Mother in her office and I could not interrupt, and then there was all the hullabaloo about Keitha, and it went right out of my head!"

Magda swung toward her, and suddenly the awareness she had been keeping at bay, all this long day, crashed over her again.

Something is very wrong. Something terrible has happened to Jaelle. . . . there was nothing specific about it, she simply knew, with a knowledge that went deeper than words, that Jaelle needed her, that Jaelle was in deep trouble; and yet when she should have kept herself open to Jaelle, she had barricaded herself and refused to accept the knowledge because she was afraid of it. She looked at Camilla in dismay, knowing that the older woman's superb barriers had kept her locked tight against Jaelle's need.

Danger. Danger, closing in on Jaelle from every direction. Red blood spilled on the sand. The dream and the bond they had shared. She had wakened in Jaelle's arms, her friend needed her, but she had fled from it, and now Jaelle was gone, running away . . . Peter was dead, and now Jaelle was gone . . .

She could hardly hear her own voice.

"Quick, Rezi! Tell me what happened!"

"Shaya—she came for her horse, and for travel-food, and her boots—I loaned her my own riding boots; I do not know what had happened to her own. She had been crying, but she would not tell me what was wrong, and then she rode away. It was before the rain started."

Magda's throat felt tight. It was not Rezi's fault. She should have known that Jaelle needed her, and she was shut up in Mother Lauria's office discussing things that could have been settled in a moment, playing diplomacy games! But that was not fair either. Cholayna could not possibly have known. She looked at the women, still laughing and joking and drinking wine with the three who had returned from Nevarsin. They were Jaelle's friends, too. Camilla was her oath-sister. . . .

Outsiders. They were outsiders. None of them understood. Jaelle had crossed over some invisible line and she was an outsider just as Magda had always been an outsider here. Even Camilla had been able to shut it out, cut

away Jaelle's trouble lest it remind her of her own. Quietly, knowing that
no one would pay the slightest attention, she slipped out of the dining hall,
hurried up the stairs. Before Jaelle was too far out of the city, she could
find her. Quickly she rolled warm stockings, extra warm underwear, her
warmest trousers and tunic, into a bundle, changed her shoes for her
riding boots. She ran down the back stairs, into the kitchen and made up a
package of hard journey-bread from the barrel, some cheese and cold meat
and a scoop of dried fruit from the bin. She hurried to the stable, quickly
saddled her horse. It was the one she had ridden into the mountains when
she went to rescue Peter Haldane; the one she had ridden to the fire lines.
She was breaking her housebound oath but she hardly thought of that.

She was about to swing into the saddle when she saw that Camilla was
standing at the stable door, watching her.

"You cannot go, Margali," said Camilla in an undertone. "Love, you
must not. This is oath-breaking."

Magda let her foot slip from the stirrup. She came to Camilla and laid
her hands on the woman's shoulders.

"Camilla, it is a matter of honor," she pleaded, and then, swallowing
hard, used the weapon she had told herself she would not use.

"We swore an oath in the mountains, before ever I came here to Thendara House," she said, her voice trembling. They had not, not in words; but
she knew now that in the truest sense they had sworn their very lives to
one another, when Jaelle lay dying with a bandit's blow, and Magda had
chosen to abandon her mission that Jaelle might live. Peter Haldane had
never mattered to either of them, against that bond, only Magda had not
known it till then.

*If I had known, if I had known what Jaelle truly meant to me, she would
never have married Peter; only I did not know. It was Camilla who taught
me what Jaelle truly meant to me, that the love of sisters means more than
any man living in this world. . . .*

"We are *bredhyini,* Camilla," she said. "I beg you—if you love me,
Camilla—let me go after her."

Camilla's face was white. "I should have known," she said, "and this is
why you would not swear to me. I—" she drew a long breath. "It does not
matter that we have been lovers," she said after a moment. "What is
important is that we shall always be friends and sisters. If it is a matter of
honor to you—" she hesitated a moment and said at last, "You are oath-
bound not to leave the House save at the command of one of the Guild
Mothers. I am an Elder here, Margali. I may command you lawfully to
go." She drew Magda to her and kissed her fiercely. "Jaelle is my Oath-
sister too," she said, "and has been like a daughter to me. Go, Margali

n'ha Ysabet, without oath-breaking. I will make it all right with Mother Lauria."

"Oh, Camilla—Camilla, I do love you—"

Camilla kissed her again. "I love you too," she said gently, "in more ways than you know. Go now. Give my love to Jaelle, and the Goddess grant you come through this safely. I do not know when we will meet again, my darling; be it as the Goddess wills, and may She ride with you."

Then Magda was in her saddle, her face blindly streaming tears as she rode past Camilla, and into the cobbled street. She did not know where she was going. Only that she was going after Jaelle, and that they had been moving inevitably toward this very moment, since that night in the travel-shelter in the Hellers.

I have not broken my Oath, Camilla has set me free. Yet she knew that she would have broken her Oath without question and without compunction, as if the Oath were a pair of old shoes that had grown too small and she had burst out of them.

Camilla does not know it, but I am no longer bound by the Guild, even as I am no longer simply a Terran. I have outgrown all these things. I do not know what I am. Perhaps, when I find Jaelle, when I overtake her where she has gone, she will show me.

She was a Terran. She was a Renunciate. She was Darkovan. She had become a lover of women. She was a *leronis,* for surely what she had been fighting away all this day was *laran.* And now she must use it to follow where Jaelle had gone. But she was no longer simply any one of these things. All her life she had believed she must choose between being Terran and Darkovan, Magda or Margali, Intelligence Agent or Renunciate, lover of men or lover of women, head-blind or *leronis,* and now she knew that she could never describe herself as either one thing or the other, she knew that she was all of these things and that the sum of them all was more than any or all of them.

I do not know who or what I am. I only know that I do what I must, no more and no less.

She rode through the gates of the city, without looking back.

Chapter Four

Jaelle did not even remember, as she went down the long corridor that led from Married Personnel Quarters, why she had such a shuddering disgust for drunkenness; she only knew that at this moment, Peter was loathsome to her. Well, she need not return, except once and briefly. Once their marriage had been formally dissolved—and she knew now that it must be dissolved, that it was as far in her past as the Great House of Jalak of Shainsa—they might let her live off base, as the Renunciate Medic Technicians were allowed to do. But if they insisted that she must continue to fill Magda's place—as if she could, as if one person could ever be an exact equivalent for another, they had been mad ever to suggest it—they would have to allow her quarters in Unmarried Personnel. Magda, after all, had lived there.

She passed the cafeteria level. She should eat something. The main cafeteria had food she could manage to eat, and all she could get later would be the tasteless synthetics of the small cafeteria up in Communications. She remembered Marisela telling pregnant women in the House that they must eat whether they felt like it or not . . . they were no longer the masters of their own destinies, they had chosen to carry their children and that was a year-long commitment to the welfare of the child's body even before their own.

So I have become no better than any of Jalak's concubines, just a brood mare to bear the next generation. No better than Rohana, for all my gallant talk about personal freedom. Somewhere in the back of her mind she could hear Kindra saying that even becoming an Amazon did not exempt a woman from universal emotions, but she cut it off with vicious self-contempt. *So now I must go into that nauseating cafeteria and stuff my disgusting body with food which revolts it, just because my wretched child, Peter's child, which I did not want anyhow, is yelling at my body to feed it.* . . . Coldly she depersonalized the child into an *it*, a thing, not the daughter Rohana had told her she would bear. . . . *Well, let her yell. Go ahead and cry, baby, nobody's going to feed you now.* She turned decisively away from the sickening smells of the cafeteria, feeling that for a day, at least, she was back in charge of herself.

Upstairs in the Communications office—for, with maddening slowness, the Empire HQ Administration had not yet assigned the Intelligence Personnel to their new office space in Cholayna's division—Bethany looked pink and chipper.

"That's right, it's not a holiday today, is it? Yesterday was some kind of enormous Darkovan holiday, I remember," she said, "and they told me that half of Montray's staff was invited to some enormous affair across the City. Actually in Comyn Castle, wasn't it?" She looked impressed, and Jaelle felt like snarling at her; the Comyn are not superhuman, they are just ordinary mortals with too much sense of their own damned importance. But she said glumly—after all, Bethany was not responsible for her bad mood—"It's a damn shame you couldn't have gone instead of me. You're prettier than I am and you probably dance just as well, and you'd have enjoyed it. Festival is no treat for me."

Bethany chuckled.

"Peter would have had something to say about that, wouldn't he? Anyhow, I went to bed at a decent hour last night, and from the long faces I see all over the department, there are plenty of you who seem to have danced till dawn. There are a few advantages to being so low down in the scale of hierarchy that you never get invited out to a Royal Command and don't have to stay up all night! Seriously, Jaelle, you look like something the cat wouldn't bother dragging in. . . . can I get you some coffee or something?"

Jaelle thanked her and declined. She didn't know what she needed, but coffee, which was not a Terran luxury she enjoyed, was certainly not that need.

"Maybe you should have put yourself on sick report and gone up to Medic," said Bethany solicitously. "After all, strictly speaking, you worked all night and should put in for overtime." It was, Jaelle imagined, one way of looking at it—she hadn't gone to Comyn Castle for her own pleasure, after all. But she only shook her head—the last thing she wanted was to be lectured by Medic about her responsibility to her unborn child—and took her place at the desk which had once been Magda's and was now hers, until she could rid herself of the unwelcome responsibility, and surveyed the unfinished language tapes without enthusiasm.

I still feel as if I ought to be doing something more important than this. But I don't know what.

She worked without stopping for more than an hour until Monty stormed in, swearing.

"Where in the *hell* is Cholayna? She's not up in Intelligence and I can't find her anywhere."

"Maybe she put in for a day of sick leave," said Bethany. "Didn't she go to Comyn Castle last night?"

Monty grinned humorlessly. "That's right she did and so, unfortunately, did the old man. My father said that listening to barbarian music squawking till the wee hours of the morning wasn't *his* idea of recreation and it wasn't what *he* was being paid for, anyhow. Could you page her in Medic and see if she registered to take the day off, Beth?"

Subtly, as something Magda might have noticed, Jaelle recognized that small matter of protocol. He would not, now that he knew her importance, ask Jaelle to do routine chores like this; while Bethany, whose whole employment was to do small routine errands which higher status employees could not be troubled to do, could be interrupted at any time. She had noticed one thing among Terran woman employees; the scramble to find a position where they were more than small-errand runners for the men. They jealously fought for these marks of status. But they also accepted this as part of the conditions of their employment. Magda was proud of being out of the main centralized office she called the madhouse; it was not a point of view Jaelle shared—if she had to work in an office at all she would rather be with the other women rather than isolated in lonely splendor with the higher-status males. She was beginning to get some vague inkling of Terran social and cultural layering and it seemed foolish to her, but she was also intelligent enough to know that social structuring was seldom rational. Just last night she had had to explain simple matters of protocol and had at least inwardly jeered at the elder Montray because he could not understand why a man who had once been his employee, the man Carr, could not be casually approached without creating the equivalent of a diplomatic incident.

Bethany was using the Communication equipment which defined her job and which it seemed to be a matter of Terran etiquette to avoid using as you went up in the ranks of employment. At last she raised her head and said, "She's not in Medic, Monty, and I even got them to page her in her quarters, in case she was taking a day but was willing to be interrupted on an overtime basis. I got a message saying she'd gone into the Old Town and would be at the Guild House of Renunciates."

Monty slammed his hand down on the desk, swearing. "Any way to reach her there?"

"I shouldn't think so," Jaelle said. *Now,* she thought with an obscure sense of having been assaulted, *I cannot even take refuge in the Guild House. Even there I find Terrans, Magda and now Cholayna have been welcomed there.*

"I'm being sent out into the field, and I need Intelligence briefing," he explained quickly.

"Lord Alderan, way up in the Hellers near Caer Donn—that's where the old spaceport used to be, before it was moved down here to Thendara —"

"I know where the Hellers are," Bethany said waspishly. "Magda and Haldane both grew up there, didn't they?"

"Haldane could help me with this—" Monty began.

"I wouldn't ask him," Jaelle said wryly, "He's up in our quarters, dead drunk and sleeping it off."

Monty said, after a minute, "I heard that he and the Old Man had a flaming row last night and Peter stormed into the city. So he came in drunk, huh? Lucky bastard; I wish I could!"

"What's your problem, Monty?"

"Going into the field," he said. "I told you a little about it—or was it Magda I told? I need to be sure I will not antagonize them, and—" he gave a deprecating smile, "I can't afford to impress them as effeminate. I need to know precisely how to dress and what to do—and what *not* to do under any circumstances. Magda made a start, but—" he shrugged.

For a moment a very clear picture of Magda and Monty in his quarters rushed over her . . . *why am I suddenly picking up all this? Why can I not push it away as I have always done before* . . . Magda, tying her Amazon knife to his waist, showing him how to move . . . she fought to barricade what she was picking up from Monty, including an overwhelmingly sexual awareness of Magda that filled her, for no reason at all, with bewildering rage. *Why should I suddenly hate Monty because he has taken Magda to bed? Magda/Margali is not my lover.* . . . Fighting to be fair through the staggering wave of resentment that made her feel physically ill, she said, "Of course I can help you, Monty. Come on up to Intelligence and tell me all about your business at Aldaran, unless it's really a secret mission."

"Not a bit of it," Monty responded. "On the contrary, when Aleki heard about it, he was all smiles; he told the old Man he'd deal with it personally as a Senatorial Representative, and you can imagine, the Old Man would have loved that!" His voice was ironic. "For once, Darkover is predictable —or that's how he saw it. Some bigwig back in Caer Donn—I'll have to look up the details, but his name is—Aldaran of Aldaran and Sca—" his face wrinkled in a struggle. Jaelle, picked it up effortlessly from his mind. "Aldaran of Aldaran and Scathfell, the old Seventh Domain of the Comyn; they're not Comyn any more."

"At war with Comyn?"

"Oh, no. Too far away for wars to make any sense. But they were once the Seventh Domain, and broke away."

"Geographically I can see that makes sense," Monty said as they went into Intelligence, looking at the map on the walls. This was something Cholayna had done, evidently. Jaelle had not seen it before. "But then, why didn't Ardais break away from the Comyn too? It seems, geographically speaking, that the country would be divided between the Lowland Domains—" he pointed, "the Aillards and Elhalyns in the lowlands, Ardais and Aldaran in the Hellers, and Altons, Hasturs in the Kilghard Hills, with the Ridenow 'way over here almost in the Dry Towns—"

"You ask me for the answer to a riddle that no one has ever been able to understand," said Jaelle stiffly, "yet the Aldaran are exiled from Comyn— perhaps for some old crime? No one truly knows; yet the Ardais have always been loyal to Comyn, though once, I am told, the Aldarans of Scathfell fought to make themselves Lords over Ardais too."

"I don't, of course, expect to understand a thousand years of the History of the Domains overnight," said Monty. "Anyhow, the Aldarans have put through a formal request to the Empire for technological help and assistance; Medic personnel, and—this is where I come in—helicopters and men to fly them. It seems that conventional aircraft are useless over the Hellers—as you may remember from that episode in Comyn Castle when we were called there to talk about the Mapping and Exploring plane that went down, they're not even really safe in the Kilghard Hills. Of course what you call hills on Darkover would be pretty formidable mountains on almost any other planet I can think of. But helicopters, and some kinds of vertical take-off-and-landing aircraft, might be usable in spite of the thermal conditions in and around the Hellers, so I am being sent to do a feasibility study. Of course I'm only in charge of protocol and liaison; Zeb Scott's going to handle the aircraft itself. And so I need a last-minute Intelligence briefing—damn Cholayna for taking this particular day off!"

"Cholayna has a right to a holiday, too," Jaelle said, so fiercely that Monty flinched.

"Yes, of course, it's damnably inconvenient for me, that's all," he said. "But perhaps you can help; find me an outfit, tell us how to arrange transport. They'll ship in the aircraft by cargo freight, of course, but we will have to have transport through the hills; foot transport. Your business, Cholayna told me once, was travel escort."

"Yes; my partner, an Amazon, and myself," Jaelle said quietly. "Let me send a message to the Guild House and my partner Rafaella can be arranging the transport." And suddenly she knew the answer to the whole complicated business. Peter could not prevent her from doing the work she had been hired to do in the Terran Zone. She would assign herself on this mission—she had enough authority for that—to guide them into the Hellers to Aldaran. And this would remove her from Peter's presence, which had been so galling to her for so long, and when she came back—which would hardly be before the autumn—she could quietly file for divorce by Terran law.

She took paper and writing stylus and quickly scribbled a note to Rafaella, to be sent to Guild House at once. "Rafi may still be sleeping. Last night was a holiday and probably Rafaella danced in the dawn. But as soon as she wakes, this will bring her, and she will start assembling people and horses, guides and pack animals. How many men will you have for escort?"

Monty gave her the details. She picked up, dimly, that he was astonished at her efficiency; he had not seen her before this in the special sphere of her competence. They talked about days on the trail, man-days of food, the best purveyor for travel clothing, which she insisted should be of natural leathers and furs rather than the Terran synthetics, and he managed to requisition purchase orders for the supplies they would need. Men had to be chosen too for the mission; Monty had access to Personnel records and knew which of the available men came from cold, inhospitable or mountainous planets and could therefore tolerate and even enjoy an excursion into the worst terrain and worst weather on Darkover.

This work was so familiar to her that by the time she had made out the preliminary listings, and arranged for Rafaella to meet with Monty at noon, she was over the worst of her ill-humor. She checked out his clothing carefully, and even went to her own quarters for the small packets of sachet that she had rubbed into the seams of her dress last night; then, hesitating, stopped to ask herself whether the scents and herbs she had used might not be unsuitable for a man's clothing. She went and sniffed the seams of the holiday gear Peter had flung on the floor, when he came in drunk. No, these were different—or as nearly as she could make out through the overwhelming smell of whisky on them.

"Jaelle!" said Peter behind her, almost apologetic. "Love, you don't have to deal with those things; you're not my valet. Anyhow, in the shape they're in, there's nothing to do but chuck them into the disposal; they're hardly worth cleaning."

She smiled and shook her head. "I'll have them cleaned in the Old Town," she said. "They'll look all the more authentic when you go into the field again. That's why I'm here—Monty's going into the field with a consignment—aircraft for Aldaran or something like that."

"Damn! Of course, as the Old Man's son he'd be in line for any favorable assignment," Peter grumbled.

"If you think he really wants to take this away from you, you are very much mistaken," she said slowly, "though there are other assignments in the field which will bring you more prestige than this. Monty would appreciate having your help in checking out his fitness for Intelligence—Cholayna seems to be taking the day off," she added artfully, and immediately he was the Terran Peter again, eager to seize the slightest advantage.

"Right; I'll go check out his kit," he said. "He'll probably have to requisition the right kind of boots." He turned to go, saying, "Meet me for lunch, will you, Jaelle?" He came back to kiss her, and her heart almost melted then. He was so dear to her. Perhaps all they needed was time, time to adjust, to grow together. . . .

"In the main cafeteria," she specified. "I simply cannot eat the synthetics upstairs," and he nodded, gently patting her tummy.

"Junior doesn't like synthetics? All right; nothing but the best for my boy," he said.

"Peter, Rohana told me it was a daughter—"

"Don't be silly, darling. Even the Terran Medics could hardly be sure about it—you're not even two months pregnant yet. We'll wait for the scientific verification, all right? If you want to enjoy thinking about a daughter, all right, sweetheart—you've got a fifty-fifty chance of being right, after all—but I'm still betting on Peter, Junior! Anyway, I'll see you in the main cafeteria at lunchtime or a little after." He kissed her quickly again with the habitual, reflex glance at the clock, and was gone.

Jaelle smothered her anger and went down to talk with the supply people about horses for the journey. They were eager to supply trucks to carry the heavy equipment across the plains, but she pointed out that there were no suitable roads, and the days in the saddle before going up into the mountains would be valuable in acclimatizing the men to the altitudes of the Hellers. "Have you no knowledge of mountain sickness, if they are transported too swiftly to higher altitudes?"

"We can deal with mountain sickness, we have drugs for it," the Transport officer said, but Jaelle insisted quietly, "It would be better not to let them depend on drugs, since they will be in the far country and away from your—" she groped for the word, to her surprise found it in the man's mind without trying, "your—lifeline—of medical help."

"You certainly have a point, Mrs. Haldane. I understand from Monty that you're coming into the mountains with us; you know the Hellers?"

"Lady Rohana Ardais is a kinswoman of mine and I have visited her in

Ardais lands many times; also, my business partner and I have led expeditions into the Hellers before this," she said. "Rafaella knows every trail in the Hellers."

"We can certainly use someone who does."

"It will not trouble you to work with a woman?"

"Look, Mrs. Haldane," he said, so seriously that for once she did not protest the refused name, "When I have to work with somebody, I don't give a cat's whisker whether it's a man, a woman or a sentient dolphin, providing it knows its job. I've worked on enough planets not to quibble with brains, whatever body they happen to come packaged in. Haven't seen many women on this one, but I understand the head of Intelligence here is a woman, and I heard scuttlebutt around the Division that they sent a woman here, because there was a woman in the Coordinator's office who had practically set up the whole Intelligence operation singlehanded by her fieldwork—you know who Magdalen Lorne was, don't you? I mean, I figured Haldane would have told you, he was married to her once. Or have I spoken out of turn?"

"No," she said. "I know Magda's work," and she wondered again if because of Peter's personal limitations she had been drawn into wronging the Terrans. They had, after all, brought Cholayna here; and had been wise enough to see that the Renunciates would be the best beginning when the people of both planets must work together.

Maybe it is not the Terran in Peter I find objectionable; maybe it is his Darkovan side which insists I must be no more than his wife and mother of his children . . . other Terran men are not like that. And if Cholayna is right I must unconsciously be a child of the Dry Towns and unconsciously wish to belong to a man, claimed as his property. . . .

The thought was so disquieting that she shoved it aside swiftly as the communication speaker interrupted them.

"For Mrs. Haldane; a personal message, a Darkovan woman at the gates." And Jaelle went to hear Rafaella's voice coming over the speaker.

"I understand I am to help you set up an expedition for these Terrans," she said, and Jaelle turned to the Transport Officer with relief.

"Come down and I will introduce you to Rafaella n'ha Doria," she said, and they went down to the Gates.

After a few minutes she could see that the Transport Officer liked Rafaella and would listen to her judgment; so she found them a map, signed Monty's Requisition order for supplies, and went to join Peter in the cafeteria.

He was gentle and solicitous as he chose foods he had seen her enjoy, but her mind was filled with knowledge of what needed to be said, and after a few bites she put down her fork and said what had been on her mind all morning.

"Peter, I'm sorry I sounded harsh the other night. But it's true and we must admit it. Our marriage was a terrible mistake. It's time to end it, dissolve it by whatever means you think suitable, and let it go."

His face crumpled.

"Oh, Jaelle, I was drunk. Can't you forgive me? There are compromises to make in every marriage—now, with a baby coming, is this any time for that kind of decision?"

"I think it is the best time for such a decision," she said, "because everything in my life will change; so this is the right time for that change too."

"And do I have nothing to say about it? It's my son too—"

"Daughter," she corrected automatically and wondered when she had begun believing it.

He fiddled nervously with his fork in a pile of some white mashed root. "Look," he said, "I admit we've both made mistakes—serious ones. But if you'll try and tell me what bothers you, I'll try and change. Jaelle, it's wrong to give up on each other now. Among other things, the kid's going to need a father. And I want my kid to have the advantages of a Terran education—"

"Surely that can be arranged without continuing to live together," she said, not looking at him. Where had it gone, all the love?

"It's a rotten thing to do," he said angrily. "I didn't think you were that kind of person. Use me to get Empire citizenship for yourself and the kid, then walk out on me—"

She started to her feet, eyes blazing, physically holding herself back from flinging her crock of soup into his face. "If you can believe that of me, then there is not even any basis for trying further—"

"Oh, God, Jaelle, I didn't mean it," he said, rising in his turn, stretching across the table to try to enfold her hands in his. She wrenched them angrily away.

"Jaelle, forgive me. Let's try again. Remember how it was at Ardais and how happy we were there?"

She did not want to remember; she felt tears raining down her face. He said, capturing her hands again and holding them to his heart, "Please, Jaelle. Darling, don't cry, don't. Not here; people will think I've been beating you—"

"If you care so much what they think—" she began, then stopped. She owed him this at least, to finish this in decent privacy. She sighed and turned to follow him out of the cafeteria. But the intercom loudspeaker device interrupted them.

"Peter Haldane, Peter Haldane. Mrs. Haldane, Mrs. Haldane. Please report to the Coordinator's office at once. Please report to the Coordinator's office immediately."

Peter swore. "I wonder what the old bastard wants now? For the love of God, Jaelle, stand by me now, don't let him get this to hold over me too!" he pleaded. She did not fully understand but picked up something from his mind, *if he thinks I can't stick out what I finish, if he knows I have nothing to tie me to Darkover,* and sighed. She said, "I won't make any decision until we have agreed on it, if that's what you mean," and let him capture and hold her hand under his arm.

"I'll never agree to let you go," he said softly. It sounded like the old tenderness. But under the veneer of tenderness she knew that he was considering what this would do to his career and she hardened her heart again. Side by side, but inwardly as far apart as if they were on separate planets, they walked toward Coordinator Montray's office.

Outside the clear glass expanse visible from the office, she could see heavy clouds hanging high in the pass. Before nightfall the city would be shrouded with it and the passes, perhaps, uncrossable. Montray was standing there, staring out into the storm, and again like a flash Jaelle caught the picture in his mind, a brilliant sun, a world of shining water and rainbows, and the pain he never allowed to surface because it would do him no good at all, marooned on this icy dark world where. . . . "This doesn't look much like midsummer to me," he said grimly, without turning round, "Tell me, Haldane, you've lived on this planet all your life, do you ever have anything remotely resembling real summer here?"

"I understand that it's much warmer in the Dry Towns and it's much warmer down on the seacoast," Peter said, "only almost no one lives there."

"I'll never understand Head Central," Montray said, and Jaelle picked up the thought, *sending me here,* and wished she could comfort him somehow, but all he said aloud was "We could have built our spaceport there and not even interfered with the natives, which would have suited *us* and suited *them* and we'd all have been happy. Only first they set us down in a place like Caer Donn, and then they move down here—Jaelle, is there any proverb on this planet which means the same as we do when we say *going from the frying pan into the fire?*"

She picked it up in his mind that Magda had been accustomed to play this game with him, and that he missed Magda though he would never let himself say it or think it. She said gently "We would say, *the game that walks of itself from the trap to the cookpot.*" For the first and last time in her life she came close to liking Russell Montray. She wondered if everyone on the face of this world, or any other, covered desperate sadness with his own defenses, harsh cruelty, nasty humor, icy stone-cold refusal to communicate—*are we all barriered from one another that way? Is there never any way to break through it? Peter and I thought we had found a way, but it was only a pretense.* She was struck with such sadness that she wanted to cry, for herself, for Peter, even for Montray, who hated the very world on which he lived and the very air he breathed, and covered it by being hateful. But she was doing it too, she only wanted to cry and here she was covering her real feelings with obedient compliance because crying simply wasn't done in offices like this one. She said, anticipating Peter by only a breath, "Surely you didn't call us down here just to talk about proverbs, Mr. Montray, we were at lunch," and then before he could answer, before she looked into the darker part of the room, she knew why he had summoned her there, and turned around to say coldly to Rohana "Lady." She bowed.

But she felt tight all over. *She has come to ask me again what I do not want to do.*

Jaelle, no one living can do only what she wants. She could read Rohana's thoughts as if the woman had spoken. *I would have liked to spend my life in a Tower. You would have preferred to be only a Free Amazon. But do you think it is only women? Gabriel would have preferred to spend his life making songs to the lute. And you know better than I what Peter wants and cannot have, and what this man Montray would rather have. . . .*

Is this what it is like to have laran, *knowing so well what everyone else needs so well that you have no time for your own thoughts and wishes?* And then Jaelle slammed off the awareness, with an effort that turned her pale and cold, while Montray was blandly introducing them to Lady Rohana.

Rohana stretched out her hand and said, "But Jaelle is my kinswoman, Montray, the daughter of a cousin who was raised with me like a sister, and of course I have met her freemate many times. He was my guest last winter." She went on to make some polite question about Peter's health and his work.

"At least I don't have to be out in the storm that's coming," Peter said, looking past Montray out the window. "I don't envy Monty one single bit, starting out for Aldaran in this kind of weather."

"Storm? I don't see any damned storm," said Montray truculently. "Dark and dismal, and nothing like Midsummer, or what I'd call Midsummer on any halfway human-type world—no offense intended, Lady Rohana, but do you *really* like this kind of weather? I suppose you must—"

"Not necessarily," Rohana said, smiling. "There is an old story; at one time the Gods gave mankind control over the weather, but he foolishly asked only for sunny days, and the crops failed, because there was no rain and snow. So a merciful God took away control again. . . ."

"On most civilized planets," Montray said glumly, "we've *got* control of the weather. That story sounds damn simplistic to me. Don't you have crop freezes, and floods, and more blizzards than you really need, and wouldn't it be a blessing if you could have the kind of weather you need for optimum crops and the benefit of your people?"

Rohana shrugged. "It would be difficult to know who could be trusted to arbitrate the weather," she said, "though I am sure you heard of the work done by people from one of the Towers during the forest fire last season, in bringing rain where it was needed. And that is one of the reasons I have come to you. I am sure you already know, for Peter has told you, that you have in your employ a young woman who is potentially material for a Tower. Jaelle—"

She whirled around, feeling trapped and betrayed. She said, spitting her words out angrily, "Rohana, we had all this out before ever I came here. I have no *laran*—"

Rohana said, very quietly, "Look in my eyes and say that, Jaelle."

That is what it is; all these last days, the laran *I barricaded so well all these years, why is it suddenly coming on me now?* "It is my life, and I have renounced that. How dare you come here, Rohana, among the Terrans, and throw this at me now?"

"Because I have no choice, Jaelle. I told you why it is so necessary that you take your rightful place among the Comyn and among the Council— and I have come here because I do not want you to say that your husband and the Terrans who have, I believe, some kind of claim on your services, will not allow you to do your duty to your kinsfolk and to the Domains."

Jaelle? A seat in Council? and at once, she knew, Peter was thinking how he could use this to his advantage. *And not even a secret now; my wife on Comyn Council and it will not demand secret Intelligence work, since Rohana has openly come here and spoken of it.*

She could no longer read Montray's thoughts; perhaps, for her, it took a moment of close sympathy, which they had shared for a moment but not now. Montray said, "I don't know a lot about the Council, Lady Rohana, but I know it's been reasonably unsympathetic to our presence here in Thendara—"

"Your presence here in Thendara, Mr. Montray, is a fact, and there is no use quarreling with facts; we must simply determine how to make these facts less traumatic for everyone. I freely admit that there are those on Council who would rather that Jaelle was neither a Free Amazon nor the consort of a Terran, but those too are facts, and must be accepted and taken into account. Perhaps I came here merely to assure myself that you are not preventing Jaelle from doing her duty in this matter—"

"We wouldn't think of it," Montray said quietly. "It's none of my business, of course, what she does with her life, but I can assure you, if what she needs is time off to take her place on the Council—"

"This is ridiculous!" Jaelle said angrily. "Why are you doing this, Rohana, and what can it possibly have to do with the Terrans?"

"As I said; the Terrans are a fact; and if one of those who would normally sit on our Council has chosen to use her work for the Terrans as an excuse for not doing her duty—"

"Once and for all I renounced—"

Rohana cut her off with a gesture; but then she sighed, looking very tired. She said, "You and Magda have spoken with me about building a bridge between two worlds; doing this by helping to place Darkovan women, Renunciates, in the Terran HQ as Medical technicians and bringing the Terran medicine, which is excellent, into the life of our city. Would this not be even a better way to build a bridge between worlds, by taking a seat in the Council when you know the Terran ways well because you have married across the wall between our people? You are not, after all, the very first—" she smiled faintly, "but of course you are not supposed to know that."

"Wait a minute," Montray said. "Another Terran—we have no record of a Terran marriage—"

"Andrew Carr," said Rohana, "your missing person. He married the Lady Callista Lanart, once Callista of Arilinn. I heard this from Damon Ridenow, Regent of Alton. It is not impossible that the Lady Callista might one day sit on the Council. And it is certain that some of this man Carr's children and grandchildren will one day do so."

"Wait a minute," Peter said. "Granted, I don't know a great deal about the Council. But one of the things I thought I knew was that women didn't very often sit on it—"

"They don't, except in the Aillard clan, where the line of descent is female; a man who marries into the Aillard clan knows that his daughters, not his sons, will succeed him, and that they will do so by their mother's name, not his own. But there are times when a woman sits on the Council. Several Keepers have done so; The Lady of Arilinn has a Council seat as of right, although Leonie of Arilinn does not always appear. I myself, as Regent for Gabriel, have taken the Council seat, until my son Kyril was declared of age. There was once a period of ten years when the Lady Bruna Leynier sat in Council for the Altons while the Heir to Alton grew to maturity; his father died a few months before he was born, and she, his father's sister, was considered a more suitable Regent than the boy's mother, who was young, and preferred to stay with her child." She shrugged. "I assure you; it is not only that we wish to make a Council seat available to Jaelle, but that we need her. It will not, when they come to consider it clearly, be a bad thing that a Renunciate should sit in Council for a time, a voice for the women of Darkover. Some of the old graywigs will be shocked, but it is not a bad thing for them to be shocked out of their complacency. Change is often desirable, frequently necessary, and always inevitable, so we can only consider which changes are best for our world, and at what rate they should come. And about that, there will always be many different opinions."

Montray had opened his mouth several times while she was talking, and closed it again, not wishing to interrupt her. Jaelle thought, without noticing particularly, that it was almost the first time she had seen Montray choose not to be rude.

He only said, "You knew all along about this man Carr? And I tried to speak with him at Midsummer, and still was prevented—"

"I did not prevent you."

"No," said Montray, with a blazing angry stare at Peter, "it was my own people who did that. Excuse me, ladies." He leaned across and pushed a stud on his desk.

"Beth. Find out for me if Monty's left yet. And tell him to get his—to get himself up here now—immediately, do you hear?"

"I think he's gone," Bethany said over the intercom, "but I'll find out, sir."

"And if he's gone, get His Excellency Li to my office, by the most diplomatic route possible, hear me?"

"Right away, sir."

After a moment, Beth's voice came over the intercom.

"Mr. Wade Montray has already left the city; Spaceforce passed him out more than two hours ago." Jaelle thought, *right after I finished with him.*

Peter said, "It was not the wisest thing, letting him out in this weather, but he's got good people with him and plenty of tents, food, and all that stuff. Weather watch were sleeping on the job, but he'll come to no harm. It's not as if he had gone alone, and with luck he'll be over the pass before it hits full strength. But the folks who were here for Festival from the Kilghard Hills—people from Alton and Syrtis—they are probably going to run into some trouble!"

"Most of them will have stayed for Council," said Rohana, and after a moment the intercom beeped again.

"We haven't been able to locate Ambassador Li, sir. He left a message that he was going to attempt to communicate with Cholayna Ares in her private quarters on a matter of extreme urgency, since she was not in her office today."

Jaelle said uneasily, "I should have been there. You made him my personal responsibility, sir—" and Montray looked at her with unusual kindness.

"He's a grown man, Jaelle. You're only responsible for him if he's off the HQ area, out in the native—the off-base part of Darkover. Don't worry about it. I heard that congratulations are in order, by the way. Check with Medic; you're entitled to all kinds of maternity leave and benefits, you know."

So he knew, too, and it was part of their damned *Records.* Was nothing personal any more, here? She felt trapped, betrayed, outraged, and behind this all was a creeping sense of guilt. She had accepted personal responsibility for Li, and somehow she had betrayed that, too.

Rohana has done this, in the hopes that when I am on the Council I shall be willing to turn over my child to them for suitable fostering, to bring up my child to Comyn. . . . so there is no freedom any more, not for me, not even for my daughter. . . .

I thought, when I went among the Renunciates, I could never be trapped into the life which killed my mother or left her to die. But now it has reached out to seek me even among the Terrans. Trapped, betrayed, she turned angrily on Peter.

"You babbler, can't you keep anything to yourself? Must you tell all my secrets like a braggart in the marketplace, so that all men can pat you on the back for your virility, as if any tomcat could not do the same little trick? You think that between you and Rohana, I will do everything I am told, like a good little Terran—or Darkovan—wife? It won't work, damn it! I am leaving Peter; put *that* into your damned record. And you, Rohana —" she swung angrily on her kinswoman, "I will see my daughter dead before I see her on your Council."

Rohana turned white. She said, "Jaelle, don't say that! Oh, don't—" and Peter said, "Jaelle, love, listen to me—Lady Rohana, she's been feeling sick, she's upset—" clearly she heard, and she knew Rohana heard. *She's sick and irrational, she's pregnant and women get a little crazy when they're pregnant, but I can talk her out of it, just let me handle her!*

Jaelle swung around, with a stableboy's muttered oath which made Rohana blanch, and stormed out of the office.

She had promised Peter the chance to talk to her about the divorce in private. But he had violated that first; he had brought out their personal business before Montray, even though he had nothing but contempt for the older man; Montray, of all people! She might have been able to forgive him, if he had told some close friend here on the base about their child—

men *did* brag of incipient fatherhood, she knew that—but to tell Montray, to put it formally into Personnel Records? *Damned big-mouthed*—she was too angry even to complete the thought. She went into their shared quarters and began slinging clothes into her old saddlebags.

A few things she must settle before she left. She would speak with Cholayna: well, she could do that in the Guild House. She should formally give over her pledged responsibility for Aleki—Ambassador Li had accepted her word and that was a matter of honor. Then she would go home.

She went to the Intercom. She had resented it; now it seemed a wonderful convenience and she wondered suddenly how she would manage without it.

"Communications, please. Bethany, has anyone managed to locate Ambassador Li?"

"He left a message for you, Jaelle. You should come and pick it up, if you can."

She looked at the nearly packed saddlebags. She was tempted to ignore it. They had, she considered, violated the terms of her employment so often, now violating even her privacy by making her pregnancy part of official record, that she felt that she should ignore it in turn.

But she would not stoop to their level. She had accepted personal responsibility for the well-being of this particular dignitary and she could not abandon him now.

She said, "I'll be right over," and left the bulging saddlebags in the middle of her bed. If he saw them when he came in, Peter would get the message loud and clear. His cozening had not worked; whatever he might now say or do, her decision was irrevocable.

Bethany, in Communications, gave her a troubled smile.

"Oh, Jaelle! Is that your Amazon—excuse me, Renunciate outfit? Are you going out in the field? Oh, yes, of course, you're going after with Alessandro Li, aren't you?"

"What do you mean, Beth?"

"I've been trying to find you all day, but you haven't been in any of the places I expected you. Li left a message here for you early this morning—"

This morning. But she had been with Monty, readying him to leave the city, and then involved in that long and stupid argument with Peter—

"You knew I was up in the Coordinator's office," she remonstrated, and Bethany shook her head.

"Li said *particularly* that this message wasn't to be given where Montray would hear about it until at least a full 28 hours after he had gone. You know what he thinks of Montray."

"This message—"

"I don't understand all of it," Beth said, "but he gave it to me; he said he didn't want it in the computer. That's against regulations, of course, but you know what it's like, the boss is right even when he's wrong. He said he had received some information about this man—" she checked a scribbled note on her desk. "Andrew Carr does that mean anything to you? He was starting out into the Kilghard Hills and would be heading toward Armida, and that you should catch him up on the way. Jaelle, what's the matter? You look sort of funny—"

Into the Kilghard Hills. Into an unseasonable freak storm, into some of the worst and most confusing terrain on Darkover. And alone? She asked, already knowing the answer and hoping that she was simply imagining things. "Who went with him, Bethany? He took some local guides and so forth, didn't he?" No; that had been what she had planned for Monty, that his well-equipped expedition should have the well-trained mountaineering skills of Rafaella and her party. But she could have planned something like that for Li if Peter had not detained her. Li knew that she had those skills and was planning to take her with him as guide and bodyguard; out of Thendara—she need not even return to the Guild House and admit her failure! But all day she had been delayed, first with Monty, then by the idiotic argument with Peter. What did she owe him? Duty came first, the clear and simple fact that she had sworn to be *personally responsible* for Li and his safety. And he had gone off alone, on strange roads with a dreadful storm brewing—at least she would have persuaded him to wait until the storm had passed.

I've got to follow him; I've got to get away fast, she thought, thanking Bethany for the message in routine words that would not betray her agitation. He was on Carr's trail, and Carr had left the Festival Ball shortly before midnight. He might have checked the weather with his starstone and realized that he must get well away to be safe at Armida—or perhaps some intermediate house of safety, Syrtis or Edelweiss—before the storms broke. Li had delayed till dawn—had he somehow heard Lady Rohana's admission that Carr was married to the Lady Callista? She wondered who the Lady Callista was and why in the world she would have married a Terran. *I can tell you, Lady, you'll be sorry. I tried it and I thought it would work, too. It won't.*

So off he had gone, to try to trace down this missing man, find out more about the Comyn, learn what had happened. . . . but he should have waited for her, consulted her. *And I failed him too! Failed in my duty as I have failed at my marriage!*

There was no sense in her first impulse, to rush madly down to the gates after him, try to stop him. He was probably well outside the City. She needed boots and clothing that would protect her in bad weather. Her horse was at the Guild House, and she could get food there too, and her saddlebags were almost packed.

On a sudden impulse, she squeezed Bethany's hand. She said, "You have been a good friend to me, Bethany. I promise you I will not forget it. I must go, now," and hurried away, not listening to Bethany's shocked question about what she meant.

Cholayna had been her friend too. All Terrans were not like Peter or Montray, wholly self-absorbed and involved only with their ambition—

The little apartment in Married Persons Quarters was still empty; good, she could get away without any further confrontation with Peter. She put a final few things into the top of the saddlebags, extra warm socks for riding, one or two small packages of the Terran synthetics which could be eaten quickly and would give fast energy and protein. She looked with a stab of regret at the bed they had shared. She had been so happy, and now—but she was wasting time. She pulled the straps of the saddlebags tight, and saw Peter standing in the doorway, watching her.

"Jaelle! Sweetheart, where are you going? I thought you said we had to talk—"

"It was you who said that," she replied precisely. "And I found out in Montray's office that you had already done too much talking, without even the courtesy to speak first to me of it. There is really nothing left to say, Peter. I am sorry; I will readily admit that it is my fault that our marriage failed. But now I must go at once. Don't worry, I am not abandoning my duty, but fulfilling it." She started to pick up the saddlebags, but he stepped forward and prevented her, grabbing her arms.

"You must be out of your mind! If you think I'm going to let you go, with a storm coming up, alone, pregnant—no, Jaelle. You're my wife and it's my duty to look after you, and damn it, that doesn't include letting you ride out into the Kilghard Hills. Li can afford to hire all the native guides he could possibly want, but my wife isn't going to be one of them, and that's that."

"I have pointed out to you already," she said, feeling her lips thinning in what she knew might look like a smile but was a grimace of anger, "that our marriage is at an end. I am not *your wife*—I never was *your wife* in that particular tone of voice, as if I were a toy you owned and could do with what you liked. I do not admit your right to prevent me from doing my duty—or anything else I choose to do. Peter, this is foolishness; I am leaving you now, whatever you do, and please do not make a fool of yourself by giving me orders which you know perfectly well I will not obey."

He reached out and tried to wrench the saddlebags away from her. "Will you put that thing down? You shouldn't even be lifting anything that heavy, in your condition. You're not going anywhere, Jaelle. There's no sun, but it must be near sunset, and rain, or even snow will be starting soon."

Yes, and Aleki is alone in it; he may lose his way, or come to grief on the trail. I do not know how well he planned this trip. "Get out of my way, Peter. I told you, I am going."

"And I said you're not," he retorted at white heat, "You're my wife and you don't talk to me that way. Put that thing down, I told you! Now, sit down, and let's have a drink and discuss this sensibly. You talk about how sensible the Renunciates are, but you are behaving like a hysterical pregnant girl, ready to rush off into a storm without even stopping to think! Does that sound like a sensible thing to do, Jaelle?"

He went to the refreshment console and dialled her a hot drink, one he knew she liked. The rich smell, something like *jaco* without the bitterness, stole into the room.

"Sit down, drink your chocolate, Jaelle. Try to see this reasonably."

"You mean, see it your way?" She accepted the chocolate; she would need her strength with a long ride before her. "Peter, can't we discuss the formalities of divorce just as well when I come back? By that time you will have calmed down, and you will see that this is reasonable. If our child should be a boy—though Rohana says it is a daughter—I will give it to you to foster; then you will have the son you want. I think that is all you ever wanted from me anyhow—"

She detected a glimmer in his mind of logical resentment; women were damned unreasonable creatures, yet a man was at their mercy if he wanted children, and how else could they have any immortality? It almost made her pity him.

"Don't be silly, Jaelle. I'm not going to let you divorce me, not with a baby coming. I owe it to my child at least, to protect and look after his mother, even if we're not getting along too well."

"And you think that I am going to sit here in the HQ and never stir myself out of doors, just because you would rather have me under your thumb? No, Peter." She set down the plastic cup so forcefully that it fell over and a little trickle of brown liquid ran across the surface of the table. "I will meet with you when I come back—in the Stranger's Room in the Guild House—and we will talk about our child, if you must. But not now; and you are delaying me; I want to be on the road before dark." She leaned to pick up her saddlebags. She had to step around him. "I'm sorry, Peter. I wish it could have been different. I—" she started to say *I loved you,* but she was no longer sure of that. She sighed and hoisted the saddlebags to her shoulder.

"No, damn it! Jaelle, you're crazy! Can't you even see how crazy this is?" He grabbed at the saddlebags and dumped them heavily on the floor. His face was flushed with anger.

"Peter, get out of the way, I do not want to hurt you!"

"I tell you, you're not going *anywhere*, not in this weather, not alone, not pregnant!" His lips thinned with wrath. "If I have to, I'll call down to the gates and have Spaceforce stop you, and you'll end up in Medic under protective restraint; I'll tell them you're pregnant and have gone crazy, and they'll lock you up until you behave!"

And he could do it; that was the terror of it, she saw herself in restraints or again drugged out of her senses; he needed only claim that she was out of her mind, meaning that she did not do everything he wanted her, as her husband, to do. She could probably prove herself sane; she was not, as a Terran wife, his property even as she would have been had she married a Darkovan. She could call Cholayna to witness that she was perfectly in her right senses, and explain her sense of obligation. But that would take time, she would have to locate Cholayna, and meanwhile she would be drugged and up in the hospital!

"And to think I believed you loved me!"

"I do love you," he retorted, "but does that mean I have to put up with every crazy idea you get into your head?"

"Peter—ah, Gods, can't you understand a sense of honor, of obligation? Can you think of no one but yourself?"

"And who the hell are *you* thinking of? Certainly not me, or your baby. If you want to convince me you're in your right mind, put down those damned saddlebags, and try making some sense," he demanded.

"Our marriage—it is my fault it failed," she said quietly. "I think you really wanted to marry *di catenas,* and though you knew my oath prevented it, you thought perhaps if you loved me enough I would change."

You and that damned Oath. For a moment she thought he had said it aloud. There was no talking to him in this mood. What could she do to prevent him carrying out his threat? He was wide open to her; she could feel his rage, his frustration, even grief for the love that had gone awry. Yet it would do no good to walk past him, even to fight her way out of the room, if the moment she was outside he used the intercom and persuaded the Spaceforce guards at the gate that his insane pregnant wife had some lunatic purpose in going out into the coming storm, and should be forcibly prevented for her own good. *My wife. She's pregnant, she's crazy, I have to keep her locked up for her own good . . .* when had those same thoughts battered her before this? *A picture of Jalak, of her mother monstrously swollen in pregnancy . . . no; surely she could not remember her mother, could not remember Jalak, she had been only a child then, without laran . . . or had it only been too painful to remember?*

"What you really want," she flung at him, in confusion and agony so great she hardly knew what she said, "is to put me in chains . . . so that I will do nothing you do not want. . . ."

"Ah, God, Jaelle, I don't want to hurt you, but you're not even listening to me," he flung at her, "and if I have to get Medic to put you in restraints I will—" and she saw in his mind a picture of herself. . . . the picture in his mind was only of a quieter Jaelle, perhaps tranquilized, perhaps tied to a bed, but in her mind she saw herself chained, *a picture in her father's mind, the young Jaelle, budding breasts, old enough to be chained like a woman, copper links binding her hands, when she was wounded in the Pass of Scaravel Magda had tied her hands so she would not tear the bandages from her wounds, she had never remembered that till this moment, she heard herself screaming and Magda had quickly untied her. All that night Magda sat by me and held my hands because of my fear of being chained. . . .*

"Don't touch me," she spat out at him, retreating backward, "if you dare—"

He grabbed her hands—and Jaelle exploded, fighting on pure instinct. Camilla had trained her both in armed and unarmed combat, how to react if any man laid a hand on her unwilling; she had forgotten that this was Peter, she had forgotten everything; she fought as she would have fought the men who would come to chain her on the morning of the day after she had become a woman. She felt the edges of her hands, soft now because she had done so little fighting in the last years, strike something soft, she felt Peter's fear, agony striking through him. . . .

And silence. Silence . . . she looked down at Peter. He was lying on the floor, and his *laran* was silent, nowhere, nowhere . . . she could not feel his presence in the room.

She knew now what she had barricaded from her mind for all these many years; she had begun to have *laran,* begun to reach out with her mind, and then, on that dreadful night when her mother bore her brother Valentine in the desert, surrounded by the Amazons, she had tried to block it out . . . too much, too much pain and terror . . .

Her mother's arms around her, her mother's pain filling her to the brim, stifling her. She could not breathe. Jaelle, Jaelle, it was worth it, it was worth it all, you are free, free . . . oh Jaelle, come here and kiss me . . . and a flood of pain and weakness and then nothing. Nothing. Nothing, her mother was nowhere in the world, was a lifeless body sprawled bloodless on the sand, blood staining the sand as the rising sun stained the rocks red with blood. . . .

And nothing, blankness, mind nowhere as Peter's mind was nowhere, he was lying before her—lifeless? Lifeless? She had killed him, then? She could not see whether he was breathing. She bent toward him, drew her hand back in horror.

She could call a Medic. . . .

And they will say that I murdered him.

The icy cold of shock flowed over her. Dead or no, there was nothing she could do now for Peter, and unless she wished to spend all the rest of her pregnancy in Medic, confined for her own good and the safety of her child—they might not be harsh even on a murderess if she was pregnant, but they would certainly never listen to her explanation that it had been purely an accident.

She must go. She must go at once, before they could stop her. He would not be discovered until the next morning, when someone missed him when he should have reported to work; the Terran obsession with clocks and with being on time for everything, especially work. They would believe he was off duty, closeted with his pregnant wife, if he chose not to appear in the cafeteria they would simply believe that they were sharing a meal in privacy in their quarters.

Resolutely, she hoisted her shoulderbag. She could get out of the HQ, they had no instructions to stop her, Spaceforce would let her through. And then the Guild House for her horse. Perhaps Magda—no; she was housebound. *I must not tempt Margali to break her oath as I have broken mine.*

And after that, the city gates and the long road to Armida, racing to catch Aleki before the storm broke. She blocked from her mind any thought of the length of the road. *There is no journey of a thousand miles that does not begin with a single step.* And the first step was into this corridor. She hesitated still, listening with her mind for some trace of Peter's awareness, some sign that perhaps he still lived . . . no, nothing. She must go, go at once.

She must get her horse, and food from the Guild-House. But Magda must not be involved.

She closed the room door behind her, slamming down a gate in her mind on the memory of Peter, their love and their failure . . . and now it had ended in murder. But she could still salvage something. Perhaps if she saved Aleki's life it would count for something in honor. *A life for a life to the Terrans.* . . .

On silent feet she went out of the building, across the great plaza, proffering her ident disk to the Spaceforce man at the gates for the last time. She hurried through darkening streets and gusty winds, the weather knowledge of a lifetime telling her that she might, if she hurried, make it before the storm.

Chapter Five

The rain was beginning, mixed with little slashes of sleet, but warmer than most of the nocturnal rains; it was after all, Magda realized, only a day after Midsummer, and the daylight lingered, even though the sun was already hidden in boiling cloud to the west. She pulled the hood of her thick riding cloak over her head; the stiffened brim kept the rain from her eyes. Her horse twitched its head from side to side, protesting this ride in the rain, evidently troubled at the oncoming night and the absence of the warm Guild-House stable, but Magda urged the creature on into the face of the rain.

Two hours north of the City she paused to consider. There was a multitude of roads into the Kilghard Hills, and Jaelle might, or might not, have seen the good aerial map of Darkover which had been made by survey. The commonest road to Armida itself was to take the Great North road as far as Hali, and turn off westward, just south of the ruined city, riding along the Lake on the road to Neskaya as far as Edelweiss; then turn southeast toward the fold of the hills where the Great House of Armida lay. This meant good fast roads all the way, and she had heard that a good rider on a really fast horse could, in dire necessity, make that trip in a single day. It would be a very long day indeed, of very hard riding, pushing your best horse to the edge of exhaustion. Riding with the fire-fighting crew they had, of course, had riders good, bad and indifferent, and had been accompanied by pack-wagons and pack animals of equipment and supplies; it had taken the best part of two days and they had not gone nearly as far as Armida. Also, they had traveled by side roads, some of them not much better than pack-trails.

Alessandro Li had been out with the fire-fighting crew though they had arrived when most of the work was over. He might have known the road they took better than the North road. Jaelle, she supposed, who had actually staffed a travel-service, would know virtually all the roads through the hills, but which one she had taken, and which one she thought Li would have taken, was still conjectural. For the first time since she had taken flight from the Amazon house, Magda stopped to wonder if she had done a reckless and foolish thing. Tracking Jaelle into the hills, when Jaelle herself was distraught and on the trail of a man who did not know the hills himself, was a blunder twice compounded. As a Terran she could have requisitioned a helicopter for a search to find Ambassador Li—or at least to make certain he was not in any danger. But with the cloud-cover and rain, it was unlikely that a helicopter could see much, and if the wind of the fierce storm she felt in her bones should actually arise, it might well blow any helicopter right out of the sky

As for Jaelle, herself on the trail of Li—perhaps she should have gone to Comyn Castle and thrown herself on the mercy of someone like Lady Rohana, to trail her with a starstone. . . . and then Magda wondered if she were going mad. How Jaelle, who detested everything to do with matrix technology, would react to such trailing, she could only conjecture.

Yet I have done a foolish thing. Jaelle was in danger; she knew it; she could feel it, like the oncoming storm, in her very bones; yet racing off alone into the storm after her, with no hint even as to which way she had taken, was not the most rational decision either. At the very least she should have asked the weatherwise Camilla, a skilled tracker and guide, to accompany her. *Camilla loves us both . . . and Jaelle is like a daughter to her.* Yet it had never occurred to her.

Why did I rush off like this alone? Try as she might, Magda could find no answer except the compelling, *Because I must, because there was no other honorable way.*

She had rushed away from the Guild House without eating her dinner. Now she took a handful of dried fruit from the pocket of her cloak and chewed on it, a piece at a time, while she let her horse take a slow jog. Soon she must decide which road to take into the hills. She could follow the present good road, the Great North Road which ran all the way up into the Hellers to end at Aldaran, as far as Hali; but if she did so, she might lose her chance of overtaking Jaelle quickly. She might not be able to persuade Jaelle that Alessandro Li could be trusted on a mission—but she could, at least, ride with her and help to find the man before his ignorance of Darkovan roads and Darkovan weather killed him.

Damn fool girl, rushing off like that. . . . would she, Magda, have done as much for her superior officer? Well, yes; in a sense she had done something nearly as rash when she had taken the road into the mountains, disguised in Free Amazon clothing, though knowing little of the Amazons, to rescue Peter Haldane. And that apparent madness had brought her here; Amazon herself, sworn Renunciate, it had been a mad choice and yet the right one on the road to her destiny. Would she have wished it undone? No, for it had saved Peter's life—and for all the ways in which she was angered by Peter, she still would not have wished him dead—and it had brought her to the Guild House, which had also been a part of her fate so inescapable that now she could not think of her life without the background of the Oath.

Even though, at this moment, she left the sworn oath behind her. . . .

No. There was no reason to torment herself with scruples. She had Camilla's permission to go, the permission of a Guild Mother in the House. Magda drew up her horse, in the fading gray light and rain, looking at the crossroads and trying to summon up in her mind—trained in eidetic memory techniques by Terran Intelligence—the picture of the map, the roads than ran into the Kilghard Hills. Where she sat her horse, three roads forked; the Great North Road running northward past Hali and later turning off to Armida, the small trail that led westward up through Dammerung Pass and into the Venza Mountains (at least she could forget about that one), and the road that turned directly into the Kilghard Hills. This road was narrow, steep, twisting and turning along the slopes of several hills—or, to put it correctly in any but Darkovan terms, fairly high mountains. No sensible person familiar with the terrain would take this road to Armida. Yet anyone who had only seen it on the flat surface of a map, since it cut directly across the hypotenuse where the Great North Road and the road from Hali were the two straight legs of a right triangle, might consider it a short cut; and Alessandro Li, as far as she knew, had spent most of his life in civilized planets and probably believed that a road marked on a map was a road as he thought of it; a surfaced artifact. If Jaelle's intention had been only to reach Armida before him, she would have taken the longer, faster, better-surfaced road. But Jaelle's concern was for Li, traveling alone and unprotected on a world whose dangers he would not recognize.

Mentally Magda rehearsed those dangers. Sleet and snow, even at midsummer, in these latitudes. Hardly banshees, unless he went astray and got on to one of the high passes above the timberline. But that was not impossible, either. And there was the ever-present danger of forest fire among the resin trees; he could set a fire himself, unless he was overwhelmingly careful about camping and cooking his food. And, if he thought of roads in the way most Empire personnel thought of roads from experience on tamer worlds, he could easily lose the trail and be hopelessly lost in country which was, except to the trained eye, trackless wilderness.

Now it would really be a help to be psychic, and know which way Li went, and which way Jaelle went after him. And did she know which way he had gone or was she only guessing? Jaelle makes a point of the fact that she has no really reliable laran, *and again and again she makes it clear that she hates and mistrusts her own* laran.

So I'll just have to psych her out and try to decide how her mind was working when she made the choice.

She was afraid of the hazards of the wild road through the hills. Yet even as she told herself that Li would not have hazarded it but stuck to the better traveled road, a picture came to her mind, Jaelle on her scrubby little mountain pony, her tartan hood bundled over her head, riding head down along a road that clung hazardously to the side of a narrow track overlooking a shadowed valley.

Hallucination? Or a genuine flash of psychic sight? Magda did not know. The picture was gone and try as she might she could not bring it back. Whichever way she chose, she would be guessing; she might as well treat her hunch as valid. She had done so before and never regretted it. Hesitating, trying to see in that strange way, she tried to cast her mind ahead and see if she could bring to mind an image of Jaelle on the better-surfaced Great North Road, hurrying along to catch up with Li—but she only saw again the steep mountain trail. She sighed and tugged at the rein to turn her horse off the main road and on to the narrow trail.

At first the road was only a little narrower, leading past isolated farmsteads with dim huddled shapes of buildings, the soft noises of animals bedded in snug barns for the night, pale firelight past the windows. Once or twice a dog barked with idle curiosity but to her great relief no one ventured into the rain to see what had aroused the creatures. Any solitary traveler on a night like this, the farm people doubtless thought, was bound on his own concerns, and in no way interesting. It made Magda think of that other trip—had it, after all, been less than a year ago?—when she had ridden north after Peter Haldane.

But after a time the road grew softer underfoot, sodden with rain, and began to climb into the hills. Thick trees, smelling of resin and wet needles, overhung the road which was narrower and narrower, until Magda knew that two horses could hardly ride abreast on the trail. The isolated farmsteads were left behind, and somewhere Magda heard the cry of a prowling night-beast of the cat-kind, hunting. The sound made her shudder; the cat-creatures seldom attacked mankind unprovoked, but if she disturbed one by accident they were savage. Then, too, in these hills there were still the remnants of the wild hominids called by early explorers *catmen;* they were sentient, probably protohuman, and very dangerous. She did not know of any Terran, except Kadarin, who explored in curious places alone, who had ever actually encountered one; but his reports had been quite enough to imbue her with a healthy respect for the creatures. Of all the nonhuman races on Darkover, only the catmen were a real threat to *homo sapiens.* And while she had heard that they no longer lived in the Kilghard Hills, only four or five years before this, a nest of them had made war on the folk of the hills, and word had come to the Trade City that many of them had been killed; there might be stray survivors, bitterer than ever against the humans who had all but exterminated them.

Strictly speaking the Terrans should have moved in to prevent genocide, if they are protohuman. Humans are the worst enemy of the protohuman cultures. Why am I worrying about that now? Afar in the hills she heard again the cat-cry and knew why it was in her mind. Well, she had a knife, and had been trained in its use, and she had sworn the Amazon oath to defend herself and turn to no man for protection. She could probably manage the catlike hunting beasts, and if she let them alone they would certainly let her alone. And since few humans, and no Terrans, had ever encountered a catman, why should she imagine she would be the first?

It was completely dark now; her horse had to pick its way, step after step, on the trail which was growing steeper and muddier by the minute. The rain beat down as if something had forgotten how to turn off a celestial spigot somewhere up there.

She began to wonder how long she could continue riding like this, Magda's horse, Lady Rohana's gift, was a good one; but Jaelle's pony was trail-bred and accustomed to these steep paths. She had no idea what Li was riding. Proof, if needed, that she had been insane to rush off without further inquiry. But she had really had no choice.

I am sworn to Jaelle. There is a life between us.

And she wondered, puzzling it out slowly between the careful complaining steps of her horse under her, just what that meant.

Jaelle was her oath-mother; had brought her into the Comhii'Letzii. That was a part of it. Jaelle was her friend—they had stood side by side under attack by bandits, they were shield-mates. Yet she could say the same of Camilla, when they had fought together on the steps of the Guild House. Further, Camilla was her lover. So why should the bond with Jaelle be stronger?

She shied away from that. She was still not comfortable with that idea. But sneaking into her mind through her attempt to turn away from it was the awareness; that too was a part of the bond with Jaelle and though she had not known it at the time—*it was Camilla who made me see it*—it had been there all along.

And Jaelle, who had married my husband, who is to give him the child I cannot. . . . Deliberately she made herself turn away from that thought. What led her after Jaelle was nothing so complex; only that she was sworn to defend Jaelle and Jaelle needed her now, when Jaelle, alone, sick, pregnant, had gone off on some insane impulse . . .

No. That was certainly what an outsider would say, but, knowing Jaelle, she knew that the impulse which had sent Jaelle after Li was as sane as her own.

Li certainly had not known what he was getting into; but Jaelle did know and had made herself responsible for him. She had done what she must, as now Magda, in following her, had done what she must.

She reached the top of the steep path and paused there. To the west there was a break in the clouds; sullen pale light shone there, and the face of the largest moon, intermittent as the swift-moving clouds covered, then blew away from the luminous disk. To the east all was dark and endless, only the deeper blackness of mountains obscuring part of the sky, and occasional flashes where lightning played around a peak. Here at the height of the pass the wind blew with such ferocity that Magda's horse shuffled around to present its sturdy rump to the wind. The rain was less heavy here, but still coming down with some ferocity. She searched the path below her as far as she could see, hoping against hope to see the small figure she had seen in her . . . was it a vision? But the road down between the hills was shrouded in the impenetrable darkness of the night, and the storm. Somewhere down there was a flicker of light. A farmstead where someone still sat by an open fire, seen through the window? The flame of a campfire where Jaelle—or Li himself—crouched for shelter? She had no way to know. A bandit pack huddled together in a lean-to, awaiting the cessation of rain?

Damn, I can see where on a planet like this, laran *would be a simple survival skill.* The thought did not seem like her own and she wondered where she had picked it up.

It was pointless to sit there, exposed in the height of the pass. She urged her horse round, sympathizing, with a pat on the neck, to the complaining beast as it faced reluctantly into the storm, and started down the slope. The road was uneven and rutted, rain washing from the heights, leaving only heavy stones and gravel under foot; even at this height most of the snow was melted, and she could smell curious flowery scents and little stings of resin and pollen in the air; the height of summer, flowers and buds everywhere rioting swiftly in the short hill-country summer. When the sun rose she would see flowers everywhere, she supposed, in the brief budding and fruiting season. An image from somewhere swept her mind, a slope covered with blue flowers and drifting golden pollen; something, perhaps, that she had seen on her travels with Peter, when they were in the field together? There was something she ought to remember about that. Well, it would come to her, no doubt.

Could she possibly press on through the night? She had had but little sleep the night before. But her horse was fresh, and for a time at least, since Jaelle was at least two hours ahead of her, she could drowse in the saddle; there was certainly no likelihood that she would pass her in the darkness. Jaelle would never try to set up camp on a steep slope like this. The rushing of water down the hillsides, to valley streams noisy with the swelling rain, was loud in her ears, and the uneven steps of her mount's hooves on the descending road. Not even Alessandro Li would have considered this a main road. Would he have realized it and turned back? No, for if he had, she or Jaelle would have met him—there was certainly, in this high trail, no place to get off the road, and it was barely wide enough for two on horseback to ride abreast. Her hood protected her face from rain, and she was warmly clad, but enough of the wind got under the hood to make her shiver and it took all her attention to stay in the saddle as the protesting animal carefully picked its way among the ruts of the trail.

A gap in the blowing clouds cast fitful light over the trail, and she gasped, pulling her beast against the cliff; normally she was not afraid of heights, but here the road, narrowing to a path, hugged the cliff and water cascaded off the trail in two places where the edge had been carried away by erosion or landslide. Well, both the man and the woman before her had passed this point; there would have been some sign if anyone had stumbled over the cliff in the ailing light. Abruptly cloud covered the moon again and she was left in darkness. Dark or light, this was not a good place to stay; with the rain still pouring, and water rushing down in ruts beside the trail, there could be another landslide. She would have preferred to dismount and lead her horse down the narrowing trail, but there was no place to get off and so she was committed to trust the beast's feet as it edged on, snorting a little.

"Your opinion of this place is just about like mine, fellow," she said softly. "Let's get along out of it. But take your time, old boy. Careful." And in a few minutes they were again safely within a darkness where both sides of the trail rose safely between heavy masses of trees. Again somewhere in the forest she heard some night beast, but she was less afraid of them than of the dreadfully exposed cliff trail which might open up again before her.

They have passed it. I can too, if I must, Magda thought, but while she was under the trees her breath came easier. Really, she should dismount here and wait till daylight. Li was not likely to travel in a strange world in the total dark—she thought he came from one of the planets with brighter suns and he would find this even darker than she did, who had lived here since childhood—and he had after all passed this way some hours before Jaelle and would have reached the comparative safety of the valley floor and camped there for the night; surely they would come up with him in the morning.

And still the rain cascaded on, flooding down from the heights, pouring in every little rut it could find, toward the valley. Most of the winter's snow must be melting on the slopes, for the rain was warm; she could already see the damage flood had done on the track and on the hillside, and once or twice she had to pick her way around a tree which had fallen during the winter storms and lay blocking the path. If a tree should come down across any point where the trail narrows against the mountainside, there would be no passage at all. . . .

Well, she would, literally, cross that bridge when she reached it. For the moment the trail was safe enough; she felt even the muscles in her scalp relaxing, and her conscious mind caught up with the subconscious enough to realize that she had passed the worst.

No need even to hypothesize *laran,* she told herself logically; the sound of water, wind and erosion, the subliminal cues in the way my horse behaves. That's all it is. Unconscious logic below the conscious threshold. I wonder how much *laran* is this subliminal adding up of unconscious cues?

It doesn't matter what it is. It probably saved my life on that damnable cliff!

She reached inside her cloak for a hunk of bread and another mouthful of dried fruit, and chewed on it. The rain blew crosswind in many places, sometimes soaking a mouthful of the bread before she could get it from fingers to mouth. Just like a man, she thought crossly, to take off into a storm; a woman would have had the sense to look at the weather and wait till it cleared.

Li could not have been expected to know what Darkovan weather was like, and after the winter snows, it must have seemed mild to him. *But he could have had the sense to ask Jaelle. That was what she was there for!*

Chapter Six

When Jaelle woke it was still raining. Fortunately she had managed to get over the pass, and down along the worst of the trail, before the light had faded. She could not imagine why Li had not continued on the Great North road at least as far as Hali, then turned west. But at least it was past. She did not want to think about what it would have been like to come down that eroded, water-washed cliff trail in the darkness.

Now, even through the rain, she felt a faint smell that tickled her nose. She had not smelled it for a long time, but no one who had ever smelled the *kireseth* flower could mistake the scent. She had no wish to ride through the rain, but it was better than ripening *kireseth* pollen, scattered by the wind.

It was early, but if she got on the road as quickly as she could, she would catch up to Li all the sooner. So far there was no danger which a reasonably good rider could not have avoided, and against all reason she clung to the belief that if harm had already come to him on the trail she would know it.

The rain was definitely slowing. Jaelle groaned and rolled out of her sleeping bag, hauling on her boots. She spread the bag on her saddle— rolling it wet would only cause it to mildew—and wished there were some way to coax a fire. A hot drink would feel very good just now, but there was no way to get it. She sniffed the dried fruit, and shrugged, thrusting it back into the saddlebag.

The ranchers out this way, usually small-holders whose main crop were the scrubby ponies or woollies, tried to keep the *kireseth* clear. But even this close to Thendara, there was a lot of wild, untraveled country, and in such sparsely settled places, there was no way to tell what might have been there. At one time during the night past, she was sure she had heard the cry of one of the catlike predators, hunting, and shivered. In years of traveling she had never met one face to face. But she was afraid of them.

The mist from the damp ground was blowing away in wisps on the erratic breeze. Jaelle swung herself into the branches of a low-growing tree, and climbed a few feet higher, looking across the valley as far as she could. No sign of Li. But he must be somewhere on this road. There was no place to turn off the cliff road, so he must have come down here, and set off across country. If she rode hard, she would surely come up with him in a few hours. There was still another mountain to cross before they reached the edge of the vast Alton lands, and another valley; a bad one, with ravines into which, she supposed, Carr's plane had gone down years before. She didn't suppose Li had come out to have a look at the wreckage of the plane, but she was no longer sure of anything a Terran might do.

She climbed down and into her saddle. She set off at a steady trot that ate up distance, and before the sun was well above the cloud layer she was climbing the steep path at the far side of the valley. Halfway up the mountainside she looked back, out over the valley. For a moment between the trees she thought she caught a sign of a solitary figure on horseback but then it was gone into the greenery again. All around her in the warmth of the day flowers were blooming, taking advantage of the short season; as she rode up the trail her nostrils were filled with their scent and her eyes with their color. Why, she was free again, did it truly matter what she had left behind her?

Piedro . . . perhaps he was not dead after all but only stunned. She must believe that. If he was dead . . . if he was dead, why, then, she had murdered him. . . . but she would not let herself think about that. Not now. It was her duty to find Aleki in this wilderness, to come up with him and escort him to Armida.

She rode swiftly as her pony could carry her, her eyes bent on the trail to spot any signs that a rider had passed this way, or camped anywhere along here. Her eyes were sharp and she had been trained in tracking; halfway up the side of the mountain she spotted crushed ferns where someone had tethered a horse, a small cooling pile of horse manure, the scrap of paper which once had wrapped some Terran ration packs. Aleki had come this way, then. She had not wasted her time on this dreadful trail while Aleki went off in some other direction. He had passed this way at least three hours before, but she was gaining on him. Surely she would come up with him before nightfall.

The trail narrowed near the top again, and once again the edges of the path were worn by water and erosion; rills of water were still taking every available rut down the mountainside, rushing down alongside the trail, taking short cuts down from worn-away dirt between the rocks. Branches of trees had come down during the storm and once or twice she had to dismount and lead her pony carefully around them. The sun was warm, and Jaelle was grateful, for her damp clothes were drying and steaming on her back, but still, at the back of her nose she seemed to smell the ominous haze of *kireseth* pollen. She had been warned about it; under its influence, men and beasts, she was told, went mad, attacked; animals rushed about madly or coupled out of season. She had been told other stories of its influence too. Well, she could not imagine that it would have enough of an effect on her that she would tear off Alessandro Li's clothes and attack him! The idea made her laugh. She was glad to have something to laugh about.

Now she began to descend into the valley. From the top of the trail she thought, again, that she saw a rider. *Peter is dead. They have sent someone to track down his murderer, bring me back to justice.* The smell of the *kireseth* was thick now in her nostrils, and she realized that her head felt muddled. Maybe she had not seen a rider trailing her, she could not see it now, maybe she had hallucinated the whole thing. Now she *knew* her mind was going, for somewhere it seemed that she could hear Magda's voice calling her name.

Jaelle! Breda! But the voice was all in her mind. Magda, thanks to the Goddess, was safe in the Guild House. She had destroyed everything else but she had not, *this* time, dragged Magda into her troubles, or involved Magda in Peter's murder.

None of this would have happened if I had not stopped to fight with Peter. I should have ignored him and done my duty as an Amazon would do it, without worrying about any man, any lover. Then I would have gone with Li, I would not be trailing him on this godforgotten road!

Her thinking was far too muddled. She had better do something about the smell of the *kireseth.* She pulled off her neckerchief and dipped it in the little stream that rushed down alongside the road, then tied it across her face. It would filter out the worst of the pollen. It was uncomfortable, blocking her breathing and clogging her breath, but after half an hour or so she could see a fine layer of yellow grains on the kerchief; so it was filtering out some of the stuff. But what about Li? Had anyone bothered to warn him about the *kireseth* in the hills? What shape was he in?

A rabbithorn loped across the road, leaping high into the air and twisting to land and scoot between her horse's legs. A *rabbithorn?* Normally they would hide in the shrubbery, and never venture out—but she was already fighting her horse, who was rearing up and plunging so hard that she had to cling to its back to keep from sliding off. She tried to quiet the frantic animal, noticing with the edges of her mind that the rabbithorn who had caused all the trouble was sitting quietly at the side of the road. It made no sense at all. She had never seen any wild animal behave like that! It must be the pollen. Not a true Ghost wind, perhaps. But enough of the stuff to affect the animals. The rabbithorn was gone. How long had she been sitting there in the saddle, staring at the sky? She pulled off the mask and wet it again. It was caked with the yellow stuff. What had it done to her horse? For that matter, how would it affect Li's horse? She did not even know if he had bought a seasoned mountain animal, or one that would bolt at the first whiff of the stuff!

The road forked, and her horse came to a halt, bending its head to crop at the green grass in the triangle formed by the roads. She got down to look for water to wet the mask, and look at the marks in the mud. Which way had Li gone?

She had tarnished her oath so many times. But at least this duty was clear. She had made herself personally responsible for this man. His safety had to be her first priority.

What would the kireseth *do to her child?* She tried frantically to recall midwives' lectures in the Guild House. They had warned about certain medicines and herbs which could damage even the child in the womb, but she had been so sure she would never want a child, she had only half listened. She looked at the roads ahead. This one must run over the peaks to the South, winding up at Edelweiss, though it was not a direct route. There were farmers living out there, and one or two little villages, and a fulling-mill where cloth was gathered in from cottage weavers who dwelt in little hillside crofts and spun and wove coarse cloth from their own woollies, dyeing it with herbs for the ancient tartan patterns. This road, when it was clear of snow, must lead by twisting hill paths to Armida, and if Li had studied the map and had a good direction-finder, this was the road he should have taken. Leading off to one side of this was a cattle trail, heavily beaten out and flat with chervine hoofs. Li would never have taken this one. She swung into the saddle again and started down the road to Armida. Surely now she would come up with Alessandro Li in less than an hour. He must be on this road. She settled her horse into a canter, but something nagged at her mind.

The width and flatness of the cattle trail. Beaten out flat and broad by hoofs. Could Li have thought this was the road? Just because it *was* broad and flat and beaten smooth. . . .

No. Surely he would have seen the hoofmarks and recognized it for what it was. He would have known that nothing on less than four feet had passed that way in at least a tenday.

Or would he? She stopped, pulling on the reins, swinging the animal around. A sharp hallucinatory pattern burst into her mind in the midst of brilliant colors; Aleki, sprawled across the trail insensible. . . .

She must go back and at least check the cattle trail for marks of a solitary horseman passing. Damn the man! Hadn't he sense enough to stay on what was clearly a road? But in the past months, among Terrans, Jaelle had seen many pictures and could now—sometimes—get a flash of what the world looked like through a Terran's eyes. As she looked at the beaten-flat cattle trail, it began to look more and more to her like a main road—more like a road than the two small narrow roads which led off to the other sides. The cattle trail led nowhere, only back into endless, bottomless ravines into which nothing could go but the surefooted chervines, into canyons and wide open spaces. But to Aleki it would have looked like a man-made, artifically smoothed road.

Surely they would have warned him in Thendara. But, no. He had probably looked at the aerial map and traced a straight cross-country route to Armida, and it might have seemed to him that this was the road. And if he had breathed enough of the *kireseth* pollen, he might even have *seen* it as a road.

Hallucinated it even, as a Terran-style paved road.

Now she was all but sure. She steered the mount on to the trail. The pony whickered, distrusting the smell of chervines, and she had to urge it on, down into the broken country, used only in summer to pasture chervines and similar cattle. There must be wild range herds out here, checked only once or twice a year, and cropped now and then for skins or for meat. There were always lush valleys tucked away in this kind of country, though she had never seen this particular stretch before, and there was certainly an inaccessible valley somewhere where the *kireseth* blossomed year by year, undisturbed. The sun was hot on her back, and the light dazzled, flickers of mirage along the trail, like spilled water. It would be all too easy to lose yourself in this country and never get out.

A solitary horseman must have passed this way, not long ago. She hallucinated a brilliantly colored picture, like a small video on one of the security monitors inside the Headquarters, of Aleki, his tall lean figure wrapped in a bright blue parka, his hair blown around his head, leaning over the back of his horse in the rain. He could not now be very far ahead of her on the trail. But it was quickly replaced with an even more brilliant little picture on the inside of her eyelids, Aleki sprawled lifeless *(Like Peter! Like Peter lying dead inside the HQ!)* arms and legs flung wide, his head lolling against a stone while at his side the horse lazily cropped tufts of grass. What to believe? And now she could hear Magda again.

She had better dampen the scarf. Her head felt fuzzy and the air shimmered. Picture succeeded picture, Aleki climbing a steep trail on foot, and

for a moment sprawled half naked beneath a strange spiky tree like nothing that had ever grown or ever would grow on Darkover, beside the
shores of a strange lake with the tree bending over him and moving in an
invisible wind. He was naked, erect, and he reached out for her with an
immediacy which made Jaelle start and blink and the picture was gone,
Aleki? Never! Surely it was the fault of the pollen, or had she picked up
some random erotic image from his mind or memory? That meant he must
be quite near. But she found that her palms felt sweaty and her heart
pounded with something like panic. She had never had the slightest sexual
awareness of Alessandro Li, would have said she could never have had,
and the fact that she had been capable of seeing that kind of mental picture, even if it was pure hallucination, terrified her. It was not hers. She
would not own to it even as a vision.

She rode for more than an hour along the trail, which slowly narrowed,
and suddenly divided into six or eight narrow paths, running in every
direction down into little ravines.

If Aleki had come along here, surely he would have realized that this
was a dead end, that it was not a road at all. Surely his judgment would
lead him to turn back. *If he still had any judgment after hours of exposure
to* kireseth. He must be lying down there somewhere, dead or incapaci-
tated, or—she remembered the sudden, erotic force of the hallucination—
wildly intoxicated with *kireseth* and not knowing what had happened to
him. Had anyone warned him about scorpion-ants or greenface leaves?
Certainly not. She had believed that she would be with him, to guide his
first essay into the field, and had relied on that. She had made herself
personally responsible for him. And now she was forswarn again.

I have failed, failed, failed, at everything and with everyone.

She looked at the sky, slitting her eyes to see it through what looked like
spiderwebs of color. Clouds were rushing across the sun. The day was far
advanced; somehow she had lost time. She looked around wildly, knowing
that she could search all her life long in this broken country and never find
a solitary man and his horse. He could starve or die out here. She had lost
him. Failed again. And the sky looked as if the rain might start again,
harder than ever. At least that would settle the *kireseth,* and her mind
would clear. Trying to see what was really there through the layers of
strange colors, she saw canyon walls rising on either side. There were caves
up there. She could try to shelter against the rain, perhaps even build a fire
—she had food with her and could brew some bark tea; it might clear her
head. If she could manage to climb, or get her pony up the trail. Yet
urgency nagged at her. Aleki, lying down in one of those ravines, unconscious but still alive.

If she had only allowed Lady Rohana to train her *laran.* She could have used it to track Aleki, to see which way he had gone. She had been selfish and arrogant, wanting none of the duties and responsibilities of Comyn.

If I get out of this alive, I will go to Rohana and beg her to teach me. It would have made it possible for me to do my duty. I have always believed I had so little laran, *yet now I know that I could have learned to use what I have. I killed Peter, I sacrificed Aleki's life, because I would not accept what I was.* It seemed that she was looking back over her whole life and finding failures everywhere, from the moment she turned away . . . turned away. . . .

She was standing on desert sand, and the sun was rising . . . *a great patch of blood lay red like the rising sun, and for the first time in her waking life, Jaelle saw, in waking consciousness, her mother's face. And she was caught up in her mother's pain and terror, and with a frantic effort she made it all go dead and silent. . . .*

From that moment I blocked away my laran, because I could not bear the terrible pain of her death. She died, she abandoned Jalak's house knowing that she would die, so that I would not be brought up in chains. She died that I could be free, and I could not accept that I was the cause of her death.

She freed me. But I chained myself again with that guilt. . . .

And now I do not know how to open what I closed away.

I killed Peter because I could not bear to remember. I struck out blindly at him, and I killed him. As I killed my mother. . . .

She forced herself to climb into the saddle again, though the effort made her whole body tremble with pain. She ached all over; she had not ridden in so long, and now she had been in the saddle for the best part of three days. This can't be the best thing for the baby, either, she thought. But then it was too late to worry about the baby. She should have thought about the baby before it was conceived. Or before she killed its father. . . .

Oh, stop worrying. You were brought up on Camilla's story of how Rafaella was caught out on the trail and barely had time to get her breeches off before she dropped the baby and rode home. The baby can take care of herself, she's nice and snug inside there. And yet it seemed that somewhere the baby was crying. Poor baby. Nobody wants her. Her father wanted her but her father is dead. What will become of her?

Surely Aleki would have gone back to the main trail, or tried to. But if he had made it back to the trail she would have seen him. No doubt he was lying down in one of the canyons, dead, or drugged with *kireseth,* or thrown by his horse and unconscious . . . she must go down there too, and search for him, it was the least she could do, it was her sworn duty. She ignored the rational voice that told her that the search for a single leaf in a forest of nut trees would be simple by contrast. She rode forward, desperately trying to force her mind ahead to see Aleki.

No. She must get back to the trail, to the main trail. If she reached one of the small villages she could bring out a search party to find him. And yet she could hear Magda calling her. . . .

No. It was the rising wind. Long trails of cloud were stretching across the sky, the trees moaning and whipping around; a branch slapped across her face; she was back on one of the smaller trails leading upward along the canyon wall. Why? What had made her choose this trail? There was only one thought in her mind, that Aleki was somewhere ahead of her, that instead of going down into the hundred little valleys of the canyon floor he had chosen to ride upward, to get a view of the valley and find out where he had lost the road. Intelligent. But if he had been intelligent enough he would never have come out alone, but would have waited for her to guide him, knowing she was sworn on her honor to keep him safe.

But he did not trust her oath either. She was a Darkovan and he looked down at her as a native from the height of his own prejudices. No wonder he had left without her. Now, when it was too late, it seemed she understood him. She had been one of those who had obstructed him from what he perceived as his duty, finding out what had happened to the man Carr, and how that fit into the peculiar patterns which Darkover made, alien to other uncivilized planets when the Empire came in.

But it was my fault, Jaelle. I mentioned Carr in his presence, put Aleki on Carr's trail; I thought Carr was Intelligence, and perfectly undercover, and I spoke out of turn. Truly, it was my fault and not yours. The voice was so clear in her mind that Jaelle actually turned and was confused not to see Magda riding at her side. She could even hear the hoofs of Magda's horse. The trail led upward, and the wind was hot in her face, like the desert wind of that journey from Shainsa that she had never wanted to remember. Kindra and Rohana had carried her little brother, wrapped in the fragments of her mother's cloak. They had tried to get her to carry him, to play with him, she would not touch him. She had never remembered that journey before, but now she remembered lying, a terrified whimpering bundle, in Kindra's arms. She had been bleeding. She had forgotten that. She only remembered that it meant she would be chained, but she could not even manage to tell them of her fears. She was only afraid they would find it out. It went away in a day or two, even before they were in Thendara, and by the time it happened again they were in the Amazon house and she had lost her fear and forgotten that it had happened before; she had learned enough, by then, to be proud that it meant she was a woman. Why did I forget all this until this very day?

My little brother. He must now be sixteen or eighteen, I have lost track. . . . I cannot remember ever looking upon his face. He has neither mother, father, nor sister; truly he is orphaned. What was it Rohana said about him? That he was sworn paxman to Valdir Alton. But if I live I must go to my brother and get his forgiveness too . . . and for the first time she remembered words Rohana had spoken on that same journey, words barricaded by her own terrible fear.

Will you not try and comfort your baby brother? You had your mother for eleven whole years. He has no one. I could have helped him. I could have been at least a sister to him, if not a mother. I have failed at every human relationship in my life, and now I have killed Peter. It would have been enough to leave him. And now it is too late. Too late for everything.

The sky was filled now with billowing clouds which seemed to move on their own, independent of any wind.

This way, Jaelle. When the rain comes there will be flood down there. Keep your horse climbing. Once again she turned to look at Magda and found her friend was not there. She was hallucinating again. She had failed with Magda too, if she had actually led Magda out to follow her here, into the wild trackless range country, where she would die.

Then she saw them.

She heard their hooves before she saw the riders, sweeping down toward her. *A Legion of mounted men, rank after rank, riding at full gallop, and over them flew Comyn banners, rippling in the rainbow wind. The colors of their robes were whirling around their horses' flanks, and they raced across the sky, their hooves pounding on the cloud as if it were the canyon floor. She could hear the pounding, the thunder of a million hooves, digging into the whirling air and sending little sprays of cloud up like dust. Then the Aillard banner stretched across the sky, and now she could see the young woman who rode beneath it.*

She was tall and red-haired, magnificent, clad in blue with golden hair like a bell of the kireseth itself, like the painting of Cassilda in the ancient chapel. Yet somehow through and over the blue shimmered the crimson robes of a Keeper. My child, my daughter, did I bear you for this? So terribly young, so perfect in her virgin austerity. And behind her pounded the men of the Comyn, led by another leronis in crimson, men and women in Tower robes of green and blue and crimson and white, racing on to drive her down, flashing knives pursuing her, driving her up the canyon, the man who rode at her side went down beneath their hooves, she saw his head explode in blood which splashed her robe. . . . She could see the horses now, hear the pounding of their hooves and smell their rank sweat, but she sat frozen, unable to take her eyes from the face of the young girl. . . .

Pain jarred through her; a cloud of dust—real dust—suddenly choked her and the world came back into focus; from nowhere a rider, kerchief tied across the face, lean and swift, swooped out on the trail, grabbed her elbow, pulled at her horse.

"Quick! This way! Jaelle! Jaelle, wake up, *hurry!* Can't you *see*. . . ." insanely, it was Magda's voice. This was another hallucination, surely, but Magda sounded angry, she had better go with her to keep her happy. Jaelle dug her heels into the pony's flank, pushed on upward on the trail. The thunder of hoofs was still there, but the riders in the sky were gone; the noise was below her, and her horse was scrambling for footing on the steep trail at the side of the gorge. But as Jaelle tried to speak, to protest this madness, the thunder and sound overwhelmed them. Chervines. Thousands of them, stampeding down the canyon floor, pounding, flying, a sea of cattle driven by the narrowing ravine into an impassable flood of horns, jammed bodies, hooves, right where she had been sitting her pony in the center of the trail!

The stampede poured past, on and on. Jaelle was shaking. *I could have been killed, I would have sat there drugged by the* kireseth *vision and let them ride right over me. . . . And Magda. Magda. She is really here and once again she has saved my life.*

The last of the herd roared past, bleating and shoving. A last straggler bawled. A few of the beasts, driven and pushed to the edges, plunged off the trail and out of sight. Then they were gone, though the noise of their passing still shook the ground. And as the sound dulled to a distant thunder, the rain began, pouring as if the heavens had opened and dumped buckets on them.

Magda put out a hand in the sudden downpour. She said, "Up this way. I saw a cave."

The light was already going as they climbed, and by the time they reached it, it was only a darkness against the cliffside, and Jaelle slid, still shaking, from her pony, and led it in. Magda followed her. She said, in a high terrified voice, "I saw you—and you were just *sitting* there—and the chervines coming down the canyon like the wind. . . ."

"What made them—stampede like that?" Jaelle heard herself say. "The *kireseth* . . . ?"

"Was that what it was? I didn't know. But there is floodwater above, pouring down into the ravine," Magda said, and put her head out. "Look."

Down where they had been riding, a wall of water was sweeping down the canyon, almost a river. Would the chervines be drowned or would they make it to higher ground? Magda thrust her head out till Jaelle was frightened as she hung over the canyon wall from the mouth of the cave, then pulled back inside.

"The high-water mark is a good four feet below us," she said. "We'll be safe here." She pulled her saddle and saddlebags off the horse. "Well, *breda,* it's better than the pass of Scaravel. At least I doubt if we'll meet any banshees here."

Jaelle's legs would hardly hold her upright. She stood holding on to her horse, unable to move. Magda turned to say sharply, "Better get your saddle off and get into dry clothes if you have any. And have you anything to light a fire? There's plenty of dry wood stacked back there—and look at the fire-ring; this place must be a regular place of resort for herd-men."

But still Jaelle's legs would not move, and finally Magda came and pushed her down on her spread cloak. "Lie down, then. Keep out of my way while I build a fire."

I am shirking again. I have failed my duty. Even Magda, even Magda I have led into my failures. My mother died for me. I failed Rohana when she would have given me my heritage of laran. I failed my brother. And my oath-sisters. And my baby. And Peter . . .

Magda had spread a blanket across the entrance for a windbreak, and was kneeling by the ring of stones, kindling a fire. Her dark hair was soaked, clinging in little wisps to her face. She had stripped off her soaked shirt and undertunic. Jaelle coughed on the smoke as the fire caught and began to blaze upward. A rough chimney had been guided through a hole in the roof of the cave. Soon Magda had a small pot rigged and was brewing bark-tea. She brought a small clay cup of the stuff to Jaelle and held it to her lips. Jaelle tasted it; it was sickeningly sweet and she shoved it away. Magda pushed it against her mouth and said sharply, "Drink it. You're in shock and sugar is the best thing for that."

Obediently Jaelle swallowed, and felt her head clear a little. She said after a minute, "You've saved my life again. How did you happen to turn up just in time?"

"I've only been trailing you for two days," Magda said grimly. "What *possessed* you to take off like that—alone, pregnant, a storm coming up? You must have been crazy."

"That's what Peter said," Jaelle whispered. "He threatened to have me drugged. Chained—"

"Peter would never do that," Magda said incredulously. "Do you think he is a Dry-towner?" Then she caught the picture in Jaelle's mind, restraints, perhaps tied to a bed in the Hospital floor—she knelt at Jaelle's side and caught the woman in her arms.

"Oh, love, they wouldn't have hurt you—truly they wouldn't—" she whispered. "I can see how afraid you were—but they wouldn't have hurt you, and Cholayna, or I could have told them you were not crazy—"

"I killed him," Jaelle whispered, her voice only a thread of horror. "I killed Peter. I left him lying dead in the HQ, on the floor of our bedroom!"

"I don't believe you," Magda said flatly. "I think you are delirious and don't know what you did, or didn't do. For now, get out of those wet clothes. We can't keep a fire in here all night—we have to save the dry wood in case it snows, everything outside here is wet." But Jaelle sat dazed and in the end Magda had to undress her like a child and wrap her in a blanket from her pack. With the embers of the fire Magda toasted some dry meat over the coals, and tried to persuade Jaelle to eat a little, but Jaelle, though she tried, could neither chew nor swallow. Magda got into dry underwear and a dry tunic, hanging her breeches near the coals of the fire.

"I was terrified," she said at last. "You must have been completely out of it—you were sitting in the middle of the trail with all those chervines stampeding down the canyon and the flood-water up ahead. And I kept seeing—I know it was only the clouds, but it looked like—well, once I saw all the Comyn lords parading down the streets in Thendara with their banners, only this time they weren't parading. They were chasing a girl—a girl with red hair, and she looked like you. Like you, Jaelle, and I thought for a moment it *was* you. And they all went galloping and galloping by over my head, and then I knew it was a real stampede through the hallucination, but you weren't up in the sky dressed in Comyn robes, you were down in the canyon right in the middle of the stampede—" She shuddered, and clutched at Jaelle.

"I saw the same thing," said Jaelle almost in a whisper, but the noise of the rain drowned her out and she had to repeat it. She had not realized that the girl in the vision had worn her face. An irrational conviction kept saying, *that was my baby, and the Comyn will kill her.*

Magda said at last, "I have heard that *kireseth* can do strange things to people's minds. There is an underground traffic in *kirian* resin in Thendara, you know. The stuff comes up from the plains of Valeron, and there are people who drink it for the visions it gives. Banned in the Terran Zone, of course, but people do go over the wall for it, the way they do for women. If we were breathing it, that explains . . . well. It's over now." She crumbled pieces of bread into the bark tea and fed it to Jaelle, like a child. Jaelle swallowed obediently. She could not remember when she had eaten last. The food and hot drink cleared away the last remnants of the fuzziness from her mind. Even the overwhelming horror of the murder receded. Maybe Magda was right. Maybe her memory was playing her tricks. If she could remember things she had forgotten since her mother died, how could she trust what she thought she knew? She could not do anything about it now, anyhow.

She said at last, shakily, "I don't understand. How is it that you are here? You are supposed to be still housebound. If you forswore your Oath to save my life—it wasn't worth it, Margali. I am not worth it."

"You're no judge of that right now," said Magda coldly. "Go to sleep. As it happens, I didn't break my oath. Camilla gave me leave to go. She loves you; you don't seem to have realized that." Her face was so grim that Jaelle could not bear it. Abruptly, in utter exhaustion, she dropped into a bottomless pit of sleep.

When she woke the fire had burned down to a dead pit of coals, the tiniest red eyes in the darkness, and Magda was curled up at her side; but Magda heard her stir and rolled over.

"Are you all right?"

"You saved my life again," Jaelle whispered. "Oh, *breda*, I thought I was so brave, and I am such a coward, and I have failed at everything— you shouldn't have risked your life for me—"

"Hush, hush," Magda whispered, holding her. "It's all right."

"Piedro—you know I killed him—"

"You told me," Magda said softly, but she could hear Magda's thoughts, like colored spiderwebs in the curious darkness, *I don't believe you did any such thing.* "Forget about Piedro."

"Why should I forget him?" she flared, "I'll forget him in my own time and my own way!" She did not know why she was filled with such murderous rage. "It's not for you to say!"

"Jaelle, I only meant—I'm sorry for him. One of these days Montray will succeed in getting him kicked off Darkover—"

It's too late for that. What was it Peter had said about Carr, *Death legally terminates a citizen's responsibilities and privileges.* Now he had no more.

"And you're all Peter has. You and the baby."

"I don't belong to him! And neither does my baby!"

"He thinks—"

"And that was why I hated him, that's why I killed him! He wanted to own me, me and the baby, like things, toys. . . ."

Magda laid a soothing hand over hers. She said, "You mustn't talk like this." *Maybe if she acted like this Peter had reason to think something was wrong with her mind. I wonder—is it even possible that she could have killed him? But even Keitha reached a point where she no longer wanted to kill her husband, but only to turn her back and walk away from him . . . and Jaelle has been a Renunciate all her life. . . .*

"No, I wasn't," Jaelle whispered. "Do you remember how you cried when you took the Oath? I never did. I—it was just confirming something I'd made my mind up to, a long time ago, and I was happy about it. I—I wasn't *renouncing* anything, I never knew till I met Peter that there was anything to renounce—I had forgotten so much, blinded myself to so much—"

Suddenly she was crying, tears raining and raining down her face. "My mother. I couldn't remember my mother's face, remember that her hands were chained, till Peter tried to put chains on me . . . that was the worst of it, he didn't know what he was doing. But I am a Renunciate, I should have seen it. I should never have let it go so far. Cholayna—" her voice choked on a sob. "I could have killed her too, if I had been wearing a knife I would have drawn it on her, when she reminded me that I was truly a woman of the Dry Towns, but it is true, true, they don't chain us, we chain ourselves." They were still in contact, their minds open to one another. *I thought it was enough to say no to all this, but that is only the beginning. All the women who had come to the Amazons, and fought and cried through the Training Sessions and left, free, having grown into freedom, but she had pretended she had nothing from which she must be freed.* She had never had any idea of the anguished battles they fought. Now she knew why it took beatings, chainings, the threat of a fatal pregnancy, to drive a woman away from her husband. She gripped Magda's wrist and felt the pain in her own arm but could not let go until Magda gently took her hand and loosened the fingers.

"They don't chain us. We chain ourselves. Willingly. More than willingly. We crave chains. . . . Isn't that what it means to be a woman?"

"Of course not," Magda said, puzzled and shocked. "It means—to be in command of your own life, your own actions—"

"And your children's lives. I didn't want this child, I did it to make Peter happy—"

How sick it was, to want to be dominated by him. . . .

"Darling," Magda said softly, "it surely wasn't all like that."

She could see herself through Magda's eyes in the first flush of passion, the warmth of her first real love. *I was ready for a love affair, it was no more than that. I would have been saner and wiser to take you for my lover, Margali. . . . Do you think he would have risked his life for me even the first time? And you . . . I knew there was a life between us. . . .*

You know I love you, Jaelle, and now I know how much, but you are sick and exhausted. . . . This is no time for this kind of decision, bredhya. She remembered Camilla saying something of the same kind to her when she had been burned on the fire-lines. She cradled Jaelle in her arms, rocking her like a small child.

Like my mother. I cannot really remember my mother, but she died to set me free, and I betrayed her by chaining myself again. . . .

Magda rocked her, gently, crooning to her. *So Jaelle is to have a child and she is no more than a child herself. I wish I could bear it for her.* But when Jaelle's sobbing quieted, she tucked her under the blankets.

"I'll make you some tea. You need it. Do you think you could eat something?"

Jaelle lay quiet, content to let Magda mother her. She said at last, "Aleki. He must be dead. First the Ghost Wind, and the stampede, and then the flood. . . ."

Magda crawled to the entrance of the cave and pushed the blanket aside. It was raining, and she looked down into the valley; Through Magda's eyes Jaelle saw the brownish, mud-swollen torrent still filling the canyon, dead trees floating, and a dead, bloated chervine, belly up and legs sticking straight toward the sky, rolling past.

"He could have found a cave before the flood started," Magda said, "Let's not give up hope yet. There are a lot of caves up along here."

Jaelle surprised herself by saying, "I think I would know if he was dead." At one time, during the *kireseth* madness, she had reached his mind. After that, surely she would have felt him die if he had died.

Magda brought her the tea and she sat up to drink it. She crawled to the door of the cave and looked down at the flood-swollen valley. She said prosaically "Thanks to the Goddess! I brought ten days' trail food; it's going to be some time before we can get out of here."

Magda felt her forehead. "You aren't fit to ride anyway; go back and lie down," she said. "There's nothing we can do so you may as well rest. That kind of hard riding can't have been good for you at this stage of pregnancy. I don't care what Rafaella is supposed to have done, you're probably not as strong as she is, and all this can't have been good for you . . ."

I never wanted this baby! It would be better if it never were born. Knowing I murdered her father—

And she believes that. That kind of obsession—she could worry herself into a miscarriage.

All the better if I did! The flood of guilt and misery was so great that Magda came and pushed her gently back on the blanket. "The best thing you can do is to rest, and not worry."

But when Jaelle had fallen again into an uneasy, nightmare-ridden sleep, Magda went again to the cave mouth and sat there, watching the endless rain swelling the torrent in the canyon. They could be there for days, a tenday. No one knew they were there. She did not like the feverish look in Jaelle's eyes, the burning, almost delirious intensity of her thoughts. She was taking it for granted now that she would share Jaelle's thoughts if there was close contact between them. Well, Lady Rohana had told her once that she had potentially strong *laran,* and now she knew that Camilla had confirmed it, in her own way, even managing to keep it barriered for her for a long time. Camilla's intentions had been good—in fact, she had done it out of the purest love—but it meant she had had no chance to learn to control it and to grow strong in its use. And now something had intensified it. Contact with Jaelle? Exposure to the *kireseth* resin, strongly psychedelic as it was?

However it had happened, it *had* happened and now she was confronted with it, with an enormous overload of new sensory data that her mind had not yet learned to process. It seemed that she saw all the way around her, as if she had eyes not only in the back of her head but in her scalp too and at several places on her body, so that she saw the back walls of the cave as well as the flooded canyon below her, the small rodents scurrying in the back walls, nocturnal mammals half hibernating in nests of sticks hanging from the ceiling. She could feel Jaelle's body as it were embedded in her own extended senses—was this what it was like to be pregnant, feeling an *other* within yourself? She could feel pain slumbering somewhere inside Jaelle ready to waken. Reaching deeper, she could feel the sleeping consciousness at a deeper level where the baby curled and sheltered within her womb, drowsing, but aware . . .

I never wanted a child. Was it only that I did not want Peter's child? I thought I did, but somewhere within me I knew I did not. And now I know that what I would feel for a child is what I feel for Jaelle, and more, and I shall never be happy now until I have a child. And that made her smile to herself, almost sadly, *for now I am certain that I am a lover of women, and it is not very likely that I shall manage to get pregnant that way! That is the only disadvantage I can think of. Maybe I should have had a baby before I decided that.* But she laughed inside herself, knowing that when she left the Guild House she had left that kind of self-definition behind her forever. *No, I do not call myself a lover of women. There are women that I love, that is all, but what may happen in the future—well, I will fly that falcon when her wings are grown.* She wondered why, in spite of their desperate situation, alone, isolated by flood, with Jaelle sick, perhaps desperately sick and perhaps insane, she felt such flooding happiness, as if she and Jaelle and the child were all one with something greater than themselves, something that beat through all the living things around them. Sky and water and falling rain and rushing torrent, trees standing to bathe their leaves in the rain, the earth opening to the flood like a woman to a lover's touch, even the little beasts burrowing in the cave and the tiny bugs in the straw were part of it. Was she still a little drugged with resin of *kireseth*? No, this was something else. She supposed if she were a religious person she would call it an awareness of God, a knowledge that everything around her had life and that she was part of it. Her love for Camilla, her intense love for Jaelle, the passion she had shared with Peter, her brief tenderness for Monty, even the sympathy she had felt dancing with Darrell, son of Darnak, even the way she had mothered old Coordinator Montray, the pain she had shared with Byrna giving birth, her own fear on the trail—all these things came together as if, for one moment, she saw her whole life pure and whole. Even as she was aware of it she knew it was beginning to fade, and she knew she must not fight to keep it, for then she would retain only the struggle. She must let it go. But it would be part of her forever.

She built up the fire, then went and lay down beside Jaelle. She, too, was still weary from the long ride, and she must build up her strength for the time when they could get out of here. She hoped Jaelle would be able to ride.

Chapter Seven

Four more times night settled down over the cave on the canyon wall; four more dawns rose red, and on the third dawn, when the Bloody Sun rose over the canyons, the rain had stopped and by that night the water had begun to go down. Magda, leading the horses out to graze on the slope, felt relieved, for though they had enough food, the grain she had brought for the horses was beginning to fail. But it would be a considerable time before the canyon was passable, and they were running short of dry wood for fires. Resin-trees would burn, even when wet, but not very well.

Jaelle was sitting up when she came back, and Magda realized that she was dreadfully worried about her. She was rational most of the time now, but she clung to her obsession that she had murdered Peter and Magda would not talk with her about it. Jaelle believed it; that was all there was to it. Magda firmly refused to believe it.

And the short Midsummer season was waning; soon they would need fire to survive. They must be ready to ride out as soon as the canyon waters went down enough so that they could get out even by swimming the horses, and for that Jaelle must be stronger. The fever hung on, and every night she woke screaming from nightmares, so that Magda had to hold and soothe her for a long time before she knew where she was; all her forgotten Dry-Town childhood seemed to be coming back to her, and again and again she woke screaming, believing herself in chains. Magda shared enough of these nightmares, with her new awareness of Jaelle, so that she insisted they should sleep at opposite ends of the cave.

"We're simply picking up each other's nightmares and reinforcing them," she said, "and we each have enough of our own, I'd think." But it was really too cold and they did not have enough blankets for that, so she slept beside Jaelle, and when the other woman woke shrieking, she would hold her and soothe her back to sleep. Magda was always grateful to see the cave begin to lighten. But during the day, though Jaelle was feverish and in pain—Magda wondered if she had caught some illness on the trail —she was rational enough. *Except for that damned delusion about Peter. Or is it a delusion?*

Yet she was equally sure Aleki was alive. "He's trapped in one of these caves, just like us," she insisted, and as she spoke Magda had a flash of him there, lying alone and filthy, unable to move. *He's hurt. And we've got to get him back to Thendara. If he dies, out here, it's going to cause a full-fledged diplomatic incident.*

"And it's my responsibility," Jaelle said quietly. "I made myself personally responsible for him."

"And I have made myself *personally responsible* for your obligations," Magda said, touching her hand lightly. "I am better fitted now than you to honor that pledge. That is what Oath-sisters are for."

"I feel a little guilty," said Jaelle after a long silence, "I wanted this mission to fail. And now it has, for we can take him back to Thendara—I didn't want him to get out to Armida and question that man Carr, or *Dom* Ann'dra, or whatever he calls himself—"

Magda smiled faintly. "From what I saw of him, *that man Carr* can take perfectly good care of himself. Between the two of them, I'd bet on Carr."

"I am not so sure. When Li is on the trail of Comyn, he is tenacious, Magda. You don't know how stubborn he is. I—I am Comyn, though I never fully realized it before. Comyn, but I am free of it through the Renunciate's Oath so I can see Darkover from both sides. Comyn and commoner. And I have seen the worlds of the Empire through their little screens. I don't want my world to be like that. And that's what Li—Aleki wants."

"And he will do it, if anyone can," said Magda. "That's what Agents are made of."

"And you are one of them—" Jaelle said hesitantly. "Do you—do you want to help him on his mission? Or will you stand by Darkover?"

Magda took her hands gently. "It's not as simple as that darling. There's no way to say, Darkover against Terra. Neither of them is all good or all bad. Let's be sure he's alive before we start worrying about his mission."

Jaelle should be getting better, if it's only a cold or a chill or some mutant strain of influenza. But she isn't. She did not want Jaelle to know how much she was worried about her.

She herself had recovered after the fatigue of travel and fear. *If this is* laran, *I am one of the fortunate ones. I have escaped threshold sickness,* she thought, not realizing how much she had picked up from Jaelle's mind. She was eager to be on their way. Perhaps it would be better for Jaelle to try to travel, even when she was sick. If they had been in the Terran Zone she would unhesitatingly have put Jaelle into a hospital. *She's really sick, and she's not getting better. So it's up to me. But tomorrow morning if she can travel at all we've got to get out of here.*

Toward morning, as cold crept into the cave from the snow outside, they began to dream.

Red sun rising over jagged rocks, blood spreading out on the sand. It was worth it, Jaelle. You are free. You are free. And then her mother was gone, was nowhere, like Peter, gone, dead . . .

No, my darling. I am here. And I am free, too. She was standing on the red sand, tall and beautiful, her red hair not braided in the loops of a Dry-Town woman but in a heavy coil caught by a copper butterfly-clasp.

Mother! Mother! Come back, mother. . . . But she had faded away, had gone to her own freedom. *And I am free too.* The crimson stain of blood on the red sands was gone, but she could still feel all her mother's pain, as the world dissolved around her. And she was a little girl, lying shivering in the bedroll of the strange old *emmasca,* who was holding her, touching her as she had never wanted to be touched by any woman . . . no, she was Magda, lying in Camilla's arms . . . it was not I. I never thought of Camilla that way. Of course not. Camilla was my mother, one of the ones who mothered me when I had lost my own mother, when I could not remember her at all. And I was the nearest to a child of her own that Camilla had never had. But Magda was not Camilla's child, she could be Camilla's lover. . . .

But the little girl was still there, a little girl who wanted so much to live . . . *No,* Jaelle said, *it's not possible, chiya, you will have to go back. To choose another mother.*

But you have chosen me and I have chosen you, said the little girl. Why could she not see the child clearly, only hear her voice? She was in so much pain. Her mother had felt like this and Jaelle could not barricade away her pain. It was too much. Too much, she was breaking apart, they were torturing her, she was screaming as she had heard screams from Jalak's torture chamber. . . .

Don't cry, mother. I'll wait for you. I'll come back again, when you want me. Such a trusting voice, a child. The little girl, in a blue dress, her golden hair curling like the golden pollen on the bell of the *kireseth* flower. Jaelle could see her walk away, into a gray world, gray silence, and it seemed to her that the little girl who could have been her daughter walked away into gray cloud like the Lake of Hali, farther and farther, and only when she could not see the little girl any more, but only the pale blue shimmer of her gown, did it strike her that this was a true parting. *Another death.*

"No! No! Come back," she cried over and over, but it was too late. The little girl was gone, and she was crying, crying because she hurt so much, so much . . . like the first time she had discovered herself bleeding and was afraid to tell. . . .

"Jaelle!" Magda, very pale, was bending over her. "You were crying in your sleep . . . what's the matter . . . ?"

"Oh, Magda, she's gone, she's dead, I couldn't call her back, I told her I didn't want her and she just went away—"

"Who, Jaelle? You had another nightmare, love. Tell me."

"My mother. No, it was my baby. And she just went away . . ." Jaelle sobbed. "I wanted to name her for you, Margali . . . oh, I hurt all over, I hurt so—"

Magda held and soothed her, believing that she had only had a nightmare, but as she held Jaelle in her arms, she realized that it was more than this. She could feel the pain knifing through the younger woman, and in a clutching terror, she realized what was happening.

I was afraid of this. She has been so sick, and under so much strain. She is miscarrying. And it is so much too early, not more than four months. Not even with the Terrans and their birth-support machines could this one live. And she, Magda, did not have the slightest idea what to do; alone, without even hot water or simple sanitation, in a filthy cave, marooned by flood-water—

Jaelle was twisting and crying out again in pain, and Magda took her hands. "Darling," she said. "Jaelle, darling, you have got to be brave, you have got to stop crying and do what you can to get hold of yourself."

I don't want you to die. And this is no place to have a miscarriage. And I don't know what to do for her. Oh, Goddess, I need help. I need Marisela or someone like that. And I am all alone with her. And I can't even let her know how frightened I am. She is frightened enough already.

Well, she would simply have to do the best she could. Jaelle's sobs had subsided to a soft whimpering. *I'll try to be brave. Like the time I fell and dislocated my shoulder riding, and Kindra was proud of me because I was so brave. I can be brave for Magda too. Poor Magda, she's been so good to me.*

My poor baby. My poor little girl. I wonder if it hurt her to die?

Magda tried to block out as much awareness of Jaelle as she could. It wouldn't help Jaelle a bit for her to suffer too. She dragged together all the dry wood they had left, and built up the fire as much as she dared. Then she put water to boil—Jaelle would need hot drinks and afterward she would need some strengthening food. She rummaged in her saddlebags and found, among the trail clothing, a couple of clean flannel nightgowns. She did not even remember packing them, but she would put one of them on Jaelle afterward. She laid the other one on top of the cleanest side of the blanket. At least it was clean. Women had been having babies, and miscarrying them, under primitive conditions without Terran-style sanitation, for centuries, she reminded herself.

Yes, and dying of it, too. She told that thought to go away and be quiet, and braced herself to reassure Jaelle, even though she was not quite sure what to do. She was sure there would be a lot of blood. She had picked that up from too many nightmares Jaelle had been having.

"The first thing you have to do," she said, kneeling down to get Jaelle's dirty and blood-soaked travel clothing off her, "is to relax and try to breathe deeply. Come on, Jaelle, you've heard more midwives' lectures than I have. *One* of us ought to remember enough of them so that I don't botch this up too badly."

Chapter Eight

Most of the firewood was gone. Magda, dead weary, dragged herself to the mouth of the cave and looked down into the valley. The water had receded still farther during the day. We could have gotten out today, she thought, if Jaelle had been able to travel. *If she had held off one more day.* . . .

It wasn't Jaelle's fault. She looked over her shoulder, tenderly, at the dark hump of bedclothes that was Jaelle. At least she was asleep now and it was over . . . at least she thought it was over. She had done her best, but she wasn't a Medic or even a midwife, and her best probably wasn't good enough.

And now she did not know how long it would be before Jaelle was able to travel. That was one extremely sick girl there. *I did the best I could, but there was no way to make sure everything was properly sterilized.* She needed proper food, and a warm bed, and good nursing. Magda put her head in her hands and cried.

And even as she wept she was conscious of rationalizing it to herself. *I'm just overtired, the strain of all this, knowing that Jaelle could still die. I love her, I'd do anything to take care of her, and I may have killed her. This whole thing is my fault. I introduced her to Peter in the first place. If I hadn't been such a rotten person back then, if I'd been able to give Peter a child, if I hadn't been so arrogant and competitive with him.* . . . *now he is dead and Jaelle may die* . . . she cried and cried, unable to stop herself, and even while the sobs continued to rack her, she remembered Marisela saying that one day she too would be able to weep. . . .

This is supposed to be good for me? Who's crazy?

It's a good thing I learned more than *that* from Marisela, isn't it? After the night past, she could have giggled; and she wiped her nose on her sleeve—there wasn't even a clean rag! and drew a deep breath, trying to assess their situation without hysteria.

Jaelle was sleeping; but she was very weak. Magda thought she had lost altogether too much blood. She needed medical attention, to be sure Magda had not botched handling the miscarriage and everything was clean. At a very minimum she needed dry clean clothes, nourishing food, and warmth. Magda could provide that, foraging for resin-branches which would burn when wet, provided she got them *now* before the fire was dead out.

Otherwise, she realized soberly, they could both die here.

If Jaelle's fever went down within the next few hours, perhaps she should simply bundle the girl on her horse, even if she had to tie her in her saddle, and pack her out to civilization, where she could organize search parties for Aleki, and Jaelle could get nursing. On the other hand, suppose they encountered some isolated farm where the woman of the place reacted like the woman who had cursed Magda on the fire-lines? That one might have been capable of turning them out to die.

If they stayed here, there was nothing ahead but starvation and cold, but she was still strong. Could she possibly leave Jaelle alone and go for help? Behind her in the cave she heard Jaelle whimper in her sleep, as if the very thought terrified her.

Jaelle, who was so strong. *Yet I have always protected her. My child. My love.*

She would stay with Jaelle, no matter what. Either she would risk taking her out to civilization, now or when Jaelle was stronger, or they would await rescue here.

The weather knowledge of years told her there was another storm on the way, but it was not yet imminent. Still, she should get in as much fuel as she could.

She bent over Jaelle, intending to whisper to her that she must not be frightened, she was not going far away; but for the moment the woman was sleeping peacefully and Magda hated to disturb her. Could she possibly reach her mind? During the aftermath of the *kireseth* storm they had spent much time in contact, and had even shared their dreams. Before the miscarriage, however, knowing she could not care for Jaelle adequately if she must also suffer all Jaelle's pain and fear, she had done something, she still did not know what, and blocked her mind from Jaelle's. Could she now reverse this process?

She tried to sink into the sleeping woman's mind; she did not know how well she had succeeded, but she tried to shape her thoughts without disturbing Jaelle's sleep; after that nightmare of pain and fumbling midwifery, Jaelle needed sleep. But she needed reassurance too.

Darling, I have to leave you just for a little while, I have to get wood, or something we can burn. If you wake up and I'm gone, don't be frightened. She repeated it mentally several times, but Jaelle did not stir and Magda wondered if she had reached her at all. Well, with luck she would be back before Jaelle woke, and could have some tea for her, and perhaps some hot porridge. It wasn't what Magda would have chosen but Jaelle had presumably lived on it before this and the stuff supposedly had all the nutritious elements needed—it was the staple travel food of the Amazons, anyhow. The fact that it tasted like stale hot cereal didn't really matter.

She pulled her hooded riding-cloak over her head, thinking that she would have felt more comfortable in Jaelle's Terran style down jacket. But Jaelle was smaller than she was and the jacket would not fit, so it was the riding-cloak or nothing. At least it was warm. She checked on the horses to be sure they had not strayed too far, patted them, gave them the last few bites of grain. Then she began dragging branches of damp resin trees up the slope. It was heavy, hard work and her arms ached, and she broke her nails on the wood. *Damn, if I could only reach an intercom somewhere. Primitive planets are wonderful, I love this one, but damn it, in an emergency like this one, what do you do? Sit marooned and die?*

She could have sent out an alarm and had Terran helicopters out looking for Jaelle before she got over the pass! She could have had a full-scale search and rescue out for Aleki before he was two hours ride out of Thendara! If Jaelle had had half a brain, that was what she would have done, instead of going racing off at night into a storm after him!

But Jaelle had killed Peter—or thought she had, Magda thought, sobered. *It was an accident. But she'd have to convince the Terrans of that.* And she couldn't have helped Aleki very much if she had been locked up in the hospital, or held for questioning.

She dragged an armload of wood to the cave mouth and went down for another one. Halfway up the slope she saw flakes of snow drifting down on to the folds of her cloak; the thick wet flakes, clumped together into little snowballs, almost, which meant it would soon be coming down hard. Some of it would melt when it hit the remaining water in the canyon, but enough would pile up on the slopes to make the trail dangerous.

That settled it. They could not be walled in here; they dared not stay. Somehow she must get Jaelle on her horse and they must make a fight to get to civilization.

The hell with all that stuff about waiting here to be rescued. A Renunciate has to rescue herself! Grimly, she dumped the wood and started getting her things together, what was left of the food. She built up the fire with the last of the dry wood and put their dried meat to boil; she would get them a good hot nourishing meal so they would be better able to travel. She packed what she could, ruthlessly discarding everything but food and blankets. She loaded them into her own saddlebags. She would put Jaelle on the horse, with her saddlebags, and ride Jaelle's pony herself. It was going to be a rough trip enough without extra weight.

If they made it out she would send a search party to seek for Aleki, or his body, in the higher caves.

By the time the soup was done, smelling reasonably edible, she knew she dared wait no longer. Already it was snowing hard, and she hesitated again; if the snow got harder yet, they could be lost in whiteout blizzard. Yet what was the alternative? To be snowed in here until they died? She drank some of the hot soup herself, and ate a handful of nuts, then poured the cooled soup into a cup and bent over Jaelle to shake her awake.

"Jaelle. Shaya, love, wake up and drink some soup. I've got to get you out of here; its snowing and we've got to try and get out of this canyon while we still can."

Jaelle stared at her vacantly, and Magda's heart sank.

"Kindra?" Jaelle whispered, "It hurts. I'm bleeding. Am I going to die, Kindra?"

"Jaelle!" Roughly, Magda shook her. "Stop that! You're here with me! It's Magda! Wake up, damn it! Here, drink this!" She held the soup to Jaelle's mouth, tilting the cup; Jaelle swallowed a mouthful obediently, then pushed it away; when Magda swore at her, shoving the cup against her mouth, she stared, not knowing what Magda wanted, letting it dribble down her chin. Magda felt like slapping her.

But it's not her fault. She's sick; she doesn't even know who I am. She checked the folds of improvised bandages. Jaelle was bleeding again. *If she loses any more blood . . .* and Magda realized that if she made Jaelle get up and walk now or ride, it would probably kill her. Her face was fire-hot, and Magda had no medicines to give her.

She could be dying. Magda looked at the heavy snow outside the cave and thought, *If we wait another hour or two it might be too late to get out before the storm, but I can't move her now.*

She tucked the blankets around Jaelle again, feeling desperate. Did she have to sit here and let Jaelle die? If only she had a way to reach Lady Rohana, who could use her starstone. . . .

If she had a way to reach Lady Rohana. . . .

But she did. She had *laran*. She was not sure how to use it, but she might reach *somebody*. The blue-gowned red-haired *leronis* who had healed her feet on the fire lines—what was her name, Hilary? Lady Callista? Ferrika, who was an Amazon herself?

Anybody. But how do you do it? I was a fool. I should have let Lady Rohana teach me. . . .

How do you yell for help with *laran?* And as she formulated the question in her mind, from somewhere the answer formed in her desperation. *You just do it. You just yell, Help!*

Well, help! Help, anybody! Magda crouched on the floor of the cave, covering her eyes with her hands, trying desperately to recapture the sureness of that moment when she had seen the whole world around her as part of herself. *Jaelle is very sick. We are marooned here by floodwater. Jaelle is sick, maybe dying, she's bleeding, we are running out of fuel. . . . Oh, help, somebody, help!*

She repeated this again and again, concentrating with agonizing intensity, trying to visualize the call going out, farther and farther, spreading in widening circles as if she had dropped a stone into the quiet around the cave.

There was a little stir in the air of the cave. Magda looked up. Dimly sketched on the air, she seemed to see faces. Women's faces, none of them familiar.

And then, without real surprise, she saw Marisela's face on the dimness. *You promised me you would do nothing rash until I could talk to you, child. . . .*

Magda said aloud, wondering if she was crazy, "I couldn't let Jaelle go off like that alone—"

I suppose you could not. It seemed now that Marisela was standing there, though she was shadowy and Magda felt that she could see the wall of the cave *through* the woman's body. *Is she really here or have I flipped out after all this trouble?* And then Marisela was gone, wholly gone, and Magda was no surer than ever that she had ever seen her. *And if she had been there,* Magda thought in indignation, *well, I must say that wasn't a lot of help, just scolding me for going away alone and vanishing again! She could at least have given me some telepathic advice about what I ought to do for Jaelle. She's the midwife!* The snow was making a soft swishing sound outside. It was just as well they had not gone into it. She should go out and get the horses inside; they probably could not endure this weather either. Wasn't there some serious disease, tetanus or something, carried by horse droppings? It was probably too late to worry about that. She and Jaelle had been handling horses enough that if she was going to get it, she'd get it. She herself had been vaccinated; she hoped Jaelle had been through a good Medic checkup lately.

There was a soft sound like the calling of crows; she felt a curious swirling in the air and looked up. The snow was suddenly gone; she was standing in a fire-blue haze—she thought of Lady Rohana's starstone—

and around her were shadowy figures, dark-robed women; she recognized none of their faces.

She is one of the pivot points of history, said a voice in her mind. She knew it was not really there.

Remember; we dare show no compassion for individuals. We are concerned only with centuries, and some must suffer and die. . . .

Magda thought; I am hallucinating that conversation Mother Lauria had with Cholayna. Only I wasn't even there. It was Jaelle.

There will be no lack of suffering, but neither must die now; she is not important, but the blood of the Aillard is important, for one day the rule of Arilinn must be broken . . .

Then will the Forbidden Tower fail?

All those who work for the hour must fail. But we must think in terms of centuries. . . .

A Terran's child in Arilinn would break their rule and their stranglehold. . . .

Do you dare presume to deny her free will? She chose not to bear the Terran's child, thinking thus to avert suffering; she has not yet learned, and so she will suffer threefold. . . .

This time we will save them both for you. But remember; it is not personal compassion for any individual. It is only that this is a point where destiny intersects with the humane thing to do. We would all rather save lives. But we cannot interfere.

Then the words dissolved into the calling of crows; and Magda found that she was standing motionless in the heavy snow, falling thickly on her face and into her eyes, blurring her vision.

She fought her way through the blinding snow. It was just as well Jaelle had not tried to ride, they could never have gotten back to the main road in this. But the horses were not where she had left them, and in panic, Magda went down farther than she had intended on the slope; her foot slipped on the wet, slushy ground and she rolled down toward the canyon's floor, crying out in protest.

Her riding cloak and breeches were soaked now, and she could see no sign of the horses. In the thick snow she could not see the cave mouth. *Jaelle! I must get back to Jaelle!* Shading her face against the thickening snow she finally made out a tiny thread of smoke where their cave opened, and struggled back up the steep grade, without the horses.

Then before her, Ferrika's snub-nosed face appeared, with eyes blue and compassionate.

Don't be frightened, sister. You have been heard in the Forbidden Tower, and someone will come to you. Don't be frightened.

And Ferrika's face was gone. Magda blinked, remembering the fragments of conversation she had heard, Lord Damon, Regent of Armida, and something about an illegal Tower. Well, they were already in trouble with the Terran authorities, if Jaelle had really killed Peter; they might as well be in trouble with the Darkovan authorities too. From what she had heard this particular Tower wasn't in very good odor with the regular Towers.

Any port in a storm, kid. She blinked, thinking that someone had spoken to her in Terran Standard. *Am I losing my mind? I had better get inside out of the snow!* Jaelle was still lying where Magda had left her, stuporous, her face burning.

Who are you?

You know who I am. I said you had guts enough for three. Make that thirty-three, kid.

Ann'dra—Andrew Carr?

I'm not great at this kind of receiving. I ought to let Callista try to reach you. No time. I saw the smoke. Don't worry. And then a picture in her mind, men turning and riding down the canyons, swarming out from what looked like a great center of blue fire . . . no, she couldn't be right . . . she couldn't expect telepathic reception to come in like television, for heaven's sake! Jaelle was muttering and moaning and throwing herself around, and Magda mended the fire and went and sat by Jaelle and drew the girl into her arms, holding her and rocking her. Jaelle muttered, "Mama? I thought you were dead, Mama. Who are these women? I'm scared, I don't want to go. Oh, Mother, it hurts—" and Magda stroked her hair and tried to soothe her.

"It's all right, Shaya. It will be all right, I promise you. They're coming, they know we're here. It's all right."

Jaelle looked at her quite clearly and said, and her voice was almost rational, "But Amazons don't wait to be rescued. We're supposed to do the rescuing. The way we did before, Margali," and dropped off into vacancy.

Magda patted her cheek. She said gently, "Even Amazons are only human, Jaelle. It's taken me a year to find that out."

But she knew the sick woman could neither hear nor understand her. The fire was dying; she crawled into the blankets and tried to warm Jaelle, holding her closely in her arms. And at last, unbelievably, she slept.

She woke to hear voices. Andrew Carr's voice, calling out in the dialect of the Kilghard hills, halloing wildly.

"Not here—not this one! No, damn it, I tell you there's got to be another cave, there are two sick women out here! Keep looking! Try lower down, along the slope! Eduin, come up here with two men and stretchers, this man has a broken leg!"

They've found Aleki. Thank God, he's alive. A picture came into her mind, as she had seen it before, *Alessandro Li, the elegant Terran diplomat, disheveled, filthy, sprawled on the cave floor, his leg bundled in an improvised splint, looking up with an open mouth as Carr grinned down at him.*

"Ambassador Li, I presume. Heard you've been looking for me," he said, and *offered a Terran handshake. Li stammered "You—you—you—" and the picture winked out.*

Magda crawled out of the blankets. The fire was dead, they could not see the smoke; it was very cold in the cave, but Jaelle was breathing and seemed all right. She pulled her riding cloak over her head and hurried to the door of the cave. The slopes were alive with men and horses and she could see a group of men, crowded around the dark mouth of a cave down the slope—about half a Terran kilometer, she supposed. She could see Carr now, a tall man with a shock of fair hair, standing a good head taller than the other men.

She shouted, knowing he could not hear her over the intervening space but knowing that he could hear her *somehow.*

"Ann'dra! *Andrew!* Up here!"

He started as if galvanized, looked and pointed; raised his hand to her in a wave, a signal.

Okay, hang on, I see you.

And Magda collapsed in the mouth of the cave, in the mud and dirt there, and began to cry. She cried and cried, as if she would never stop, knowing suddenly what Marisela had meant.

Some day you will cry and be healed.

She was almost unaware when a man, quiet and deferential in the Ridenow colors, came up the slope; but she heard him call "They're here, *vai dom!* Both of them." He cleared his throat, *"Mestra—"* and she quickly scrambled to her feet, clutching some dignity, some remnants of composure. A poor pretense, she knew; her face was blotched and swollen.

"Mestra, are you all right?"

She said quickly, "My friend. She is sick; you will have to get a stretcher to move her, too. There is nothing wrong with me."

"We have a stretcher," he said. "Down there. As soon as we can get him into a horse-litter, we will come up and move her," and Magda saw, at the cave mouth farther down the slope, men carrying a prone form on the litter, carrying it down the hill to waiting horses and men. And then Andrew Carr was striding up the slope to the very mouth of the cave.

He smiled at Magda, a good-natured grin and said quietly, so that the man could not hear, "It's all right. They know I'm Terran and they don't really care. I've been racking my brains to figure out who *you* could possibly be. Lorne of Intelligence, aren't you? I knew you by reputation, but I don't think we ever actually met each other—"

And, incongruously, they shook hands.

Then he was bending over Jaelle.

"Miscarried, has she? Well, we'll have her down where they can look after her. Ferrika's still in Thendara for Midsummer, but *mestra* Allier from Syrtis can look after her. God knows Lady Hilary's had enough of that kind of trouble. We'll take her to Syrtis, and when she's well again we can move her to Armida." He laughed. "Somehow I think you and I have a lot to say to each other. But it can wait."

He bent and scooped up Jaelle in his arms. He was so tall he lifted her like a child. She could see, without knowing why, the picture in his mind of a beloved woman who had recently suffered such a loss, and his compassion and enduring sadness; but when Jaelle cried out in pain and fear he spoke gently to her, and Jaelle quieted at the touch of his hands and perhaps, Magda thought, of his *laran.*

The other man's hand was on her arm.

"Mestra, let me help you—"

She started to say, "I can walk," and then realized she couldn't. She let herself lean on him, and stumbled toward the horses in the valley. She should be there when Jaelle recovered consciousness.

Epilogue

Alessandro Li, still holding himself erect between two crutches, managed to give the impression, though he hardly moved his head, of bowing deeply over Magda's hand.

"I am truly grateful to you. Jaelle, I hope your recovery is swift and complete." He spoke a polite phrase which Magda recognized as a formal farewell in his own language, but it was one of the Empire languages of which she had only a smattering. "My Lord—" another of the gestures which somehow implied a deep formal bow, to Damon, "I am thankful for your hospitality."

The Great Hall of Armida, with its massive beams and the huge fireplace, was warm and snug around them; but a chilly draft entered the hall as the doors opened. Outside it was snowing softly. Andrew murmured, "This way, sir," and Aleki followed him, hobbling on the crutches, two or three men on either side. They would escort him to Neskaya, where he would be picked up by Terran helicopter.

Lady Callista said quietly to Magda as the door closed behind him "I hope he will not make trouble in the Empire," and Andrew, striding back into the hall, said, smiling, "He won't."

"How can you know? What he did while he was a guest in this house might be very different—"

Andrew chuckled. "Don't worry about Li," he said. "I know his kind. He'll dine out on the story for the rest of his life, about his hairbreadth escape on a primitive planet, and enjoy being thought the expert on Cottman Four—which means he'll have to tell himself how wonderful it all was."

"But he did promise to get rid of Coordinator Montray," Magda said quietly, "and to put in a Legate who knows the planet and appreciates it. He even offered to put in a word for me if I wanted the job."

"You should take it, if only to spite them," Jaelle said. She was lying on a sofa, wrapped in a frilly soft blue house robe which looked very unlike her. She had some color in her face again, but it had been a long, hard fight against weakness and infection, and even earlier that day, Aleki had tried to persuade her to come back to the Terran Zone so that the Medics could give her a thorough going-over. "We owe you that," he had protested, but Jaelle smiled and told him that by now she was perfectly well again, and Magda had heard the unspoken part of that as well as Jaelle; that she had not the slightest intention of returning to the HQ, now or ever.

Magda did not believe that she was perfectly well—only when she was flat on her back and delirious could Jaelle ever admit any weakness at all—but she was over the worst. She had been desperately ill when they carried her down to Syrtis, and for all they could do for her, she seemed to have lost the will to live.

She had begun to recover only when Magda, knowing at last what was troubling her, gathered with the *leronis.* They called Lady Callista, the Regent, Lord Damon, and Andrew, at their invitation, and gone out in their *laran* circle to seek out Peter Haldane's fate in the Terran Zone. He was alive; he had been found lying in a coma and carried down to the Hospital floor, but now he was recovering.

"You struck him with your mind as well as your hands," Lord Damon had said soberly to Jaelle. "You could easily have killed him; it was only an accident that you did not. Perhaps it was the grace of some God with whom you are on better terms than you know."

And from that day Jaelle had begun to sleep without nightmares and to eat and gain back a little of the weight she had lost.

That hour within the matrix circle—and Magda knew she had taken a full part in it—had somehow made her part of them; Andrew and Callista treated her like a sister and brother, and she felt as if she had known Damon all her life. She felt somewhat less close to the pretty Lady Ellemir, who said forthrightly that for these years while the children were young she wished to give them her full time and attention. She was sitting now at the far end of the hall, the children of the household gathered around her. Magda still did not have them all straight, though she knew that the seven-year-old, curly-haired redhead they called Domenic was the oldest son of Damon and Ellemir, and her only surviving child. Lady Callista had two daughters somewhere between four and seven, one dark and serious— Magda thought her name was Hilary, a name she remembered because of the *leronis* who had healed her feet—and one fair-haired and giggly, but

Magda never could remember her name. There were several other children who were explained offhandedly as fosterlings of the House; the smallest of them Callista explained blandly as Andrew's *nedestro* son, which seemed strange—no one could possibly mistake the deep devotion between Callista and Andrew; Magda had never seen such a devoted couple—and the others were small redheads who had, Damon explained with equal casualness, some Comyn blood somewhere, had been born to small-holders and farmers, and were being brought up where they could be properly trained when their *laran* surfaced. Magda and Jaelle too were astonished at the way in which this was taken for granted. Ellemir mothered all the children indiscriminately.

"It is pure self-indulgence," she admitted, "but they are little only such a short time, and Callista is my twin—she has *laran* enough for two, so for these precious years while they are so tiny, I take delight in them while I can. We come from a long-lived family; I shall have forty or fifty years to come back into the circle and master my *laran* after they are grown." Now she was telling them all some kind of story, the littlest one on her lap, the others clustered around her knees.

Jaelle sighed as the sound of Ambassador Li's escort died away outside. She said, "I do not suppose Peter will make any trouble—now—about giving me a divorce. Aleki promised to set it up so that I need not—go back." Her eyes were shadowed, and Magda knew without needing to touch her mind what she was thinking. Jaelle was still easily depressed, and cried easily, but Ellemir had privately assured Magda that it would pass in time.

"I know," Ellemir said sorrowfully, "I have lost three; and the last only this season. Just before Midsummer." Magda remembered Ferrika, crying in Marisela's arms. Having been, though briefly, part of the circle, she understood the bond, and knew Ferrika was a very real part of this matrix circle—the only one on Darkover which was not hidden, guarded, shielded behind Tower walls. And Ferrika, though commoner born, was as much part of it as Lord Damon himself, or his brother Kieran, or the aristocratic Lady Hilary, who was married to Colin of Syrtis. Hilary's one son Felix was somewhere in the circle of children around Ellemir, but Magda had forgotten which one he was.

You never wholly cease to grieve, she had said to Jaelle. *But you learn to live with grief, and find a way through it. And you try again. And you open your heart to other children.*

Jaelle had said, very low, "As Kindra did. And as Camilla does still," and from that day she had begun to sleep without nightmares of the little girl with red hair, walking away into the gray irrecoverable mists of the overworld.

Now Andrew came and said, "I am going to ride out and see that everything is well with the horses before the storm shuts down. Who wants to come with me, lads?"

All the boys, except the tiny one in Ellemir's lap, raced out after him. They all called Andrew by the word which could mean Uncle, or foster-father, just as all of them—including her own two daughters—called Lady Callista by the intimate nickname meaning auntie, or foster-mother; but Lady Ellemir was simply "Mama." Not only to her own and Ellemir's children but to every child on the estate of Armida.

One of the girls grabbed down her cloak and demanded to be taken too. Ellemir said deprecatingly "Oh, Cassie—" but Andrew only laughed, picking up his younger daughter.

"You shall come if you like, Cassilde n'ha Callista," he said, setting her on his shoulder, and Callista explained, with a laugh, "She is Ferrika's favorite, and Ferrika always said she had the making of a Renunciate! Andrew, you should not call her that, she might take it seriously!"

"Why not?" Damon asked, "We shall need rebels some day," but Ellemir shivered. She said in a low voice, "Don't, Damon. Time enough for that—" and Damon patted Ellemir's shoulder and stood close to her for a moment. It seemed to Magda that she could hear the curious rustle of the dark robes and the far echo like the calling of crows, as if the fates were flying overhead. Then Andrew went out with his brood; Ellemir called a nurse and had the other children taken upstairs to the nursery suite, and Lady Callista came to sit by the fire between Magda and Jaelle, fingering her *rryl*. She said, "Had I ever heard of the Renunciates, I think I might never have gone to Arilinn!"

Damon laughed and said, "They would not have accepted you in a Guild-house, Callie. I was in Council the year Lady Rohana stood before them and pledged herself for Jaelle, that she should be freed—"

Jaelle began dripping tears again, though she bent her head and tried to hide them, and her awareness of failure was painful to everyone in the circle around the fire. But Damon only said quietly, "Well, you must take you own seat there until you choose—what is it you say, *in your own time and season*—to bear a daughter for the Domain of Aillard. And if you do not, no doubt the Hastur-kin will survive, as they have for centuries." But again Magda had the flickering vision of the little girl with red hair, running in a storm of autumn leaves behind the girl Ellemir had called Cassie. She did not understand it, but accepted.

Her *laran*, so recently wakened, was still not wholly under her control. She saw again the curious circle of women's faces under their dark hoods and the sound of the crows calling far away, and her mind slipped away. *We are not concerned with the good of the Comyn, nor yet of the Terrans, nor of the Renunciates; we must think in terms of centuries. So many of the Comyn are loyal only to their own caste, and most of the Towers have become only their instruments, where once they served all for the common good. That is why the Altons and the Forbidden Tower have become our instruments for the moment. They too shall suffer for the moment, although in the centuries they shall attain perfection and enlightenment.*

Magda whispered, almost aloud, *Who are you?*

You may call us the Soul of Darkover. Or the Dark Sisterhood. . . .

"Magda, where are you?" asked Jaelle, and the vision faded swiftly, even as Magda sought to hold on to the awareness, the last fading words, *We are instruments of fate, even as you, sister. . . .*

Callista touched Jaelle's hand. Magda had been among them long enough to know what a rare gesture of intimacy this was. She said, "I was Keeper long enough to know how you feel, Jaelle. I did not share Ellemir's acceptance of the duty to bear children for the Domain——"

"Duty?" declared Ellemir with a touch of annoyance. "Privilege! Anyone who would willingly refuse to have a child—well, I can only imagine she must be mad, or I am very sorry for her!"

Callista smiled affectionately at her twin. It was evidently an old argument between them. "Well, I promised you that you might bring up all of mine, and I have kept that promise," she said, laughing. "I am fond enough of my children, and of yours too, and some day I suppose I will resign myself to give Andrew the son he wants, though it seems unfair that I, who would be richly content if I never had a child, bear them so easily, while you, who would like to have a child in your arms every ten moons— no, don't deny it, Elli—can have them only with so much trouble and suffering."

And loss. . . . They all heard it, but none of them spoke it aloud. But Ellemir said quietly, "The Alton blood is a precious heritage. I am proud to be the instrument of transmitting it."

Jaelle said ruefully, "You sing the same song as Lady Rohana, and to the same tune. And yet you are a potential *leronis,* which must be very like being a Renunciate—having something better to do than other women——"

"I do not see how it can be better," Ellemir said, "A racing mare, no doubt, is proud of winning all her races. Yet if she does not transmit that bloodline she might as well have stayed in her stable eating hay. We need the brood mare as well as the racing filly."

"I will do my duty," said Jaelle quietly. "I know, now, why I must." The women around the fire seemed very close; to Magda it was like the peace that sometimes came at the end of Training Session, when they had argued and cried and fought their way to peace. Callista, she sensed, had fought longer and harder battles than any Renunciate, yet she seemed even more serene.

"And yet you are sworn to Jaelle, Margali," said Callista. "Will it not trouble you if she turns from you to a man—since, as yet, there is no other way to bear a child, and Jaelle has promised this?" Callista was rehearsing in her mind the Oath of the Amazons, wishing there had been some such way for her as a young woman, and at last it burst out of her.

"Andrew and Damon are bound to one another, I think, by a stronger bond than to either of us. Men may swear such oaths. And yet for women, such an oath is always taken, it seems, as a thing for untried girls, and means only, *I shall be bound to you only so long as it does not interfere with duty to husband and children.* . . ."

Jaelle turned and took Magda's hand. Memory flamed between them of the bond tested by the very edge of survival in the canyon; and of a night, during Jaelle's convalescence, when they had turned to one another and each, taking her Amazon knife, had exchanged it with the other; the strongest bond known to women. Close as Rafaella was to Jaelle, and even though they had been lovers for a time, they had never exchanged knives in this way, and Magda knew it was a bond as close as marriage.

"Only one bond is closer," said Ellemir, just audibly.

Callista's fingers began to stray over her *rryl* again, and she said at last, "Can it be that a woman's bond to a woman is not overturned by her commitment to others, just as her bond to a single child is not overturned when she bears another? I thought, when I bore Hilary, though I had not wanted her, that I loved her as I had never loved even Andrew, or you, Elli. And yet when Cassie was born, I loved her no less . . ."

As I love Andrew no less because my bond with Damon is eternal and strong. . . . Magda could hear Callista's thoughts, and Jaelle said softly "Is it possible—that women can love without needing to possess what they love? Every woman knows that one day her child will leave her." And for the first time without pain, she understood her mother's dying words, without guilt.

It was worth it all, Jaelle. You are free. With great pain, Jaelle had seen her own daughter leave her, and had known she would some day have courage to free her, again, to live her own life and bear her own risks.

"Peter—he wanted to possess me and the child," said Jaelle, and Magda nodded, and Callista, her face still bent over the *rryl,* said, "It was a long time before Andrew understood . . . and even now . . ." and could say no more.

Ellemir said softly, "But Damon is not like that." And for a moment all of the women in the circle knew who would father Jaelle's child for the N49

Aillard clan; because he would have no need to possess woman or child, but could leave them free to their own heritage and destiny.

The silence and the crackle of the fire and the soft, absentminded sounds of Callista's hands on her harp were broken by Andrew's laughter. "No, no! No more! I am not a chervine to carry you all on my back! Run to the kitchen and find some bread and honey, and let me talk to the grown-ups! Yes, Domenic, I promised that you and Felix should ride with me tomorrow unless the snow is too bad, and if it is, when it clears! And yes, Cassie, you may come too! Now, for the love of heaven, run along, all of you. I saw some apples in the kitchens—go and get them."

The children scattered and Andrew came back into the hall. He said something to Damon about the stock and pasture shelters for the snow, then joined the women at the fire.

"Play for us, Callie," he said, and she began to sing an old ballad of the hills. Damon and Ellemir were sitting close together on the foot of Jaelle's couch, and Magda felt a moment of deep strangeness. It was as if a door had slammed between herself and the life among the Amazons that she had loved and sworn to. The Terran life, too, was gone, and she felt cold and alienated. She was sworn to Jaelle, yet she could see that this bond held no promises of security, either. And though she knew the strength of the *laran* circle, she did not know if it would be enough.

Andrew leaned over, and put a friendly arm around her.

"It's all right," he said, hugging her close with a brotherly smile, "Listen, girl, do you think I don't know how you're feeling?" Magda's Amazon spirit recoiled at that careless "girl"; I am a woman, she thought, not a girl, but then she knew it was only Andrew's way; like Ellemir, he had the habit of protecting. Like herself, he would have made a good mother.

Are Andrew and I going to spend the next ten years trying to decide whose business it is to protect all the rest of us here in the Forbidden Tower? Magda wondered, and gasped at the knowledge of how much that implied.

Andrew said gently, "But that's what the Forbidden Tower is all about, Magdalen." He alone chose to use her full name, without shortening it. "There isn't one of us here who hasn't had to tear up our old lives like waste paper and start over again. Damon's had to do it two or three times. It isn't safety, or security. But—" his arms tightened around her for a moment again, "we've got each other. All of us."

And for a moment, again, Magdalen Lorne heard the faint far calling as of distant crows—or fates?—and the rustle of wings.

A note from the publisher concerning:

THE FRIENDS OF DARKOVER

So popular have been the novels of the planet Darkover that an organization of readers and fans has come into being, virtually spontaneously. Several meetings have been held at major science fiction conventions, and more recently specially organized around the various "councils" of the Friends of Darkover, as the organization is now known.

The Friends of Darkover is purely an amateur and voluntary group. It has no paid officers and has not established any formal membership dues. What it does have is an offset journal called *Darkover Newsletter,* published from four to six times a year which carries information on meetings, correspondence concerning the aspects and problems raised in the Darkover works, and news of future Darkover novels and critical commentaries.

Contact may be made by writing to the Friends of Darkover, Thendara Council, Box 72, Berkeley, CA 94701, and enclosing a dollar for a trial subscription.

(This notice is inserted gratis as a service to readers. Neither DAW Books nor the Science Fiction Book Club are in any way connected with this organization professionally or commercially.)